THE GREEN
AND
THE BLONDE

~◞

An American Journey

by
John Thomas Baker

Lyric to "*Box of Rain*" by Robert Hunter.
Copyright by Ice Nine Publishing Company.
Used with permission.

Cover Design: Michael Hale, Artist (A.F.G.F.)
Book Design: Marsha Slomowitz
Maps by Mary Rostad / Everett, WA

ISBN: 978-0-9890336-0-2
    First Edition

Lost Wages Publishing Company LLC
PO Box 1051
Port Townsend, Washington
98368

For my mother, Helen, and sister, Gail,
    whose devoted emotions run deep,
for Buster and Laurie,
    who allowed us all to be together,
and for Charlotte,
    whose quiet understandings always remind …

"It's just a box of rain
I don't know who put it there
Believe it if you need it
or leave it if you dare.

But it's just a box or rain
or a ribbon for your hair
Such a long long time to be gone
and a short time to be there."

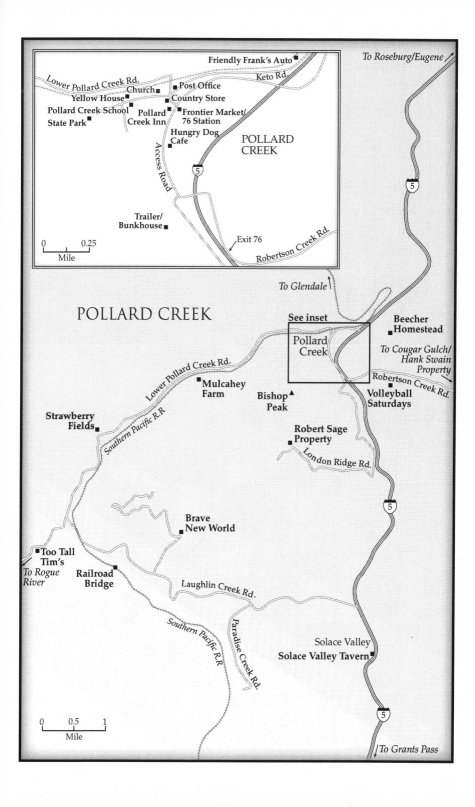

Inset map:

To Roseburg/Eugene

Friendly Frank's Auto

Lower Pollard Creek Rd.
Keto Rd.

Church
Post Office
Yellow House
Country Store
Pollard Creek School
Pollard Creek Inn
State Park
Frontier Market/76 Station
Hungry Dog Cafe

Access Road

POLLARD CREEK

5

Trailer/Bunkhouse

Exit 76

Robertson Creek Rd.

0   0.25
Mile

Main map:

POLLARD CREEK

To Glendale

See inset

Pollard Creek

Beecher Homestead

To Cougar Gulch/Hank Swain Property

Robertson Creek Rd.

Lower Pollard Creek Rd.

Mulcahey Farm

Bishop Peak

Volleyball Saturdays

Southern Pacific R.R.

Strawberry Fields

Robert Sage Property

London Ridge Rd.

5

Brave New World

Too Tall Tim's
To Rogue River

Railroad Bridge

Laughlin Creek Rd.

Southern Pacific R.R.

Paradise Creek Rd.

Solace Valley
Solace Valley Tavern

5

0   0.5   1
Mile

To Grants Pass

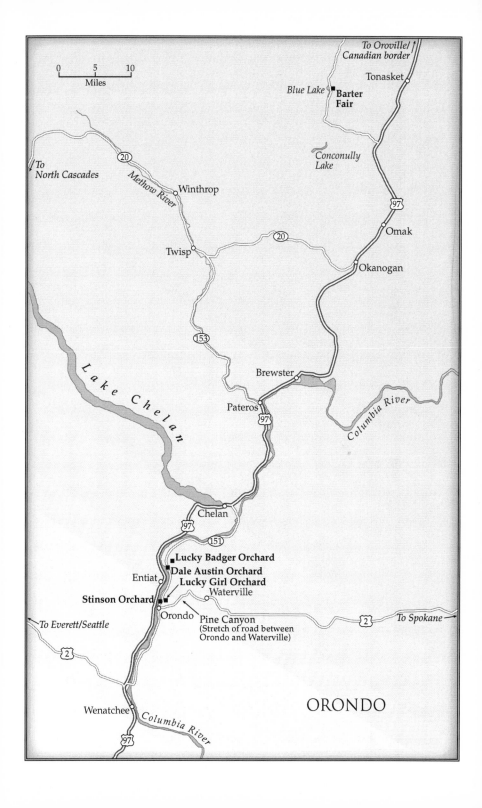

0 5 10
Miles

To Oroville/
Canadian border

Blue Lake ■ **Barter
Fair**

Tonasket

*Conconully
Lake*

97

To
North Cascades

Methow River

Winthrop

20

Omak

Okanogan

20

153

L a k e   C h e l a n

Brewster

Columbia River

Pateros

97

Chelan

97

151

■ **Lucky Badger Orchard**

■ **Dale Austin Orchard**

Entiat

Lucky Girl Orchard

Waterville

Stinson Orchard

Orondo

Pine Canyon
(Stretch of road between
Orondo and Waterville)

2

To Spokane

To Everett/Seattle

2

Wenatchee

Columbia River

97

ORONDO

Part One
An Unfixed Course

"Destiny is what you are supposed to do in life.
Fate is what kicks you in the ass to make you do it."

- Henry Miller

CHAPTER ONE

WHILE MY GUITAR GENTLY WEEPS
Wilmington, Delaware / June, 1968

SEAN MCALLISTER'S BODY JOLTED UPRIGHT, involuntary, his eyes open in a semi-conscious rise. What was it? He fought himself awake. Outside his bedroom door, quick heavy footsteps passed by, rushing staccato down the carpeted stairs to the floor below. When it came again, he knew. An inhaled breathless cry winced the morning air. His mother! McAllister ripped the sheet cover off his legs. His feet swung to the floor, standing. He jerked on the pair of shorts lying nearby. Throwing open his bedroom door, he followed down the stairs.

McAllister found his mother in the family den. She sat hunched on the edge of the couch, her head resting on clenched knees, hands pressed between her thighs. His father stood over her, his right arm reaching across her shoulders, pulsing up and down with the shudder of her weeping. His father's face held hard, his gaze transfixed toward the television screen across the room.

"Mom?" her son questioned. McAllister's eyes turned toward the television, seeing the black and white images of men reporting news. At the sound of his voice, his mother's sobbing softened to a whimper. Slowly, she raised her head and looked his way. Her face appeared as if someone he didn't know, distorted, stricken.

"They killed him," said his mother, her voice anguished. "Now they've killed Bobby, too." She turned away, weeping again into the side leg of his father. Sean McAllister's stomach sank, the impact of her words holding him still.

For a long moment no other words were spoken, only the crying sobs of his mother, while the images and voices of the reporting continued on the screen. The grip of some distant tragedy emanated from a rectangular box on the other side of the den. Going to his mother, he sat beside her on the couch, holding close against the cloth of her robe. The stark and measured tones of the news cut like a knife through the humid morning air.

Robert Kennedy, younger brother of John, lay dying in a California hospital, shot in the head at close range in the early hours of a west coast morning. Moments before the shooting, Robert Kennedy had spoken words of victory and hope in a Los Angeles hotel ballroom, winner of the Democratic primary, a candidate for the Presidency of the United States. "On to Chicago, and let's win there."

Hours before, his mother had gone to bed, her spirits high, her anticipations swollen with pride. They had stayed up late together to watch the results. Bobby Kennedy was leading, and it looked as if he would win California. Now the unimaginable, the shock. His mother's hand found his own, grasping it tight. McAllister felt the strange warmth of her skin.

A car horn sounded outside the house, as if breaking a spell. It forced the reality of the day upon them. His father went outside through the garage, telling the carpool to his job to continue on without him. His mother began to draw herself up. "I've got to get to going," she said. "Mickey, you need to get ready for school." Wiping tears away with the back of her hand, his mother went upstairs to dress. His father returned inside. He looked at his son, shaking his head. "This goddamn mess of a country. This goddamn killing, when will it stop?"

A short time later, McAllister stood in the driveway to his house, watching as his mother backed away in the car. Somehow she had willed herself back to the mom he knew, trying to act like it was just another normal morning. But it wasn't. Her voice was different, as if forcing each word about the breakfast cereal, the orange juice, the shirt he needed to get for graduation. Over her objections, he had declined a ride to school. Although he would be late by choosing to walk, he didn't care. He felt sick and in no hurry. And today he would have no better excuse.

The morning sun was bright, the temperature rising. He ambled slowly through the suburban streets of Northland Hills. People were already off to work, other kids off to school. It was that in-between time when the large homes and lawns seemed vacant of humans, like a science fiction movie where everyone had disappeared. In the pressing heat, he could hear the sound of sprinklers watering grass, the hum of an air conditioner stuck in a downstairs window.

Sean McAllister felt a peculiar numbness in his chest. In his mind, he could still hear his mother's crying. He vainly hoped that Bobby Kennedy would not die, that everything would be okay. But the news reports had been hard and resigned, as if the truth of the telling had to be done. His mother, Constance Doyle McAllister, had already sensed the outcome. Two months before, Martin Luther King had been shot down on the second-floor balcony of a Memphis motel. It seemed like only yesterday that President Kennedy had been murdered in Dallas. Today, his younger brother Bobby might meet a similar fate. Any thoughts of hope didn't have much of a chance.

Bobby Kennedy. How does one cope with the devastation of this family loss, this killing of one of your own? The financial and political success of the Kennedy family had become an icon of an ethnic Irish ascendancy in America. Before Connie Doyle became his mother, she had grown up in the Irish wards of Holyoke, Massachusetts. The Doyles' were part of the immigrant poor. His grandfather worked the mills along the Connecticut River. But to the Doyle clan, and many others like them, the Kennedy family represented an emotional extension of their own Catholic faith and ancestry, a larger world beyond their meager circumstance.

The Kennedys' were a tether for thousands of Irish Catholic Americans. It was a story of personal acceptance and graduation towards the American Dream. The Kennedys' had become their reach toward acceptance on the national stage. Irish hearts would always be with them, right or wrong. For Sean McAllister's mom, Bobby Kennedy was the sweetest of them all. She loved Bobby Kennedy with a constant and particular devotion.

The numbness began to give way, but was replaced by a rush of anger. A desire beset him to strike back against something, to defend this attack against his mother, this terrible pain inflicted upon her and her family. McAllister felt strangely uncomfortable in his clothing, the brown loafers he wore on his feet, the khaki pants and paisley shirt that seemed so stupidly draped upon him. He wanted to turn away from school, to simply not give a shit for a change. Unfortunately, he had nowhere else to go. He would have to stay on track. This high school thing was almost over. He was days away from graduation. He was bored, ready to move on toward a different life. Bobby Kennedy was dying, and there was nothing he could do.

As Sean McAllister reluctantly continued his meander toward school, it occurred to him that indeed his life would be changing soon. For some odd reason, past images of a childhood innocence played within his thoughts. The days of teddy bears and Santa Claus were fading farther and farther away. The tooth fairy no longer came as he slept at night, leaving a dollar under his pillow. Other innocent pictures rendered before him. There was the family move from North Carolina, when he had to leave behind the open fields and friends of his ten-year-old world, including the little girl Stephanie, who his heart had beat for every day. There was the image of his grandfather, laying forever silent in a suit of clothes, the casket later shut and carried with his body inside, dropped into a hole in the ground, covered with dirt. There was the night President Kennedy came on the television, speaking to the nation. The President showed pictures of tall missiles in Cuba, pointed at the United States ready to fire. He recalled the images of people living in bomb shelters, dug underground in their own backyards, of families having to live there just to stay alive.

He remembered the day in junior high school, standing by his locker, the voice of the school intercom sending them home. Later that afternoon, tossed from a truck, a bundle of newspapers it was his job to deliver. The man in the truck threw the bundle onto the lawn, McAllister watching as it came to rest, the headline reading in bold black print, KENNEDY DEAD. He recalled the images of Mrs. Kennedy, the blood of her dead husband scattered over her dress. On that following Sunday morning, he could see the black and white frames of the killer, Lee Harvey Oswald. There was the bulky man, Ruby, wearing a black hat, shooting Oswald dead. Days later, he witnessed the horse drawn funeral carriage, the sound of their hooves clomping on the pavement, the twenty-one gun salute.

Sean McAllister wasn't sure why these thoughts were coming to mind. They didn't feel particularly good. For the first time, he felt like the world might forever continue to be an unjust and dangerous place.

In his World Problems class, there was no getting away from the reality of the shooting. The teacher, Mr. Biglelow, tried to put the tragedy in perspective, allowing the students to express their worries and fears. But nobody had much to say. It was if everyone wanted to keep any feelings to themselves. As far as anyone knew, Bobby Kennedy was still alive. A quiet hope remained. Mr. Bigelow seemed tight with anger, as if he wanted to shout out the bad things about America. But he kept his tongue. Mr. Bigelow had said that Bobby Kennedy's campaign for President had been less than three months old. The Kennedy campaign had continued to stir the ongoing national debate among Americans about the war in Vietnam, as well as the poverty and injustice facing poor children and families throughout the United States.

As he had often droned before, Mr. Bigelow began to tell the class that America's future would be counting on them to make things better. For McAllister, those words didn't carry much weight today, as if it was his job to fix this mess. But the quote Mr. Bigelow read from Bobby Kennedy had its own ring of importance.

"Few will have the greatness to bend history itself; but each of us can work to change a small portion of events, and in the total, of all those acts will be written the history of this generation."

The day at school had been long and hot, the teachers dazed and unfocused. Everyone seemed restless, distracted. When the end finally came, McAllister met his teammate Jody Morrison in the parking lot at school. They went for a ride in Jody's MG convertible. With the top down, Jody raced the car through the light rolling hills of the Brandywine Valley. They felt the full flush of a green and blooming countryside, the heated June wind rushing through their hair. It was a chance for McAllister and Jody to finally be away from the recent months of baseball practice and games. Late in the afternoon, Jody dropped McAllister off at home. His mother was in the kitchen preparing food for dinner.

"Oh, there you are. How was your day? Only a few more left before the big one." Her voice was back to normal, trying to be cheerful, seeming more like his mom.

"All right, I guess." McAllister opened the refrigerator door and peered inside.

"We're going to eat soon, Mickey," she said firmly. Mickey was his family nick name. He closed the refrigerator door and looked at her as she reached for dishes out of the cabinet.

"Mom, any more word on Bobby Kennedy?"

His mother paused for a moment, holding the dishes in her hands, before turning to the kitchen table to place them down. "It's critical. They performed very difficult surgery on his brain. I'm afraid the outlook is very bad." Connie McAllister spoke like the hospital administrator that was her job every day, not the woman who earlier this morning had been emotionally undone. Standing over the table, she continued. "I still can't believe it. And for Ethel, and their children, I'm…. I'm…." McAllister saw his mother begin to weaken. He stepped forward, embracing her. She rested her chin against his shoulder, sniffling again with tears. "He could have been a great President, Mickey. He would have done so many good things. It's just so hard," she sighed, "so terrible. I can't bring myself to understand."

McAllister held his mother in his arms. It was something he rarely did, unless going away for a trip to the beach or camp. Always before, it was she who did the hugging. She released herself, wiping her tears away with a napkin. "I spoke with your Grammy, and your Aunt Marie. They're so sick at heart. And your sister called just a little while ago. She is very upset."

"Mary Jane? So what did she say about it?" McAllister asked.

"She is very very hurt and sad, and wanted to be close. She asked if she should come down any sooner. I told her no."

"I suppose she'll want McCarthy to get his delegates," McAllister stated. "To vote for him now against the war."

"Mickey, don't be that way. It's a terrible day. For everyone, including your sister."

His mother was right, and he was wrong to say what he said. His sister had caused a ruckus not long before. Mary Jane was up in Boston at college. She had announced that she was for Eugene McCarthy many months ago, long before Bobby Kennedy had gotten into the race. But when Bobby got in, she had stayed with McCarthy, saying that Bobby was an opportunist, and had only gotten into the race because McCarthy was doing so well against President Johnson.

Those words had hurt, and McAllister had tried to defend his mother when Mary Jane insisted so strongly against the Kennedy campaign. McAllister wanted just the opposite, for McCarthy to support Bobby, but McCarthy said he never would. Perhaps now, it would make no difference. Bobby Kennedy was going to die, or at least be a vegetable. In two more weeks Sean McAllister was going to have his birthday, to turn eighteen. He would have to go downtown and register for the draft. He agreed with Mary Jane about the war, just not the person to stop it.

"Mr. Bigelow, in World Problems class, said some nice things about him today. I could tell he was really angry, but he didn't let it out. He read some statements from Senator Kennedy. He read the speech after the killing of Martin Luther King, and another one about the future of America."

"Which one was that?" his mother asked.

"I can't remember exactly," McAllister answered. "Something like the small things you do for the world, will all add up and make a difference in history, something like that I think."

"They can," his mother responded. "I believe they can. With or without him, maybe they can."

A short time later, McAllister's father came home from work. The family sat down for dinner. The sad events of the day hung like an unspoken secret. With her son's graduation from high school only one week away, Connie McAllister talked about the family gathering to be held after the ceremonies were over. Grandma Doyle, his mom's sisters, Aunt Marie and Aunt Teresa, his uncles and lots of his cousins would be coming down from Massachusetts. Uncle Joe and Uncle Franny, his dad's brothers and their families from the McAllister side, would be present as well. His sister, Mary Jane, would be coming home from college the night before, her school year over for the summer. Family friends and neighbors would also attend. It would be a reunion of sorts to commemorate the big day.

For McAllister himself, the event felt like much ado about nothing, something he would have to endure. He was ready for high school to be over, to be free like his sister Mary Jane, away from home and going to college in the fall. Things would all be new and different. He was hungry to feel older and away from home. But this celebration meant a lot to his mom and dad. He felt obliged to show his gratitude and appreciation, which he did, just not so much.

When McAllister rolled and rubbed his right shoulder for the second time at the dinner table, his father looked at him seriously. "Is that still hurting you, Mickey?" he asked.

"Just sort of achy, I guess," McAllister answered. "I think it's getting better. It just feels tight sometimes."

"Well, if it doesn't feel better in the next week or so, we should have it checked out. Something could be torn up there. I still can't believe that coach of yours. For crying out loud, he should have known, using you the way he did. It sure didn't help."

"Dad," McAllister answered flatly, "it wasn't Coach Spencer's fault, it was me. I told coach I could go, and the team needed me. It just didn't work out, Dad. They were the better team anyway, you know that. We did the best we could."

"I just wish you had been healthy," his father grumbled. A familiar look of frustration was etched upon his face.

Bill McAllister, his father, had been a good baseball player and athlete in his time. He had always hoped his son would be as well. And McAllister was very good for awhile. But things had evened out over time. Actually, McAllister was okay with it, but he knew his father had his own solitary dreams invested in his son.

Since McAllister had first started playing baseball, he and his father had spent hours together pitching and hitting till darkness drove them home. His dad had watched him almost every game, before commenting and analyzing every play. Together, they had gone to games at Connie Mack Stadium in Philly, watching the best. There was Robin Roberts, Richie Ashburn, Willie Mays, and Hank Aaron. They had even driven to New York to see Mickey Mantle at Yankee Stadium. For a time McAllister shared his father's dream, playing hard and wanting to make his dad feel good. But as everyone got older, you sort of knew where you stood.

McAllister's right arm began to betray him before his senior season. The year before, several junior college coaches had come to his games. They had introduced themselves, telling him about their schools. But the shoulder started to hurt in summer league, although he continued to play. He never said a word to his dad. But he knew the next spring, things weren't getting better. Before the injury, his two-seam fastball always had this cool late break in the strike zone. But after, it had begun to flatten out and started getting hit. Without the fastball, McAllister couldn't set up his curve. So the hitters sat on the fastball whenever they could. He tried to gut it out with location and changing speeds. He tried throwing different pitches in different counts. He tried anything to get by. But the junior college coaches that had spoken with him the year before, now only said hello. Nothing more.

When it came to the district final against Franklin High in late May, his good friend Jody Morrison would get the start, and Jody deserved it. McAllister would play first base. But Jody was wild that day and couldn't find the strike zone. He walked himself into trouble and Franklin took advantage. A few big hits later and they trailed four to zip. In the fourth, Coach Spencer went to McAllister. It didn't matter. McAllister tried to pitch around the big Franklin hitters, but they waited on the fastball and raked him pretty good. The damage was done, losing the game eight to one. The season was over. He and Jody Morrison had played together since Little League. On the drive through the Brandywine Valley that afternoon they had talked about the loss. In a weird way things had happened for the best. He and Jody had gone down together. It's always a good thing not having to share your failures alone.

For Sean McAllister, his baseball dream was ending. In most cases, players generally know where they stand with each other, and why things happen the way they do. But for those that love them, like his dad, it's a little harder road. Sean McAllister was sure his father understood the nature of things. It was just tough, and would take a little longer to put to rest.

His dad worked as an engineering executive for the Dupont chemical corporation. The Dupont Company, as well as the Dupont family, ran and ruled the city of Wilmington, including the State of Delaware. It seemed like almost everyone in Wilmington worked for Dupont. The corporation cast a long shadow over the employment and lives of so many citizens. The state was like a feudal aristocracy. The Dupont family liked it that way, and they weren't about to change.

McAllister knew his dad wasn't much happy with his job, overhearing the complaints to his mom from time to time. But work was part of life in this world, a teaching Sean McAllister had been trained to understand and perform. You shouldn't bite the hand that feeds you, his father would often say, but never with much conviction. His mother and father got up and went to work every weekday morning. Sean McAllister would be expected to do the same.

Bill McAllister was a child of the Depression, and a veteran of the Second World War that followed. He was an honorably discharged pilot in the United States Army Air Force, and a good one. He had been so good that he managed to have never flown a combat mission overseas. Instead, they had made him a flight instructor. During the war, he had crisscrossed the skies of the American Southwest, teaching men to fly and pilot B-17s. For many of the men he taught, Bill McAllister had become a friend as well as mentor. But Sean McAllister knew that his dad had taught many who would never return.

Only on rare occasions had McAllister ever heard his father speak about his service during the war. Sometimes he would talk with his brothers, all three who had enlisted together after the bombing of Pearl Harbor. Other times, he might speak with one of his other buddies who had served. But he never spoke directly or soberly with his children.

Still, there had been those occasional nights when his father would be buzzed with whiskey at the kitchen table. He would sit, either half-angry or half-maudlin, telling a disjointed story of a guy's forehead expanding at certain altitudes, or crash landing in some driving rainstorm. Sometimes, he would mention the names of men with whom he had flown. One particular night, his father flashed a memory of one of those friends, before breaking down in tears. But the next day, not a word was said. There was one thing McAllister did know. His father had never again piloted an airplane. For the most part, the war was a closed chapter in the McAllister family history, unspoken and emotionally unknown. Things had happened that were better left alone.

McAllister excused himself from the table. He picked up his plate and utensils, rinsed them in the sink, placing them in the dishwasher. "Mom, I'm going to the mall tonight, to look for that dress shirt I need. Okay?" he asked.

His mom looked over to his dad, "Mickey needs something better for his graduation. I told him he should get something."

"Are you taking one of the cars?" his father asked.

"No, I'm catching a ride with Reggie."

"With who?" his mother questioned. "Reggie Disalvo? Reggie hasn't been to this house in the longest time. Where did you see him?"

"I ran into him on the way home today," McAllister answered. "He's graduating next week, too. From Pike Valley. He's got a really cool new car. I told him I needed to go shopping at the mall. He said he'd cruise me up there."

"What kind of car?" his father asked absently.

"A Buick, I think. A big black one. It's really sharp."

"Well, you make sure he comes in and says hello when he gets here," his mother said. "I want to see him."

"Okay. I've got to call and let him know I'm ready. I'll tell him."

Sean Michael McAllister may have begun to lose the innocence of his youth as his eighteenth birthday approached. But in exchange, he was becoming practiced in the art of deception. The trip to the mall was true, but only half the story. McAllister hurried upstairs to his parent's bedroom and quickly made a phone call on the bedside phone. His old friend, Reggie Disalvo, answered the call.

"Mickey boy," Reggie greeted him, using the childhood nickname McAllister no longer allowed outside of family. But Reggie went too far back to change.

"It's Mr. Mickey to you, Disalvo, you pizza-eating greaseball."

"OK, cabbage-eater, what's up?"

"You know, Disalvo. Can we go? Do you think things are cool in the city, with the Kennedy shooting and all?"

"I guess we'll find out. I talked with Leonard a little while ago. He didn't say nothing about trouble. You ready to go?"

"Yeah, but remember, I got to go to the mall, okay? And mom wants you to come in the house and say hello. I guess she misses you. Don't ask me why?"

"Mrs. Mac! She's the best. No problem there. I'll see you in twenty. The Black Bomber is ready to roll."

Reggie Disalvo and Sean McAllister had been friends since they were ten years old, when the suburban neighborhood of Northland Hills was first under construction. McAllister's family had just moved up from North Carolina, and Reggie's folks had moved out of the Brownsville section of the city of Wilmington. In the early days, they and a few others had been the only boys in the neighborhood. For several years, their afternoons were shared having dirtball fights around the construction sites, collecting pop bottles out of the housing starts, catching salamanders out of the creek, or playing war games in the woods nearby.

But as time passed and school life turned into junior high, their time together diverged. McAllister occupied most of his time playing sports, and hanging with the other kids that played the same. Reggie was into go-carts, motor bikes, eventually cars. Reggie wasn't much for school. He often worked for his father, a cement contractor, to make money for the machines he liked to buy. Instead of going to high school with McAllister, he went to Pike Valley Vocational, learning auto repair and construction skills.

Reggie was stocky and tough, but a jokester at heart. He had smooth Italian skin, and jet-black hair that glistened with a *Brillcream* look. Reggie was ever confident, never afraid to try and fix something or take a chance. He had a steady girlfriend named Teresa. She still lived in the city, and so Reggie spent much of his time back in the old neighborhood. Although he and McAllister had drifted apart in their youthful social worlds, the friendship that they shared as boys ran deep, one for the other whenever they met.

Working for his father, Reggie shoveled and finished concrete. He carried hod and drove trucks throughout the city and suburban enclaves of Wilmington metro. Reggie was connected to the vices and rhythms of an adult world. Reggie could get things that McAllister and his other friends were unable to procure. Reggie Disalvo was the right man for the mission ahead.

It wasn't the first time that they had made the run. Reggie and his older colored friend, Leonard Woods, had worked on numerous jobsites. Leonard lived in a section of town near the center of the city, an area that had given way to the exodus of white working-class Americans fleeing the urban neighborhoods. These families were being replaced by Negroes from farms and towns deep to the south. Wilmington was becoming a mostly colored city, its row houses and front stoops peopled by a different ethnicity from the Irish and Italian neighborhoods of only a few years before. Niggertown was no longer just the ghetto flats down by the Delaware River. It was spreading outward every day.

McAllister's mendacities were not totally untrue. The two young men rumbled in Reggie's spacious black Buick Roadmaster out to the

Westover Pike, then north to the mall. McAllister found a new dress shirt that fit him, purchasing it with the money his mom had pressed into his hands. Afterwards, he and Reggie walked through the mall's interior, checking out the girls passing by, killing time until the onset of early darkness. Returning to the Buick, Reggie pointed the car into the city of Wilmington. With the windows down, the night air was comfortably warm, fresh with the odors of spring and the summer ahead.

Reggie skirted the Buick through traffic on the higher edge of downtown. Off to the southeast, McAllister could look down on the districts toward the Delaware River. In the distance were the warehouses and docks, the marine terminals and chemical plants. On the river itself, the ships moved quietly along, their signal lights in a slow-motion cruise, north to Philadelphia, or back out to sea. In the foreground below. McAllister could see blocks and blocks of city streets crisscrossing through a vacant landscape. The area had been stripped of houses and buildings, everything torn down and removed. The scene appeared like a strange planetary desert of pale dust and destruction, as if an atomic bomb had fallen from the sky. Urban renewal it was called. But in the darkening evening light, it looked vacant and forlorn.

Reggie steered the Buick into the near silent streets of downtown, beneath the towering Dupont buildings and the corporate banks of the city. He pulled the car over to a parking spot just off Washington Avenue, then shut down the engine to wait.

"What's up?" McAllister asked.

Reggie turned down the music on the radio, leaning back in the driver's seat. "We'll wait here until the combat forces go by," Reggie answered. "They circle the perimeter in their jeeps all night long. But Leonard says they never go inside the 'compound'. That's what he calls it. He told me to wait until they pass by on Washington, before crossing over. From here, we can see them come through."

For the first time that evening, McAllister felt anxious about the mission ahead, about possibly getting caught and what might happen. He had done this trip before with Reggie, but not in the months since baseball season started, and not since Martin Luther King had been assassinated. And tonight, on the day that Bobby Kennedy lay dying in California, it did not seem like a good time to be here. But Leonard had said things were okay, so here they were.

When Dr. King had been shot, Wilmington, like so many other cities in America, went up like a Roman candle. Market Street, just a few blocks over, had been smashed and looted all that night. There were not as many fires as other cities, but angry mobs of Negroes had swept through the downtown, taking out their retribution against the city and the police. The Governor had wasted no time in calling in the National Guard. And even though the trouble had passed, the Guard remained, patrolling the streets of Wilmington like an armed occupation. According to the news, the Governor had no intention of pulling them out. There would absolutely be no more looting he said, and if anyone cared to know what that meant, the military presence spoke for itself. The Governor came from the southern part of the state, and there was no mystery about how he felt about things up north. At night, the downtown business core was empty. The boys sat waiting for the jeeps to pass.

"So the college boy is going to Washington D.C., to be a diplomat, or a senator or something. Maybe he'll be famous one day. Maybe, he'll be the next Bobby Kennedy, or someone like that."

McAllister turned and gave Reggie a harsh look and held the stare. "Hey, don't talk like that, Reg. Not today." McAllister didn't blink.

Reggie got the message. "Hey, sorry man. I didn't mean it that way, you know that."

McAllister leaned over toward the radio, accepting the apology. "Do you think we could shit-can the soul music for awhile, maybe a little rock music instead? I know you still want to become a member of the Four Tops and all, but damn." McAllister put his hand out toward the radio dial and held it, looking at Reggie.

"No, go ahead. Do your thing." McAllister fiddled with the dial and found the station he liked. The Rolling Stones' song "Mothers Little Helper" began to fill the car. McAllister sat back in his seat. Reggie turned toward him. "I've got a Hermin's Hermits album you could borrow."

McAllister let out a laugh. Reggie Disalvo was a regular Eddy Haskell. For a time, they sat together in the car, enjoying the friendship they had missed for awhile.

"Yeah, college." McAllister breathed out the words. "I haven't really thought about it much since I got accepted. I suppose I'm ready to go. It just feels like a long way off right now. I've got to sign up for the draft in a few weeks. At least I'll get a deferment from that."

"It will be great, Mickey," Reggie said. "I bet you'll like it a lot. You're smart, man. It will be a breeze for you."

"What about you, Reg?" McAllister asked. "Are you going to keep working for your dad?"

Reggie Disalvo looked ahead toward Washington Avenue. "I'm not sure," he paused, "helicopters, maybe."

McAllister rose quickly off the seat and looked at his friend. "Helicopters?" he questioned. "You're not thinking about…."

Reggie interjected, nodding his head toward the cross street ahead. "There they are!"

McAllister swung his gaze toward Washington Avenue. A green military jeep cruised in front of them. One soldier sat behind the wheel. Another uniformed guardsman stood up in the back, a rifle held vertical beside him. The helmets looked almost too big for their heads, and their faces didn't look much older than McAllister and Reggie. Watching the jeep pass, Reggie started up the Buick, pulling into the street. Reaching the corner, he looked left and waited as the jeep went up another block, passing through a light. Then he gunned the Buick across Washington Avenue. For several blocks they drove through the commercial part of the city, passing buildings with restaurants, delicatessens, and other retail businesses.

"Yeah, I'd like to either fly or work on the birds," Reggie continued. "They're probably going to come and get me anyway, so why not choose something I'd like to do."

"Fuckin' A," McAllister breathed. "Shit, Disalvo, are you sure?"

"Nah, I ain't sure, man. But I'm thinking about it."

"Mary Jane would be sure. She'd be trying to talk you out of it. She's been working for a draft counseling service at school. They help people go to Canada if they can't get out of the war. My parents don't know about it, but that's what she's doing."

"Mary Jane? Mary Jane McAllister? She's up in Boston, right? Your older sister is hot, Mick!"

"Hot?" McAllister queried. "Hot? More like a hot pain in the ass if you want my opinion. I'll be sure and mention that to Teresa the next time I see her. Does Teresa know what you are considering?"

"Don't do that, man. No, Teresa doesn't know, nobody knows. It's just something I been thinking about, that's all."

"Well, maybe it is something you should keep thinking about,"

McAllister returned. "Those things get shot down all the time over there. It's dangerous fucking shit, Reg." McAllister paused. "Hell, I don't know. You'd be good at it, I know that."

The conversation trailed off as the street narrowed, lined with parked cars on either side. Brick row houses were now pressed together one by one, set off from the sidewalks, each with a front stoop, all the same. In the heated dark of evening, colored people sat and lingered outside, kids playing along the pavement in the humid night air.

Unlike the prior booze runs he and Reggie had made before, tonight there seemed to be a quiet restraint in the city. It lacked the normal edge and tension of being in this section of town, of being a white face. There seemed an almost silent passivity, as if people were waiting for something to happen. For McAllister, it felt like one of those weird Atlantic calms, bobbing in his father's fishing boat, having pushed many miles deep into the ocean's waters. There was always that hushed feeling of danger in the graying sky, but nowhere to be seen.

Reggie slowed the car up to one of the snug concrete stairways, idling in the street. He leaned out the window and asked for Leonard. Someone pointed down the block to the corner, just a few houses down. Reggie gently pushed the car forward, catching sight of Leonard on the sidewalk with several other men. When Leonard noticed the car, he stepped out into the street, pointing. "Take the left, then pull into the alley." Reggie rolled the car around the corner, steering the big black sedan into the entrance. Leonard walked along with Reggie, urging the car forward until telling him to stop. As Reggie and McAllister got out of the car, two other Negro men approached.

Reggie and Leonard exchanged greetings. "Sorry we're a little late," Reggie apologized. "We had to wait awhile for the army to go through, like you said. You remember my friend, Sean. He's been with me before."

McAllister and Leonard shook hands. McAllister thanked Leonard for helping them out. But he could feel a nervous energy in his voice as he spoke.

"That's cool," Leonard said. "Getting some juice for the graduation parties, Reggie tells me." Leonard pointed towards his friends. "This is Satts, and this is Big Arthur." The men all shook hands. "So what do you got?" Reggie went over the purchase list with Leonard, pulling out the money that McAllister had given him. Leonard ran through the cash in his hands. "Looks like it's more than enough, but we'll see. If we need more to take care of us, I'll let you know. You're good for it, right boys?"

"Sure, Leonard, you know that," Reggie answered.

Leonard gave Reggie a fake punch to his shoulder. "Yeah, I know that," he said, smiling. "We're going down the alley to the next block, then around to the package store. Your dad's old finish man, Billy E., is working the package store part time. He knows we're coming. You brothers wait here till we get back." Leonard, Satts and Big Arthur walked down the alley. Crossing the street, they disappeared into the darkness beyond.

Reggie and McAllister got back in the car and waited. As he sat in the car with the window down, McAllister didn't speak. The waiting part was always the worst, especially being an unarmed white kid in a colored section of Wilmington. He could smell the intense odor of rotting garbage in the alley. In the ambient electric light of the evening, the backyards of the row houses were cluttered with broken and discarded appliances. Tall weeds grew through bent and rusted chain link fences. Broken mortar lay in pieces along crumbling foundation walls.

It was kind of strange to think about the fear he felt inside. Sure, he was worried about getting caught buying alcohol underage, and the hell he would have to pay at home if it happened. But he had done this trip before. He knew the risks, and he wouldn't be killed for his crime. And nobody had been robbed or beaten up this evening, at least not so far. There were no gunshots or sirens exploding into the air, prompting a person to be alert for their physical safety. There had been no acts of anger or hate. No threat of bodily harm had been aimed at him, none of these things. And yet the fear of all these things consumed him, feeling tense.

McAllister wondered if it might be the perception of all these unknowns that distracted him, not the reality of their actual occurrence. Nothing had happened, and yet the fear of these things was palpable and sharp, as if placed inside him by something outside himself. It was if he was made to feel this way by certain presumptions he had learned to suspect. Still, in another way, he was almost glad to be here in this place tonight. It was an adventure so different from his everyday life. Perhaps this was why he came here, to feel the risk, to take on the challenge of something unknown.

"Kinda crazy sitting here in jigaboo land like this," Reggie said, breaking McAllister's nervous reverie. "Here we are, a couple of honkies, just sitting in the back of a dark alley, minding our own business, waiting to get mugged. I think I'm ready to get out of here."

McAllister was about to agree, but a shout from behind interrupted him. Reggie jumped from the car, looking down the alley. He went to the back of the Buick, opening the trunk. The three men closed in on the car, each carrying a case of beer, with brown paper bags resting on top. McAllister got out and watched as they loaded the booze, then Reggie closed the trunk.

"Enough dough for everyone," Reggie asked?

"We're cool," Leonard answered. "You boys should have a damn good house party with this here stash. A real good time."

"It's not like we get to drink it in a house, Leonard. More like the beach, or the woods, or someplace outside," Reggie joked.

"Well, next time come on down to my place here. We'll have a party at my pad. Nobody will be looking for you boys in this neighborhood. Ain't I right brothers?" Leonard looked over at Big Arthur and Satts.

"No shit about that, cuz," the man Satts concurred. All three colored men laughed together, filled with a particular knowledge it was only their own to share.

"Well thanks, Leonard," Reggie said. "That would be cool sometime, a party in the city."

"I'm game," McAllister answered.

All the men grasped hands in brotherly handshakes, saying goodbye. "Just head straight out the way you came," Leonard advised. But as the boys turned for the car, Leonard spoke again. "Hey, wait a minute, what do you boys hear about Kennedy? He still alive, or dead?" The question suddenly changed the moment. McAllister answered.

"My mom says they did a long surgery on him today, but he's still critical. She said it doesn't look good."

"He's a dead man, I bet," Leonard stated. "Fuck man, first they got Martin, now Bobby Kennedy. This country's got some heavy shit, brothers. That man was good to us, he cared about us."

"My mom's got a broken heart," McAllister volunteered. "She cried and cried this morning."

"Mine, too," Leonard said. "Mine too. She hasn't eaten all day."

Reggie rolled the car down the alley and onto the streets. They crossed back over Washington Avenue without incident. Reggie kept to the speed limit as they climbed the last hill out of town, heading back to the suburbs of North Wilmington. He detoured to his father's business office and construction yard. There, they stashed the booze in an old equipment shed that Reggie said was safe.

"Whew," McAllister breathed as they turned onto the last street before home. "I'm glad that's over. Kind of takes it out of you. I'm bushed."

Reggie pulled the Buick over to the curbside next to McAllister's house. McAllister grabbed the bag with the shirt he'd bought at the mall, climbing out of the car. He leaned into the open window. "Well, thanks Disalvo, you criminal. We couldn't have done it without you. We owe you one."

"More than one, Mickey boy. And don't forget, I still got the key to the booze locker, remember that."

"I haven't forgotten. I'll give you a call." McAllister stood outside the car, but he paused for a moment and held his gaze at Reggie. "Are you really thinking about this army thing? What the hell, Reg, you could get killed doing that shit. I mean, that's all you see on television these days, guys getting blown to shit and coming home dead. My sister gets back on Monday. You could talk to her if you want."

"Listen, Mickey. I ain't going to Canada and shit. That's for fucking pussies, man. But I'll take a date with Mary Jane anytime. Does a bear shit in the woods, or what?"

"Come on, man, I'm trying to be serious right now."

"Yeah, I know. But hell, Mick, they're going to get me anyway. Especially if I don't go to school, which I'm not planning on doing right now. And if they do get me, then I might as well enlist. That way, there's at least a good chance I'll get the helicopter job."

"All right, never mind," McAllister agreed. "Anyway, the Black Bomber here is one fine ride. Thanks for the run. I'll be in touch." With the farewell, Reggie Disalvo hummed his shiny black sedan into the night.

Sometime later, Sean McAllister lay in bed, needing only a sheet as cover in the close heated darkness of his room. Outside his open windows, the sound of a mockingbird sung in the night. Images of the day crossed through his thoughts. He saw the desperate and tearful look on his mother's face earlier that morning. He saw the shuttered and empty homes on the walk to school. He recalled the hard edge of frustration in Mr. Bigelow's eyes, and Reggie Disalvo's cool persona while driving through the city streets. There was Leonard Woods, in his sleeveless white tee shirt, his muscled brown arms smooth with perspiration. And Leonard's buddy, Satts, with his pork pie hat and rounded brown face. Finally, there was the image of Bobby Kennedy, brushing away his hair as people pressed around him, seeking a touch. Finally, he drifted into sleep.

In the early morning hours, while McAllister slept, three thousand miles away, a man struggled to hold his emotions. He walked to a podium microphone, delivering a prepared statement. With his words, the prayers of a nation lay in vain, awakening to a future of grief and distress.

> *"I have a short announcement to read, which I will read at this time. Senator Robert Francis Kennedy died at 1:44 A.M. today, June 6, 1968. With Senator Kennedy at the time of his death, was his wife, Ethel; his sisters, Mrs. Patricia Lawford and Mrs. Stephen Smith, his brother-in-law, Stephen Smith, and his sister-in-law, Mrs. John F. Kennedy. He was 42 years old."*

The first week of June remained hot and humid. Saturday, June 8th, 1968, began no different. Sean McAllister got up late, ate breakfast, before going outside to mow the family lawn. Some of his friends would be headed for the beach down south. Normally, he would have been with them. But on this day, he stayed behind. His father, Bill McAllister, had gotten up early, loaded his golf clubs and gone to the course. Both his wife and his son had said he should go. It was a reversal of sorts, after years of toting his boy to one ball field or another. On this particular day, it was not Bill McAllister's responsibility, he had done enough.

Connie McAllister busied herself that morning, cleaning the house and doing the laundry. The television kept solitary company in the family den, the funeral of Robert Francis Kennedy in progress. In between the routine of their Saturday life, McAllister and his mom watched the ritual of the services. They heard the sad words of praise and loss. They viewed the tortured faces of the Kennedy family, masked by a shock that held them still. After the services, a procession of cars left St. Patrick's Cathedral in New York City, headed for the funeral train to Washington D.C., and the later burial at Arlington National Cemetery.

After lunch, his mother went upstairs to dress. McAllister changed out of his grass- stained pants and shoes. He put on shorts and a shirt, returning downstairs. His mother wore a white sleeveless blouse, blue skirt and shoes. He watched as she put her rosary and sunglasses in her purse. Together, they walked out into the bright heated afternoon. McAllister drove the car several miles east toward the Delaware River, to a small commuter station where the funeral train would pass.

The station platform was already crowded with people. McAllister and his mother walked down along the tracks with others, the hot black cinders of the railroad bed crunching under their feet. Reaching an embankment that adjoined an overpass, they climbed up the rise, standing on the weeded rough ground. They began to wait.

Waiting. The hot afternoon sun bore down on the crowded line of Americans, north and south as far as the eye could see. McAllister found a piece of strewn cardboard. He placed it on the ground so his mother could sit. He looked out upon the tenement buildings across the tracks. He thought of the night in Leonard's alley several evenings before. The view was a reminder of the hidden side of a poverty he did not have to live. Nearby, there were Negro men dressed in white shirts and dark shoes, colored women in summer shorts, their hair pulled up tight above their heads. A young white boy stood beside his father holding an American flag. A policeman walked the tracks, keeping people back with the wave of his arms.

Finally, a wind of human sound carried down from the north, catching the expectant attention of the people. The crowd stirred. Connie McAllister rose to her feet, her rosary beads in hand. McAllister leaned forward on the slope of the hill. He could see the train moving slowly down the rails ahead. He felt a rush of anticipation, followed by an empty dread as the train moved ever closer. When the train began to pass, some people waved, others remained perfectly still. Men took off their hats, pressing them over their hearts. The young boy raised and circled the flag in the air. The policeman straightened his body, holding in full salute.

McAllister looked over at his mom. She held her votive hands together, the rosary beads clenched and hanging in-between. The sound of the train engines encompassed the crowd, the rails creaking as it slowly and deliberately passed before them. One by one, the passenger cars moved by, filled with human faces looking out upon the people. McAllister could feel the overwhelming presence of a man he'd never met, an imagined persona before him, flushed with an emotion that swelled within him as he stood on the hill. But inside the train, a body was dead, a voice silenced. It lay in a covered casket, draped with a flag.

Then it was over, the last car pulling away to the south. A man stood on the rear platform of the train. He was dressed in coat and tie, waving back at the crowd. Children and others ran behind. Their arms were outstretched, grasping the air, as if reaching for something lost in the breeze. McAllister watched as his mother's gaze followed the trailing car, her hands still clasped, tears welling on her cheeks. Her hero, Robert Francis Kennedy, was leaving her forever. Forever alone without him. Constance Doyle McAllister was forty-two years old.

CHAPTER TWO

LONG TIME GONE
Bethel, New York / 1969

THE SHOCK AND SORROW OF JUNE 5TH 1968 passed quickly. Bobby Kennedy was dead. The war in Vietnam lived on. By late August the mourning was over. Anger returned, the divisions continued to grow. The shit hit the fan in Chicago.

With a hurricane of political and social change in America sweeping around him, Sean McAllister continued to live his days in a youthful naiveté. He registered for the draft, getting his 2-S student deferment. He got a summer job doing labor in one of Wilmington's many chemical plants. He went to the beach on weekends, swimming, water skiing, hanging with his friends. The cocoon of a middle class innocence sheltered him. College lay ahead.

His sister, Mary Jane, didn't stay long at home. After McAllister's graduation, she returned to Boston. She seemed older to him, impatient, at odds with their parents on so many things. Like any older sister, she had always been a pain in the butt. But lately Mary Jane hadn't laid any trips on him, she was busy with her own life. The only advice she delivered, about the time she was leaving, was to stay in school. "Mickey, just don't drop out, whatever you do. Those assholes will get you. They don't care who you are, or what you think. Once they've got you in their grasp, you're screwed."

He had mentioned to her the deal with Reggie, how he was thinking of going into the military, how he wanted to fly or work on helicopters. "Sure, I'll talk to him," she responded. "I'll tell him he's nuts. But if he's not in school, that's not good. If he ends up 1-A, they won't waste time.

He'll be a goner. They like them young and eager to fight. If he really wants out, which I don't think he does, then he can come up to Boston. I will get him to some people that can help."

"Canada?" McAllister asked.

"Better than coming home to Dover in a body bag," she answered.

Dover Air Force Base, just an hour south of Wilmington, was where many of the war dead were sent. The base dealt with coffins returning in huge transport aircraft, an assembly line of dead soldiers. Dover was a government sponsored funeral home.

McAllister hadn't seen Reggie since they picked up the booze before graduation. And Mary Jane was gone before any kind of discussion could be arranged. Everyone was doing their own thing, whichever way it might turn. For McAllister, it was kind of hard to think about leaving school when you hadn't even got there yet. And Reggie wouldn't be much excited about being a draft dodger. He only wanted an excuse to hang out with Mary Jane. All his buddies thought Mary Jane was hot. They were like dogs in heat whenever she was around. Mary Jane would feign interest in them, she liked the attention, but McAllister knew she could care less. As for Reggie, if he really wanted to fly helicopters, he'd make a good soldier. McAllister knew that much about Reggie. What McAllister didn't realize, was how much he would miss his sister, once she returned to Boston.

In August, came Chicago and the Democratic National Convention. People like Mary Jane and her friends had gotten their heads and bodies pounded with night sticks by the Chicago police. McAllister hadn't known his sister was in Chicago until she told him sometime later. Mary Jane didn't get arrested, so their parents never knew. McAllister had only watched the drama on television, somewhat angry, mostly confused. It wasn't just black people now, raging through the streets of America, it was white people, too. It wasn't solely the nightly television scenes of soldiers shooting guns and carrying the wounded on stretchers, fighting the Communists. It was broken glass and fires in the United States. Sean McAllister didn't know how he felt, everything was coming so fast. Chicago was a turning point, but which way to turn. The footage and feelings about the Vietnam War were troubling his world, as he made his way to college in Washington, D.C.

McAllister could not have made a better choice, although he had no idea at the time. In 1968, if it was the politics of the United States government and its national impact you wanted to be around, step right up. Perhaps other locales like UC Berkeley or Madison, Wisconsin would be a close second or third. But unlike those towns, all the really heavy hitters were here, right down the street in Washington D.C. This was Sean McAllister's new home, the center of the American political universe.

The nation's capitol had its own particular billboards. They were made of smooth white stone, large monoliths of pillar and history, august and severe in their presence, expressive of certainty and power. Washington was a city trimmed with bordered reflecting pools, cherry trees that blushed in spring, the Potomac River flowing peacefully through its domain. In the daytime, the city ran with the hum and discourse of doing America's business, its institutions working with a machine-like presence and decorum. Washington D.C. conveyed a forceful and encompassing first impression of American strength.

What one couldn't see was the cover of hypocrisy that hid underneath. In the underground bowels and secretive back rooms of its fortified structures, in the K Street offices linked to Wall Street lobbyists, or the kitchens and porticos of cocktail gatherings in Georgetown homes or Virginia estates, the real business of the United States was being delivered and done. The arrogance and influence of American policy was shaped and polished in places no pedestrian tourist was ever invited to visit. Like the imperceptible bass line of a popular song, it was present, but hidden, and rarely ever heard.

Within this milieu of the nation's capitol, Sean McAllister began to learn many things. He learned the basics of constitutional government, the history of how ancient civilizations rose and fell. He learned how to do research and write long papers. He read important American literature, discerning the authors' symbolic expressions of human behavior. He delved into theology and philosophy, encouraged to understand the thoughts of famous men and women regarding the human condition. Within this context of his campus life, he became exposed to the wider array of socio-political issues facing both America, as well as the university of which he was engaged. He wasn't in Berkeley or Madison. He wasn't in New York, Boston, or San Francisco. He wasn't in Chicago. But he was close to the pulse that beat cold and constant on each end of Pennsylvania Avenue in Washington, D.C.

He learned other things as well. How young men like himself could be so different in their personalities and priorities in daily life. He met straight-laced Jesuit prep boys from places like Cincinnati, or hardened public school boys from throughout the Northeast. He learned how to drink beer by the bucketful. He inhaled Mexican dirt weed, laughing at the silliest things, while devouring a package of cookies in no time flat. His curly brown hair grew longer. He learned how to study all night, drinking instant coffee until his stomach cut inside him, meeting last minute deadlines or cramming for a final exam. He spent hours playing stupid board games in the dormitory lounge, reading Zap comics, or listening to music he had never heard before. He learned how faculty and Jesuit administrators, the supposed beacons of adult authority, had strange personal lives, including secret sexual inclinations of which no one openly spoke.

In addition, he learned how to meet women without knowing them first. He learned how to overcome the worry of putting his own self-doubts on the line, how to overcome rejection and stay intact. He began to learn that first impressions of beauty and attractiveness sometimes left a lot to be desired.

He learned all these things, all this new information and input of a college and individual life, an understanding of a larger world while coming of age. Still, there was one thing he could not learn along the tree-lined walkways and safe stone edifices of an academic world. He could not learn war. He could not learn how to overcome the fear of death, the heaviest absolute in the history of man. This was something you could not learn in school, or ever be taught to comprehend.

The coffee brown station wagon rolled up the New Jersey Turnpike heading north, McAllister behind the wheel. The August sky was heavily overcast, the temperature outside seasonally cool. The weather was atypical for this time of year. It wouldn't have been a good day at the beach, but that was just as well. Unlike most weekends when McAllister didn't have to work, the beaches of southern Delaware or New Jersey would not be his destination today. On the bench seat beside him was a thermos of coffee and a much needed map. He and his two passengers would head up the turnpike. Somewhere short of New York City they would cut off and steer northwest, finding their way near where the borders of New Jersey, Pennsylvania and New York appeared to meet.

Sitting next to McAllister, a wiry black-bush of hair on his head and face, his arms covered in the same, Snark Rosenbloom, the hairiest man alive. If you had asked McAllister twenty-four hours earlier if he would be running this car on the turnpike this morning, with Snark Rosenbloom by this side, the answer would have been a definite negative. McAllister had never really cared for Steve Rosenbloom. Snark was a munchkin Jewish guy who only stopped talking when he had to take a breath. He was a motor mouth, a guy that didn't fit. The kind of guy that seemed to be around all the time, but was nobody's real friend.

But that was the Snark. Steve Rosenbloom could appear out of nowhere, whenever something was up. He had a way of inviting himself to any event or gathering of the boys. By virtue of some scientific law regarding consistent proximity, Snark was part of the greater group. In other words, you couldn't get rid of the guy. If something was happening, Snark always was able to suddenly appear, but nobody was sure how he ever got the word.

Yet on this Saturday morning in August, Snark Rosenbloom was becoming a blessing in disguise. The radio didn't work in the car, and if McAllister's right ear could hold up without getting paralyzed, at least he had someone to listen to. As far as the other passenger was concerned, that big slug lying in the back seat of the car, well, he wouldn't be any help. Mike Taylor, nicknamed the Bruiser, was already laying his lineman-sized frame across the seat, snoring away. McAllister and Bruiser went way back to the neighborhood. Back to the days of front yard football games on the McAllister's lawn, where the Bruise had graduated from innocently breaking everybody's new Christmas toy on day number one, to later breaking your bones whenever he tackled you. However, when it came to the Bruise, there was never any purposeful intent. He was more like the Lennie character in Steinbeck's *Of Mice and Men*. The guy just didn't know his own strength.

No, Snark and Bruiser were unlikely candidates for this trip, but Sean McAllister didn't have a choice. He had wanted to get a couple of other buddies to go, but they had bailed on him weeks before, and

McAllister didn't want to make this trip alone. In fact, he had pretty much given up on the journey. When he made one final casting call at a summer party the previous night, Bruiser had said 'what the hell', and the Snark had immediately jumped in with both feet. So here they were, dodging traffic on a Saturday morning, the Bruise comfortably in dreamland, and the Snark waiting on any topic to expound upon. Meanwhile, the destination itself remained as uncertain as this trio of travelers coming together.

Talk about two diametrically opposed personas. Snark was a walking-talking book of knowledge on history and current events. He was like boiling water over a pot. Bruiser was deeper and slow, with a simplicity and common sense it was good to have along. Throw in the added dimension that Bruiser was one big dude, and he was the kind of friend it never hurt to have by your side. Providing of course, that you could wake him up in time to save your ass.

When McAllister finally got a word in edgewise with the Snark, he briefly mentioned his first year in Washington D.C. That was all the Snark needed to hear. He was off to the races. McAllister unconsciously took his index finger, clearing an eardrum.

Snark began with the outcome of World War II, and how the victory over the Nazis and the Japanese had put the United States on a whole new agenda. Fear of communism as a serious threat to democracy had become the primary matter at hand. According to Snark, this fear dovetailed perfectly with the corporate arms machine that had been built up to fight that war. The munitions and armaments industry needed a way to sustain itself. As a result, an American foreign policy that was in concert with that need was just the right prescription. The United States would continue to build its defenses against threats to its national safety, both external and internal in source.

But winning sometimes has unintended consequences. Being the big stick on the block means having to worry about keeping and protecting the big stick. Constitutional liberties at home needed to be put aside, when challenged by the fears of nuclear war and government socialism. Such threats require an internal authoritarianism demanding loyalty to the cause. Public displays of treason against the republic would be handy tools for the job. So cue up Senator Joe McCarthy and the House Committee on Un-American Activities, where blacklisting and other nefarious devices could offer necessary constraint.

The only wild card, Snark explained, that might derail this plan would be a struggling American economy. And the blue-plate special to keep that concern from happening was one thing, and one thing only. Oil and gas. Oil and gas had become the nectar of the gods in the second half of the twentieth century. As long as the United States could control the countries that had this resource, and control them before they could ever control themselves, the American economy would grow. It would keep money in people's pockets. It would keep jobs in the cities and farmlands of America. Everyone would prosper. At least everyone who was white. As for the niggers, well, they would perform the dirty work no one else wanted to do. According to Snark, this was the perfect imperial scenario.

To keep the operation going, it was paramount to maintain the people's fear of ultimate death and destruction. This was an ancient yet proven modus operandi. Still, you needed to cut everybody a small piece of the pie. To insure their silence and passivity, you needed to keep them believing that things were getting better than before, that opportunity and prosperity would always be at their doorstep. And you needed to give it a name. So why not call it the 'American Dream', that's a catchy appellation. But in the end, cheap energy would be the meal ticket to success, allowing the big boys to carve off most of the spoils.

This is damn good, McAllister thought. Snark is on a roll, the miles are clicking off down the road, and Bruiser is probably dreaming about some ex-cheerleader he met at a fraternity party. The big lug remained prone in the back of the car, snoring away. Snark even quoted President Eisenhower during his farewell Presidential address in January of 1961.

> "In the councils of government, we must guard against the acquisition of unwarranted influence, whether sought or unsought, by the military-industrial establishment. The potential for the disastrous rise of misplaced power exists and will persist. We must never let the weight of this combination endanger our liberties or democratic processes. We should take nothing for granted. Only an alert and knowledgeable citizenry can compel the proper meshing of the huge industrial and military machinery of defense with our peaceful methods and goals, so that security and liberty may prosper together."

Ike was a little late with that advice, Snark complained, since he was conveniently leaving office at the time. Eisenhower had spent the eight years of his two Presidential terms keeping the Red Scare alive, holding the United States in Korea long term, and had begun to finance and prop up an anti-communist regime in Indochina. The French colonialists were only too happy to let the United States hold the Asian line, Snark said, and they booked it fast. The results were becoming a grand design to engender a new American destiny, to make the world safe for democracy. It was imperative to keep those Commie dominoes from falling, for at least as long as cheap tungsten and rubber were available.

McAllister couldn't believe the Snark. He knew Steve Rosenbloom was a history major, and could stick his head in a book like no one else. That is, whenever he wasn't talking in between. But for now, the Snark was on a run.

"Snark, you got a photographic memory or what? You're unbelievable, man."

"Yeah, I do," Snark answered. "You didn't know that."

Before McAllister could respond, Snark returned to his Saturday morning treatise.

Of course the Beats were hip to the whole thing in the fifties, Snark continued. But their opposition was more emotional and personal in nature. Their criticisms were focused on the rigid social structures and homophobia of the American state of mind. The Beats were mainly writers, musicians, and artists. They were old enough to have experienced and understood the Red Scare tactics and propaganda of the late forties and early fifties, the hysteria of the McCarthy era. A hell of a lot of talented thoughtful Americans had lost their careers and personal self-respect as a result of lies and half-truths during the witch hunts of that period. And it was really a time not so long ago.

The Beats were the vanguard of the hippies. They traveled by rail and hitchhiked like Kerouac. They rebelled against the values of materialism, lock-step patriotism, the empty sameness of this so-called American Dream. They desired to keep some sort of expressiveness in culture alive. But for most of them, politics really wasn't their thing.

Snark went on. With the onset of the Free Speech Movement at the University of California in Berkeley, a new political movement was beginning to form. It picked up on the civil rights movement already underway in the South. The FSM fought to bring political advocacy and protest onto the college campuses, opening the American university system toward becoming a more progressive force. No longer would the colleges be simply a knowledge and research factory for the government and corporate America. Serious issues of inequality and government policy would be discussed and challenged in an open forum by the youth of America. The post-war youth of this country wanted a voice. The authority of an imperial and reactionary governance would continue to be challenged.

This movement picked up quickly across campuses throughout the country. In 1964, when President Lyndon Johnson used the phony Gulf of Tonkin incident to escalate US military aggression towards a full-fledged war effort in Vietnam, the protests grew. Subsequently, the last few years had been a constant battle against this machine and power of state; the military draft, civil rights, nuclear proliferation issues, the murders of Martin Luther King and Bobby Kennedy, and recently last summer the police riots in Chicago.

"The shit just keeps going," Snark muttered with distaste.

"Geez, Snark, you should be a history professor or something," McAllister interjected.

"Not much else a history major can become," Snark answered. "At least the draft can't get me for awhile."

Yeah, the draft, McAllister thought to himself. For the time being, going back to school was a darn good proposition. And he hadn't thought otherwise. Still, a lot of guys his age didn't have that luxury. A lot of guys were either ready to join up and fight against the Commies, or they were somewhere between a rock and a hard spot. He thought about Mary Jane, what she had told him over a year ago, and continued to say whenever she came home. Stay in school, little brother. Maybe having an older sister wasn't such a bad thing after all.

McAllister pulled the car off the turnpike to get some gas. After Snark's soliloquy, he felt a measure of guilt filling the tank. But hell, they weren't going to get to their destination hiking the rest of the way. Bruiser woke up, and all three men took a turn at the station restroom. After driving over to a grocery store to get more coffee and food, McAllister studied the map. He decided to take the next exit at New Brunswick, before working their way north and west.

"How much further do we have to go?" Bruiser asked.

"I'm not sure," McAllister answered, "maybe a couple hours or more."

"Do you really think we'll get in?" Bruiser continued.

"I don't know, Bruise. But we're giving it a shot. If we don't, well shit, at least we tried."

"We'll get in," Snark said firmly. "We'll get in. I got a good feeling." McAllister fired up the station wagon, steering out of the parking lot, back on the road. The sky remained gray and overcast, but no rain fell. For McAllister, getting to their destination mattered a lot, although he quietly feared the outcome might be in vain. Still, taking this chance was far better than another weekend at the beach. As much as he loved the ocean, the warm sand and water, the body surfing and boating, lately the whole scene with some of his old buddies was growing old. The trips to the shore had become more like a repetitive fraternity party, with the same jokes and cut ups, the same games of football on the beach, the same evening rides to Ocean City to goggle at the girls. He longed for something new and fresh, other adventures to stimulate his life. And this had been a trip he hadn't planned to miss. He put gas to the accelerator, settling back into the drive. "So, tell me more, Snark, you're like a walking encyclopedia on this stuff."

"What stuff?" Bruiser grunted, sipping his coffee. "Snark, are you making speeches again?"

"Uh oh, another country heard from," McAllister cracked. "Careful, Snark, you wouldn't want to put too much pressure on the Bruiser's brain. It's a small and delicate thing."

"Chuck you, Farley," Bruiser croaked. "Last night, Mac, you were practically begging me to come along on this trip, this drive to nowhere it sure looks like to me. Now, you're kicking my ass."

"It's all right, Bruise," Snark said. "We're just talking politics, that's all."

"You mean, you're talking politics," Bruiser retorted. "You're always talking politics, Snark. History and shit. And Mac's only listening because the radio never works in this piece of tin. Ain't that right, Mac?"

McAllister laughed. "Come on, Bruise. Snark knows more about history than both of us put together. He graduated with honors and stuff. "Capitalism, Snark, tell me about capitalism? Inquiring minds like me and Bruise want to know." Bruiser only grunted, peering out the window at the flattened fields and mixed woodlands of central New Jersey passing along.

Capitalism was dead, Snark began. Capitalism was just a tool now, a tool of the rich. The game was over, really. As Eugene McCarthy and many others had reminded, 70 percent of the wealth of America was now owned by 10 percent of the population. So do the math. That meant 90 percent of the American population was struggling over the remaining 30 percent. And it will only get worse, Snark cautioned, as time goes by. Capitalism by its nature eventually has winners. And once the winners have won, they're not about to give it up. But they'll surely keep feeding you this garbage that there remains a free enterprise system alive and well in this country. Yeah, it's alive and well all right, alive and well for them no doubt.

Sure, there will always be a few entrepreneurs that create new products that Americans will want to consume, or devising new technologies that will become commercially successful. But they are just the wild cards in the deck. And their success works, because the big boys can point to it and say looky here, a self-made man, a rags to riches story. Didn't we tell you the American ethic of hard work and sacrifice is alive and well, that it can happen for you. Sure, it can happen for you, but the actual chances of it happening are maybe like one in a million. So all the big boys really need to do is just keep the dream alive. Keep you thinking you might be that special one in a million. But don't be fooled, the game is really over for most of America.

And don't think for a moment that those one in a million guys, once they got a bigger piece of the pie, are going to behave any different. Greed is an insidious element of the human condition, even for a guy with twenty bucks in his pocket. The concept of 'enough' becomes a relative variable. It slowly starts growing along with a perception of 'need'. It grows to the point where you need a million dollars just to be safe and whole, and not run out. Sure, maybe you give some away, and it makes you feel better, but you're going to keep most of it for the kids and the rest of the family. It's just good old basic human nature, that's all it is.

The problem is the real 'greed merchants'. They can't stop themselves once it gets in their blood. It's like a drug. They will kill every buffalo because it's there to shoot. They will cut every tree because it's there to cut. The *Treasure of Sierra Madre* is like the best 'greed' film ever made. Humphrey Bogart was awesome in the movie, and John Huston was equally as great, but it was the guy that wrote the book that really nailed the story. He used a pseudonym named B. Traven, and he was a

German adventurer and writer they say. But no one ever really knew who he was. Still, both the book and movie illustrate the inherent flaw in capitalism. It begins and ends with the letters G-R-E-E-D.

"So my chances of getting rich are like my chances of hitting a Nolan Ryan fastball," McAllister mused. "That would be like a million to one, no question there."

Bruiser cracked up on that remark. Snark just looked perplexed. "Leave it to you, Mac, to look at things that way," Bruiser said. "Hell, I wouldn't even get in the batter's box against that guy."

"That's what I mean, Bruise. No fucking way." Snark inhaled a little extra oxygen and continued onward.

So America, despite what you might be told, is not a democracy, at least not an economic one. The country is slowly and surely becoming a plutocracy, a government of the wealthy. It's not quite there yet, but it's on its way. And that's only because there is still enough wealth available for a middle class to exist. As long as a significant majority of Americans have more than they had before, then a democratic political reality will continue to operate, or at least a semblance of one. And thanks to leaders like Franklin Roosevelt and others, some of that wealth is being dragged down through taxes to keep things going.

You would think that the wealthy would be happy to pay taxes, to keep the capitalistic ruse alive. But no, they aren't happy, not one bit. Instead they whine and complain. Like I said before, they got all these symbolic tools at their disposal. They got words like patriotism, the land of the free and the home of the brave. They got a Protestant religious ethic like Calvinism, where material success looks good in the eyes of God. They got the Communists infiltrating your neighborhood. They got the crackers hating the niggers, the niggers hating the spicks, the whops hating the micks and vice versa. They got everybody hating the kikes, the japs and the camel jockeys, even the goddamn French. You'd think they would have enough. But no, they aren't feeling so good. They want to have it all. The treasure, they've got to have all the treasure.

And now these hippies and long-haired anti-war types are causing a ruckus with their protests and new ideas. The sticky problem here is that these kids are predominantly white. So the big boys got to say to themselves, we better be careful with this one. We need to add a few more diversions to keep the lid on. How about we plot the old versus the young, the working-class versus the college student, the parents against their own kids. We'll make the social welfare system seem like the bad guy, when it really should be the good guy. No doubt about it, they have raised treachery to the highest form of art.

One of these days they will go too far. They will run out of wars to fight, and the resources to run them. The middle class will go bankrupt, and the government will have become so strangely perverse under their influence that all hell will break loose. But ironically, the government will not have been the enemy. The real enemy will always be those 'greed merchants' who just had to have it all.

"Damn, Snark, I think you've had enough coffee for one day," McAllister ventured. "What do you think, Bruise, did you get all that?" McAllister turned his head toward the back seat, giving a quick look to Bruiser. Bruiser's face was expressionless, like he was lost in a strange neighborhood, and had no idea where he might be. That really wasn't unusual for the Bruise, but this countenance was longer and deeper. "Snark, snap your fingers at him. I think we got overload," McAllister laughed.

Snark turned, snapping his fingers twice in front of Bruiser's face. Bruiser's expression changed, coming out of the trance. "What….? You fuckers," he rasped. "Suck my ass. I was…, I was just thinking about something else."

"I hypnotized you, Bruise," Snark cried. "I did. I hypnotized you."

"Snark, you hairy little fuckhead. You and your crazy shit."

McAllister howled, trying to keep his eyes on the road. But as the hilarity died down, a long pause ensued. Some road trip fatigue was beginning to settle. Bruiser sank back in his seat, closing his eyes. Snark sat quietly still for a time, sipping his coffee.

"So have you seen the movie Easy Rider?" Snark asked.

"No, Snark. Have you? I heard about it, though. Is it good?"

"Oh yeah. I went up and saw it in Philly last week. It's great, especially the music. Bummer ending, though."

"Well, don't tell me too much about it. Something tells me you could probably repeat the whole movie line by line."

"Hey, let me tell you about one part of it okay?" Snark asked. "This one particular scene kind of fits what I've been talking about."

"Okay, just as long as you don't give away the story."

"I won't, I'll just tell you this part. So Captain America, that's Peter Fonda, and his buddy whose name is Billy, are riding their motorcycles to New Orleans for Mardi Gras. Anyway, they are riding through the south somewhere, and they come up on this town that is having a parade. So they kind of wheel into the parade with their bikes, having a laugh. But the redneck cops don't like their long hair and what they're doing in the parade, so they bust them for disturbing the peace and throw them in the city jail."

"So there they are, locked up in the slammer. But in the cell next to them is some guy lying in a bunk, sleeping off an all night drunk. When the guy wakes up, one of the jail guards comes by and talks to the man real nice, bringing him a cup of coffee. Anyway, Billy can't figure this whole thing out, but this guy must be okay with the cops, so maybe he can help them get out of their jam."

"Turns out this guy, George is his name, not only knows all the cops, but he is a lawyer, too. So George helps them to get cut loose later that morning. Peter Fonda appreciates what George did for he and Billy, so he asks George if he wants to ride along with them to Mardi Gras. At first, George says no, but then he figures why not, he's never been to Mardi Gras. So the guy climbs on the back of Peter Fonda's bike and off they go."

"Anyway, they're going along, camping out at night and stuff, and George is just this really funny dude. On the second day or so, they are getting real close to New Orleans. They stop in this hick southern town in Louisiana, where they enter this little restaurant to get something to eat. But with their long hair and hippie clothing nobody will serve them. Anyway, to make a long story short, there is a cop and three rednecks in a nearby booth, talking loud enough so the guys can hear them. They keep calling them fags and stuff, you know, like the racial slurs I was talking about a little while ago. I'm not going to tell you all that happens, but the guys eventually get the message and split the restaurant."

"Later, they are just sitting around the fire, camping out again, and Billy says something bad about the rednecks, how those rednecks are scared of them and such. But George says no, they aren't scared of you, they're scared of what you represent. Billy doesn't really understand what George is getting at, and he says something like all we represent to them is somebody who needs a haircut. But George corrects him. He tells Billy that what Billy really represents to them is freedom. Billy is a little confused at this remark. But freedom, Billy asks, that's what it is all about, right?"

"And then George says, yeah that's what it's all about. But talking about freedom, and really being free are two different things. However, George cautions Billy, reminding him that he better not start telling those rednecks they ain't free, because that's when they will start beating the shit out of you, just to prove they are. Those kind of people will talk to you all day long about being free, George says, but when they see a truly free individual, it scares the shit out of them."

"So Billy thinks about that for a minute, and then he says something like, it sure don't make them runnin' scared."

"No, it don't, George agrees. It only makes them dangerous."

At that point, Snark ended his recollection. McAllister didn't respond right away. Boy, that was good, he thought to himself, good enough to want to see the movie as soon as he could.

"I'm not going to tell you anymore," Snark followed, "I don't want to spoil it for you. But it's just like what I was talking about before. About this whole freedom and liberty thing they sell in this country. It's like a black slave reading the Declaration of Independence. It sounds really good, just don't try to live it. Or maybe some poor Vietnamese cat living in South Vietnam, surrounded by a bunch of white faces telling him they are making his world safe for democracy. But first, they've got to burn down his village and destroy his crops. Trust us, they tell him, we're in your corner on this democracy and freedom thing. We're here to help you be free like us. Fucking bullshit is what it is, just a bunch of fucking bullshit words."

McAllister kept driving. Snark was done for awhile. He laid his head against the car window and closed his eyes. If Bruiser was listening, he didn't let on. For McAllister, it was like Snark had taken him on this weird political journey of sorts, painting another picture of America he was trying to understand. It was like all the bits and pieces were finally falling together, but in a way he would have to think more about, to try and get clear in his mind. He had exited the Jersey Turnpike sometime back, wandering northwest through upstate New Jersey. Pretty soon they would be in the neighborhood. He sure hoped they could pull off the mission ahead.

The August sky remained gray, static, as if the weather was at rest for a day, before moving out to sea. The journey reached the border junction of three states, New Jersey, New York, and Pennsylvania. At Port Jervis, the station wagon crossed the Delaware River into New York. At a turnout on the road, McAllister pulled over and stopped the car. Snark and Bruiser came alive. McAllister spread the map onto the hood of the car. The trio huddled together as McAllister pointed to a spot.

"I think we are here," McAllister said. "We will head up this way to Highway 17, then out toward Monticello. At that point, I think we are close."

"But hey, Mac, the town of Woodstock is further north up there," Bruiser questioned, putting his finger to a place away from where McAllister had drawn his route.

"It's not really at the town of Woodstock," Snark corrected. "They had to move the site. I think Sean is right, it's more like where he says."

"That's what I was told," McAllister returned. "When we get up to Highway 17, we can stop and ask someone. They showed Highway 17 on the news the other night. The road was jammed with cars everywhere. Let's go that direction for now, and see what happens."

Their route picked up Highway 17 at a town called Wurstboro, turning due west toward Monticello. Closing in over a ridge on the highway, suddenly the traffic slowed to a crawl as if an accident was ahead. Then, along the shoulders of the highway, as well as the green median strip between them, appeared multitudes of parked vehicles stretching as far as the eyes could see. There must have been thousands of vehicles, most deserted and left behind. For a time, McAllister idled the car slowly ahead, bumper to bumper, excited by the incredible scene.

Snark rolled down his window, asking someone how they could get to the site, how far away. It was still miles away they were told, and probably no chance they could get there going this direction. McAllister felt a sense of desperation, the nervous anticipation of missing out on something big. He pulled the car into an open spot on the median strip, checking his map. Then, turning the car back onto the highway, he headed back the way they had come.

"We've got to try another way."

"Mac, I don't think we can get there, man," Bruiser worried. "This is unbelievable. I've never seen such a mess. What are we going to do?"

"I want to give it one more shot, Bruise," McAllister answered. "We'll circle back from the south. If we can't get close from there, I guess we're screwed."

As the travelers returned back by the route they had come, McAllister began to feel the anxiety and fatigue of a wasted trip. But they still had a little time, it was only pushing mid-afternoon. Driving all the way back to Port Jervis, he picked up a road that snaked along the Delaware River. There was very little traffic on this road, but the drive remained many miles south of their intended destination. Reaching another highway junction, they turned due north away from the river. The road would come out somewhere west of Monticello if they could possibly get that far.

After another rush of anxious miles, the woodlands of the country pressed right to the side of the road. But looming in the distance before them, McAllister saw other vehicles halted on the highway, blocked by the blinking lights of a police car. His stomach sank. Slowing the car down, he pulled along the narrow gravel shoulder flanked by the trees. It was indeed a roadblock, about a half mile ahead. He could see the policeman standing by a stopped vehicle, a line of other cars behind. The station wagon idled as the men watched the first car back up, before turning around in their direction. It appeared to be a hopeless situation. McAllister moved the car slowly along the shoulder, expecting the worst. As the first car passed them by, he watched as the policeman repeated his movements with the next car in line.

Then something caught McAllister's eye. Just ahead, a narrow dirt road fell off to the right, turning into the trees. Moving forward, he kept his eyes on the cop, watching as the officer continued to converse with the next car in line, his attention diverted. Reaching the dirt road, McAllister slowly bumped the station wagon down and into the trees. Snark and Bruiser became alert and silent in there seats. The car bounced into the woods, the road rutted, trees limbs scratching against the doors. The road dropped in elevation down to a small creek, before veering left along its banks. McAllister continued to follow along.

If the road ended anytime soon, there might be no way to turn around. He kept moving forward, everyone tensely silent but for the whacking of the brush against the car. At this point, McAllister had stopped hoping for getting to a concert. Instead, he began wishing for an open space where he could gratefully give up this adventure and still get home. But shortly, the trees began to give way to an open meadow, and he felt himself able to breath. The narrow road began to vanish into the field, which was pocked with large rocks half in the ground.

Taking one last shot, McAllister turned the car up the incline of the meadow. He careened the wagon slowly around and over the stones, trying to keep speed as the car climbed upward across the field. Finally, the car bounced over one last hump at the edge of the highway, the hood and front wheels of the vehicle nosing onto the asphalt.

McAllister looked left down along the road. Holy shit, they were behind the roadblock. He could see the cop at the roadblock, looking the other way. Quickly pressing down on the accelerator, the car jolted onto the pavement, before righting itself and speeding down the road. Snark let out a yell as he and Bruiser looked through the back window of the station wagon, watching the cop. McAllister peeked into the side view mirror as he floored the vehicle, trying to get away. As the car sped around a slight curve, they were out of sight. Still, he kept his foot on the pedal, moving fast. The road was empty, not a vehicle to be seen. The station wagon raced down the asphalt, as everyone looked behind. No one appeared to have seen them.

McAllister exhaled. "Fuckin A, man. I can't believe it." He looked over at Snark Rosenbloom. Snark appeared as if he was levitating in air, looking down on McAllister, wearing a wide-eyed grin.

"You did it, Sean. You got behind them. I told you we would make it. I knew we would. We're going to fucking Woodstock."

McAllister just smiled, shaking his head, the car flying further down the road. He couldn't see Bruiser, but the Bruise was more than likely speechless again, a dumbfounded look upon his big round face. Then, McAllister felt the warm firm grasp of a large hand press upon his shoulder. It remained there for a moment, strong in its grip. "Fuck you, Mac," a voice exclaimed. "Fuck you, you lucky son of a bitch."

McAllister nodded up and down, full of affirmation. "I think we're going to make it, Bruise. I think we are going to crash the show."

Ramparts Magazine, that's where McAllister had seen it a month or two before, a single column advertisement for the festival. Three Days of Peace and Music it read, with a lineup of bands and musicians it was difficult to believe could be in one place at any one time.

But hell, the damn concert was somewhere in upstate New York. Meanwhile, he had been working five days a week doing road construction. Every day was spent setting up and breaking down forms, pounding long rusty spikes with a sledgehammer, shoveling and spreading heavy concrete coming out of a chute. Every day his feet were chafed red from rubber boots heavy with mud, his hands nicked and bleeding, dry as a bone. So whenever Friday came, he did what he always did this time of year. He headed for the shore. He'd lie on a hot summer beach full of sand and sun, or body surf like an arrow through rolling Atlantic breakers. He'd hang with his buddies on warm delicious boardwalk nights, watch giggling exotic college girls walking by, a perfect elixir for the weekdays in between.

Still, as time went by, he'd begun to feel like he was missing something, something he wanted to be part of, feeling left behind. He had mentioned the concert, but nobody wanted to go. Nobody wanted to break the constant summer routine. As a result, his desire began to wane. He had given it up, letting the adventure fade from his mind.

Until he'd watched the news on television, seeing thousands and thousands right where he wanted to be, descending upon and becoming what he had so much wished to encounter. A hair went up his ass. In a last minute comeback, there's always the Bruiser, the one guy who lacked any understanding of future orientation, the one guy who lived completely in the moment, if not by choice. In other words, the Bruise didn't have any plans. And of course, the Snark, that hairy little Jewish political genius, with a photographic memory and no real friends. Well, Snark certainly had a friend now, McAllister agreed. Sometimes you just don't know who they are until they are chosen, and McAllister was happy to oblige. If there is one thing instilled from his Irish mother, you're loyal to those who are loyal to the cause. Today, the Snark was definitely in, and in tight.

Some miles ahead, the road was fully closed, but who the hell cared. Hundreds of cars and other modes of transportation were scattered everywhere along the roadway, or parked upon the adjoining stubbled hayfields that stretched beyond. The men parked the car in an open spot, got out and stretched. To the west lay another dirt road with open meadows on either side. Tents and makeshift camping areas spread into the distance. Snark found out quickly they still had a couple miles to go. But it would be an easy hike forward into the fading afternoon sky. The trio quickly figured what baggage they could carry, sleeping bags, a ground cover, coats, some water, and a little bit of food. McAllister opened the spare tire compartment, fishing out a single bottle of wine and a small bag of pot that Snark had been able to provide. He locked the car and the pilgrimage began.

And such a strange pilgrimage it would become, a veritable city of hippies everywhere as they hiked on down the road. Men were laughing or yelling, selling pot, or asking for drugs and booze. Others simply hung around their campsites, intent with their own space and friends. There were vehicles of all shapes and creations, flying flags of peace. The scene looked like a refugee camp of thousands, scattered amidst the fields and pocketed groves of trees, everything outlined in shadowed form against the graying western sky.

Slowly, the campsites gave way to larger groups of people moving en masse one direction or another. In the distance, the tops of the speaker towers came into view. The men stopped for a moment, suddenly realizing they could lose each other in the swarming movement of the crowd. McAllister and Bruiser couldn't stay all day Sunday. They would have to return for work. Should anyone get separated, they would meet at three o'clock the following afternoon, back at the car. Snark would be on his own if he didn't show.

The mud grew softer, thick and heavy under their feet. Everyone had ankles and footwear splattered with its remains. The dusky sky hung on, the air cooling further as the evening grew close. Finally, they could see the reflected lights of the stage below, a hillside angling down in elevation. Over the bobbing heads of the crowd, one could catch glimpses of an expanse of humanity, spreading up from the stage like a wide sea of darkened forms. There would never be words to describe it. In this one single moment, Sean McAllister knew where he had come, seeing it with his own eyes. Woodstock.

Throughout their final approach, there had been no spoken announcements projecting from the stage, just the murmured hum of this human din, spiked by raised voices or cries in the sky. But then, the sound of several guitars began to tune, the occasional short rolls of a drummer, clear and distinct.

Slightly down from the crest of the hill, they could go no further. Seeing a vacant spot of flattened grassy mud, they asked the surrounding people if things were okay to settle there. Sure, no problem. The men spread their ground covers and put down their gear. Behind the towered speakers and lights of the stage, a thin slice of bluish sky wedged itself between the charcoal clouds and timbered distant hills to the west. Shortly, a loud amplified voice bellowed into the night. "Ladies and Gentlemen, please welcome, Canned Heat." Like a sudden gust of wind bracing throughout the valley, an incredible aural roar spread across the outlined hills of southern New York, and electric music rocked the fading sky.

Mountain, Grateful Dead, Credence Clearwater Revival, Janis Joplin, Sly and the Family Stone, The Who, all through the Saturday night. The bottle of wine, the pot, a trip to the sanitation cans ankle deep in muck. At times, people nodding off in restless moments during the early hours, as the music played on and on. Hours later, as the blackened sky gave way to the soft pale of a Sunday morning, a new dawn beginning to rise, Gracie Slick and the Jefferson Airplane.

They couldn't stay. The final scheduled acts would not begin until late on Sunday. The men made the long hike out, before driving down through the Delaware River Gap, south toward home.

Monday came early, to another day of work clothes and muddy boots, the smell and smoke of diesel trucks, the idle push of road graders, the pounding of sledgehammers in a labored August morning. Unbeknownst to Sean McAllister, several hundred miles away, in the discarded hills and dairy farms of where he had been, the searing screams of a black man's guitar bombed through the air. It was to become a foreboding national anthem of protest and change for America, falling not only upon the remaining concert goers' ears. The anthem spread out across the hills of Bethel, New York, and further across the breadth of an American nation. A Woodstock Nation, its history complete.

CHAPTER THREE

RUNNIN' BLUE
Los Angeles, California / 1968 -1969

Jack Gruden hesitated before shutting off the engine to the car. He hoped it would start quickly the next time he turned the key. The starter bushings were worn. There was a chance the engine might not turn over right away, which would not be good today. Shifting his large frame in the driver's seat, he began to wait. His bushy reddish-blonde hair was tied back in a pony tail, his broad shoulders resting heavily against the front seat, his powerful legs cramped to the floorboard. Jack Gruden felt the obvious anxiety of his current mission, but there was no other recourse. It was something he had to do.

The early morning sun was low in the sky, its light shining through the gaps in the downtown buildings. Yet, the center city of Los Angeles was clearly awake, beginning another day of clamor in the daily drama of Southern California. Looking through the windshield, there was not a green growing thing in sight, only paved streets, parking meters, sidewalks, stucco glazed structures, all metal and glass. Downtown Los Angeles was modern man's testament to his triumph over nature, his control over the ground below. Jack Gruden was certain he would never return here, to this amplified volume of a city. One day he would seek a place where the land could breathe. It would not be today. But sometime in the future there would come a chance for his escape, away from this cement-hard reality he had lived most of his life.

Jack Gruden was taking steps, one at a time. With only a few more months of school at Cal Poly in San Luis Obispo, an animal husbandry degree in hand, he could begin to work his way out. Jack enjoyed working with animals and livestock. He was at his most comfortable with them, learning how to tend to their needs for nutrition, medication, and care. They allowed him a quiet communication and sense of control he didn't have with the others, the human kind. The life of people had always been a harder thing, a struggle he was challenged to endure. It was a rigorous responsibility put upon him, without the necessary tools to fix.

Jack Gruden could fix about anything. That is, just about anything that couldn't speak or find a way to hurt your feelings. His difficulties had started early, by a circumstance he could not control, the sudden death of his father. Jack had been six years old when the family tragedy struck. A terrible accident the electric company had reported, the power lines were supposed to have been shut down of current, but they weren't. In seconds, a man was left lifeless by this simple mistake. So simple, that the electrical problem could be easily repaired, the power turned on again. But for a small two-bedroom bungalow in the Gardena section of Los Angeles, the consequences were eternal. Forever is a long time, as long as memory allows it to last. Left behind was a working mother with two young boys, amid the painful loss of a man they would never see again. Jack Gruden had learned an early lesson in life. Things that appear simple are not often as they seem.

The stutter, the speech impediment as the doctor kindly gave it definition, took hold shortly thereafter. As hard as he tried, Jack Gruden could not spit them out. The words stuck, they fluttered, pounding against him time and again. Finally, he would push them through, but the damage was done. The results were understandable, the teasing, the embarrassment. He became a quiet child.

Fortunately for Jack, he had grown big and strong, imposing in his presence. At least his size was something to manage the consequences. He accepted becoming the big strong silent type, although he desired to say so much more. It was easier to stay mum, to learn and engage in things that did not require human interaction, to avoid the troubles his disability ordered upon him. The unspoken activities of mechanics and machines were a sanctuary, as well as surfing the constant waves of the Pacific Ocean. These were activities that did not oblige the dictates of conversation. And now, in college, he had found the lives of animals. They were carnal beings who could hear his broken words without judgment or some patient kind of sympathy. These near speechless vocations became his forte.

The wait was getting longer. Jack felt the outcome might not be as planned. His brother, Derrick Gruden, was somewhere upstairs in the building across the street. When Derrick returned to the car, Jack would drive them back to the house in Hermosa Beach. There, another car would be packed and ready. They would say their good-byes. Derrick would drive away to Toronto, Canada and a future unknown. That was the plan.

Still, today's outcome would be whatever it would be. Some things in life were not Jack's to decide. Even if he could speak to those things with an articulate eloquence, people would not understand. Derrick was his older brother, the daring and extravagant force that lived within him all the time. Derrick had been his childhood protector, the voice in his world of reluctance, his leader in times of crisis and personal decision, speaking the words that Jack could never convey.

Derrick had taken over the reins early on, stepping into the void when a family shattered by his father's death could have careened off the rails. Derrick had assumed the mantle, in ways even their mother could not foresee. He became the captain of the Gruden ship, and he steered it with words of direction and assurance both Jack and his mother were willing to accept. Desperation has a way of creating trust, an emotional loyalty, whether for good or bad, right or ill. In desperation, there is no analysis, no weighing of the pro or con. It becomes a patriotism of survival impossible to explain.

So you sit in a car, parked on the street across from the Los Angeles Army Induction Center, and you wait. You prepare for an unknown outcome. Derrick Gruden was joining the United States military this very morning, although it would not be for long. Whether it was today, or tomorrow, or the first opportunity, Derrick would go AWOL, away without leave. That was a fact. Derrick had not registered for the draft. When the Feds finally began to get close, he went to an attorney to discuss his options. Surprisingly, the attorney said the penalties for not registering were more serious than desertion from the army, but who would have thought. Consequently, somewhere in that building across the street, Derrick Gruden was stepping forward and taking an oath:

"I, Derrick James Gruden, do solemnly swear, that I will support and defend the Constitution of the United States against all enemies, foreign and domestic; that I will bear true faith and allegiance to the same; and that I will obey the orders of the President of the United States and the orders of the officers appointed over me, according to regulations and the Uniform Code of Military Justice. So help me God."

As far as Derrick Gruden was concerned, not a word of it was true, unless perchance God had something to say about it. And God wasn't talking. Following the oath, Derrick would look to escape from the line of men, ditch the building and jump in the car. Within hours they would be on the road to Canada.

The word 'they' did not include Jack Gruden. For sitting beside him in the front seat of the car, a beautiful young girl waited quietly, a two-month-old child held sleeping in her arms. Darla was the girl's first name. Jack Gruden didn't even know her last. Glancing at her, she seemed encased in a fathomless innocence that bore no comprehension of the circumstances that might be upon her. But Jack did not question her presence. Surely, Derrick could have left her and the baby at the house in Hermosa. But Derrick always had a reason for things, often unknown to Jack.

Jack did know that Darla was a Canadian. She had a dual citizenship, and it would make a difference when it came time to cross. She was less than a year out of high school, and now the young mother of his brother's child. Darla had moved into the Hermosa house to have the baby. Other people lived there as well, others that Derrick had found or recruited to join him in living together. Derrick had given the house a name, a funny name that Jack couldn't remember, but it was some kind of extended family, with Derrick as its leader. But Derrick, Darla, and their baby daughter, Jessica, would now be leaving, perhaps never to return.

Moments later, a young man, his long red hair catching the glint of the morning sun, stepped quickly out of the building. Catching sight of the car, he headed briskly into the street. Jack turned the key, feeling relief as the car roared to a start. Derrick Gruden threw open the back door, sliding inside, laying down on the floor boards out of sight. Jack quickly pulled the car into the traffic of a Los Angeles morning, motoring away.

Derrick Gruden's escape to Canada did not last long. Living a long frozen winter by a lake north of Toronto was not how Derrick Gruden saw his life becoming. By the following spring of 1969, the family slipped back into the United States. Jack Gruden finished school in San Luis Obispo. Through friends, Derrick and Jack found an old farm property in the coastal hills above Santa Cruz, California. The brothers changed their last name to Mulcahey, arranging a new identity. They started a garden and landscaping business in the local area. And Darla, pretending that her husband was missing, began to receive welfare from the state for her and the child.

For public consumption, Derrick James Gruden no longer existed. But Derrick Mulcahey would not hide away. He was accustomed to being a leader, of directing things the way he liked them to be. The family would build a self-sustaining farm under his tutelage. Jack would procure the animals and supplies, as well as fix the vehicles. He would become the family front man for whatever needed to be done. Much like the house in Hermosa Beach, others could come and stay, helping to work the land. Derrick gave the farm a name, Shamrock Ridge.

Derrick Mulcahey exhibited a confidence born out of tragedy, the demands of a childhood survival. The circumstances had brewed a fierce element of anger and resentment in Derrick, at a world that had taken his father so long ago. But Derrick had learned how to hold those feelings close to the vest. They would become a power he could use over others when necessity might demand. A power and influence both his brother, Jack, and his young wife Darla had come to know too well. One did not cross Derrick Mulcahey without a response.

The US government was another matter. They had a hammer Derrick Mulcahey did not possess. For Derrick, this called for a different type of survival, the cleverness of a fox. The FBI was out there somewhere. They might be clumsy, but not to be underestimated. Derrick Mulcahey was not a fool. He kept his own counsel, and his eyes peeled.

CHAPTER FOUR

MAGGIE'S FARM
Washington D.C. / November – December,1969

A FIERCE WIND WHIPPED THROUGH THE STREETS of the Capitol city. In the early darkness of a November afternoon, it wrestled the tree limbs along the banks of the Potomac River, scattering the last cover of dying wet leaves. Sideways rain pounded the pavement, glimmering in the reflection of wavering street lamps. The washing sound of passing tires splashed the deluge over concrete curbs, like ocean breakers attacking the beach. The wind's ferocity pushed human torsos backward against the onslaught, yanking umbrellas inside out. It chipped against raincoats, turning ungloved hands red with cold.

Climbing up the long narrow M Street steps above the Potomac, Sean McAllister and his friend, Chris Huggins, hustled toward higher ground. The two young men forged steadily forward, heads down, busy with getting home, seeking shelter from the storm. Amidst the swoon, a message was clear. Old Man Winter was now in power. He would be staying until the next election. No peep of human dissent would be tolerated, until a wishful American spring could muster the votes to overcome his reign.

The evening forecast: a time to sit in lighted dormitory rooms, the wind buffeting the window glass, reading the next assignment, or news of politics and sport. Perhaps one might lay a towel across the bottom of a doorway, smoke a bowl, listening to the wail of rock music hidden under ear phones. It was a time to drift away in reflective dreamy thought, while the storms of the world swirled outside.

Earlier in the day, McAllister and Huggins had witnessed Supreme Court Justice William O. Douglas. As part of their constitutional law class, they had taken the bus downtown to visit the Court in session. Sitting in the gallery of the large ornate hearing room, the Justices entered in their dark robes, the lawyers nervous, the argued case obscure. Douglas sat beside the other Justices, seemingly uninterested in the matter before him, busy with his own notes and thoughts. He asked only one question of the attorneys. But Douglas' presence had been riveting. This particular Justice overshadowed the rest. He gave the impression of an old hand, a man comfortable and detached, like any forty-year veteran of a career might seem. Douglas was an aging man now, it showed in his movements. Yet, his persona was unshaken, larger than life.

Washington D.C. was a place where noted political figures could be seen in the flesh. It was a town where familiar photographic or televised images were distilled into human shape and appearance, whether exiting a downtown restaurant, walking the street, or stepping out of a limo to enter a Georgetown home. The aura of their notoriety surrounded them, giving one pause. It was a unique dynamic to encounter, where imagined perceptions and everyday human reality crossed against themselves. These occasional sightings were not a conjured event staged for official presentation. Instead, they might be the singular happenstance of sharing a line in a corner grocery store on an early Sunday morning, an everyday human event.

A few weeks before, McAllister had stood behind Senator William Proxmire of Wisconsin. Dressed in jogging shorts and tennis shoes, Proxmire held a cup of coffee and a *Washington Post* in hand, waiting his turn to pay. There were no Secret Service men in dark glasses hiding in the candy aisle. There was no excited buzz in the room, no hushed voices, no autograph seekers pressing behind a cordoned security line. It was nothing more than the regular Sunday routine. Such occurrences made the nation's capitol an unusual place, a political Hollywood that was no big deal. Yet, soon enough, another major blockbuster was coming to town, not giving a hoot how famous or unknown one might be.

By Saturday morning, November 15th, the storms had given way to a clear angled autumn sun. The sky spread with an inspired pastel blue, sharpened by window frosted cold, crisp with glorious yellow light. McAllister dressed in his long johns, hooded sweatshirt and rugged pants. He tied back his shoulder length hair, lacing up his heavy soled boots. A navy surplus pea coat, a pair of smooth leather gloves and black beanie cap lay nearby on the dormitory bed. He took an old washcloth near the sink, rinsed it heavy with hot water, stuffing it into a plastic freezer bag, before placing the bag into the pocket of his coat. He would carry no wallet today, just his driver's license and a few bucks in hand. He considered taking the old battered construction helmet in his closet, but declined. The helmet wouldn't fit over his beanie cap, being just one more thing to carry along. He vaguely hoped that he wouldn't regret the decision.

On most Saturday mornings, the long dormitory hallway would be quiet with students sleeping late. But this was not a normal Saturday. Rumbling with activity, small groups of students began heading into the brightness of the morning sun. The campus stirred with anticipation, the human energy rising. McAllister and Huggins met in the hallway, exiting the building, walking toward a woman's dorm not far away. There, McAllister met his sister, Mary Jane, and several of her friends, who had driven down from Boston the night before. Banding together, they joined a growing exodus leaving the campus periphery. Deliberate with intent, the throng made its way through the tree-lined streets of Georgetown, towards the bus lines off Wisconsin Avenue, their destination today the center of the capitol city.

McAllister was pleased to have his sister by his side. Mary Jane put her arms around him, holding him close. He felt carefree and warm in her grasp, secure with a new sense of camaraderie they had never shared before. Today, he might get to be her protector, to show his brotherly love through his knowledge of the terrain, to make important decisions on her behalf. Striding along with her, a confidence grew inside him, the adventure beckoning. The morning blue spread forever brilliant in the sun. The colors and temperature of the streets buzzed with people and activity. There was nothing more to do but smile, feel good, take in the day.

To engage and share in something that matters has an addictive pull, closing the gap of separation in people's lives. It can soften the uncertainties of an individual existence, promote a sense of oneness, of being a part of something greater than yourself. McAllister had read about these things, but they don't hold water until you get to ride the wave. Woodstock had given him a taste, a morsel of the drug. He had felt the festival's attraction, and by force of his desire and the breaks of unintentional fortune, he had drunk from its well. At Woodstock he had only been an observer, the new kid on the block. Still, he had been allowed to feel a larger sense of belonging he had never known before.

The bus ride downtown was packed and chattering with citizens, heading for something important. There were people the age of his parents, families with young children, students and friends. It was a cross section of America, sharing a similar conviction and cause.

The city began to fill, from Virginia, Maryland, and many other states. Traffic slowed and many chose to disembark the buses. Thousands upon thousands were taking to the street, heading to the US Capitol for the beginning of the march. McAllister was not part of any one brigade. He watched as the large and well-known Yippie contingent formed nearby. He and Mary Jane breathed it all in, it didn't really matter who was where. The incredible numbers and exuberance of the crowd warmed the brisk November day. There were signs and flags representing multitudes of organizations against the war. People were dressed in costume, amidst shouts and chants throughout the crowd. Slowly, the human mass leaned forward, step by step toward the White House and Washington Monument, filled with an intoxicating sense of purpose as far as the eye could see.

The sweeping panorama of protest pressed together, moving along Pennsylvania Avenue, their signs held high, the colorful flags in perpetual wave. Chants and slogans combined in unison, drowning out the sounds of the city. Bystanders lined the street, as if watching a parade. Others hung from storied windows above, waving and cheering, as if the World Series had been won. As the wide corridor of human emotion pushed forward along the route, the police stood ready. Dressed in their white helmets and heavy black leather, they seemed quietly withdrawn against the peaceful spirit of the crowd, yet watchful for its intent.

The march grew more strident with each step toward the White House, the symbol of the Presidency, where the evil Richard Nixon sat fortressed in his lair. Nixon had earlier scoffed at the movement before him, vowing to ignore the protest by watching college football, content in his arrogance toward the forces that surrounded him. It didn't matter. He could not stop its coming. Despite his false public bravado, he was a man trapped in his own home on a lovely Saturday afternoon.

The march veered to the hardened grounds of the Washington Monument, swelling out like a congregation surrounding the pulpit, a church of American dissent. McAllister, Huggins, along with Mary Jane and her friends, broke off from the crowd, finding their way as close as possible to the front of the White House. They watched as a dedicated line of protesters filed past its gates, each stopping and shouting out the name of an American soldier dead from the Vietnam War, state by bloody state.

A month earlier, McAllister had carried a poster board sign, inscribed with the name of a deceased Delaware soldier, during a candlelight vigil to honor the dead. Anderson was the soldier's name. Sean McAllister did not know the young man in life, nor the circumstances of his untimely loss. He only knew Anderson in death, a statistic, an imagined finality. Somewhere back home in Delaware, a family grieved the loss of a son, perhaps a brother, or lover and friend. And yet, there was one thing certain about Anderson, as well as thousands of other young American men. For them, this blue cascade of autumn sky would never again be crossed.

Returning to the monument grounds, the speeches began, challenging the authority and overwhelming power of a government lost in its insolence and deceit. Each speaker unmasked the charade of Nixon's 'secret plan', opposing his vacuous policy of 'Vietnamization', his vapid phrases of 'peace with honor'. They challenged the 'silent majority' of America, whose support for the conflict continued to send their precious young sons home for burial. Equally, they suffered for the millions of Vietnamese civilians who had been killed by the bombs of war, or horribly burned by naplam and white phosphorus heat. These were human citizens of the world, who were witnessing their village homes destroyed, their culture eviscerated, all in the cause of a shallow propaganda perpetrated by fear.

As the mass gathering came to a close, John Lennon's message of hope, his elemental lyrics of aspiration, sang across a palette of white stone monuments and leaf fallen trees. Under a crisply bright afternoon sky, the words seemed to carry like a prayerful wind, over the bridges of the Potomac, out across the American continent. They carried over hills and farms, along dusty dirt roads, over mountains and desert canyons, to the shores of a western sea far beyond. With arms raised high, and palms outstretched, flowing to the rhythm of a half a million hearts, they sang. "All We Are Saying, Is Give Peace A Chance. All We Are Saying, Is Give Peace A Chance."

The main event was over, the sun beginning to trail in the mid afternoon. The many thousands, having made their statement against the Vietnam War and the social injustices of the time, began to disperse. With a deep sense of conviction, they would return to their homes and individual lives, strong in their beliefs of peace and non-violence, of the freedom of speech and assembly, certain in their growing cause against the policies of a government of which they were a part. They were happy with the outcome, with their togetherness of purpose on a sun-struck autumn day.

But the true heartbeat of America is a fierce and complicated pulse, as diverse in its myriad beliefs and behaviors as snowflakes in a winter sky. The dark and hidden forces that seek to control its destiny are forever constant, and never far away. These forces, confident and surreptitious, know time is on their side. Divide and conquer is their game plan, and they are purposeful in its execution. A half a million Americans on a Saturday afternoon are certainly a concern, but there is more than one way to skin a cat.

The American anti-war movement had been in a state of fracture for some time. For many, after Chicago and even before, the policies of peaceful protest and civil disobedience had given way to a deeper frustration and anger. The lack of results in stopping the war, of changing policy in the halls of national leadership was clearly apparent. A growing minority wanted to 'bring the war home' to the streets of America. Militant resistance was on the rise. Early in the summer of 1969, policy splits at the national convention of Students for a Democratic Society (SDS), had proven the divide. The trial of the Chicago Eight for conspiracy to disrupt across state lines, to violently riot at the 1968 Democratic National Convention was now underway.

Meanwhile, the powerful enforcers of government order were

not standing idly by. Nixon was in the White House, his crony John Mitchell at Justice. And arguably the most dangerous man in America, J. Edgar Hoover, controlled the levers of domestic intelligence. These men remained intent on destroying any opposition that might gain a stronghold of support.

And so the Yippies and other militant cadres were saying, 'not just yet'. Chicago was not going to be forgotten, not today. We are going to take over the strong arms of Justice, not tomorrow, not next week, but this very afternoon. The word went out amongst the dissolving mass of human persuasion. However, most would defer.

Mary Jane did not take up the cause. She had seen enough of what could happen. McAllister's sister and her friends would meet them later back on campus, planning to return to Boston on Sunday. But Sean McAllister had not been in Chicago. The adventure of seeing a street fight remained unknown to him. His dorm friend, Chris Huggins, had been more than ready, suggesting the packing of the washcloth in a plastic bag. Together, they joined the broken ragtag army of assault toward the Department of Justice, several blocks away.

Alongside the brownstone walls of America's great hall of order and control, the crowd got what they came for. The cops and civil defense units of the Washington metro police were armed and ready for a fight. Loud militant chants began, amidst the screams of 'off the pigs' crossing the void between the opposing forces. The angry crowd mobilized in front of the hulking structure. McAllister watched the firing of red paintballs against the building, streaking like tears down its side, the color of blood.

With that assault, the chase was on. Tear gas canisters coursed through the air, landing and whirling across the pavement, spewing the acrid cloud of their contents, like skidding little campfires rising into the sky. The protestors fell back, breaking into small groups away from the smoke, or grabbing the canisters, and with outstretched arms heaving them back the way they had come. But the troopers were masked, moving forward against the crowd.

McAllister felt the thrill of the danger, the sheer weighted power of force against the agitated crowd. He moved away from the spiraling gas, the washcloth in hand as necessary, quick on his feet to dart at any instant. Back and forth the battle surged in the blocks surrounding Justice, running away, then returning, as the cops surged in all directions.

There were probably a few arrests. But as the afternoon waned, the action became more of a dance than a fight, pushing one way, then another, short of direct engagement. There was no reason to get caught, unless one had a dying need to feel a stick on his head or spend a night in jail. Unlike Chicago, the metro police were in a primarily defensive mode, dispersing the crowd their singular intent. In time, the protest melted away, blending into the streets of the city. Another day of action in the nation's capitol had come to an end. It would be time for everybody to go home for dinner on a Saturday night. Or that's the way it felt, like actors on location, heading for their trailers after shooting a scene.

McAllister and Huggins rode the bus back to campus. They spent the evening drinking beer and eating pizza with Mary Jane and her friends, watching local television coverage of the demonstration in the student lounge. As he escorted his sister back to the women's dorm, they pondered whether the events of the day would make a difference in stopping the war. Had the enormity of the event changed anyone's mind? It was difficult to say.

Mary Jane was leaving in the morning. McAllister felt a truly special bond with his sister. They were now attached in a new and different way. The bond no longer had anything to do with their lives growing up together. It was now shorn of the patterns of big sister and little brother in a suburban world they were both leaving behind. He and Mary Jane had always been close, but a deeper relationship was forming. The best part of the day had been sharing these things with her.

As he lay in bed that night, arms folded behind his head, McAllister reflected on the events engaged upon only hours before. It wasn't so much the politics of the moment that amazed him. Sure, the purpose of the day was of great importance. He was part of an historic moment, alongside thousands of other Americans, protesting an inhumane policy of unjust killing and destruction in a world so far away. He felt morally and intellectually secure in his dissent. But more inviting was the drama of human theatre that played out in the streets of this capitol city on a resplendent November afternoon. It was the spirit, the energy, the actual events of life and adventure that stuck with him. There were the cinematic colors, the sounds and multitude of human expressions that ran like a movie beneath his weary eyes. That was the high, almost habitual in its sustenance. Woodstock had been overwhelming in its size, the character of its impact. But Woodstock lacked the contention of this recent afternoon, the emotion of battling an opponent that deserved to be vanquished. This was a different form of electricity, one he looked forward to feeling again.

The November 15, 1969 demonstration against the war came and went. The beauty and togetherness of that frosted clear-blue day, the peak of its abbreviated high, slowly sank against the ongoing conflict that would not end. The dark clouds that had given way for one moment in time, closed in upon the country. Nothing changed. It only got worse.

Within weeks, in Los Angeles, California, the investigation into the horrific Tate-LaBianca killings of the previous August had broken with the arrests of the Manson Family. The national horror at their murderous rampage inflicted a terrifying scar on a generation of young Americans, whose belief system spoke to a more humane and ethical world. The terror of such a hate-filled and demonic psychosis, masquerading behind the notions of freedom and love, mirrored the extremism of the time. The murders were as blatant and unforgivable as the Massacre at My Lai, the strafing of napalm and Agent Orange upon innocent civilians, the incessant bombing of North Vietnam. A dangerous rage was burning. A country was splitting apart within itself.

The peaceful summer interlude of a Woodstock Nation, its cultural reflection sacred and shining in the national mind, now, only four months later, became disgraced by the bigoted domestic violence at Altamont Speedway. In San Francisco, the hope and music of the 1967 Summer of Love had been ruined by malevolent greed. A generation was at a crossroads. It could no longer look at itself with a righteous intent. It now was forced by circumstance to look at its own failings, with no one else to blame.

As disappointments grew, the dangerous minds of state continued their operations of disruption and deceit. Fred Hampton, a burgeoning young black leader in Chicago, was murdered in a hail of early morning gunfire without direct provocation. The Chicago Eight Trial continued amidst a theatre of anger and contempt, its outcome dangerously apparent. Leader after leader of American dissent and outcry, had been assassinated, murdered, imprisoned, or threatened by traitors of infiltration. Their strategy was clear. Cut off the head, and you can kill the snake.

All the while, the Nixon propaganda machine showered the silent ones with accolade. It anointed them as champions of liberty and faith. Nixon calmed their uncertainties with words of honor and patriotism, while reiterating the necessity of their safety and protection against a provocative and dangerous world. He used all the same timeworn imagery. They were good Christian soldiers, loyal, and filled with righteous intent. Somehow they never seemed to notice as he marched them willingly into the sea.

The first day of December 1969, was a Monday. McAllister dragged himself out of bed, dressed and attended an early class. The morning was cold. Overhead, charcoal black clouds roamed the city sky, backlit by a pale white background, threatening snow. Students moved about campus with resigned purpose. They trudged along with the uninspired responsibility of school, the return of a weekly routine. After class, McAllister grabbed some breakfast at the dining hall, before going to the library to work on a research paper due the following week. Finals were approaching. It was time for the last minute push. He went to another class in the afternoon, then down to the old brick field house for some intramural basketball. Returning to his dorm room, he lay in his bunk, nodding off between pages of a textbook.

As the late afternoon gave way to winter night, the men's dormitory hall picked up its normal buzz. Voices rose in the hallway, stereo music beginning to play. Usually, if a door was closed, a neighbor was probably at work on their studies, or simply wanting to be left alone. An open door meant one was looking for social contact, to hang out and bullshit with the guys.

McAllister put down his book, got up and went out into the hall. His roommate, Gage, was hardly ever around. In fact, Gage was the perfect roommate. Gage had a girlfriend, spending a lot of his time over at the woman's dorm. He was also on the crew team, having to get up at five am for training or practice on the Potomac River. So McAllister never had to entertain the troop of other night owls like himself. He could visit the various dorm rooms of friends in the evenings, before disappearing into the quiet of his own space. He would tip toe by a sleeping Gage in his bunk, back to some late night reading or sleep himself. Gage's necessary routine allowed McAllister a unique cover of peace and solitude, one that a different roommate would never have provided.

Down the hallway, Ronnie Davis' door was wide open, his big bad stereo cranking away. A few of the other boys were inside, lounging on the bunks or standing idly making conversation. Ronnie Davis had a lot of toys, including a color television. Ronnie was a Jesuit preppie out of Cleveland, but was more like a party animal most of the time. His father owned a big Dodge dealership in Shaker Heights. And Ronnie had the latest off-the-line Dodge Challenger resting in the student parking lot. During his freshman year, McAllister had taken a ride to Cleveland with Ronnie, and Ronnie probably had broken the world speed record in getting there and back to D.C. It was the kind of trip where as a passenger you just closed your eyes and pretended you were asleep. It was surely better than witnessing your own premature death in a fiery vehicular catastrophe. Meanwhile, Ronnie was never worried a lick. He was loose as a goose, talking and steering all the way, foot heavy on the pedal, blowing through the Pennsylvania and Ohio countryside, immortal as hell.

By no means was Ronnie Davis the brightest bulb in the room, but he was a carefree and fun loving guy, and honestly generous with his riches bestowed. Most times, he had plenty of weed, so poor little lemmings like McAllister would generally stop by to see what was up. And on this particular Monday night in December, 1969, something very big was up.

After McAllister arrived, they closed and sealed the bottom of the door, opening the window to the cold night air. Ronnie pulled out his newly purchased water pipe. He filled it with the sticky blonde hashish he had procured from a connection down on Wisconsin Avenue. The water bubbled as long smokey hits ensued. One coughing fit after another hacked through the room. Stoned to the gills, the group stumbled out together, bouncing and laughing down to the dining hall for dinner. Although they hadn't discussed the coming event that evening, they might easily have appeared like a gaggle of death row inmates, ingesting a last supper before their fate would later be sealed.

With dinner over, they returned to Ronnie's room and turned on the television. At eight o'clock the vigil began, the young men all watching the program together. But deep down inside, they would each view these proceedings very much alone. On the television screen, old white men in forlorn coats and ties stood over a glass tumbler drum. The drum was filled with plastic capsules inside, three hundred and sixty-six in all. Nope, not even a leap year baby was going to escape this little show and tell. As if that wasn't enough, the good ole boys had brought in a so-called jury of your peers, fifty young men from fifty states, sympathizers necessary to give this charade an oily sense of credibility. They were Nixon's hand picked youth advisory committee for selective service.

In dorm rooms throughout the country, in bars and cheap apartments across the nation, a sense of reluctant anxiety hung suspended in air. Young men watched as the first capsule was pulled from the drum, a pair of nervous hands separating its parts, drawing out a small rolled piece of paper with a calendar date inscribed.

September 14th. McAllister and his friends exhaled in the dorm room. At least no one here had become the ultimate prize, the first pick in a lottery that no one wanted to win. But a sudden cacophony of shouts erupted down the dormitory hallway, far off in another wing of the building. Word of mouth rushed down the halls, one guy in the dorm had become the first. Later, they would see him on the television screen, as the local Washington stations wanted a body, someone to represent that day of birth in human form, for the emotional impact it might produce.

For McAllister, in his rational mind, it really didn't matter. The US government could have all their pomp and circumstance. He would never go. He would choose to face the consequences when they had to be faced, but he would not fight their bloody illegal war, or ever subscribe to their authority. They would not determine his fate. He would not be a pawn in their deadly noxious game.

But the rational mind and the emotional mind play by a different set of complexities. Your birth date, your goddamn moment of delivery to this world, was now something that they could use against you, something they believed they could control. Your life, your liberty, your pursuit of happiness, had come with a definite kicker. The human dynamic of national sovereignty and civilian order demanded a ticket stub to stay in the theatre. And once inside the theatre you couldn't just yell 'fire'. Self-professed anarchy cannot be tolerated when the movie is underway. There is a level of constraint and responsibility that must be met for the benefit and safety of all.

Where in hell is that line in the sand they call personal conscience? And when is it crossed? And what truly is the greater good? Was it God that said the war in Vietnam needed to be won? Did God say that burning Vietnamese children to the bone was a necessary evil to protect the domestic public welfare? Had God given his holy consent to Hitler and other genocidal maniacs on behalf of a better world? No fucking way. The one true fact is that there is a line. But it's a line that is always moving, either north or south, east or west. It is a line moved by men, for purposes of their own. And human beings either step over it, or they don't, and that will never change. It is a line created by men, not some superior being, otherwise all of us would know.

Ronnie Davis went first. Number 52. Ronnie Davis was the one student who could have cared less about politics of his world. The one child who could probably have most anything he wanted, he only had to ask. But Ronnie couldn't change this number tonight, no frigging way. McAllister watched Ronnie's expression. He observed a short moment of recognition, a quickly passing veil of understanding, of what it might read. Perhaps it said to Ronnie, maybe this is serious, maybe I should pay some attention, maybe I should get to class tomorrow. Ronnie Davis quickly covered his fear. Fuck, shit, piss, Ronnie Davis began to say, who are these guys anyway? But McAllister had witnessed the Passover. He saw Ronnie's sudden flicker of awareness, as if a fun-loving exercise of boyhood expression had suddenly met its match. The immortality of Ronnie's youth was getting a slap right across his face. Ronnie Davis was priceless in his naïve exuberance of life, and he shared it in spades with his friends. Ronnie was the poster child of thoughtless innocence and spirit. Such innocence and spirit now shaken and lost by a tiny roll of paper inscribed with a birth date. The overall effect was nothing less than a goddamn crime.

McAllister fell next. June 17th, number 73. For a moment, his mind went blank, his stomach doing that usual sinking thing whenever fear would get the best of him. Cocksuck, motherfuck, he said to himself, no fucking luck today. Immediately, he had to move. He pulled himself up, making for the hallway. The concrete block corridor stretched away, aching fluorescent lights flickering above. He was still pretty stoned from the hash. The dorm appeared like the hallway of a mental hospital, an asylum, an involuntary commitment. Further down, a mirage of doctors appeared huddled together in white smocks. They rubbed their chins in discussion, before nodding in confirmation, definitely no chance of release.

McAllister gathered himself and returned to the room, putting on a face like Ronnie's, making the best of a bad situation. The dates and the numbers droned on, every so often somebody else taking a fall. For those who had survived past number 195, things were projected to be safe. You could go on with the rest of your life. Chris Huggins, his partner in crime during the Yippie melee at Justice only two weeks before, pulled number 259. Unlike many others, for whom the anti-war movement meant very little, and for whom such a high number would mean less so now, Chris Huggins certainly deserved the reprieve.

And goddamn Bruiser, that big lug of a homeboy pal, whose birthday was June 29th, a whopping 353. McAllister knew the Bruiser's birth date well, as they had shared its proximity together for many childhood years. The Bruise, that lucky ball-busting son of a bitch. Then he thought of Reggie Disalvo. Reggie had not joined the military, or yet been called to the fray. McAllister was unable to remember Reggie's birthday, but perhaps it wouldn't matter. If it was low, he guessed Reggie would enlist. If Reggie did that, he had a better chance of getting what he wanted. Or so they often promised.

But for Sean McAllister, the die was cast. Any thoughts of dropping out of school were done. He would have to make the college deferment last as long as he possibly could. Either that, or be forced to confront other decisions he simply was not ready to face. In reality, he was so much luckier than most. Tonight, there were guys out across America, whose immediate personal fate stood menacingly at attention, staring them right between the eyes.

What McAllister didn't know, as he journeyed home for Christmas a few weeks later, was that another holiday present awaited him. It would be a surprise gift from the University, given in the spirit of the season.

Bill McAllister stepped down off the bus at the entrance to Northland Hills, walking with his briefcase down the street toward home. The December evening was cold and dry. Christmas lights adorned many of the houses and yards, some decidedly overdone. Others, like the McAllister home, appeared more minimal, as if required to unwillingly participate. Nevertheless, Bill McAllister had performed his annual duty for the family.

Connie had yanked out all the decorations, hanging the wreath on the door, the candle lights in the windows, placing the nativity scene and other knick-knacks throughout the house. Together, they had purchased the tree over the weekend. Bill had put it up in the living room, spending a Sunday afternoon wrangling with lights and boxes of bulbs rising from the basement storage. In recent years, it felt more like a mundane expected exercise, his holiday spirit lacking. The kids were grown now, and wouldn't be around long enough to care. Still, it remained important to Connie. All in all, it would have been even stranger to not have made the effort.

Walking along, his mind was burdened with thoughts of his damn wayward son, who more than likely would be home from college when he got to the house. Bill McAllister had been stewing about the damn situation since the arrival of the letter last week. Tonight, he would have to confront the kid about the damage done. Part of him was ready to lose his temper, the other part wishing he didn't have to deal with the problem. Connie had been angry, too. But like the mother she was, she feared spoiling the holiday, wanting her son to be happy at home.

Damn these two kids. Mary Jane was one thing. She was like her mother, strong-willed and independent, purposeful about everything she engaged, but emotional to a fault. Much like Connie, you couldn't control Mary Jane once she got something in her head. He'd given up on that a long time ago. It wasn't worth the effort. And he sort of admired the spunk his wife and daughter displayed, their personal adherence to one thing or another, no matter what others might think.

But this circumstance with Mickey was a different expectation, his one and only son. Mickey wasn't necessarily a troublemaker, but he could often find trouble without realizing the consequences. There had to be a different standard in his particular case, and the young man needed to know that reality.

It certainly wasn't cheap, this having two kids in college at good universities. He'd been taking the bus the last couple of years to save on the parking downtown. He had borrowed against the house when Mickey had started school. And this goddamn job was growing old.

He was over fifty now, and the writing was on the wall. There would probably be no more promotions coming his way. Younger, faster-talking men were coming into the company. And he wasn't doing research any longer. Instead, he was having to deal with people. But you don't pass up the chance for more money, not with two kids in school, regardless of what you yourself would rather do. Management paid more, and now he knew why. Yet, he could feel the last rung on his corporate ladder had been reached. Pretty soon, this newer blood would pass him by. In the years ahead, he would have to suck it up and continue on.

Mickey didn't understand these things. He didn't understand that his record would speak for itself. The world was an unforgiving place. One could pay dearly for their sins, despite their own opinion about what's right or wrong. But how the hell do you tell a young kid about something he doesn't see? The boy could blow his future, and he needed to know the ramifications.

This academic probation ruling might follow his son around for a long long time. Employers would see that kind of behavior. And even though they might accept the explanation as a vagary of youth, if there was a tie in the qualifications, they would always take the safer bet. So he would have to confront his son about the situation. He would let Mickey know in so many words this was serious big trouble, and he better get the message. And Bill McAllister knew he had to do it right away, before Mary Jane arrived in a couple of days. She would defend her younger brother, and Christmas would be a mess.

Bill McAllister was damn tired of this season called winter. The golf course was shut down to protect the greens, his boat out of the water and covered up till summer. There was no place to escape from this thing called work, this thing called life. He had come so far from the way things used to be. These years, he could hardly remember much from the row house days of growing up in Wilmington. Those Depression times were hard, but just as hard for everybody. The big war was a different story, those memories were more acute. Next to his wedding day with Connie, and the birth of his kids, getting his pilot wings had been a peak event. Outside of a few moments in baseball, it had been his first serious success as a man.

Unfortunately, that success had come at a price. Bill McAllister had been better than most at flight school. He was smart and easy to get along, so they had made him a flight instructor. One might have thought that was a lucky break, he would not be sent overseas. But the job had an unanticipated form of consequence. You taught young men like yourself how to fly. Men who were mostly long forgotten now, except in those dreams when you would see them again. There they were, sticking the landing of a brawling B-17 at the desert airbases of California and New Mexico, when you knew they were ready to go. They would strut away from the aircraft, happy and proud, immortal in their readiness to make it alone. You celebrated their camaraderie and fearlessness, until some months later came word that they would never return.

Bill McAllister had never anticipated the pain of their subsequent loss, nor the guilt he would feel when they didn't come home. These were memories that did not go away. They became invisible scars you could only share with yourself. They would always be there, those faces. In a way he was glad for that circumstance. Within him, these men would continue to be remembered, not forgotten with the passage of time. Yet, it did not extinguish the emptiness that sometimes welled, or the guilt he felt for staying behind. Even more difficult were the following days of teaching another group of willing recruits. Carrying inside the knowledge of their possible fate, a fate of which you could never speak. Bill McAllister was lucky to have stayed stateside in one piece, to have come home and met Connie, to have found a good job and a raised a family, a safe place to continue his life. But these memories would always be there, and he felt obligated to share the cost of their pain and sadness.

Connie loved that weathered picture of him as a flyboy. She kept it loose in a small treasure box of keepsakes on her dresser. It was the picture of him in his leather flight jacket, standing on the desert airfield at Lancaster. It sure would be nice to be that age again. His face was young, his hair dark and full. Now, his hair was thinning, his face sagging and creasing with age, his suit coat and tie bearing like a weight on the walk to the bus stop each and every day.

Connie knew he was growing tired, that much of his desire was spent. Thankfully, she was happy being herself. She had her friends, her sisters, and her constant responsibilities at work. He knew she was missing the kids. And so did he, but not in the same way. As for himself, he had his brothers, and his buddies from work and school days. Many had returned to Wilmington after the war. He and Connie still enjoyed their life together. The best parts were the summer evening boat rides they would take at the shore. They would race through the light swells of Rehoboth Bay, tasting the spray of salted air. Then he would cut the motor, where they would enjoy a beer or gin and tonic, bobbing in the quiet roll, far away from land.

Approaching the house, Bill McAllister wished that his son might not yet be home, that he wouldn't have to play the angry and disappointed father. But if so, it needed to get done. He'd let the boy know how he felt, that this was dangerous behavior, the trouble it could mean for his future. He would remind him how much it worried his mother. Mickey needed to begin thinking of others, not only of himself. But really, in the end, Bill McAllister just wanted to see his son, to talk about sports, to have his boyhood friends come by the house, to enjoy this time of the family being together once again. Mickey was a good kid, just terribly naïve, like all the kids his age.

The whole family drama caught Sean McAllister by surprise. His father, his mother, the disciplinary action. He sat at the kitchen table, his father standing against the drain board, his mother trying to act like she was cooking dinner, which she was, but sort of scurrying about. Those goddamn cowards at the University had never informed him. Instead, they had sent a letter to his parents, right before the holidays. The letter lay on the kitchen table. McAllister had only half-assed looked at it, but now he knew what it said. Disciplinary action, academic probation, a cease and desist order, or he would be expelled from the University. The charge, the disruption of a legitimate and approved course of curriculum, classes of the Reserved Officer Training Corps, better known as ROTC. These Jesuit chicken shits were smart. They would scare the hell out of his mom and dad by forcing the trouble into his parent's home. They would threaten him by making it a family issue. The bastards!

McAllister tried to explain, but it wasn't going well. How do you tell your mother and father that this has to be done. That bringing the war home through tactics of resistance, especially when the very agents of the war machine are right on your campus, is a conscious and necessary act. That these methods are similar to the tactics of keeping corporate recruiters like Dow Chemical off the campuses, the companies that are making napalm, Agent Orange, and other weapons and devices of war.

The time for writing letters to your elected representatives, or your local newspaper editor had long ago passed. And walking down the street with a sign in your hand, begging for beneficent leaders to recognize and agree with some greater moral authority, had gotten absolutely nowhere. It was ludicrous. Sure, it might make you feel good for a moment. Gee, you are exercising your constitutional right of freedom of speech. Your ninth grade civics teacher would be proud of you. But the moment doesn't last. You begin to realize that nothing is happening. They aren't fucking listening. They're watching football games. Thanks for coming they say, we understand your concerns. But you just don't understand the bigger picture of things. Trust us, and everything will be okay.

Meanwhile, the bombs keep raining, the villages keep burning, the children keep crying for their dead mothers and fathers. Young men your own age come home silent in a flag- draped box. Others lay howling in a Veteran's hospital, waiting on a flesh-colored plastic appendage that is supposed to make them feel all better. We appreciate what you have done for America's freedom, they crow. Here's a nice shiny silver medal. Good luck down the road. Well, looks like halftime is over. It's time to get back to the game.

So you go into a nice little comfortable classroom setting, and you simply say, wait a goddamn minute. You toy soldiers aren't going to continue waltzing in here anymore, at least not on this campus, pretending that its business as usual. There will be no more pretending like you aren't responsible, that you are just doing your job. Fuck that shit. No, today you're going to try this on for size. We're scrapping the lesson plan today. Today, we are going to deliver a lecture of our own, built on a different set of facts, a different set of assumptions. We're going to shake the goddamn tree.

Obviously, they are not very pleased. But hell, you didn't blow up their home, or beat them over their head with a night stick. You didn't ransack their dorm room, or steal their stereo and cash, nor call their mother into question. No, you just pissed them off for a day or two. You let the air out of their tires, disrupted their regular routine for awhile.

Maybe you made them defend their own behavior, and by having to make such defense, perhaps a few other questions would arise.

"You don't understand, Dad."

"You're saying I don't understand?" his father shot back. McAllister's mother continued to be on the move, re-setting the table for like the third time. "If that's what you mean, you're goddamn right," his father continued. "But I do understand a few important things. I understand that you are disrupting the other student's freedom of speech. What gives you the right to do that? And I sure understand what it takes in order to write a big check for your education down there twice a year. And I sure know I have to go to work every day. Meanwhile, you're prancing around Washington, D. C., eating food and buying books, and probably missing classes that you're mom and I are paying for. I think I understand that pretty well. I also understand that your mother is hurting and worried about you. Maybe you should understand that she and I are working hard so you can get the kind of education that we had to struggle for. Here in a country that allows you to go to school, and say all these things you feel you need to say. No, I understand a few things, Mickey. So, what do you say to them apples?"

McAllister felt caged. His dad was right. What do you say to them apples? Maybe in this situation, it wasn't a case of not understanding, more of a case of things that couldn't be understood. But McAllister was in a corner now, and he knew it. And there was definitely something dark in the back of his mind. Something that was too damn scary to think about. It was the number seventy-three. So, who was the chicken shit now?

"Well, maybe I shouldn't take your money. You're right. You shouldn't have to pay for all this. But it remains important to me. And I don't like being told that I can't act on my beliefs. As crazy as that might sound to you."

"Now, that's enough," Connie McAllister burst in. "That's enough, we have to sit down and eat. No more the rest of the night, Bill. Our son is home."

McAllister's dad pushed himself off the drain board. "I need a drink. Of whiskey, a stiff shot." Bill McAllister turned the corner to the family den, opening the closet door, reaching up for his bottle of bourbon."

"Bill," his mother said, "Bill, we are going to eat."

"Just one, honey. Please don't argue with me now. Just one."

Bill McAllister returned to the kitchen and fished in the cupboard for a glass. With his father's attention turned away, McAllister's mother pointed at her son, like she had done for so many years. In a whisper, her finger gunned at his face, she mouthed the words so he could easily read her lips. "Your father loves you." The pointed finger said the rest. "And don't you forget it."

McAllister didn't know why he said it. The words just came out. "I'll have one, too."

His father halted for a moment, before pulling down another glass. "Yeah, that's right," Bill McAllister responded. "It's time for a drink with my son." His father turned forward, the bottle in one hand, the two glasses squeezed between the fingers of the other. He set them on the table before sitting down in his kitchen chair. Unscrewing the bottle, he poured out the bourbon, pushing the first glass toward his son. Pouring his own, he sat back in the chair, staring at his boy, one man to another. His expression relaxed.

"It's like what Uncle Franny always says," raising his glass. "A man should never drink alone at Christmas."

Sean McAllister picked up his whiskey and did the same. It wouldn't be the first time he had swallowed a drink from the liquor closet. Nevertheless, it would be the very first time he ever shared a drink with his Dad.

CHAPTER FIVE

WHAT ABOUT ME?
Washington D.C / Winter-Spring, 1970

THIS TIME, THEY MADE THE LIQUOR RUN themselves, he and Bruiser. Just said 'fuck it', drove down into the city, parked near the package store at the corner of Second and West, walked right in and bought the booze. They knew that Reggie's old friend, Billy E., would be working the register, so things went fast. A case of beer, a bottle of bourbon, a jug of wine, and out the door. They quickly packed the trunk, threw a blanket over the stash, before jumping on the interstate, heading south. If they got busted, so be it. Yeah, you could get conscripted and sent off to war, but you were still an underage criminal if you had a beer in your hand, in some states a lifer if you got busted with a joint. Sean McAllister was now old enough to know that the world was unfair, that justice in America was not some grand moral arbiter where innocence was presumed. Rather, it was based who you knew and how you looked, and it didn't hurt to have a roll of bills in your pocket to help cover your tracks.

At the off-campus apartment in Newark, near the University of Delaware, they were welcomed like Olympians. Not for their athletic accomplishments, but for the gold they held in their arms. The faces were older, heads longer with hair, jeans torn or patched, dresses lengthened, colors alive and bright. *Abby Road* played on the stereo, the smokey odor of marijuana passed in the air from hand to hand. It was New Years Eve, 1969.

A thumbs-up handshake or bear hug had become a common salutation between men. The words 'brother' and 'sister' were filled with new meanings. Inside the apartment, posters hung off walls, candles burned in various places. Black lights hummed in the bedrooms, a lava lamp nearby. The kitchen was like Grand Central Station, voices drowning out the music. Hard liquor and wine bottles sat on the countertop, the refrigerator filled with beer. Everyone had a story to tell. The nucleus of the party consisted of old friends from high school, but there were new people as well. McAllister was a stranger to some, but part of the larger gathering. This was the new world of which he now belonged.

She stood in the corner of the kitchen. McAllister caught her eye contact before looking away. He slowly moved within the crunch of bodies to get a better view. While engaged in other conversation, he watched her. Straight brown hair to her shoulders, a long print dress stretching down below her knees, her legs hidden by the long underwear she wore beneath. A small pair of hiking boots enclosed her feet. Her cheeks were pronounced with a smooth reddish glint, her breasts appeared firm and perfect for her size. Like a thief he stole one glance after another, sensing her openness. No longer would getting high be the purpose of his evening, a more important necessity prevailed.

A short time later, while she was speaking with someone he knew, he found his chance. He still lacked the courage to break the ice on his own. Sliding into the conversation, he went through the standard greeting with his friend, but honestly he could less how things were going. For crying out loud pal, introduce her, you knucklehead. Thankfully, she held there watching him, as he faked being nice.

Her name was Mad, short for Madelyn. A funny name for a girl, but he liked it. McAllister tried to keep her attention, asking questions about her life, something he had learned from Mary Jane. 'Don't ever start talking about yourself with girls, little brother. Show your interest and concern. Make them feel like you want to get to know them.' Well that wouldn't be hard. She was a student here at campus, hailing from the outskirts of Philly, a freshman, a year younger than him. McAllister found her another glass of wine, and she didn't move away. He talked about his school in Washington D.C., but purposely avoided the things that were weighing heavier on his mind.

When midnight struck, she found him again, as everyone hugged and celebrated. She planted a short kiss on his lips, catching him off guard. As he tried to respond, she slipped away, and before anything more could ensue, she was gone. As the party slowed, people began to evaporate into the night. McAllister sat on a couch with a final shot and a beer. He wasn't drunk, yet stilled with a desiring numbness that wouldn't pass. Bruiser sat in a chair across from him, as usual, drifting into a laid back sleep. Finally, McAllister shook himself back to the moment, rousting Bruiser from his slumber. They stepped out into the biting cold of a new year, a new decade, making the drive back home.

He awoke late to New Year's morning, overcome with the dreams of a night before. He wanted to head back south, to find the girl, to slip into her arms, simply drift away. A host of sensibilities pursued him, confusing his already uncertain future. He let them go, unwilling. In a matter of days he was back in his dorm room, the academic probation upon him, his father's unhappiness and the money issue causing a restless anxiety he was unable to shake. The number seventy-three might as well have been tattooed to his forehead. It reminded him of its dictate. He had nowhere else to go.

The eastern winter of 1970 struggled on, hard and unnerving. The Sixties were over, but the beat didn't change. The Vietnam War continued. The national anger settled into divisions no one could abate, the country splintering as a result of its inability to bring the trauma peacefully to an end. The Beatles had fallen apart. Chicago turned ugly as the conspiracy trial spiraled out of control. The recent murder of Black Panther leader, Fred Hampton, was paraded by the Chicago police as self-defense. Daniel Berrigan, a Catholic priest, had been found guilty of destroying draft records in Catonsville, Maryland, then sentenced to jail. Berrigan disappeared before sentencing, refusing to report for incarceration, but was eventually caught and imprisoned. The Weatherman faction of SDS went underground, vowing a more violent response against the state. Meanwhile, the Nixon regime continued its paranoia, its defense of the indefensible. Culturally, a broader America grew harsher and more at war. For almost every adult American, there was no choice but to take a side.

McAllister thought often of this girl he didn't really know. She was out there somewhere, far off in this imagined place he could not reach. But her vision sustained him, amidst a loss of purpose in his own daily experience. College had simply become a place to hide out, to weather a winter of carelessness and persistent unconcern. At school, he did enough to get by. In between he smoked weed, drank with his friends, took LSD and mescaline, all to avoid the boredom of the day to day. At some point, he would have to make some decisions. But decisions are based on choices, and choices require options from which to choose. He was stuck between a rock and a hard place. There was little to do but wait things out.

In the midst of his quandary came the David Nolan incident. Noles, as he was called by his dorm mates, was a spirited eccentric guy, much like McAllister's friend Snark Rosenbloom. He was another student with a genius-like mind, but with an off-the-wall personality that rubbed against the grain. Noles didn't fit, a square peg looking for the round hole. But much like Snark, he was part of the greater group. Noles could play the game of Risk for days in the student lounge, or come up with the most outlandish comments in the middle of a conversation. He dressed in loafers and sweaters. Noles appeared born to disturb, challenging any inane conversation with serious intent. Whenever Noles was around, there was always a strange sense of tension, as if he might take any conversation haywire, whatever the subject. But that was Noles. And like many group dynamics, be it summer camp, a sports team, or some other social context, a men's college dorm was a place where the personalities of certain individuals were thrown together without particular choice. Noles was just another hand you were dealt.

Until the acid trip that got him. It was a normal Friday night, with nothing more on the schedule than to find out what anyone else might be doing. Ronnie Davis had scored and was looking for company. So McAllister and Chris Huggins said sure, why not. Noles wanted in as well. They slipped some blotter acid under their tongues, smoked a bowl, drank a beer, listening to Ronnie's stereo, waiting. Within an hour they started to come on. For McAllister, an acid trip was always precipitated by a strange sensation beneath his jaws and the gums of his teeth. Whenever he got that feeling, he knew he was on his way.

Then it hit, the shapes of the dorm room changing, the fixation on the smallest weirdest things. The way Huggins mouth moved as he spoke, the mattress sinking up and down like an ocean as McAllister shifted position while sitting on Ronnie's bunk. Everyone trying to maintain conversation until something pulled them away. The music, the nausea in your stomach, there was no turning back. The four students went outside into the evening, hiking to the package store for more beer to drink. Returning, they wandered along the boat canal bordering the Potomac River. They drank a beer, listening to the jibber jabber of their voices in the moonless night. Except for Noles. He was quiet. Under a street lamp, McAllister thought he saw a face in pain, etched with duress.

Severely under the influence, the men went back to the dorm, visiting around. They injected themselves into the straighter world of a Friday night, trying to appear in control. Unnoticed, Noles had slipped away. Suddenly, anguished wailing cries came from his dorm room. When the others reached his door, Noles lay on his bunk. He had taken off his clothes, wrapping himself in a white sheet, his breath seething, his face contorted in torment. He began shouting people's names that no one knew. The situation scared McAllister as straight as he could get. Noles was on a bummer, a bad trip, and nobody knew where it might go. He lay naked in his bed, the sheet askew, talking in gibberish, wrestling with demons that now overcame him. Suddenly, like a cat, he jumped up with a snarl, heading toward them as if physically ready to attack. Stopping short, he began staring deep into their eyes.

McAllister and Huggins tried to calm him, to no avail. The ruckus made waves and others started to congregate in the hallway. The dorm resident arrived just as Noles tried to climb out the window, McAllister and Huggins pulling him to the floor. "What the fuck. Keep him down," the resident shouted, before bolting away. McAllister and Huggins held Noles as he shook and cried out. The trauma seemed to last forever. Finally, two hospital guys arrived. They strapped Noles to a gurney and gave him a shot. Taking over, the medics held his arms, talking to Noles in muffled tones. "What did he take?" one of them yelled, not looking up. "Some bad acid," McAllister volunteered. The whole scene felt like a never ending dream, like a camera out of focus until the injection took effect. Noles' body gave up the fight. Surrounded by a crowded hallway, the hospital men carried Noles away.

Ronnie Davis had split. Only McAllister and Huggins remained in the dorm room. They knew the resident, his name was John. He was usually cool, but not this time. "How do you know it was bad acid?"

John asked. He said so, was their response. "If this shit comes down on me, and I figure it will, then it's coming down on you for sure," John demanded.

"You know Noles," Huggins said. "He does his own thing."

"I know dilated pupils when I see them," John said in response, looking into their eyes. "Clean up his room and get the hell out of here."

McAllister and Huggins tidied things up, closing the door. Noles currently didn't have a roommate, the guy had left school at semester break. They went to Ronnie's room and knocked on the door. They received only silence. That was enough for McAllister, he was angered straight by now.

"Open that fucking door, Ronnie, and give us the beer, you goddamn Jesuit chicken shit. Or I'll tell them it was your idea, and right where it fucking came from." The door unlocked, opening wide enough to push the beer out with a foot. "I'm not feeling so good, Sean," Ronnie implored. "I got to lay down for awhile. Noles is going to be okay, right?" he asked.

McAllister bent down and picked up the beer. "You do that, Ronnie. You lie down and get your beauty rest. Noles is fine, Ronnie. He's dead, but feeling a whole lot better." McAllister grabbed the door knob and pulled it closed. Huggin's roommate was out of town. They got out of the hall and went to his room to disappear. As they tried to come down, they worried about what might happen next.

Later, as McAllister lay in his own bed, he remained wired from the acid, unable to sleep. He didn't know if there would be serious repercussions, if the police would investigate. He was out of pot, so he didn't have to worry about ditching his stash. And the beer was legal in the District. He was clean. As for Noles, who was to say? Hopefully, he was coming down and would be okay. McAllister would try and check on him tomorrow. If the shit came down, which it could, McAllister figured he'd be done. Out of school, out on the street, and what that would mean. He thought about the girl, Mad. At least he could go home and try to find her. Or maybe he'd go up and see Mary Jane in Boston, perhaps find a job up there. His mind whirled, his body still nerved from the trip. He tossed and turned, finally drifting off to sleep.

Sometimes in life, you never get the full story, the things that happen behind the scenes. David Nolan never returned. Not even to pick up his things. It was as if Noles had vanished into thin air. McAllister lived on pins and needles for a week. Nobody had any information, only that Noles had left school. At some point his possessions were removed from his room. Somebody came and got them, but no one was around. It was all a crazy mystery, but not one McAllister, Huggins, or Ronnie Davis were inquiring to resolve. Was it the family, the University, no one knew. It was as if the incident had never happened. Noles had come from somewhere in Western Pennsylvania, but he was so fly by night nobody really knew him well. For a time, McAllister waited on an outcome, figuring something had to give. Surely, sometime, there would be a knock on his door, and all would be revealed. It never came.

For the old, memories grow longer with time and experience, before slowly beginning to disappear with the senility of decline. For the young, memory is barely a point of reference. It carries no nostalgia. The road is still unfolding, the future filled with wishful thinking. The present tense surrounds the young. It is the moment that prevails. The memory of David Nolan remained written in a history book that no one had time to read. There was always the next moment coming.

In late February, the verdicts came down for the Chicago Seven, formerly the Chicago Eight. Charges against Black Panther leader, Bobby Seale, had been separated from the other defendants. Seale had been bound and gagged in the courtroom of Judge Julius Hoffman, then jailed for contempt after vociferously demanding his right to self-representation. Although the remaining seven were found innocent of the conspiracy charges against them, five were found guilty of crossing state lines for the crime of inciting to riot at the Democratic National Convention eighteen months before. It was well known in some circles that the outgoing Johnson administration in late 1968 had pressured Mayor Daly and his prosecutors to drop or lessen the charges, to let things fade away. Too many Americans had witnessed the bloody response by the Chicago police.

But Richard Milhous Nixon had won the Presidency. Nixon, and the newly elected Republican administration, with John Mitchell as

Attorney General, had pressed forward to punish the movement and jail its leadership. The trial had become a spectacle of youthful dissent against authority, a clash of cultures put on display. The hard line by those in power and control had won again, the jury had spoken. There had to be a response.

Sean McAllister had never heard of the Watergate apartment complex, nor the business development of which it was a part. Built along the Potomac River in the Foggy Bottom section of the city, the Watergate had become the home for many of the Nixon cabal, the "Republican Bastille" as one journalist had coined it. One of its famous residents was the Attorney General himself, along with his crazy southern belle of a wife, Martha. Mitchell and the Justice Department had been the target of the Yippies and others as the Chicago trial had progressed. It only made sense that the Watergate would be a deliberate location to express a purposeful counter-attack.

The march to the Watergate was more of a local protest, several thousand at best, on a cold dry February afternoon. It wouldn't get far. As soon as the authorities knew of its plans, the government mobilization was heavy. There was the usual D.C metro police presence, but they were now backed by a powerful new quick strike force called the Civil Defense Unit, or CDU. The CDU was a combined element of elite trained personnel from departments throughout the region, an all-star team of sorts, aggressive and battle ready. It didn't take long for McAllister, Huggins, and the other protestors to realize that this one could be serious trouble.

Marching down the street, the Watergate complex could be seen in the distance, blocks away. It would remain so. A phalanx of heavily equipped police met them early and didn't waste time. There had been no issued permit for the taking of the street. As a result, one or two bullhorn demands to immediately disperse, before the tear gas projectiles began to fly. The crowd was pushed quickly in all directions through this residential section of the city. It became readily apparent that this would not be the cop's only strategy, to simply defend the target and hold a firm line. The CDU appeared in full attack, vehicle after vehicle racing through the narrow tree-lined streets intent on securing their prey.

McAllister and Huggins were pushed by the gas into a side street. Mistakenly, they were caught off guard watching the long string of police cars, with lights flashing and sirens blaring, racing by as if headed for another destination. Only they weren't heading anywhere. The line of cars suddenly came screeching to a halt, their doors flying open, with heavy blue bodies the size of football lineman pouring out onto the pavement. Although McAllister didn't mouth the words, the thought of 'holy shit' shouted inside his head. He was caught flat-footed, leaden with the surprise of the moment. The large dark body of a hulking officer, the black nightstick raised above his head, bore down like a specter of immediate pain and capture. McAllister got his ass in gear.

He gained momentum, pushing off the balls of his feet on the sidewalk, picking up speed. He could hear the jangle of metal and handcuffs behind, the heavy pounding of boots keeping pace. The whoosh of the nightstick caught McAllister's right shoulder with a glancing blow. But the swinging action caused the cop to stumble and lose his balance. McAllister kept picking up speed, pulling away. He angled out and cut across a street corner, scattering a couple of school kids with books in their arms, dodging an old lady toting a grocery bag, accelerating down the block. Cutting between two parked cars into the side street, he raced down its center in full retreat.

At the next corner he stopped and looked behind. There was no sight of the cop on the advance. He must have pulled up. McAllister bent over and breathed heavily, his hands on his knees, but kept his head up, searching down the block. Standing upright, his breathing began to slow. He had gotten away, but it had been too damn close. Looking around the neighborhood, no one else was running. On the corner of the next block he watched a group that looked like demonstrators, pacing together, as if deciding their next move. Sirens continued to blare in the distance. The Washington locals, who had gotten caught up in the melee, stood looking in all directions, wondering which way to go. Chris Huggins was nowhere to be seen. And that was it. McAllister wandered a few blocks looking for Huggins, before slowly heading through the streets of Foggy Bottom, pacing toward the bus line that would take him back to campus. He'd had enough of the fight for one afternoon.

As he walked, the gray winter day was waning, dimming its way toward dusk. McAllister passed through the ordinary streets of office buildings and shops, with men moving briskly in coats and ties, woman in long coats and high heels, children playing innocently in a nearby park. He was struck by the strange ironies of this life. In his beanie cap and long ponytailed hair, his green army surplus coat pinned with a peace button, his ragged corduroy pants and worn heavy boots, he felt a mix of uncertainty about his own place in this world.

He was part of a good cause, no doubt. Of that he was certain. For all the reasons he didn't have to review. Yet here he was, surrounded by this other world that lived side by side with him everyday. It was the straight world of a steady America, with families like his mom and dad, people with jobs to do, kids that had to be fed, clothed, and sent off to school on time. There were cars to be driven and pumped full of gas. There were people in taxis, hurrying off to somewhere important. At the transit stop, he joined the bus ride of a regular working day, a journey of purses and satchels sitting on pressed knees, riding toward solitary destinations, alone together, both young and old. Each person would have their own story to tell. As for himself, here he was, bumping along on a fading weekday afternoon, one step from a bloodied head and a jail cell for the night. Outside of that possibility, nothing would have changed. The busy buzz of a regular world would have kept on going right along.

It disturbed him to begin pondering about a purpose in his life, a multitude of identities to choose from, or directions to take. Did he really have a choice in these matters, or was it more like being a victim of circumstances you could not control. Had all the people on this bus really made a conscious choice to be here? Or was their presence in this place somehow destined by choices they had made before, and now could not escape? Or worse, had such choices been made by others, and by such resulting consequence had brought them to this moment. It was heavy shit to think about. One thing for sure, the number seventy-three still had a hell of a consequence. He could certainly take that one to the bank. Patience is often said to be a virtue, but by the same token, it wasn't all it was cracked up to be. Sean McAllister could certainly vouch for that declaration.

Riding along, he worried about Huggins, hoping he got away. Geez, the pigs were getting more serious than ever. Nixon, Hoover and Mitchell, and all their puppet surrogates were locked and loaded for bear. Guys like Hoffman and Rubin, Davis, Dellinger and Hayden, were going to get theirs one way or another. There was no question where the ammunition lay, and how it would be used. Unfortunately, one extreme casts its die to the other. The repercussions would only get more damaging as the desperation grew.

McAllister got off the bus near campus, walking the last few blocks toward home. He felt tired, a little depressed. Again, the girl found her way back into his thoughts. In the last few weeks she had faded a bit, as that usual mandate called time wedged its way in between. But solace and loneliness always desire some company, and the mystery girl named Mad would have to do for him. At least his imagination could go there, without any responsibility to attend. She could occupy these empty moments inside him, providing a comfort not otherwise near. He was thankful for the wishfulness it allowed him to possess.

The winter of 1970 felt like a hangover, the dull beat of a headache and queasy stomach, shuffling with a listless lack of focus. A funk. McAllister was growing with a discontent that shadowed him through the stale daily routine of his college life. More and more mornings he slept in late, missing classes became a regular weekly circumstance. Life in the dorm had lost its attraction and novelty. Its social life now became repetitive, most of the prep school boys and their antics seeming redundant and juvenile. His light brown hair was long and shoulder length. The jeans and ragged clothing he chose to wear identified him as a different student from the rest. Not that he was alone in his appearance and perspective. He didn't stand out much in that regard. He just felt constricted by his surroundings, a silent sense of alienation creeping within.

No doubt there were things on his mind. And that was the problem, he had too much time to think. If he had a girlfriend, that would be one thing. But he felt unwashed with some of the ones he had met. Most of the university girls were straight in their attentions, their motivations and interests so mundane to him, as if life after high school, now college, continued unabated. It was hard to let things go, his personal discomforts and fears continued to hold sway.

Throw in the money thing. He felt a persistent guilt about the cost of school, the amount his dad and mom were putting up for him to be at this distinguished institution. They were sacrificing every day. Meanwhile, he rolled over in bed, caring less about the academic studies, a higher learning he was supposed to feel was an opportunity to be reached. His expectations coming out of high school, of a serious education and career orientation had withered away. He held a deep sense of negativity toward his country, his government, or any structured roads to financial success. All this shit simply exasperated him. He wanted to extricate himself from these demands, to find something new in which to engage. But he was cornered by a lottery number that rested like a bull's eye on his back. He wanted out. But the truth was clear. He lacked the courage to make a move.

The news from Chris Huggins only added to the ennui. Huggins, his protesting partner and political mentor, the one guy with whom McAllister felt a particular kinship of intent, was leaving school at the end of the semester. Huggins would return home to Connecticut for either work or another school. Huggins number was 259, currently safe enough from the draft. He would be able to pull up stakes and look around. Huggins, like McAllister, had come out of the public schools. They had come to realize along the way, that most of the public school kids were the ones who had taken up the cause against the war. They were often the ones who spoke up in class, who had disrupted the ROTC routine last fall, who enjoyed looking at the dust in the corners for what they might find.

The Jesuit prep school boys were a different lot. When it came to parties and mischief, or traditional dating with girls, they were crack operators. When it came to school, they generally matriculated to the easier courses, particularly to the general college studies or business curriculums. They embodied the traditional Catholic conservatism of their parents, a youthful republican view. College was for them a frat-boy mentality, a time to have fun before settling down to the framework of a good job in the family business, the right girl to marry, a predictable future ahead. They were sideline participants when it came to challenging the powers that be. Unaccounted risk was not their forte. They were followers in the most convenient sort of way.

The University was built and financially supported by this type of ancestry. Although the Jesuit mystique was heralded for its history as warrior defenders of the faith, marked by a freedom of intellectual curiosity and spiritual debate, the University knew which side of the loaf to butter its bread. Particularly in Washington D.C., the University's alignment with the US government was palpable, its anti-communist agenda in sync with the national obsession and the standards of behavior required. The University's purpose was to deliver highly-educated personnel to the cause, people who could take the reigns of government and maintain the status quo. This mandate wasn't so different from other academic knowledge factories across the country, universities whose financial prosperity depended on the production of able minds and bodies for a corporate or bureaucratic necessity. In Washington D.C., it was simply more local, to train the political and administrative resources that needed to be supplied. And if the University had its druthers, anti-government sentiments need not apply.

Now Huggins was going on the lam, and McAllister felt even more alone. Chris Huggins was another well-read political and cultural junkie, full of opinions, but armed with the facts and history to back them up. Huggins understood how the Tet Offensive the year before had changed the course of the war in Vietnam. He was the first to speak about the Massacre at My Lai, months before its dramatic revelations in the press. Huggins was well-versed on the directions and plans of different elements of the American anti-war movement. He was familiar with its leaders and the changing strategies they sought to employ. Huggins spoke to the deliberate government strategy as well, including the insidious illegal attempts to discredit the movement and jail its leaders. He was a wealth of information and knowledge. McAllister had become a willing listener, and had learned so much.

But even more than the political side, Huggins was a guitar player with a love of music. He turned McAllister on to the American blues, the migration of its roots from the sharecropper regions of the Mississippi Delta, north to Chicago and other urban cities in America. He spoke to its impact on British bands like the Beatles and the Stones, of John Mayall and the Bluebreakers, Fleetwood Mac, and Eric Clapton. Huggins spent every dollar he could find purchasing used albums down on Wisconsin Avenue, bringing them home to the dorm. McAllister would listen to them with his friend, while they smoked pot and drank a few beers, killing off both the winter and the academic world that surrounded them.

As McAllister reflected more about his future, perhaps Huggin's intended move made sense for him as well. Part of him still enjoyed living in Washington D.C. The experience and adventure of its political dramas remained appealing. The Capitol had become his new home. Any thoughts of leaving, of going back to the even more conservative University of Delaware, back home to the State of Dupont, was an alternative with little attraction. Having to make such a retreat would feel like losing a game, of having to accept defeat, enduring the consequences of a personal failure and a damaged self-image. The whole thing sucked, pure and straight.

On the other side of the coin was the reality of things. Financially, it would be much cheaper to stay in school. His parents would be disappointed, but they would never know the entire sad story. And his father would be relieved, not having to write the big check each semester. McAllister had some good friends in Delaware. Perhaps they were not as political, but they were otherwise engaged in different adventures of which he could join. It would simply be a different place to hide for awhile, while he kept the student deferment as long as he could. Such a move would buy him more time, and maybe ease his fractured state of mind.

And the girl, yes the girl. He tried to make himself stay away from that purely emotional wishful thinking. Such feelings were a foolish anticipation, devoid of any reason. For crying out loud, he'd only met her that one night. He didn't really even know Mad, or what she might be like. She would be living her own life, and other guys would be checking her out. McAllister wanted to slap himself out of it, to bury this crazy irrational desire. It was not a blueprint for any kind of important decision. But deep down, he knew better. It would not go away until this wanting was either answered in some direct understanding, or forgotten and replaced by someone else. It was useless to fight the obvious. These imagined enchantments were the one thing that kept him going each and every day.

In March of 1970, a Greenwich Village townhouse blew out its doors and windows onto a smoking Manhattan street. The concussion pounded across the American anti-war movement from coast to coast. Unlike the murders of three college students in the dark mind of the Mississippi flatlands some years before, the carnage in New York City sung a different tune. The incident revealed a turning point, a proclamation that there would be no more mister nice guys, no more lyrical pleas to give peace a chance. Events were moving toward an unwanted but predictable extreme. The faces in the newsprint photos of the *Washington Post* were young, educated, and very very white. Unlike Mississippi, the frank realities behind those photographic images were no longer innocent. They reflected a new intent, a strategy born of a desperate frustration to battle back, to fight fire with fire. A new rationale was finding expression. To allow the United States government to commit violence day after day, and do nothing about it, was a violent act itself.

Sean McAllister felt a similar consuming anger. But he was a choirboy compared to the passionate response others were willing to take upon themselves. The Vietnam War was making people crazy, forcing some to step over a line from whence they would not be able to return. The Weatherman faction of SDS had convinced themselves of a necessity they were willing to meet. The result was a revolutionary identity, and the methodical journey such a created self-image would require. But you better know the playbook if you are going to take the field against the Green Bay Packers. Unforced errors will kill you in a game for all the marbles. Three dead individuals had paid the ultimate price for their mistake. Blown to smithereens.

No doubt, the ante had been raised. It was no longer the revolutionary rhetoric of the Black Panther movement, the understandably serious fright of 'niggers with guns'. If there was one group of citizens who had the stone-cold reasons for a revolutionary response to a racist economic repression, it was Black America.

Even the most bigoted Klansman would understand that if you hang a nigger from a tree, and other niggers got guns, you better be ready for a response. That was a given. The key would be to make sure you kept your superiority of force at all times. It was Power 101, a mandatory requirement for graduation with a degree in keeping control. However, the portent of a white woman with a bomb in her purse was a whole different kind of offensive strategy. That would be a game changer. Such premonitions mandated a time out on the field. The coaches needed to think fast and come up with an adjustment.

With all the personal uncertainties confronting Sean McAllister, trying to emotionally rationalize the human enigma of violence against your fellow man, well it was simply an unwanted exercise. On one hand, it went against any tradition of human hope and goodness, the teachings and belief systems where the ultimate goal was peace on earth. On the other hand, could any one human being seek the excuse of being an innocent bystander, especially when confronted by such unwarranted aggression against these tenets of personal morality. Tenets the better part of the human enterprise needed to cherish and sustain.

World War II was not about the Germans or the Japanese. It was more about the dilemma that Nazism personified, the greed of a superior race of humans, whose survival and ascent had allowed for a perverse code by which the human practice of 'any means necessary' was made moral by the presumptions it could create. Hitler and the Nazis were nothing new in the history of the world. They were just another version of the horror that beset the human condition, the devil in all mankind, asserting their drive for the dark absolute of acquisition at any cost. Greed and fear, in whatever color you chose, was always the heart of the matter.

So if you blow up a building, and in doing so you kill an innocent bystander, who was culpable? Was it you, the individual, who in defense of a greater cause, committed this act? Or was it the tyrant, whose quest for superiority and control had created the circumstances that forced you to respond? Did you perpetrate the act out of a love in your heart for a better world, holy in your defense of saving that love, while destroying the evil that threatened its existence? Or did you perpetrate that act out of anger, out of a dogmatic agenda inspired by others, for reasons that gave you the sustenance of revenge, or of claiming your own sense of power? Or would it always be something terribly in between?

The envelope please! And the winner is …? The winner is to put down the *Washington Post*, to roll a fat one, to light it up and suck deep, exhale as you turn on the stereo, let Jimmy Morrison and the Doors wail into the night. "This is the end, my only friend, the end. Can you picture what will be, so limitless and free, desperately in need of some stranger's hand, in a desperate land." No more questions, at least for today.

Spring in Washington D.C. is truly recognized by one thing, and one thing only. When the cherry blossoms along the National Mall reach peak bloom, their pale pink and white flowers unfolding under the warm sun of a cloudless afternoon, all the vagaries of a difficult winter melt away. The Tidal Basin reflects blue against the backdrop of marbled white monuments. Deciduous leafy hardwoods bless the contours of the city. The body loosens itself from the constraints of colder days, softening in the heat. Life unburdens itself for a time.

April unwinds with thoughts of summer. Women blush in colorful displays of beauty and attraction on serene campus mornings. Windows open to the sounds of the street, prompting distractions of love and desire, of green grass and laughter, in hopes of a future shorn of discontent. For a moment, Washington D.C. sheds the imprint of its colossal magnitude of power, its stale redundant conformities, its truculent undercurrent of political arrogance. Like a train pulling out of Union Station, spring begins its journey on a one-way ticket to the sun. Sean McAllister was ready to go along for the ride.

April 30th, 1970 was one of those days, resplendent with the intoxicating odors of lilac and fresh mown grass. It was a time to be outside, whatever the choice. At the dorm a couple of the prep boys mentioned golf and McAllister became all ears. He hadn't been on the course in a long time. They headed for a public course that rested on a flat strip of ground surrounded by the Potomac River, not far from the middle of the city and the National Mall. From the fairways on the course, the Lincoln Memorial stood brazen white in the foreground. Deep behind, the obelisk of the Washington Monument rose like a missile, its phallic point piercing a blue streaming sky.

Playing the game and being outside in the warmth of the sun raised McAllister's spirits. It reminded him of afternoons with his dad, just the two of them spending time together. The weather seemed to promise the end of the school year, of the summer ahead and new things to do. Dreamy thoughts of his future, which had forsaken him for so many months, began to cater with inspiration. Driving back to campus, the car windows open to the soft textured evening of extended light, he felt the hint of romance in the air, and better times ahead. If only they would last.

Sadly, this was not to be. Some hours later, the axis of an American nation was to tragically shift again. Richard Nixon, his gross complexion speaking before the nation, added one more nightmare passenger aboard his hellbound train of war. The United States would now officially invade another sovereign nation. Appearing like an evil lord, he announced the military incursion of Cambodia, further spreading the disease of a conflict that seemed to find no cure. Four days later the train would enter the station, reaching the gates of a national conflagration.

On college campuses across America, the student killings at Kent State were like a Molotov cocktail thrown into fifty-five gallon drum of gasoline. A symbolic wave of combustion spread throughout the land, singeing with its heat even the most apolitical agnostic. Once again, the explosive battle resumed. Universities across the land were overwhelmed with a greater mass of their students stepping forward in dissent. No longer was it the perceived guilty fixed in the target of the crosshairs. With Kent State, the innocent bystander had been killed. Every American parent with a child in college rose up and out of their Lazy Boys. No longer would any child be safe. Across the nation, business as usual came to a halt. Student strikes erupted and hundreds of colleges began to close.

On the following Saturday, a hundred thousand descended upon the city. Washington D.C. turned in a free-for-all as the demonstration grew ugly. Cars and storefronts were smashed, as small cadres of vandals found an excuse to destroy property and wreck havoc. Despite his continuing frustration and anger, Sean McAllister could not raise a hand to destroy and vandalize this place he called home. Answering the cops was one thing, but in this instance he still could not pull the trigger of his hate to go so far. It served no greater purpose in his mind. But did he do anything to stop it? No. His courage continued to run thin.

Reflecting on the hysteria, McAllister wanted nothing more than to just go home. But not to the campus that for most of two years had served that purpose. Suddenly, the angst and uncertainty which had grated inside of him over the last several months became more compelling. He was overcome with a sense of fatigue, the kind of feeling one gets when the opponent has buried you on the field, when defeat has sapped your purpose and self-confidence, leaving you to yearn for the clock to expire. Sean McAllister was feeling beaten, desiring only a quiet place to lick his wounds.

Despite his own personal exhaustion, the strength of the Kent State uprisings had a momentum of their own. The University had also seen enough. For reasons unknown, whether for its own particular safety, or a similar sense of weariness, the University capitulated to the shutdown and called it a year. It set a date for the dorms to close. Sean McAllister packed up his belongings. He called his old friend Bruiser up north, who came down to D.C. with his car.

McAllister said his goodbyes, particularly to Huggins. Packed and ready, Bruiser moved the car through town. Slumped in his seat, McAllister caught glimpses of the skyline, the pensive Potomac River flowing ever the same. Deep down, he could sense this leaving might be his last. He was exiting this worldly white city, with its strangely self-indulgent beat, its dangerous fenced ghettos, its confederate southern influences, its myopic sense of self. In a singular way, Washington D.C. was a planet all its own. But, in many other ways, it wasn't hurting him to go.

CHAPTER SIX

YOU AIN'T GOIN' NOWHERE
Newark, Delaware / July, 1970

MCALLISTER SNUGGLED HIS HEAD into the back of her shoulder blade, his right arm resting over her brown summer torso. His legs followed the shape of her slightly fetal position, the back of his feet rubbing gently upon the tops of her own. She stirred, turning over to face him. Strands of hair lay across her softly flushed cheeks, the lips moist. She slid her arms under his, her small firm breasts engaging his chest. They kissed, holding each other close. Pulling away, she looked into his eyes, smiling. "Good morning", she said. He returned the salutation, kissing her again.

They lay together in her single upstairs room, the summer morning sun rising outside the open window. Birds chirped in the green leafed trees beyond, the background sound of vehicles purring by on the street below. McAllister lifted his head, seeking the clock on her night stand. He slid back down, his head resting on hers, licking her ear. "I love Sundays", he whispered. She pulled herself closer against him, concurring. Touching him with her thin restive fingers, his manhood grew hard once more. Slowly, cautiously, deliberately, they made love a second time, sweeter than the passionate rush of attraction only hours before.

Sometime later, they showered and dressed, speaking in low tones so as not to disturb the others in the rooming house. Walking hand in hand through the subdued campus streets, they shared a Sunday breakfast at a diner on Main. He began getting to know her in a different way. She was funny and sweet. When she laughed, the soft red of her cheeks blushed with color. Walking back to her place, they strolled through the vacant campus sidewalks. McAllister felt like he was on vacation to a faraway place.

Returning to the house, he called his parent's home, telling his mom that he had stayed over with friends the previous night. He gave her a ruse about an apartment that might be available in the fall, asking if he could keep the car the rest of the day. Per the usual, his father was at the golf course. But his dad had caught a ride with his buddies, so his mother had a car. Things were copasetic.

"Bring your bathing suit," he said to Mad.

"My bathing suit? Where are we going?" she asked.

"It's a surprise," he answered, "but it's a cool place, you'll dig it."

Packing a lunch, they drove northeast out of town, toward the uneven hills of the Brandywine Valley. McAllister weaved through the narrow paved roads, past lightly populated residential driveways, scattered amongst the shaded dense woodlands. Near the Pennsylvania border, he found the turnout he was looking for. Parking the car, he gathered up the suits, towels and food into a back pack. With a bota bag over his shoulder, a section of rope in his hand, he led Mad through a path in the woods. Eventually the trail opened to a grassy hillside meadow full of sun and sky. At the apex, stood a rounded cement structure with a slightly angled roof surrounded by a chain link fence.

As they approached Mad remained perplexed. "What is it, Sean?" she asked.

"You'll see," McAllister answered. "Just take your time, and I'll help you over the fence." He hoped she would be game for the task. They went slow and easy over the chain link barrier, then he hefted her up to a metal ladder on the side of the building. She climbed deftly to the rooftop. McAllister tied the rope to the straps of the back pack and bota bag, before tossing the length of rope to the roof. He jumped to the ladder's first rung, pulling himself up, climbing the rest of the way. Mad sat away from the edge of the building, watching as he pulled the bags up with the rope, handing them for her to hold. He went over to a shiny tin cover on the roof. He lifted off the lid, checking down inside. "Come, look," he called.

Mad got up, went over and peered down into the darkness. "Water?" she questioned? McAllister laughed. "It's an artesian well," he answered, "it comes right from the ground. We call it 'the 'tank." McAllister paused to look across the fields that surrounded them, but in all his trips to this place he had never seen a soul. "I don't think you need your suit," he said, unless you want to wear it. My guess is that we are trespassing on one of the Dupont estates, but no one has ever been around."

"You go first," she said. McAllister took off his shorts, tee shirt and shoes, then smiled broadly as he placed himself on the inside ladder rungs, lowering inside. Mad watched as he let himself go, falling back into the water with a splash. "Yeow," he cried, and the sound of his voice echoed inside the well, rising through the hole of light. "Come on," he said, "just one quick splash. You won't regret it." He paddled himself in the cold water, waiting. Then two lovely feet stepped cautiously through the hole until Mad was below the roofline. "Just push off and let yourself go," he said calmly to quiet her fear.

Mad let go and splashed into the darkness, followed by a scream of delight that bounced inside the building. The look on her face was electric, eyes wide, her face bright with the shock of the chilling cold pool. She swam right at him, and they clutched into each other's arms. She held him tight for a moment, speechless, before pushing herself away back toward the ladder, grabbing it to hold on. "You're crazy," she gasped. "It's freezing." She pulled herself up quickly, her mouth open. The light through the top of the hole illuminated her gaze back toward him within the darkened interior. "But refreshing, right," he laughed. She pulled herself up on the rungs, back toward the heat. "Be careful," he said. "Go slow."

The couple sat on the roof with their towels spread, eating the sandwiches, passing the wine bag between them, alone in the pure heated sky of a July afternoon. In the distance, dense trees bordered the open fields of burnished dry grass, the sun warming their goose pimpled skins.

"How did you find this place?" she asked.

"We found it in high school," he answered, "just roaming around."

"Have you brought anyone else here?" she asked, looking away toward the fields below.

"No, you're the first," he said truthfully. He paused. "I'm glad you came."

"Me, too," she said. She turned and looked at him, her eyes seeking his.

"I'm glad I'm the first, it's a beautiful place." Leaning over, she kissed him, the taste of red wine on her breath, warm with the sun.

In the early evening, they sat on the front steps of the rooming house, the heat of the day waning, continuing to share the individual histories that neither knew of the other. McAllister would return to his parent's home in North Wilmington, back to his summer job with the road construction outfit he had kept from the year before. Mad would stay on campus. She had a job with the University administration, doing file work and miscellaneous things for the registrar's office. McAllister did not want to leave her, everything else seeming so trivial in necessity. The prior evening and this day were so momentous, so perfectly rare and at ease. Still, they were both tired, with things to get done. He would call her when he could make it down again.

Driving home he couldn't believe his incredible fortune. He felt so lucky that she was unattached, at least enough for them to come together and meet this way. Sexually, it was not his first time, but it had been months and months since his last encounter. He was relieved to have performed so well. And Mad had made it easy, she had been as willing as him. The day was drifting into a soft pleasant summer night. Sean McAllister couldn't recall if there had ever been a day better than this.

He had refrained from telling her about his hitchhiking trip to California, only several weeks away. Until today, he had been excited about the journey, the adventure ahead. But finally meeting this girl, the thrill of her presence and companionship, seemed to lessen his intent on going. Part of him didn't want to leave her so soon. Consequently, he had kept those plans silent in his mind.

Johnny Howard was another old buddy from the neighborhood. Johnny and he had gone through school together, playing ball and spending summers at the beach. Like McAllister, Johnny was home from college until September. Neither had been to California, expressing a similar desire to travel west. McAllister knew he wouldn't back out from making the trip. He just hadn't anticipated this new distraction that pleased him so much.

In the middle of the week, McAllister drove back down to see her. They spent the evening together, making love again, before heading back home late into the night. He was hoping to return for the weekend, but

Mad was catching a ride north to her parent's home in Pennsylvania, so that was out. He was disappointed. He was becoming willingly attached to this new beautiful companion in his life.

Mary Jane was coming down from Boston for a short week, to visit at the beach with their parents. McAllister had expected to beg off with one excuse or another, but with Mad unavailable, he decided to go down for the weekend to be with his family. On Friday night after work, his parents packed up and drove down to the shore. McAllister waited for his sister to arrive. They would follow behind on Saturday morning. That evening, he and Mary Jane lounged in the kitchen of the empty house, sharing a bottle of wine. It was the first time in a long while they had spent some time together.

"Mom says that Dad is disappointed you are leaving school. He wanted you to stay and finish what you started."

"I know. But now he won't be able to hold it over me so much, the money it costs," McAllister answered. "I'm just not into school these days, Janie. But like you said, I got to stay as long as I can. Coming back home will be cheaper. I think I can make it without much help."

"Have they accepted the transfer?" Mary Jane asked.

"Pretty much," he answered. "They won't accept the theology credits though, can you believe that? Theology was actually one of the better courses. If they had just called it comparative religions, it probably would have been okay. But heck, I guess they figured it was like going to mass on Sundays, or something like that. So I lose six credits and that sucks."

"What about the academic probation thing? Is that a problem for you?"

"I never said anything about it, and I don't think it was on the transcripts they sent. The University is just as happy to be rid of me, and guys like Huggins. I think they're pissed they accepted guys like us in the first place."

"Your friend, Chris? He was so nice last fall. How's he doing?"

"Oh, I didn't tell you. He's leaving, too. He went back home to Connecticut. He got a high lottery number, so he's okay. But with him going away, it made it easier to decide."

"Will you miss it? I mean, being in Washington and everything."

"Yeah, some." A fleeting thought of Mad crossed his mind. "Coming home to a straight town like Newark doesn't exactly make me jump up and down. But it will be all right. I just met a girl down there, she's really nice."

"Mickey, a girl?" His sister's voice raised in pitch. McAllister already regretted the remark. "Little brother's got a girlfriend?" Mary Jane picked up the wine bottle, pouring more into each glass. "So tell me more, what's she like?"

If McAllister could have kicked his own ass, he would have. "Janie, I just met her, geez. I don't know, she's pretty, she's going to school down there. I met her on New Year's Eve, but I didn't really meet her until a couple of weeks ago. I like her though, she's easy and fun to get along with."

"Did you sleep with her yet? Did you have sex with her?"

McAllister unconsciously picked up his glass of wine and took a big gulp.

"Did you just ask me if I slept with her? Am I expected to answer that?"

"Mickey, I'm your sister." Mary Jane's voice turned a little more serious. "Is she on the pill? Did you use any protection?"

McAllister caught the drift. A worried consequence stripped across his mind. "Sure, I guess. I mean we didn't talk about it or anything. Like I said, we just met."

Mary Jane sipped her wine, leaning back in the kitchen chair. "Well, you just need to talk about it the next time," she warned. "It's important not to make a mistake. It can change things in a big way. Take it from me is all I'm going to say."

McAllister's head was staring down at the tablecloth. But hearing those words, he rose up and looked at his sister, uncertain. "You're not…?"

Mary Jane closed her eyes, shaking her head. "No. But I know what you might be thinking. You can't say a word, Mickey. Not a single word."

McAllister understood. "No shit," he mumbled. A quiet pause grew between them, hovering with discomfort. "I'm good," he said, easing her concern, "never a word. But don't you be telling Mom about the girl, either. I hardly know her yet. I don't want Mom getting all squirrelly about things. Is that a deal?" Mary Jane's eyes slowly opened, as if waking from a memory that still pursued her. She nodded. Silence was indeed golden, especially when the truth would have been like a train wreck derailing into an Irish Catholic world.

"Deal," she answered. "We can change the subject now. I mean, I just want you to be careful, it can be a hard thing. By the way, what's her name, your new friend?"

"Mad. It's short for Madelyn."

"Huh, it's different," Mary Jane said. "I kind of like it. Hey, whatever happened to Reggie Disalvo? Did he ever enlist, or get drafted up?"

"Reggie, oh yeah," McAllister answered, pleased to move away from the worry of the moment. "No, they never called him, don't ask me why. He never did go to school or anything. And then he got this really high number in the lottery, like over three hundred or something, the lucky stiff. I think his girlfriend Teresa talked him out of the helicopter thing. They've got an apartment together downtown these days, and planning to get married, I hear. He's still working for his dad, making the good money. I saw him briefly after I got back home. I offered to trade him draft numbers and stuff, but he wasn't buying." McAllister laughed. "No, Reggie Disalvo is flying free as a bird."

"I'm glad," Mary Jane said.

"Me, too," McAllister agreed. "Real glad."

The next morning, Mary Jane drove her car down to the beach cottage that their parents shared with several other friends, exchanging its use on varying weekends throughout the summer. McAllister sat alongside his sister in the car, paging through a recent copy of Rolling Stone. They crossed the bridge over the Delaware and Chesapeake Canal, into the southern part of the state, heading toward the ocean beach towns that rimmed the state's southeastern border.

"I can't believe that your school got shut down," Mary Jane said. McAllister looked up from the magazine.

"I know. Me, too. But I think we just wore them out. The city was nuts. Everybody just wanted to go home. Finals were optional, you could either take them, or just take the grade you had at the time and split. I split. This cranky old English professor gave like everybody a 'D' in my Shakespeare class, just because he was pissed about the whole thing. Mom and Dad weren't too happy about that particular grade. I tried to explain the situation, but it didn't help much. Didn't do much for the transcript either."

"Couldn't you appeal or something? That's bullshit."

"The old fart has been a professor there probably since the Revolution. And I couldn't avoid the course, as the other options were already full. He had a reputation for being a low grader anyway. No sense in fighting it. If you took the final, maybe you got a 'C' at best. That's what Mom and Dad don't understand, spending all that tuition money, then not getting the courses you want to take, and ending up with assholes like him. It's just wasn't worth it."

"Yeah, it's only a democracy these days if you are on their side," Mary Jane stated. "Sometimes the arrogance that inhabits them makes my blood curdle. And all the rest of the suckers just follow along, waving the flag and wearing their hard hats. In their evil minds, the four at Kent and the two at Jackson got what they deserved. I don't know what it's ever going to take for this war to end."

"It says here, the Ohio National Guard fired off sixty-one shots in thirteen seconds." McAllister held up the copy of Rolling Stone. "That's a fair fight, don't you think," he remarked sarcastically. "I don't know. It looks like things might get worse. The march after Kent really got out of hand, people busting up cars, smashing windows and stuff. I just can't get into that shit. But what should they expect when the cops start shooting at you with guns."

"I'm not sure what I want to do when I graduate in December," Mary Jane followed. "Nine more credits. Part of me wants to get away, maybe move up to Vermont. But David got accepted into law school at NYU. He wants me to go with him to New York."

"David seems like an okay guy, although I just met him that one time. Is he the one? I mean…."

Mary Jane didn't respond right away. "Yes, he's the one. And he was good about it. We shared the cost, but it definitely shook him up. It would have changed so much. Still, it was my decision. It just wasn't the right time for us, but no less hard. That's why you need to be careful, Mickey. Some girls will want to have the baby, and your life will change in a very big way."

"I hear you, Janie," McAllister agreed. It worried him some that the damage might already be done. But he also felt confident that Mad would not have put herself in that situation.

The drive took them through the corn and soybean fields of southern Delaware, along the back roads and small farms of a rural

America. Each town appeared white on the inside, often black on the outside. They passed little clusters of shanty wood cabins along the highway, cut out from the fields.

Equality in the United States was a cherished turn of a phrase, a word that could flow eloquently from the mouths of men. Men like Martin Luther King and Bobby Kennedy, who believed in the spirit of its meaning. But replacing those dilapidated shacks with a real house of running water and security against the weather was a fact of life that belied such intent. These shacks were the self-evident truth, a truth that the use of eloquent words could not mask. McAllister wondered how many of these African-American sons were now crawling their way through a dense humid jungle, an automatic weapon clutched in their hands, fighting for their lives, based on words like these. The hypocrisies of his country continued to stand out to him. Somehow, these shacks could be easily ignored, while driving by on a Saturday morning, before leaving them comfortably behind.

This soft flat farmland country reminded McAllister of his childhood years growing up in the black river and peanut region of North Carolina. He remembered the Negro housekeeper who came once a week to look after he and Janie. She would clean the house as his mother ran errands or went to a social gathering. Della was her name, and she had a son she was forced to bring along at times. His name was Bo and the boy was McAllister's age. He and Bo would play together in the big backwoods of pine trees, or climb the large piles of peanut brush after harvest. They would sit there together, crunching open the light brown shells, chomping on the raw green nuts inside.

Until one day the three Charles brothers came along. They chased Bo away, screaming the words nigger and coon at him, trying to catch him as he ran back toward the house, escaping into his mother's old car. They banged on the roof of the car, as McAllister trailed behind. Bo's mother came out on the porch, yelling at them, but they paid her no mind. When McAllister caught up, he pushed the older Charles boy, telling them to go away and leave them alone. But the older Charles boy rose up and struck him, knocking him to the ground. McAllister grabbed the boy's feet, but the kid kicked him loose and ran away, calling him a 'nigger lover' as he lay beside the car. McAllister's eyes ticked involuntarily as the memory became complete, recalling the hurt and confusion he had felt. To this day, the word 'nigger' had its own special meaning for him, always one of hate and injustice. His young friend, Bo, never came with his mother again.

Mary Jane broke the spell. "Mom says you are talking about hitchhiking to California next month. What's that all about?"

"Yeah, me and Johnny Howard. We're going out to visit his cousin. She goes to school in Berkeley."

"Mom's worried as sin, you know. I think Dad is, too."

McAllister sighed. "I know, I know. But what are they going to do, try and stop me or something. I've never been to California, or across the country. I want to get out of here for awhile, that's all. See something new."

"I was just asking," Mary Jane responded. "I think it's great. How long will it take? You have to be back at school, when is that?"

"I've got a little over three weeks to make the trip. Registration is in mid-September. If I get stuck, I'll take a bus back. Johnny is going to go up and see some college friends in Seattle, Washington, and probably catch a ride back with them. He doesn't have to be back as soon as me."

"You're going to hitchhike all the way back by yourself?"

"Yeah, I guess so. Or catch a ride somehow. I haven't thought about it much."

Mary Jane turned her head and smiled. "Really, Mickey, I'm just jealous more than anything else. It should be fun, a real adventure."

"Thanks," McAllister said. "You can just keep telling Mom it will be okay, if you would. I'll be calling her when I can."

In the early afternoon they reached the beach house. They spent the rest of the day on the sand, laying in the sun with their mother, their father taking a long nap inside the cottage. The ocean had a decent swell, body surfing the waves a good hit. McAllister spent a long time in the water, his sister and mother either chatting together under the umbrella or reading their books. Lolling in the waves, he thought about Mad, how much fun it would have been to have her here. Later, the family barbequed and spent the evening together. Everyone stayed away from talking about politics or the future.

On Sunday morning, McAllister got up early with his dad. They took their coffee and surf rods, casting over the waves for an hour or two. They stood knee deep in the white foam of the ocean, breathing in the salt air, the constant refrain of the rolling surf playing in their ears. After a late breakfast, McAllister spent the rest of the day reading, swimming, or sleeping in the sun. Finally, showering the sand and salt off his body, he helped clean up the beach house. With the cars packed, they headed home. It had been a typical weekend at the shore, something the family had always loved and shared.

Retracing the drive north, McAllister listened as his sister pondered her future, sharing bits of personal expectation, and the realities that lay before her. Mary Jane, so often sure of herself, so pragmatic in her convictions, seemed less certain about her life ahead. She wondered openly about what she might do when she graduated, whether or not she should follow her boyfriend to New York. Some of her friends had finished school. But instead of looking for jobs, they had relocated to a large farmhouse in Vermont, rejecting the life of the city. He sensed in his sister a measure of doubt, as if a burden of sorts was upon her, an answer that would not come. It was a circumstance new to McAllister, a side of his sister he had never engaged.

"I still wonder sometimes, if I made the right decision," she said.

McAllister turned toward her, seeing something sorrowful in her face, a hurt she was trying to convey. At first, he was oblivious to know the reason. Then it dawned on him, a realization he had never considered, a remorse he now tried to understand. She glanced his way, two thin tears hanging liquid on the edge of her eyes.

"You mustn't ever tell Mom and Dad. Please, Mickey, for my sake."

"Never," he said to assure her. He felt the pain in his sister's voice. He felt for her a deeper affection than ever before. He felt the returning fear of his own thoughtless calculations, and he felt himself older than he might ever want to be.

CHAPTER SEVEN

RETURN OF THE GRIEVOUS ANGEL
West / August, 1970

Day One

THE EASTERN SUMMER DAY IS HOT AND BRIGHT, a good day for sunglasses against the late August sun. Sean McAllister and Johnny Howard stand alongside the Pennsylvania Turnpike, dressed in tee shirts and heavy boots, their arms tanned brown with the color of the season. Their backpacks, loaded with gear and strapped with sleeping bags, lean against a tall metal light stanchion. In thin scratches on the silver post are the markings of others who had come before, archeological idioms of life on the American road.

'Denver or Bust', 'Stuck here for five hours, June 1969', 'Fuck Tricky Dick', 'Billy loves Peggy', 'Suck My Cock', or 'Jesus Saves'. Nearby, a cut out piece of cardboard lays cast aside in the roadside brush. In faded magic marker, a destination is scrawled in ultimate simplicity, 'West'. McAllister picks up the sign. He holds it against his chest, his right arm outstretched with thumb pointing up. The journey is underway.

With this beginning, the trip from east coast to west has no scheduled itinerary, the process of its telling a complete unknown. The future must be left simply to imagination. Only the destination can be confirmed, where sooner or later something will happen, something that will push one further toward the Pacific rim of America. Johnny Howard sits nearby, his curly blonde hair raving about his head. With his handsome baby face, he looks like Roger Daltry of the "Who", a rock and roll first impression to the hordes of rushing vehicles passing before them.

McAllister, a blue bandana tied back over his head, watches the high speed race of a mobile America flying across the national domain, encased in their private metal spheres. They are a multitude of human strangers, fueled by petroleum and wasting with exhaust. Speeding by, they are singularly preoccupied with their own thoughts and purposes of intent, their internal conversations becoming surprised for a moment by the roadside distraction of two young men, soliciting for some curious reason to enter their personal worlds.

Despite the numbingly high odds of two long-haired men catching a ride with most of America, ultimately the theory of sentimental probability increases with each passing car or truck. Then suddenly it happens. There is the sound of a motor breaking down, the distinctive aural change of rubber on the road. It is a sonic that raises the antennae of all hitchhikers, causing them to look behind. The fast moving vehicle touches down on the roadside shoulder, scattering gravel and dust before shuttering to a stop. As the dust clears, a flashing red turn signal beacons like a buoy far down the highway beyond.

For an uncertain moment the hitchhikers stand frozen by the event, as if waiting for a punch line. For a quick standstill click of time they wait. Is it stopping for them, or some other vehicular reason? Meanwhile, the vehicle sits like a creature in the distance, idling by the side of the road. Nonetheless, the scramble begins. Sticking stuff in pockets, the heavy packs are swung up and over the back, traipsing with their load hurriedly toward the beast. As the men approach, a car door opens. Someone steps out on the shotgun side, waving them along. Expectations rise. The initial ride has begun.

The phenomenon of hitchhiking is a peculiar human interaction, a social compact between individual strangers, layered with a multiple of personal motivations, some simple, others more complex. For McAllister, ever since his first time out, it was like a coloring book of adventure, waiting to be filled with a mysterious palette of crayons. Perhaps there is an expected outcome, but the construction of which no one knows for certain. And therein lays the mystery, so often missing in other parts of daily life. Hitchhiking is an exciting distraction where the process of form is as important as the form itself. It is social science at its most creative. It is Henry Miller's *Tropic of Cancer* on the streets of Paris, a day in the life, to be ravaged or loved, or placed somewhere in between. Hitchhiking is novelty, fresh and inventive, original in its unfolding. It becomes an exciting thing to do.

That's not to say there are no rules or conventions one can purposely ignore. Hitchhiking often demands the required elements of exchange. Should the driver require conversation, or perhaps a forum for his views of the world, then payment for the transport necessitates a listened response. Good hitchhikers understand the dynamics of fair trade, that giving time and ear is part of the bargain. The automobile might rightfully be described as America's second home. And should a hitchhiker become an invited guest for a particular duration, there are some common courtesies involved which are never too much to ask. Excepting of course, that the driver is not some form of raging psychotic, or wants to fuck you up the ass. In that case, all bets are off.

The early rides carry them through the Susquehanna, the Allegheny, on toward the state of Ohio. A Christian family with three kids in a large station wagon; later, a van full of hippie travelers like themselves, headed for a party somewhere in Western Pennsylvania. The darkened evening takes them northwest to Interstate 80. When dropped off at a rest stop south of Cleveland, they lay down their packs near a fence line, away from the busy parking area of trucks and cars.

Stretching wearily on the dark picnic grass, they are serenaded by the lullaby of refrigeration units in the big rigs humming nearby, the irregular shine of passing car lights, the sounds of diesel engines gearing down to take a piss and stretch the legs. Car doors slam, rest room toilets flush, dogs are walked along the great American highway that never sleeps. For Sean McAllister, it feels good to lay his body down, to be out of his boots. He thinks of the girl he has left behind, caressing her in his thoughts before falling into sleep.

Day Two

McAllister awakes to morning dew and the rising heated sun of early light. He rubs his eyes, pulls himself from the cocoon of the sleeping bag, feeling the wetness of the grass on his shoeless feet. Yawning his way to the rest rooms, the highway noise of the previous night remains unbroken. Packing their gear, he and Johnny Howard walk through the parking lot of tractor trailers, thirsty for coffee and a friendly morning face. Johnny Howard approaches a trucker, but is waved away. The pair continue their hike out the exit ramp to meet the highway. Putting down their packs, they begin the second day of the job ahead.

Ohio. It is the land of Kent State and a gunshot 'middle majority', numbed by television and the daily routine. It is the province of a 'love it or leave it' mentality, the dogmas of a conservative Midwest. They catch a ride to Chicago, passing through the sedated farmlands of Indiana and bread-basket cultivation. In the distance, one sees the industrial stacks of metal and smoke that is Gary, Indiana. This is the world of economic production, overtime and the night shift, where men work from daybreak to dawn, sleeping away the weekdays of their lives. Further images of a commonplace America come pouring in. Out on the highway, perhaps a new pick-up truck from Detroit, with a handgun under the seat, or a fat complaining wife with kids on a sugar rush. These are the visions of a meat and potatoes future as haunting as any episode of the *Twilight Zone*.

In the blurred haze of a late summer morning, the Vietnam War goes on. On a city street of bungalow homes with green bordered grass, an American flag hangs lazily in the still humidity, a symbolic gesture of belief. At a nearby street corner, an unmarked car makes a silent turn, pulling over to a curb. Two men in uniform push themselves from within, bending out with an unwilling task. At the front door of a modest house they will deliver the official news. Another neighborhood son will not be coming home for dinner. The vanquished prayers of a mother's faithful love have gone unanswered, and a shattered second death begins. It is the kind of human finality that has no escape. The kind of death that the survivors must forever carry on.

McAllister changes the subject of his reverie. He forces himself to dream of other images, of happier expectations. He begins to envision the crashing blue waves of a Pacific beach. He sits with legs crossed, smoking a bowl on a rocky cascade head, as a huge orange sunset dips below the horizon. He watches the ocean breakers swell, hears the strum of an acoustic guitar, inhales the salted air of an ocean breeze. The evening gives way to a starlit night, soft in the sand of rolling dunes, out of the wind, clear and free.

"Well, this is it, boys. I've got to drop you before the toll booths. Welcome to Chicago."

Chicago, Illinois. So much for any more California dreaming. Instead, you step out into the brutal sun of a mid-afternoon, amidst the grip of an insane highway interchange on the outskirts of the metropolis. Thousands of vehicles jockey their way through a long string of payment stalls, the high-energy confusion of a frenzied urban commute. Ahead, another dozen hitchhikers are strung up the shoulder of the road. It looks like a tough spot that could take some time to escape.

But before McAllister and Johnny Howard can get their bearings, another kind of heat is upon them. A police cruiser is rolling up the shoulder, a loudspeaker atop the patrol car. Two cops are seated in front, a solitary figure in back. They come to announce an unexpected type of departure. "Leave this highway now, or join this man in the Cook County jail. Get off this roadside immediately, or be subject to arrest."

Easy for them to say. There is nowhere to go but for an eight-foot chain link fence rising behind them. And so another scramble begins, looking like a zoo full of human monkeys wrestling up and over the barricade. The harsh fencing waves under their weight, fingers branded by the pressure of its links. Backpacks are raised and pushed over the top. Bodies land roughly onto the other side. They are a band of young Americans, appearing like innocent refugees from a culture war they didn't commit. The cops sit inside the cruiser, enjoying the scatter, getting their afternoon kicks.

Now the travelers are stuck in a light industrial section of the city's regime, the jurisdiction of one Mayor Richard J. Daley, home of the bloody Democratic Convention of 1968. McAllister has arrived. He is two years older and two years late. Most likely, little has changed. At least today, everyone's head is still in one piece, and one supposes they should be thankful for that. The afternoon heat is intense, the humidity draining, the location unknown. A long slow march begins without direction, through uncaring streets of human device. Several hours later, they are back on the road. Although tired and heavy, they are at least moving on. They continue riding until nightfall, to another rest stop somewhere in western Illinois. Hiding under some trees, they fall easily to sleep, weary from another long day.

Day Three
Mid-morning of the following day, they cross the Mississippi River. The river's broad sweep is marked by barge and tugboat traffic, imbued with the histories of explorer, pioneer, and the mythic imaginations of

Huckleberry Fin. The crossing becomes something of a demarcation point in their adventure, a watershed deliverance towards purple waves of grain. On the other side comes Iowa. The riders pass miles and miles of perfectly green cornfields, tall and ripe in the afternoon sun. Barreling through the torso of a continent, the mileposts flash by, further on through the bluff country of Iowa's western border, before fording the Missouri River into the state of Nebraska.

Skirting the city of Omaha, the rides continue past Lincoln, pointing like an arrow straight across the farmland plains. As the light of the day begins to fade, they take an exit off the interstate, directed to a quiet county park on the edge of a husker town. Far to the west, large dark clouds rise across the evening horizon. They appear like huge anvils in the sky, threatening the first rain of the journey. The two men unload their packs on picnic tables within the empty silence of a summer night.

At the park, a phone booth stands alone between the bathrooms. McAllister drops a dime, making a collect call. The phone rings, followed by the answer of a female voice on the other line. The operator asks for Mad, and the female voice says just a minute. After a time, her voice comes on the line, accepting the call.

"Hi there," he says. "I'll pay you when I get home, but I wanted to call, like you said."

"Oh, Sean, it's okay. Where are you? Is everything all right?"

"Somewhere in Nebraska. Everything is good."

"My gosh, so far already," Mad says. He tells her about the trip so far. She tells him that nothing important has happened at home, just the normal life of day to day. The sound of her voice is comforting, against the night of this faraway place. "I miss you," he says, feeling the long vacant distance between them. "I wish you were here. I've never seen so much corn in a single day."

She laughs. "I miss you, too. When you get home, you will tell me all about it." They say their good-byes. The click of the phone feels like the rope of a life raft cut away from the ship. The moonless sky is black. Rumbles of thunder pound in the distance. Slicing white light refracts along the treetops in a suddenly lonely world.

So strange are these tugs of competing emotion. Wanting to be with her, yet wanting to be in the here and now. He and Johnny Howard share the last of some crackers and cheese, an apple, the end of their food until the next opportunity. They spread their rain ponchos over the picnic tables, weighting them down with rocks. Underneath, they make their sleeping quarters, hoping the storm will miss them. Rustling in his sleeping bag, McAllister wills his thoughts to caress her, imagines a soft mattress sinking below him, home in her arms, the smell of her hair, dreaming away.

Life on the road can be a hell of an inconvenience. McAllister awakes to thunder and rain breaking overhead, the pounding of hard drops on the picnic table, sheets of wind rushing through the nearby trees. He pulls himself tight, holding hard to the shrinking dry ground below the table, awaiting the floodwaters. Eventually, the storm passes, leaving behind the sound of falling drips of moisture, the musty odor of flora swelling in the darkness of the night.

Day Four

Morning rises and begins to warm. Rolling over, McAllister stretches his bones. The birds are busy jabbering in the trees, a nearby creek hustling with the runoff, the sound of vehicles swishing along on the highway above. Green wet grass steams in softening mist as the day slowly heats. McAllister struggles from his damp sleeping bag. Johnny Howard does the same. They pack things up and continue on.

Matted and damp, looking like two dogs washed by a garden hose, the young men hold out a thumb to the sultry traffic rolling by. The Nebraska locals pass in their cars and pick-up trucks. Dressed in their farm shirts and cowboy hats, they slow down to take a gander. Their expressions appear more curious than derisive, but no one stops. An hour later, a step van of hippies finally pulls over, taking them to an exit back by the interstate. At a truck stop restaurant, they replenish themselves with breakfast and coffee before trudging back to the highway.

Things remain slow, as they sometimes often do. Surrounded by corn fields under Nebraska sky, the cars and trucks fly past in a high-speed chase across the flatlands, ignoring their presence and solicitation. Johnny Howard keeps his thumb upraised, walking back and forth on the gravel of the shoulder, performing the first shift of the working day. McAllister takes the time to rearrange and tighten his gear, thankful to be drying out in the growing summer heat. Sitting on his pack, he sifts handfuls of gravel through his hands, killing time as Johnny paces the roadside. With impatient desperation, Johnny points his outstretched arm toward an approaching vehicle, before letting the arm follow as the car speeds by, watching as the vehicle disappears into the distance.

Hitchhiking in America demands no routine. It follows only the fateful course of circumstance. The first three days had gone pretty well, the waiting not too long. Outside of the Chicago diversion, they had not been bothered by the police. But patience is a necessary emotional tool of the road. On this day, as the sun begins its fall from a midday peak, very few miles have been left behind.

A big blue sedan pulls off the secondary highway, turning onto the entrance of the interstate. Instead of accelerating toward the road ahead, it rumbles slowly up the ramp. McAllister's first thought is that it might be an unmarked police car, preparing to pull over and give them some anticipated grief. The car slows further as it reaches them, before stopping beside. An older man with a large crew-cut head, leans over from the driver's side, rolling down the window of the idling car.

"What are you boys doing out here?" the man asks.

Obviously a stupid question, but McAllister remains courteous. "Trying to catch a ride, sir."

"Catch a ride," the man repeats. "Most people in these parts use a car for that." McAllister steals a quick glance at Johnny Howard, raising his eyebrows.

"Where you catching a ride to," the man asks, "you know, if you had a car?" Johnny Howard steps beside McAllister, peering in the window.

"California, sir," Johnny answers. "We're hitchhiking."

"California? Well, you're a long way from there without a car." The man's expression changes. He chuckles to himself, as if responding to his own peculiar joke. "Well, get in boys, before I change my mind."

McAllister and Johnny Howard push their packs into the backseat of the car, climbing in front. They thank the man for the ride. He accelerates the vehicle onto the interstate, settling in behind the wheel.

"People call me Duke," the man says. "What do they call you?" The men respond in kind. "Well, I'm headed over to Scottsbluff," the man Duke says, "a couple of hours or so from here. But I reckon you're on the right road for California." Turning his head toward McAllister, the man smiles. Duke's head was as square as a block. His shoulders were broad, with powerful hairy forearms. He looked like a drill sergeant, the size of a man who could take care of himself.

"You boys are lucky today," Duke says. "Most times I've got a wagon load of samples in this rig. Mercantile products. And if those things could drive, even I wouldn't be here." Duke laughs again to himself, but looks over toward McAllister for approval.

"What do you do?" McAllister asks.

"What do I do? I sell things, son. You name it, I sell it. From Lincoln, Nebraska to Denver, Colorado. Sundries, mostly."

"Sundries? What are sundries?"

"Just about everything you don't eat or drink," Duke answers. "About everything you can buy in a drug store except the drugs. That would be one way to put it, I reckon."

"I guess that would mean a lot of samples," Johnny Howard confirms.

"Yesirree," Duke answers. A lot of samples. But these days, I just carry the new products that come onto the market. In the old days, I did both, deliver and sell. Nowadays, I just visit the establishments and let people know what is good to buy."

"You must travel a lot," McAllister says.

"Yessiree, all over this country. I'm drivin' all the time. Good thing I love to drive." Duke keeps his gaze on the road, beginning to whistle a tune, before speaking again. "Beautiful day, isn't it boys. Beautiful country, too. You know, around here you can see a church steeple six miles away."

McAllister tries to contain a laugh. The land was as flat as a pancake. There was nothing in the distance but fields of farmland and forever sky. This guy, Duke, was a trip. "Have you lived here all your life?" McAllister asks.

"Yessiree. Except for my days in the service way back when. Buffalo country, that's what I call it. Good people in these parts. What you see is what you get. You treat them right, they treat you right. It's a damn fair place to live. As I said, I like to travel, to see new things and people. But this is home. No need to go someplace where somebody is trying to cut your throat."

"Do you have a family?"

"Sure do," Duke says. "Two boys and a girl. And the wife of course. She does the thinking and I do the driving. My little girl is still at home, but the boys are grown up and gone. My oldest works in sales like me, a regional manager for General Foods. He's back in New York these days.

He's the youngest regional manager they have ever promoted. I like to say I taught him all he knows. The other boy is a newspaper man in Los Angeles. He's more like his mother, kind of quiet and serious. But he's a damn good writer, I'll tell you. You boys going to Los Angeles?"

"Maybe," McAllister answers, "but mostly San Francisco to start."

"My boy went to school in San Jose before getting the job in Los Angeles. He doesn't like it much, but he's got his wife and my granddaughter, so there isn't much he can do. A job is a job when you got mouths to feed. You know, a couple of years ago he interviewed Senator Kennedy just a day before he got killed."

McAllister sat up in his seat and turned his head toward the man. "He did? Bobby Kennedy?"

"Yessiree, he and two other reporters. They met with the man for like forty-five minutes, about the campaign for President and his visit with that farm worker guy. What's his name?"

"Cesar Chavez?"

"Yeah, that's the guy. Anyway, my son told me Bobby Kennedy was as good as gold with them. He didn't go on like all those other politicians, just told them what he felt and what he saw, a lot about farm labor issues and such. Then my son reported on the big parade in Los Angeles where thousands of people were climbing all over the guy. They were pulling and touching him, wanting to be near him like nothing my son had ever seen. You know, Kennedy could have been killed right there, but they just couldn't keep the people away."

McAllister tried to picture Duke's description, thinking of the television footage he had seen in the past. Images of that morning with his mom, as well as the funeral train came back to him.

"And the next day he was dead, just like that. My son still chokes up when he talks about it, every time he tells the story. Like I said, he's the quiet one in the family. But it sure had an effect on him."

Duke drove on, talking and telling stories all the way. Although he didn't have much interest in politics himself, his father-in-law had actually started the first farmer's cooperative in the state of Nebraska. His wife's family was part of the progressive farm and labor movement in America. They were conservative in their view of the world around them, but democratic when it came to the equality of work and money. Duke was telling a story about the farming people of the land, a rural ethnos and state of mind that McAllister had never encountered. It was a Woody Guthrie kind of experience, of catching trains and looking for work, of honest people helping those in need, of respect for the soil and faith in god. It was like going back in time, when compared to the pace and cynicism of life in the east.

"You boys take care of yourselves, now," Duke said as he let them go. "And next time, get yourselves a car." McAllister could see Duke chuckling again as he drove away, keeping himself amused. As he went whistling down the road, Duke had everything he needed in this flattened silent land of dirt and sky. There hadn't even been a radio in his car.

Soon after the ride with Duke, afternoon thunderheads built across the western Nebraska sky. In the distance, McAllister and Johnny Howard could see the wind and cool rain come pouring across the flats. They huddled with their backpacks on a ledge just under a highway overpass. When the storm passed through, they slid down the embankment, standing back from the highway as an occasional vehicle jetted by, splashing water off the pavement. There was not a farmhouse or homestead in sight, just miles of silent loneliness across the open range. Before they were able to catch another ride, a Nebraska state trooper was upon them, checking their identifications. He booted them off the interstate onto the secondary road above. Fumbling with their map, they tried to figure which way to aim.

An old pick-up truck motored by, stopping to let them ride in the back. The highway followed a long flat river meandering beside them, crossing into the state of Colorado. Sitting with his back against the front cab of the truck, McAllister gazed at the flatland expanse, admiring the soft curves of this treeless plain. He began to feel his first sense of being in the American West. It was easy to imagine the buffalo roving in dark herds across the country, or perhaps an Indian camp of tee pees settled by the river's edge. This was the earth of the Native American tribes, who had been forced to give way to white men on horseback, driving cattle across the land. It was a vision of pioneer wagons and stagecoaches, pulling their own dreams of freedom further west. Somewhere nearby perhaps would be a town, where rustlers and railroad hands were drinking in a busy saloon, waiting for a gunfight or a community hanging on a Saturday afternoon. These were cinematic historical images of a time now gone.

The truck entered the city limits of Sterling, Colorado, a one-story town plunked down on this high prairie of distant range. The old days of the west had now given way to tractor supply and feed stores, of two-bedroom bungalows and mobile homes, of grocery stores with parking lots, of cars and trucks on paved asphalt streets. The town was complete with a baseball field, its overhead lights blazing in the twilight dusk of a summer August evening. Back on their feet, the two travelers began to reorganize themselves, but were drawn to the game nearby. Laying their packs against the aluminum grandstand, they could feel the crowd stirring at their presence. They were a couple of long-haired strangers definitely from out of town. They were perfect strangers in a perfectly strange land.

As they settled in to watch, they were surprised to see that it was not a baseball game, but rather a fast pitch softball contest, played not by men, but by women their age. There were girls with their long hair tied back behind their heads, alluring in their uniform shorts and rubber cleats. This was something you wouldn't see much in the east. For the first time in a long while, it made Sean McAllister miss the game he loved, aching to play under the lights on a warm summer night.

As an inning or two went by, it became apparent to the nearby fans they were not a threat, and with that understanding their curiosity began to grow. Johnny Howard became engaged in conversation with a couple nearby, other people listening in. When the game was over, the couple gave them a ride to a Dairy Queen so they could buy some food. After stopping at a convenience store for beer, their hosts drove them to a small county park on the western edge of Sterling. Sitting at a picnic table in the tepid summer darkness, they talked with their benefactors, telling of their travels, while listening to the stories of a Colorado life.

As McAllister lay in his sleeping bag under the midnight stars, this was what it was all about. This adventure of the road, of meeting different people, of seeing places in America he had never seen before. Each day was unexpected, each happenstance solely in the hands of fate. He and Johnny had passed beyond the halfway mark of their journey. McAllister was happy. Twenty-four hours earlier, there had been a slight missing inside him, of the girl he had left behind. Tonight, in the warm soft grass and nocturnal coolness of a Colorado evening, he could only think of tomorrow, and where it might lead.

Day Five

The next morning was slightly chilled, but the day rose quickly with summer heat. Hardly settled upon the roadside, they caught a ride to Fort Collins with two women in the back of a VW station wagon. In the distance, the Rocky Mountains appeared to the west, their snow-capped peaks jutting toward the horizon. It was another demarcation in their journey, another spectacular geographical image of America being witnessed before them.

The women offered to let them stay in the back yard of their home in Fort Collins. Life felt different in so many little ways. There were women playing softball like men, these Fort Collins' girls picking up hitchhikers, letting them stay over. Everything appeared so casual and open, a refreshing ambience from the more traditional conventions of life back home. After four days of riding in vehicles, breathing exhaust fumes, hiking along the highway and sleeping on hard ground, their little backyard camp seemed like an oasis. They took showers in the house, read the books they had brought along, before taking a walk through town. Later, they shared an evening dinner with the women, before slipping into their bags for a good night's sleep.

Day Six

Packing up again, after cereal, coffee, and some thankful goodbyes, it was back on the road. Having checked their map, they would aim north along the foothills of the Rockies. Eventually they would cross the border into Wyoming. There, they would once again intersect with Interstate 80, before pushing further west toward San Francisco. After a day of rest, it was time to try and get as far as they could.

A Volkswagon bus pulls over. Two men are in front, a woman in back. McAllister and Howard push their packs through the sliding door, climbing inside. The woman tells them they are camping up the Poudre Canyon, located high on an awesome meadow looking out over the Continental Range. The woman asks if they want to join them, promising to give them a ride back to the highway the following day. The invitation engenders the first difference of opinion of the trip. McAllister is ready to move on, to continue heading for their destination. Johnny Howard is more cavalier, maybe taken by the girl's particular interest in him. McAllister can feel the dissonance, but agrees without discussion.

Heading up the canyon road away from the highway, the girl tells them the group has just dropped some LSD, and would they like a hit for themselves. McAllister is reticent, but Johnny is willing, so he goes along. For McAllister, it is hard to let go of what he really wants to do. But he doesn't want to be a party pooper, feeling there is little choice in the matter. The VW slowly chugs up the canyon road, climbing higher into the mountains. McAllister tries to relax, to let go of a nagging uncertainty as they ride further and further away from their intended route.

After the long slow drive of many miles, the bus turns onto a loose graveled road, spitting its way higher for another mile, before cresting to a wild open meadow of grass and rock. McAllister can feel the acid trip coming on, but as they exit the vehicle the sheer awe of the vista overtakes him. The mountain meadow runs away toward an incredible opening in the distance. Miles of white-capped peaks spread to the horizon, surrounded by a blue sky as clear and deep as he has ever seen. Tall spires of ponderosa pine reach high along the meadow's boundaries, glittering in the morning sun. He feels a shortness of breath in the scarce pine- scented air. Taking in this heavenly vision, he is wowed by the intensity of natural color and beauty. So this is what they call the high country. It is an overwhelming sight.

But as he and Johnny gaze upon this Rocky Mountain masterpiece, the darker sound of a human voice enters into their conscious thoughts. They can feel it right away. It is the anger of a man in high-strung aggravation, talking fast, spiked with a flurry of words. "Who are these people, and what are they doing here?" the voice demands. "They've got to go, they can't stay." McAllister turns back toward the voice. He watches as a small wiry mustached man, dressed only in denim shorts and hiking boots, stomps towards the folks who have brought them to this place. The people try to calm the man, but he waves his arms wildly, continuing his rant, appearing out of control. Suddenly, McAllister knows. He's been here before. He looks toward Johnny Howard, who is standing nearby.

McAllister gives Johnny a pissed off look, shaking his head. "Fuck", he breathes to himself, "not fucking again." He quickly searches the ground, sees a nearby rock, reaches down and picks it up. Johnny

Howard looks at him curiously, stilled by the sight of the rock in McAllister's hand. Johnny's mouth drops open, not sure of what might be going down.

McAllister turns toward the group, pushes his way forward, the adrenalin rushing over him. He raises the rock in his hand.

"You!" he shouts at the man. "Get the fuck out of here, or I'll bust your head wide open, right here and now. We're leaving all right, but shut your goddamn trap, and get the fuck away."

McAllister sees the change of expression on the man's face. The sudden response has frozen him cold. McAllister takes advantage, raising the rock higher as the man steps back. The driver of the van starts to speak, but McAllister turns to him, staring intently. "He's tripping, right? Now you're going to get back in this van and drive us back to the highway right fucking now. There won't be any more trouble. Johnny, get back in the van, we're leaving." McAllister continues to stare at the man. "I said get back to your camp until we're gone, buddy, and I'm as serious as shit."

The driver returns to the bus, starting the engine. McAllister can hear the woman crying words to the angry man to please let them go. He backs up to the vehicle, holding the rock high as he enters the shotgun side. The VW circles away, heading back down the gravel road.

"Hey, man," the driver says, "he was just on a bummer, you didn't need to …."

"That's right, he was on a fucking bummer," McAllister interrupts. "Now, I'm on a fucking bummer, you understand."

"But, Sean," Johnny Howard starts to say, "we could have just gotten out of there. You didn't have to …."

"I'll explain it to you later, Johnny, when we get back to the road."

At the intersection of the gravel road and pavement, the driver tries to beg off on going further, but McAllister tells him, "Fuck that, we're going all the way back." No one says a word the rest of the ride, a dead silence continuing between them. When they get back to the highway, McAllister jumps from the bus, throwing the rock hard into the ditch. He helps Johnny pull out the packs, before slamming the door. The bus turns around, slowly driving up the hill. The sun was already striking midday, rising high overhead. The sky remained a clear Colorado blue, the grass along the highway waving upon a soft summer breeze. It was supposed to be another beautiful day. But now, hell, he was really coming on, and angry enough to kick his own ass. Until this acid trip wore off, he would be on a bummer himself, feeling like shit.

It was the first bad experience of the journey. But no way was McAllister going to go there again. He was not about to deal with another troubled asshole losing his mind. Not that his student friend David Noles had necessarily been an asshole. But being fifteen miles up in the mountains with no food and little water was another fucking thing all together. McAllister fought like hell not to let the acid trip overtake him. He hadn't trusted the driver from the gate. The dude had displayed a sense of arrogance about himself as they had driven up the hill. Tripping on LSD was supposed to be fun, to let the hallucinations take you wherever they might go. But the fear of being stuck up in the Rockies without escape, a raving lunatic on the loose, that wasn't going to happen. He tried to will himself against the electrical verve that was surging through his body, holding hard against its presence within him. Johnny Howard was quiet. McAllister tried to explain. But after that, they didn't speak. Dealing with the event and the effects of the acid would be enough for both of them.

They got lucky. A man picked them up, headed for Laramie, right where they needed to go. McAllister let Johnny Howard climb in front, and Johnny managed to fake it pretty good. McAllister sat in back and simply endured. He silently looked out at the desolate foothills of the Rockies, the rangeland beginning to climb toward the higher Wyoming plateau. He could not stop the trails of color. He saw himself on horseback, the reins clutched in one hand, guiding his ride through high rock and ridge tops, braced against the wind upon this forbidden and lonely frontier. Not surprisingly, he was riding very much alone.

At Laramie, they reached a windswept high plateau. Wyoming was a barren desolate terrain, stretching toward a rim of shadowed mountains far to the horizon. Laramie appeared like a town that had no business being there. It looked like a junkyard of debris, scattered carelessly across a hardened brown territory of blowing crusted dust. It appeared forsaken and forlorn, as if the harshness of winter prevailed, even on a summer day.

Another tough ride continued onward to the city of Rawlins. Rawlins was an irritable cow town of dirt covered pick-up trucks and gun-racked windows, of long-haired obscenities shouted by angry young men jacked up by hate. Wyoming felt like the curse of western

America. Its only saving grace would be marked by the remarkable beauty of Yellowstone, far to its northwest corner. A beauty which this alien humanity would certainly never deserve.

Talk about a bad trip. McAllister had never wished so much for an evening to come, to blot out this distempered scar of a land that was forcing itself upon him. Tired, hungry, and finally coming down, he and Johnny hoofed along the commercial access road into Rawlins, searching for food. Entering a diner, the mistakes of the day continued. The busy din of the restaurant suddenly shifted to a low murmured hum as they entered and lowered their packs.

The diner counter was built in the shape of a horseshoe, and there were no two empty seats together. Johnny Howard had to take a stool on one side, McAllister the other. Trying to concentrate their thoughts, they waited. And waited. For McAllister, it became a strenuous test of defeating paranoia. But no menu came, no water, eventually no way. It was an *Easy Rider* moment, just waiting for an excuse. McAllister looked over at Johnny Howard. Slowly, a strange shit-eating expression evolved on Johnny's face. He cocked his head sideways and opened his mouth, then started pointing a finger toward it with his right hand, before silently shaking his head back and forth. McAllister burst out laughing. With this response, the harsh dark spell of the day was broken. Simultaneously, they quietly stepped off their stools, picked up their gear, closing the door behind them, hoping no one would follow.

McAllister's felt relieved, a burden was lifting. Things would be okay, he could let it go. The acid trip was descending. The guilt about his behavior, the fear and anger that had overtaken him earlier in the day began to absolve. Wyoming was just Wyoming, a place to simply remember and leave behind. He and Johnny were good again. It was all just a bad moment of circumstance, a bad trip. They finally got to the exit ramp on the other side of town, catching another ride in the dark. Somewhere deep in the Wyoming night, they had the driver leave them at a large busy truck stop. Finally, once again, they were just a couple of long-haired hippie travelers out on the road. You saw them all the time. They took a booth in the truck stop restaurant. Famished from the long anguished day, they cleaned their plates to the very last crumb.

After the meal came the next decision. The truck stop was located far off the interstate. It was a lighted compound oasis, surrounded by dark shadowed mountain peaks against the blue-black sky. Standing in the chilly parking lot of vehicles and trucks, McAllister could feel the emotional fatigue of the day, the heaviness of a full stomach. The journey was beginning to take a toll. It would be good to find a place to lie down and close their eyes. But there was nothing to do but hike back toward the exit ramp, hoping to find some little nook or cranny along the road to rest until dawn.

Luckily, fortune steps in and finds them. A car pulls up and the driver asks which direction they are headed. The same. He is driving to Salt Lake City. Just the break they needed. They will get out of this high rugged Wyoming plateau, down into Utah only a few hours away. On the road again, Interstate 80 began its descent from the Continental Divide, falling sharply towards the Great Basin below. Sometime later, amidst the blackness of the midnight evening, what looks like a bonfire appears in the distance, growing larger as the headlights of the car steer down the curving grade. Upon approach, halide illuminations shine upward into the nocturnal darkness, surrounded by the unseen pitch-black of the mountains above. It is Little America, the late-twentieth-century icon of the American road.

Little America is a place where the forces of natural evolution and native history have been replaced by ribbons of cement road beds, surrounded by trails of monoxide exhaust, rising into the atmosphere of planet earth. Little America is a neon and fluorescent world, born of the of the internal combustion engine, a devoted way-station for the vehicular mobility of the times. Little America beacons the weary travelers of America to rest and restore themselves, before forging onward to the destiny of their continental journeys.

If only Lewis and Clark could see things now. They would have been able to injest a country fried steak and gas up their rigs. They could have bedded down for the night on firm motel mattresses, with synthetic linen pillows, resting on carpet-fibered floors. They could have taken a warm shit, a shower and a shave, before paying a visit to the largest gift shop on earth. Perhaps they would purchase a key chain of remembrance, a talisman of good fortune, before moving on to the manifest destiny of the new imperial state. God Bless America, they might have sung, and everything it has become. Sean McAllister had been up for hours. He was as dinghy as a bat in a barn. The clock struck midnight, Wyoming crossing into Utah. His eyes closed, slipping away.

Day Seven

McAllister was aroused from sleep by voices speaking in the front seat before him, a shifting of bodies, as if something was up. Looking through the windshield, thousands of lights spread for miles across a limitless valley below. It was Salt Lake City, the righteous capitol of the great Morman theocracy. Before the driver was to leave them by the side of the road, he asked if they would like to see the Morman Temple in the center of the city. It was one-thirty in the morning. They are driven off the interstate into a desert American kingdom of wide empty avenues, of long city blocks that seem to reach forever.

The Temple grounds are bordered by iron fencing, perfectly trimmed in flora and trees. Intense spotlights shoot upward, illuminating the tall spires of the Temple, which rise shining into the night, piercing the sky. McAllister had only seen St Patrick's cathedral in New York. The Temple seemed grander in scope, a palatial dominion, a gated city of Oz. As the driver circled the extent of its ramparts, McAllister could feel the other-worldly sense of authority that this edifice implied. He was at the center of the Morman universe, so mysterious and secret in its ultimate control.

And yet the mythic images that the Temple sought to project, lay trapped inside the irony of a secular America residing at its base. Unlike Oz, it towered not over fields of flowers or even a desert wasteland. Instead, the edifice stood like a sore thumb amidst the urban streets, the parking lots and modern architectures of the city, appearing to lose the aura of its absolute command. It was if western civilization had overcome its power, spreading like a cancer of non-belief right to its very doorstep. From this perspective, the Temple looked no more than a museum piece of history, waiting silently for morning, and the next walking tour of tourists to enter within its sanctum.

However, it would be a grand mistake to engender such a presumption. For inside its fortress of testament and icons of devotion, the Temple had garnered another power it would be forever able to play. And that power was money, a whole hell of a lot of money. The Morman Church had acquired a horded green cache of financial strength and political control that would sustain its hegemony far into the future. Although the impact of its theology might lessen over time, the economic armor of the Deseret would insure its survival, including the global influence its missions would continue to project. One thing was undoubtedly for sure, the Catholic papacy had nothing on these guys, and their Morman religious cartel.

Feeling like outlaws amongst the holiness and certainty of the initiated, it was time to get out of Dodge. Back to a desolate entrance ramp on the edge of the metropolis, cut with a raw desert chill. It was sometime past two in the morning. The hitchhikers had been on the road for eighteen hours, and all the crazy stuff that had occurred in between. While Johnny Howard stood guard over their backpacks, McAllister pawed the ground and brush nearby, hoping for a spot to make a camp, at least until the light of day. The ground was rough and uneven, hard with rock and desert scrub.

Surprisingly, a lonely car pulled onto the entrance ramp. McAllister watched from below the road as it pulled up beside Johnny Howard, its engine continuing to run. He watched as Johnny opened the car door and spoke to the driver. Then Johnny gestured toward him, calling for McAllister to return. He scrambled up the bank to the car. Johnny pushed the packs into the back seat of the vehicle. As he shut the door, he leaned toward McAllister, whispering into his ear. Two words. "San Francisco!" Enough said. The young men climbed into the front seat of the vehicle, heading again ever forward down the road.

"*Pizza Hut*? Never heard of it," McAllister said to the driver. The driver had said his name was Kane. McAllister didn't know if it was his first name or his last. He guessed Kane to be about thirty-five. He wore a golf shirt. His hair was nicely combed. He was a businessman, driving west.

"It's a fast food franchise," Kane answered. "The company is opening a new location in Portland, Oregon. I'm meeting with the regional manager in San Francisco. Then I go to Portland. I make sure they set up the new operations according to the company's specifications. The home office is back in Wichita, Kansas. Fast food is big business now."

Wichita, Kansas? Pizza? Not exactly an Italian stronghold, McAllister thought to himself. He shifted in the middle seat. Johnny

Howard sat shotgun beside him, his head leaning against the window glass, eyes closed. Both men had fallen into sleep shortly after the ride had begun. Now, the sun was coming up behind them. The morning light revealed a flattened desert of white scratched pan, the salt flats of northwestern Utah. Kane was pushing ninety on the speedometer. Although McAllister knew that he was still in America, the landscape could have been another planet in another world. He rubbed a stiff neck from sleep, his body heavy and tight. There are times when a man would give anything for a soft mattress in a dark room. But such small pleasures weren't likely anytime soon.

Passing the exit for the Bonneville Salt Flats, Kane pulled off the interstate near Wendover. They had reached the Nevada state line. Johnny Howard wrestled himself awake. The men got out of the car, stretching their limbs. Kane filled the vehicle with gas. Entering a nearby restaurant for coffee, McAllister saw slot machines for the very first time. Returning, he caught sight of Kane popping a couple of pills with his coffee. McAllister had a good guess, but didn't ask. Back on the highway, Kane again flattened the accelerator up to speed, ripping across the desert floor of sand and rock, the sun rising ever higher in the dawning sky.

"Either of you got any grass?" Kane questioned. McAllister said no, they couldn't afford to carry it, too dangerous if they got searched by the cops.

"Yeah, I guess so," Kane said. "So what are you going to do in San Francsico, pick up some hippie chicks and hang out for awhile? Get yourself laid?"

The hitchhikers laughed at Kane's suggestion. "I've got a cousin that lives in Berkeley," Johnny answered. "We're going to visit with her, then figure things out from there. But we'll take whatever comes along, I guess."

"So you wouldn't turn down a summer of love," Kane quipped. "Well, neither would I, if you gave me the chance."

"I think we're a little late for that," McAllister responded. "But I do want to see the Haight-Ashbury, and Berkeley for sure."

"I'd do the same if I could," Kane said. "But duty calls. I got obligations these days." McAllister and Johnny Howard did not respond, sipping on their coffee.

"So what do you think of the war?" Kane asked. "You against it, like all the other hippies?"

Uh oh, McAllister said to himself. Here comes the red flag. Be very careful. You got a ride all the way to San Francisco. Don't blow this scene, and end up in the middle of bum- fucking Egypt. Both he and Johnny were way too tired for that potential outcome. But how does one respond?

"Were you there?" McAllister asked.

"No," Kane said. "I got out long before the buildup. United States Marines. I was lucky, I suppose. But I would have gone for sure. I mean, for four long years, that's what they trained me to do. To have put in all that time and not get a chance to fight, it kind of leaves you with mixed feelings. It doesn't matter, though. I'd had enough of the military. I just wanted to go home. But we've got to support the guys who are over there, no question about that."

McAllister and Johnny Howard didn't answer. A vague silence hung in the air.

"Hey, listen," Kane said, "I'm not going to bust your balls on this. I'm just curious. If I had a shit-ass attitude toward you boys, I would have never picked you up in the first place."

McAllister had to respond. "Well, I don't have anything against the guys who are over there," he began. "That's a bunch of crap, that the anti-war movement hates the soldiers. We understand that most of them didn't have a choice. Or maybe, if they did have a choice, it was because they wanted to serve their country, or felt obligated by their families, or they just needed a job. In my mind, it's just the government and the press making us out to be anti-American, or cowards, or whatever you want to call us. Sure, there are always a few assholes that have laid the 'baby killer' tag on the soldiers, but that's not the point. The point is the policy, and why the heck are we in Vietnam anyway. You got all these people getting killed or bombed to shit because of it. That's what I'm against. Not the troops."

"Well, what about that policy?" Kane asked. "Don't you think it's important to keep the Commies from taking over Southeast Asia, threatening our interests in the world? Isn't that important to protect?"

McAllister wasn't sure if he should continue. Kane was up to a steady ninety again on the speedometer scoreboard, the Nevada desert flying by the window like a bat out of hell. "Are you sure you're okay with this?" McAllister asked. "I mean, we really appreciate you picking us up, and taking us all the way to San Francisco. So I don't want to piss anybody off, especially over something we can't do anything about."

"No," Kane answered. "Like I said, it doesn't matter that much to me. Don't worry about the ride or me getting bent over your opinions. It's okay. I just want to hear your side of it, that's all."

McAllister sipped more coffee. "Well, how about I put it this way. So you're standing on a street corner in your own neighborhood, hanging out with your friends, minding your own business. And this gang from across the street is heaving bottles and bricks at you. They're hitting your kid sister and maybe even your mother. Well, screw that. Eventually, you're going to cross that street, you're going to fight back and kick some ass, right? And that's a good thing, it's a necessary thing to do."

"But pretend you're the bad guy, going into somebody else's neighborhood. Maybe you're the one causing trouble, acting like it's your turf, just because you say so. Can you blame those people for heaving shit back at you in response? You're not wanted, man. And you're going to continue to be their enemy until they finally chase you out. Really, what the hell are you doing there anyway? And that's a damn good question. Those people were just minding their own business until you showed up. Am I making any sense?"

"I don't know," Kane answers. "Got to say I never heard it put that way before."

"But that's my point," McAllister continued. "It's not your neighborhood. So why the hell are you there? Is it because you were afraid they might come into your neighborhood? Well, they never have. Or maybe it's some other reason. Maybe they've got something you want, something you think you need. And it just so happens, you got more sticks and more guys than they got. So what do you do? You go get it, that's what you do. Cause you're the bad guy. Meanwhile, you make up a lot of silly excuses as to why you have to be there. You con everybody in your own neighborhood to believe that they are the bad guys, not you. And damn if it doesn't work." McAllister paused for a moment. "Are you still with me?"

"Yeah, I'm with you," Kane said. "Go on."

"Some people might call this whole deal 'imperialism', but I don't know about that. Except, that after awhile, a lot of your own guys are getting pretty hacked up on this little excursion, and don't have much to show for it. But shit, somebody has got to be getting something out of this, or why the hell would we be doing it. And that's the sixty-four thousand dollar question. Who the hell is getting something out of this thing?" McAllister paused. "Anyway, that's sort of my two cents on the whole damn Vietnam deal, for what its worth. I just know I still got two good arms and two good legs, and I'd like to keep it that way."

"Huh," Kane said. He didn't immediately respond, keeping his hands on the wheel of the car, looking straight ahead. Then he spoke. "Is that it?"

Johnny Howard leaned forward in his seat, looking at Kane. "So how much further to Reno do you think?" Johnny asked.

"I know one thing," Kane insists. "I don't like that flag-burning shit. Right or wrong, that shit don't sit with me. But I'll agree with you, a lot the guys are sure getting pretty fucked up over there. Maybe you got a point. Maybe I don't know the reasons why."

Amen, McAllister says to himself, but holds his tongue. The flag-burning story is a whole other deal, and never seems to have a happy ending. He sips the last of his coffee. Reno is a few hours away, miles and miles of inhospitable desert blur in the distance ahead. McAllister has said too much already, but Kane had sort of asked for it. Silence or distraction might have been a better choice at times like this, no matter what anybody says about speaking your mind. For the moment, California was getting closer with each speeding click of the odometer. And with Kane juiced up on whites and behind the wheel, damn if things weren't flying by fast.

"The Biggest Little City in the World". That's what the sign read, arching over the downtown city street of Reno, Nevada. The town was the home for cut-rate, down-on-their-luck gamblers. It was a way-station for temporary visiting residents, looking for a legal escape from the unforeseen consequences of marital bliss. Reno was the gilded palace of sin, McAllister thought, like the album title of the Flying Burrito Brothers band that Mad liked to play so much. Mad was infatuated with Gram Parsons. McAllister knew if Parsons would have been anywhere in the vicinity of Mad's particular neighborhood, McAllister would have easily become yesterday's news.

In a weird reflection, the people on the streets of Reno looked similar to the urban racetrack crowd McAllister used to observe in high school, while hanging out on summer evenings at the Brandywine Raceway. He recalled the women at the track, with their puffed up platinum heads and heavy doses of mascara. They dressed up in nylons and spiked heels and spoke with their nasal-hard Philly accents. He could also see their men, with slicked-back hair and pointed shit-kicker Italian footwear, their wide shirt lapels and jewelry hanging open at the neck. They were men with a cigarette hanging long out the corner of their lips, reading the nightly racing form like a bible, a two-dollar salvation only one bet away. But he could also recall the lonelier souls as well. They would walk with their slackened shoulders hunched forward, dressed in soiled wrinkled pants, with electrical tape wrapped around their shoes. These were men on the last rung of the ladder, praying for the longshot to make that closing run, in one final play at the last chance saloon. Much like the track, Reno was an image of America where the chance for opportunity and wealth had been reduced to the fortunes of Lady Luck. The only difference was location, under a high-blue desert mountain sky.

Kane had an agenda not open to discussion. He rented a room at a cheap motel, taking a suitcase inside. McAllister and Howard loitered in the parking lot, waiting by the car. When Kane came out, he had showered and changed his clothes. He tossed McAllister the keys, putting the suitcase back in the car.

"It's all yours. I'll be back in a couple of hours. Unload your stuff. Get cleaned up and rest for awhile. If you're here when I get back, I'll take you into Berkeley."

There was no deliberation. McAllister went down the block for food while Johnny Howard showered. Upon returning, McAllister did the same. They stretched out on the two queen beds, eating, watching television, nodding off, waiting hopefully for the last ride to come. Kane didn't disappoint. Wherever he went, or whatever he did, mattered little. He showed up and they repacked the car.

In minutes they were out of the city, climbing the High Sierra, the Truckee River glistening in the evergreen sunshine below. Cresting the peak of Donner Pass, they headed down into California, a long awaited mission soon to be realized. It would be one damn ride all the way from Salt Lake City, and thirty-plus hours since waking up in a small backyard in Fort Collins, Colorado. Through it all, there had been the dark mood of the Poudre Canyon mistake, the rugged acid journey, the Wyoming redneck freak scenes, the Mormon Temple dream state, and the long desert run with Kane. They were reaching the land of beach boys and surfer girls, of hippie chicks and rock roll musicians. It would be a world of mythic images, perhaps soon to be dispelled. Still, for Sean McAllister and Johnny Howard, a youthful dream had been realized. They had traversed the great American continent, like so many others who had come before.

CHAPTER EIGHT

PIECE OF MY HEART
San Francisco / October, 1970

"JANIS DIED FOR OUR SINS". The homemade sign, the letters printed in black against a rainbow colored background, hung loudly off a second-story patio railing on a somber October morning. Valerie Williams, like many in the city she called home, remained suspended in shock. Two days before, Janis Joplin had been found dead in a Los Angeles motel room, a reported victim of a heroin overdose. For Valerie, the emotions of hearing such news, then trying to accept its impact, refused to merge.

Valerie sat on the couch of her Noe Street apartment, a cup of coffee in hand, her young son crawling at her feet. Images and thoughts of Janis in life would not let go. She could see the wild hair and presence that Janis could command. She could hear the boom of her laughter, feel the heat and sweat of the Carousel ballroom. And there was always the voice, the gutsy thrill of a Joplin' performance, the unstrapped emotion that could pierce your heart and hold you still. To imagine Janis gone was impossible to believe.

Two nights previous, Moonglow, Valerie's upstairs neighbor, had knocked on Valerie's apartment door. Moonglow was distraught, disbelieving. She needed to talk. Only months before, Janis Joplin had shared the apartment with Moonglow, prior to moving to her new home in Marin County. That evening, Valerie had done what she could to comfort her friend, trying to understand. How could it be?

Although Valerie Williams was simply the neighbor below, she had been surrounded by the proximity and aura of a rock and roll heroine rising to fame. There were the musicians who mistakenly had come to her door looking for Janis. On occasions, Valerie had visited Janis' apartment above, even seeing her large round bed and the crystal chandelier of flowered lights that hung from her ceiling. Janis had never been home that often, hers was not an ordinary routine. Janis would spend weeks on the road, performing, recording, or staying at other places. Valerie knew well that harder drugs and alcohol had become a troubling mix for Janis at times, but that was a scene in which Valerie did not engage. For Valerie was a mother these days, having a young son to love and care for. She might still have her pot and a glass of wine, but she would never consider sticking a needle into her arm.

Janis Joplin had always been friendly and good to her. Valerie and Moonglow had made Janis a large wind chime mobile for her new home in Marin. They had presented it to Janis at her housewarming. Janis had adored the gift, and had looked forward to hanging it somewhere close. But Valerie would never know if that had been done. The housewarming party had been the last time Valerie Williams had seen Janis Joplin alive. These were the thoughts that made the reality of the news so difficult to accept.

Moonglow was convinced that Janis had been murdered by the CIA, coming so close to the sudden death of Jimi Hendrix only weeks before. It was certainly not a circumstance to be discounted out of hand. Paranoia could not be easily dismissed as a consequence of a drug induced state of mind. The Kennedys', Martin Luther King, now the icons of rock and roll, it was not that far-fetched when strung together to believe. Still, those notions and fears did not matter today. Janis would be gone forever. The pain of losing someone you know, whose accepted presence felt so close to your own personal mortality, was singularly enough to bear. Valerie sipped her coffee, watching her young son fumble with his toys on the hardwood floor. She worried for him, about his world to come.

The sudden death of someone close demands such reflection. It challenges the deeper emotions of self-preservation, of protecting yourself and the ones you love, whose safe keeping you are obliged to ensure. Valerie felt something stir within her. It was more than the

expected obligation of protecting her son. For the first time, she began
to realize that keeping him safe might mean doing the same for herself.
This was a recognition she had rarely entertained. The stubborn
fearlessness that marked her own personal identity was not something
she had previously questioned or assessed. But on this morning, she
felt a crack in the hard crust she had constructed around her world.

Valerie didn't need that deadbeat father of her child. When she had
told Carl of the pregnancy she had been filled with a hopeful outcome.
She had let herself slip into a loving and dreamy expectation of things,
of having a family and someone to share her life. His response had hurt
her deeply, and caught her by surprise. He assured her he could not
be party to the circumstances. Only then had Valerie learned that he
already had another child from a previous relationship, from which he
had already run. She had taken the punch hard, her innocence lost. But
stubbornly she pulled herself up. Despite the situation she would not
abort. She would fight back against the odds, have the child. Carl could
go to hell. She would make her own way.

Carl was true to his word. He disappeared shortly thereafter.
Valerie birthed her son, Canyon, at the Noe Street house. Two midwives
attended, her close friends nearby. Valerie gave her son a Christian name
as well, Matthew. This would appease her mother and the Catholic
religious ancestry that marked her own past. She signed up and took
the welfare money she needed to survive on her own. Motherhood
would become her new occupation. Valerie took to it easy and without
regret. She was twenty-one years old.

Everything had happened so fast. Valerie picked up her baby son,
breast feeding him for a time, before laying him into his crib. It seemed
like only yesterday she was a seventeen- year-old high school student
from the Richmond District, an adolescent child of the city, but living
a second life. Valerie had pretended to conform to the edicts of a
Catholic girl's school education, but the draw of the dramatic events
that surrounded her had been too much to resist. Along with her good
friend, Susan, they had slipped into the burgeoning culture of the
Haight-Ashbury, the new world of peace and love. They began hanging
out on Hippie Hill at Golden Gate Park, smoking pot and meeting new
friends. They passed out flowers and bubble gum on Haight Street.
Valerie loved dressing in her purple tights, peasant dress and floppy
hat, including a long fur coat she borrowed from her grandmother.

As her parents became aware of her terrible new influences, her father moved the family to the suburban enclaves of the East Bay. But the damage was already done. When Valerie graduated, she immediately returned to San Francisco, running away from her parents and the life they wished her to lead. She went to City College, working as a file clerk in between. She and Susan found an apartment at 22nd and Dolores. The apartment became a way station and crash pad for all her friends who lived at home. Most nights were a party, smoking pot or dropping LSD. They made trips to the Carousel or Avalon ballrooms, danced to the music of the Jefferson Airplane and Grateful Dead, Big Brother and the Holding Company, where she had first seen Janis Joplin in earlier days. On calmer evenings Valerie rested at home, or dutifully attended Stephen Gaskin's Monday Night Class.

As quickly as this aura had come, it came to an end just as fast. Suddenly, the Haight-Ashbury was overwhelmed with outsiders. Each day turned meaner and more dangerous with their coming. The rock bands became famous, leaving the club scene for bigger venues. Harder drugs and alcohol cast their net over friends and loved ones. People with bad intentions masked themselves behind long hair and a hippie veneer. The joy of the early days was replaced by a vibe of self-destruction. The Haight had become an ugly shell of its former self. Harsher realizations pressed upon Valerie's heart. This world, a world she once loved and thought would last forever, was coming to an end. Confused, she felt a sense of isolation, threatened with a reality she would be required to accept.

On this morning a hollowness inside beset her. She missed her friend Susan, wishing her to be nearby. But Susan had moved out to West Marin, living near the beach, away from the pulse of the city. At their Delores Street home, Susan had been commuting to college over in Berkeley. There, Susan had taken up the cause against the Vietnam War and the military draft. She had begun to speak of women's rights and other political change. Things in Berkeley had always been different from the city, more serious, less about having a good time. The focus was on 'revolution' as Susan called it, turning over the government, words like economic equality and social justice. Valerie believed in all those things, but she was not political. She preferred the music of togetherness, a world of peace and harmony, not the conflicts that others chose to fight.

But soon came the hated California governor, Ronald Reagan, and the People's Park bloodbath. Susan had been injured in the government's response, hit hard with the butt of gun and sickened by tear gas. The hate and anger of those events had scared Susan away. That summer, Susan quit school. She had moved from the apartment on Delores to be with her boyfriend, escaping to an old farmhouse near Point Reyes out on the coast. Recently, Susan had spoken of moving farther north to Arcata, or perhaps to Oregon. Susan would begin a new way of living she said, apart from this society she now despised. It seemed so far from the fun loving days that Valerie and Susan had spent in the city not so long ago.

Valerie's memory drifted back to those nights at the Presidio, the military installation near Golden Gate Park. In high school she and Susan had become Red Cross volunteers. Each Thursday night they would meet with other girls from school at the hospital annex. For an hour or two they were expected to visit with the returning wounded soldiers, to try and entertain them in one activity or another. Valerie's heart had swelled with a deep sadness and sympathy for the young men she had met there.

These were boys only a year or two older than she, many parked in wheelchairs with a missing arm or leg, waiting to be sent home to small towns and cities throughout America. Others had minds deadened from shock. Each and every one had endured some singular catastrophe, then sent back to America from an alien world thousands of miles away. For an hour or more the volunteers would talk, dance, or play games with these confused and isolated boys. She and Susan would tell them about their own lives in San Francisco, just outside the hospital walls. Sometimes, they would dress in their best hippie finery to impress the soldiers, these men who knew nothing of this new exterior world. When the hospital night was over, she and Susan would immediately sneak over to the Haight, smoking pot with older friends who lived in the neighborhood. But those visits to the hospital had left their impressions. Valerie remained heartbroken at the memories of these injured and powerless soldiers. She and Susan had seen early the tragic remains of war.

Now Janis was dead. It seemed like the oxygen of San Francisco had been sucked out its streets. A blandness of intent surrounded her, the bright colors of the city seeming to pale with a tarnished wear.

Valerie felt the urge to cry, to return to her bed, to pull the covers over her head, to mourn the loss of her dreams. But no, she would not allow such weakness to ensue. She would dress and make ready for a shopping trip, force herself into the day. She would overcome this sadness that sought to pull her down. But deeper in her heart, Valerie understood there was something she would eventually have to confront. There would be choices she would have to resolve. Choices for herself, as well as her young son who slept nearby. Somehow, together, they would find their way to a better place.

CHAPTER NINE

COMING INTO LOS ANGELES
Arizona / Mexico / California / Oregon / Winter 1970 - Spring 1971

THE DESERT CARAVAN WANDERED MILE AFTER MILE over the bumpy dusted roads of the Sonora Desert, searching their way. Somehow the lead driver had missed a landmark further back. It surprised the driver to have lost his direction. He had made this trip numerous times in the past. At the next junction, he checked the compass glued to the dashboard of the van. He made a right turn north, the second van following behind. They had plenty of water, and enough gas for a few more mistakes. Still, it was difficult to fix one's position in this forbidden land of cactus, rock, and unhindered blazing sun. After another mile or two, a familiar side road intersected. The driver recognized the little pile of rocks stacked on its corner. It confirmed the route they should have been traveling. Relieved, the driver pressed forward.

Several miles later, a cattle gate came into view. The two vans pulled up, idling while the driver found the keys. He got out of the vehicle, unlocked the gate, swinging it open. The vans drove through, crossing the border. They were now on the US side of the Papago Indian Reservation. Taking in the scabland horizon, no other vehicles or human activity appeared in sight. This was per the usual, like so many other trips. The driver knew the rest of the way home.

Unfortunately, a detour was about to ensue. A reservation police vehicle accosted them at the highway junction. The driver made his girlfriend quickly change places up front with Jesse, the fourteen year old kid who had accompanied them on the trip. Two heavy-set Indian policemen waved the vans over, requesting their permits. The driver explained to the policemen they had only entered the reservation the evening before. Having camped overnight, they were planning to get the permits today. The officers requested them to follow the six miles to the stationhouse. They could get the permits there. Upon arrival, the police station was a solitary ramshackle building, sitting alone amongst the vast desert scrub. A second police vehicle was parked out front. The vans rolled to a stop, shutting off their engines. The driver got out to acquire the permits, hoping it would be routine.

No such luck. The first two officers exited their vehicle, holding ground. Immediately, four other uniformed men stepped out of the building. In their gripped hands were sledgehammers and sharply ground cold chisels, the shiny tips gleaming in the afternoon sun. The driver's stomach dropped, curse words escaping his lips. His present occupation was about to end. The gig was up.

Jack Mulcahey answered the ringing phone. He normally didn't answer the phone unless no one else was in the farm house at Shamrock Ridge. And that was the case this evening. On the other end of the line was his friend, Tim Moore, the owner of the Santa Cruz property. Jack Mulcahey listened nervously to the news. Busted in Arizona. The customized vans had been hacked apart, the contraband seized. Six adults were holed up in two cells in the Arizona desert. But young Jesse had been driven to Tucson, to a juvenile detention center located there. Tim Moore was already dealing with the adults, arranging for legal help and bail.

Jesse was a different situation. They needed to find his mother and fast. Jack would have to call her and explain the circumstances. Tim Moore was already in Los Angeles. When Jack reached Jesse's mother, Moore would pick her up and drive to Tucson. They would spring Jesse as soon as they could. Jack felt some serious guilt for allowing the young boy to take the trip. He made the call to Jesse's mother, Betsy. Although surprised, she was predictably cool. Betsy would be ready when it was time to go. Jack hung up the phone, wondering what would be the outcome for this fatherless young boy, who had practically become his own son.

Jesse Simmons was no ordinary kid. He was the oldest of three young brothers. The boys and their mother had shared a home two blocks up the hill from the house in Hermosa Beach, where Jack's brother Derrick had lived before his escape from the draft. At his early age, Jesse had already been growing up on his own, much like Jack and Derrick had done only years before. But unlike Jack and Derrick's own mother, Betsy Simmons was not likely to be getting any nominations for mother of the year. The kid was a harbor rat during those days in Hermosa, walking past the house with his fishing pole or old scuba mask, often on his own. Derrick had adopted him first, taking Jesse fishing and giving him chores to do in exchange. Jack had met the boy while visiting his brother from college. He had enjoyed watching Jesse scamper through the avocado trees at the house, pulling down the high ones for everyone to eat. The kid had become all eyes and ears for Jack and Derrick. The brothers were welcome substitutes for the missing man in Jesse's life.

When the shit came down on the draft, Derrick had gone to Canada with his young wife and daughter. Jack had continued at school in San Luis Obispo. But Derrick and Darla's time in Canada became lonely and unfamiliar. They didn't stay long. Derrick had taken his chances and returned across the border. At Derrick's insistence, the brothers changed their last name to Mulcahey, hoping to take on a new identity. Jack finished school. Eventually, they had found their way to the Shamrock Ridge farm, perched above Santa Cruz. There, they operated a garden and landscaping business. Recently, Jack had started a small feed and hardware store next to the food coop on the edge of town.

In the two years since his underground life had begun, Derrick had stayed in touch with Jesse Simmons. Derrick and Jack had let Jesse come up to the farm for the summer, working with them in the business. When the school year began, they would put him on a bus for the return trip to Los Angeles. But at the end of the second summer, Jesse said he didn't want to return. His mother, Betsy, knowing how much it meant to him, let Jesse stay. At first, the brothers made Jesse go to school in Santa Cruz. And Jesse did, but he never wanted to be there, he wanted to stay close with Derrick and Jack.

In the adult world, things were changing on a number of fronts. The FBI was getting closer to finding Derrick any day. The Feds had already been to the feed store in town, and once to the farm. The farm itself had been purchased with the money from pot smuggling. That alone made everyone worried. Just last month, Derrick had convinced Tim Moore to help them buy some land in Oregon. Moore would buy the land in his name, then Derrick and Jack would pay him back. Derrick had found a forty-acre piece in Southern Oregon. Returning back to Santa Cruz, Derrick began making preparations for moving north. He would be the first to go.

The reality of things generally played out on a different course. Derrick always made the plans, Jack and Jesse did most of the work. So Jack and Jesse ended up making the trip to Oregon with Derrick. Fighting the winter rains, the two men and Jesse cleared brush and cut out possible building sites. They fashioned a cabled swinging bridge to get over the raging creek, then roughed out a shelter for Derrick to live. Finally, Jack and Jesse headed back to Santa Cruz, with the intention of making the final move in later spring. With a vehicle and a little bit of cash, Derrick remained behind in Oregon.

In the months that followed Jesse's trouble, the court demanded that Jesse return to Los Angeles and live with his mother. Jesse was shaken, heartbroken. He didn't want to leave. With Derrick's approval, Jack approached Betsy, asking if she and her two younger boys would consider a move north to Santa Cruz, then onward to Oregon. Betsy agreed and the family expanded. Meanwhile, Jack and Jesse had become like two peas in a pod. They were as close to a father and son duo as any real life possibility.

Derrick Mulcahey always had this dream in his mind. It was a dream of a large self-sustaining family, with Derrick at its head. Derrick had a way of painting the picture. He would color the painting in a manner that would include those he needed to convince. Derrick's wife Darla was pregnant with their second child. Jack had his girlfriend, Christine. Along with Christine's college friend, Jerry, Betsy and the boys, the Mulcahey family began making arrangements for the final move.

With the advent of summer, everything was packed and ready. They rest of the family headed north across the border, leaving sunny California for the mountains of Southern Oregon. A new adventure lay before them. They would carve a communal farm out of this marginal land of timber and rock. The prospects were exciting, and Jesse Simmons was on his way. He would continue to have a home and family he could call his own.

CHAPTER TEN

EASY RIDE

California / Baja, Mexico / Oregon / 1971

Tom Sullivan's nightmare wrestled awake on the motel bed. Jumping up, he bolted from the covers. He made sure the front door of the room was locked, the security chain latched in place. He stumbled into the kitchenette, checking the locks on the rear door of the unit. Returning to the front room, Sullivan pulled the blanket, sheet and pillows off the bed, spreading them on the worn carpeted floor. He lay down there, covering himself again. But the danger wouldn't pass. They could come from either side, he was simply too exposed.

Tom Sullivan kicked off the bedding, hurriedly threw on his clothes and boots. His gun was missing. He unlatched the back door, opening it to the sound of the ocean beyond, the waves crashing on the rock and beach below. He stepped outside into the darkness. He felt naked without a gun in hand. He forced himself stealthily toward a grove of trees that led to the bluff. His eyes began to adjust to the night. He found a spot to set up the perimeter. He would put an LP there, another one down to the left, another one deeper down to the right. Still, this was not a secure position. The patrol remained dangerously exposed. He sat down on his haunches and waited, listening intently for the sounds of their coming. Sullivan remained confused by the consistent pounding of the sea beyond.

His breathing slowed. A moment later a strange voice rose inside his head, challenging the instincts that held him still. Silently, he listened to its rebuke. "What the hell are you doing, man?" the voice cried. "Are you fucking crazy, or what? You're in California, asshole. Three hours north of the city, along the Pacific coast. You're back in America, soldier. There ain't no VC out here tonight. You're home. You're goddamn fucking home."

Sullivan tried to ignore the voice. He felt the ocean breeze against his face, smelled the salted brine of a thin mist in his nostrils. But the voice roared again inside his mind. "It's all over, man. It's all fucking over now. Get back inside, before some old lady sees you out here shouting orders in the night, before she calls the cops."

Sullivan stood up and looked both ways. Nothing moved, just the pounding of his chest against the north coast air. The nightmare began to pass, some clarity of thought returning. Okay, he said to himself. You just lost it for awhile. It's just another flashback, another bad dream. It will be okay. He went back inside the motel, switching on all the lights. He fumbled in his jacket for a cigarette. He saw the near-empty fifth of bourbon resting on the nightstand. Reaching over, he took another hit. He sat down on the motel bed, leaning his back against the headboard, smoking. Yeah, I guess I'm still fucked up he reminded himself. I'm still goddamn way fucked up.

Sullivan finished the cigarette, stubbed it out. He got out of his clothes, turned out the lights, returning to the floor. He wrapped himself in the bedding one more time. Then it came to him. In the morning he would get up and call Marty Johnson in Santa Monica. Sullivan had the phone number. Marty would be home by now. He had said to look him up. Sullivan would drive down and see Marty for a few days. He needed to keep moving, wherever it might lead. He needed to see a familiar face. Eventually, things would get better. But he knew with little doubt, there was still a long ways to go.

In the morning, Sullivan threw his gear in the car. Checking out of the motel, he drove to a pay phone. He called Marty Johnson at his father's home in Santa Monica. It took a few moments for Marty to remember him. They hadn't served together in the shit, but had met while bar hopping in Sydney on an R&R break. Marty Johnson had been on short time when their trails had crossed, on his way out of the bush. Sullivan had been on break from regular army. The two of them had hit it off easily, both having a connection to California. Marty had entered the Marines right out of high school, Sullivan sometime later. But both were combat patrol leaders, Marty up north, Sullivan south. They had traded addresses to get in touch when Sullivan got back. Sullivan wasn't quite sure why Marty had come to mind. Maybe because there was something that they shared, or maybe because Marty had been out for awhile. It would be someone he could actually talk to about returning home.

Marty said he was currently in school at a local junior college in Orange County, getting the VA cash but not going to class much. So come on down. Without a single plan of his own, Sullivan turned around and headed south. He steered clear of San Francisco, driving east over the coast range to pick up Interstate 5 for the straight shot to Los Angeles. There was no reason to retrace his steps back to Redwood City, where his parents lived in his old hometown.

He'd only been out two weeks, processing out of Oakland upon his return. They had given him a Class A uniform off the rack to wear outside the door. What a waste. He had immediately gone to a thrift store, trading it for some civilian clothes. He headed into the city to get drunk with friends. The next day he went down to Redwood City to see the family. But it only took a week for home to feel like a prison. He bought a car, packed his duffel bag, driving north along the coast. He thought he would get up to Oregon, but now he was turning south instead.

When Sullivan got to Santa Monica, things were good. Marty's dad was pretty cool for an older guy. Mr. Johnson said he was an original Okie. His family had come to California with the dust bowl migration, landing in Santa Monica. There were a lot of Okies in Santa Monica he joked, because that was the end of the road for the old Route 66. And dumb Okies like his dad couldn't get any further away unless they had a boat. Mr. Johnson had served in the Pacific theatre during World War II. Upon coming home, he had used the GI bill to get an education, before making a career with McDonnell-Douglas in the aerospace industry.

What Sullivan didn't know, was that Marty Johnson had spent most of his youth in Tulsa, Oklahoma, where his mother had returned after the divorce from his father. Marty had nothing kind to say about his stepfather, only that the guy had said Marty would never amount to anything. So Marty's fastest way out was to join the Marines, determined to show the stepfather he could make it on his own. Marty had entered the recruiting office intending to make it a career, signing up for a twenty-year hitch. Fortunately, the recruiting officer talked him down to a four-year enlistment, saying if Marty liked it then, he could opt for more. It was a blessing in disguise Marty said, as it didn't take long for four years to become an eternity.

Marty did his tour in Nam and managed to survive in one piece. That was enough, but he still had almost two years remaining. Back at Pendleton, there were too many returnees and not enough jobs. Marty would either go up to Hollywood on weekends or down to Mexico. He would drop acid and party with the other jarheads who also were killing time. When the Corp finally realized he could give a shit, they cut him out eleven months early. It was the happiest day of his life.

Now Marty's hair was long. He had a young hippie girlfriend from Huntington Beach, a car and a healthy stash of weed. Marty had met the girl, Celia, at the community college. With Sullivan's arrival, Marty found the perfect excuse to pull the cord on that deal. Not the girl, but the school. After a week of hanging out with Marty, Celia, and their other friends, Marty Johnson said let's go to Mexico, and so they did.

Driving out of Los Angeles, they crossed the border at Tijuana, heading for Ensenada. At Hussong's Cantina they got slammed on Mexican beer and shots of tequila, mixing with the jarheads out of Pendleton, some whose days were numbered. Sleeping in Sullivan's old sedan, they woke in the morning with a hangover. Making the peso exchange, they gassed up the car, pushing south. They found another motel bar by the beach in San Quntin. They drank the night away, trading shots with a group of expatriate Americans living by the sea in broken down trailers with no running water or electricity. After closing the place, they slept in the sand outside the car.

Sullivan awoke to the compression sound of the ocean waves pounding in the distance, the cranky cries of gulls bitching in the sky. His head thumped heavy with the consequences of his behavior, dehydrated, his stomach nauseas and inconsolable. Surprisingly, these distractions were beneficial. He had actually slept for several hours without waking in anxiety, uncertain of where he might be. He couldn't recall any dreams, and that was a good thing to be without. He rolled out of his sleeping bag, wandering to the water, a black notebook and pen in hand. He sat on the beach, watching the white frothed waves break onto shore, the foam sizzling in bubbles as it slid across the sand. He crossed his legs in the morning sun, writing down the names of towns and bars, of people met, or other objects and incidents since the trip's beginning. But no deeper thoughts or reflections found their way to paper. He was remained bound up with nothing to say.

The trip zig-zagged its way down the Baja Peninsula, over the rough pot-holed asphalt strips of highway, dodging roadside cattle and slow moving trucks, passing young Federale conscripts with machine guns in their hands. The car bounced through dry arroyos, crossing the desert terrene, bordered by the magnificent azure blue of the Pacific. Turning east, they climbed the high Sierra of ponderosa pine, before descending down through daring mountain canyons to the windswept Sea of Cortez. Southward they plunged, through Loreto and Muleje, before crossing again back to the west, then down the narrow gut of dry terra firma to La Paz.

Making one final zag back to the Pacific, they settled down fifty miles north of land's end, just south of Todos Santos, setting up camp with what little they had. For ten days, they smoked joints with the surfers, struggled in broken Spanish with the locals, ate fresh fish with beans and tortillas. They wore shorts of cut-off denim, with pint bottles of tequila stuck in their pockets. On wide empty beaches, they battled the dangerous undertows, beaten down by the close breaking waves, the salt air drying their skins, their bodies tanning in the heat. By campfire at night, under breathless starlight and moon, they drank and smoked cigarettes, before nestling close to the fire in the tight cold desert air.

Tom Sullivan began to feel himself coming to, as if awakening to a new sense of self. The constant buzz that had continued to wire through his body began to give way. An ease and calm began to flow, he was less on edge. Sleeping on the ground soothed him. He slipped into longer and deeper slumber, the worry of life without a weapon growing less intense. Waking in the early blue-black mornings of dawn, his body no longer jumped alert. He could roll over in the sand, fall back into a heavier rest until the heat of the rising sun brought him sluggishly back to another day. Was he beginning to feel safe? Could this feeling last? He wasn't sure. But he knew it was better. Even the slamming of a car door, or any loud shout or sound, began to become more cushioned in response.

Marty Johnson didn't appear to have these similar transactions of physical discontent. It was as if Marty had left the memory of the movie behind at the theatre, as if he could walk right out of the afternoon matinee without having to shield his eyes. Marty no longer even looked the part. He was a handsome man, his long brown hair glistening in the afternoon sun, his tall lean stature steeped with a confidence that Sullivan could not yet feel. Sullivan still felt the weight of something alien inside him, but not Marty Johnson. Between them, there had been no real talk about the war. There was no need to emotionalize what so recently had been left behind. Sure, they continued to trade funny stories about guys in their platoons, known only by their nicknames, and how they had got them. They could share talk about asshole battalion commanders, or NCO's who didn't know their ass from a hole in the ground. But the deeper shit was left unsaid, and that was just as well.

Marty Johnson could easily have been just another surfer on the beach, as indifferent to his past as any flunky who had never served in-country. Sullivan wondered if Marty's remarks about his stepfather, the need to leave that situation behind, had hardened Marty Johnson in some peculiar way. It was as if Marty readily understood the bullshit when he saw it, and could easily deal with any outcome. As if things were simply what they were, and if you stayed alive, you just went on. Like any other person, Marty Johnson could complain about life, even pass a judgment or two. But his complaints sounded like he was ordering off a menu in a restaurant, with nothing emotional at stake. There was no degradation in his voice, no condescension or prejudice, as if he never took anything personal. He was like a lawyer arguing a case for a defendant who was guilty as sin. You just did your job, and then went home. No, Marty Johnson didn't seem prone to beating himself up very much, or anybody else for that matter, whether he was right, or whether he was wrong.

One night a surfer named Ronnie came by their camp fire. When Ronnie learned indirectly that Sullivan and Johnson were recently out of Nam, he started in with the questions. The kid wasn't pestering, just curious. But Sullivan found himself disliking Ronnie's inquiries. It wasn't something he wanted to discuss, unless it was with a brother who had been there. But Marty Johnson was perfectly frank about things, as if he was repeating nothing more than name, rank, and serial number.

"You guys been getting any shit since you been back," Ronnie asked?

"Well, you know," Marty began, "it ain't like I been wearing my uniform all around town everywhere I go. But if you mean like the 'baby killer' shit, I wouldn't say that. Most of my friends know the score, they understand what went down. Sure, the brass boys and the lifers would always try to make us feel like the draft dodgers and war protestors hated us. That they would spit on us upon returning home. In fact, a lot of the assholes who had served in-country had bought into that pinko-commie coward stuff. But most of the regular guys knew the score. I imagine a lot of guys had to travel to duty stations, or had to wear full uniforms to get a ticket home, or perhaps carry orders on civilian flights. It wouldn't surprise me that those boys caught some shit from time to time. But as far as I can tell, most people just felt sorry for you. Although that's a bunch of shit as well. Whatever, it is what it is."

"Are you glad to be home," Ronnie asked?

"Fuck, yeah," Marty Johnson answered. "At least out of fucking Nam. Are you kidding me? But now, that shit is all over for me. I'm done. It' time to get on with other stuff. Ain't that right, Tommy? No more Semper Fi."

Sullivan lay on his side by the fire pit. He took the last puff of a cigarette, pitching it into the flames. "Yeah, it's over," he responded. But the tone of his answer was said without confidence.

"Tommy's only been out a few weeks," Marty Johnson advised, speaking to Ronnie. "He's straight off the goddamn transport. So you don't need to be asking him too many questions, you understand?" Marty Johnson lifted the pint bottle of tequila to his lips, taking a long swig before handing it to Sullivan. Sullivan did the same, holding the bottle in his hands.

Ronnie the surfer, his blonde hair bleached white from the sun, sat with his legs crossed, his young face framed in the light of the camp fire. "Sorry," he said. "I was just curious about things, I don't mean to pry."

"Are you safe from the draft, Ronnie? You got a way out," Marty asked.

"I got a high number in the lottery last year," Ronnie answered. "I was in junior college at the time, but I dropped out to spend the winter down here. I guess I don't have to think about it anymore. And

I sure hope that doesn't change."

Marty Johnson pulled a small canister from the breast pocket of his tee shirt. He opened it up, beginning to roll a joint. "They'll let you know if it does," Marty answered. "But I wouldn't worry about it too much, Ronnie. They're trying to slow the damn thing down anyway. And believe me, there are sure enough dumb shits out there like me and Tommy to probably cover your ass." Sullivan had to snicker at that remark.

"I'm not sure what you mean?" Ronnie asked.

"I mean dumb shits who thought they wanted to be somebody. Hard line fuckers who bought the sales pitch that they were needed to fight for freedom against a bunch of communist gooks. Those guys were all spit and shine and brave, until one day somebody took a shot at them. I'll tell you one thing, Ronnie, that sure will make you change your mind in a hurry. Take it from me, at that point you forget about everything else and just start counting the days. You just start living in order to fucking survive."

Marty Johnson finished rolling and licking the joint. He fired it up with his lighter and took a long hit. Leaning over, he gave it to Sullivan, taking the bottle of tequila from his hand. Ronnie sat still without speaking.

"Tommy will tell you, it's a damn fucked up place to be. Everybody's talking about the guys coming back, how they can't handle shit when they get back home. And they're goddamn right about that. A lot of guys are a fucking mess, me included. Hell, I got one buddy whose been living in his parents garage for like six fucking months. He still hasn't come out. He shits and pisses in a bucket everyday. But you want to know something, a lot of the guys were pretty screwed up even before they got there. For them, it was either do time in prison or sign up for boot camp. Or like a lot of the niggers, they didn't have a pot to piss in. There were guys who had lost their girlfriends, so why not be a hero. Or they simply got drafted. But once you get to Nam, all that shit goes out the fucking window. You screw the damn circumstances or how the hell you got there. At that point, you got nobody else but each other. And so everybody does what they can just to make it till tomorrow."

Marty Johnson stood up, wobbling a bit. He reached down and took the joint from Sullivan, walked around the campfire, handing the joint to Ronnie, who took a hit and passed it back. Marty continued around the fire pit, plopping himself back down. He took a final drag on the roach, before stubbing it out.

"Only problem is, for some of those poor unlucky fuckers, that tomorrow never comes."

Sullivan felt that familiar anxious buzz surge back through his body. He shifted quickly in the sand. "That's enough for tonight, Marty," he stated. But Marty Johnson had caught the buzz and didn't respond.

"Don't worry, Ronnie. As long as you're not a Joadie, you'll be okay."

Ronnie the surfer sensed the tension in the air, getting up to leave. "A Joadie? I'm not sure what you mean."

Marty Johnson laughed. A slur took over his voice. He turned his head toward Sullivan. "Get your ass in gear, soldier," he mimicked, almost shouting. "You little faggot, Joadie's got your girl." Then he laughed again.

"Thanks for the beer and the smoke," Ronnie said, getting up to leave.

"Sure, Ronnie," Sullivan answered. "We'll see you in the morning."

As Ronnie the surfer, turned away, Marty called after him. "You ain't no Joadie, Ronnie. But you're a damn good surfer. Catch a big one for me in the morning, you hear."

As Ronnie slipped into the night, Sullivan got up, banking the fire, placing a few more pieces of wood to keep some warmth. He grabbed Marty Johnson's sleeping bag, handing it over to his drunken friend. Then Sullivan slipped into his own, pulling himself closer to the fire. "You jarheads talk too much sometimes," Sullivan aimed. He rustled himself comfortable, laying his coat beneath his head for a pillow. "It's time to get some sleep."

Marty Johnson slowly capped the bottle of tequila, struggling to lay his sleeping bag nearby. "Only when I drink, brother Tommy. Only when I drink."

⌒

The plan was hatched the next morning, over coffee and clear Baja sunshine. A white fog hung off the Pacific shore. Brown pelicans cruised the cusp of the ocean breakers, fishing for breakfast, the persistent thump of the waves pounding the solitary distance of desolate open beach. The plan had been incubating through the course of the trip to Baja. Now, on this beautiful blue agave day, some necessary reasons for a future needed to be born.

Sullivan would be the point man. He would head first to Oregon, acting as reconnaissance. He would probe the territory for a suitable outpost to set up the operation. Marty Johnson would remain in Los Angeles, see if he could wrangle enough provisions for the assault. In the case of this mission, that would be the money. Marty was sure his girlfriend, Celia, would be more than willing to go. They had already dreamed of such a move. So that was the blueprint, a purposeful design that would give tomorrow a whole new reason to come. For Sullivan, it would be another excuse to remain on the road, with a hopeful destination to reach.

Sullivan sipped his coffee, a pleasant moment of satisfaction warming within him. A slight upward rise lifted from the corners of his mouth. A smile? An emotional response shorn of cynicism or required expectation? Perhaps so. He got up, digging into his pack, pulling out the notebook. Not to record any emotion of course, but to make the necessary list of duties ahead.

With a reason for being, the rest of the journey home was a breeze. He and Marty worked their way back north, retracing the way they had come. Todos Santos and Pescadero were left behind, perhaps to return another day. The shock at the US border was to be expected. They re-entered the amphetamine American madhouse, a nation constantly speeding its way toward death. But Tom Sullivan would only be visiting now. It would simply be a matter of dodging all the rats, racing along in their perverse pursuit of the American Dream. They would appear only as moving objects it was now his mission to avoid. He dropped Marty Johnson off in Santa Monica. Celia was happy and excited with the news. Everything was good. Sullivan pulled off in Redwood City, dealing with the obligatory concerns of family. There is nothing that can't be overcome when the imagination is inspired. It was only a matter of fueling up, before getting back on the road again.

On a Saturday afternoon, Sullivan packed his car with the normal essentials. He headed south from Redwood City, crossing the San Mateo Bridge to Hayward. Traffic was light. He aimed north toward

Concord to pick up Interstate 80. There, he would make the diagonal
cross to Sacramento and Interstate 5. From that point, it would be a
straight shot to the Oregon border. At an exit near Walnut Creek, he
pulled off for a tank full of gas. As he pumped the fuel, he noticed a
woman on the corner of the entrance ramp nearby. She stood with her
thumb upraised. Sullivan went inside the station, paying the attendant.
Returning outside, the girl remained by the exit ramp. He walked across
the pavement, shouting to catch her attention.

"Where you going," he called?

"Martinez," she yelled back. He waved her to come. She was bogged
down with a small pack over her shoulder, a big dog on a leash in one
hand, the grip of a small child in the other. He walked toward the
woman as she slowly approached.

"You've got a handful," he said, as they came within distance to
speak. He smiled at her as if to make things feel safe. She was attractive,
with long dark hair to her shoulders, her blue jeans adorned with a
myriad of patches sewn down her legs. A long colored blouse stretched
to her hips. She was definitely a hippie chick, no doubt about that.

"Yeah, I guess so," she answered.

He took the dog leash from her hand, asking her to give him the
pack. She picked up the child, a small young boy. They walked the rest
of the way to the car. Sullivan made room in both bench seats of the
sedan, the dog in back, the woman and child in front.

"Thanks for the ride," she said. "You're going as far as the Martinez
exit, I hope."

"A little further than that," Sullivan answered. "Oregon. By the way,
I'm Tom."

"Really? Oregon? I'm Valerie, and this is Canyon," she responded.
"And that's Fillmore in the back. Do you live up in Oregon?"

Sullivan placed his hand on top of the boy's head. "Hey, Canyon,
how you doing?" Returning to the wheel, he drove over to the entrance
ramp, heading north. "Fillmore. That's a good name for a dog. After
the street?"

"Not exactly," the woman answered. "More for the ballroom,
I suppose. The Fillmore West."

"Oh, the music hall," Sullivan said. "You know, I've never been
there. A lot of good bands I bet. Do you go there a lot?"

"I used to go there a lot," Valerie answered, "when I lived in the

City. I grew up in San Francisco, in the Richmond / Sunset."

"I'm from Redwood City," Sullivan responded. The woman turned to look at him.

"You're from Redwood City, and you've never been to the Fillmore West?"

Sullivan shifted in his seat. "No, I've never been able to make it there. I've been out of town for awhile."

"Oh, Oregon. Sorry about that, what was I thinking," Valerie responded, turning his way.

"Well, not exactly Oregon." Sullivan paused for a second, but went ahead. "In the service, I just got out of the military." The woman turned back, looking straight ahead.

"Vietnam? Did you have to go to Vietnam," she asked nervously?

"Fourteen months," Sullivan answered.

"I'm sorry," she started. "I mean…. I don't mean I'm sorry, I mean…." She halted for a moment, collecting herself. "I mean I'm glad you're home safe, that's what I was trying to say." Then she turned back to face him, expressing a soft look of concern.

"It's okay," Sullivan responded. "I know what you meant. So, do you live right in Martinez? It's no trouble for me to take you to your home. That way you won't have to walk or catch another ride. I'm not in any hurry really, not with such a long way to go." Sullivan began to open up. "In fact, to be honest, I'm not even sure where I am going in Oregon, if you can believe that. Some friends and I are hoping to buy some land up there. I'm just headed up there to look around."

"Wow, no kidding? That's cool," she said. "And thank you, my house is not very far from the freeway. It will be easy for you to get back."

Sullivan turned off the exit at Martinez, driving only a few short blocks to the woman's home. Valerie asked him if he would like something to drink before he got back on the road. He accepted. Sitting at her kitchen table, he waited while she put her son down for a nap. Returning, she poured them both a cold glass of iced herbal tea from the refrigerator, occupying a chair across from him.

Sullivan listened to her story. She had lived in the City for several years, but had gotten pregnant and birthed her child. Sometime later, she had hitchhiked to Colorado to find the boy's father, although she wasn't sure why. Unfortunately, he couldn't be found. Coming back home, she stayed for a time at her parent's home in the East Bay, trying to figure out her next move. Shortly thereafter, she had contracted mononucleosis, becoming racked with fatigue and losing weight. It had taken months to recover. Only recently had she found the place in Martinez, with the money from welfare and help from her family. She still had many friends in the City, but San Francisco had gotten too expensive. In time, she was hoping to find another place to live. Perhaps she would move out towards West Marin, or farther north along the coast. She got up from the table, finding a map of Oregon in her living room. She spread it out for Sullivan to view.

"My best friend, Susan, lives out near Point Reyes. But she told me about people she'd met who have purchased land in a place called Solace Valley. It's somewhere north of Grants Pass, I think." She peered at the map, then pointed to a spot for Sullivan to see.

"Wow, that's coincidental," Sullivan said. "I was planning to scout around for places between Grants Pass and Eugene. It's right along Interstate 5. Do you know what the country looks like?"

"It's in the mountains, I think," Valerie answered. There are lots of forests and not many people. But mostly, the land is cheap."

"Well, thanks for the tip," Sullivan said. "I do think I'll go there. It will be a good place to start."

"Will you be coming back down if you find something," she asked?

"Oh yeah, either way," Sullivan answered. "It's pretty much just an idea for now, not much more than that. We've got to hustle the money to buy something as well. And my friends would have to see it for themselves. For now, it's just something for me to do. To be honest, I really don't know what's going to come of it. I just got out about six weeks ago."

"Would you mind stopping by when you come back down," Valerie asked? "It would be cool to know what you found, to know if you liked it and such."

"Oh yeah, sure," he answered. "I'll come back by and tell you the story. That would be great." Valerie stood up, found pencil and paper, writing down her address and phone number. Sullivan slipped it into his wallet. Then he got up to go. Valerie walked him to his car. He wanted to touch her as they said good-bye, but withheld the urge.

"I'll light a candle tonight, and say a prayer of good luck for you," she said. "A prayer that you will find a beautiful place for yourself and your friends."

Sullivan chuckled at the statement, but smiled at her, showing his gratitude. "Every little bit helps, I guess. Well, thanks so much for the direction. I'll call you when I get back down." They waved to each other as he pulled away.

A short time later, he was settled on the freeway, heading north. He was more excited about the mission than ever before. He could feel himself wanting to hurry the trip, to find a place to buy, so he could rush back down to tell her all about it. Not so much for himself, or even for Marty and Celia for that matter, but for her. His romantic imaginations, which had been dormant for so long a time, ran crazy with anticipation. He looked for another hitchhiker to pick up on the road. He decided that tonight he would sleep in a motel. He would welcome a good night's sleep in a soft bed. Tonight, he wouldn't be worried about his dreams or fears. Tonight, he would look forward to thinking of her.

The jeep pulled off the paved road, before sharply descending down a bumpy drive to a creek bed below. The real estate agent got out and turned the hubs on the front wheels, putting the vehicle into four-wheel drive. He surveyed the depth of the rushing water before climbing back inside the cab. The truck plunged into the creek, the water rising to the sideboards, bouncing over large river rock to the other side. An old logging road ran narrowly through the evergreen timber, passing over a single set of railroad tracks that cut through the property. A hundred yards later, the road reached a large meadow open to the sky. A dilapidated one-room cabin rested nearby.

Sullivan and the real estate agent got out of the rig. Sullivan listened as the agent looked at a county map, pointing out the approximate boundaries of the property. The creek appeared to border the land on three sides, in the shape of a horseshoe, except for a narrow point that extended beyond the county road across from where they had entered. The bulk of the land swept upward toward a hillside, tight with second growth fir and pine. The northern boundary dropped off sharply into a canyon, where the creek ran deeper below. The creek would eventually fall towards the Rogue River, about fifteen miles to the west.

"A week ago, we couldn't have crossed Laughlin Creek," the agent said. "Short of someone building a bridge, driving across the creek is the only access. So from November until about now, there is no vehicle access at all. Unless of course you cross the railroad trestle by foot. From what I understand, that's what the former owners would often do. It's also the reason why the property is priced as listed."

"The trestle?" Sullivan asked. "Where's that?"

The men got back in the truck and returned to the railroad tracks. Parking again, they walked along the fire road that paralleled the rails. Shortly, they reached the canyon abyss. Black steel girders rose high from blasted cement pilings deep below them, supporting the bridge. On each side of the single track, galvanized grating served as a walkway, guarded by strings of cable about three feet high. The cables would be the only barrier preventing a falling death hundreds of feet down to the creek. Sullivan was exhilarated by the sight. The trestle crossing itself must have been two football fields in length. Below him, the canyon carved its way deeper through cliffs of steep-faced rock, with miles of spreading timberland rising higher above.

"This is some bad-ass country," Sullivan said, as if to himself. "It's beautiful."

"No one will bother you here," the agent responded. "Sometime back, some old guy thought it was a mining claim, but he never bothered to check. That's how the cabin got built. But a timber company legally owned the property, running him off when they made the cut. The old bridge over the creek washed out years ago. The current owners were planning on making themselves a homestead, but they never did. They're getting too old now, I gather. They have been trying to sell for quite some time."

The surrounding afternoon was quiet. Early spring clouds hung lazily against a backdrop of blue sky, the cool sun playing hide and seek in between. The men returned over the creek and onto the county road. But the agent turned the jeep in the opposite direction from the way they had come. A short distance down the road, he stopped and pointed to another dirt turnout. "You can enter here," he said. "Then drive through those trees and you'll find the access road by the tracks. You can double-back up to the trestle and walk across. I did it once before. It will tighten your balls, I'll tell you that. Be sure to listen for the train. You can hear it miles away, so not to worry. But you wouldn't want to be caught in the middle if you know what I mean. Anyway, just in case you wanted to come back and see the land again."

Further on, they crossed a small bridge. A somewhat smaller creek rumbled below. "This is Pollard Creek," the agent began. "It ends a short distance to the left, merging with Laughlin, and eventually to the Rogue. We turn right here, and I'll take you up to Pollard Creek. The property is sort of located between the two communities. At Pollard Creek, we can take the freeway over to Solace Valley to get you back to your car. You might as well see the whole neighborhood."

The road up to Pollard Creek wound around curve after curve for several miles, the large timber draping like a canopy along its edge. After a time, the road opened up into a narrow valley, following the railroad tracks off to their right. Along the way, other dirt roads angled off into the trees, marked by mailboxes here and there. Some standard looking houses were set back from the road, but other more rough-built structures could be glimpsed hidden in the trees.

"A lot of young people like yourself have been buying acreage up this way. Some people might call them hippies. But me, I just call them buyers, if you know what I mean."

Minutes later, the Pollard Creek road passed under a tight railroad overpass, opening up to the town itself. There appeared to be a post office, a small grocery store and gas station. Off to the right, surrounded by a green lawn and flowering trees, there stood a large white wooden building with a pillared porch out front, looking something like a southern plantation. The building had a rundown appearance, its porch and the balcony above slightly askew. A neon beer sign hung in one of the windows.

"What's that building?" Sullivan asked.

"That's the Pollard Creek Inn," the agent answered. It was once an old stage-stop hotel, built in the late eighteen hundreds I believe. It's still a bar for the locals, but I don't think they rent the upstairs rooms out anymore."

"It's a cool looking place," Sullivan said.

"Needs a lot of work, and probably cold as hell inside," the agent said. But, I did hear a rumor it might go up for sale one of these days. I sure don't know who would buy it though. Being so rundown, and with so little business around these parts, it would be a really tough go. But you never know, there's always somebody who will give something a try."

The men drove through the rest of the town. They passed by a truck stop before entering the freeway and heading south. The jeep motored over a steep mountain pass, before descending into the wider stretch of Solace Valley. The agent took the exit, returning Sullivan to his car. Agreeing to meet again in the morning, the agent continued south on the freeway, back to the city of Grants Pass, fifteen miles away. Sullivan stood by his car, viewing the open fields of Solace Valley, the timbered mountains rising high in the background. Making up his mind, he jumped into the car, heading back on the freeway north toward Pollard Creek.

Tom Sullivan retraced his path back to the access road by the railroad trestle. Listening intently for the sound of a train engine, he dared himself quickly across the bridge, high above the canyon. He felt a weird sinking feeling in his stomach, a flush of vertigo as he traversed across to the other side. For another hour or more he wandered the property, amidst the timber and silence of the land. He heard only sounds of the rushing creek below, the occasional chatter of birds, the distant muffled grind of a car engine on the county road, the quiet rustle and creaking of the trees in the cool afternoon breeze. There was a sense of distance and repose to the property, both unnerving and yet settling at the very same time. It would be a hell of a project to live on this land. But it sure would be a place to disappear from the rest of the world.

Sullivan hiked out, returning to Pollard Creek. At the truck stop called the Hungry Dog Cafe, there were several motel rooms separated away from the restaurant. He paid for a room, before unloading his toiletries and clothes. Driving over to the market and gas station, he decided to fill up the car. As he reached for the gas pump, a grizzled old man in coveralls came out of the station. "Hold up, son. Can't let you do that. Not in Oregon." The man took the pump handle out of Sullivan's hands. "Fill her up?"

"Sorry," Sullivan apologized. "I forgot. Kinda hard to get used to. Yeah, you can fill her up. Thanks."

"Happens all the time," the man said. "Pain in the ass, if you ask me. You're from California, huh. I see your plate. Where you headed?"

"Well, sort of around here," Sullivan answered. "Sure is beautiful country. Maybe looking at some property to buy. Just kicking around, I guess."

"Plenty of that, I reckon," the old man said. "No work, but plenty of ground. You got some hippie friends up here?"

"Excuse me? No, I just got out of the service. Don't know a soul."

"Vietnam?" the old man asked.

"Yeah, Vietnam."

"Well, plenty of you boys around here. You won't be alone."

Sullivan stepped aside as an old green pick-up truck pulled along the other side of the gas pumps. Two men about Sullivan's age stepped out of the rig. The driver was a husky man, with blondish red curls and a full-bearded face. His passenger's hair was a brighter red, running shoulder length, wearing wire-rimmed glasses on his face. In the back of the pick up, Sullivan could see a stack of feed bags, a roll of black plastic pipe, groceries, and other miscellaneous hardware. Sullivan nodded to the red-haired man, who smiled and raised his head in acknowledgmen, before walking off toward the market next door. The bearded man got out of the truck and stretched. "Fuh, fuh, five dollars worth, Sid," he stuttered to the man, before he too headed for the market.

As they walked away, the old man spoke. "The Mulcahey brothers. They got a hippie farm down on Pollard Creek. Like I said, a lot of hippies coming to this town lately. Don't get me wrong, it's good for business now, but I sure as hell can't figure why. People around here so broke, they can't even pay attention. Unless you're working the woods or driving over to the mill. But the scenery is getting better when their women come to town. Not a bra to be found. My wife gives me the evil eye every time they come by for gas." The old man winked, smiling up at Sullivan.

After eating a solitary dinner at the Hungry Dog Cafe, Sullivan retreated to his motel room. Sitting on the bed, he called Marty Johnson down in Los Angeles. He told Marty about the properties he had seen, going into detail about the one near Solace Valley and Pollard Creek. Sullivan would look at another piece or two the next day, before returning south. It would take some time to figure things out. They would have to rustle up the financing, get some others to go in on the deal. But Marty remained excited about the prospects and that was good.

Either way, Pollard Creek was becoming a draw for Sullivan. In the morning, he would check things out a little more, perhaps talk to a few people if the opportunity arose. He pulled out the worn journal book from his pack. Propped up on the motel bed, he wrote down notes of recollection and other items of information. He would definitely stop in Martinez on his way back south, see if he could find Valerie. He would tell the woman his story, maybe get to know her better. Things were beginning to look up. Oregon felt good. By summer, one way or another, he knew he would return. His recent past was beginning to fade, lost in the distraction of his current intentions. Putting down the journal, he slept long and well, deeply through the night.

.

CHAPTER ELEVEN

I LOOKED AWAY
Strickersville, Pennsylvania / August, 1972

SEAN MCALLISTER HUNG UP THE TELEPHONE. The recording on the Longshoremen's message line had favorable news. The regular weekly freighter from Costa Rica would dock by morning. Chances were good a long day of work lay before him. It would be a decent payday if his number was called. For most weeks during the summer, he had gotten to work the boat. It would be a twelve-to-sixteen hour run, stacking forty-pound boxes of green Del Monte bananas into tractor trailer trucks, until the freighter was empty and turned back to sea.

The Wilmington Marine Terminal was always busy with traffic. There were meat ships from Chile. There were auto ships from Germany, filled with Volkswagens and Audis, sometimes a Porsche mixed in between. Each and every week, a ship full of bananas arrived. The union Longshoremen would work the freighter, the Teamster warehousemen handling the flat. Whenever the Teamsters were stretched thin, scab laborers like McAllister and Johnny Howard would get their numbers called. They would work long and hard until told to go home.

McAllister left the Strickersville' farmhouse, running his pick-up into town. He stopped by the off-campus apartment where Johnny Howard had been living with his girlfriend since his recent graduation in Vermont. The men arranged to meet at 5:30 am the next morning. McAllister gassed up the rig and bought a few groceries. He purchased a big cup of coffee and a *Washington Post* at the magazine shop, then steered back to the farm. Sipping his coffee on the front porch of the house, the August morning was beginning to warm. He began to read the front page stories of the newspaper. It had now been over two years since leaving school in D.C., but he still read the *Washington Post* whenever he could.

This Watergate break-in story was getting more interesting by the week. The reports were like reading a good mystery novel, a page-turner waiting for the next revelation. Two unfamiliar journalists for the *Post* carried the by-line. Each installment was intermittent and difficult to follow, yet strangely addictive to read. McAllister was hooked. There was something going down here, and these two reporters were definitely on to it. But it was a story no one else was paying much attention. Clues to the mystery kept popping up, a thread of possible deception here, another there. Officially, nobody was copping to anything, so it had become a story that was hard to tell, and even further to believe. If truth sometimes be stranger than fiction, this story might just be the poster child for that little aphorism. For the most part, the Watergate break-in remained a weird single event. The investigation didn't have legs as they say in the trade. So McAllister followed the newsprint drama seemingly alone in a conspiratorial world.

His reading complete, McAllister drank the rest of his coffee, enjoying the full flush of a summer sun. It came to mind that almost two years ago this time, he and Johnny Howard had been on the road across the country, bound for California. All in all, it remained a pleasant memory. The hitchhiking trip had opened his world to the rest of America. He had seen Berkeley, San Francisco, Big Sur and Los Angeles. However, in the end, the Golden State had not been as expected. It was surprisingly populated and very fast. Still, with its warm and sunny skies, its beautiful geography of mountains and coastline, the journey remained imprinted in his mind. It beckoned him to return. Maybe not so much to be in California, as to one day be out of here.

He was now free to go. It was an odd feeling for sure, after four years of killing time in school. He had managed to get his diploma, the exact number of credits to graduate, not one hour more. Upon his graduation there had been no ceremony. He had chosen to skip all the straight mumbo jumbo. He had simply gone down to the administrative offices a week later, picking up his blue covered piece of parchment paper, its recognition signed off inside. There had been no excitement or drama, no gown or tasseled hat thrown high into the air.

Although the college degree meant little to him, it had at least provided an escape from the draft. For that he was thankful, if not much else.

McAllister had become one of the fortunate ones, born of time and circumstance. In the last two years, he had gone to counseling as a conscientious objector to the war, to at least be on the record. But he knew it wouldn't fly, he was too honest for that particular mendacity. He was essentially a political objector to the Vietnam conflict. Religious reasons, or any passive resistance to violence had nothing to do with it. Canada seemed like the only alternative. Although his sister, Mary Jane, had moved to New York City, she still had contacts in Boston who could advise him as necessary. He had ignored investigating those possibilities, waiting instead to face the potential reality of conscription whenever it would arrive.

He hadn't known then, but the politics of the war would save his ass. Even though the military draft remained in effect, it was coming to an end. Everyone knew the underlying story. It was just a way for Nixon and the government hawks to dampen the intensity of opposition to the war. Slackening the draft had become a political ruse to keeping the war funding alive while promoting a different strategy. The government was reducing troop levels, shifting the fight from a ground war to an air campaign over North Vietnam. For some time Nixon had been conning the nation with the bullshit that the South Vietnamese would take up the battle for their own sovereignty, with United States assistance. This tactic had been called 'Vietnamization'. Meanwhile, the US military continued to bomb the holy hell out of the North. They believed this plan would eventually forge a satisfactory 'peace with honor', before hightailing out of this Asian mess whenever it looked good to go.

So Sean McAllister was off the hook. A constant personal fear and conflict in his life had been erased. But the war wasn't over. In fact, the outright murder of Vietnamese innocents persisted. McAllister's hate for Richard Nixon had not diminished. Nixon and Kissinger's incredible arrogance and righteous moralities turned like a knife in his gut. Nixon had been an underhanded cheap-shot artist from the gate. The 'Tricky Dick' moniker was a rotten apple falling not far from the tree. Nixon's 'secret plan' for the war was not so secret anymore. But he owned the bully pulpit, and his 'moral majority' scheme played well across an indifferent American republic, untouched by the tragedy of the time. One had to give Richard Nixon some begrudging credit for the self-indulgent manipulations he was able to convey. Just don't ever turn your back on the man, or forever pay the price.

In the two years since Kent State, McAllister's political idealism had bounced back and forth like a tennis match. Some days he had a cynical sense of apathy, a careless feeling of futility against the powers that be. Other days, charged with a hopeful wishfulness and belief that something might change. Good people of respect and conscience were doing what they could to solve the riddle of this desperate division in the American character, this wide gulf between self-image and truth. For years now, emotions had run every which way, dividing families and friends, co-workers and neighbors, congregations and institutions, lovers and loved. The Vietnam War had become a raw and dramatic convergence of cultural forces, so alive, and yet so exhausting in its effect. It was a battle of wills, a country in outright rebellion against itself.

Into that breach, two events had begun to turn the wheels of salvation closer to a forced resolution. The first was Daniel Ellsberg. Ellsberg had risked his own personal freedom to inform the people of his country the factual truths of American policy in Southeast Asia. Ellsberg unmasked the hidden history and secret agendas of a post-war American government, revealing an imperial policy of influence and control, shorn naked of any moral compass or democratic intent. Under the surreptitious guise of national security, this policy was being kept secret from the lighted eyes of an American democracy. It was a policy that by its flawed vision and purpose, had caused the useless loss of over fifty thousand American citizens, as well as the untold deaths of millions in an undeserving nation far across the world.

Heck, few people sat down at night and read the Pentagon Papers. The divisions of mind amongst many Americans had become too hardened to make a difference. Thankfully, the American media had stepped up to the plate, ignoring the government's attempt to criminalize the documents' publication. The ensuing revelations threw off the veil of lies and untruths that were being perpetrated on a so-called trusting American public. Finally, some representative leaders were catching the drift. A coffee pot of greater dissent had begun to percolate. A larger portion of the American populace was squirming in their televised lazy-boy chairs.

The second event became equally as troubling. Many American

soldiers were now coming home. As the shock and solitary tragedies of their experience in Vietnam began to taper, they found themselves alone together amidst an uncaring and distracted homeland. With the memories of their experience so fresh, and some clarity of their minds restored, these soldiers stepped into the void of a waning protest movement, giving it renewed life. Amongst them, they had a terribly honest and horrific story to tell, filled with unbelievable truths that any self-respecting American needed to hear. Hippies and cowards they were not. Instead, they were the very young men who had battled for the cause, the actual defenders of freedom that Americans had pledged by their faith to support. These were men whose dead and disabled companions were a telling reminder of the heinous consequences of war.

The Winter Soldier testimonies of February, 1971 were largely ignored by the press. But like a seed they grew within a generation of dispossessed and forgotten men, men who had seen so many die in vain. They were no longer believers in the righteousness of the task. They were men who had survived an insane masquerade, living only for themselves and their brothers, fighting against an enemy who had more at stake on their own turf. But fight they did, in every way, to survive, to avenge the loss of those companions, to take out their rage on others and make it through another day. They were fighting to simply get out alive.

But after their service, when suddenly removed from the madhouse of Vietnam, they were thrust onto the surreal streets of an alien terrain, a terrain they once called home. And everything had changed. For most of these men, there were no parades, no celebrations. Back at home, the war had become a drum beat no one wanted to hear, filled with silent pulses of guilt that were easier locked away. America had grown too big to truly feel the pain and emptiness of the human wreckage its government could cause. These were men left behind. They were left behind to bandage their own wounds, mend their own fences, handle their solitary nightmares alone.

How could Sean McAllister not go to Miami Beach, to take to the streets in solidarity with these homeless comrades. A deeply felt anger still stirred within him. The Vietnam Veterans Against the War would be there, fighting now to bring the remaining brothers back. Equally important was to stop the bombing, this insane remote-control killing and destruction of innocent lives. The bombings' only intent was to save the face of defeat, to force a ridiculous outcome called a 'negotiated peace'. The nausea and obsession of Vietnam refused to let go.

McAllister was not a McGovernite, some hopeful young American who believed in the democratic process to redress the grievances of government policy. Fuck that shit. Richard Nixon, and all he represented, was clearly more devious than any heartfelt democratic devotions. A political and economic war machine now owned America, and its very survival was at stake. McAllister wanted to believe that this wasn't the case, that perhaps a saner and more progressive alternative could find its way into the nation's political understanding. But a darker narcissism now clouded his vision, day after fraudulent day.

The screen door to the farmhouse porch opened behind him. Bruiser stepped through, rubbing an eyeball with one hand, a cup of coffee in the other. He sat his large shouldered frame into an empty chair on the porch, pulling himself awake to the day. "Hey," was all he could say. "Hey, yourself," McAllister answered. Each drew another sip off their coffees, a momentary silence between them.

"Did Mad call here last night?" McAllister finally asked. The evening before, he had driven up to North Wilmington to have dinner with his folks, before stopping for a late night beer in town and returning to the farm.

"No, not that I know of," Bruiser answered. "And I was here all last night. But Jimmy Knox called. Said he heard we were going to Miami, and he wants you to call him."

"Jimmy Knox, no shit. Geez, haven't seen him since high school. He's back from Nam again, right? Wonder what that's all about?"

"I think he wants to go," Bruiser said.

"Well damn, that would make four of us," McAllister responded. "We could travel in pairs. That would work real good. You and Mookie are still in, right?"

"Yeah, you know, Mac. Whatever. Mookie is all jacked up to go, so I guess so."

Bruiser hadn't changed much. All you had to do was pull on the cord to his light bulb, and he would turn on. Making decisions was still not Bruiser's forte, but he was always easy to have by your side.

He and McAllister hadn't been on any big road trips since they had crashed the Woodstock festival a few years before. Bruiser was pure gold. If you needed a companion for something, he was usually good to go, although he never showed must excitement about the allegiance he displayed.

"I left Jimmy's number by the phone," Bruiser yawned. "And Dutch Rollins came by looking for you and Willie. He was with some guy I didn't know. They were all wired up on some shit. We drank a few beers waiting to see if you would show up, but then they split. That fucking Dutch is crazy man. He pulled a gun out of his shirt, asking me if he could shoot a few rounds on the property. I said, no, are you crazy? So he put it away. What's with that guy anyway?"

McAllister's body went tense. "You remember the other guy's name, was it Eddie?"

"Yeah, that's him, Eddie. He kept looking around the place. Strange dude, Mac, I didn't get a good feeling about that guy."

"Did Dutch say if he was coming back?"

"Nah, they just got up and left after awhile. Just said to tell you he came by."

McAllister wanted the fear thing to go away, but it was worried enough to stay. "I don't know, Bruise. I think Dutch is getting into some weird shit these days. And I'm beginning to feel the heat around him or something. But geez, a gun, that's getting scary. I agree with you, I don't know about that Eddie guy. I think they're getting into the coke thing, not just dealing weed anymore. We don't need that stuff around here. Definitely not the gun act, that's for sure. I'll talk to Willie about it. But if Dutch calls for me, just say I'm not around, at least until we figure this out. We don't need any heat around this place, and Dutch and Eddy sure feel like heat."

"Whatever you say, Mac."

Dutch Rollins was an okay guy, or at least he used to be. McAllister had met him through his housemate, Willie Chambers. Willie Chambers and Mookie James were guys he had met while going to school, living in a rooming house near campus, after he had transferred up from school in Washington D.C. And the three of them had rented the farmhouse together here in Strickersville sometime back. Bruiser was crashing at the house for the summer until he went back to school. The Bruise had another semester to go before finishing up. Stephen

"Mookie" James was cool, a good student and a serious guy. He shared McAllister's politics and they got along well. For Willie Chambers, it was less so. Willie had dropped out of school but had stuck around town. He was a small-time pot dealer, and that's where Dutch came to the party.

Dutch Rollins was Willie's connection during the days at the rooming house. And even McAllister had gotten into the game from time to time. McAllister knew a lot of the frat boys on campus, back from his high school days and playing sports. Through Willie Chambers, Dutch Rollins would front McAllister a kilo from time to time. McAllister would weigh and bag up the pot, keep a little for himself, then deal the rest to the frat boys and make some easy money. It didn't take much effort. It was just another way of making a few bucks between the jobs he worked at the dining hall, the banana boats, and working for a painting contractor he had gotten to know.

But Dutch was getting a little wacko lately. Perhaps he was getting a little too big for his own good. Dutch had a new car, and he wasn't just selling weed anymore. He'd graduated to Quaaludes, speed, and now it was a good guess, cocaine. Lately, Dutch was more fucked up when he came around to the farm. And now, for Christ's sake, he was carrying a gun. It wasn't a good sign. Willie Chambers was still involved in the whole thing, acting kind of secretive and usually not around. Throw in this Eddie guy, who always seemed to be with Dutch whenever they came over, and things were beginning to feel pretty tight. McAllister hadn't paid much attention before. He'd been doing his own thing, and spending time with Mad whenever he could.

It's hard to describe those times when you feel the heat. And you're never really sure that it might not just be your own paranoia. But this Eddie cat, along with Dutch acting more like a loose cannon, well, the temperature was rising. McAllister was beginning to feel the vibe big time now. He'd have to talk to Willie Chambers when he could find him. But what the hell do you say? At least no more guns on the property, that was for sure.

McAllister and Bruiser made some breakfast and another pot of coffee. Afterwards, Bruiser grabbed the newspaper, found the hammock swinging in the yard, laying back to read. McAllister started a load of laundry, before sitting down to give Jimmy Knox a call. Bruise was correct. Jimmy Knox wanted to go to Miami. He wanted to join the other Vietnam Veterans that were planning to protest Nixon's nomination for a second term at the Republican National Convention. With Jimmy Knox coming along, the group of four could now pair up. The plan was to start hitchhiking toward Florida the following Sunday.

Jimmy Knox was as taciturn on the phone as McAllister remembered him in high school. He was a man of few words, with a voice that didn't rise or lower all that much. If Jimmy was excited to go, you would never know by his vocal expressions. McAllister knew very little of Jimmy's time in Vietnam, except what Bruiser had heard through the grapevine. The word was that Jimmy had done one tour as a point man and squad commander on patrol in the jungle. He had eventually come back home to the states. But then he suddenly turned around, volunteering to return. The second tour had been cut short by an addiction to heroin. Jimmy had been sent to rehab and managed to clean up. That's all McAllister knew.

McAllister gave Mad a call at her place. Nobody answered. He wondered where she could be. He couldn't remember if she had traveled home to see her family. Mad hadn't been happy when he told her he was taking the trip to Miami. Things had gotten kind of distant between them this summer. She loved her music thing, going to concerts and clubs with her girlfriends. But mostly, they were both always working a lot. Mad still had her summer job with the university, and McAllister had been all over the neighborhood, either working with the painting contractor up in the Lancaster area, or working the long days at the docks when the opportunity arose.

In addition, he and Bruiser still enjoyed playing ball, and they had hooked up with a league team in town. The summer before, Mad had come to every game, being a fan with the other girlfriends who attended. But this summer she hadn't come at all, preferring to stay home sewing or finding free music venues around campus. Mad was good at taking old bargain clothing and making garments she liked to wear. Neither of them were giving up the things they liked to do. As far as McAllister was concerned, it was no big deal.

However, he hadn't been able to reach her in over a week. It seemed like she was always somewhere else. At least that's what her roommates said, whenever he called. Things didn't feel quite right, and she seemed to call back whenever he wasn't around. He sort of knew they needed to talk about things, but it was easier to just put things off, hoping any uncertainties might simply fade away. Still, they had been so inseparable for such a long time. Things felt different today, and it worried him to think about.

McAllister hung out his washed clothes. Then he and Bruiser pulled a few beers from the refrigerator, driving the back roads to the tank for an afternoon swim. They jumped the fence, climbed to the top, swam inside the cold artesian water, before laying on its roof, smoking a joint and drinking their beer. McAllister thought about his first trip with Mad, how warm and enticing it had been for them. Today, it seemed like such a long time ago. He tried to push it from his mind. Before the trip to Miami, they would have to talk, and he would see what he could do.

Returning to the farmhouse in the early evening, McAllister called her again. This time she was home. He asked her where she had been.

"I told you, Sean. I went up to see my parents. And then my sister and I went with friends into Philly for the Poco concert. You said you were going to your folks for your Dad's birthday on Saturday."

"Huh, I did? I guess I don't remember. You mean friends from up at home?"

"Yes," she said.

McAllister asked her about the concert. She was brief. She didn't ask about his father's birthday. He mentioned that he probably would get a long day's work at the docks tomorrow, but he would come by Tuesday after she got off work. Mad said she was getting together with the girls on Tuesday to eat pizza and have a sewing thing. Wednesday would work better. Willie Chambers came into the house, entering through the kitchen while McAllister wrestled with Mad. Moments later he passed through the dining room, a sandwich in hand. Chambers was looking narrow and thin. His kinked out hair was wide about his head.

"Tell Mad, I said hello," he spoke, walking on by and heading upstairs. His voice was louder than usual, his face turned away.

"I've got to get off the phone. Rebecca needs to make a call. You can call me on Wednesday after work, and we can get together then. When do you leave for the protest thing?"

"Sunday," he answered.

"I'll see you Wednesday. Just come to the house and I'll make dinner here."

"Okay," he said, then paused. "I miss you, sweetheart."

"I know you do, Sean. Have a good day with the bananas."

The world is full of crazy places, full of crazy states of mind. There are so many people to either encounter or observe. Life can be full of contented moments, beneficent in their grace and fulfillment. The world can hand you the keys to a new Cadillac, a shiny silver blue one. You can drive it all around town and feel pretty darn swell. But darn if there isn't that other side, when life turns against you. It can clobber you with certain situations of which you cannot contend. It can force you to become a victim of circumstances so out of your control. So feeling good on a warm summer night you decide to take the Caddy out for a spin. But as you step outside your front door, shit if the goddamn automobile hasn't disappeared. It's been stolen right off of your block, right in front of your own home. There are few feelings comparable to being the victim of a theft. It makes one feel empty and violated deep inside. It's personal. Worse yet, despite all the sympathy that others might give, the pain of your loss must be suffered alone.

Union longshoreman, Clarence Johnson, was today's circumstantial victim, his new blue Caddy stolen from his street in the bright light of a Wilmington day. There wasn't going to be much a couple of young honky brothers could say to comfort the man, but, "Damn, Clarence, that's a fucking bummer for sure. The insurance will take care of it, right?"

"Insurance? Don't be talking that shit," Clarence spits. "Insurance? That's something only white people can get to protect their lily-livered assholes. Insurance in the 'hood'? Get the hell outta here, man. Yeah, I got an insurance policy, with Lloyds of Fucking London. You white boys can suck my one-eyed trouser snake, you hear me." Suffice to say, longshoreman Clarence Johnson was not a happy camper, early on this banana boat morning.

If there was one sure thing about working the Wilmington docks, there was rarely a dull moment to be had. At least that was true for a couple of white boys who only got a chance to visit from time to time. So cue the scene with a massive freighter from Costa Rica tied to a wharf. A large open warehouse rests nearby. Inside that warehouse, a freestanding loading platform stretches down the building's center. A dozen tractor trailers are backed up to each side of the platform. The heavy smell of diesel exhaust hangs in the air. Bright lights are strung from the rafters of the dark interior. The warehouse seems to glare like a Hollywood movie set, which was never far from the truth.

It was a movie all right, a heavy industrial grinder of a film. And every actor had a speaking part, with a bad-ass personality to match. Throw in a heavy dose of extras, thousands and thousands of them, dressed in rectangular cardboard boxes. The boxes are yanked off a conveyor belt by men like Clarence Johnson. They slide down sections of removable metal roller stanchions, pieced deep into each trailer. These rollers carry the green bananas down into the rigs, where they are packed and loaded ten high, pushing the working Teamster actors out the back. When the truck is full, the driver latches down the doors. He fires up his semi-truck, pulling out of the warehouse. Immediately, another empty trailer is backed up to the platform. Every two hours there is a ten minute break, lunch after four, and overtime after eight. The show doesn't finish until the freighter's holds are empty, the heavy ropes untied, the ship sailing back to sea.

The job was a kick, a whistle to whistle hustle from start to finish. The Wilmington Marine Terminal was a world where scabs like Sean McAllister and Johnny Howard were known only by their number, rarely a name. It was a black man's world of tough talk and profanity, the bitch-blasting humor of personal degradation, yet mixed with a grudging mutual respect. The docks were a place where your hair or your race was never an issue, as long as you carried your weight. Working the docks was observational cinema, but more than anything else, it was another crazy world to be. As the August summer twilight fell across the land, McAllister and Howard threw their lunch pails into the back of the pick-up truck, heading back to their white hippie universe and post-college lives. As the film credits begin to roll, a pissed off Clarence Johnson can be seen catching a ride with some of the brothers, angry and alone with his unfortunate loss.

"So when do you leave?" Johnny Howard asked. McAllister steered the truck away from the security gate, guiding them home.

"Early Sunday," McAllister murmured. He was beginning to feel some fatigue from the work day, his thoughts turning to other things. "I sure hope we don't get stuck on the way down. We're going to be cutting it close."

"You don't sound all that excited about it." Johnny Howard questioned.

"Oh yeah? I guess I'll manage to get up for it by the weekend. I've just got a lot of work and stuff to do before we go. I've got to go back up to Lancaster for a few more days. They've got a couple more units that are ready to paint. I need to get that done before I go."

"How's Mad doing?" Johnny asked. "I haven't seen her in awhile."

"You and me both," McAllister answered. "I don't know. It hasn't been going well lately. It doesn't feel like things are good between us right now. It's been kind of going that way since I finished school in June."

Johnny Howard turned his head toward McAllister, showing surprise. "Really? You two always seem so good together. What's up?"

"Not sure. She just seems distant lately, unavailable. She hasn't come up to the farmhouse in weeks. And I've been busy trying to make some money. In fact, she seemed pissed off when I told her about the Miami trip. And whenever I start talking about going west together after she finishes school, I get a cold response. I thought she would be excited about the adventure. But lately, she's not interested in that discussion. So I haven't mentioned it again. But things feel real different, I can tell you that."

"Well, she probably can't think that far ahead right now," Johnny advised. "It might be best to leave it alone for awhile."

"Yeah, I suppose you're right," McAllister whined. "But you know, Johnny, I just want to get out of here whenever I can. I guess I figured Mad would feel the same. But maybe that's the issue, she can't see it right now." McAllister wanted to change the subject. "Hey, did you ever meet my Uncle Franny?"

"Yeah, I think so. Isn't he the uncle that works at the refinery in Delaware City?"

"Yeah, that's him," McAllister affirmed. He's the shipping superintendent down there. He handles the tankers that come and go. Anyway, Uncle Franny said he could possibly get me some work on one of their ships. It would be some real good money. I've been thinking I could work it hard while Mad was still in school. That way I could pay off most of my college loan, and we would have plenty of dough to hit the road together."

"Did you tell Mad about that, too?" Johnny asked.

"Yeah, I did," McAllister answered. "I mean I was just trying to make some plans. But now the way you are asking, I don't know."

"Well, they're your plans, Sean. They're not Mad's. Sounds like you and her better talk it out a little. It's not like I'm trying to give advice or anything, but Mad has never struck me as the adventurous type. Although she is pretty hip in a lot of ways, she seems more like the Philly homegirl type deep down. A lot like Liz as a matter of fact."

"So how are you and Liz, anyway?"

"Hmm. To be honest, I may have moved into this thing a little too fast. Of course, I needed a place to stay at the time. But she really wanted this whole deal more than me. You know, sometimes I'd like to think I could go back out west, too. But it may not be in the cards right now. Liz is really great, don't get me wrong. But things are sort of confusing most of the time, like where things might be headed and stuff."

"Confusing, no doubt about that," McAllister mumbled, as if to himself. "I guess I got to get this situation straightened out, one way or another. It just doesn't feel good right now, and I'm not sure why. But don't mention any of this to Liz, okay? You know what I mean, right?"

"Not to worry," Johnny answered, "the lips are sealed." The conversation ended for a time, driving along toward home.

Then, Johnny Howard let out a laugh. "Well, you know, Sean, we're a whole lot better off than Clarence is today." He mimicked the old longshoreman. "Insurance? Insurance? You can suck my one-eyed trouser snake!"

The two men laughed together. For a moment, it brought back to mind the hitchhiking trip he and Johnny had shared so long ago. Ever since that journey, they would joke from time to time about the man Duke from Nebraska. Whenever they might be in mutual company, and somebody said they were hitchhiking somewhere, one of them would throw out Duke's funny response about getting a car.

"Hey, Clarence," McAllister began humorously. "What are you doing there by the side of the road? You say you're going to work? Heck, most people in these parts get a car for that?" McAllister cracked up at his own joke.

Johnny Howard picked up on the repartee. "So what the hell does it look like Duke? Like I got Lloyd's of Fucking London? Hey Duke, get the fuck outta here, you hay-eating son of a bitch." The two men continued in character, laughing away. It was just something to do on another road trip home, a way of pushing deeper concerns into the closet of obscurity.

Wednesday came, and McAllister was stuck up in Lancaster, Pennsylvania. If he was going to get both apartment units sprayed and trimmed out by Friday, he would have to work late. He took a break, went to a pay phone, calling Mad at the rooming house. One of her roommates answered. He left a message that he had to work late, not to worry about dinner. He would try to call her when he finally got home. But it would be way past dark when he pulled into the farmhouse. Bruiser was on the porch, drinking a beer. He sat petting the farm dog, Meatball, who lay sprawled by his side. McAllister grabbed a beer out of the refrigerator, sitting down beside them. Meatball got up and greeted him, before lying back down.

"Nice and quiet here at home," McAllister said. He rested back on the porch chair, drinking the beer. He could hear the crickets singing by the pond on the adjoining property, the lightning bugs flashing pale red beacons in the yard.

"Willie was here for awhile, working on his car," Bruiser said. But he got a phone call and said he was going into town. Also, Jimmy Knox called and said he would get a ride down Saturday night from Wilmington. He asked if he could crash here overnight. Mookie went to borrow a backpack from some friend for the trip. He should be back in a bit."

"I guess Mad didn't call?" McAllister asked.

"Not that I know of," Bruiser answered. "But I didn't get back home until about six or so myself."

McAllister didn't respond. For some reason, a nervous hurt feeling swept over him, as if something might be wrong, wrong in a big way. The thought forced him up from the porch chair. He went and got his lunch pail out of the truck. He had to eat and get ready for tomorrow. He fixed a can of chili with a bag of potato chips, made some lunch for the following day. He drank another beer, wrestled through a drawer, found a cigarette and smoked it. He decided not to call Mad tonight. But he worried all the same. She could call him for a change.

Lying in bed, McAllister tossed and turned. He heard cars pulling into the driveway, the sound of voices downstairs. This thing with Mad was keeping him awake. On the other hand, in a few days he'd be out on the road to Miami, in another world all together. Somehow he slowly drifted into sleep.

On Saturday night, McAllister, Bruiser, Mookie James, and Jimmy Knox sat in the farmhouse living room, drinking beer and smoking weed. McAllister took the lead on plans for the trip. They all looked at a map, locating Flamingo Park in Miami Beach. Bruiser and Mookie would hitchhike together. McAllister would travel with Jimmy Knox. Once they got down to Miami, McAllister would make a sign for Delaware. Bruiser and Mookie would look to find them. As long as they were able to get to Flamingo Park, eventually they would find each other. The phone rang about nine o'clock. McAllister didn't budge. Bruiser got up to answer.

"If it's Mad, tell her I'm already in bed. And we're leaving early in the morning."

"What?" Bruiser asked. He looked at McAllister quizzically. "You mean tell her you're not here?" Mookie and Jimmy Knox remained silent.

"Please, Bruise," McAllister said firmly. "I'll explain it to you later."

"All right, Mac, whatever. But I don't like it." Bruiser went into the kitchen and answered the phone. Mookie felt the unease, asking another question about the trip, but everyone could hear Bruiser's voice relaying the message. Then Bruiser came back into the living room, sitting down. McAllister looked over, and Bruiser nodded his way.

"Thanks, Bruise," was all McAllister would say.

CHAPTER TWELVE

BALLAD OF A THIN MAN
Miami Beach / August, 1972

SOME CHOICES IN LIFE DON'T ALWAYS MAKE SENSE, at least on first impression. Going to the state of Florida during the month of August might qualify as one of those decisions. Initially, the 1972 Republican National Convention was not intended to be held in Miami Beach, Florida. San Diego, California was originally designated to be the convention site, a breezy warm ocean city, close to Richard Nixon's west coast residence at San Clemente. But things had gotten dicey on the Pacific side, when Jack Anderson, a nationally syndicated investigative journalist, had broken a story that International Telephone &Telegraph, one of the largest corporations on earth, had offered to spice up Nixon's garden party with a four hundred thousand dollar gift to the Republican National Committee.

International Telephone & Telegraph had a dark corporate past, as far back as investments in the German war machine under Hitler. So anyone in the know wouldn't have been surprised by these latest shenanigans. The quid pro quo in exchange was to let an anti-trust investigation currently inside the US Justice Department die a quiet death. And with Nixon's Attorney General, John Mitchell, at the helm of the criminal justice system for the United States of America, it wouldn't take a wild guess to figure out how that inquiry might turn out.

To further complicate matters, the anti-war movement on the western side of America, was preparing en masse to flood San Diego with up to 750,000 demonstrators. Such numbers descending on San

Diego would make the 1968 Democratic Convention in Chicago look like a Boy Scout camp. So the Republican hierarchy had made a quick switch to Miami Beach, where Nixon could still sleep in his own bed at Key Biscayne. Although the number of protesters might be down in size, it promised to be no less intense.

Efforts by the Nixon administration and J. Edgar Hoover's FBI were continuing to disparage and marginalize the movement against the war in Vietnam. Even the CIA was suspected of engaging in domestic intelligence, in express violation of its legal purview and charter. Stolen documents from an FBI field office in Media, Pennsylvania had revealed the existence of an illegal domestic operations unit, known as Cointelpro, under Hoover's specific direction. Shortly before the Convention, Vietnam Veteran organizers in Gainesville, Florida had suddenly been indicted on conspiracy charges to disrupt the Convention and murder public officials. As well, John Lennon, who had further taken up the cause for peace from his new home in New York City, was facing deportation charges from the United States. Major anti-war organizations, along with the Black Panthers and other dissident groups within the US, had become the victims of infiltration and harassment. There were ongoing efforts to demonize their leaderships as violent and extreme. Meanwhile, in Cambodia, the U.S. government continued secret bombing missions, in express disregard of Cambodia's sovereignty and the required Congressional approval.

More and more Americans were taking up the cause against these threats to constitutional liberty. Yet, the bulk of America's citizens preferred to ignore their evidence and impact. The words 'protecting national security' had become the catch phrase for rationalizing such illegalities. What was really needed was not a revolution on the streets of the United States, but a revolution in ninth grade civics classes across the land. The effects of the war in Vietnam were not only claiming the lives of thousands of American soldiers, or eviscerating a sovereign nation far from it borders. Consequently, it was further destroying the basic tenets of a republican form of government and representative democracy. McCarthyism had not been defeated. Twenty years later, such nefarious devices had simply become a horse of a different color.

On Sunday morning, the August sun inched higher in the sky. Sean McAllister once again returned to an interstate highway entrance ramp, his arm outstretched, his thumb up. Bruiser and Mookie had caught the first ride. McAllister and Jimmy Knox would follow. Destination, Miami Beach. For McAllister, it was good to be back on the road, distracted for a time from his concerns with Mad. He felt bad for not having spoken with her the night before. His anger toward their situation had gotten the better of him. But deeper down, he knew it was not just his anger that was presenting itself. It was more a brooding sense of fear he was unwilling to face, a fear of possible consequences over which he had no control.

Jimmy Knox sat silently on his haunches, smoking a cigarette. His red frizzy hair was growing out below his baseball cap, the freckles of his youth beginning to disappear with age. Jimmy looked strong and fit, his forearms etched with purple vein. No doubt this journey would be a different trip for Jimmy Knox. Anti-war protests had not been on Jimmy's docket the last few years. But you had to figure the dangers of protest would be a piece of cake for him, compared to his recent past. It was impossible for McAllister to imagine where Jimmy Knox had been just a year ago this time.

People can wax poetic about almost anything in life. They can make up a lot of fancy words and images to describe one thing or another. They can let their imaginations have a go. But until you felt the whispered sound of a bullet whizzing by your ear, or felt the thundered impact of the earth shaking beneath your feet, you didn't know shit. Until you truly had met and accepted the perverse realization of your own mortality, you weren't at liberty to say. How does anyone manage to emotionally overcome the fear of certain finality, and yet continue to perform his duty as if that fear did not exist?

Obviously, it was humanly possible to do just that. Men had chosen to make war since the beginning of time. Still, no literary words could ultimately describe such fear. You had to be there, and that was it. Jimmy Knox had been there. In today's morning sun, Jimmy Knox squatted on a highway roadside below McAllister, alive and in one piece. But deeper questions remained. How does one ever return to a larger world that would never understand?

When Jimmy Knox came home the first time, there was no parades, no ribbon cutting ceremonies, no high fives for getting out alive. Instead, there was just a hell of a lot of personal confusion. Oh, and one other minor thing, an addiction to heroin. For Jimmy, it probably had started as some form of coping mechanism. Coming home had not been what he expected. There was a good chance everything previously known about his life had changed for Jimmy Knox. And expectations are just that, expectations. Coming home becomes just another place you have to deal with. Consequently, one begins to yearn for a world they do know and understand, something familiar. Maybe there's only one place a man like Jimmy Knox can think of going. Going back.

Jimmy Knox returned for a second tour. But the heroin addiction had won the battle inside. Jimmy was shipped back home. He cleaned up, got out a second time. There began a new battle he wished to wage. Whenever they reached Miami Beach, Jimmy Knox had told McAllister he would join with the Vietnam Veterans Against the War. Jimmy would eat, sleep, and march with the VVAW, until it was time to leave. McAllister knew that Jimmy Knox had stories to show and tell. Only he would not be the person to hear them.

The hitchhiking rides began to come, down through Maryland, Virginia, the Carolinas and Georgia. With each border crossed, anticipation grew. They hitched through Florida to urban Miami, finally traversing the water causeway to the beach city that shared its name. They found Flamingo Park, the staging ground and headquarters for the protest ahead. McAllister put up the sign, where Bruiser and Mookie found them. Setting up their makeshift camp, they shared stories of the road. Jimmy Knox went off to find the VVAW base camp. It was a shirtless summer night, hot and humid close.

Things had already been happening. That evening, a tense calm hung in the air. Strategically, Flamingo Park was a safe haven, but would it be for long? McAllister's antennae vibrated with a sense of apprehension, elevated by the heat and the redneck state of Florida. One thing felt certain, everyone on both sides was here for a reason. Tomorrow, each side would surely continue on their appointed rounds. No one would sleep well in the nights to come.

At first light on Wednesday morning, McAllister slipped out of his sleeping bag and left Flamingo Park. To the east, some blocks away, the sun was beginning to rise. The ocean had to be near. He needed to get his bearings. McAllister loved the edges of the day, those times when the routines of daily life felt quiet and sparse. He walked through the city streets, away from the encampment. In the distance, sliced between some buildings, he could see thin shards of ocean blue.

Crossing several blocks, he observed balding old Jewish men shuffling along, scrawny little apartment dogs leashed to their hands. These men were locals, yet keeping to their daily rounds, despite the unwanted mystery of the day before them. Normally, August would be a pensive time of year, the winter tumult of vacationing tourists gone for the summer months. The locals would be left alone with their coffee and bagels, living out their remaining days. These men were dressed in pale pants of relaxed print, with colored golf shirts open at the collar. They puttered along, against a backdrop of square stucco buildings painted in white and pastel shades, under an awakening Atlantic sky. They purposely chose to ignore him, adorned in his dusty tee shirt and denim shorts, his heavy boots, his long hair swept back with blue bandana. Still, he could feel their disdain. They were branding him a troublemaker that they preferred would go away.

The locals had a reason to be concerned, as well as McAllister himself. He was wary at every crossing street corner. Newspapers lay on doormats in the growing angled light, their headlines announcing the forces that would further engage the city in the hours to come. As he neared the ocean, the buildings to the north grew tall and narrow. Hotels were pressed together side by side, almost every surface washed in stucco white to reflect the midday heat. On most days, it might be a beautiful summer morning of palm trees and freedom from worry, a city safe and proper in its comfortable security. There was no doubt about it. Miami Beach, Florida was a strange and ironic locale for the heightened divisions ahead.

McAllister found his way to the beachfront. He removed his boots, pushing his feet through the soft white sand to the ocean's edge. Breathing in the salted air, he looked out upon the disappearing mist at the edge of the Atlantic horizon. Dark blue waves rolled and broke courteously before his him, the soft white foam enveloping his ankles. The water simmered over the brown wet sand, then withdrew. How many times had he stood here before, enjoying the peace and solitude only the ocean could bestow? He thought of the many times he had fished with his father amongst the patterned repeat of the Atlantic's swell, the sound of their lines singing off the reel, plunking behind the breakers into the surf. Perhaps a sea trout or flounder would jerk their hooks, before flopping onto the flattened sand as they cranked them home. It would always be a pleasant memory, easy to receive.

But of course the woman found her way into his thoughts, like he knew she would. He could see Mad's wet blissful smile as she stumbled out of the water towards him, the languid torso of her hips exciting him as she approached. She appeared happy and carefree, encased in the moment as he welcomed her into his arms. But today, this was a memory of another time. A sense of impending loss controlled him. McAllister turned away, steeling himself against the premonition, wishing there was something he could do to make the past return again. How does one overcome this approaching emptiness inside?

He began his return to Flamingo Park, the city beginning to arise. There were more cars and people on the streets. It was hard to feel much sympathy for this city or its inhabitants, including the greater mass of a country that allowed their government to continue this insanity called Vietnam. It was a nation that had bargained away its individual culpability or its claims of defensive innocence. At this very moment the United States of America was raining clusters of bombs and destruction on terrified women and children, on aging human beings no different than these men nearby. Men, who by their silent affirmation, had granted a collective credence to leaders like Richard Nixon, devoid of conscious shame or personal regrets. McAllister refused to be sorry for these people's inconvenience. A basic truth remained. There would be nothing in Miami Beach falling from overhead today. There would be no fiery reign of terror that would obliterate their homes or community, shattering their lives in burning horror or death. They could damn well suck it up for a day or two, before returning to their safe and protected physical lives.

On the afternoon march to the Miami Beach Convention Center, McAllister, Mookie, and Bruiser followed the contingent of Vietnam Veterans Against the War. These were young men of similar age, dressed in camouflage and field shirts, patched jeans, heavy boots and berets. Some wore the VVAW tee shirt, an upside down rifle with helmet, a symbol of soldiers killed in action. The insignia was dyed in the national Vietnam colors of yellow and red. Many of the men wore sunglasses with dog tags hung around their shirtless necks. They were rugged and angry, fearless in their intentions. Unafraid, they hoisted an American flag upside down, exhibiting a frank response to the deceptions they had endured. Other signs were held aloft, 'Stop the Mad Bomber', 'Bring the War Home', or 'I Killed for Tricky Dick'. They shouted and cried, "One, two, three, four, we don't want your fucking war", or "Ho Ho Ho Chi Minh, the NLF is going to win". They referred to themselves as 'The Last Patrol'. These young Americans were the survivors of a present day holocaust. They were as tough as they could come.

Somewhere amongst them would be Jimmy Knox. McAllister wondered how it must have felt for Jimmy, to be back with his brothers in a new and different cause. During their encampment in Washington D.C. the year before, the VVAW had spiked the anti-war movement with a burst of energy and tremendous validity. They had somehow overcome their own defeat of coming home to an indifferent America. Disabled in mind and body, they had taken their message to the streets. It was something to see. Even more, it was something to respect.

The opposing forces of authority had surrounded the Convention Center with a barricade of empty buses and a heavily armed presence. The protest became a madhouse afternoon of unstructured speeches and broken cadres of protest, separate one from the other. There were some incidents of vandalism, amid pockets of pro-war response. Richard Nixon would be re-nominated for President that evening, in a perfectly planned love fest of Republican hegemony. An effort was being made to spoil their fun. The protestors would try to block access to the Convention Center wherever possible. McAllister and his friends pushed and shoved with the crowd, trying to stay together, making their voices heard.

Seemingly out of nowhere, a band of Cuban men pushed dramatically through the street. Surprised, McAllister got caught watching the contingent passing by, trying to figure out who they were. Suddenly, the men attacked the crowd. Before McAllister could react, a man from the group lunged at him, swinging his fists. A staggering blow caught McAllister's forehead. He grabbed the man's right arm, holding on as they fell to the pavement. As the man pounded him with his free arm, trying to pull away, Bruiser was on top of the man, pounding on his midsection. Then someone else was on top of Bruiser and the melee was on. Other protestors defended themselves, shouting and fighting back. Just as quickly as the attack ensued, it was over, the Cuban men retreating up the street. The nearby police moved nary a muscle to intervene.

McAllister got up slowly, the left side of his forehead bloodied by the initial blow, the skin on his elbow ripped open from hitting the pavement. A medical team descended on the injured, helping to clean the wounds. Although the head strike had been a glancing blow, it was deep enough to require stitches. There must have been a ring or perhaps brass knuckles on the attacker's hand. McAllister sat on the curb, holding a towel compress to his head. He had been dazed by the impact, but otherwise okay. Bruiser was fine, just shook up from the incident and mad as hell. "Provocateurs" they heard someone say in the crowd, and it only made sense by the way it went down.

In the evening, back at Flamingo Park, McAllister received further treatment. The wounds were further cleaned and bandaged, the stitches sewn. He felt lucky that was the worst of it for him. Others had suffered far worse over the years. Mostly, he kicked his own ass for getting caught off guard. Always before, he had managed to stay just out of reach. There would never be any glory in becoming an innocent victim. It was a form of recognition that would never make sense to him.

Thursday would be the finale. Richard Nixon would get his coronation, amidst the lily-white chants and colored balloons of 'Four More Years'. The protestors would once again answer by blocking the Convention Center so no one could get inside. Bandaged and ready, McAllister, Bruiser, and Mookie found themselves near the head of the march, just behind David Dellinger and Renee Davis of the Chicago Eight. Sometime before six o'clock on a humid Florida afternoon, the final push headed north up through the hotel district. Protestors were lined up by the thousands, following behind. There was only one question before them, where it all might end?

The answer came soon enough. Blocks away from the Convention Center, the militarized opposition appeared loaded and ready. Hundreds of uniformed police in riot gear loomed ahead, halting the march. There came one perfunctory announcement to disperse, and then the tear gas canisters started to fly. The main street of the Miami Beach hotel district was very narrow, with parked cars lining both sides of the street. Pressed together, the crowd was forced to retreat from the barrage. Attempting to run back from the assault, it was difficult to disperse. A tear gas canister flew over McAllister's shoulder, landing and skidding on the pavement, its white smokey gas spewing directly in front of his escape. There was nowhere to go but through the gas, this time without a washcloth to assist. The putrid cloud doused him with its poison.

McAllister stumbled against the parked cars in the street, his vision impaired by stinging watery eyes. A weakening nausea overcame him, further slowing his retreat. Steadying himself against the trunk of a car, he was able to see a grassy lawn area to his right. Crawling up a sloping bank of ground, he collapsed on the grass. His eyes burned fiercely, the nausea overcoming. He lay prostrate on the hotel lawn, trying to recover. Shortly, a woman in a white smock kneeled over him, flooding his eyes with water, soothing his face with a cloth and words of support. Quickly, she was gone. He continued to lay prone on the lawn of the hotel, waiting for the nausea to pass.

Looking up to the sky, he could hear the sounds in the street beyond, the bustle of shouts and voices surrounding him. Sirens wailed in the distance. Then strangely, he also began to hear a different aural sonance rising amongst the hubbub. It sounded like a chant, a peculiar background hum lifting into the evening air. He realized the chant was the sound of 'Om', the sacred mantra of the eastern religions. Feeling better, he slowly raised to his feet, his vision clearing. Beside him, others protestors remained on the ground, immobilized from the gas. He headed across the lawn, following the chant. Bruiser and Mookie were nowhere in sight. Reaching the edge of the elevated ground, he looked down upon the street below.

A hundred or more protestors sat on the pavement, their legs crossed, with voices chanting in unison. Behind them, a U-Haul truck was backed up to their rear. Uniformed police were dragging the limp contingent one by one into the boxed vehicle, pushing them rudely inside. Sitting at the front of the group, a bearded man was dressed in a white robe, a long beard and straggly hair hanging off his balding head. He was unmistakable, it was Allen Ginsberg. Amid the shouts of the demonstrators along each side of the street, as well as the curious attentions of frightened tourists and locals, the Miami Beach police roughly yanked and pressed the deadweight bodies into the truck. Throughout this slow and deliberate task of arrest, the chants mockingly continued in the twilight ocean sky.

McAllister watched the proceedings. The early evening theatre had begun to be backlit by the buzzing sound of street lamps beginning to flicker alight. The white hotels became framed against the twilight sky and distant ocean horizon. Beside him, an old Jewish man and his wife stood transfixed by the events before them. The man was smartly dressed, the woman heavily laden in jewelry and mascara. The moment seemed imbued with a certain sense of unreality, as if viewing a surrealistic painting, full of color and images of incongruity. The man turned to his wife and spoke with a measure of resignation in his voice, "I think I have seen everything, now," he said. McAllister had to laugh at the comment, but also agree. Miami Beach, Nixon, the cops, Allen Ginsburg, veterans of both war and holocaust, all here together, as if posing for a snapshot of America no one else in the world could ever comprehend.

McAllister attempted to find his way toward the Convention Center. With Bruiser and Mookie nowhere to be found, he joined other rogue groups in the streets trying to head north. But the Florida National Guard was out in force, chasing them down, arresting anyone they could get their hands on. McAllister had to respect the civil disobedience tactics of groups like Ginsberg's, those that would spend a night in jail for a justifiable cause. In the end, such tactics might be the most admirable method of gaining neutral support, a Gandhian non-violent expression of human principle against the controlling powers of the state. Such strategic political behavior was far better than smashing storefront windows, or rolling over the car of some unsuspecting citizen. Those were the kind of tactics that would never get the silent ones running to your cause.

The outright violence of bombing or gun play was out of McAllister's league. He didn't have the balls or the belief for that level of commitment. But he could understand that every method of response is capable of devising its own rational construct. Much like the American government, any one person or group can build a case to justify their deeds, their particular means to an end. But unlike the government, such violent responses can eventually put the perpetrators within their powerful grasp, at the mercy of their superior control, one's individual freedom captive to their ultimate disposal. Sean McAllister preferred playing keep away in the streets, disrupting the daily routines of their authority, before running for the hills. And yet, amidst the insane craziness of the times, what else could one say, but to each their own.

Bruiser and Mookie were back at Flamingo Park upon his return.

Things didn't settle down till very late. They managed to get a few hours of sleep before packing up in the morning. Bruise and Mook headed out first. McAllister would see them at home. Meanwhile, he would wait for Jimmy Knox to return. He sat and watched as the bedraggled army of protestors made preparations to leave. He tried to imagine what a neutral observer might ask. What difference had you made here, how many minds had you changed? The answer was simple. It really didn't matter. The bottom line was crystal clear. You had to do something, whatever it might be.

While McAllister waited, he found a copy of the Miami Herald newspaper. Nixon got all the headlines, no surprise there. Business as usual would continue. George McGovern, the Democratic nominee, was a damn good man. He believed in halting the war. As a US Senator, McGovern had done his best to stop the violence in the past several years. But McGovern was already on the ropes with the Eagleton vice-presidential fiasco. In addition, the old-school Democrats were pissed at their loss of power in the party. People like Hubert Humphrey, Richard Daley, and AFL-CIO union boss, George Meany, were hanging McGovern out to dry. McAllister had a vain hope that the Watergate stories he'd been reading in the *Washington Post*, might halt the Nixon victory train sometime before election day. Perhaps the events would cause America to reconsider. But McAllister would have no expectations, he knew the chances were slim.

There were sidebar stories of the protest in the paper. It would be the usual there as well. The focus was always on the numbers, the arrests, and violent acts of a few. Never would there be a discussion of the moral outrage that was at the source of this frustration and dissent. Still, there was one little sidebar that caught his attention. It was a report that when Allen Ginsberg had been brought before the judge at booking, he had been asked to give his home address. His answer had been typical Ginsberg, both erudite and wry with humor. "The Universe", Ginsberg had answered. Despite the certainty of such an overwhelming ineffectiveness, Ginsberg's response had to make one smile.

McAllister's elbow scrape had lost its bandage, the cut painfully tightening as it began to heal. His head wound was clearly visible on his forehead. He would have to get the stitches removed once he got home. Jimmy Knox approached, hauling his pack. The pair began the

long trudge to leave Miami Beach. But Jimmy was more spirited, as if
the adventure of the last two days had invigorated him. Perhaps Miami
would give him a sense of belonging to something for a time, a means
for finding his way back home. As for McAllister, a darker personal
mystery would be waiting upon his arrival, a possible future loss he
would be required to confront. It would undoubtedly be an unwilling
task, but a situation from which he had no choice. He would have to
see it through.

The long trip home would cover almost twelve hundred miles.
The entrance to the Florida Turnpike was one big mess. Dozens of
hitchhikers were strung along the road in front of the toll booths.
The August sun was bearing down with heat. It could be hours before
catching a ride. But fortune, sometimes good, sometimes bad, is never
far away. A beaten tractor-trailer rig pulled slowly to the side of the
road. The driver, a husky black man, appeared at the rear of the truck.
Unlatching the doors, it revealed a trailer bed without a roof, the four
metal sides open to the sky. The driver said something to the hitchhikers
nearby. Then quickly there was a beckoning wave, and with that a wild
scramble ensued.

Along with a host of others, McAllister and Jimmy Knox grabbed
their gear and climbed up into the rig, maybe thirty or more by the time
the driver shut the doors. Nobody was sure where they were going, but
going they were. The tractor-trailer geared slowly onto the highway.
It paid the fare at the toll booth before rolling onto the interstate.
Somebody said Orlando. It was surely not their intended direction, but
at least they were on the road.

The weird ride was much like being in a general lockup, although
short of arrest. The wind of the highway swirled overhead. Hitchhikers
shouted at each other to make conversation, while bouncing off balance
with each bump in the road. Sitting was impossible. The midday Florida
sun beat down heavy on the journey. McAllister watched as one rider
pulled his head over the side of the truck, waving to a speeding car
below. Shortly thereafter, a can of beer flew over the side of the truck,
then several more, having been tossed up by a passing car. Sixty-mile-
an-hour Budweisers had become suspended in the air, before being

quickly cracked open and shared amongst the group. Several hours later the ride reached Orlando. McAllister and Jimmy Knox worked there way back to I-95, crossing into Georgia by the end of the day.

On Saturday, the Deep South journey was god awful slow. Sections of Interstate 95 remained incomplete. Georgia was a land of red clay, dotted with speed trap towns and brutal heat. It was not good to be a longhair, despite being white. But the pair made it through without incident. In South Carolina, a young overweight girl picked them up in a large sedan. She was sweet and sadly alone on a Saturday night. As sometimes happens in hitchhiking, she took the travelers miles and miles out of her way. With midnight's passing, they reached the North Carolina state line. There, once again the interstate turned into secondary highway. Having met the limits of her generosity, the young woman said her farewell. Circling her car around, she headed back home. She was a solitary angel of feminine beauty, more than deserving of her own dreams to share.

When dropped off so late in the middle of nowhere, McAllister and Jimmy Knox went through the usual roadside discussion. Whether to give it up and find a place to lay down, or to wait awhile longer, to perhaps get lucky and catch one more ride. The clear night sky was black and moonless, loaded with stars. Although there was no overhead lighting above, the exit onto the secondary road was a good spot to be, as traffic had to slow to pick up the narrow highway ahead.

Before they could decide, an old sedan rumbled through the curve. Slowing further, the vehicle pulled halfway off the road. The car's engine idled softly in the dark, its headlights peering into a thin black mist, the brake lights glowing red behind. No one got out of the car to beckon them forward. McAllister and Jimmy slowly approached. A man sat in the shotgun seat of the car, his window open. He spoke without looking at them. "Get in the back if you want," he said in a heavy southern drawl. The car was a four-door, so McAllister opened the door on the nearest side and Jimmy went to the other. They pushed their way into the car, cradling their packs on top of themselves. The men in the front seat remained silent as the car began to move, picking up speed.

As was the custom, McAllister thanked the men for the ride. But the men did not immediately respond, the car driving forward in silence. Finally, the man in the shotgun seat posed a question. "Where you boys coming from," he asked? The tone of his cracker voice was flat, hard with an edge. It was indeed a question, but not spoken with the curiosity that cared to have an answer. "Florida," McAllister answered, although he never said Miami. The man in the shotgun side adjusted his position. He wore a jean jacket, its sleeves cut off at the shoulders. He raised a powerful tattooed arm, resting it on the top of the seat. "A lot of people got fucked up down there," the man said.

McAllister didn't answer. Jimmy Knox was stone-cold silent. The car began to descend a grade on the highway, its headlights illuminating a dark forest of thick trees hugging the road. It appeared as if the car was entering a long tunnel far ahead. Reaching the trees at the bottom of the hill, the car began to noticeably slow. McAllister's adrenaline surged. He slowly reached for the door handle, holding it firmly in his grip.

The car began to pull over to the shoulder, nearing to a stop. McAllister kicked open the door with the side of his foot. Leading with his pack, he burst out into the night. Moving quickly away from the car, he turned back to see if Jimmy Knox was doing the same. Jimmy had jumped out too, but as he rounded the back of the car, McAllister heard the force of a military command.

"STAY TOGETHER!" McAllister halted as Jimmy Knox caught up to him. Jimmy grabbed McAllister's arm and pointed him toward the woods. They rushed into the darkness, crashing through brush towards the tree line, trying to see. Once inside, Jimmy pushed him down, then sticking his face close to McAllister, he raised a single finger to his lips. McAllister held still, the beating of his heart racing against his chest.

The car remained by the side of the road, the engine continuing to idle, the headlights peering down the highway. They watched as the car backed up slowly, turning so the headlights poured into the forest. McAllister lay pressed against the ground, watching. The car moved again and again, the headlights swinging into the trees. But each time it missed their location. It finally backed up slowly down the road, coming to a stop. The engine shut down, the headlights disappearing. The night was totally black, silent but for the creaks of the car engine cooling down, amidst the piercing calls of cicadas, sounding like an army in the forest night. McAllister tried to listen for any human sound, but the beating of his heart was like a freight train in his ears. Had he heard a car door slam? He didn't know for sure.

Time went by forever. McAllister searched for a flashlight in the woods, or any sound of movement in the brush. Infrequently, other cars went speeding by. Had the car driven on, they couldn't tell. McAllister grew weak with exhaustion, his eyes wanting to close. But he forced himself to stay awake. Jimmy Knox never said a word. Several hours passed. At very first light, McAllister could see Jimmy Knox lying on the ground nearby. Jimmy lay on his back, his knees up, his eyes closed. Sean McAllister knew then something he might never forget. A man could be capable of resting without ever falling asleep. McAllister knew where it came from. It was a learned survival skill that Jimmy Knox had by necessity acquired, an animal response that Sean McAllister would never share. Thank god for Jimmy Knox, for the man he had become.

McAllister waited until Jimmy Knox opened his eyes. They were now able to see their way. They continued to hike through the woods, away from the scene. Reaching a meadow, they waited as the highway traffic grew in regularity before returning to the roadside. The old sedan was nowhere in sight. The sun was beginning to rise toward another blue summer morning. It would be a day called Sunday, a damn good day to praise the Lord.

CHAPTER THIRTEEN

TRAIN LEAVES HERE THIS MORNING
Pennsylvania / Delaware / 1972-1973

THE ROUTE FROM LANCASTER, PENNSYLVANIA south to the Strickersville' farmhouse was usually a pleasant drive, meandering through sixty miles of back roads and open rolling hills of Amish farmlands. The course was marked periodically by tiny village hamlets, whose historical geographical presence had been created by the mere fact of two roads coming together. Still, it was a long working commute. Having returned from his Miami adventure, Sean McAllister continued his labor for a local painting contractor who had gotten the bid on the new apartment complex. But the project was coming to an end, and further work remained in doubt. The lengthy travel days to Lancaster would soon be over. With the eastern summer retreating, the early September days were fading with light, giving portent of an Indian summer to come. Although this time of year was often a beautiful season, it would also be one on the brink of change.

McAllister was not looking forward to the evening ahead. Upon reaching the farmhouse, he showered, put on a clean tee shirt and jeans, before combing out his long rustled hair. He paused in front of the mirror. A shadowed resignation looked back at him, as it had for several weeks. He tried to imagine feeling good about his life, but it would not come. Mad would be at the rooming house, waiting. They would finally talk it out. Perhaps things would be okay, but he couldn't help expecting the worst. Either way, there was no predicting the outcome.

He drove into town. The campus streets remained quiet. It was the calm before the storm of a new academic year, now only days away. Tonight, this small college community appeared strangely alien to him. It was almost as if he had suddenly grown old in some way, its purposeful academic world no longer part of his life. He pulled the truck up to the curb in front of the house. For a moment he sat in the cab, struck by the nervous energy he felt inside. How ironic this feeling, almost as if calling on a girl for the very first time. Although the evening's particular circumstances would be different in kind, he knew what the feeling meant. It was the fear of an ultimate rejection that pursued him, a fear that any young man would hope to avoid. He forced it out of his mind, there was no turning back. It was time to face the music, whatever it might be.

The front door opened. There she stood, the one person in his life he had relied upon for so long a time. She embraced him, clutching for a long moment before kissing him on the cheek. Letting go, she stepped back. Noticing the discolored scar on his forehead, she asked what happened. He mumbled something to dispel the question, to avoid a long answer. In the past, he might have gone into great detail about the circumstances, explaining all the events of its consequence, like so many things they had often shared before. But tonight, the story seemed trivial and beside the point. No one else was home. They went into the living room, sitting down on the couch together. Their knees touched, but felt so far apart.

What followed was like living through a bad dream, of becoming a character in a theatrical script you did not wish to play. Hearing words that traveled through the air, but wishing not to listen as they spilled towards the heart. We had grown apart, the words said. Or perhaps she had grown apart was closer to the truth. It had seemed to her like he had gone to other places. He had been caught up in his draft concerns, or his constant talk of travel and new places to live. He seemed to be making plans that did not concern her, pursuing his own interests, only wanting to be with her in the times between. She had begun to feel abandoned, not part of his life. This wasn't a bad thing she said, just the way it had become. For her, it was best to be apart for awhile, to let things take their course. They should continue as friends, to see where it would lead. She loved him very much. These were the words that hung in the late summer air.

That dreaded word, 'friends'. He felt the plunging of the knife hit its target, the final fateful stab. He tried to recover. He'd had a lot of work to do, he began, to pay for everything from school to rent, for all the things to live. Yes, he had been distracted by the draft worries, but they were over now. And yes, he did want to travel out west, but never alone. He had always wanted her to be by his side, an adventure they could share together. Maybe he had been distant from time to time, not willing to share the things that she liked to engage. But that could change. He could try to be with her more often, finding a way to make things better. He forced everything out on the table, including the kitchen sink. He tried anything not to lose. But he could feel himself sinking, with an internal bleeding that could not be stopped.

She cried. Like a man, he held her close, but he was dead inside. Finally, as she wiped away her tears, he became selfish and had to know. The suspicion had hung for weeks, battling to have an answer. Out of respect for her, and the inherent honesty he wished for himself, he had fought back the temptation. But now, the self-indulgence of the moment took hold of him. He had begun to weaken against the pain. Was there somebody else? The ensuing seconds of silence were deafening. She crashed into her lap, sobbing. The word 'yes' never needed to be said.

McAllister didn't ask. He was sure he already knew. The puzzle pieces fit. He stood up in the room, hard as a rock. "I've got to go."

Mad looked up from her tears. "Please, Sean, please stay. How can I make you understand?" He looked down upon her misery, then quickly away. He walked to the door, opened it, before turning back toward the room.

"I understand," he said firmly. Stepping outside, he closed the door behind him. It was the boldest falsehood of his twenty-two years of life.

McAllister dialed the number. The phone rang several times before picking up. A familiar voice came across the line. "Hello."

"Uncle Franny, hey, it's Mickey."

"Well, hello young man. How the hell are you?"

"All right, I guess. You got a minute?"

"Sure, son. Everything okay?"

"Oh, yeah, everything's fine. Uncle Franny, I was wondering if it was still possible to maybe apply for some work on the ships. I'm finished with school now, and this painting job I've had is coming to an end. I need to look around, and I'm not sure what's next. I figured I'd call you, maybe see if there were any openings down there, like you had mentioned before."

"Well, Mickey, I'm not sure. But I'll see what I can do. When can you get down to the refinery? You'll need to fill out an application. You'll also need to get a Z-card up in Philly before anything can happen. And you can't get the card these days unless we say that we are going to hire you. So you would need to do those things first. Still, son, there's no guarantee of work right away. But at least you'd be on the list."

"I could come anytime you say."

"Tomorrow?"

"Yes, sir," McAllister answered.

"All right, come down tomorrow at noon. You can fill out the application. We'll type the letter and you can take it to Philly as soon as you can. But there is one other thing, Mickey. Is your hair still as long as Jesus Christ?"

McAllister bit down on his lip, but he had expected the question to come. "Don't worry about that, Uncle Franny. I'll see you tomorrow at noon."

On the final day of December, 1972, Sean McAllister stood on the bow of a six hundred foot oil tanker. The ship was fixed at anchor in New York harbor, surrounded by the incandescent glow of a midnight skyline. Firework displays exploded in myriads of bright color before disappearing from sight. The calendar was shedding its page, a new year was ready to begin. Throughout the world friends would raise a toast, strangers would cheer together, and lovers would kiss sweetly with champagne breath. Beyond him, out of reach, millions of human souls would share the intimacies of new beginnings. Somewhere back home, Mad would be one of them, held in the arms of another. Three years before, she had planted her lips upon his, giving him a reason for hope, and the imaginations that one day might transpire. Now, tonight, time had brought him here, to this harsh and desperate place. He felt like the loneliest man in the world, left adrift with only a single resolution. That somehow, some way, his life might go on.

'Future orientation'. Sometimes words or phrases can pop into one's head, not knowing where the hell they came from. Much like the lyrics and melody of a song recently heard, they keep playing over and over in the brain. You might not even like that particular song, but somehow you keep humming it, driving yourself nuts. Finally, it slips away, replaced by other thoughts until the next time around.

Sean McAllister knew something about the phrase. It had to do with time, and how human cultures perceive it. The concept implied having a prospective view of life, of anticipating what tomorrow might bring. Did you see a new future in front of you? And if so, were you willing to perform the necessary tasks of the present time in order to realize that future? Or were you only concerned with an immediate orientation, of living purely in the moment, never paying attention to what tomorrow might bring? This was something of a fatalistic view of life, that events will simply be as they will be. 'Que sera, sera'.

McAllister knew one thing. It was damn hard to have a future orientation when most of your days were stuck living in the past. Hell, you could forget any present tense, that was more akin to sleepwalking. The present tense these days was nothing more than a 'going- through-the-motions' experience. Wake, dress, eat, work, undress, sleep. Then do it again and again. The future was missing in action, and the past was nothing more than a stone-cold monkey on your back that just wouldn't go away. As for the present, well, it was a lot like the merchant marine.

So you get up in the morning, put on your work clothing, eat eggs, pancakes, and sausage. This is followed by four hours of ordinary maintenance, scraping and painting the vessel, checking rope, fixing whatever needs to be fixed. Eat a hamburger for lunch. Go to your bunk and take a long nap. Have meatloaf for dinner. From eight p.m. until midnight, you perform the four hours of watch. The last two hours are spent on the bow of the ship, battling the dark wind and sea, ringing in anything that might lie ahead. Finally, you return to your bunk for more sleep. Wake up tomorrow and repeat the redundant mantra. They call you an 'ordinary seaman'. No doubt they had adequately nailed that particular job description.

On the next trip, maybe there's a transfer to the steward's department. But it's the same routine, just different tasks. Wash dishes, serve food to the officers, clean their private quarters and make their beds in the morning. Otherwise, report to the wheelhouse for various instructions. One has dutifully become a highly-trained college-educated gofer, day after boring day. One thing for sure, having a 'future orientation' wasn't a necessity, stretching only as far as the next regular paycheck.

'Que sera, sera'. You're a twenty-two year old man, healthy and strong, but wasting your free time sipping whiskey with old retired navy guys. Your social life is spent with merchant marine lifers, men who are perfectly happy living each day in an insulated world surrounded by water. In between, you slip into the fictional creations of dime-store western novels, until you've read every one in the ship's library. Once you realize what you're in for, you eventually manage to procure some literature. You travel the streets of New York and Paris with Henry Miller. You go on a road trip with Kerouac and Dean Moriarty. You open the door of perceptions with Aldous Huxley, or slip into the intimate sexual dreams of Anais Nin.

Eventually, you take on the blessed spiritual advice of Baba Ram Dass, to be here now. But Richard Alpert definitely hasn't been on an American flag tanker for most of nine months, hauling thousands of barrels of highly explosive gas and jet fuel. A job where the only land you might discover, is confined to a smoking industrial province of petroleum refineries and tank farms, always discreetly located out in the middle-of-nowhere. Be here now? As if there was a choice. To hell with that prescription. All in all, it certainly gives a man a darn good reason to develop a 'future orientation'.

'Killing time'. Hadn't he just finished that performance, by staying in school, trying to avoid the draft. Guess not. His love for Mad, and his reliance on her, had distracted any serious life intentions. Yet, he couldn't have been more content with that reality. But looking back now, maybe he had started to coast on certain things. Maybe he had taken her for granted as he sought to create a future for himself. Still, it had always been a future of which she would be a part. But he had taken his eye off the ball, and that is never a good thing. Then the roof caved in on his heart, splintering all his pre-conceived notions of where his life might go. Once again, expectations are just that, expectations. When they don't work out, it's best to be prepared for the consequences.

In late May of 1973, after nine long months, he was making his last trip at sea. Killing time, part two, would be over. He would somehow go on with his life. His college loan was paid in full. He had money in the bank. He had left the Strickersville' farm shortly after the deluge, writing off Willie Chambers and all he had stolen from his soul. He had returned to live with his parents until the seaman call had come. Bruiser had gone back and finished school. Now he was back in Wilmington, working in his father's liquor distributing business. Johnny Howard had remained in the off-campus apartment with his girl, managing to work almost full time at the docks. During McAllister's absence, Dutch Rollins and his crazy partner Eddie had gotten popped in a big bad way. They had been arrested for trafficking in marijuana and cocaine. The news had made all the papers. More than anything, he sadly had not seen nor spoken with Mad since the evening of their fall.

The time and distance had not fully erased his loss. He still could not think of her without those empty feelings inside. But somehow, the excruciating love sickness had finally passed. Gone were those mornings when it seemed impossible to get out of bed, or those moments before sleep when nothing seemed to matter. Slowly, it had become easier now. He had begun to laugh again. But he knew how gruesome it would be to see her, especially with someone else. He wondered if there would there ever be a time when he could think of Mad without this pain, when the sound of her name might not disrupt him in such a difficult way. Might there be a future time when he could listen to a beautiful Gram Parson's ballad, and not have the beauty of the lyrics drain the blood right out of his heart? Nonetheless, he was getting better, and ever more positive about his life moving on.

In early June, he walked off the ship's gangway in Delaware City. He purchased an old Dodge panel truck with a reliable slant six engine. Mookie James, his good friend from both the rooming house and the Strickersville farm, had moved to Boulder, Colorado. Boulder would be a good place to start. And Meatball, the farm dog in Strickersville, had traveled with Mookie. It was funny how the thought of a dog could bring pleasure to one's wandering mind.

A few days before his leaving, the first summer hot spell struck the east coast. McAllister, Bruiser, and Johnny Howard had a little going away party. They drank alcohol before taking some mescaline late, putting an all-nighter in progress. In the early hours of a warm June morning, they drove the back roads of Brandywine Valley, hiking to the water tank for one last swim.

They sat without clothes on the roof of the tank. McAllister could see the gentle hallucinations of animals moving in the nearby trees. He felt the rising sun grow warmer on his skin. Suddenly, over the rim of the meadow came two people on horseback, an older man and a beautiful young girl. They were dressed in equestrian clothing. The older man, a black riding hat on his head, a small buggy whip in hand, held the girl back before approaching. There was nothing to do but sit and watch him come, naked as jay birds in the summer morning light. The man told them they were trespassing. Once he returned to the girl, they were to dress themselves immediately, to leave and to never come back. For Sean McAllister, this little piece of wonder had finally been discovered. The three men dressed and did as told.

Taking one last look from the rim of the water tank, it occurred to McAllister that a fitting ending might be at hand. He had taken Mad to this place on their first day together. Now it was over, a paradise lost. Two days later, he was out on the road. Although she followed in his heart, he tried not to look behind.

CHAPTER FOURTEEN

BITTER CREEK
Boulder, Colorado / 1973-1974

"Santa Barbara?," McAllister questioned. "What? You're moving to Santa Barbara?" Mookie James stood over the kitchen drain board, pouring two cups of coffee out of the pot. The September morning sun shone through the window of Mookie's Boulder apartment. "I thought you were working on getting your residency here, to go back to school."

"I've changed my mind," Mookie answered.

The news surprised McAllister. He had just arrived in Boulder earlier in the summer. He had just settled in, gotten a job and a place to live. Mookie James was leaving? Heading for California? "You've changed your mind?" he questioned with emphasis. What the hell's up, man?"

"Annie wants to go to school there, instead of here. And she wants me to come along. I started giving it some thought, then decided what the hell, why not." He handed McAllister a cup of coffee. The men sat down at the kitchen table.

"I'm kind of blown away," McAllister whined. He took a sip off his coffee. "I guess I thought you would be here for awhile." Once again, he could sense that vacant feeling of being left behind. "Are you sure? I mean, that it's the right move and all? When would you be leaving?"

"Pretty quick," Mookie answered. "Annie's leaving next week. She's been accepted for the winter quarter. She's going to find an apartment there. I'll give my notice at work, then get a U-Haul and drive our stuff back. Things are going pretty good for us, Sean. Staying here in Boulder just doesn't seem important anymore. Sure,the town's okay, but it's not like I want to live here the rest of my life. I'd rather be with Annie for now, maybe go back to school there at some point. Hey, do you know anybody that might want to buy my car?"

McAllister reluctantly shook his head, genuinely hurt by the news. "Guess I'm sort of spooked, Mook. I didn't realize you and Annie had gotten so tight? Geez, it's going to be kind of lonely around here without you. Damn!"

"Sorry, Sean. I'll miss you being around, too. But things will be okay. You've got friends here, now. And Faye, she's always been a pretty nice chick. How's that going for you?"

McAllister remained distracted. "Listen, Mook, I'm just trying to get my head around this thing, your leaving and all. I suppose it's got me thinking about being here, too." He tried to answer the question. "Yeah, Faye. She's pretty nice, a good person. But it's not like I'm serious about anything. After the whole darn thing with Mad, it's not like I'm wanting to get involved." McAllister continued shaking his head. "Did I tell you she doesn't even know how to swim. I wanted to go up to that swimming hole on Boulder Creek last Saturday, and she told me she'd never learned."

"A lot of people can't swim around these parts," Mookie answered. Faye came here from Kansas, right? A lot of these folks never grew up around water, so they never had to learn. Pretty weird, huh. But I guess it's understandable when you think about it."

"Yeah, weird is right," McAllister mused. "Man, at least you're going to be back on the ocean. I can certainly tell you one thing. I sure have missed the shore this summer."

"I'm with you there," Mookie answered. "But whenever we get settled, you can come and visit. We'll hit the beach like we used to do back home." There was a pause between them. Then the tone of Mookie's voice went serious. "Sean, by the way, I wanted to ask you a real big favor. See what you thought about it."

"What's that?" McAllister asked.

"I was wondering if you would consider taking Meatball for a period of time? You know, while Annie and I get things set up in Santa Barbara. I don't think they allow dogs at this first place we're going to rent. But once I got things together, we could get him out to California.

Would that be possible?"

"Meatball? Meatball could stay?" McAllister questioned. "I know he's sort of your dog and all, but he's like my dog too. Sure, no problem at all. I'll just tell my roommate I have to take him for awhile. The upstairs neighbors have a dog, so it must be okay. It would mean a lot to me to have Meatball around, a hell of a lot."

"I'd want to keep him here until I go, of course. But thanks a million, brother. What a relief. I wasn't sure what I was going to do, if you said no."

"Geez, Meatball is family, Mook. We got to keep him close." McAllister yelled for Meatball to crawl himself off the couch in Mookie's living room. The dog panted into the kitchen. McAllister reached out, rustling the dog's head and shoulders. Meatball would stay with him, at least for a time. McAllister didn't let on to Mookie how much it really meant.

Driving home from Mookie's apartment, McAllister couldn't help but feel sorry for himself. He couldn't blame Mookie for making the move, but the news sure had come as a big surprise. The ride out to Louisville, Colorado was ten miles east of Boulder, a town high and flat on the edge of the Great Plains. Louisville had been about the closest and least expensive place McAllister could find to live. He was sharing a two-bedroom apartment with a guy named Eric. It was a duplex apartment with another apartment upstairs. The apartment was by no means the Ritz, but at least it was a place to eat and sleep at night.

He'd recently gotten a job at a printing plant, a low-paying gig running a machine all day. McAllister would take piles of subscription letters off the presses, then machine-fold them to letter size for eventual envelope posting. It was a redundant and frustrating job. You spent most of each day fixing the damn folding machine, screwing with the rollers and crease adjustments. Plus, the damn moisture in the paper was always working against you. All these headaches for the enriching price of two and a half dollars per hour. Boulder had so many young people looking for work, McAllister was supposed to feel lucky for having a job. One thing was for sure, luck had a hell of a lot of confusing definitions.

Now, Stephen "Mookie" James, his one true friend in Boulder, was checking out to California. Since their meeting at college in Delaware, Mookie and he had easily gotten along. They had shared the same interest in politics, music and sports. But more than anything, Mookie was a good guy, a special friend. Bruiser and Johnny Howard were homeboys from his high school days. They would always be a given. But Mookie was one of those guys you meet and the friendship just fits like a glove. He and McAllister had grown really close, ever since their very first day.

Mookie's original intentions had been two-fold. One was to get out of the east for awhile. Like McAllister himself, to find something new. The other was more goal-oriented, to establish residency in Colorado, then go back to school. Mookie was a smart guy, the kind of guy with a few things in mind. He had found a job tending bar at a nice restaurant in Boulder. That's where he had met Annie, and the two of them had immediately hit it off. Still, McAllister hadn't expected the surprise he got this morning. Mookie would soon be out of Boulder, leaving McAllister behind to figure things out on his own.

Boulder, Colorado was a beautiful setting. Nestled north of Denver, it was a small city, tucked into a lovely spot on the Front Range of the Rockies. Boulder was a college town, a hustle and bustle community for young people from lots of different places. Sean McAllister had been enjoying his new surroundings. He was away from the boredom and conventions of the east coast, away from the emotional scathing of losing his girl. About the rest, he wasn't rightly sure. He wasn't much into thinking of his future, just trying to live day to day was enough of a pursuit. But today, the thought of Mookie's absence began to raise certain doubts that he preferred not to confront.

Boulder, Colorado. In passing conversation, someone once called it "a rest home for the young". When one thought about it, the characterization sort of rang true. There were young college students from everywhere. There were ski bums, rock climbers, spiritual seekers, you name it. There were people from all over the Midwest. There were refugees from both New York and California. And there were more Texans than you could shake a stick at. It was a whole new world in so many ways.

McAllister had spent most of the summer hanging out with Mookie. Whenever Mookie was tending bar, McAllister would stop by for a drink after work. From time to time they had gone to music clubs together. They had camped up in the Rockies near Estes Park, and traveled down to Denver to see the city. But without much money to spare, they mostly hung close to home. Annie worked in the restaurant portion of the hotel. That's where McAllister had met her friend, Faye. Things had been going along okay. Okay, till now.

Within days, came news of Gram Parson's tragic overdose and death at Joshua Tree in the desert of California. Mad would be heartbroken. Once again, another loss was at hand. Parson's death seemed to signal a further reminder of something he would never be able to retrieve. A week later, Mookie packed up a truck and headed west. October arrived. The Rocky Mountain autumn began to cool the high western plateau. In the foothills, the white barked aspen trees turned to a golden quivering yellow. By November, cold winds out of the north blew down across the Front Range. With the onset of darkening afternoons, white flurries of mountain snow began hurling in the air. McAllister, and his new partner in life, Meatball, hunkered down in Louisville for the mile-high bitterness ahead. There are times when a man's warmer dreams must be put on hold, a time to suck things up and endure. You got yourself a job, a television, a cold bed, and a dog to keep you company. There's a bar down the street and nowhere else to go. They have a name for times like this. It's simply called winter in America.

The February wind sliced its way across the high plain of a Sunday afternoon. A wild blue sky was giving way to streaks of twilight orange and paling white. Off to the west, the sun began its early descent behind the white-capped Rocky Mountains. Football season was over, leaving America with a solitary question. Where in the hell was kidnapped heiress Patty Hearst?

McAllister kept his eyes focused on the sidewalk, his face taut and stinging from the steady afternoon breeze. He watched for ice as he trudged the four blocks toward the main street of Louisville. The snow in the yards was knee deep. It had become crusty and hard-shined from a thin melting of its cover in the earlier midday sun. Rock-hard barriers of snow packed the street's perimeters, corroded by gritty sand and blackened by auto exhaust. The winter could grow ugly fast, the initial beauty of its pristine fall so quickly spoiled by the cold hard facts of age. The prairie wind gusted, pushing McAllister off his gait. He recovered by bending forward, his gloved hands steadying his balance, before pressing on.

When he reached the corner of Main Street, he headed down the block to the Louisville Tavern. His roommate, Eric Nordberg, had left a note on the kitchen table that he was meeting with friends, and to come on down. They were folks Eric had known while living in the mountains above Boulder, before his recent move down to Louisville. McAllister had nothing better to do, short of taking a Sunday nap. He figured he might as well find some company. It would help to kill the rest of a boring winter day.

At the turn of the century, Louisville, Colorado had been a bustling coal mining town. But the coal lacked the quality of other regions, and the community drifted into decline. It was a little hard to imagine coal mines in this barren province of flattened earth. The surrounding countryside looked like nothing more than windswept territory to the naked eye. But in those early days, Louisville was a rough community of Italian immigrants, its residents working mines that were drilled deep below the ground. Although the mines had long since shut down, Louisville had remained alive by becoming a destination point for Italian food. Most of these noted restaurants were located on Main Street, with people coming from Denver, Boulder, or smaller towns to partake of its fine cuisine.

Outside of that single attraction, Louisville was a weathered burg of small bungalow homes. It was a cheap working-class community, a place where hippies could beat the higher rents of Boulder. 'Spaghettiville' was a moniker that Eric Nordberg and other locals called the town. In other words, despite the good eats, there wasn't much to say for the place.

The same few words could be said for the Louisville Tavern. The bar was a long narrow meeting ground for ranchers and other down on their luck locals, who found solace and company inside its dark interior. Upon entering, a long wooden bar stretched down to the right. In the rear, two pool tables glowed under fluorescent lighting. The best part of the tavern was the regulation shuffleboard table that ran down its left side. McAllister enjoyed the challenge of sailing the weighted pucks down the lengthy hardwood board, coming to rest in the scoring area at its opposite end. It was sort of like pitching strikes in baseball. Shuffleboard didn't require the macho image and hard-ass persona of an eight-ball pool game, where somebody was always trying to put you out and remain king of the table. People were more relaxed and engaging when playing shuffleboard.

Coors was the official beer in the state of Colorado. And the
Louisville Tavern was a Coors establishment. Back on the east coast, it
was always a big deal to find a six-pack of Coors. The eastern beers were
frowned upon in Colorado, even the Budweiser brand was treated with
an air of disgust. So when in Rome as they say, McAllister stepped to
the bar and ordered the home state draft. At a table in the back of the
barroom, alongside the pool tables, he could see Eric Nordberg sitting
with a man and a woman. McAllister paid for his beer, walking down
to meet them.

Eric's friend, Charley Tucker, was a rough looking dude. His face
was pockmarked, his skin veiny red as if from too much drink. A
healed scar etched his cheek on the left side, his nose crooked from a
previous break. The dark oily hair under his cowboy hat was straggly
and medium length. He was not a handsome man. His broad shoulders
and large frame gave him the look of a biker minus the leather jacket.
Instead, he wore a leather vest over a blue denim shirt with pearl snaps.
The brim of the hat was circled in animal hide, beaded and hanging
over the back. A necklace of pale white bone hung from his thickened
neck. When McAllister was introduced, he felt the grip of strong meaty
hands, his fingers soiled under the nails. Charley Tucker looked older,
maybe over thirty. He carried the presence of a man who had walked a
hard and dangerous road.

Sitting beside Charley Tucker was a young woman about
McAllister's age. Sharon was her name. She wore long auburn hair
and exhibited a similarly tough demeanor. She wasn't exactly pretty,
but there was something about her that made you want to look at her,
perhaps to find the hidden beauty of a woman that lurked inside. She
was friendly enough, but carried that familiar first glance of suspicion
that some women show when meeting other men.

Sharon's apparent lack of interest reminded him of Faye, the
woman McAllister had met when visiting the bar at Mookie's old job.
Faye had never given McAllister a second look the first few times he was
in her presence. Like Annie, she had been a cocktail and food waitress at
the restaurant, attractive to his sight. But Faye had shown him nothing
more than the indifferent facade women in her trade had to wear to
make it through the night. And that was the case, until one night at
closing time. While sitting late one evening with Mookie and Annie,
Faye had stopped by to join them. All of a sudden, Faye was inquisitive

and inviting, and the next thing he knew he was sleeping in her bed. Sometimes with women, you just never knew.

Two men were playing pool nearby. Charley Tucker had a quarter on the table, waiting his turn. When he got up to play, McAllister was able to gauge more of his persona. He was about McAllister's size in height, an inch or two over six feet. But unlike McAllister's long thinner frame, Charley Tucker was solid and firm, like a well sunk fencepost. He carried himself with a sense of possible aggression, exuding a confidence that made one pay attention, wary of where things might go. He seemed to command a particular deference in his words and behavior. There was definitely an edge to the man one couldn't ignore, as if trouble might have just strolled into the room, but you couldn't exactly be sure. If McAllister hadn't just met the man, he more than likely would have kept his distance.

Charley Tucker was a Colorado hippie mountain man, or at least a dude playing the part. A marijuana leaf was sewn into the back pocket of his jeans. Attached to his belt was a sheathed knife on one side, a small suede pouch on the other. He wore ankle high work boots with high rubber heels, greased black to defy the snow. In McAllister's humble opinion, there was nothing about this man that would make you want to fuck with him, unless you were blitzed to the nines and on a suicide kick.

As Charley Tucker played his pool game, McAllister sipped his beer and listened as Eric Nordberg and Sharon engaged in conversation, catching up on their time apart. Sharon's initial shell-like persona upon McAllister's initial introduction, had given way to a youthful exuberance when talking with Eric. They reminisced about Sharon and Charley's unforgettable wedding party earlier that summer. From the telling, the reception at been held at a tavern in Rollinsville, Colorado, where Charley had walked the full length of the bar before crashing to the floor. Rollinsville was where Eric had met them, while living in a mountain cabin nearby. But employment in the high country could be as thin as the air, so Eric had retreated to Louisville to find a job and keep a place to live. He had advertised for a roommate, and that's where McAllister had come along.

Charley Tucker had secured a job on the Union Pacific railroad, working the high stretch of track through the Continental Divide. He and Sharon now lived in railroad housing at a place called East Portal, the eastern entrance to the Moffat Tunnel. The tunnel was a six-mile bore through the Rockies at an elevation of nine thousand feet. Sharon said it was like living at the top of the world. She encouraged Eric to come visit for a weekend, to party again with all their old friends. Eric agreed to make the journey soon. Then Sharon turned to McAllister for the first time, saying he was welcome as well. McAllister felt gracious to be included in the invite. It would give him a chance to see another part of this Rocky Mountain country that loomed over his world in Louisville, to encounter a new topography he had never seen before.

The couple stayed for another hour or two, everyone enjoying a few more drinks. Later, out the back door of the bar, they stood in the bitter cold, smoking a bowel of pot, compliments of the pouch that hung off Charley Tucker's waist. 'Chas', as Eric and Sharon referred to him, told McAllister that he would never live down on this flatland hardpan of Colorado plain. The high country would always be his home. 'Flatlander' was a pejorative term in Colorado. It was a slur used by the mountain people who lived above, separating themselves from the prairie mediocrity of those that lived below. McAllister had recently heard the expression, but now he understood the prejudice the word intended. In his own way, he looked forward to finding out how these mountain people lived. His curiosity had been raised.

Back at the duplex, McAllister and Eric heated up some cans of chili, gulping down their meal with slices of white bread and cheese. Sitting at the kitchen table, McAllister inquired to know more about these friends of Eric Nordberg. It's wilder up there, Eric would say. And Chas Tucker could be crazier than the rest, especially when he got to drinking hard. It was rumored, Eric explained, that Chas had done prison time back in the state of Kentucky, but for what crime nobody knew.

In the Rollinsville Tavern days, Charley Tucker was one of the few who had a good job, and he would often buy the bar a round. Such generosity secured his status if not his reputation. But Chas could be dangerous, Eric advised, if you happened to get on his bad side. It didn't happen often, but it was best not to fuck with him. By the looks of first impression, McAllister was not surprised. Eric had actually known Sharon before she hooked up with Charley. It was through Eric's friendship with her that Charley's acquaintance had sprung. Every mountain town had a guy like Chas Tucker, Eric mused. And in most cases, it was better to be on their good side, as not. Sean McAllister understood.

The Colorado winter was not in an accommodating mood. One storm after another hauled ass over the continental range. Clear sunny days would fork their way in between, fighting back. But all the weakened sun could do was create a thin patina of melting water on top of the packed snow and ice. By nightfall, the roads became a hellish episode of automobile Ice Capades, capable of steering cars and trucks into ditches with astounding technical skill. The skating judges ran out of placards numbering ten. Olympic champions were everywhere, sporting their gold medallions, while driving along with crushed fenders of twisted metal and chrome. For McAllister, getting the panel truck to work and back had become a treacherous pastime, far more dangerous than the printing job itself.

As for the rest of his life, the winter days were nothing more than a highlight reel of hot dogs and baked beans, of rent, heat and electric bills, with a scratchy black and white television screen on cold lonely nights. Toss in gas for the panel truck, or a few shots and beers at the Louisville Tavern for entertainment, and there was little money left for anything else. If Sean McAllister might have once pondered dreams of an exciting new life, a brazen Colorado winter had certainly put such foolish notions to rest. Meatball's life was decidedly worse. Imprisoned on most days in a near-freezing apartment, with nothing more than a bowel of crusty dried food and bitter cold tap water, Meatball fought to survive. To think that Meatball could have been frolicking in the warm Southern California sun, chasing sticks through the gentle waves on a Pacific Ocean beach, was definitely a bummer. Mookie James should have been brought up on numerous counts of animal cruelty, for leaving the poor dog behind.

To make matters worse, Meatball now had a rap sheet of his own. The Louisville dog catcher was good at his job. Meatball had been arrested and jailed two times on the canine felony of 'dog-at-large', then dragged into court. His court-appointed attorney was the well known barrister, Sean McAllister. Dressed in long hair and blue jeans,

Meatball's attorney looked more like the defendant than the poor dog himself. The pooch would have probably had better luck going 'pro se'. And whenever the verdict did come in, it was always the same, guilty as charged. But for Meatball, there would be no court-ordered social rehabilitation. The dog was forced to return to his old neighborhood and the bad influences that surrounded him. McAllister was sure the next time Meatball was arrested, he would opt for doing time in the joint. Three squares at the Louisville dog pound were looking better every day.

As for McAllister, his own symptoms of cabin fever were all too apparent. The previous winter, during the tanker run, he had already exhausted every book he could read. This time around, there was nothing to do but wear out the grooves of his album collection, whether it be Neil Young, Little Feat, Steely Dan, or the Grateful Dead. His personal theme song for the winter season was Commander Cody's "Down to Seeds and Stems Again". The sad winter picture was more than complete.

As for women, any thoughts of Mad were dealt with swiftly, his sentence for the crimes he had committed. There would be absolutely no presumption of innocence, no trial before his peers. Instead, he would be simply lined up, tied to a post and shot dead, execution style. McAllister had spoken with Johnny Howard sometime back. Johnny had run into Mad, and she had asked about him. One would think such news might make him feel better about things. Instead, it only scraped an old wound he was trying to heal. Any thoughts of what an answer might have been, made McAllister want to lie through his teeth. He sarcastically would have had Johnny Howard deliver a response, which read:

"Oh, he's really doing great. He's become an under-assistant west coast promo man. He spends his idle days skiing with big Texas oil men and Hollywood starlets. In the evenings, he goes to fabulous cocktail parties, or hangs backstage with rock stars. And of course, there are always the private after-hours parties, where he dances all night until the sun comes up. He's having such a full and adventurous life, he's already begun to write his memoirs. And surprisingly, Mad, you're not included. So I've got to tell you, he's doing pretty swell". The real story, ever so sadly, was a badly written Shakespearian tragedy, far too depressing to ever reach print.

After too long a time, he'd gotten in touch with Faye. The reason was primarily out of loneliness, of not having met someone else. And Louisville, Colorado wasn't exactly crawling with chicks. Nor was it the kind of town a woman would go looking for a man, unless losing at love happened to be her idea of having a good time. McAllister liked Faye. She was hardworking and sexually attractive on first encounter. But after several episodes, she had no longer inspired him. It was nothing personal, just the way he felt. Faye was a little too college-like, a practical somewhat dour Midwest girl. It was not a bad thing, just not a good fit. So out of desperation, when he did finally call, the news was curt and unavailable. The rejection had stung for a moment, but he took it in stride. Anyway, he still felt like a loser, so why not embrace such emotion. Or to characterize Richard Farina's novel, *Been Down So Long It Looks Like Up To Me*.

Then there was Angie, who lived in the duplex across the street. A man's mistakes don't usually come in single occurrences, more often in multiples when things get rolling along. Angie was a girl who seemed to live in her apartment all day and night, appearing to have no visible means of support. She wasn't bad looking upon first impression. But more often than not, Angie would sit curled up in her chair, surrounded by astrology texts, doing charts of everyone who came through her door. It was as if she lived her own life through the lives and fates of others. One particular evening, after too many shots of schnapps at the Louisville Tavern, McAllister stopped by Angie's place with devious intent. Angie welcomed his unannounced visit. But despite his alcohol glazed hunger, he immediately realized the error of his ways. Before Angie had even completed her first dissertation on the complaints of her life, McAllister found an excuse to exit stage right. When it came to Angie, Meatball would make better company. In addition, an early morning extraction would never have to be imagined.

By the middle of March, there were signs of spring in the flatlands. The thaw brought warm days in the sixties, the foothills of snow melting with haste. With little prospects for their futures, McAllister and Meatball joined Eric Nordberg for a Saturday morning trip to the high country. They would visit Charley Tucker and his elevated mountain home. Driving west, they ascended the steep torso of the Rockies, climbing almost three thousand feet above the city of Boulder in less than twenty miles. At over eight thousand feet, the sun shined bright, but the cold and snow remained. Reaching the little town of Nederland, they headed south to Rollinsville. Turning onto a rough unpaved road, they pointed due west towards East Portal. They passed through a flat open valley, the drive bumping along on packed snow, dodging sections of muddy potholes and scattered broken rock. Surrounding them, the massive peaks of the Rockies reached high into a clear blue sky.

Eric Nordberg was a young man from the great plains of South Dakota. He had attended the University of Colorado for a time, before dropping out to live in the mountains near Rollinsville. According to Eric, the mountain life was a different scene from the cultured academic city of Boulder that rested below. The old mining towns of Ward, Nederland, and Rollinsville were not necessarily a peace and loving kind of world. The harsh weather and even harsher landscape created a more serrated edge, a rough and tumble personality. Many of the residents were as extreme as the milieu they had to endure. The air was thin, the mood temperamental, not conductive to the softer soul. This lifestyle imbued a rough pride and prejudice for those who took to it. There was a meaner and more severe articulation, as if its history demanded a scarred individualistic sensibility. For some, it was a home for rebels without a cause. Sean McAllister didn't know this country, but he could feel a sense of the survivalist mentality, where a lack of warmth created a different breed of character.

Halfway down the access road, the snow pack grew deeper, the car beginning to slide and spin. Eric stopped his vehicle. Stepping outside into a steady cold wind, they put on the chains. Meatball took the opportunity to romp in the breaking snowfields, at times almost disappearing into the drifts. Their chore complete, the car powered onward the last few miles. Approaching East Portal, one could see the entrance to the Moffat Tunnel. It appeared like a large black hole piercing into a barrier sea of white. Looming above them was an omnipresent wall of snow and rock. They had reached the great Continental Divide.

Off to the right, several faded two-story bungalows rested side by side. Wood smoke raced from their chimneys, before disappearing with the wind. Large metal equipment sheds stood further off near the tunnel. Four wheel drive pick-ups, jacked high with suspensions, rested in front of the homes. Other vehicles were scattered nearby, some with snow as high as their door handles, taking the winter off. Trails of packed snow led to each house. Eric Nordberg pulled his car into an open spot, shutting down the engine. The men exited, stepping again into the stiff breeze, shielding their eyes from the bright glare of snow and sun. The blue of the sky was so utterly clear and deep. It reminded McAllister of his prior visit to Colorado several years before. Sharon's previous words rang true. It felt like a person was at the top of the world.

Sharon answered the door. But instead of a warming welcome, there appeared an unhappy woman. She weakly hugged Eric, who asked her what was up. "I'll tell you later," she answered. Sharon turned and pointed herself at the bottom of the narrow stairway that led to second floor of the house. "Chas," she yelled. "Chas Tucker. Get your lazy ass up. Eric's here." There was no question about the anger in her voice. "Sit down," she said, "I made a pot of coffee." She left the living room, passing through a curtain that led to the kitchen. McAllister looked at Eric Nordberg with a questioning expression. Eric simply raised his eyebrows and shoulders, but began taking off his coat. McAllister did the same. They took seats on the couch in the living room, beginning to wait. McAllister figured they had walked in on something, wondering where it would go.

The time was shortly after noon. Sharon returned with coffee in two tin cups, handing them out. "Chas," she yelled again.

"I heard you, damn it," a voice responded from above.

"Sharon, tell me, what's up?" Eric asked. "It looks like a bad time. Maybe we should go."

Sharon's face showed fear. "No, please don't. You've come all this way. I'm sorry, but please stay."

McAllister had to interject. "Sharon. Eric said it was okay to bring my dog. He's out in the car, I'm a little worried…."

"No, please bring him in," she answered. "Our dog died last month, so please bring him inside."

"Jester? Jester is dead?" Eric asked with shock in his voice.

"Chas got fucking drunk at the bar. He left him in the truck. Jester froze to death."

"Is that what all this is about? I can't believe it," Eric asked, with anguish in his voice. McAllister stood up and put on his coat, heading for the door.

"No, that isn't what it's all about. That's just a part of it," Sharon stammered.

McAllister went out the door. He hustled down to the car, letting Meatball out into the snow. Shit, this didn't look good. He was ready to turn around and head back home. Whatever the trouble, it was none of his business for sure. He took the gloves and beanie out of the pocket of his coat, deciding to stay outside for a while. He walked down toward the railroad tracks and the entrance to the tunnel.

The words Moffat Tunnel were inscribed above the entrance. The years 1923-1927 were etched below, presumably marking the starting and ending dates of the tunnel's construction. It was hard for McAllister to believe what it took to build such an engineering feat, the ingenuity and foresight necessary to construct such a project. It must have been incredibly dangerous work, boring over six miles through a mountain of rock. He marveled at the enormity of the task, the project accomplished in such a short period of time.

McAllister and Meatball rambled around the site for a while, until the sharpening cold became too much. He didn't really want to return to the house, to have to engage in the difficulties of someone else's problems. Didn't all of us have enough of our own? But right this moment, he was about a hundred miles from nowhere and freezing his ass. There was little to do but hang around and ride it out.

As he knocked and then entered the house, Charley Tucker was sitting in a cushioned chair across from the couch. The interior of the home was toasty warm. Charley was shirtless, his feet bare, wearing only his patchwork jeans. Eric remained on the couch. Charley greeted McAllister, before turning his attention to Meatball, petting the dog with his large rough hands. Charley Tucker looked hung over and short of sleep. His greasy brown hair strung down to the top of his bare shoulders, his white skin weighted with a raw flabby strength. A tattoo that read 'Triumph', superimposed on a marijuana leaf was pasted to his left arm. McAllister heard footsteps upstairs, figuring that Sharon had retreated above, keeping away.

McAllister did not know how long Charley Tucker and Eric Nordberg had been speaking, or what it might be about. But they seemed to have gone silent upon McAllister's entry. A strange quiet continued to hover in the room. Eric Nordberg did not look his normal self, his face projecting a concern he could not easily hide.

Charley Tucker broke the spell. "Well shit, if it ain't beer-thirty already. Time for a cold one." He threw down the last of his coffee before walking into the kitchen. McAllister looked over at Eric Nordberg, who grimaced in acknowledgement, shaking his head. Charley returned with three bottles of beer, handing one to each of his guests before sitting down.

"*Heinekin*? Not bad Charley," Eric admired. But before Charley could answer, Sharon came clomping loudly down the stairs, dressed in a heavy coat.

"Nothing's too good for my friends," Charley said, taking a swig off his beer. Sharon, her face frozen in anger, strode by him toward the kitchen. She stopped at the curtain.

"Did he tell you it's stolen," Sharon demanded. "Cases and cases of it, right out of the Nederland Tavern. He's got most of it stored at the house of his whore girlfriend over in town. Isn't that right, Chas Tucker. Tell them, why don't you. Tell them, if you're man enough!" Sharon turned her gaze toward Eric Nordberg. "That's right, Eric. You know, don't you? It's the same old shit. He's a goddamn fucking thief in the night. And now, he's a liar and cheater as well."

"Shut the fuck up, bitch," Charley Tucker roared. Sharon turned back from the kitchen, heading for the front door. As she passed by him, Charley Tucker stood up, grabbed her by the back of the shoulder, roughly spinning her around. Then, with an open hand, he slapped the woman across the side of her face. Sharon screamed, falling back toward the front door.

McAllister yelled, "Hey, hey." Bolting off the couch, he caught the woman in his arms, pushing her away. They stumbled against the door frame. Meatball sprung up from the floor, howling. McAllister kept the woman in his grasp, turning her sideways, away from her husband. McAllister stared at Charley Tucker. "You don't hit a goddamn woman, man! That's fucking chickenshit!"

Charley Tucker stared at him, as if in disbelief. But his eyes steeled as his fists clenched. "Don't you fuck with my business, buddy. I'll kick your fucking ass."

McAllister ignored the threat. He quickly opened the front door, pushing the woman outside onto the porch, slamming the door behind him. But once outside, she broke free of him, racing down the steps, before crossing the snow towards the house next door. There was no time to think. He pushed back through the door inside the house. Meatball ran past him, spilling outside. Eric Nordberg was up, trying to push Charley Tucker away, enough time for McAllister to grab his coat.

"You ever fuck with my business again, and I'll gun you down," Charley Tucker warned. But the man did not move forward to attack.

"You'd let somebody hit your sister like that. That's fucking bullshit, man."

"I don't got a sister, asshole." Charley Tucker shouted, staring hard into McAllister's eyes.

McAllister stared right back. "Well, I do, brother. And that's enough for me." McAllister jumped out the door, again slamming it shut. He bounded down the steps, throwing on his coat, trudging quickly away in the snow. Eric Nordberg came out onto the porch, yelling to him.

"Pick me up on the road, I'm out of here," McAllister returned. He headed into the Saturday afternoon, his adrenalin pumping. He was scared as shit, hoping to get as far away as he could get.

"Fuck Colorado," McAllister said only to himself. He and Meatball had struggled far enough down the road to finally begin to think. Jesus Christ, he thought, what the hell just happened back there? Is this crazy fucker coming to get me, or what? If Charley Tucker did come, what would he do? Would he hop over the snow bank and run through the drifts? Good luck with that escape. He could feel the bitter cold starting to harden his face. Come on, Eric, for crying out loud. But looking back, he could still see the car parked near the house.

McAllister kept hustling down the road, getting further away. Sooner or later, Eric Nordberg would have to come by and pick him up. He was counting on that. The sun was still high, the wind pushing behind him. In the distance, on the timbered edges of the wide naked valley, he could see an occasional ranch or two. Time remained to get out of this jam before nightfall, and hopefully not freeze to death. As he pushed himself forward, walking fast, he tried to settle down.

Damn, things were not going well here. Life was beginning to suck. He thought back to that time when he and Johnny Howard had hitchhiked into that weird deal up in Poudre Canyon. That was the last time he had really acted out. And shit, if that wasn't Colorado, too. Sure, there were a lot of good people here, nice people at work, acquaintances he had met and so forth. But now this fucking asshole was in his life, and whatever else might occur. He needed to make some decisions, whatever they might be, try to figure something out. The problem was where to go, and how the hell to get there. He didn't have a clue.

He heard a vehicle behind him, the chains crunching in the snow. Turning back to look, it was Eric's car moving slowly in his direction. McAllister hoped that nobody else was with him, certainly not Charley Tucker, or even his crazy wife, trying to escape. McAllister just wanted to be done with this whole deal, to get his ass back home. He moved over to the snow bank as the car began to approach. He called for Meatball to be near him. Looking back again, it appeared only Eric Nordberg was inside the car. He kept walking, but began to relax. The car pulled up beside him. McAllister opened the back door, letting Meatball jump inside. Then he climbed in front, pulling the door closed. The interior of the car was warm.

"Hey, Sean. I'm really sorry, man. That was fucking nuts. Are you all right?"

"Yeah, Nordberg. I'm all right, as long as that big fucker isn't coming to get me." McAllister turned his head and looked at Nordberg.

"Fuck, I never seen him like that before," Nordberg answered. "Nah, he's not coming to get you. At least not now."

"Oh, that makes me feel a whole lot better," McAllister said sarcastically.

"Hey, listen man, he's usually a pretty good guy. I've never seen him do that kind of shit. I guess things are pretty bad between him and Sharon. Talk about bad timing."

"Yeah," McAllister blistered, "a pretty good guy. A pretty good guy who cold cocks his wife in front of god and everybody. Yeah, that's a pretty good guy. Damn, Nordberg, you don't hit a woman like that. There's no excuse for that kind of bullshit."

Eric Nordberg didn't have an answer, letting the rebuke pass. Then he spoke. "I went next door, talked with Sharon before I left. She says he's sleeping with another chick in Nederland. He tells her he's been out on a call, dealing with work. But when the other guys come home from the job, he doesn't show. She says he and another dude stole a bunch of beer out of the back of the tavern in Nederland. Listen, Sean, I know Chas has got a bad side to him. But hell, he's always been good to me. And Sharon and I have been friends from Rollinsville, way before she even met him. I didn't know what to tell her. She still loves the guy, I guess."

"She'll go back to him, I bet," McAllister said. "He'll apologize and promise it will never happen again. He'll sweet talk her. Then after awhile, he'll just do the same damn thing. It's called domestic violence, Nordberg, and it happens all the time. But unlike today, it rarely occurs in front of anybody else. I had a course about it in college. And something similar happened to my sister once, with one of her boyfriends. Mary Jane, she was smart enough to get out of it right away. I'm not sure about Sharon, she probably doesn't have anywhere to go. But she's in for a big surprise if she thinks its going to change."

"Maybe you're right," Eric Nordberg answered. "I've got to reach her on Monday, when Charley's working. I'll see how she's doing. She said to tell you thanks for helping her. I'm sorry, Sean, it's a big freaking bummer. I was hoping we would have a good time."

"What did he say?" McAllister asked. "Is he still going to shoot me?"

"I tried to talk to him, you know, tell him he can't do that kind of shit. I tried to remind him that Sharon was my friend, too. But hell, I wasn't sure he might not freak out on me. He just said don't ever bring you around again. That's all."

"He can count on that," McAllister agreed.

The Colorado spring finally arrived with the fullness of bloom. The aspen trees began to leaf out, the hardwoods in Boulder and Louisville doing the same. The snow pack drained away, the creeks and rivers flushing with whitewater. Birds began to sing. The sun's heat returned, warming the skin on pleasant afternoons. The days reached longer into evening, the nights shining crisp and clear.

Patty Hearst had not been hiding in the Rockies. Instead, she was helping the Symbionese Liberation Army rob banks in San Francisco. The better news was that Richard Nixon was heading for a fall. The newspaper reports in the *Washington Post* that McAllister had followed so long ago finally had a name. They were calling it the Watergate Scandal. For McAllister, the particular irony of that moniker would have to be shared only with himself. Events were surely moving forward to the precipice of a possible Presidential impeachment. It would be too late to help George McGovern, but better late than never for that criminal of a President. Already, Nixon's buddy and personal hatchet man, Vice-President Spiro Agnew, had been taken down. Agnew had been caught with his grimy hands in the political till, having taken illegal kickbacks on construction contracts while governor of Maryland. Sometimes, if one is patient enough, karma gets to have its day in the sun.

Maybe there was hope for America to find its better progressive way, to return to the honor and integrity of its original beliefs. The exhaustion of the Vietnam War was ending. The rights of gender and color were gaining. Focus on the pollution of the environment was growing. Perhaps the war mongers and greed merchants could possibly be overcome. Although cynicism toward the government ran deep on both sides of Main Street, maybe the ethical elements of the American character might catch a break after all.

Sean McAllister needed some sort of break in his own life, and it eventually came in a letter from Mookie James. Mookie had met a guy in Santa Barbara who was going to visit a working commune in Oregon. Mookie had gone north on the trip and checked out the scene. Apparently, he was hooked. He had returned to Santa Barbara, suddenly planning to pack up and move to Oregon. Annie would even be coming up when her school was out. It would be a good place for Meatball, Mookie wrote. And for McAllister as well, if he wanted to come.

Mookie had no idea how much the content of this letter meant to him. McAllister had been waiting for an opportunity, for a new place to go. He wrote back immediately, asking Mookie to inform him if things were cool to come.

This new possibility put a spring in McAllister's step. He kept working at the printing plant, putting some extra money aside. He ate cheaply and stopped drinking at the bar. He'd also met an old house painter in Louisville, starting to work on the weekends to make some extra cash. Early in May, word came from Mookie that he was back in Oregon. The tone of the letter was bright with excitement. Mookie was helping to plant a huge garden at the commune. The people were great. And with some money he had saved, he was planning to build a cabin on the property. He urged McAllister to bring Meatball and check it out. Everything was cool.

McAllister gave his notice at work. He would have two weeks to go. He informed Eric Nordberg about the move. Eric Nordberg had been drinking a lot, spending more evenings at the Louisville Tavern. Much like McAllister, for Eric Nordberg, the daily life in Colorado had fallen into a pattern of uncertain ennui. His mountain days were done. The woman, Sharon, had actually left Charley Tucker. On a recent weekend, Nordberg had gone back up to Rollinsville to say his good-byes. Sharon was leaving for Los Angeles to be with her sister. According to Nordberg, Charley Tucker had quit the railroad job, moving in with the other woman in Nederland. Eric had seen him briefly, but Charley Tucker had been drunk and uncaring. So the gig was up. The events only seemed to prove an elemental fact of life. People and things can change, as time and circumstance go by.

Two nights before McAllister's departure, Eric Nordberg had stumbled into the duplex, drunk on his heels. McAllister had been reading in his bedroom. But objects were crashing in the kitchen and McAllister could hear Nordberg talking to himself. He found Nordberg slumped at the kitchen table, slurring his words, a bag of potato chips spilled before him.

"Hey, brother. You okay? Maybe you should get to bed."

Eric Nordberg raised his head slightly from the table, his blurry eyes finding McAllister. "Huh," he said in a buckled voice. "He's dead man, he's fucking dead."

"What do you mean, he's dead? Whose dead?"

"Chas, that's who," he blurted. "In Nederland. Somebody shot him. Dead as a fucking doornail. That's who."

McAllister tried to listen for a time, but Nordberg was wasted pretty bad. He was able to get his friend to bed. The next morning, a hung over Eric Nordberg told the rest of the story. Charley Tucker had been shot and killed in the Nederland bar the weekend before. The story had been in the news, but neither he nor Eric had seen the papers or been watching the television. Nordberg had found out through the grapevine only the day before. The consequence had become just another excuse for Nordberg to tie one on. But Eric didn't know the circumstances, only the result. "Fuck getting another roommate," Eric said with anger. "Enough is enough. Maybe, I'll just go back home." Somehow, he managed to pull himself together, heading off to his job.

McAllister spent the day winding up his affairs, finishing his packing. He had to chase the painting contractor all over creation to get a final check. As soon as it was written, he went into Boulder to cash it, before it might be stopped. Eric Nordberg didn't come home that final night. Early the next morning McAllister loaded the panel truck, leaving Eric Nordberg a final good well note. If there was ever a time to leave, this was surely it. People say that sometimes it's better to leave well enough alone. Perhaps it can be equally said for the opposite condition, to leave bad enough to its own device. Either way, it really didn't matter now. For Sean McAllister, it was time to move. And for a second or third time in his life, it wouldn't be necessary to look behind.

CHAPTER FIFTEEN

DOCTOR MY EYES
Oregon Road Trip / May, 1974

RICHARD MILHOUS NIXON HAD STEPPED into a deep pile of political dung. For more than thirty years, Nixon had managed to sustain his very own political confidence game. Years later, his deliberate treacheries were catching up to him in a big way. A little snowball had begun rolling down the hill. By May 1974, the avalanche was roaring down the mountainside. Watergate was no longer just a Republican condo hotel and commercial complex on the banks of the Potomac River. The name had become a linguistic idiom, a synonymous word for deceit in the history books of a powerful nation state. Watergate was a real-life suspense novel, with Tricky Dick Nixon as its evil protagonist. The chickens were coming home to roost. Nixon's karma was a retribution he couldn't avoid. Perhaps best expressed in the parlance of the time, 'what goes around, comes around'.

The triumph of personal ethics over expediency certainly needed a victory in the win column. Impeachment proceedings against Nixon in the United States Congress were beginning to move forward. Like many other Americans, Sean McAllister felt the false exhilaration of a necessary and deserved revenge. But such emotions are best reminded of another particular human imperative. 'Revenge is a dish best served cold'. This type of celebration should never be an end in itself. It is often better to let the weight of the man's own misdeeds befall him. Still, one had to be pleased that Richard Nixon's crimes had caught up with him during his lifetime. There was no question the man had earned his present comeuppance. And should jail time for criminal conspiracy happen to be in the cards, such a consequence would result in a sufficient vindication of its own.

There is one common advantage of driving the highways of America alone. It gives you time to think and reflect on who you have become, or where your life might be going. However, it should be noted, such a solitary personal enterprise must be exercised with caution, for sometimes feelings of doubt and uncertainty can be the unintended result. It can throw you off track, raising troubled questions of insecurity. It can interfere with your anticipations, the desires of your own private dreams. It can screw with your positive self-image, ushering in a series of wanton self-denials designed to protect yourself from harm. Serious thought and reflection can sometimes muck you up pretty good.

For almost two years, Sean McAllister had done a pretty good job dealing with his own denials. He had pushed the pressing loss of his girl deep into the closeted back rooms of his conscious mind. He had sucked up his defeat, endured the pain of its impact, moved on with his life. Yet, from time to time, the emptiness of losing at love pushed its way back into his thoughts, despite his best efforts to lock it away.

He knew that some men could manage these troubles better than others. There were men who could fill the void created by such loss with substitutes of one form or another. Most often, they would immediately find another woman. Others found solace through the numbness of alcohol, or the false euphoria of similar intoxications. For McAllister, his substitute had primarily been the escapes of time and separation, the distance that days and geography could provide. Unfortunately, sailing the waters of the Atlantic Ocean, or scuffling amongst the high plains and mountain beauty of Colorado had not fully done the trick. Although his dreams of Mad remained dead, the medicinal prescription of passing time had only softened the corners of his hurt. A sense of regret still tugged at his persona. From time to time, the memories of his loss had weakened his strength of self, challenging his confidence in the choices he had made.

Today, heading the panel truck north out of Boulder hadn't helped those memories. McAllister had considered heading directly into the Rockies, before driving up through Steamboat Springs and onward toward Wyoming. Instead, he decided the truck would be better served by skirting along the Front Range of the mountains. So he drove north to Fort Collins, finding the old highway he and Johnny Howard had hitchhiked together several years before.

He passed by the turnoff to that crazy acid trip up in Poudre Canyon, reminding him again of the fear and necessary anger he had been forced to display. But despite that difficult recollection, he would pass through the absolute beauty of the high foothill country near Virginia Dale. He would head once again toward Laramie before turning west. He wanted to sense that rangeland divinity one more time. Neil Young's soft and warm instrumental "The Emperor of Wyoming" played inside his head.

Memories, the good and the bad. His earlier journey across America had been full of adventure. At that time, everything had been new and unexpected, filled with those unadulterated youthful feelings of being on your own. Behind it all, there had been the security of a beautiful companion waiting upon his return. Mad had been the first real love of his life. But today, he was again driving toward another unknown, his past disappearing further with each mile in the rear view mirror.

A quiet surge of guilt swept over him. McAllister hadn't seen or spoken with Mad since that fateful evening. He hadn't been man enough to take the bad with the good and put it behind him. He hadn't been able to settle the reality of their separation, the respect of their time together, the cherished value of her presence in his life. He had acted like a jerk, a grieving loser who had left it all behind. These thoughts now challenged his own sense of integrity, his need to be a better human being, a stronger man who could accept his loss without the emotions of revenge and a sulking retaliation. Right then, he knew he would have to write to her, to apologize. He would have to make peace with his past, if only for himself.

This belated decision began to calm his doubts, making him feel somewhat better. He expressed its confirmation by verbally telling Meatball his intentions. Meatball got up from the mattress in the back of the panel, sticking his head between the seats of the cab, acknowledging McAllister's attention. McAllister rustled Meatball's head with affection. The dog yawned before returning to the mattress, circling back to his sleepy canine world. Meatball lived in a dog's world, where bad memories only came in dreams. But they were the kind of memories that simply came in the front door, and then went right on out the back. In Meatball's world, the future was always a clean slate, vacant of doubt or worry. It was a world where only the present moment dominated the conscious mind. It was the *Be Here Now* philosophy of existence, exhibited in its truest state. Yes, a dog's life. Some days, maybe the most comfortable place to be.

The trip motored onward. Back through Laramie, then west on Interstate 80, riding high on the desolate Wyoming plateau. But San Francisco, California would not be the destination this time around. Just past Rock Springs and Little America, McAllister's latest trail would turn away from the interstate, heading northwest toward Idaho. New contours now occupied McAllister's vision. His reflections upon Boulder, including the strange visualizations of a man he had known being shot to death in a bar, began to draw further away. He was now homeless on the open road, left only to wonder what would be next?

At least his good friend, Mookie James, would be on the other end. This knowledge heartened his intentions. The rest would be a gamble, but a gamble he was ready to take. Still, it was a little nervous to think about. He was going to a commune to join with people he had never met. What if he didn't fit? What if he was asked to leave? Look at it this way, he thought to himself, you're delivering Meatball to his new home in Oregon. You're going to a state you have never seen before. Summer is coming. You will meet new people. You're going to 'God's Country' in the best time of year. Within these thoughts, his confidence began to return, his expectations growing with each mile rolling under the wheels.

There was plenty of time for other thoughts. He had spoken with his mother on Mother's Day. She and his dad seemed to be doing okay. He knew that Connie McAllister worried about her son, as all good mothers do. So it was always important for McAllister to create general mendacities to keep the waters calm. He was fine, he said. The job was okay, it was beautiful in Colorado. It didn't make sense to tell her that Boulder felt like a dead end, that a man he knew had been murdered, or that a sense of loneliness had been dragging on his life. He hadn't told his mother he was quitting his job, or striking out again to find something new even further away. There was no need to plant such uncertain fears in a mother's heart.

As for his father, always a different story. Whenever McAllister called on the phone, his father didn't have much to say, which in one regard said it all. He could sense a measure of frustration in his father's voice, an aggrieved silence that spoke a thousand words. But he could hear his dad's unspoken refrain all the same. "What the hell are you doing? It's time to grow up and get serious about life. Bumming around has never been part of the McAllister heritage. It was time to get down to business. Financial security was an important value to make happen in this world." Bill McAllister never spoke those words, but his concerns echoed over the wires. Yet, at the very same time, Sean McAllister felt as if a certain tinge of jealousy hung in the air. As if his dad wanted to be out on the road as well, off the beaten track of his everyday American life. No doubt, Bill McAllister would never cop to such a particular affirmation. That wasn't part of a father's job description. Rather, it was to protect his son from the dangers of a youthful indiscretion which could harm his future in life.

Nonetheless, Bill McAllister always had a hard time reciting those rules of the road, and his son was now old enough to know. There was indeed a strange thread of wanderlust in Bill McAllister, one his generation and the times had never allowed. Instead, his father had found the panacea for such unfulfilled aspirations on the open fairways of a golf course, or bobbing in his boat far from the shores of a busy predictable world. It wasn't in Bill McAllister's repertoire to say 'how's it going kid, what the hell is it like out there'. The best he could say to his son was 'talk to your mom', not realizing that Sean McAllister would surely have to spare her the truth. It was something of a sad thing, that the experience and adventure of his own life, this journey on which he was traveling, could not be shared with his dad.

Thankfully, there was Mary Jane. In recent years, McAllister had found a friendship with his sister he valued very much. As siblings, they had always been close by proximity, but it was a relationship that as kids that had been completely unknown to them. Mary Jane could still be somewhat self-possessed, independent in her feelings, and as children she had always been in charge. But nowadays, it was if their consistent absence from each other had somehow joined them in ways they had only recently begun to realize. Mary Jane's admission about her abortion sometime back had set the stage. This revelation had allowed McAllister to become part of her personal life, not just the baby brother to whom she only offered strict advice and opinion. It was if Mary Jane had begun to let him in, and in doing so, granted him the security of being honest with her. Since then, they had built a trust and understanding. They now could share much of their personal lives, their disillusions and issues, in addition to the mundane realities of their everyday concerns.

From time to time, McAllister would write a long letter Mary Jane. He told her of his life on the oil tanker, as well as the deep hurt that he felt over the loss of Mad. And lately, he had expressed his dead-end uncertainty about things in Colorado. In exchange, Mary Jane had shared with him her growing ambivalence about her relationship with David in New York. She still enjoyed the energy of the city, but something was missing in her life, she just didn't know what. They both looked forward to seeing each other again. But neither had the surety of when it might occur. McAllister promised himself to write another letter soon. He would tell her about the shooting death of Charley Tucker, of leaving Boulder for Oregon. But he would wait until he was more certain of where he might be. And heck, that was surely an open question today.

As far as the homeboys went, Reggie Disalvo had gotten married to Teresa back in Wilmington. Reggie had bought a little row house in the city, and he and Teresa had a baby on the way. Reggie continued to work in his father's construction business, and more than likely would take it over someday. McAllister and Mike Taylor, the Bruiser, remained in touch by phone from time to time. Writing a letter would not be an activity one would expect from the Bruise. Such an exercise would require the Bruise to string together too many consecutive thoughts at one time. It was far too heavy a load for McAllister to expect. Actually, the Bruise was a pretty smart guy. But his was a tangible intelligence, born more of the body and common sense than any handwritten flow. His dad owned a beer distributorship. And the Bruise, like Reggie, was working for the old man.

Through his contact with Bruise, McAllister knew that Steve Rosenbloom, the Snark, had remained in Madison, Wisconsin. Snark had begun teaching as a graduate assistant. He was pursuing his PHD in history, and might one day be a professor. It only made sense. The Snark was right where he should be. He would now have a captured audience of students, and be able to proffer his opinions for hours on end. Some people, like the Snark, just seem to find their calling in life. But McAllister had to smile at such a thought. With the Snark, a pair of ear plugs would be a handy accessory to bring to class.

As for Jimmy Knox, the veteran of Vietnam, not much was known. And you could figure that would be the way Jimmy would prefer it to be. Bruise thought he had heard that Jimmy got a job with an oil company. He had taken up commercial diving, and been sent to the Persian Gulf. That sounded like Jimmy Knox. Courting some form of danger was right up Jimmy's alley. Whatever the challenge, Jimmy would be the right man for the job.

Johnny Howard, his dear friend and hitchhiking partner, had remained in Newark since McAllister's departure to Boulder. Johnny was still working almost full time at the docks, but he was changing gears and looking at chiropractic schools. The list included a school in Boulder, Colorado, a fact that held its own sense of irony. Unfortunately, wherever Johnny was accepted, his girlfriend would not be going along. He would be leaving Liz behind. McAllister could only wonder how much easier on the heart that being the leaver might be.

Finally, there was some word on Mad. She was still in Pennsylvania with Willie Chambers. What did it matter, she wasn't with him. When he wrote his letter, he would send it to her parent's home outside Philly. He certainly would not ask about Willie, that skinny-ass chump could make his own way. With Mad, in all this time gone by, he had written a million feelings inside his head, but none had ever been put to page. The things we say to people in our heads are never the same in translation. They sometimes might be more honest and true, but they never really help the cause, or change the situation. What's done is usually done.

McAllister pulled the panel truck off the highway, the twilight May evening growing closer to dark. The location, Kemmerer, Wyoming. At nearly seven thousand feet, Kemmerer was a community high on a desolate plateau. Somewhere nearby, was located the largest open-pit strip mine in the United States, the nation's biggest hole in the ground. Wyoming was such a god forsaken region. It was a place where Mother Nature was expected to take it up the ass, all for the good of America's electrical energy needs. It was a land where coal-fired power plants polluted the sky day and night. But it was a place with a civilized purpose. For it allowed unsuspecting American consumers like Sean McAllister to comfortably take a warm shit in a well-lighted room.

Tomorrow would be Idaho, and then onward to the state of Oregon. The past was just that, the past. Cherished memories or unresolved regrets were the incidental remains of its passing, the remnants of a time gone by. Somewhere in your being, if the total is greater than the sum of its parts, you are generally not accustomed to know. Perhaps that is the mysterious wisdom of experience in life. Only with time will such particular secrets be revealed. Only with time is the tree of one's perspective able to grow.

McAllister got up early out of Kemmerer, found some coffee, fed Meatball, getting back on the road. They skirted the northeast corner of Utah, crossing into Idaho. At Pocatello, he picked up another interstate, joining with the Snake River Plain, heading further west. The panel truck was running well, the old Dodge slant six making its way. But with the cost of gas, oil, and food, McAllister knew he would get to his destination with little leftover cash. The money thing worried him some, but there wasn't much he could do. At a rest stop near Twin Falls, another travel day on the journey came to an end.

The next morning, he picked up a couple hitchhiking to Boise. The man sat in the shotgun seat. McAllister set up the cooler so the woman could sit between. They had been visiting friends in Twin Falls, but would be working on a fire crew for the summer. The city of Boise would be their home base. They were hippies like himself, originally from Salt Lake City. They referred to themselves as Jack Mormons, those who chose not to abide by the traditional tenets of the Utah theocracy. Per the usual, everyone shared their individual stories, while the miles went rolling by.

Dropping the couple off in Boise, the drive continued. As another twilight evening began to descend, the panel crossed the border into Oregon. A sign by the side of the road read, 'Welcome to Oregon / Enjoy Your Visit'. The natural features were nothing like McAllister expected. The surrounding country remained raw and barren, a desperate land of harsh terrain and distant mountains, shadowed against the sunset horizon. There was rarely a person or vehicle in sight, only the sound of the wind amongst the isolation of fence lines and telephone poles as far as the eyes could see. This was definitely not the Oregon of

Sean McAllister's projected vision, the expected realm of lush green timberlands and rain driven rivers coursing to the sea. Under a blazing milky way of stars, he and Meatball pulled over at a roadside turnout, sleeping once again. They still had a ways to go.

McAllister awoke at first light, continuing southwest across this solitary Oregon desert, which appeared to stretch forever toward the horizon. As the afternoon pealed away, in the distance a rim of higher darkened mountains began to take shape, running from north to south in his peripheral sight. Scattered pine and juniper trees grew in greater numbers, the beginnings of a thick forest rising beside the highway. He was approaching the Cascade crest. The panel truck whined, climbing in elevation. In the cooling light of later afternoon, with his window down, he breathed in the distinct perfumed odor of fresh cut lumber. Evergreen trees soared high towards the cumulus sky, the underbrush thickening in yellow Scotch broom, the rocky volcanic ground red with pumice. This was more like it, the picture of Oregon he had often seen and believed in his mind's eye. He was getting close.

Driving upward into the darkness of the evening, he reached the high divide, before descending into the town of Medford. There, he found the intersection with Interstate 5, the great north-south corridor of western America. He could feel the proximity of the Pacific Rim, the crash of ocean waves somewhere beyond. Boulder, Colorado now lay distant, far to the east. Even further behind him, there remained a faraway place he once called home. Turning the panel truck north, McAllister passed through Medford, reaching the outskirts of Grants Pass. There he found a rest stop for the night. He was only thirty miles away.

He slipped into the back of the panel, heavy with fatigue. Tomorrow he would reach his destination, his mission complete. His excitement to find Mookie James merged with the doubts about his arrival. But at the moment, he was too tired to care. He closed his eyes, sleeping long and hard.

Part Two

Pollard Creek
(The Green)

*"Look...Reality is greater than the sum of its parts, also
a damn sight holier. And the lives of such stuff as dreams
are made of may be rounded with a sleep but they are not
tied neatly with a red bow. Truth doesn't run on time like
a commuter train, though time may run on truth. And
the Scenes Gone By and the Scenes to Come flow bending
together in the sea-green deep while Now spreads in circles
on the surface. So don't sweat it. For focus, simply move a
few inches back or forward. And once more....look."*

- Ken Kesey, Sometimes a Great Notion

CHAPTER SIXTEEN

GOING UP THE COUNTRY
(A BRIEF AND UNSUBSTANTIATED HISTORY
OF POLLARD CREEK, OREGON)

The first residents of Pollard Creek, Oregon were a transitory group. Often, they did not hang around for long periods of time, but needed to travel for various reasons. Archeologists and historians say they first came to town from the north, migrating south over many generations. It was believed their ancestors originally emigrated from Russia, passing over a land bridge way up in Alaska. Eventually, they wandered their way down the North American continent to the Lower Forty-Eight.

As time went by, some would make Southern Oregon their home. Others kept moving in various directions. They tended to form in small groups, like a big family of sorts. It was easier to look after each other that way. Because eating food was the most important job in their lives, they had to spend a lot of time rustling up the grub. Southern Oregon had a lot of animals living in the woods. In order to survive, they would try to surround and corner the animals, then have to kill them. But these people had no malice in their hearts when committing this necessity. Instead, they said prayers of thanks to the animals, for helping them to live.

When these residents did move around, they liked to be close to water. They would set up camp near the creeks and rivers, often in a flat spot nearby. There, they would settle in for a period of time, particularly in winter. They would build shelters of roughly cut sugar pine bark. This helped them to stay dry and warm and out of the rain. In the spring, when the steelhead fish swam up from the ocean, the residents would catch and eat them, or dry them on sticks for food later on. Sometimes the group might travel to the ocean, to live by the sea for awhile. As the weather got warm, they would start moving higher into the timbered hills, following the snow line as it melted away. This is when they would hunt for the animals. But they also harvested plants, berries, nuts, as well as certain roots that were safe to swallow. Sometimes when they were sick, ingesting some of these roots made them feel a whole lot better.

Because the group spent most of their days together, it wasn't often they ran into other groups of residents doing the same. But when they did cross paths, they mostly got along with each other and were happy to see other residents doing the same. They might exchange gifts, or perhaps cut a deal on something one group had that the other group needed. These special events would break the monotony of the daily routine, and everybody felt good.

Back at home, it wasn't like the group didn't have differences between each other. Indeed, there existed the normal social structures of gender and strength. But all in all, these local residents didn't necessarily let it get out of hand. Historians say that these people believed in the oneness of all things. They did not think of themselves as different from the lives of the trees, plants, and animals that surrounded them.

Like most human beings, they celebrated their group identity by adorning themselves with the bones and teeth of animals, or coloring their skin and clothing with natural pigments found in plants, flowers, and even the residues of burnt rock and clay. They liked to wear basket hats on their heads, woven from cedar bark and spruce root. This headwear helped to keep them dry on those rainy Oregon days.

But don't be mistaken, for these first residents of Pollard Creek, life was difficult. The group had to endure cold mountain snows, penetrating hot summers, the dangers of flood and fire. Still, this was the only life they knew. And everyone learned to be content with the cycle of its permanence. They bore children and buried their dead. They looked after each other the best they could. Sadly however, there came a time when everything began to change. Their natural world, as they had come to know it, took a turn for the worst. Suddenly, strange people with white skin began trucking through their woods.

These original residents of Pollard Creek had gotten word through the grapevine that bad things were going down. Eventually, they got their firsthand look when the Applegate brothers carved a new southern route for the Oregon Trail. The Applegate's were seeking an alternative circuit to avoid dealing with the dangers of running the rapids of the mighty Columbia River. Tragedy had struck the Applegate clan as they neared the end of their westward migration. Three children and a family elder were swept away and drowned in the waters of the Columbia. It was a terrible family loss, having occurred so very close to their final destination. After settling themselves in Oregon's Willamette Valley, the grieving brothers felt compelled to find a safer way for others to reach the new territory.

Forging south from the Willamette, the brothers blazed a new route down through Southern Oregon. Turning east across the Cascade Range, they were able to connect their tracks to another spur trail heading southwest from Idaho. Unfortunately, it was the increasing use of this new route that began to bring other white people into the mountains and valleys of this land our original residents called home. The discovery of gold in California only made things worse, as prospectors from the Willamette Valley used this new trail to head south to try and make their fortunes. This new breed of white man began to refer to our first residents as 'Redskins', or 'Savages'. These were words of contempt that the current residents had never heard before.

These new people were not very nice. They acted like they owned the land and could do whatever they desired. Finally, this continuing infiltration of white settlers forced the native peoples, now referred to as 'tribes', to respond in defense. They picked up whatever weapons they could find and fought to protect their homeland. They battled so hard and well that the new white settlers called them 'Rogues', a French word for 'fierce'. But their small bands were no match for the newcomers. The tribes were pushed and cornered into the narrow canyons of the Rogue River that led to the sea. Defeat followed, and no mercy was shown. Most of the survivors were driven to constricted reservations of land in northern Oregon, far away from the wandering indigenous surroundings they had come to know and love.

As a result of this historical consequence, the first residents of Pollard Creek, Oregon were now banished and gone. Immigrant white Americans took their place. These alien people continued their angry and careless feelings toward the land. They would seek to plunder this rugged country of evergreen and rock. Pollard Creek, by its own peculiar location, became a way-station for these many travelers, part of a stage line and supply route, humping north and south through the rough mountain barriers between Sacramento and Portland. Many of the miners returned, always searching for the golden colored rocks. They scattered themselves throughout the narrow surrounding watersheds, sluicing for nuggets and flake, for the money it could bring.

One day, a giant beast called the railroad steamed into town. The railroad's appearance raised the opportunities for greater resource extraction. Men with soft hands and paper money, called investors, showed up in Pollard Creek. They brought with them other slant-eyed people called 'coolies' to help dig the ditches. The coolies would channel the readily abundant sources of Oregon water into huge pressure-filled pipes. Immediately, the white men began to hose away the hillsides with hydrologic power, before scavenging the rocky remains for gold and other metals. Concurrently, new camps of people, called towns, grew up in the wake of these industrial expeditions. Thousands more white people came, looking for work and dreams of wealth.

But these Southern Oregon hills did not have enough mineral bounty to give. After a time, the soft-handed investors, with their fat wallets heavy, left Southern Oregon for other places to play. Just as fast, the town folk scattered. The miners began to disappear, their makeshift towns left behind. Soon these towns became occupied by invisible ghostly inhabitants, marked by empty wooden shelters, silent but for the sodden dripping of winter rains. Also abandoned, were expansive fields of useless exposed rock spreading across the valley floors. Placer tailings they were called. These rocky fields looked like remnants of some ancient planetary world, forbidden and lost.

Although there wasn't enough gold in these Southern Oregon hills, goodness gracious, there were still the mighty forests. In this heavily timbered country, where the Siskiyou and coastal mountains merged, the area now became a gold mine of a different extraction. Watered by Pacific rains and moderate temperatures, it was an evergreen paradise of Douglas fir, ponderosa pine, hemlock, and cedar. Money did grow on trees in Southern Oregon, and with the Southern Pacific Railroad, a way to get them to market.

Over time, mountain hamlets like Pollard Creek became the

home of tree fallers and horse loggers, choker setters and high-line operators. These were strong, stout, and brawling white men, performing dangerous work. In the mill towns, logs were cut to size and length, sorted and packed on the railcars, then hauled away to a building America. Southern Oregon became a hard-hat country of gyppo logging families and company stores, with timber as far as the eye could see.

With the invention of the internal combustion engine and chain saw, the economy of the Southern Oregon roared ahead. Earth movers plowed roads deeper and higher into the forest. Shovel equipment loaded the product onto trailers, and log truck drivers hauled ass down the mountainsides. The more trees that could be cut and delivered, the more money that could be made. It became a highballing economic time.

But as some people say, sooner or later all good things must come to an end. The first-cut virgin timber began to slowly fade, becoming harder and harder to find. The job market dulled. For many years, nobody had bothered to re-plant the resource of trees, there had always been so much more to harvest. Others simply didn't care. The land wasn't much good for anything else. Southern Oregon was marginal sloped ground, hard with rock and clay, fertile only for trees. And by this time, the big lumber companies and railroads controlled the industry. They cut deals with the government for more land and contracts. But the boom days were over for most of the men that had worked the hardest in cutting down the woods.

Smaller land owners knew the jig was up. The trees that remained on their parcels of ground were of little commercial value, not worth the cost of a selective cut. In addition, they knew they would never live to see the monetary benefits of a necessary reforestation. So what the heck, if somebody wanted to buy a ragged piece of logged over timberland, why not sell. If some dopey buyer came along, one would happily cash out, even carry the contract to pay if necessary. The dollars received could easily be used for any number of family needs.

What happened next couldn't exactly be explained. And it certainly wasn't expected. Suddenly, a whole lot of new strangers began to appear in Pollard Creek. Men were showing up at the '76 station or the Country Store with long hair and blue jeans, some adorned in scarves or headbands of all different colors. And their women folk wore long dresses with beads around their necks. And by god, sometimes you could see the tops of their breasts in full open view. Even their kids were practically naked most of the time.

However, most of the hardcore residents of Pollard Creek weren't born yesterday. They had their televisions and newspapers. They knew quite well who these people were. They were the hippies, most of them from California no doubt, that immoral land of Sodom and Gomorrah to the south. What the hippies were doing up here in Southern Oregon nobody knew. But here they were nonetheless, buying groceries and gasoline, or driving by in Volkswagon busses and battered pick-up trucks on Lower Pollard Creek Road. They were turning into the properties like the old Crocker place, which had recently sold.

"They look like a bunch of fucking gypsies," one of the good old boys said the other day. "Not gypsies," another corrected. "Indians. They look like a goddamn tribe of Indians to me."

CHAPTER SEVENTEEN

YOUR MOTHER SHOULD KNOW
Main Street / Pollard Creek / May 1974

VALERIE WILLIAMS AWAKENED to shards of morning sunlight slicing through her open bedroom window. Warm spring air carried the perfumed odor of lilac on the breeze. Valerie stretched her sleeping torso, a fading dream slipping away, replaced by conscious thought. A pair of blue jays squabbled in the trees outside, drowning out the other song birds, announcing the busybody business of another Oregon day. Those stellar jays never sing, Valerie thought to herself, always fussing over something. Their wise-assed cries reminded Valerie of all the people in the world who spend their lives never finding peace. Those unsatisfied human beings who rush through their daily existence always stirring the pot, unable to leave well enough alone. She didn't like those blue jays, or those people. They seemed to be everywhere in one form or another, pushing and shoving their way through life. But she also knew they would never go away.

Her son Canyon lay sleeping beside her. Even though the boy had his own little bedroom, each night he would wander in and find her, snuggling close before going back to sleep. Canyon was growing older each day, yet the tether of their bond remained tight. He was the most important person in her life, the focus of her being since the very first day of his wondrous birth.

Valerie wasn't sure she had made the right decision. To come here to Oregon, to this little mountain town called Pollard Creek. But Tom Sullivan had wooed her with its anticipations. He had prompted her with its evergreen beauty, its potential freedom from the angst of her California existence. Truthfully, she had wanted to come, to seek the shelter and warmth of a smaller world, to make new friends. Perhaps she was hoping to find a good man to love, to build a life in the country, peaceful and different from the lonely separated world she had begun to live. But dreams are fickle expectations, often short of fulfillment. Valerie was no longer shocked by the vagrant consequences of her reality. By now, she had seen enough of life's contradictions. She had felt the pain of their singular betrayals enough to know. She smiled to herself, thinking of the aphorism a friend had once pronounced, 'if wishes were horses, even beggars would ride'.

Tom Sullivan was a good man. For a time Valerie had thought maybe her man, but she and Tom had realized together that friendship would be the better alternative. They had slept together in California, needing each other for the intimacy it might provide. For Valerie, it had been mostly for the companionship of a man. For Tom, the necessity for some stability, an anchor from the troubling effects of coming home from war. But Tom Sullivan was in no shape to be a provider, or to take on the responsibility of a woman and a young son. He was not settled enough to give himself over to that kind of future. Still, the loyalty and care that was part of him could not be mistaken. Eventually they had talked it out, understanding together what was best.

Getting the property in Solace Valley with his friend Marty Johnson and others was where Tom Sullivan needed to be. His homebuilt cabin was almost finished now, and she could sense his calming down. There were moments when he still withdrew, quietly serious and distracted, as if leaving for a place no one else could know. But those occasions were diminishing. Valerie sensed Tom's head and heart were getting lighter, his dry sense of humor and outlook finding its way. Oregon and the property they called Railroad Bridge was good for Tom. Acting as his confidante now, rather than his lover, Valerie could feel him coming home to himself.

Despite the recognition that it wasn't their time, Tom Sullivan felt compelled to look after her and the boy. When the Railroad Bridge property was purchased, Tom Sullivan had made the move north. But from the very outset he had wanted Valerie to come. At first, Valerie suspected it would be a rough go. She couldn't see putting Canyon through such a difficult change. She wasn't ready to struggle on that level of daily life. The Railroad Bridge property was no piece of cake. Most of the year, everyone had to hike across the train trestle with their food, propane, and other supplies. Sometimes they had to run like heck when they heard the train engines rolling through the forest. It was scary enough just to walk cross the trestle, even with nothing in hand. During the dry season, the men could ford the creek with their vehicles. But they often got stuck in the rocky bottoms of stone and gravel, having to winch the trucks back onto land. It was not a place for a woman or kids, and rarely had Valerie stayed for long.

Hearing about the yellow rental house on Main Street, Tom had called to her in California, and she had taken the place sight unseen. Tom drove south to Martinez with the big flatbed truck. He packed her up and they headed north. She, her son, and her dog Fillmore, followed behind in the station wagon. Valerie was taking a chance on something new. It had only been last September. What she hadn't considered in her haste, and in Tom Sullivan's particular conviction, caught her by surprise. It was called the Oregon winter. For a girl from San Francisco, the shock of months of mountain rain and snow was an unanticipated challenge. But once again, Valerie had dug in and persevered. She learned to chop wood for the stove and drive her car in snow. She managed to endure the cold and rain, even the persistent fog that hung in the valley like a tomb.

But with days like today, the payoff had come. Beautiful spring mornings were upon her, the sun warming her skin. The hills were glorious with wildflowers, full of purple vetch and white oxeye daisy. There was the bright yellow invasion of scotch broom, glints of light shining off the budding green trees. Valerie had her backyard garden underway. A hot summer of cloudless blue skies lay ahead. She rolled back the covers, anxious to greet the day.

Valerie rustled her son awake, watching as he rubbed the sand from his dreamy blue eyes. She made them breakfast. Going outside, she kept her eye on Canyon as she worked the garden beds. She watered her starts under the glass covered hotbox that Tom Sullivan had built for her. Nearby, the row of ragged little houses on Main Street was coming to life. A car and truck passed on the narrow paved street. Down the block, a lawn mower fired up its engine. The sounds of the nearby Pollard Creek Elementary School rose high with children at play.

Taking a break from her chores, Valerie placed her lawn chair in the sun. She sipped on a second cup of coffee, watching Canyon playing with his toys nearby. Fillmore lay at her feet. He licked himself, before closing his eyes to the warmth of the sun. Just behind the house, she heard the predictable roar of the morning freight train braking on the tracks, its cargo of lumber and wood chips grinding to a stop. Valerie could see the railroad men as they walked by at the end of the block, heading for the Hungry Dog Café, taking a welcome respite from their job.

Valerie turned her face to the sun, closing her eyes, feeling its growing heat. Upon hearing the voice of a child, she looked down to see her friend, Darla Bloom, walking along the street. Darla held her young son Caleb in her arms, her daughter Jessica beside her, making their way. It came as a pleasant surprise, Darla Bloom having her children in town. Canyon would have some early company. The two women embraced upon arrival. Valerie made another pot of coffee. Grabbing an extra lawn chair, Darla and she returned to the yard, settling in to talk, enjoying the day. The children hopped and played amongst themselves, the youngest, Caleb, trying to keep up.

Darla Bloom was a long story. Tall, dark, and striking, she had come to Oregon with the father of her children, Derrick Mulcahey. She had recently been part of the Mulcahey Farm, a large extended family located three miles down the Lower Pollard Creek Road. The family had come up from Santa Cruz, and like Tom Sullivan's friends at Rainbow Bridge, they had cut themselves a home out of these rocky timbered hills. The property was a working commune of people and animals, of rough sheltered barns and cabins, as well as the biggest fenced garden Valerie had come to see. The Mulcahey Farm was known to be the hardest working, the most serious attempt at self-sufficiency in Pollard Creek. And there was no uncertainty as from whom such inspiration and intention had founded its communal purpose. It was Derrick Mulcahey. The Mulcahey Farm had a reputation for trying to make good on homesteading the land, and proving it could be done.

But as Valerie had gotten to know Darla, she learned that things are not always as they seem. Darla's time had not been easy. Derrick Mulcahey may have believed in the oneness of family living, in a democracy of consensual community spirit. But when you cut to the chase, things at the Farm would be done Derrick Mulcahey's way. And no person understood that reality better than Darla Bloom. She had lived at the foot of Derrick's personal kingdom almost every day, as the dutiful wife and mother. Only Derrick's younger brother, Jack Mulcahey, had lived longer under Derrick's influence. But as time passed, Darla had reached the end of her perseverance. Darla made a decision to leave the Farm and her relationship with Derrick. This decision had slowly conspired with her maturation from a teenage mother and wife, toward the awakening of her own spirit and personal identity.

But getting away from Derrick had not been easy, and the price had been very high. Almost too high for any woman with children they love. Darla could leave, Derrick had commanded, but the children would stay. There would be no further discussion, no arbitration that would ever take place. One did not cross Derrick Mulcahey without some resulting consequence. Perhaps you might win a battle, but you would never win the war. The children would not be leaving the Mulcahey Farm.

According to Darla, Derrick had never resorted to physical control, but his angry verbal attacks were like slaps across the face, pointed and debilitating. Derrick could sense the weakness and personal fears inside her, then use that knowledge to silence her and make her question herself. He was brilliant in his manipulations. Darla's fear of losing her children was certainly enough of a threat, but the fear of being a target of his controlling power constantly hung in the air. Darla clearly understood the consequences of an authority that others tried to avoid. The confusing irony was the other side of Derrick's intentions. It was the charm Derrick could use to soften you, to make you feel wanted and important to him and his cause. But in the end you would have no say, and you were mistaken to believe you did. Derrick Mulcahey was a mastermind of personal influence, and he was dangerous as a result.

Valerie Williams had gotten the picture, although it was something she had already learned. Trust could be a volatile commodity. It could often be disguised by the theatrics and emotional impacts of language and hidden motivations. Many other men had similar methods of survival and dominance. But unlike Derrick, their actions were often unconscious in expression. The patterns of manipulation they displayed were often concealed, even from themselves. In a strange way, these men were not responsible for their exploitations. Their behavior was simply an involuntary and oblivious pattern of control. Yet, although such actions might not necessarily be intended, it was control all the same.

Just ask any woman who had been the target of such manifestations. In Derrick Mulcahey's case, it felt like something more. His need for control had become a necessary tool of artful deception, in order to manage and preserve his survival, and thus to maintain his uncertain hegemony in a tenuous world.

Finishing their coffee, the two women gathered up the children, walking together up Main Street to the Pollard Creek Post Office to get the daily mail.

Sean McAllister was nearing his new destination. Traveling north out of Grants Pass, the panel truck climbed a long mountain pass on the interstate highway. The big semi-trucks rumbled slowly up the grade, the faster vehicles flying by swiftly, barreling away. At the highway's peak, the elevation was only two thousand feet, yet the vista of hump-backed mountains in the distance made it seem much higher. After months of living on a flatland prairie at better than five thousand feet, the Rocky Mountain pinnacles elevating twice as high, it was an unusual sense of relativity stretching out before him. Nonetheless, he was invigorated by the obvious beauty of this surrounding geography.

The interstate curved its way down the mountain, opening to a wide green valley below. The exit sign read, 'Solace Valley'. Traffic continued flying down the descending grade into the valley floor, before climbing again up another timbered ascent. Reaching the crest of the second mountain pass, the interstate sharply dipped into a narrower depression below, as if falling into a pit. At the bottom of this descent, an exit sign suddenly appeared, approaching very fast. McAllister quickly broke his speed, gearing down toward the exit ramp below. He swung the panel truck off the highway, continuing to slow toward a stop sign ahead. So this was it, exit number seventy-six, Pollard Creek, Oregon.

At a roadside junction ahead, a green horizontal road sign pointed left toward Pollard Creek. As McAllister slowly made the turn, he could feel the butterflies in his stomach, much akin to those familiar pre-game jitters he had not experienced in quite some time. The road passed under the freeway, before turning onto an access road that led into town. McAllister spoke to Meatball, announcing their arrival. The dog raised his head, stirring awake. Mookie James and Annie would be somewhere nearby. The access road passed a truck stop café and gas station called the Hungry Dog. A line of semi tractor-trailers were parked alongside the shoulders of the road. Beyond him, to his right, McAllister could see what looked like a market store with a large parking area out front. Across the street to the left, stood a large white building that looked like a Southern mansion hidden in the trees. A sign across its driveway announced its identity, the Pollard Creek Inn.

McAllister brought the panel to a halt. The motor idled in the market parking lot as he tried to survey the scene. Further to the left, across a triangle confluence of dissecting roads, he saw a building that appeared to be the post office. Driving on past the Pollard Creek Inn, he pointed his vehicle into the post office lot, before parking the truck. Climbing out of the panel, he stretched his body in the midday sun. Meatball followed immediately behind, jumping through the driver's seat into the day. All around them, a forest of evergreen hills rose sharply above, ebullient in green, against a deep blue sky. All seemed quiet and well, a beautiful place. Oregon.

As he watched Meatball pander and sniff in the nearby grass, the post office door opened. Two women stepped outside, surrounded by several children. The women were dressed in peasant dresses, their long hair falling below their shoulders, sandals surrounding their feet. The women's presence aroused McAllister's intentions. As he approached, they looked his way.

"Excuse me," he introduced. "I'm looking for the Lower Pollard Creek Road." The women stopped and observed him. One of the women pointed over his shoulder. Her reddish brown hair shined in the sunlight. The features of her face were narrow and sharp, her figure lean. After days on the road, this woman was nothing less than a lovely sight. McAllister turned and looked behind, where a road headed under a railroad overpass. He pointed in the same direction, as if to confirm. "That a way," the woman said. "That's Lower Pollard Creek. How far are you going down?"

"A place called the Mulcahey Farm. Do you know it?"

The two women looked at each other and smiled, as if sharing a secret between them. The second woman was equally as attractive, with straight black hair, a more mature expression gracing her face. The brown haired woman continued.

"Are you the friend of Mookie and Annie's, from Colorado?"

Sean McAllister's head cocked with surprise. "Well yeah, I am. Geez, how the heck did you know that?" The brown haired woman pointed at his license plate.

"We know everything," the dark haired girl answered beside her, laughing softly.

"They said you were coming," the brown haired one continued. "I used to live there. "My kids live there," she said, spreading her arms above the children at her side.

McAllister shook his head, looking down at the children. "Hey there, kids. My name is Sean." He waited patiently as each child bravely announced their names. Looking back up, he spoke to the women. "Wow, what a trip. I guess it's nice to be expected." He reached out his hand to make acquaintance.

The brown haired girl reached out first. Her hand felt warm and delicate in his grip. "Darla," she returned. "And this is Valerie." McAllister let go, shaking the other woman's hand the same. "We know Mookie and Annie. Derrick Mulcahey is my ex-husband, so I'm down at the Farm from time to time, visiting the kids."

McAllister had a lot of questions, but didn't begin. For now, this extraordinary moment spoke for itself. He felt his whole body relax, as if coming to a place where things were known and safe.

"Are you just visiting, or coming to stay?" Darla asked. She looked at him intently with the question.

"I guess I don't know for sure. I have Mookie's dog to deliver." McAllister turned to check on Meatball, who remained nearby, wandering in the grass. "Then, I guess, I'll see what's next. But I have no plans to return to Boulder."

The women gave him directions. Darla told him to look for a turnout after the mile marker three, where there would be a parking turnout by the road. He should park there, then follow down the fire road along the railroad tracks. He would come to a cabled walk bridge over the creek. That would be the place. She pointed to the Pollard Creek Inn across the street, saying she lived in a school bus behind the building. Valerie pointed to another street nearby. She lived in a small yellow house at the end of the block. McAllister took in the ease of their presence, as if they had known him for a long time. Thanking them, he said his good bye. But the woman, Darla, stepped forward, becoming close.

"You'll meet Derrick," she said. "He and others won't have nice things to say about me. But he has another woman now, so things are better. If you stay for awhile and get a chance, come to the Inn. I'll show you around."

McAllister thanked her, returning to the truck, Meatball jumping inside. The women, with their children in tow, crossed the street and waved as he turned down the road. He couldn't have asked for a better beginning. Slowly, he steered the truck through the narrow railroad overpass, heading down the road. The uncertainty of his arrival had begun to lessen with this encounter. He drove forward with the anticipation of finding Mookie James, his old homeboy friend. A reunion awaited him. He was excited for whatever was next to come.

CHAPTER EIGHTEEN

SPACE ODDITY
Mulcahey Farm / Pollard Creek / May, 1974

SEAN MCALLISTER FOLLOWED DOWN the Lower Pollard Creek Road, heading for the Mulcahey Farm. To his left, a single set of railroad tracks cut through the timber. Below the tracks, he caught periodic glimpses of a whitewater creek running in his direction. At the sight of mile marker three, McAllister began to slow the panel. Ahead was the vehicle turnout the woman Darla had mentioned. He parked the truck by a single lone automobile. Exiting the panel, he and Meatball crossed the set of tracks, before walking down the fire road. Parked along the road were two old pick-up trucks and a battered station wagon. McAllister could hear the sound of hammering in the trees beyond, the occasional calls of human voices remaining unseen.

Strung between four large evergreen trees, two on each side of the water, a wooden platform walkway was suspended by thick strands of metal cable. It hovered across the creek divide. He and Meatball stepped up onto the bridge, swinging their way steadily to the other side. Returning to firmer ground, a path led off to the right. He walked past a two-story homemade structure. The path continued toward a large round building shaped like an octagon. This building was set on large tree stumps serving as the foundation, a black stove pipe pushing through its top. This structure sat alone in a bare open area. A tall log-framed woodshed and picnic table stood nearby. Two dogs appeared, barking and coming forward. Meatball slowly and deliberately moved toward them. The dogs reached each other without undue consequence, circling and smelling each other in canine greeting.

As McAllister neared the building, a man stepped out of the door. McAllister introduced himself. The man's name was Darius. Similar to his unexpected welcome at the post office, Darius also was aware of McAllister's arrival. Darius led him through a gap in the trees, opening to a wide vegetable garden exposed to the afternoon sun. There, about a half-dozen people were scattered throughout the expansive fenced area. McAllister caught sight of Mookie James, standing shirtless with shovel in hand. His dark hair hung much longer than the last time McAllister had seen him in Boulder. Mookie's eyes lit up with recognition. Laying the shovel aside, he walked swiftly down a path between the raised beds of the garden.

"Meatball," Mookie James cried excitedly. The sound of Mookie's voice brought Meatball's head up, his tail wagging. Dog and man met at the garden gate. Mookie fell to his knees, rustling his long lost friend in heartfelt welcome. McAllister walked forward to join them.

"Brother," Mookie James began. Standing back up, he and McAllister shook hands and embraced. "You made it, man. I can't believe it, Sean, you're here."

"Mook," McAllister responded. "Yeah, the Meatball delivery service has arrived. Man, what a trip. Wow! Geez, this place?

"Yeah, Mac," Mookie affirmed, smiling broadly. "We're not in Kansas anymore."

"No shit about that," McAllister answered.

Annie had followed behind. Although McAllister had not gotten to know Annie well in Boulder, she too greeted him with a strong embrace and warm kiss on the cheek.

The rest of the day took on a life of its own. Mookie walked him throughout the property. McAllister saw the barn and other outbuildings for the animals. He witnessed Mookie's cabin site foundation, as well as the other personal structures in varying degrees of construction. He continued to meet the other folks who lived on the forty acres of property, trying to remember their names. He met Jack Mulcahey, the younger brother of Derrick. Jack Mulcahey's reddish blonde hair was tied back in a pony tail, a full beard hugging his face. He was a man of muscular dimension, his quiet taciturn words stuttering when he spoke. Shortly after, he met the man called Derrick, his orange red hair blazing in the sun. Derrick Mulcahey's greeting toward him was warm and engaging, further easing McAllister's earlier concerns about being an unwelcome guest.

In the early evening of extending daylight, chores were performed, the animals fed. McAllister helped Mookie tote water from a spring box down to the octagon building where he had met the man, Darius. The eight-sided building was the Farm's communal kitchen. Inside the structure sat a large propane cook range, a smaller freestanding wood stove in the opposite corner. In the middle of the room was placed a long flat burl of wood, surrounded by tree rounds close to the floor.

According to Mookie, each day a designated pair from the group would prepare the evening meal. As dinner was served, everyone sat together around the low wooden table, eating a meal of vegetables, rice, and early spring greens. Fresh cow's milk was poured from gallon jar containers, or chilled water from the propane refrigerator that sat outside. McAllister spent part of the meal answering questions about his trip, explaining his past friendship with Mookie and Annie. But mostly, he listened as others spoke of projects underway, or chores to be shared the following day. Derrick Mulcahey seemed generally to direct the discussion, inquiring information from various people, but without a sense of command. Still, McAllister could sense the seniority of his presence, evidenced by the deference from others it appeared to confer.

After dinner, with Meatball running alongside, Mookie led McAllister back across the swinging bridge. Returning to his panel truck, they drove a short distance down the paved road to the driveway of a neighboring property. There, a crossing allowed him to drive the panel truck over the tracks. Turning back, the panel truck bumped along the fire road, doubling back to the Mulcahey Farm. Pulling the rig into a grove of trees, a campsite appeared. The camp had been Mookie and Annie's home for the past six weeks, since Mookie's arrival at the Mulcahey Farm. Mookie's VW camper van was open wide. Next to the van, Mookie had built an open pole structure covered in tarps. Underneath, he had placed a picnic table covered with lanterns, flashlights, and other camping accessories. Nearby, three lawn chairs were set by a fire pit circled with large gray river rocks.

McAllister busied himself with setting up the panel truck for the night, finally having a chance to collect his thoughts. The day had been non-stop since his awakening along the interstate earlier that morning.

He felt some relief to be away from the hubbub of so much new experience. Mookie tidied up the picnic table, checked the oil in the lanterns, before setting the lawn chairs toward an open view through the trees. He pulled two beers out of the cooler in the van, placing himself down in one of the chairs. McAllister walked over and wearily sat down beside him. Mookie James uncapped the beers, handing one to his friend. They looked out upon the paling white sky to the west.

"So, what do you think, brother, pretty cool scene, huh?" Mookie James asked.

McAllister took a hit off the beer. Laughing at the question, he rested back in the chair. "Man, what a day. Geez, Mook, how the hell did you find a place like this?"

"I brought Jerry up from Santa Barbara. He's the guy that told me about the Farm. I really wanted to see the place."

"Jerry? The frizzy-haired short guy?"

"Yeah, that's him. Derrick and Jack said I could come back and stay if I wanted."

"But what about school, Mook? What happened there?"

"I don't know, Sean. I'm just tired of the college thing, I guess. I had been planning to start again this fall. But once I got up here, I didn't want to leave. When Annie said she wanted to come, that kind of sealed the deal."

"Did Annie drop out or something?"

"Yeah, right in the middle of the quarter. Her parents are seriously pissed. I'm sure as hell on their shit list. But once we got to Santa Barbara, Annie didn't much like it. California is a weird place, Mac. It's certainly beautiful and warm, and there's the ocean and all that stuff. But I don't know, maybe too many people, too slick, too busy, something like that. Anyway, I just couldn't feel settled there. Oregon feels a whole lot better. Lots of good people here at the Farm, and always something to do. Right now, Annie feels the same."

"Well, I can't argue with you," McAllister agreed. "Pretty awesome what you guys are doing here. And I can't believe this country, Mook. It's beautiful."

"You're going to stay for awhile, right?" Mookie asked. "Maybe you could stay here and help me build the cabin. See if you like the Farm."

McAllister lifted himself out of the lawn chair, pacing out toward the gap in the trees, looking up, taking in the sky. He turned back toward Mookie. "I guess so," he sighed. Although I haven't had time to really think about things. I suppose Meatball and me were just trying to get here. I mean, I'm done with Boulder, that's for sure. But what the hell is next, I don't know. Pretty quick, Mook, I got to get some work. I'm really low on dough. To be honest, right now, I couldn't get that far anyway."

"Ah, don't worry about that for tonight," Mookie answered. "You can get some food stamps in town. And I got some extra money stashed away if you need some. As long as you're here on the Farm, things will be all right."

"What's the money trip here?" McAllister questioned.

Mookie James got out of his chair, taking a last swig of his beer. "Want another?" McAllister nodded. Mookie went to the cooler, grabbing two more beers, handing one to McAllister. "I'll roll us a number when Annie gets back. Well, the money thing is kind of loose. The Farm is not like other places where you are expected to turn over everything you own, make a vow of poverty and all that shit. So far, you just kind of contribute when you can, and if we get a job together for a day or something, it all goes into the pot. But everybody works doing one thing or another, either here on the Farm, or perhaps somewhere else. And we trade for stuff as well. So far, things are working out I guess. But right now, there's a lot to do on the land, so things are pretty busy here at home, especially with the garden and stuff."

The two men sat back down in the lawn chairs. "Well, just tell me what you or anybody needs for awhile," McAllister requested. "Kind of help me along if you would, until I figure things out a little. I'd appreciate that."

"No problem there. Everybody's pretty cool, Sean. It will all be fine."

"So, do the two brothers own the property?" McAllister asked.

"I think so. Actually, I think one of their friends legally owns the place on the deed, but they're paying him off when they can. I'm not really sure. Derrick and Jack kind of keep certain things pretty tight when it comes to some stuff. In some ways, it's sort of their thing here. But Jack is great. He doesn't say very much, but once you get to know him, he's the best. Derrick's a little trickier to figure out. Sometimes you're not sure where he is coming from. One minute, he acts like your best buddy. The next, he might be questioning you about what you're doing here, what you think about the place. He's one of those guys that sort of keeps you on edge. Nobody really likes that stuff, so we just try and stay away from it. But don't sweat it, brother, it's just Derrick being Derrick."

"When I got to town today, two women at the post office gave me directions to the Farm. One was named Valerie, the other, Darla. The one, Darla, said she was married to Derrick and used to live here at the Farm. She had her two kids with her."

Mookie laughed. "Well, you didn't waste time getting into town, Mac, did you. Yeah, Darla originally came to the farm with Derrick and the kids. But I guess she'd had enough of him, and maybe just the whole move from Santa Cruz. I wasn't here of course, but I guess the shit hit the fan when she wanted to move and tried to take the kids. Derrick didn't let her. Then another time, she did take them and headed for the coast. I guess Derrick found her and convinced her to come back. But that didn't last long. Finally, she just moved to the Inn, when the folks from Strawberry Fields bought the place. And the kids stayed here. I guess they sort of got it worked out now. And Derrick has Marlene these days, and as you can see, she is pregnant with another kid. Darla is all right, although you can figure she doesn't think much of Derrick. But at least she has the kids from time to time, so that's good."

"She said that no one thinks much of her down here," McAllister said.

"I don't know about that. Maybe Jack and his woman, Christine. Jack's pretty loyal to his brother and all. But I don't think anyone else really feels that way. Darla is pretty cool, really. She'll probably be down here tomorrow, bringing the kids back. By the way, Sean, I need to tell you something. Derrick is wanted by the FBI. They were here again, just the other day."

"The FBI? What the hell for?" McAllister asked.

"Derrick's still dodging the draft, if you can believe that," Mookie answered. "He's been on the run for a number of years. That's why everyone moved up to Oregon. I guess the Feds almost caught him in Santa Cruz. And now, lately, they've found him up here. You should know about that, in case they come again. When they ask, you can go ahead and say you know him, but you haven't seen him around in a long long time."

"So what does the FBI do when they show up at this kind of place?"

Mookie laughed again. "Sean, you won't believe it. It was just like on television. Here come these two suits, parking in the turnout in an unmarked car, even wearing their sunglasses. They come stumbling across the bridge, but by the time they get to the other side, Derrick has run halfway up Bishop Peak. So the two guys just stand on the property looking around, like they can't believe what they are seeing. They ask if anyone has seen him. Everybody says he hasn't been around, not sure if he is ever coming back. I'm certain they don't believe it, but they turn around and leave. I'm not sure they really want to catch him. Jack told us that Sheriff Haines, the local cop in Pollard Creek, took him aside one day. He let Jack know that the Feds were snooping around for his brother. I guess there isn't much love lost between the local cops and the Bureau, at least for Sheriff Haines."

"No kidding," McAllister responded. "Geez, Nixon and his boys are half in the slammer themselves, and they're still out here chasing people down. Where the heck does the FBI come from around here?"

"Medford maybe, possibly Eugene, I'm not sure. But you'd think they would be a little more undercover, wouldn't you. I mean, Derrick doesn't drive much, but he still drives into Pollard Creek, and into Grants Pass every once in awhile. It's not like he's hiding out in a cave. Weird story, huh?"

"Yeah, I guess so. But damn, who the hell would want to go to jail at this point in time? Most of the guys are finally coming home, and Nixon is on the run himself. It would be a hell of a bummer to get caught now."

There was a rustle in the bushes behind them. Annie came into view. It was almost dark, the late May twilight giving way to night. With the mountain air cooling, McAllister got up and put on a light coat. Mookie James lit the lantern. They sat down at the picnic table while Mookie rolled a joint. Together, the three friends sat for another hour catching up and reminiscing. The conversation turned to their times in Boulder, and Mookie and Annie's move to Santa Barbara. They exchanged updates on others they knew in different places. Then it was time for bed. Meatball was confused. After so much time with McAllister, the dog wasn't sure which way to go. But Mookie made a bed for him on the floor of the van. McAllister felt a little tinge of loss inside. Meatball, his solo partner for so many months and miles, was now moving away.

Lightly stoned and very tired, McAllister lay down on the mattress in the back of the panel truck, the rear doors open to the near quiet of the chilling night. He heard the sound of a car barreling down Lower Pollard Creek Road, rushing by. In the distance, he could hear the muffled downshift of semi-trucks climbing the interstate pass several miles away. Somewhere, an owl hooted a nocturnal soliloquy in the forest beyond. So here he was, his destination reached, another chapter complete. The recent past days stretched behind him, fading into the darkness of an Idaho, a Utah, a Wyoming, a Colorado state of mind. Further east, he thought of Mad's sleeping torso, somewhere in a Pennsylvania dream.

When he had awakened at the rest stop earlier that morning, the melodic other-worldly essence of David Bowie's song, "'Space Oddity" could be heard playing on a nearby radio. The ethereal melody and lyrics of the song had accompanied him throughout the day. The music continued to perform in his head as he closed his weary eyes. He sort of felt like Major Tom, stepping into the unknowns of outer space, the Oregon stars shining beyond.

For the next four days, Sean McAllister did not leave the Mulcahey Farm. He helped feed the goats in the barn corral, as well as the crazy pigs in their torn up pen near the edge of the property. He retrieved eggs out of the chicken coop, hauled water from the spring box to the kitchen. He watched as Annie and Christine baked bread in the oven. He dug beds in the garden, mixing in shovels of manure, lime, and blood meal, planting starts for zucchini and squash.

All the while, he continued to meet and chat with the people. He further got to know the older woman, Betsy, and her three boys. There was Darius, Derrick's pregnant lady Marlene, Christine's friend, Jerry, and a number of others. He listened to the stories of how each had gotten to the Mulcahey Farm. The core group has come up from Santa Cruz, from a farm they called Shamrock Ridge. Jerry had gone to college with Christine, Marlene had met Derrick picking fruit near Medford. Darius had simply been picked up while hitchhiking on Interstate 5. McAllister continued to view the cabins under construction, each unique in style and varying in progress. One evening, he helped Mookie and Annie cook dinner for the group. He heated water for the dishes, learning where things needed to be put. Each step he took was fresh and uncertain.

Back at the campsite with Mookie and Annie, he had begun to set up his own personal world. He built a makeshift table, constructed a plastic rain cover set on poles near the panel truck. He strung a clothesline and hauled over some tree rounds for a place to sit. He made a list of things he needed for whenever a shopping trip would come.

In the evenings he sat with Mookie and Annie, smoking a joint and talking about many things. He mostly listened and asked questions about the Farm, the town of Pollard Creek, hearing the names of other communes like Strawberry Fields and Railroad Bridge further down the narrow valley. Everything was a whole new world waiting to be experienced. But he was beginning to settle in.

On the fifth day, he and Mookie drove into Grants Pass on a town trip. With Mookie planning to get some lumber joists for his foundation, they drove one of the old pick-ups fixed with a lumber rack. Stopping in Pollard Creek at the post office, McAllister paid for a postal box. He stamped and sent himself a letter with a blank piece of paper inside. He would now have an address. With that complete, he could get an Oregon driver's license and apply for food stamps on the next trip to town. For the first time since his arrival, he viewed again the center of this little roadside village called Pollard Creek. Mookie accelerated the truck onto the interstate, heading for the city, twenty miles south.

The trip climbed over the first mountain pass, down into Solace Valley. After traversing the second higher peak, they hit the wider valley floor stretching towards Grants Pass. Not having to drive, McAllister took in the geographic dimensions of this rugged country called Southern Oregon. The Rogue River Valley lay surrounded by the humpbacked intersection of the coastal mountains and the Siskiyou Range, the whitewater river slicing its way through the steep narrow canyons on its way to the Pacific sea. To the east, the Cascade Mountains ran north and south toward the Sierras and the border with Northern California.

In this apex moment of burgeoning spring, wildflowers spread across the hillside meadows, the forested timber gleaming in deep budded green. The morning sun picked its way through lazy cumulus cloud formations, broken across the sky. Southern Oregon was a dramatic and beautiful country, possessive in its reach.

Taking the exit at Grants Pass, a large brown figure of a caveman sculpture stood brooding at the entrance to the town. The shoulders of the figure slumped forward, its demeanor boorish, the arms hanging, weighed down by a club in hand. Mookie explained the sculpture's representation. It symbolized the ancient Oregon Caves geologic formations that were located at the far end of the county. But Mookie joked about its possible truer representation of the Oregon locals themselves.

Entering Grants Pass, the route became a two-way strip of low slung commercial buildings and enterprise, leading to the center of town. When they reached the city center, a sign crested above the width of the one-way street. The words of the sign read simply, 'It's The Climate'. After seeing the sign, McAllister shook his head and looked at Mookie.

"What the heck does that mean?" McAllister asked.

"I'm not sure," Mookie laughed. "But everybody says that whoever came up with that slogan, must have never spent a winter here."

Mookie turned the truck off the main arterial. They drove further on toward a feed co-op business, backing the vehicle up to the loading dock. Inside, Mookie checked the farm list. They loaded hefty bags of animal feed, and a number of bales of alfalfa hay, beginning to fill the bed of the truck. After paying, they drove on to the lumber yard. There, Mookie purchased his framing joists, as well as miscellaneous hardware items. At the local food coop, they continued to stuff the truck with large sacks of rice and flour, a five-gallon bucket of honey and other items. Finally, it was on to the regular grocery store, the truck so full that grocery bags surrounded them on the bench seat of the cab.

Returning to the interstate, the truck veered left and right on the highway, struggling with the heavy load. Mookie slowly chugged up the freeway, sliding to the shoulder as they crept over each mountain pass. Arriving back in town, Mookie turned the truck into the front parking area of the Pollard Creek Inn, saying it was time for a beer. The men exited the truck, walking toward the pillared front porch at the entrance to the building. McAllister looked up to see a man sitting on the outside balcony above, strumming a guitar. Trading eye contact, each of them nodded hello.

Inside the Pollard Creek Inn was a small room that acted as a hotel lobby. To the left, a doorway led towards the human voices of a modestly sized barroom. Straight ahead of them, another door opened to a restaurant seating area with lots of empty dining tables and chairs. Further in the back of its large interior, stood a pair of swinging doors that must have led to a kitchen. In between the barroom and the restaurant sections, a narrow wooden stairway rose to the second floor. McAllister followed Mookie into the barroom, where a woman stood behind the bar. Several patrons were seated on a line of bar stools facing her. In the middle of the barroom was a pool table, surrounded by additional table seating. Mookie went to the bar. He said hello to the bartender by name, ordering a couple of beers. The two men sat down at one of the tables. When the woman came over with the beers, Mookie introduced McAllister. Her name was Laura. She said hello, before returning to her station.

"I'm still trying to get to know everybody myself," Mookie said. "I really haven't gotten off the Farm much since I got here. Especially since Annie showed up."

"I can dig that," McAllister answered him. "It's not like you've got a lot of time to hang out, that's for sure. So what's the deal here, you said some people from another commune bought this place?"

"Yeah, the people from down at Strawberry Fields. Their property is further down Lower Pollard Creek another mile from the Farm. But a lot of the people from their place have moved upstairs, working the business and living here. Pretty cool building, huh."

"I'd say," McAllister said, taking a sip off his beer.

"Someone was telling me the Inn is one of the original stage stops on the early road from Sacramento to Portland. So there is a lot of history to this building." Mookie paused, drinking down a swallow, before wiping his lips. "So, what do you think now, Sean? I mean, about the Farm and all. Oregon?"

McAllister leaned back in his chair, beer in hand, thinking for a moment. "Like I said, Mook, it's a trip. I suppose I'm still breathing it all in, kind of taking it day by day. Otherwise, I really haven't had much time to think about things. It's so cool what you're doing. And it's certainly not Boulder, and it's definitely not back home. I'm thinking I'd like to stay for awhile, what with…."

Suddenly, a loud voice interjected across the barroom. "Hey, girlie!

How about a couple more over here." Two men sat at a table in the back corner of the bar. The tone of the man's request sounded more like a demand.

McAllister had stopped in mid-sentence, looking in the direction of the voice. Both men wore dark suede cowboy hats, circled with leather strips hanging off their brims. Long hair straggled down the sides of their faces. The men were dressed in tee shirts and jeans, with rugged boots on their feet. McAllister caught sight of a sheathed knife fixed to the side of one of the men.

Two other men were sitting at the bar. They shifted in their seats. These men were dressed like twins, both wearing black suspenders over light gray shirts with thin vertical stripes. One of the men was burly in size, with broad packed shoulders. The other man was longer in height, with a lean hard physique. The broad man turned, looking back at the men at the table, staring. He had jet black hair and a pudgy face. "Her name is Laura," he announced. There was a harsh edge to his response. "And I don't believe I heard the magic word. You know, maybe Laura's been on her feet all day. Maybe one of you could get off his ass and give her a break."

The woman behind the bar, Laura, tried to halt the exchange. "It's okay, Hank," she said, "I got it." She turned and reached into the bar cooler, bringing out two more bottles of beer.

The man who had yelled for the beers had leaned back in his chair, a strange smile on his face. "Thank you, if you please, Laura. I reckon we're just a little tuckered out ourselves today."

The broad man, Hank, turned back toward the bar. Laura cocked her head at Hank, as if to tell him no trouble was necessary. The look didn't stop him. "Yeah, like I said, tired from sitting on your ass all day."

The man next to Hank began to shake his head, suppressing a laugh. McAllister turned toward Mookie, as if asking what was next. Mookie had his lips pressed together, also trying not to laugh at the remark.

"What's that Hank?" the man in the corner asked.

"Nothing you need to hear, fella," Hank said to the mirror behind the bar. But he turned again toward the man at the table. "Guess I'm just an old stickler for courtesy," he remarked, continuing his stare. Laura swept around the bar to the table. She put the beers down, picked up the empties and returned.

John Thomas Baker

"It's all right, Hank," the man said. "I didn't mean nothing by it." But the strange smile never left his face.

The exchange ended, as if nothing had happened. McAllister couldn't help but think of Charley Tucker back in Colorado. The demeanor of the guy at the table reminded him clearly of the dead man back in Nederland. He hadn't yet told Mookie about that weird incident. It really wasn't necessary. But here it was again, men challenging each other, often over nothing in particular.

Mookie and McAllister finished their beers, returning outside to the warm afternoon. Stepping off the front porch, they walked out to the open lawn area beside the building. McAllister looked up at the Pollard Creek Inn's large size and breadth. Across an alley was the Pollard Creek Country Store. Chipping in together, he and Mookie bought several quarts of beer and a pack of smokes. But as they returned to the truck, the woman named Darla was standing in the yard. McAllister was taken with her attraction. Her long reddish brown hair glided off her shoulders, her bare feet showing softly in the fresh cut grass.

"Hey, Darla," Mookie James greeted her. "How's it going?"

"Hi, Mookie," she answered, but her gaze pointed at McAllister, their eyes meeting.

McAllister pointed at himself with his finger and smiled. "Remember me?" he asked.

Darla smiled back. "Uh huh. I guess you found the Farm all right."

"Yeah, I did. And thank you so much for the directions. You made it easy for me."

"Your welcome," Darla answered. "So, are you staying for awhile, or just visiting?"

"I guess I'm here for at least a little while," McAllister responded. "Maybe stick around and give Mookie a hand with his cabin project. At least for now."

"That's good," Darla followed. "That way I don't have to say good-bye."

"Nah, he's not getting away that fast," Mookie interjected. "He's got to stay for the summer at least, don't you think?"

The threesome chatted a bit longer. Darla walked with them over to the truck. She pointed to a sign taped on one of the windows that fronted the Pollard Creek Inn. "Did you see the poster about the dance next Saturday?" she asked. "Mookie, you should bring Annie and come in for it. You too," she said to McAllister. "There's always a good crowd of people. It should be fun."

McAllister nodded to her through the open window of the truck. "Sure, that would be great," he answered.

Mookie started the vehicle, McAllister waving to Darla as they pulled away. Mookie gave McAllister a glance, raising his eyebrows. The truck snaked under the railroad overpass, bumping down Lower Pollard Creek back to the Farm. On the fire road, Mookie stopped the truck, putting the purchased beer in the cooler by his van. They continued down to the swinging bridge, where Mookie parked the rig. In the next hour, with the help of others, they hefted the feed bags to the barn, brought the food to the kitchen and larder shed, before trudging the lumber up to Mookie's house site. After dinner, McAllister helped clean up the kitchen before heading back to his campsite. Along with Mookie and Annie, they drank the beer and smoked a joint, before taking an evening walk along the tracks. The twilight sky was burnished in streaks of red out to the west.

The trio strolled along the rails, flanked by the high-timbered stretch of conifers above. The land was silent for a time. But then, the distant sound of a vehicle could be heard barreling on the county road, heading for town. Through a gap in the trees, the automobile flashed into sight above them. The car was painted in red and white, but the vehicle was missing its doors, and had no roof on top. Two men sat in the front seat, their hair flying behind them. The car looked like a convertible missile flying through space. Sean McAllister stared at the sight, his expression awed, his jaw dropping in comic expression. He started to laugh as the vehicle roared onward, disappearing into the trees.

"What in the hell was that?" McAllister spluttered, trying to contain himself. But his laughter couldn't stop. Mookie and Annie gazed at him, but his stricken loss of control was infectious. Mookie read his mind, comprehending the cause of McAllister's hilarity, and began laughing just as hard at him.

"The boys…," Mookie James tried to spit out, "the boys from Loco Landing."

McAllister bent over, holding his side. He couldn't stop his hysterics. "Lo … loco Landing," he ached. "No, … not the boys from Loco Landing?"

Mookie was useless too, his eyes tearing with each word. "Yes," was all he could say, "the boys...."

Annie could only stand back, gawking in disbelief at these two crazy men losing themselves, sharing some ridiculous male understanding she was unable to share. Finally, the two men pulled themselves together, their comic appreciation beginning to calm.

"Whew," McAllister breathed. "I really don't believe this place. It's a goddamn hoot." As he began to settle down, McAllister could not remember the last time he had laughed so foolishly hard.

Annie continued staring at the both of them. "You two," she admonished sarcastically, "it's time to go home." They all turned, heading back for the Mulcahey Farm.

CHAPTER NINETEEN

MY BEST FRIEND
Railroad Bridge / Pollard Creek / May 1974

TOM SULLIVAN FINISHED HIS COFFEE, closing his black journal book with pen in hand. He stood up from the old cushioned chair that sat near the wood stove in his cabin. He placed the journal book and coffee cup on the round spool table nearby, before stretching his six-foot frame. A light spring rain descended outside the cabin. He could hear the familiar sound of dripping water off the roofline hitting the ground. The warmth of his late morning fire was beginning to abate. There was no reason to stoke it further. He intended to go to Glendale to get some laundry done. Then he would return to Pollard Creek for gas, food, and propane. The trip would take up most of the day. He would start a new fire upon his return.

Tom Sullivan packed up the things he needed for the trip. He stuffed the laundry bag with dirty clothes. He put laundry soap, a flashlight, and other items in a small backpack, including a towel, shaving kit and toothpaste, his container of Dr. Bronner's soap and a luffa sponge. He planned on stopping by to see Valerie at the yellow house on Main Street, taking a shower there if she was home. He donned his green rain slicker and beanie hat. Outside the cabin, he found the wheelbarrow. Unhooking the ten gallon propane cylinder for the kitchen stove, he lifted it in. He wedged the cylinder with a couple pieces of split fire wood, bunching the load together with the laundry bag and pack. Pushing the wheel barrow forward, he made his way down the worn path from his cabin, out across the meadow, then further down the road to the railroad tracks.

For the past week, Sullivan had been the only person on the upper portion of the property. Marty Johnson was down in California, on a mission Sullivan was worried Marty might not be able to fulfill. Marty's longtime girlfriend, Celia, had left the property the previous Christmas. Celia had returned home to Los Angeles, to work and stay with her parents. She had vowed to return in spring. Now it was late May and she had not come back. Marty had gone down to check on her, with the intent of bringing her home to Oregon. Tom Sullivan wasn't so sure that would be the outcome.

Railroad Bridge was simply not an easy place to be, especially during the dark Oregon winters. Summertime was a breeze in comparison. Early on, the property had been alive with people, helping build up the land, sleeping in tents and campers. At the outset, everyone believed this was the beginning of a long and exciting adventure together. Railroad Bridge would become a new communal formation. Spirits were high. But the eventual duress of the Oregon rains limited access to the property. The lack of electricity and indoor plumbing began to take its toll. As time went by, the population of Railroad Bridge had withered to four. There was Marty Johnson and Sullivan, Celia's younger brother, Little Kenny, and Marty's close Vietnam buddy, Freddie Jones.

Little Kenny was somewhere up north, working for a Hoedad tree planting crew out of Eugene, but he was expected to return. The nickname, Little Kenny, was indeed a misnomer. Kenny was a twenty-year old, six-foot-three strapper of a kid. Little Kenny had fixed up the old miner's cabin at the edge of the meadow. He had become fascinated with growing the weed. Sullivan was tending to the starts until Kenny and Marty returned. Little Kenny was a bundle of youthful energy, happy to be on his own. Railroad Bridge was no problem for him.

Reaching the tracks, Sullivan could hear Freddie Jones pounding nails, working on his cabin down by Laughlin Creek. Freddie was a keeper as well. Another Vietnam vet like Sullivan, Freddie was happy to be as far away from the world as possible. He rarely left the property unless it was necessary. When Marty had found the money to purchase the eighty acres, the group had arranged for Hank Swain's logging crew to cut some of the remaining bigger timber off the land. Although most of the money had been used to pay down the land debt, Freddie convinced them to use some of the money to purchase an Alaskan mill and several bigger chain saws. As a result, the group had cut and milled most of the rough cut dimensional lumber for their structures. It was slow deliberate work, but Freddie was the mechanical genius and energy force to make it go. Sullivan had learned a lot from Freddie on how things worked. Freddie Jones was an indispensable member of Railroad Bridge.

Sullivan had visited with Freddie the night before, getting his shopping list for a big can of Top tobacco, beer, groceries, as well as a few hardware items from the Coast to Coast store over in Glendale. Sullivan turned the wheelbarrow down along the tracks. At the trestle, he stopped and listened for the sound of the train. It generally wasn't due for another forty-five minutes, but one would be a fool not to check. Below him, the water in Laughlin Creek was still running high with winter melt. It wouldn't be too much longer before they could drive across the creek again, to be able to get in and out with the vehicles. Everyone was more than ready for that opportunity. Summer was right around the corner.

Sullivan pushed his cargo along the metal grating strip next to the tracks. The trestle towered over the narrow canyon below. Three hundred feet down, the rushing creek thrashed its way southwest through steep timbered hills and canyon rock, toward its meeting with the Rogue. Sullivan looked forward to the opportunity to run the river once the summer arrived. During the winter, he had met a rafter in Grants Pass, who had said he would be happy to take Sullivan on a three day trip. On the other side of the trestle, Sullivan lifted the tire of the wheelbarrow over the shiny silver rails of the track. He humped his load down the banked grade of the railroad bed, reaching his pick-up truck parked on the fire road. Loading up, he drove through the trees to the county road, heading for the freeway at Pollard Creek.

After several hours, the laundry and supply trip to Glendale was complete. Sullivan returned south over the pass and back into Pollard Creek. Driving into town, he thought about stopping for a beer at the Inn. But first, he would see if Valerie was at home.

Valerie. What was there to say about her that he hadn't said to himself so often in the past? Valerie Williams had helped to save his stupid ass, in ways the woman didn't even know. But Tom Sullivan knew, and he knew it well. He could still recall the first time he'd seen her, walking across the gas station parking lot on a sunny Saturday afternoon. Valerie had been loaded down with her son, her dog, a day pack strung over her shoulder, her long black hair reaching to her patched jeans below. No, Valerie would never really understand in the same way as he, how her grounded presence and concern had lifted him from his darkness inside. Quietly, without the necessity of something in return, Valerie had given him a future, when so many things had been confused with doubt.

Valerie had loved him when he needed to be loved, yet accepted the reality that he couldn't go much further. It was if she said that everything was okay, let's move on. With that particular understanding, amidst the uncertainties which could have prevailed, he had become deeply loyal to her. It was a loyalty and abiding promise which he intended to keep. Perhaps at times, a strain of sexual desire still inhabited a small corner of his manhood. But he knew better, and so did she. Their platonic relationship had become the best thing for the both of them, without the responsibilities that an expected love might demand. They were good for each other in a way that was difficult to explain. Was this called friendship, or something of a family tie, he didn't know. But it was something he surely didn't want to lose.

When Valerie opened the door, they embraced, each happy to see the other. He brought her some chocolate candies and a grocery bag of items he knew she could use. It was accepted on the surface as a fair exchange, for the hot shower he was about to take. Yet, it would always be more than a simple barter between two parties. Rather, it was the knowledge that someone you could trust would be nearby if things got tough, someone you could call on when trouble or loss ensued. He needed that particular support more than she, but he would always be there for her should such circumstances demand.

"You know, you shouldn't feel like you have to do this for me," she said directly, referring to his gifts.

"Yes, I do," he said equally as a matter of fact.

"Well, take your shower. I have some wine. After you're done, we'll sit and catch up."

Sullivan took the hot shower. It had become such a rare event the last few years of his life. Those years included the long stretches of time in the jungle bush of Nam, where at base camp they would rig up fifty-five gallon drums on platforms to get clean. Those times had been followed by his last two years at Railroad Bridge, where indoor plumbing did not exist. Sullivan brushed his teeth, put on clean jeans and a tee shirt, repacked his toiletries. Looking around the bathroom, he could feel the surroundings of a woman and child's place in a normal home. He returned to the living room, warming himself by the trash burner woodstove, as Valerie poured glasses of wine in the kitchen. An album by the Youngbloods played on the stereo. Valerie owned an impressive collection of records stacked on the floor between a set of concrete blocks. Much of it contained the music of the San Francisco and Bay Area bands she knew so well. Sullivan was aware of Valerie's history in the City, of her proximity to Janis Joplin and others during the early years of the Haight-Asbury scene. That history was part of who she had become.

Valerie handed him the glass of wine, before slipping down into an overstuffed chair. Sullivan took a seat on the couch. Her son, Canyon, was spending the day down at Mulcahey Farm. They conversed with each other about the normal events of their lives. He told her how his cabin was coming along. Valerie had her garden underway, and along with a friend was teaching preschool kids a couple of days each week. But Sullivan could tell something was bothering her, although Valerie didn't speak to it right away. He waited. Eventually she told him of her unease.

A pick-up truck with two men had driven by the house the day before. There had been a rifle resting across the back window of the truck. The men had come up from the state park at the end of the Main Street, the driver yelling something like you hippies better get out of town. The man's shouts had been mean and scary. Although Valerie tried not to show it, she had been frightened by the incident.

Who wouldn't be frightened, especially a young woman with a child to protect. Still, the truth of the matter was clear. There were people in Pollard Creek with an axe to grind. It had been going on for some time. Not often, but often enough. And everyone knew it was there. When Sullivan, Marty Johnson, and Freddie Jones had first set up camp near the county road at Railroad Bridge, somebody had shot at them from the road below. Luckily, Marty had his pistol nearby, firing back. They had managed to get a good look at the rig before it roared away. Nobody was hurt. Nevertheless, for the next several weeks the men had packed either a rifle or pistol wherever they went. They had also quickly moved their camp to the other side of Laughlin Creek, deeper into the property.

At that point the bar at the Pollard Creek Inn had not yet been purchased by the folks from Strawberry Fields. It had been owned by an older husband and wife, and patronized by loggers and the other locals who drank there. One evening during Happy Hour, Sullivan, Marty, and Freddie had walked into the tavern and ordered beers. Although they had already figured out who the shooters had been, they hadn't let on. Indirectly, Marty Johnson told the bartender what had happened. Raising his voice he said they knew the truck. And if anyone wanted to know, if they ever saw it again down near their place on Laughlin Creek, they would blow the fucking rig right off the road. They were Vietnam veterans, Marty said, and they didn't want any trouble in town. But if the truck ever came their way again, next time they wouldn't shoot high. They would shoot to kill. Marty had spoken loud enough for everyone to hear. The men quickly downed their beers, walking out.

One of the loggers, a large broad shouldered man with jet black hair, followed the men outside. He introduced himself as Hank Swain. Swain told them not to worry. Instead, he laughed, telling them that when they shot back, the word had gotten around. Getting to know Hank Swain and his three brothers had become a good thing for Railroad Bridge. And it was surely the reason they had ended up with Hank Swain's crew cutting their timber and becoming his friend. No one had fucked with Rainbow Bridge since that day. But now the hippies had taken over the Pollard Creek Inn. Sullivan guessed that particular reality wasn't going down well with a number of folks. It was hard to figure what might happen next.

Sullivan asked Valerie if she would consider having a gun. Emphatically, she said no. She firmly responded that she would leave Pollard Creek before ever living like that. Sullivan had already expected the answer, but he had to ask. Seeking to calm her fears, he reminded her that the situation was just a few assholes, that most of the town was okay. However, if she saw the truck again, to remember it, get the plate number if she could. She had a telephone, so she should use it to call Sheriff Haines if things got weird. Then he quickly changed the subject. They sipped their wine together and spoke about other things.

Driving back home to Rainbow Bridge, Sullivan expected that Valerie would deal with whatever might confront her. He knew she enjoyed living on Main Street in many ways. She had the house. There were other children nearby, and now lately, the people at the nearby Inn.

She was making lots of friends and the best of summer was coming. But he also understood that Valerie needed a man in her life. Until the right one came along, the care of her son would be her world. Still, he had listened to her concerns about the elementary school. In another year or so Canyon would enter first grade. Jordan County was generally a poor and difficult rural community. The Pollard Creek School had good people trying hard. But when it came to education, it was not California.

Part of Tom Sullivan felt a sense of personal guilt. He knew that Valerie Williams needed a safe home and a man by her side, a happy and educated child. At the time of her coming to Pollard Creek, Sullivan had believed he was rescuing her from the sad prospects of an isolated suburban existence. He was intent on rescuing her from the solitary and troubling reality of a single-parent mother in a world that didn't have time for her. For those reasons, he had encouraged Valerie to join him in this new adventure which he had chosen for himself. It was a new world filled with people who were choosing to live away from an America where only status and money prevailed. But today, he wasn't so sure.

His guilt extended further than this singular concern. Maybe it was he who had needed Valerie nearby, because she meant something more to him than just a friend. Perhaps she represented something he needed for himself, something predictable and necessary that demanded his attention. Yet, for many other reasons, he couldn't go that far. There was no doubt he was feeling better about his life. But the responsibility of love, and the necessary requisites for its survival, remained too burdensome for him to endure. He still needed to be alone with himself, to figure out why he was still alive. And why the others were not. It was going to take more time.

CHAPTER TWENTY

TREAT

The Dance at the Inn / June 1974

RICHARD MILHOUS NIXON COULD NOT BE SLEEPING WELL at night. The boogie man stood outside his bedroom door, silently waiting. It wouldn't be long now. America had begun to turn against the man, the same America that was willing to buy his demonstrations of power and arrogance only eighteen months before. Presidential impeachment proceedings were grinding forward in Congress. A large number of self-righteous political sycophants were getting caught with their pants down. They were high tailing it away from Nixon's criminal odor, while yanking up their drawers from behind a Capitol pillar. No doubt the winds had changed direction in America. In response, so-called men of honor were quick to get it behind their butts, quick to find a lifeboat as the ship was going down. For Richard Milhous Nixon, nobody knows you when you're down and out.

Meanwhile, in the eyes of the authorities, the kidnapped newspaper heiress, Patty Hearst, had become a bank robbing terrorist. Patty had somehow avoided the murderous firebombing barrage of the infamous Los Angeles Police Department. The stand-off between the LAPD and the members of the Symbionese Liberation Army had been viewed by most of a televised nation. Perhaps the war in Vietnam was beginning to wind down. Nonetheless, the effects of the war's insanity would take a longer time from which to recover.

A particular type of leaving had been going on for most of five years, back to the land, hiding in the hills. Many young Americans were separating themselves from the mental illness that had diseased the American mind. They believed there had to be a better way, an alternative destiny, a different and more peaceful American Dream. In July of 1969, a month before Woodstock, Life Magazine had published a story about a hippie commune in Oregon. The story was titled "The Youth Communes / A New Way of Living Confronts the US". Perhaps most of a propagandized America did feel confronted by such youthful choices and behavior. But for those personally engaged in the emigration, 'escape' would have been a truer choice of words. For them, the confrontation days were over, it was time to disappear. The magazine had agreed not to report the location of the commune. But for those in the know in Pollard Creek and Solace Valley, you didn't have to ask.

Hippies, the counterculture, the greening of America. Everything in the good ole USA needed a label, a particular definition in which to preconceive itself, to create a mythos, to sanctify, then later to criticize or eulogize. But more than anything else, to advertise. The most important thing in America was to tailor a fashion in the marketplace, and by that medium foster an economic following. Capitalism needed only a new idea in order to capitalize. And when opportunity knocks, you couldn't be late for the show. Genuine reflection, intellectual and moral inspiration, a confirmed belief in a more progressive and peaceful social order, these were simply not the point. There was no money to be made in speaking the truth. Those types of ideals would only upset the apple cart. And for sure, the big-time marketing boys couldn't have that. So get out there, men, and advertise. Never forget the first commandment of a consumptive world is this: 'Money talks and nobody walks'. Amen.

The Saturday morning in early June awoke to a pastel soft blue, clear of a single cloud. The sun rose alone over the ridge tops of Southern Oregon, drying the wet coolness of the dew within its growing reach. Human hearts welcomed the day with summer anticipations and things to do. Across the tellur of Solace Valley and Pollard Creek, there was a happy and expectant stir about. It was time to get the chores done, then pucker up and head for town. The day of the dance had come.

At the Pollard Creek Inn, everyone began the preparations. They stocked and cleaned the barroom. They threw open the windows, cleared the dining room and set up the bandstand. In the big kitchen, they prepped and readied food to sell. Someone got the lawn mower running, cutting and raking the yard outside, before placing tables and chairs in the fresh green grass. Every which way, the buzz of human activity passed amongst them, with a single purpose in mind.

At the Mulcahey Farm, Mookie James and Sean McAllister worked shirtless in the midday heat, nailing off the subfloor of Mookie's new home. At Railroad Bridge, Tom Sullivan and Freddie Jones rolled logs onto the Alaskan mill, measuring and running the chainsaws, cutting rough one-by siding for Freddie's cabin. On Main Street, Valerie Williams planted starts in her garden, before baking some cookies for the kids, and making a potluck salad of fresh greens. She washed her blue flowered dress, hanging it off the clothesline to dry. Back at the Inn, Darla Bloom finished her work in the kitchen, before tidying up her school bus home parked behind. Throughout the narrow valleys of Pollard Creek and the more open meadows of Solace Valley, people made ready for the afternoon and evening ahead.

As the time of consequence arrived, pick-up trucks and rough battered cars bumped along pot-holed dirt roads toward the paved arterials that led to town. Women and men, with kids scrambling into the back of truck beds, began making their way. They picked up others walking toward Pollard Creek. An early summer pilgrimage was underway.

When the chores were done, a number of people from Mulcahey Farm packed themselves up, driving the three miles to town. Upon his arrival, Sean McAllister was surprised by the incredible number of people that had descended into the center of this small logging community. Parked vehicles surrounded the grounds of the Pollard Creek Inn. Other cars and trucks overflowed down Main Street, or filled the post office parking lot. Young children ran everywhere through the open yard. Tables were stocked with potluck food, coolers sat alongside lawn chairs, iced with beer and other fluids for the kids. People sat in circles or small groups, lazily commiserating amidst the warm afternoon.

McAllister felt like an unknown visitor, a bit overwhelmed by the presence of so many people he had never seen and did not know. He sat on the grass, beer in hand, watching the throng, holding close to Mookie, Annie, and the others from the Mulcahey Farm. A group of musicians gathered with their instruments, beginning to play and sing together.

The woman, Valerie, whom he had met at the post office on the day of his arrival, came by and said hello to the Mulcahey conclave. McAllister had gotten to know her son, Canyon, from his regular visits to play with Derrick Mulcahey's children. Shortly thereafter, Darla Bloom herself came over to the group. Once again, her long loose reddish brown hair glinted in the afternoon sunlight, the dark narrow features of her face smooth against her deep brown eyes. Darla was adorned in a sleeveless one-piece white dress, her long tanned arms soft in attractive contrast, her breasts gently exposed. McAllister said his hello, and after a moment of salutation with others, she sat down beside him.

Several weeks had passed since McAllister's introduction to this new and provocative world. When Darla had told him about the dance the week before, he knew he would come, even if he had to walk the road or railroad tracks to get into town. Now, here he was, with this beautiful woman sitting beside him. Was she older than him, he didn't know for sure. She seemed so relaxed, so experienced in her interest. On the contrary, he felt just the opposite, nervous in her presence. His gaze fixed upon her long brown legs, the lean fingers of her hands, while trying to avoid her eyes. He was forced to remind himself. This was the former wife of Derrick Mulcahey, the charming and eccentric ringleader of the property where he now uncertainly made his home. He knew Darla had a long and unknown history with the Farm, as well as this community he was just beginning to know. She was a mother with two young children. If he dared to look into her eyes, he couldn't be sure what he might find, or where things might go.

Still, when Darla asked him if he would like to see the upstairs' rooms at the Inn, he jumped at the chance, if only just to move. She led him across the lawn to the back of the building. As he walked, he could feel the gaze of other men upon him, wondering perhaps who this stranger might be. It was something you didn't have to see. Perhaps other women were staring as well. However, it would be the men with whom he would have to measure himself in this new and muscular land, to show he was worthy at some future point in time.

As Darla entered the Inn to go upstairs, she pointed him towards her current home, a stubby multi-colored school bus parked in the rear, the windows curtained, a line of potted plants and flowers growing outside. The second floor of the Pollard Creek Inn was like a wild hippie dormitory. The hallways were tight and narrow, the rooms small. Each room was like a crash pad of makeshift beds, posters, colorful tapestries, stereos, musical instruments, and half-burned candles sitting on fruit boxes. The Inn was like a co-ed fraternity of individuals, living upstairs, and working down. According to Darla, three men of individual means had purchased the property. They had originally lived at the commune called Strawberry Fields, further down Lower Pollard Creek Road. Darla spoke their names as if he might know them, or would soon enough. At the end of the long hallway, a door opened to the upstairs balcony at the front of the Inn. Outside, they stood together in the shaded sun, looking down at the parked vehicles, at the people coming and going, and the paved road that led to the freeway. For a moment, McAllister imagined a vision less than a hundred years before. It was one of gold miners and timber men, of rutted roads and stage coaches, of kerosene lamps, and a dry place to sleep for the night. He could only think to himself, what a cool place to live.

Returning downstairs, Darla allowed him to look inside the school bus. Stepping into the entrance of the vehicle, he peered down its narrow interior. A sink and small propane cook stove lined one side, a benched seating pad on the other. In the rear, beyond a small closet, a large bed was built waist-high off the floor, topped with pillows and comforter. Worn Persian rugs carpeted the passageway, the window curtains sewn in burgundy fabric. The décor gave the impression of a warm and cozy cave, secure from the world outside. As he stepped away from Darla's home, their eyes met. He felt stronger now, his nervousness more in check.

"Wow, what a nice little home. Is it yours?"

"You like it?" she asked. "It belongs to a friend. He's gone back to California for awhile. At least I have a place to live. It's temporary of course. One day soon, I hope to get a house where the children can stay."

"I guess that's a long story?" McAllister questioned.

"Too long for now," Darla answered. "You've met Derrick. But one day you will come to know him. I'm not so sure you will like what you find."

McAllister did not respond. There was indeed a certainty in her tone, as if she could say a whole lot more, but not today.

As the swirl of the evening began, McAllister returned with her to Mookie and Annie. He visited for a time with Valerie, getting to know Darla's friend. Later, he and Mookie took to the barroom of the Inn. Once inside, they drank with some of the men of Pollard Creek. McAllister was introduced to a few, listening to their stories, hearing of projects on their land or in the woods.

With the onset of nightfall, the band began to play. The large dining room filled with those of drinking age, the kids playing outside or looking through the windows. When the music rose, almost everyone in the dining room took to floor. There was no choice to be a wallflower at the Pollard Creek Inn. If you were, you either returned to the bar, or snuck outside to smoke. Everyone danced together, sometimes paired, sometimes not. McAllister danced with Annie, with Valerie, and soon enough with Darla. At a break in the music, he shared a joint with Mookie, enjoying the warm evening sky, beginning to catch a buzz.

As the party began to wane, Darla came by and took his hand, pulling him again outside under the stars. There they kissed. His hands followed the torso of her back, her slender hips, feeling her breasts close against his chest. As Mookie and others loaded into the truck to return to the Farm, McAllister took his friend aside, saying he would stay behind. For the first time in what seemed like years, he found the passion of love, the sentient touch of a woman's skin, the ecstasy of his manhood that had been missing for so long. Hours later, he awoke to the morning light, the perfect sun rising above this unknown land, the birds singing the chorus of another beautiful day. The stretched naked frame of a brown-skinned woman rested in his arms.

Yet, just as fast, the moment had come and gone. Darla quickly got up, dressed, telling him she had to work the Sunday breakfast detail. She now appeared distracted and matter of fact. He thanked her for the company and their time spent together. She said she would see him again, before disappearing out of the bus. McAllister dressed and tied his boots, exiting the bus into the day. With no particular plans of his own, he decided to forsake walking down Lower Pollard Creek Road, opting for the railroad tracks and the long walk back to the Farm.

Walking between the rails, the Sunday morning was quiet and still, but for the insects buzzing in heated chorus deep within the weeds.

Again, with time for reflection, he tried to consider where he was leaving from, and where he might be going to. But today, he could make no sense of either. For the first time in his life, or at least his thinking life, his past seemed lost to him, an empty and forgotten book. There was nothing but the faint smell of a woman's breath on the collar of his shirt. As for the future, it was way too early to tell. Perhaps something was out there waiting for him, something he couldn't see. But he felt damn good. The desire of his masculinity had been satisfied. With no strategy of expectation anywhere near his head, the future stretched only as far as the next railroad tie ahead. Then the next, the stitching of worn steel rails curving into the distance. Today, only the moment prevailed, until another moment might take its place. Was this what Ram Dass was speaking to, was this what it meant to 'be here now'? He didn't know for sure. He just kept going along, before he caught sight of Meatball's tail wagging down the tracks.

CHAPTER TWENTY-ONE

SPIRIT IN THE SKY

Sunday Services / Main Street / Pollard Creek / July, 1974

WHOSOEVER INVENTED SUNDAYS deserves to be congratulated for their effort. In Christian societies, the big chief upstairs generally gets the credit. As the old story goes, on the seventh day God rested, after working all week creating the world. One thing for sure, the invention of Sundays was definitely good for America. At least there was one day a week where the people could take a break from running hirsute down the road of life. Sundays acted as a short reprieve from working your ass off toward getting closer to death, towards that mythical place called heaven, where every honest dream in your heart would finally come true. Then and only then, you could spend the rest of your presumed eternal life living happily ever after.

So thank god for Sundays. If not for that day, America would be a very sad place indeed. There would be little room for any amount of human reflection, no time to enjoy the natural world, to stop and smell the roses. No time for pondering the mysteries of life, whatever they might be. Without Sunday, every day might become a full tilt boogie toward conquering the earth, of mastering some safe and secure moment, until death did you part.

Unfortunately, way back in the past, some unidentified bullshit merchants had gotten a hold of a bullhorn. They had begun to pronounce that paradise was not of this world, but of the next. So it was best to be a good boy and girl, to do what you're told, and your reward would be in heaven. And who's to argue? It's not like one could prove otherwise. To be honest, if one took a real hard look, any wayward thoughts of heaven on earth sure didn't appear to be a very safe bet. So why not join the crowd and get with the program. Take a minimal chance, and perhaps be on the good side of fate. Like the preacher says, roll the dice on eternal salvation and you won't be forsaken. Still, it was surely a hell of a wager, putting all of your eggs in one basket, gambling on the certainty of eternal life. On the other hand, what did you have to lose?

Meanwhile, back here on earth, the really big serious mullah, the 'good shit' as they say, was flowing to the top. It was hard not to notice that those boys with the bullhorn were driving around in silver Cadillacs and living in fancy shacks. Somehow, they had become experts at defining the devil's work, while honing their skills in the artful manipulation of divide and conquer. It wasn't your fault the world was such a mess, they proclaimed. Don't worry, you soon would be saved, for you were part of the Almighty's chosen few. The real problems in this world were caused by those godless neighbors of yours, living down the block. They were the devil's children, beware of their temptations. Paradise is at your doorstep, your salvation awaits its deliverance. Just one more thing. Before you leave today, reach into your pockets because the collection plate is on its way. Remember the first commandment for eternal life. It is always holier to give, than ever to receive.

The Pollard Creek Alliance Church was a simple rectangular framed building. The exterior clapboard siding was painted white, its standard-sized windows trimmed in Oregon green. A modest steeple was mounted above the gabled roof of the structure. A single religious cross was fixed to the small porch that led into the church interior. Inside the hall of worship, wooden pews stretched forward to a raised platform stage, where the pulpit stood. Further back to one side, there sat a small organ and chair for the organist. Two large speakers hung in the back corners of the modest sanctuary. Behind the pulpit, a brass-plated crucifix faced the holy brethren, where the Son of God hung in mortal distress.

Reverend Roland Whitman stood at the pulpit on this summer Sunday morning in mid-July. The number of people in the congregation was larger than most summer Sundays, which pleased him greatly. Behind the church, connected by a short open breezeway, was a small two bedroom home, where Roland kept quarters with his wife and his single daughter. Roland Whitman had grown up in the city of Roseburg, about forty miles north of Pollard Creek. The faithful flock of this small mountain community was not unlike those of his old home town. These were people of the woods, the hard-scrabbled timbered hills of Southern Oregon. They were people of ordinary means and simple ways, much like the church in which they quietly sat this morning. They were very much like the man Roland Whitman had become.

Roland Whitman had never crossed the borders of the State of Oregon, not even to California. After finishing high school, Roland had moved directly to Portland for his divinity education. Upon his graduation and ordainment, he became an assistant pastor in the farming town of McMinnville, located in the Yamhill Valley, southwest of Portland. There he had met his wife, Melissa. They soon married and birthed their daughter, Penelope. For several years, Roland carried on the work of the church. But when the opportunity arrived to become a pastor in Pollard Creek, he returned with his family closer to home. Although Roland had never worked the woods, his pale thin frame certainly not meant for such an occupation, he understood the hardened challenges of the timber faller's kind, their sometimes rough and tumble ways. He understood their occasional failings with sin. He could speak to them, helping to quietly shelter them under God's forgiving wing. At times, this was not an easy task, but it was a calling with which Roland Whitman was familiar, a duty he felt compelled to fulfill.

For in Roland Whitman's mind, there was a right way and a wrong way in the secular world of man. And Roland, as a man of God, was obligated to distinguish between the two. Mercy was a tool that could be used to confront the dangers of sin. Forgiveness could only be granted to those who chose to be forgiven. Tolerance was the grace of God that men of faith could dispose towards those who wished to be saved. They could enter into the House of the Lord, and be sanctified within His flock.

But sadly, there were others for whom the Devil held sway. These were the evil sinners of the world, for whom all chance of redemption was unattainable. For these lost souls, there could never be a divine resolution. They were a scourge and danger upon God's green earth. And they must be vanquished by any means necessary. It was imperative to protect the holy cause of God's children, to save them from the evils that sought to engineer their fall from grace.

Today's sermon would speak to those dangers. Roland would announce the devil's appearance in Pollard Creek. Currently, there were evil spirits whose presence could contaminate his flock with their sinful ways. Roland knew that the roughneck logger, Jake Beecher, and his crusty wife, Shirley, would not be in the congregation this morning. Their own particular salvation might take some time for Roland to convince. But the Beechers' fears and hardened opinions were stirring the community, and Roland needed to speak to his troubled flock today. As they were insisting, Pollard Creek was facing an onslaught of sinful newcomers. These people were a godless horde of disturbed youth, who by their sordid ways of living, threatened the moral fiber of this holy town. And so he began.

"A disease of the soul has infected Pollard Creek" Roland Whitman intoned from his pulpit of influence and authority. "There are strangers amongst us, whose activities threaten the fabric of our moral conscience, the god-fearing sanctity of our common good. Within earshot of where we sit today, we hear the drumbeat of the devil's march, the evil sounds of a sinful cancer that seeks to invade our body of Christian health. We are overwhelmed by the unwashed minions of a nation under siege, the ungodly sickness of an atheistic intent. Within an arms reach of our children's safety, our very own elementary school, we hear the music and immoral drumming of this careless tribe, who smoke the devil's grass, who carry on throughout the day and night. These desperate Pharisees ignore the righteous ethics of our Christian lives, and by their purposeful lack of respect, they disease the holy contract we make with almighty God. They seek to sever our cord of sustenance with everlasting life."

"Today, only footsteps away from our sacred and devout church of faith, where we sit in honor and grace this very morning, a house of red lights brashly beacons in the night, calling men and women to violate God's law of stricture and chaste. Day after day they parade down the center of our streets, the heart of our village life, unrepentant in their immorality, snubbing their noses at the decency of our virtuousness in the eyes of the Lord."

"We are called upon by the necessities of this abrogation against our reverence, to respond to the challenge of this sinfulness in our midst. Under both the laws of God, and the laws of man, we must do so with kindness and restraint, but do so we must. As Jesus Christ cast the wayward from the temple of Jerusalem, we must concert together to do the same, to rectify this intrusion within the heart of our community. We must vanquish their temptations. We must sanctify again our temples and our homes. We must remove from the vision of our creator this unsightly tumor that continues to grow. May God bless you, my brethren, in the communion of this holy mission."

Sean McAllister stepped out the kitchen door of the Pollard Creek Inn. The late Sunday morning was heating fast. Darla Bloom had fixed him some breakfast, after his sleepover with her in the school bus the night before. Darla again had a shift cooking the Sunday morning brunch. Consequently, it was time for him to walk down Lower Pollard Creek back to the Mulcahey Farm. As he crossed the green yard of the Inn, Laura Hale, one of the several women who lived upstairs, was practicing her skills on a pair of conga drums. McAllister took a moment to say hello. Ever since he had begun spending time with Darla, he was beginning to meet more of the people who lived together at the Pollard Creek Inn.

Today, McAllister decided to walk the road, hoping to catch a ride, rather than walk the railroad tracks all the way back from town. There had been no necessary reason to break down his camp set-up at the Farm, simply to drive his panel truck into Pollard Creek. Most of the time, it was easier just to catch a ride from somebody at either the Farm or up on the road. In fact, this travel chore had become a good way to meet people heading in and out of town. He was slowly becoming familiar with more and more of the community, in this place he might be calling home.

At the intersection of Main Street and Lower Pollard Creek, he waited as a dusty sedan pulled up to the stop sign. Inside the car, an older man sat behind the wheel, his wife beside. They appeared to be wearing clothes that reflected a Sunday morning attendance at church. McAllister waved a silent hello as they passed in the car. But in return, he received a distrustful and hated look of disgust from the woman, a harsh response of contempt that surprised and unnerved him. There was no question of her staring intent. It was an intolerant and pointed expression of distaste, loaded with a prejudice impossible to ignore.

McAllister had heard that there were people in Pollard Creek who had no time for the hippies who now resided in their town. But this was the first time such an obvious rebuke had been directed at him alone. Although this unanticipated castigation had caught him off guard, it would not be the first time he had experienced the hated look of others at the way he was perceived. He had done enough hitchhiking and protesting over the years to know well those looks of hate. But on this beautiful summer morning, he had not been prepared for its effect. He tried to let it go from his mind as he walked further toward the railroad overpass. But being the object of hatred has a way of hanging around for awhile, of disrupting one's otherwise oblivious equilibrium. Its unanticipated appearance leaves an image in the mind that demands some response, even if that response is simply to try and forget. Subconsciously, Sean McAllister carried this insult the rest of the way towards home.

Margaret Benjamin treaded down the porch steps of the Alliance Church, following the cement sidewalk out to Main Street. People from the services were gathering outside on the tiny front lawn, making salutations and small talk amongst themselves. Margaret would not be one of those people, especially today. In fact, Margaret Benjamin was quietly upset. Pastor Whitman's sermon this morning had been like an arrow to her heart. She had sat through his dangerous provocations to the very end, afraid of leaving in its midst, and thus by doing so, bringing attention to herself. But this was not the kind of sermon she had come to hear. It was not the type of Christian missive she had sought upon awakening today.

Margaret Benjamin could feel a strange sense of nausea in her stomach. She wanted so much to be part of the Pollard Creek community, to be a member of its greater amalgamation. She desired to share in its spiritual responsibilities, to be a helpful participant in aiding its public need. Pollard Creek, Oregon was a very poor human circumstance, with many economic and personal tribulations. Margaret wanted to be of service in her time here. Her own personal faith required her to do so. As a practicing Christian, she believed in the responsibility of the church to do good works, to help people who couldn't help themselves. She trusted in human understanding and love for all mankind. But this pastor, Roland Whitman, appeared to hold a different view. It was a view that spoke of retribution and separation. And even more so today, a view that was completely untrue.

Margaret Benjamin could easily have been labeled as a target today. And she felt as much. She and her husband, Bob Benjamin, had moved to Pollard Creek to forge a new life experience, to forsake the materialism and negativism of an American culture that had lost its way. They had come to raise their children in a different climate of simplicity, to become closer to the earth, amidst a community of people that shared the same intents. Together, she and Bob had bought their small homestead on the edge of town for that very purpose. And for Margaret, the church would always be part of that calling, an institution of justice and generosity in the attainment of those beliefs. But these beliefs were not the words she had heard this morning.

Margaret Benjamin reached the pavement of Main Street. Turning left would be her way back home. At the end of Main she would walk past the Pollard Creek Inn, before passing through the open triangle that rested in the center of town. She would cross the access road that ran to the freeway, before walking past the '76 Station to a small dirt road leading to her farm behind. Her husband, Bob Benjamin, would not be waiting for her today. Indeed, things in their own life had changed. Bob Benjamin had become a wanderer, either back to California, or to one place or another. Sometimes he would come home for a rest, before eventually becoming absent again.

For most people, when reaching your mid-forties, you generally would have settled down, made Oregon your home, put down your roots. But for Bob it had become just the opposite. Bob and Margaret had grown up in a time when you went to school, graduated, got a good job, before settling down to raise a family. And this was what Bob and Margaret had done, after meeting and falling in love in San Francisco. But as time went by, other needs began to assert themselves. Bob had begun to look behind his own particular age and generational peer group. He had begun to witness the young people that were following behind him, young people who were forsaking the expected routines of adulthood, and choosing other ways to live. Bob had become intoxicated with their new lifestyles, convincing Margaret that they must pursue this different path. As for herself, Margaret had been uncertain. The kids were early teenagers, needing the stability of a normal home. But for Bob, the die had been cast. They ended up selling everything, before moving to Pollard Creek to begin a new life.

Since that time, Margaret had worked hard to keep the family together. But Bob's restlessness had only become more acute. He was not a homesteader, woodsman, or farmer. Once unwound from his past and the standards of society, he became more and more ethereal, a dreamer and thinker, a lover of the occult. With these changes, his marijuana habit grew each day. Then began his wanderings, sharing his passions for astrology, numerology, and the world of the spirit. Margaret let him go. Her husband was a good man, an honest man, but a man who could no longer cope with the everyday. Upon his leavings, Margaret became just the opposite. She dug in. She planted a huge garden. She allowed young people looking for a place to live to share her home in exchange for work. She had home-schooled the children, canned and dried vegetables, sewn her own clothes, raised chickens and goats. All the while, she maintained her faith in the teachings of Christ, in her fellow man, and the necessity of community service. Bob Benjamin was on his own path of realization, and Margaret was content with hers. But whenever Bob returned, he would always have a home.

Although the walk back to her farm turned to the left, Margaret had no choice but to turn to the right. She slowly paced down Main Street toward the state park at the end of the road. She remained disturbed by the sermon and its terrible fabrications. She was quietly compelled to share its implications with Valerie Williams. For Margaret Benjamin did not need to be told as to which house Pastor Whitman had been referring, with his charges of prostitution a short time ago. Valerie Williams deserved to know what Roland Whitman had proclaimed. Not only of its specific untruths, but more so for the safety of the woman and her child.

Pastor Roland Whitman had tarnished his position as a man of god. These young people at the Pollard Creek Inn were not agents of the devil. They were simply young adults living their lives like many others in America. Perhaps they were careless and foolish at times, filled with opinions born of inexperience, but they were nothing close to the evil presumptions of which the pastor had proclaimed. In fact, for Margaret, it was the opposite perspective that was more to the point. There had recently been those dastardly written signs on the telephone poles in town, or the cries of 'hippie faggots' from pick-up trucks driving nearby. And now, Pastor Whitman's cruel and mendacious accusations were adding fuel to this fire. These were the flames of intolerance that threatened Margaret's community. But to accuse a poor defenseless woman of prostitution, this sad situation had gone much too far.

Margaret Benjamin and Valerie Williams had become friends during their time in Pollard Creek. Valerie was a beautiful young woman, a good mother to her child. Yes, many young men and women came by Valerie's house, sometimes to visit or take a hot shower, but mostly to drop off their kids. Margaret had helped Valerie with her notions of setting up a preschool for the children in town, including the communal children who lived in the surrounding hills. Certainly at times Valerie could not be missed. She liked to dress in her colorful clothes and floppy hat. Being from San Francisco herself, Margaret understood. Valerie was a former flower child of the Haight-Ashbury. And she could sometimes be intensely outspoken, exhibiting the freedoms of expression of which she truly cherished and believed.

But this was not the Haight. This was Pollard Creek, an under-educated land of woodsman and paternalistic mores, a land of mountain hamlets far from the progressive urban enclaves of San Francisco. For many in this community, California was a demon land of sinners or smarty pants pinheads who thought themselves better than you. Margaret Benjamin had reached the accustomed wisdoms of middle age. She had seen and comprehended the insecurity and fears that beset the white natives of these timbered mountains. She could see the negative emotions and response that these young people were creating in Pollard Creek. Reactions they themselves could not see or understand, or were only becoming to recognize. Today's sermon spoke to those irrational perspectives, now being further fueled by Pastor Whitman's careless accusations.

It was not difficult to comprehend, if one could see the view from the other side. Hundreds of people so different from yourselves, invading your neighborhood, acting as if they had lived there forever, unconsciously brazen in their particular view of themselves. It was a sure-fire recipe for prejudice, and the dangerous confrontations that prejudice can cause. Valerie needed to know to be careful, to be cautious in her innocence, vigilant to the possible results of circumstances she might not be aware.

Valerie Williams did not waste time. She roamed nervously around the house, finishing the dishes, straightening up the living room, making up the beds. Distracted with her anger, she bumped from one chore to another like a pinball, inefficient in her movements, thoughtless to the tasks at hand. She wished she could telephone Tom Sullivan, tell him of this second crazy circumstance that had just landed in her world. But Railroad Bridge, like so many other properties in Pollard Creek, did not have a phone to the outside world. No matter, she insisted to herself, it was not Tom's problem. She would confront this news on her own, as she always had to do.

Margaret Benjamin had found Valerie sitting in her front yard, the garden watered, enjoying the Sunday sun before seeking some shade from the heat of the day. Margaret had been dressed in a modest summer outfit, her hair bunched up cleanly above her head, wearing nylons and brown pumped shoes, a small church book in her hands. Margaret displayed the appearance of an old farmer's wife, a woman of the land and a time gone by. She was an older woman with a generous loving soul. But on this Sunday morning, Margaret Benjamin had acted like a schoolmarm, serious in her presence, delivering cautionary news of the preacher's sermon just up the street.

Valerie had not shown the emotion of worried fear that coursed through her heart upon hearing Margaret's report. Instead, she refused to let it show. She thanked Margaret for her dedicated telling, before letting her go. But now, Valerie's anger was building as the effects of the words sank in, dictating a required response. But she needed to settle down, get her act together before challenging the situation. The house work was helping, but not very much.

Why her? What the hell was this fucking redneck town to her, these crazy people and their hateful intents? Part of Valerie wanted to run away, to escape such unadulterated misperceptions, such outlandish lies and malfeasance. A part of her wanted to pack up the car and her child, to immediately leave these poisonous fools behind. But hell no, that was not her way. She had a house and a garden. She had many new friends. She had a young boy enjoying his precious childhood time. She would stand up and face this bigotry and deceit. And she would do it alone, like she had always done before. However, a weaker part of her wished to see Tom Sullivan, to help give her some support.

The mix of anger and fear is a strange concoction. It can prompt such a multitude of consequences, some unintentional and dangerous, others brave and liberating in their effect. Valerie steeled herself calm, washed her face and hands, combed her hair. She changed out of her torn jeans and halter top, put on a plain summer dress with a higher neckline, yet lacing up her work boots to strengthen her intent. Her son, Canyon, had stayed overnight at the Mulcahey Farm, playing with the kids down there. She would pick him up later in the afternoon. Valerie decided to walk over and see Darla Bloom at the Pollard Creek Inn. It would give her time to build her courage, before going to the church. But Darla, and the others on the Sunday brunch crew were busy with the kitchen work. There was nothing for Valerie to do but head for the church.

Valerie crossed back towards Main Street. Pastor Whitman was out on the lawn with a push mower, cutting the small green area that bordered the entrance to the church. He subconsciously looked up and saw Valerie coming his way. Furtively, he put his head down, staring back to his work. From Valerie's perspective, Pastor Whitman was a thin, pasty white man, with a cropped receding hairline. He was dressed in a short sleeve collared shirt and long cotton pants. He was as straight as they come. Upon seeing his body language and his attempt to ignore her, Valerie was emboldened. Her fears disappeared in an instant, replaced by a surging confidence and spirit. She had him pinned down, and she knew it. Valerie walked right up on the lawn, standing before him. Roland Whitman did not look up right away.

"Pastor Whitman," she stated. He stopped pushing the mower, raising his head to face her, trapped.

"Yes, yes I am. What can I do for you?" he acknowledged. He tried to summon his authority with an impression of calm understanding, but Valerie saw through the veil.

"Pastor Whitman, my name is Valerie Williams and I live down the block. I've heard about your sermon this morning, and I need to get something straight. I believe you know what I mean."

"I'm not sure I understand," he started. "Miss Williams did you say?"

"You know very well, Pastor Whitman, the house with red lights. The house of prostitution as you referred to it. My house," she said emphatically. Valerie watched as the Pastor held himself still, searching for a response.

"I'm not sure, I'm not sure I know…."

"You're not sure what you said," Valerie interjected? "You're not sure of your own words. About the whore house down the street. About the red lights blinking in the dark. About people coming and going all hours of the day and night. Is that what you're unsure about, Pastor Whitman?"

"No. I mean yes, I mean…dear woman."

"No? Yes? Which is it, Pastor Whitman? And don't 'dear woman' me today. You don't know me, and you don't know my life. And you don't know that it's not a red light in my house at night, but a blue light. A night light, Pastor Whitman, for my son to find his way to the bathroom, or to my bedroom when he awakes from a bad dream. No, you don't know that I have a lot of friends. Friends who come by to use my phone, because they don't have one of their own. Friends who come by to take a shower, because they have no hot running water. Or friends who come by to drop off their child to play with my son. Friends who come by to visit, just like every other house on this street, including yours. You don't know me, do you Pastor Whitman? But you think you do!"

"I wasn't necessarily referring…."

"Yes, you were, you know you were. Enough to make your congregation believe the lies you wanted them to hear. Enough to speak those lies in your own house of God. And that's what they are, Pastor Whitman, lies and untruths. And you know it, you know it very well."

"I was told, I was told by someone I trust, that these events were occurring. It was my duty as pastor to bring them to light. Perhaps…, perhaps I should have spoken with you, brought these reports to your attention. Perhaps…."

"No, you weren't. You made them up yourself. You made them up because it fit your sermon. It fit how you and others want yourselves to believe. Now I want you to know, Pastor Whitman. You remember this. I want you to know, if anything happens, if anything happens to my son, you will be responsible. That it will be your lies and hate that caused it. And I will talk to Sheriff Haines tomorrow, and tell him what I believe. Do you understand? I am a mother with a young son, living here and raising my child. I am not a prostitute, or whatever you might say. And I expect that next week, you will tell your people the truth, and not the lies you have spread today."

Valerie turned, starting for the street, walking away. She had said her piece, and that was enough. As she reached the pavement, she heard the man try to respond.

"I never said anything about hurting anyone," Pastor Whitman attempted.

Valerie stopped, turning back to face him. She stared at his wilted figure, the worried expression that hung through his face and eyes, the uncertainty of possible consequences that might seek to betray him.

"Hurt anyone?" she questioned. "Hurt anyone?" she repeated. "You already have!" Then Valerie Williams strode fiercely away from this poor sick man, heading for home.

CHAPTER TWENTY-TWO

TELL ME ALL THE THINGS YOU DO

Letter to Mary Jane / July, 1974

Hey Janie,

How goes it these days? How's life in the Big Apple? Bloomingdales, huh? Design and fashion work. Who would have thought? Are you still going to every second-hand store in the universe? I bet. In a way, I guess it makes sense. You've always liked to dress weird. And you know I mean that in a good way.

Sorry to hear you and David didn't make it. Is he still around? Did he finish law school? Is there anyone else, although you've never had a problem with the boys. Damn if you didn't get all the looks in the family. But did you have to get all the brains too? It just isn't fair.

I spoke with Mom and Dad last week. I called from a pay phone in this little Oregon town. Spoke to Dad for like thirty seconds. I guess he is still bummed that I appear to be a drifter and wasting my life away. It's a bit of a bringdown for me, because I'd like to tell him about all my travels. But he just says 'talk to your mom', then hands the phone over to her. So I just tell Mom that everything is great and not to worry. When you get this letter and talk to her, just tell her it's all going well. Which is actually the truth, and not a lie for the most part. I suppose they both are getting used to us not being around that much. As long as Dad has the boat and his golf clubs he should be okay.

Well, where to start? I've been here at this commune in Southern Oregon for about two months now. My good buddy Mookie James is here, as well as his girlfriend Annie. I don't think you ever met Mookie, but he is a friend from college. I'm helping him build a cabin on the property. I'm also feeding pigs, working in this huge garden, and help cook meals about once a week.

The two brothers that started this place really want to make it a sustainable farm. I'm learning a lot. The one brother, Jack, is this big quiet guy. He doesn't talk much, mostly I guess because he has a stutter, but he sort of knows everything from animals and farming to fixing trucks and equipment. The commune would be lost without him. The other brother is the talkative one. He's got the big ideas for the farm, always looking for deals and trades, and what to do next. In a way, he's sort of got a power trip going from time to time, but not like some religious ethic or anything. Still, everyone tries to stay out of his way, including me.

I know when you think of Oregon, you think of lots of rain. But it's actually high summer now, hot and dry every day. There are probably twenty or more people here, all coming from one place or another, but mostly California. I'm still living out of my panel truck, but I've got a nice camp set up. And I met a girl in town that I've been seeing from time to time. Her name is Darla. Through her, I've met other people who live in the town. There are maybe seven or eight other communes in the mountains around here. Some are pretty strong in their efforts. Others are more like a crash pad where everybody does their own thing. All in all, there are a lot of cool people everywhere, especially a lot of women with kids. Everybody is just living off the land here so to speak, or at least trying to. Although if people didn't have some welfare money and food stamps coming in, it would be pretty hard to make it here. There's not much regular work.

I don't know how long I'll stay. I've got a little of my own cash left, but not much. Some of the commune folks are planning to go up to Washington in late August to pick pears and apples in the orchards up there. I'd like to do that, too. I've never been to Washington, the state, and I definitely need to make some money. In a couple of days I've got a job loading hay, so that will help. Whatever money we get from the work, we give some of it to the Farm, then keep a little for ourselves. That's kind of how it works around here, at least as far as I can tell.

As I write this letter, it's early afternoon, and believe me it's hot. Not hot like the east coast, we don't get the high humidity that occurs back home. But it's more than hot enough. Some of us are going over to the swimming hole down on Laughlin Creek pretty quick. It's a really cool place. Got a deep spot where you can climb up high on the rocks and jump in. But Mary Jane, you got to dig this, you can't really wear a bathing suit or you would stick out like a sore thumb. Nope, it's like a 100 percent skinny dip scene all the time. You can imagine that took some getting used to, with all the girls nearby. But somehow I'm managing. Snicker, snicker. Hey, I've got to stop now. I'll write more tomorrow, before I send this off.

Okay, I'm back. The next day, but a beautiful evening now. It really cools down in the mountains at night. But today was another hot one, just like yesterday. Not a single cloud in the sky. It's getting so dry that the loggers have to shut down working in the woods by one o'clock. The fire danger is already off the charts, and it's just the middle of July. Speaking of the loggers, that's pretty much the economy around here, working in the woods. A lot of the local men wear black denim pants with suspenders, and gray shirts with vertical lines called hickory shirts. They have heavy black boots with spikes on the bottom they call 'corks', so they don't slip while walking on the logs. There are a couple of lumber mills in the next town over the mountain, called Glendale. Some of the locals in Pollard Creek work there. They mill the logs into lumber of all different sizes. It's really hard work, but not as dangerous as cutting the trees. There are a few of the hippie guys getting into the work, but mostly just on the land they own. It's not like the locals are especially fond of the hippies taking their jobs.

It seems for the most part, everyone tries to get along. But there are some folks who really want to run the hippies out of town. They have been putting up signs on the telephone poles, saying the longhairs need to go. It's not like there's all that much trouble, more like you just don't know who is thinking what. I guess there have been some shooting incidents in the past, and guys trying to run hippies off some of the old mining claims further down toward the Rogue River. But most of the hippies pretty much keep to themselves, especially those of us at the Mulcahey Farm.

But you never know, from time to time you can feel the tension in town. A group of people from one of the communes, called

Strawberry Fields, bought an old bar and hotel right in the center of Pollard Creek. A lot of the people from that commune are now living in the rooms at the hotel, while they work the bar and restaurant downstairs. It's the only bar in Pollard Creek, so you can figure what that means. Nothing bad has happened yet, but it makes you wonder sometimes if it will.

Yeah, it's pretty much a crazy scene here. Hippies, loggers, gold miners and such, all living in the same place. And a lot of Vietnam vets, too. As you might figure, those guys pretty much just want to be left alone. I couldn't tell you how many, but a lot for sure. Most everyone has a gun or rifle somewhere, either hidden or on display. It sort of feels like the Wild West here sometimes, or maybe Easy Rider, take your pick. A long way from life in the east coast, I'll tell you that.

But you'll dig this story, too. One of the Mulcahey brothers, Derrick, the one I mentioned earlier, the leader one, damn if he isn't still running from the draft. The FBI has been chasing him for years. He went to Canada at first, but then went back home to California. But they got onto to his trail down there. That's pretty much why the brothers bought this land here in Oregon in the first place. But now the FBI has even been coming to the property looking for him. When they do come, Derrick just hides in the woods until they leave. Shit, you'd think the FBI would have better things to do, with the war finally winding down. Some people say the Feds are really looking for Patty Hearst, and looking for draft dodgers like Derrick is just an excuse. Who knows for sure, but I thought you'd appreciate that little tidbit.

So what do you think? Is Nixon finally going down? I don't get to see any television, although I do pick up a newspaper from time to time. The people who do have electricity and a television, they get like one or two channels out of Medford, and not very good reception. I hear it's pretty funny to watch the local news. It's like the minor leagues for news reporters. Some of the guys at the Pollard Creek Inn tell me they like to smoke a joint and watch the newscast, just to see the reporters screw up. Like I said, this place is a long long way from home.

Anyway, I guess I'll close for now. Don't be telling Mom about this stuff, please. Let's just keep it between you and me. As far as Mom needs to know, it's a beautiful and safe adventure, with lots of good things going on. I'd like to think I could get back home for Christmas. And

Mookie has talked about it too. He's from Cherry Hill on the Jersey side, just outside Philly. Anyway, maybe we can pull it off. I know I can't make it through an Oregon winter camping out like I am now. So it's hard to say what the future might bring. But for the time being it's a great place to be.

So be well and take care of yourself in the meantime, and write me whenever you can.

Your brother,
Mickey

CHAPTER TWENTY-THREE

BAD MOON RISING

Troublemakers / Pollard Creek / July 1974

JAKE BEECHER NEVER WENT TO CHURCH, but that damn sure didn't keep him from knowing God's will. And it was damn sure time for God to get off his ass. That's exactly what Jake had told Roland Whitman, that milk-toast preacher down on Main Street, and anybody else who would listen. People had to listen to Jake Beecher. Because even if they didn't care to, they damn sure would hear it anyway. The devil himself had arrived in Pollard Creek. And damn if he wasn't drinking, smoking loco weed, and cavorting with women, right in the middle of Jake Beecher's private town.

Jake Beecher didn't have much time for right or wrong. That was beside the point. Or even the law for that matter. Those were damn sure things that just got in the way. You didn't let the deer eat in your garden, you didn't let the coyotes or the cougars get into your chickens or livestock, and you didn't let no government man come on to your property with some silly papers in hand. Hell no, that wasn't how God or Jake Beecher intended things to be. More than anything, you damn sure weren't going to let a bunch of ragged faggot longhairs from San Francisco or wherever, take over this place. Damn sure about that.

Now, the worst had happened. A few of those hippies had some serious money, and shit if they didn't up and buy the Pollard Creek Inn. There was a whole shitload of them faggots from one of those communes down on Lower Pollard Creek, living right smack in the center of town. Hell, a man couldn't even go in for a shot and beer without some dirty longhair taking his money with a stoned out smile on his face. But Jake Beecher would damn sure fuck the lights out of one of their welfare mommas, if he ever got the chance. He'd check for crabs and fuck her good. Teach those little faggot boys a lesson or two on how to be a man in these parts.

He'd gotten the wife, Shirley, to make up all those signs. Shirley put them up on telephone poles at night, right in the middle of things. 'Keep Oregon Cleen, Chase A Longhare Out of Pollard Creek', and other good sayings. Shirley was likely down at the Inn right now, having her afternoon wine with the girls. She'd be sitting right there in their own fucking living room, and nobody would know the better. Sooner or later, some of those boys would pay for laughing about her spelling, damn sure about that.

Deputy Bill Haines would get his, too. That asshole sheriff was too damn kindly to those people. Must be back about two years ago now, there was Haines, coming up on Jake's own goddamn property, asking him, Jake Beecher, if he knew anything about the gunfire down on Laughlin Creek. Pretty much telling him, that Jake and his nephews, Solly and Jed, might be suspects if any more trouble might come of it. Solly and Jed, those two damn lamers, they had protested high and low that they didn't spill the beans. Hell, according to Solly and Jed, it wasn't the law that was making them lay low. It was more that those goddamn hippies from the Railroad Bridge had started firing back. Word was that those hippies knew who done it, and the next time they wouldn't miss. Then Solly and Jed started whining that old Jake should have told them that those boys from Railroad Bridge had been in Vietnam. What the hell did that matter, a hippie faggot is a hippie faggot, Vietnam or no Vietnam.

Then that damn Haines also starts warning Jake that rumor had it that Jake Beecher was the one threatening that really tall boy down near the river. Trying to chase the boy off his claim on the Tujunga Mine. I'm just doing my job, Jake, Bill Haines had said, saying a crime is a crime and all that bullcock. Haines was just giving Jake a warning he said. But Jake Beecher wasn't about to forget the messenger, damn sure about that.

For too long these long-haired boys, and all their women and kids, were buying up the land or filing mining claims with the BLM. They were like a horde of cockroaches taking over the damn territory. This was Jake Beecher's home, his state, his country. They were strutting around talking all that peace, love, and commune crap about making a better world. Well, it wasn't a better world for Jake Beecher. It wasn't a better world living next to a bunch of draft dodgers, faggots and dykes, pot smoking hippies and welfare mothers. All with their goddamn kids running around half-naked every day. It sure wasn't a better world seeing them animals down at the swimming holes on Laughlin Creek, lolling around with their dongs and tits hanging out. Just like Jake told that puny-ass preacher the other day, enough was enough. It was time to circle the wagons and save this town.

Crazy Randy Halston set his feet, pulled the rifle barrel to even horizontal, firing. The empty beer can popped straight up in the air, did a couple of three-sixty degree flips, before bouncing off the tree stump onto the ground. The sound of the gunshot echoed through the valley of Cougar Gulch. Halston aimed and fired again, another empty can doing the same. He brought the rifle down, holding it in his left hand. A cracked wooden table was placed just to his right, its paint peeling away. On it, a half-full can of beer sat next to his ammo box. Randy downed the beer in one raised gulp, tossing the container onto the ground. Wiping the frothy remains from his mouth, he reached into the ammo box to reload.

Buck Thornton stood behind Crazy Randy, beside the table. Buck filled a bong pipe with another pinch of weed. He raised the pipe to his mouth, clicked a cigarette lighter, drawing in deep. The bong gurgled with the intake, the smoke exiting away as he drew a hit deep into his lungs. Buck Thornton began coughing hard as Crazy Randy pushed the bullets into the chamber. He handed Randy the pipe and lighter. Randy Halston put down the rifle, repeating the ritual, holding the smoke inside. He breathed it out strongly without a cough. Placing the bong back on the table, Randy once again picked up the gun, turning away toward the targets. He fired two more rounds exactly as before, with the same results. Then, Halston put the gun back down on the table, reaching into the pocket of his flannel shirt for a cigarette.

The two men stood next to each other in the rough stumped meadow, behind a dilapidated mobile home, surrounded by the rusted solid waste of broken machinery and automobiles. Attached to the mobile home was an unpainted plywood addition, roofed in tar paper and shredded blue tarps. In the distance below the men, they could look down upon Cougar Gulch. The road cut a potholed and pounded-gravel path deep into a narrow mountain draw amongst the timbered hillsides. Scattered along its way were other residences and trailers, some in better shape, some not. There was only one way into Cougar Gulch, and one way out. Rumor had it that strangers were not invited, and sometimes never returned.

The two men wore holstered pistols on their right side, sheathed buck knives belted on their left. Each had straggled long hair underneath buckskin brimmed hats that were soiled with sweat. Their teeth were yellow and at a premium, their blue jeans torn over rough heeled boots. Crazy Randy Halston let the burning cigarette hang from his lips, as he gazed across the valley. A soft afternoon breeze pushed cumulus clouds above, temporarily blocking the sun.

"So, are we going down to the bar?" Buck Thornton asked.

"Sure, why not." Crazy Randy answered.

"When do you want to go, man? We need some more beer and smokes. And we need a loaf of bread to go with the venison stew."

Crazy Randy drew off his cigarette, letting the smoke blow slowly from his lungs. "I don't care, it don't prefer me. We still got whiskey?"

"A half fifth, I reckon," Buck answered. No need to go to Glendale today. But I got to tell you something, Randy, something important. That skinny-assed Jew boy down at the Inn asked me real nice yesterday to start leaving our heat outside the bar. I told him we'd think about it. He said we were scaring some of the other customers and the girls working the place."

Crazy Randy shot a look over at Buck Thornton. He took a last drag on the cigarette, before pitching it away. "Fuck those people. I'll do what the fuck I please. What the fuck, they get some idea they own the fucking place."

Buck Thornton laughed at Halston's joke. "Shit, Randy, they do own the fucking place, like it or not. Hell, you want to get eighty-sixed out of there or what?"

"Fucking whiny little creeps. There's too many people, always telling you what to do. Fucking reminds me of the joint. Lights on, lights out, clean you're fucking toilet. Eat now, eat later, strip down to your ass. I've had enough of all that fucking shit for one lifetime.

"Whatever, man," Buck pleaded. "I'm just telling you what they said. They got little kids running around the place. Hell, Randy, you know those folks are all right. They don't want no gosh darn trouble."

"They're still fucking people," Randy Halston answered emphatically. "All the fucking people, all the time telling you how to live. They can all suck my lily-white ass."

The men went inside the mobile home to get their money. Returning outside, they climbed into Halston's dented blue four by four, its primer spotted paint job covered with red summer dust. The truck roared to a start, bouncing down Cougar Gulch until they got to the paved county road. Randy Halston floored the truck hard, taking the men to town.

CHAPTER TWENTY-FOUR

U.S BLUES

The Powers That Be / Grants Pass, Oregon / July, 1974

Jordan County Commissioner Wilton Parker didn't have to be a mind reader. He knew what the several men and one woman in this room thought of him. As far as they were concerned, Wilton Parker was just another downstate good-old boy. Just another stick-in-the-mud they had been sent here to deal with, in order to enforce the legislative gospel emanating from the Oregon state capitol up in Salem. The group sat in the jury room of the Jordan County Courthouse. The jury room often acted as a meeting room when the Superior Court was not in session.

The lone woman was from the State Board of Health, and Wilton Parker was a little confused why she was here. Also present was State Police detective Barry Walton. Not sure why that arrogant little asshole was here, either. As for the others, Wilton Parker had a good idea. The head honcho of this little gathering was Assistant Attorney General David Hinson. Sitting beside Hinson was the regional director for the new State Building Department, Craig Benson. Benson was another piece of work, a real flamer. Wilton's only friend in the room, if you could call him that, was County Prosecutor Jeremy Morris. Morris acted as legal counsel for Jordan County when things got dicey with the people from state.

It was a mid-July afternoon, pushing over ninety in the direct sun. A worn air conditioner sat in one of the jury room windows, its fan motor beginning to whine, trying to keep things cool. The other two Jordan County Commissioners were conveniently on vacation, one with her family rafting down the Rogue River, the other probably running his quarter horses at a track somewhere in eastern Oregon. So it would be left to Wilton Parker to take this different blast of heat coming out of Salem. Assistant Attorney General Hinson wasted little time in getting to the point.

"As you know, Wilton, this is simply a statewide mandate. And Jordan County is not moving expeditiously toward the statutory application and regulatory enforcement of these new standards. Mr. Benson, as our representative down here, feels that the County is dragging its feet on this matter. He believes that there is evidence of a steady and persistent amount of non-compliant building construction occurring in your jurisdiction, particularly on private residential property."

Wilton Parker knew that he and the other Commissioners were somewhere between a rock and a hard place. But he would give it his best shot. "Let me remind you, Mr. Hinson," Wilton began, "Jordan County prepared a comprehensive county-wide zoning plan that took almost two years to complete. As you well know, that plan was put before the voters of Jordan County, and was roundly rejected. You must understand that Jordan County is not Portland or Salem, or even Eugene or Medford for that matter. As a result of this defeat, the County is essentially back to the drawing board on these issues. We are being diligent in attempting to fashion a zoning and growth plan that will be both acceptable and fair to the people of Jordan County. We have not been stalling on these difficult circumstances."

Wilton Parker continued. "We are indeed making progress in Grants Pass, and should have something appropriate in the coming months. The rural communities of Jordan County are obviously more resistant. The people of these areas are generally opposed to public regulation of their land and property. Not everyone mind you, but most without a doubt. We are not dragging our feet. We are aware of the need for some element of public control that protects the property rights of all concerned. But this is not an easy task. It takes a lot of understanding and patience in order to establish a blueprint for growth. At the same time protect the private rights of our citizens. We are moving forward down here the best we can. But any premature expectations by the State of Oregon for a swift resolution, only makes the job more emotional and difficult. This is what I'm telling you."

"I understand some of the difficulties you face, Wilton," Hinson answered. "The State of Oregon is fully aware of the time and effort necessary to put a comprehensive zoning ordinance in place. And Jordan County, like all the other counties in the State of Oregon, has a significant amount of leeway in establishing those parameters for growth. You have a generous amount of discretion and variance under the current statewide zoning laws. But Wilton, you are missing the point. These zoning issues are not necessarily why we are here today, although they are certainly a concern. Our primary purpose this afternoon is the lack of a proactive approach by Jordan County in regard to the recently mandated state building codes."

Wilton Parker had figured the smokescreen he had tossed out probably wasn't going to work. He had tried to get this guy Hinson on another track, but the man was returning to the real issue for which they had come.

"Let me attempt to be as clear as possible," Hinson continued. Any building to be constructed in the State of Oregon, will now be required to go through a permitting process. And that process is going to require that each and every building in Jordan County meet accepted industry standards in regards to structural integrity and safety. Now, it is Jordan County's responsibility to establish certain particular policies and procedures within the confines of these state mandates, in order to effectively enforce this legislation. Local zoning issues obviously are significant in establishing the types and number of buildings that would be compliant on a particular piece of property. But according to Mr. Benson, there appears to be reluctance by Jordan County in moving forward with the application and subsequent enforcement measures under the new state law."

Hinson went further. "It is important that you understand that Mr. Benson is ready to assist the Board of Commissioners in establishing these measures of compliance. However, in the interim, I have accepted Benson's request for pursuing a process of assessing the degree of the problem. That is, identifying particular building projects that may be underway, especially those that might be in direct violation of the new state code. I have advised the Attorney General in regard to this matter, and he agrees. Enforcement of the law needs to begin, while your board moves forward toward establishing its own procedures. As far as our offices are concerned, this can be done quietly and without undue public discussion or debate. I hope I have made myself clear. This is now Oregon law, and we expect it to be applied statewide.

A rock and a hard place, forget that. What this suited lawyer from Salem was insisting Wilton Parker to do, was going to get him thrown right out the courthouse door, flat on his proverbial ass. Wilton Parker was well aware that a lot of hippies had come into this county in the last several years. They were building one crazy structure or another upon the land they had purchased, as well as the mining claims on which they were squatting. Nobody would have a problem with shoving a stick up their butt if possible. But Wilton's real problem was the other side of the coin. Whenever you start telling every farmer or rancher in Jordan County that they got to stop building a barn or tool shed on their own property, well, that's a horse of a different color. You start telling them that they've got to come into Grants Pass with their hat and wallet in hand, begging for a permit to build on their own goddamn homestead, well, nobody needed a picture to figure that result. Wilton Ambrose Parker would be DOA, dead on arrival in the next election cycle. No doubt about that.

And Wilton had no illusions about Craig Benson. This guy wouldn't waste a minute before running around the county red-tagging every resident with a hammer and nail in his hand. Wilton Parker's only hope for re-election would be that Craig Benson, or one of his surrogates, might get shot full of holes on their first misadventure. He looked over at Jeremy Morris, the local prosecutor. Morris had been around long enough to know the deal. But Morris just sat there quietly shaking his head.

Hinson started up again. "Now, there is one other matter today that we would like to discuss. It concerns the Pollard Creek Tavern facility in Pollard Creek. We have begun to receive some complaints at the state level in regards to alcohol and health compliance issues at that particular establishment. Have you been aware of any similar complaints by residents in that community concerning its operation?"

Wilton Parker had a funny feeling that something else was up today, or why would this woman from state health be along for the ride. Again, he looked over at Jeremy Morris, as if to ask what he might know.

Morris, the prosecutor, cleared his throat. "Well, yes, we have had some calls. We looked into it, and we spoke with our local deputy Bill Haines in regard to those complaints. The Pollard Creek Inn, or Tavern as you call it, was recently purchased by a group of young people in that community. According to Deputy Haines, there exists a small element in Pollard Creek who are not particularly happy with that situation. However, based on our initial assessment of the problem, the complaints are strictly personal in nature. In small communities like Pollard Creek, something as simple as a change in business ownership can often create animosity amongst the residents."

Morris continued. "Now it is true, that here in Jordan County we have had a large influx of young people in the last several years, particularly from California. Some people may want to call them hippies, or longhairs, or whatever. But if these people are not committing crimes, or otherwise threatening their community, then there is no legal prerogative to become involved. Certainly, Pollard Creek has a reputation for being what one might call a reckless community. But unless we have evidence that certain crimes are being committed, we have no direct cause to become involved. Specifically, in regard to the complaints to which you are referring, this does not seem to be the case. In fact, according to Deputy Haines, the opposite may be closer to the truth. Any incidents of harassment in Pollard Creek appear to Haines to have been instigated by this very same group of residents who are lodging the complaints."

There was a long pause in the jury room. Wilton Parker sensed that the assessment by Prosecutor Morris was not exactly what the state people wanted to hear. Hinson broke the silence. "As you may know, the Pollard Creek Tavern has been determined to be of significant relevance in the history of our state. It is one of the last remaining stage stop locations, dating back to the late 19th century. Some time ago, the Oregon Historical Preservation Commission noted this particular significance, and when the previous owners offered the property for sale, the State of Oregon expressed a desired interest in purchasing the site. Unfortunately, the owners chose not to engage in that potential sale. Instead, they chose to sell to the current ownership. This was obviously disappointing for all concerned.

Hinson went further. "Now, less than a year ago, the new ownership made a formal request for a liquor license with the Oregon Liquor Control Board. And as part of the process, the Control Board received a favorable recommendation from the Jordan County Commissioners concerning that application...."

If ever there was a light bulb to go off in Commissioner Wilton Parker's head, right now it snapped on like a flood lamp. If he hadn't been certain before where this whole little confab might be going, it was now barreling into his eyes like the headlight from a freight train.

"Yes," Wilton interjected, "we reviewed that application as part of the process. The background checks and other relevant information, as presented by the Control Board itself, showed no evidence of criminal history, nor any particular conflicts of interest, which of themselves would have posed a concern. There were no circumstances that would have prevented anything but a favorable recommendation from the Board." Wilton Parker could feel his blood starting to run. "Tell me, Mr. Hinson, just where in blazes are you going with this matter?"

The Assistant Attorney General pushed himself back from his chair. He looked over at State Police Detective Walton before answering. "Commissioner, it has come to the attention of the Oregon State Police that a number of public health and safety violations have been occurring at this location. According to Detective Walton's investigation, there appears to be a number of incidents that pose obvious legal concern. The state liquor control inspector has reported that on several occasions children have been seen passing through the barroom area of the facility. These children have either been unsupervised, or clearly after the requisite hours normally allowed for their presence. Detective Walton has also been advised that a number of individuals are currently living in the upstairs portion of the premises. Many are assisting in the operation of both the food and beverage sales without the required health department certifications. Also, that these same residents are preparing food for themselves in the commercial kitchen area, without adequate oversight, and in direct violation of health department rules."

"More serious and problematic have been reports received of armed weapons being carried by customers into the establishment. These weapons have been witnessed both inside and outside the facility. Now, I will admit, none of these reports has led to any formal agency complaints. Nor have there been any criminal charges against either patrons or owners of the establishment. Nonetheless, these reports are a grave concern to both the state police, the state board of health, as well as certain members of the Pollard Creek community. We felt it was important to bring these concerns to the attention of the Board of Commissioners, as well as the Sheriffs' Department and Prosecutor Morris."

Commissioner Wilton Parker shot a glance over at Detective Barry Walton. He wanted to get up and wipe that pretentious smirk off the little man's face. Little men with little dicks, Wilton thought to himself, that was Walton. This particular state cop had caused more trouble during his tenure in Southern Oregon than he would ever hope to find. It was getting difficult to find good quality policing in this part of the world. Good local men who would take on the job. Good men, like Bill Haines up in Pollard Creek. In most cases, you had to settle for rogue cops out of Los Angeles County, who had surreptitiously retreated to this part of Oregon. Wilton knew that those cops out of LA had ended up in his neighborhood for reasons that didn't show up on their application resumes. Those boys down south always protected their own, regardless of their previous conduct as officers of the law.

Was Hinson sending a message? Goddamn right he was. Did the State of Oregon want another shot at the Pollard Creek Inn? Hell, nobody had called it the Tavern for years. Damn right they did. Wilton Parker wasn't born yesterday, he understood this deal. The State of Oregon was setting things up, just waiting for the right opportunity. And no doubt in Pollard Creek it would come, with all the flakes and crazies in that part of Jordan County. It was only a matter of time. When it did finally happen, the state would immediately pull the license, slapping a bunch of liquor and health violations right behind. The state would throw as much mud as they could muster up against the wall. And you could bet they would fully expect Wilton Parker, Prosecutor Morris, and the other two Commissioners to give them the appropriate cover.

In the end, it was a simple no-brainer. The state would cut the owners off economically, essentially starving them out. Shortly after, they would come along and offer them a deal they couldn't refuse. It wasn't that Wilton Parker was any fan of a bunch of dope smoking hippies from Pollard Creek. The State of Oregon owning the Pollard Creek Inn wouldn't necessarily be a bad thing down the road. And perhaps Hinson might go a little easier on this building inspection trauma that was definitely going to kick Wilton Parker's ass. But it surely didn't make Wilton Parker feel any better about the world, this new goddamn world of political influence and gratuitous deceit.

"Well, thank you for bringing this matter to our attention, Mr. Hinson. You can be assured that we will look into this information from our end. Now, I think it's time for Mr. Morris and myself to get back to our duties for Jordan County. But Wilton Parker couldn't help but express his true feelings in some personal way. He gave both that little prick Walton, and that compulsive 'yes man' Benson, a stern look. It was a look that said, 'Kill'!

CHAPTER TWENTY-FIVE

IN THE HEAT OF THE NIGHT
Pollard Creek / July, 1974

THE '53 CHEVY PICK-UP BUMPED ALONG the Lower Pollard Creek
Road, returning to the Mulcahey Farm. Mookie James steered the
truck. Sean McAllister sat beside him, holding two silver milk canisters.
One was held in McAllister's arms, the other between his legs on the
floor board of the truck. The two men had awakened very early, driving
down to the nearby pasture and milking barn where the Mulcaheys'
kept their two Jersey cows. The Mulcaheys' had bartered for the use
of the property from an older retired couple now living in Pollard
Creek. The exchange was for a regular delivery of milk and eggs. Twice
a day, every day, someone at the Farm had a large chore to handle.
For farmers who owned dairy cows, there were no weekends and no
vacations. Mookie James had gotten the hang of the milking routine.
For Sean McAllister, it was a whole new ballgame.

Hand milking dairy cows was not an easy task. It took an acquired
skill to grab two female teats in your hands, squeezing and pulling the
milk into a pail with one easy motion. McAllister was beginning to get
the rhythm of it, but there were distractions aplenty. One had to get
accustomed to the cow's tail occasionally slapping your face, or perhaps
worry about a disgruntled hoof knocking you out. If it wasn't your
head getting cold-cocked, then it might be the metal pail, with the milk
spilling lost on the barn room floor. Often, the cow might decide it
was the perfect time to relieve itself, letting go with a huge green cow
pie slapping the deck. There was nothing quite like a gooey piece of

slime finding your lips. With the chore complete, the teats were greased with bag balm, before rousting the cows from the barn. It was a most unusual way to begin a summer morning.

Reaching the Farm, the men poured the milk into gallon jars, wrapping the tops in cheesecloth with a rubber band. There, the jars would sit, letting the cream rise to the top. Later, once the cream was scooped, someone would take the jars to a refrigerator at the Harkness' place next door. The Harkness' place had electricity, the Farm again bartering with the neighbors for the use of additional refrigeration, as well as some freezer space to store their meat and other perishables.

About a week before, McAllister had met someone new at the Pollard Creek Inn. This person had referred to the Mulcahey Farm as a 'Viking camp'. McAllister could surely now understand their perspective. All you had to do was take one look at Jack Mulcahey, with his broad football shouldered frame, his wide face, his blonde red beard and curly hair, and you didn't have to be convinced. Throw in an outhouse, no electricity or running water, and the Viking picture begins to come into focus. Add a few chickens getting their heads cut off, with boiling water and feathers everywhere, and who could argue. The Mulcahey Farm was something of a pioneer lifestyle, as old as the history of America. One thing for sure, the current expression of 'going back to the land' might have an idealistic earthy ring to it. But one better be prepared for some blood and guts, the constant smell of animal manure, and a lot of dirty work to perform every single day.

Mookie brewed a pot of coffee in the kitchen. McAllister sat on a tree round, idly paging through a recent copy of Mother Earth News. On a bookcase sat a variety of cookbooks, *Joy of Cooking, Diet for a Small Planet,* the *Tassajara Bread Book,* and others. Stacked in a pile below, sat a worn copy of the *Whole Earth Catalog,* several *Foxfire* and gardening books, and a few heavy texts. The texts were books on animal husbandry and farming techniques, the last remains from Jack Mulcahey's college days at Cal Poly in San Luis Obispo. All were informative elements of practicality, related to food preparation and the farming work at hand. However, they were not the only books on the Mulcahey Farm.

On the far side of the property, a small wooden building, sheathed in barked quarter poles, acted as the library for the Farm. Inside the library was an old cushioned chair, a kerosene lamp and night table, surrounded by shelves of various reading collected over time. Books were a mainstay on the Mulcahey Farm.

The first warm body to arrive in the kitchen was the oldest kid, Jesse Simmons. Jesse was seventeen years old, with a long straight ponytail running down the length of his back. Thin and wiry strong, Jesse was a bundle of human energy, blessed with the smart aleck confidence of a kid his age. Jesse was Jack Mulcahey's right hand young man, a workaholic dynamo ready to perform whatever farming task might need attention or result. McAllister really liked Jesse Simmons. The kid had a brash sense of humor that poked fun at you. He was always trying to make you a little uncertain of your place. But Jesse's irreverent jabs were always delivered with a love of fun, laughing along with his intents. There was never a sense of meanness or complaint with Jesse Simmons. He was simply a wise-ass kid taking his shots.

Jesse Simmons was far from book smart. He was a school-age boy who had become hidden from the rest of the normal adolescent world. For years, he had played the role of Derrick and Jack Mulcahey's adopted farmhand servant, but not necessarily in a manner of control. Jesse was a willing participant in his position. He was always ready to please the two men who had taken him under their wing at a very early age. Jesse had begun to call Mookie James and Sean McAllister the 'college boys'. It was obviously a jab meant to unnerve them and their inexperience in a world Jesse knew so well. But both Mookie and McAllister took the barbs in stride, knowing the boy meant no harm. It was just his way of standing tall. Perhaps it masked a sense of youthful insecurity for Jesse, a response to an ordinary childhood he would never get to engage. There was a good chance Jesse Simmons would never receive an academic degree of any kind. But for such a young man, he was already the magna cum laude of a real and practical experience. He had become the ultimate survivor at a very young age.

In the hour that followed, more and more of this loose band of communal adventurers made their way to the hub of the Mulcahey Farm. With the summer in high arc, the population of the Farm had grown in number, as friends, family, and other wayward travelers had come to visit. More coffee and breakfast ensued. People traipsed in and out of the kitchen, either engaging in conversation, or making work plans for the day ahead. Sean McAllister was beginning to feel a sense of belonging, of being part of something bigger than his own singular life. He was now sharing with others the duties of a daily survival, the preparation of food for immediate sustenance or winter preservation, the building of shelter, the learning of skills necessary for living together.

At the Mulcahey Farm, there were no rules written on a stone tablet that met you upon entry to the community. There were no commandments or oaths of allegiance and fidelity for which you had to swear. The goals and structures of the Mulcahey Farm appeared to be unspoken. You could come and go as you pleased, with the understanding of what needed to be done being your only responsibility. The Farm appeared as a unique consensus of expectation and common commitment, willingly shared. It was indeed an intentional community, but without rules or regulations requiring adherence to a cause. Rather, it was more a feeling of expectation and shared aspiration, of which you wanted to be a part.

At least up to a point. Webster's Dictionary defines utopia as 'an imaginary and indefinitely remote place', or the even harsher definition, 'an impractical scheme for social improvement'. Thanks a lot, Webster's. Talk about a categorical bubble-bursting expression of eventual doom. Did the people at Webster's just have a bad day at the office? Did they lose their wallet or car keys, or get stood up on a date? But more than likely, maybe something called history was tragically at play. The people at Webster's needed a word for something that is perfect, but that can never be attained. And the word 'utopia' seemed to fit the bill. Whatever its etymological determination, the word was definitely a bummer when looked up in the dictionary.

But perhaps in the instant case there is another way of looking at things. For example, take a simple deck of playing cards. Take them out of the pack and shuffle the deck. Now remember, somewhere inside the deck is a card you can't control. It is a card that will either bless you or curse you with its presence in the game. It is a card that might fulfill your dreams and expectations, or shatter them with its play. There is a name for this card. It's called the 'wild card', or the 'joker' to be more precise. The Mulcahey Farm appeared to have been dealt a clean hand. But the joker, the wild card, it had to be out there somewhere. And it just might be lurking under another term, an alias perhaps, a name called Derrick Mulcahey.

Meanwhile, at the Pollard Creek Inn, one summer day simply blended into the next. Not that there wasn't a calendar nearby, just that it didn't get much attention unless to fix a date. Every day was a holiday in most people's minds, so who the hell needed a chronological road map to distinguish one day from another. Each day was the mantra of the moment, with the next one coming right behind. Someone once said that innocence is bliss. They must have been referring to the Pollard Creek Inn.

Most of the Pollard Creek Inn's new residents had emigrated from Strawberry Fields, a loose confederation of hippie wanderers, mostly from New York or San Francisco, or refugees from the long continental American highways that stretched in between. Albert Krieger, a tall man with a delicate and generous heart, had purchased the eighty acres off Lower Pollard Creek Road. Albert had given the land its name. In three years time, Strawberry Fields had become a phantasm of communal experience, a free and mystical land of peace and love. It was a collection of tents, campers, and tee pees, and eventually a towering house of log and lumber, simply called the 'Big House'.

The Big House may have been a place that allowed for the privacy of mind, but certainly not the privacy of person. Everyone slept or lounged in the huge sleeping loft upstairs, while communing during the day in the spacious living area below. If the phrase 'come together' ever had a meaningful physical manifestation, Strawberry Fields met the requirement. The Big House was the ultimate communal test-tube baby, right down to the expansive clothes closet which everyone shared.

People came and went, left and returned, coupled and uncoupled, alone or together. But as time went by, the test-tube baby began to grow and shed its skin. By most accounts, it was a late-twentieth-century creation, and its genetic makeup was scientifically confirmed. In other words, the baby needed its own space. The roots of its genealogy were born of the melting pot, bred from a pluralism of the American experience. But equally as necessary, it needed to assert its individualism, its own singular expression. The facts of the matter were simple, the baby eventually wanted its very own room.

And so the Pollard Creek Inn was the perfect alternative. The Inn would provide the virtues of a common collective reality. But in addition, you could now have your very own cave in which to retreat and dwell with yourself. Privacy can be a beautiful thing. Not to mention hot running water and electric light, or the luxury of a black and white television set, where you could watch Johnny Carson late at night. As a result, most of the core of Strawberry Fields packed up and headed for town. They were ready for another adventure, but one which included the personal space to be their private selves.

Albert Krieger had much of the dough, compliments of a family trust. The other partners who invested in the purchase were probably a little less legal, with some quiet laundered cash to seal the deal. There would be a bar and restaurant to run, a job to do in their own communal way. But at the end of each day, one would be able to retreat upstairs to their personal time and space. As a result, the fun and games were about to begin. Call it a fraternity or sorority house, whatever you choose. The Pollard Creek Inn was as old as America, living upstairs and working down, a hippie business enterprise in the center of town. Whatever its ancestry, it was something of a magical gas.

Jimmijay Connell sat on a sturdy limb of a large spreading oak tree, smoking a joint. The tree stood just outside Jimmijay's second-story bedroom window at the Pollard Creek Inn. The limb had grown close enough to the window of Jimmijay's room. He was able to work his way onto it, then scramble further into the leaves, sitting unnoticed by the world below. The July afternoon temperature was hot. Jimmijay's room was hot. It was a wee bit cooler in the shade of the tree.

The weekday afternoon was almost silent in the heat. The only sounds to be heard were the buzz of insects in the yard, the muffled tires of an occasional automobile passing by, or the slow grinding acceleration of a tractor-trailer pulling out of the Hungry Dog Cafe. It was siesta time, or swimming-hole time. Work in the woods would be shut down for the day, with people seeking the shade and darkness of cooler places, out of sight.

There were probably a few loggers drinking an afternoon beer inside the bar. Tired from their heated work, they would be conversing quietly about their jobs, or perhaps the other trivialities of daily life. Later, the night shift would be a completely different story. When the scorching Oregon sun finally fell behind the timbered hills, the comfort of evening would be warm and captivating, inviting people into the night. Jimmijay Connell didn't have to work this evening, but he more than likely would check out the scene. The bar promised to be busy, with lots of people to engage.

Although most people didn't know, Jimmijay Connell was one of the founding members of Strawberry Fields. Not by choice, but rather the circumstances of fate. At sixteen, he had run away from his Chicago family, hitchhiking west. Hitchhiking is often a long forgotten story, but its destinations are generally remembered. For Jimmijay, his runaway journey ended at a house on Broderick Street in San Francisco, his last ride taking him there. San Francisco had become a city accustomed to young kids wandering its streets far from home. Albert Krieger, who had been renting the house on Broderick Street, generously let him stay. Shortly thereafter, when Albert and others headed north to Oregon to look for land, Jimmijay was allowed to tag along. Within a month, Albert Krieger had purchased the Strawberry Fields property, and Jimmijay Connell spent the rest of the summer camping out on the land, helping to begin the foundation for the Big House.

But one day in August, Jimmijay Connell got a message that his older brother was about to be sent to Vietnam. Afraid it might be the last time he might see his brother alive, Jimmijay Connell returned to Chicago, leaving Strawberry Fields and Oregon behind. A year later, Jimmijay was himself in the Marines, destined for Vietnam. And as fate would have it, almost four years to the day that he had first walked upon Strawberry Fields, he knocked on the door of the Pollard Creek Inn. To his obvious delight, Albert Krieger hugged him as if a long lost brother. After Albert's consultation with the other residents, Jimmijay was invited to stay. He sometimes wondered where he might be if the decision had been negative. What a long strange trip his life had become.

Jimmijay Connell was ever the prankster, and the Pollard Creek Inn allowed him the freedom to live out his full personality. The Marines had only been another way to get out of the house and on his own. The military had done their level best to harness his spirit, but his wits prevailed, and so here he was again in Pollard Creek. Jimmijay was a clever comic of mind. He loved the eccentric musical compositions of Frank Zappa and Captain Beefheart. They had become his heroes of brash sardonic humor and cultural rebellion.

On restless nights, Jimmijay Connell made up radio shows, making tapes of recorded music, acting as the disc jockey in between. He wrote wild radio advertisements, playing the different voices, inserting them between the songs. In the mornings, he would play the tapes in the kitchen of the Inn, the men cracking up at his jokes, the women just shaking their heads as they prepped food for the day. He had created a radio personality for himself, a disc jockey and stand-up comedian ready to burst upon the public stage. His alter ego now became known as 'Jerry Fisher'. Day by day, 'Jerry Fisher' was beginning to replace Jimmijay Connell in both name and persona. Jimmijay welcomed this personal transformation. He was ready to become a heralded figure, if only in his very own mind.

Sitting in the oak tree, Jimmijay Connell watched as a familiar young teenager walked down below. The boy sat down under the shade of the tree, pulling out a suede stash bag and loading his pipe. Jimmijay silently watched as the kid took a big hit, holding it in his lungs, before breathing out the smoke in a long smooth exhale. Jimmijay knew the kid. He was Margaret Benjamin's wayward long-haired son. More than likely, the kid had probably crossed the access road from his mother's farm, seeking the perceived protection of the Pollard Creek Inn to smoke his weed. Jimmijay stealthily changed position on the tree limb, letting his torso hang down from the limb with his arms. Then, steadying himself, Jimmijay let go, falling to the ground. He landed with a thud next to the kid.

The teenage boy virtually levitated about three feet to his right, rolling over in the grass, leaping up, his heart in his throat. "What the...." was all he could get out. Upon landing, Jimmijay had crashed sideways to the ground, breaking his fall. But Jimmijay quickly pushed himself upright, smiling at the boy with a Cheshire grin. The kid backed away several steps, before halting and trying to speak. "Where the hell did you come from?" he stuttered, his eyes still wide with the remnants of his shock.

"Excuse me, young man. I didn't mean to frighten you. But can you tell me, is this planet earth?"

"What?" the boy implored.

"Planet earth. I've just arrived from Venus on a very important mission. I must see your President immediately."

The Benjamin kid backed away another step. Shaking his head, he began to collect himself. "Are you crazy, man, or what?"

"Yes, young man, I am crazy." Jimmijay Connell paused. "But come to think of it, I'm also thirsty. Would you happen to know where a Venutian like myself might obtain some liquid refreshment? I believe the people on your planet call it 'cold beer'. Jimmijay Connell knew he had the kid suspended somewhere, but Jimmijay never once cracked, observing the first rule of comedy, never laugh at your own routine.

The kid tried to dismiss him, but his surprise and uncertainty prevailed. He silently raised his right arm, pointing towards the front of the Inn.

Jimmijay Connell raised his left arm and pointed in similar direction. "There? Inside? I believe your people say 'thank you', am I correct?" Jimmijay paused again, tilting his head, the thin smile still crossing his face. "Yes, thank you. And have a nice day!"

Jimmijay turned and headed for the front side of the Pollard Creek Inn, leaving the Benjamin kid scrambling for his stash bag and pipe, and perhaps another big hit. But for Jimmijay Connell, it was just another heated afternoon at the Pollard Creek Inn.

The air was cool inside the Hungry Dog Café. Outside, the hot afternoon sun was descending in a slow decline, its direct heat beginning to temper. The dinner hours were underway. Tractor-trailers lined both sides of the access road in front of the truck stop, pointing north and south, the sound of their refrigeration units droning in the oven-baked heat. The air conditioner and restaurant compressors whirred at a higher pitch, working overtime.

Jake Beecher sat on a stool at the Formica counter, sipping his iced tea, smoking a cigarette. Before him lay the remains of a chicken fried steak, mashed potatoes and green beans slurped into his gut. Jake Beecher drew on his smoke, his thinning gray hair pressed toward the back of his head, his face tobacco red. A pack of Lucky Strikes hung in the chest pocket of his white tee shirt. His black cotton pants were cuffed above white socks and black shoes, his heels hooked over the lower rung of the stool. The waitress, gum chewing in her mouth, picked up the plate, slipping the billing ticket onto the counter. Jake Beecher paid her no mind.

A passing driver sat a vacant seat away, dressed in cowboy hat and blue denim shirt. His collar was open, exposing the marked line of his white chest against a tanned neck. He sipped a cup of coffee held in his hand.

"Here tell, a boy can get a good piece of ass over there," the trucker said, as if asking the question more than stating a fact.

"Or he could get it up the ass," Jake Beecher grunted. "Whatever your flavor."

"There's word on the radio you can get a slim little hippie chick that will do whatever you tell her," the trucker inquired. "A slender piece of prime with all the trimmings."

"Yeah, probably comes with a side of the crabs," Jake Beecher answered with a mean chuckle in his voice. "Good chance she'll give you the burn, fella. I'd advise sticking with some lipstick on the dipstick, if you know what I mean. Like I said, keep an eye on your cupcakes, they got a few washroom faggots wandering the place. You married?"

The trucker laughed. "Yeah, but what's that got to do with it?"

"Nothing, I guess. Just wouldn't want to take it home, I reckon."

The trucker finished his coffee, stood up, pulling out some tip change, pressing it on the counter. "It's an occupational hazard, what can I say. Maybe I'll check things out next time through."

"You might want to make it sooner rather than later," Jake Beecher responded. "It just might not be there for long."

As the trucker left the restaurant, Jake Beecher sipped on his tea. Out the window of the café, he caught a glimpse of Hank Swain's four-wheel drive pick-up passing between the parked tractor rigs along the road. So there goes that fucking asshole, Jake Beecher thought to himself. Fuck you and your dead brother, you hook-tending piece of shit. There was no love lost between the Beechers' and the Swains', and if Jake Beecher had anything to say about it, it would always stay that way. Jake Beecher always had a hell of a lot to say.

The Swain brothers could kiss his lily-white ass. Hank Swain more than the rest. It had been that way ever since the day on that King Mountain show. The day when that young sucker puncher put he, Jake Beecher, down for the count. It had been Jake Beecher's show, and he was the bull. And goddamn, despite what Hank Swain claimed, Jake had never dropped that yellow-bellied pine anywhere near the kid. But the kid thought so, and his brothers took Hank's side. When Hank had knocked Jake cold, the four brothers had all looked down at him laughing, as if there might be something funny somewhere. But there was never nothing funny about it. "Make them out" those Swain brothers had demanded, and they had forced Jake to pay them off right there. It was the last time a Beecher ever worked with a Swain, that was for damn sure.

Now, all these years later, Howard Swain was dead. Killed in his airplane down in California a few months ago, smuggling that marijuana shit out of Mexico. Howard had tried to go low, skirting the radar at night. But sure as shit, Howard had buried himself right into the side of a mountain. People said Hank hadn't been the same since. They said the deal had all been Hank's idea, his connection. Ever since, the guilt was really wearing Hank down. Well, good riddance to that damn buck. Eventually the chickens always come home to roost. You fuck with a Beecher, and somewhere down the line, you goddamn well gonna pay.

Twenty-year old Larry Cathcart finished the last of his French fries, swirling them in a pile of ketchup before sucking them down the hatch. In a few more minutes Larry would have to do this bullshit stupid job. But the result would be less probation time on his sentence. And he could definitely handle that. At least that's what the twerpy state police guy had promised, during a meeting earlier this afternoon in Medford.

Larry had been busted for possession of amphetamines and reds a few months back. He'd gotten sentenced for time served in the Jackson County jail, as well as a fine he would have to pay off, plus the probation. But then comes this offer from his probation officer, and that detective guy named Walton a few weeks back. Larry's probation time would be reduced if he would work with this liquor control man named Smith. All Larry had to do, was go around to different small markets and convenience stores, trying to buy beer and wine without an identification.

Larry had scored booze at two different markets in the Medford area, and this guy Smith seemed happy with his work. But earlier today, they had met with the detective Walton, and this particular job seemed more important than the others. It would be Larry's first time trying to get served in a bar, and Walton seemed really anxious to make this one happen. Walton had made Larry dress up in a white tee shirt, with suspenders that hooked to a pair of black jeans. On his feet they gave him a heavy set of boots with raised heels. He would wear a baseball hat on his head, labeled with the name of a chain saw on the front. In this hick mountain town, they wanted Larry to look like a logger.

The liquor guy, Vance Smith, waited till Larry's plate was clean before going into his spiel. Smith said he would remain here in the booth of the truck stop restaurant. Larry would walk about a hundred yards down the road to the big white building they could see out the window of the café. He would go inside the bar, acting like he had been there before. He would step to the bar and ask for a Blitz tall, trying not to meet the bartender's eyes. The bartender might be a woman, Smith said. If the bartender asked for identification, Larry was to tell the bartender that he'd left it in his car over at the truck stop. He was here only for a quick beer before getting back on the road home. If anybody asked, he'd been setting choker and working on the rigs for the Davis logging show up on Cow Creek. He was just now making his way home.

"If they serve you, pay for the beer with the dollar, and tell them to keep the change," Smith said, "Take a quick swallow or two, then ask the bartender where the men's john is located. Go to the john and take a leak, then return to the bar, take another swig, then say thanks and you gotta go. Get a good look at the bartender after you are served, so you can identify them. Ask for their name if you get the chance. Walk back here and you're done."

Larry Cathcart departed the truck stop restaurant, walking in the hot evening air along the shoulder of the road towards the Pollard Creek Inn. He stepped onto the pillared front porch, entering through the open door of the building. Inside was a small room like a hotel lobby. To the left a loud rush of human voices spilled toward him, the barroom. He could see a pool table sitting in the middle of the room, with chairs and tables surrounding. To the right of the pool table was the bar itself. It was a short bar with only four or five stools, all occupied with rough looking men. A couple of the men sat facing toward the bar. The others were turned toward the pool table, watching the game.

Larry Cathcart hadn't expected such a busy scene. He grew nervous as he edged his way into the barroom. Standing by the end of the bar, he had to wait, while a number of unfriendly sets of eyes looked him up and down. The bartender was standing at one of the tables, talking to the patrons, before picking up some empties and returning to the bar. He walked down toward Larry's end, putting the empties into a cardboard box near where Larry stood. The bartender caught sight of him, but kept moving back to the taps, grabbing a glass pitcher, filling it with beer.

"What can I get you?" the bartender asked, turning his head toward Larry.

"I'll have a Blitz tall," Larry Cathcart tried to say over the din of the room.

"What's that?" The bartender was about medium height, with a bushel of long black hair tied back in a pony tail. His face looked pudgy and kind of pockmarked. Larry Cathcart made note of the man's appearance, as Smith had requested.

Larry Cathcart grew more nervous. He pointed at the cardboard box with the tall empty bottles. "I'll have one of those," he responded.

The bartender watched his movements, giving Larry's face a long look. He topped off the pitcher of beer. "You want an empty," he said sarcastically. "That will cost you five cents." A couple of men at the bar laughed along with the bartender, looking Larry's way.

"No, I just want a tall, whatever you got. I'm sort of in a hurry."

The bartender looked him over again. "Me, too," the bartender answered, before grabbing a couple of clean glasses with his free hand. "I'll need some ID," he said as he went back around the far end of the bar and into the crowd, delivering the beer.

Larry Cathcart cursed to himself without speaking, but patted his rear pockets as if looking for his wallet. A long-haired man, who sat on the stool closest to him, chuckled and sipped his beer. As the bartender returned behind the bar, somebody said, "Hey Slick, I'll have another." This time the bartender headed right toward Larry.

Larry tried to beat him to the punch. "Hey, my ID is in my buddy's car over at the truck stop. I just wanted to get a quick one before we hit the road."

The bartender tilted his head and raised his eyebrows. "Sorry pal, can't do it unless I see some ID. If you want to go over to the Hungry Dog and get it, I'll be here when you get back." The bartender moved toward the beer cooler behind the bar.

Larry Cathcart had to think fast. With the bartender turned away, Larry grabbed one of the tall empties in the box nearby. With nobody looking, he stuck the bottom of the bottle into the front pocket of the jeans, before turning to leave the bar. In the lobby area, another door opened to a large dining room empty of patrons. He stepped into the room. In the far corner, a guy sat at an old piano, hitting the keys wildly with his hands. He looked like a mad scientist fingering the keys. But he caught sight of Larry and stopped. "Was looking for the bathroom?" Larry asked.

"You can use the one down there to the left," the man said, before returning to his playing.

Inside the bathroom, peeing in the toilet stall, Larry Cathcart tried to figure out his predicament. He had the bottle. He had the bartender's first name. He would lie to Smith, tell him that the bartender served him without ever asking for identification. Larry Cathcart would tell them anything they wanted to hear. As he looked at the wall alongside the toilet, he read the words that someone had written in black marker on the side of the stall.

"To the brothers and sisters at the Pollard Creek Inn. Thanks for the overnight stay, and the delicious meals you were so kind to provide. You are true heroes of the revolution. I look forward to coming back soon and staying for awhile. Off the pigs!" The bathroom note was signed with the name 'Patty Hearst'. Larry Cathcart began to relax, nodding to himself. He would tell that cop Walton a story he just might buy. Larry Cathcart left the Pollard Creek Inn, heading back to the Hungry Dog Cafe.

Sean McAllister sat in an old cushioned chair at his camp site on the Mulcahey Farm. The warm summer evening was blending from dusky twilight to darkness. It was that time of night when the birds chat with themselves before settling down to sleep. That time of day when the buzz of human activity begins to wane. Occasionally, there might be the solitary sound of a car going by on the road above, a raised voice calling for their dog, or the distant bark of a coyote preparing for the hunt. McAllister was tired. And for the first time all day, he was alone as well. Mookie and Annie had taken their sleeping bags up to the new cabin being built. They had found an old mattress, placing it on their newly finished floor of plywood. They could now sleep under the stars at the site of their future home.

McAllister got up, pulled a beer from the cooler, punched in the eight-track tape player he had set up to run off an old car battery. He picked up the roach clip that sat nearby, lit a kitchen match, smoking the last of a joint. The eight-track clicked to a start, the music of Fleetwood Mac's *Future Games* album replacing the silence of the night. He sat back down in the chair. He would drink this beer and relax for awhile, before calling it a night. He'd been up since five o'clock with the cows. He and Mookie had performed the evening milking as well. Tomorrow, he could sleep in a little longer. Jack Mulcahey and his partner Christine would be making the morning run.

McAllister sat back and listened to the music. He really liked the recent albums of Fleetwood Mac. A lot of guys, like his old buddy Huggins back in the D.C days, preferred the early Peter Green influence of the group. Those albums were more bluesy and traditional. McAllister actually preferred their more recent sound of the band, the Danny Kirwan and Jermey Spencer influences. *Kiln House, Bare Trees*, and *Mystery to Me*, along with *Future Games*. It was kind of funny how the music of certain songs or albums, could return him to places in time. *The White Album* and *Abby Road* went back to his first years in college. Hearing songs by Gram Parsons, Neil Young, or Poco, always ushered thoughts of Mad into his mind. It was Derrick and the Dominos and Steely Dan at the Strickersville house, and Little Feat during his time in Boulder. He wondered now if Fleetwood Mac might mean the same for Oregon. Upon moments of reflection and memory, he was beginning to accumulate certain markers of time in his life. Was this a sign of age? He wasn't sure.

Resting in the old chair felt good. He had found it for five bucks at a second hand store in Grants Pass. It hadn't rained a drop in almost a month, making it a breeze to live this makeshift camping lifestyle for the summer. But eventually things would change when the Oregon rains returned. In another month, he would head north to Washington for the apple harvest. After that, he would have to make some decisions. He would either figure out a way to remain on the Farm, or find some other place to go. Right now, he would be happy to stay if he could.

McAllister hadn't seen Darla since the previous weekend. She was a beautiful woman, and the opportunity for sex was certainly an event that made him feel better about himself. But he could sense her becoming less interested, and perhaps himself as well. There was no question that sleeping once or twice a week with Derrick Mulcahey's ex-old lady was strangely unnerving. Even so, Derrick had yet to say a word to him about it. Derrick continued to act friendly towards McAllister, as if nothing else was up. But McAllister couldn't feel sure that suddenly a shoe might drop, and it might become an issue. Derrick Mulcahey was the unspoken but surely recognized director of this otherwise communal enterprise. To end up on his bad side would obviously change McAllister's circumstance. For now, there wasn't much he could do about that possibility. It was funny how one could find time to worry about things not in their control.

Listening to the music, McAllister let the concerns slip from his mind. The late July evening remained warm, the stars beginning to fill overhead, a perfect summer night. Tomorrow, he and Mookie, along with Jack and Jesse, would be heading over to the Railroad Bridge property, to look at some lumber for sale. McAllister knew of Railroad Bridge, but had yet to see the place, or meet any of its folks. So much of Pollard Creek remained unknown to him. Each day was like another page turning over in a book, another adventure waiting to be engaged. Being part of the Mulcahey Farm had given him a presence in Pollard Creek. It had begun to provide a fixed point from which he could be identified, an entry into the community, to share in its daily existence. For now, he was certain there was no other place he'd rather be.

CHAPTER TWENTY-SIX

HOT SUMMER DAY
Railroad Bridge / July 1974

Tom Sullivan stood in the meadow of the Railroad Bridge property, the rising summer heat beginning to burn. Pulling off his tee shirt, he bunched it like a towel, wiping a moist sweat from his face and eyes. The skin of his upper torso shined with a copper glaze. Overhead, the cloudless sky spread in a deep metallic blue, marked in contrast against the thirsty evergreen hills. He continued to shovel sawdust from under the platform of the Alaskan mill. Filling the wheelbarrow, he spread the remains along the garden paths nearby. Finished with the task, he started up the boom truck, moving it out of the sun.

It would be another scorcher today, any kind of cool place would be very hard to find. For most of America, the image of Oregon is framed in the cool gray mists of coastal waves crashing against ocean pillared rocks. The image would not normally be one of oven-baked temperatures, in tinder-dry mountain valleys, at the very height of summer. Even Tom Sullivan had not known such heat waves existed in these otherwise green forested mountains west of the Cascade Crest. 'Rattlesnake weather' was the name some locals had coined it. And the description spoke to more than the dry summer heat. Rattlesnakes were indigenous to this Southern Oregon country, and never more dangerous than on a hot summer day.

Jack Mulcahey was due to come by the property before noon, looking to buy some cedar and pine siding that Freddie Jones and Sullivan had recently milled. If it met with Jack's satisfaction, he would purchase with cash. Sullivan looked up at the blazing sun peaking in the sky. It wouldn't be too long now. He walked over to the shade of a nearby oak tree, grabbed his plastic container of water, sitting down in an aluminum beach chair to await Jack's arrival. Rolling a cigarette out of his pouch of Top tobacco, he leaned back in the chair and smoked.

Sullivan was impressed with Jack Mulcahey. He was a quiet brawny man, who had a speech impediment, and stuttered when he first spoke. Like Sullivan and the others at Railroad Bridge, Jack Mulcahey and his brother had cut out a homestead on marginal land, without the benefits of electric power and running water. But unlike Rainbow Bridge, which was more a loose association of individuals living on the same piece of property, the Mulcaheys' were driven by a desire to create a communal sustainability. They were a dozen or more people working together as a single unit. They were raising animals, sharing meals and projects on a regular basis, trying to grow their own and live off the land.

The reputation of the Mulcaheys' was that of a working farm. The brothers were rarely seen in the social world of Pollard Creek, keeping mainly to themselves. Jack Mulcahey appeared to reflect a presence of almost religious conviction. He looked like a cross between a mountain man and an Amish farmer, strong and stoic in manner. Sullivan had met Jack's brother Derrick only one time. Derrick was more talkative and excited about things, a definite contrast between the two men. But from what Sullivan had heard from Valerie and others, Derrick Mulcahey apparently had a more difficult persona, one that belied his first impression.

According to Valerie's friend Darla Bloom, Derrick was the constant manipulator and director of the Mulcahey Farm. Derrick decided who came and who stayed, what was to be purchased and where the money spent. The reputation was that Derrick did the thinking and his younger brother Jack did the work. However, Sullivan had never even visited the Mulcahey property, only viewing it while passing by on Lower Pollard Creek Road. So any more truthful perspectives were unknown to him. As far as Sullivan was concerned, that was just as well. There was at least one thing Tom Sullivan had learned in his time here. Even though these hills were sparsely populated, and the towns of Pollard Creek and Solace Valley particularly small, everyone seemed to know everyone else's business in one way or another. Rumor and innuendo were often the primary topic of human conversation, with the truth more often than not trailing somewhere far behind. So the trials and tribulations of the Mulcahey Farm were none of Sullivan's concern. Right now, Railroad Bridge had enough of its own. Marty Johnson, his long time friend and partner since their returns from Vietnam, was not doing well. He had come back from California last month empty-handed. And if one wanted to be clever with words, empty inside as well. Marty's girlfriend, Celia, had not been with him. She had decided to stay in California, to work and return to school in the fall. Marty, as usual, had acted like it was no big deal, which was always Marty's way of dealing with things. At least on the outside. On the inside, Tom Sullivan knew a darker ship often sailed the seas.

Since getting back home, Marty had little time for working on the property, which was unlike his normal routine. Marty Johnson had initially found most of the money to buy Railroad Bridge. And along with Freddie Jones, Marty had been the primary energy in building up the place. Sullivan knew that he himself had also been a big part of the effort, but Marty had been the catalyst early on. With Celia by his side, it was Marty's inspiration that made things go.

But it might have been for naught. Living in this backwoods country day after day, with little to look forward to beyond the necessities of survival, Celia had begun to wear down. As others drifted away with the coming of winter, Celia had toughed it out, but Sullivan could sense her long-term misgivings. During the second winter, when she had left for the holidays, Sullivan had made a silent guess she might not return. Unfortunately, he had been correct.

Lately, Marty Johnson was drifting. He spent most evenings at the Solace Valley Tavern, playing pool and hanging with the hardcore locals who frequented the place. Other nights, he might go to the Pollard Creek Inn. He was drinking too much, that was a fact. Worse, a terrible looking skin rash had taken over Marty's upper chest and back, a burning and itching that seemed to put him in a constant state of distraction. Was it the anxiety or stress of his personal situation, Sullivan didn't know. Could it be the result of Agent Orange? Maybe. Whatever the cause, Marty Johnson was becoming a far cry from the confident and singular dude who had once appeared to have endured Vietnam completely unscathed. Sullivan quietly worried about the situation, but there had to be limits to his concern. It was simply a world of live and let live around here. So he and Freddie Jones had agreed to let Marty work things out on his own. But if Marty ever needed help, or found himself in trouble, they would be ready for the rescue.

As for Sullivan, things had gotten somewhat better with time. He still had nights when the nightmares would raise him out of his sleep, tingling with sweat. But they were coming fewer and farther between. The flashbacks were all but gone. Moving to Oregon, and the Railroad Bridge adventure had become the necessary medication. That experience, and perhaps the distance of time itself. Sullivan liked the prospect of getting up every day with something to do, of recording the objective diary of his work in his journal book each morning. His beneficent relationship with Valerie Williams had helped to settle him. Valerie had become his closest confidante and friend. Each day, he felt a little easier about stepping back into his life, while leaving the unwanted memories behind.

Sullivan heard a truck gearing up the road from the creek bed, and another following the first. He got up from the lawn chair, stepping out into the heat of the sun. The sound of the trucks slowed as they crossed the railroad tracks, before coming into sight at the end of the meadow. A large flatbed and a Chevy pick-up pulled up near the piles of lumber, before shutting down their engines. It was time to do a deal, and hopefully get some cash.

Later in the hot afternoon, Tom Sullivan sat next to Valerie Williams on the sandy beach of the Laughlin Creek swimming hole near Railroad Bridge. Valerie kept her eyes on her son, watching as he tried to keep his balance on the rocks by the edge of the water. Other children swam nearby. Adults lounged in the shallows of the creek, keeping an eye as well. Valerie's dark hair lay wet on her brown shouldered skin, her breasts exposed. She sat with her knees pulled up, her thin feet digging into the sand. Sullivan shook out his hair from a swim, reaching into the cooler nearby, snapping open a couple of beers.

"Did you know he is sleeping with Darla in town?" Valerie asked. She took the beer in hand, keeping her eyes focused on her son.

"Who, the new guy, Sean?" Sullivan returned. He swallowed a hit of the beer, turning his head toward Valerie. "How's that going down on the farm, I mean with Derrick Mulcahey being her ex-old man and all?"

"I guess no problems so far," Valerie answered. "Derrick's got another woman living with him for the past few months, so he probably doesn't care."

"Yeah, maybe," Sullivan answered. "Well, he seems like a pretty good guy. While Jack and Mookie did the wood deal with me, he and the kid Jesse pretty much walked all the property. They checked out the cabins and the mill. They even went down and visited Freddie. After we loaded the lumber, Jack and Mookie pulled out in the flatbed. But he and Jesse sat in the shade with me for awhile. He seemed like a pretty nice guy."

"I like him, too," Valerie said. "He's an old friend of Mookie's from back east. He lived in Colorado before coming here. I don't know, but I think Darla is just having a time with someone new, like meeting a stranger or something like that. She's pretty flighty these days."

"Hopefully he understands that reality." Sullivan paused for a moment, looking at the creek. "I mean I can understand Darla, too. I remember that one time when she said that living with Derrick was like being in a prison camp." Sullivan chuckled at his own remark. "She's probably just getting her own kicks, making up for lost time."

"Oh, hush," Valerie responded. "You darn, men. It's always the girl that's running around, is that it? When you know full well that it's just the opposite most of the time." Valerie turned her head, giving him a smirk.

"Yeah, you're probably right," he said with tongue in cheek. Sullivan leaned forward toward her and winked.

Valerie smiled, still keeping her attention on her son. A short silence occurred between them, then she turned toward Sullivan with serious intent. "There is something I need to tell you. But you have to promise me that you won't get upset."

As Valerie's story unfolded, Sullivan remained calm on the outside, but he was burning within. If he had made a promise to her, it was extremely doubtful it would be one he would keep. In the images of his own mind, that fucking redneck pastor had the crosshairs of a rifle scope aimed directly at his forehead. He might soon be a dead man, with no chance for any last words or good-byes to his family. That's the way it would be. That would be the frontier justice his fucking crime deserved. Sullivan could feel an adrenaline rush of anger coursing through his frame. If he did commit such an act, he wouldn't stop there. He might as well drive up and find old Jake Beecher, and those two lug-nut nephews of his, and finish the fucking job.

It took everything he had for Sullivan to not let on, to frighten Valerie, or worry her to death. But it was hard for him to speak, to fake things, to let her think he understood. "He's just a little weasel of a man," she said. "I've thought about it some. They're just scared. Of what, I really don't understand. But that's what they are. And I'm okay with it, I really am. I made it very clear to him that enough was enough. You don't need to be angry or upset about it."

Sullivan let Valerie have her way. He boxed his anger up tight, keeping it close. But later, in the remaining light of evening, with the red-stripped sky giving way to dusk, he cleaned and loaded his handgun. He fired a few rounds at a garden post across the meadow. He did the same with his rifle, before placing them in his truck.

Where the hell was Marty Johnson when you needed him? The Marty who would tell him "not to worry, just let it go". The Marty who whenever he saw Jake Beecher in town, would simply give Jake a crazy smile and say, "How's your aim, Jake, any better? Tell me, where do you live again?" Then Marty would leave things right there. He would go smiling out the door of the market, leaving old Jake Beecher scratching his balding head in fury. That Marty, the old Marty. Not the new Marty. Sullivan couldn't tell him now. The new Marty just might go off kilter, and all hell would break loose. No, if something got done, it would be Sullivan's way. But he had to think about this, for himself, and for Valerie and Canyon as well.

CHAPTER TWENTY-SEVEN

DREAM A LITTLE DREAM OF ME
Pollard Creek / Late July, 1974

MAMA CASS WAS GONE, her body found in a London hotel room, the result of a heart attack. Some reports said she choked to death while eating a sandwich. Whatever the cause, the sound of her beautiful voice had been stilled forever. There would be another vacant hurt, another tragic loss. Laurel Canyon would never be the same. Mama Cass was so much more than a fat woman who could sing. Her fun-filled personality reminded everyone that true beauty remained deeper than the skin. One always felt a certain kind of sympathy for Mama Cass, that she had gotten the raw deal. She deserved to be as astonishing beautiful as Michelle Phillips, as much of a heartthrob as any woman could be. Her voice and her generosity toward others would always belie the errors of first impression.

Any former east coast boy could tell you, that the Mamas and the Papas hit single, "'California Dreaming", had been the siren's call. It had planted the seed of a generation, to eventually pack your bags and wander west. For many, like Sean McAllister, you had no choice in the matter. The pull had been that strong.

Meanwhile, America was becoming a nation of dishonest persona, full of presentation and false projections. As Marshall McLuhan had theorized, it would continue down a road of advertised myth for whatever ends necessary. America was becoming a country built on illusions, proffered by others with something to sell. Cass Elliot did not fit such a necessary image. Yet her voice and persona were too much to ignore. Still, the battle was being lost, and Cass Elliot's unfortunate passing did little to help the cause.

Thankfully, Richard Milhous Nixon was definitely on the ropes. His trainers and corner men were either under indictment or quietly backpedaling their way out of town. As well, previously loyal sycophants were undergoing incredible personal transformations. In other words, they were out there saving their own skins, acting as if shocked by Nixon's unforgivable behavior and criminal intents. Politicians were seen jumping ship as the Titanic went down. As for Nixon himself, the escape hatch was closing. He might soon be headed back to San Clemente. And maybe, just maybe, an all expense paid trip to Leavenworth would eventually be in his future. There was a darn good chance two names would forever rub Nixon raw. Their pictures would be pasted on a dart board, hanging in his cell. Two names that would live in his own personal infamy, now and forever more. The names would be 'Woodward' and 'Bernstein'. Enough said.

The real problem would be the resulting outcome. The attention span of America was lessening each day. Nowadays, it seemed like a crook only had to lay low for awhile, get a good publicist, and he'd be back on top in no time flat. He only had to throw in a few sincere and heartfelt mea culpas. He would do his time in rehab, then return to business as usual, with nobody knowing the better.

As George Santanyana once wrote, "Those who cannot remember the past, are doomed to repeat it." But Santanyana could never have known the power of cultural media, or the incredible influence it was beginning to confer. The memory of America had become shortened like never before. And with it, the boys in charge now had a new weapon at their disposal. A weapon they would learn how to use in order to maintain their hegemony. It went something like this; "So don't sweat the small stuff, boys. Give it a little time. Just throw in enough cheeseburgers and circus acts, and soon they won't remember a goddamn thing. Then we can crank it up again, just like we have always done before."

Deputy Sheriff Bill Haines was finishing his police report. The prior evening, someone had tried to set fire to the Pollard Creek Country

Store. Fortunately, the fire had burned itself out, only blackening the side of the building. But this hurried attempt at arson had been a very close call. With the Oregon summer so hot and tinder dry, Bill Haines figured the Country Store might have gone up like a matchstick, maybe even the town. Things were damn lucky, all in all.

The fire investigator sent out from Grants Pass had looked things over for a couple of hours before heading back to town. The investigator hadn't said much, but it appeared to Bill Haines like some paper and scraps of wood had been doused with gasoline, the perpetrator lighting the fuel before dashing away. It wasn't a professional job, and the minimal amount of gasoline used had probably saved the day. As Haines sat in his police cruiser, writing up the last of his report, Ralph Swanson, the owner of the Country Store, approached.

"Well," Ralph Swanson started defiantly, his head at the window, "are you going up to arrest him, or what?"

"I told you, Ralph, we've got to take this one step at a time. If we find the evidence we need, we'll take care of it. Until then, you just have to be patient."

"Patient? That's easy for you to say," Ralph Swanson argued. "Patient? You mean before that asshole burns us out of house and home. I told you, Bill, Randy Halston is the son of a bitch who did this. And he needs to be arrested before he tries it again. If you don't do something, then I'll do something my goddamn self."

"No you won't," Bill Haines demanded. "You hear me, Ralph. You aren't going up there to Cougar Gulch and get your own ass shot over this. We will handle this in the proper legal manner. If you do go up on that gulch, you might find your own ass in jail. Now settle down."

"Well then do something, Bill. And do it fast. Or I'll hold you and everyone else responsible. Betty is out of her mind scared, and I won't have that shit."

Bill Haines watched as Ralph Swanson huffed his way back toward the store. Tossing his clipboard onto the seat beside him, he fired up his vehicle, turning for home. Despite his own frustrations, he could hardly be angry with Ralph Swanson. The man had a right to be nervous and upset, especially for his wife. And there was little doubt that the man to whom Ralph Swanson was referring was indeed a culpable suspect.

Randy Halston, 'Crazy Randy', as he was labeled by everyone in Pollard Creek, was a troubled and dangerous character. Haines was aware that Halston was an ex-con out of Stockton, California. Halston's rap sheet included a stint in Folsom for a string of burglaries and illegal weapons possession. And Halston had threatened Ralph and Betty Swanson that very same evening. Ralph had confronted Randy in the store, telling him he needed to start making good on his credit bill, cutting him off from charging any more groceries. Halston hadn't taken the news well. He reportedly told Ralph Swanson he better watch his back, before violently kicking the door as he stormed from the premises. Although it was a disturbing incident, it hardly rose to the level of a convictable crime. But an arson attempt was an entirely different matter. And coming on the heels of the argument that evening, 'Crazy Randy' was at the top of the list of suspects.

Deputy Sheriff Bill Haines had worked the north end of Jordan County for almost twenty years. And that amount of time was long enough to have seen just about everything there was to see. Pollard Creek had never been a bowl of cherries. It was a town with very little soup, and a whole lot of nuts. If it wasn't some drunken loggers fighting with each other simply for the hell of it, it might be a crackpot miner blasting away with a double-barreled shotgun at some imaginary thief trying to steal his gold.

Over the years, Pollard Creek had seen plenty of desperate men on the run, hiding from the law in these Oregon hills. There were the anti-government Bircher types, fortressed up on their sacred private property, sensing conspiracies around every corner. Hell, their so-called cherished homesteads looked more like solid-waste garbage dumps than anything else. But damn if they wouldn't post their precious ground anyway, before anxiously awaiting some nefarious government agent to stroll on by. And now in recent years, this hippie invasion of long-haired kids and draft dodgers, buying up the logged-over timber tracts, or registering gold claims while smoking pot and running naked through the creeks.

Deputy Bill Haines was the only law for miles and miles. And although Haines was not a man to say he'd seen it all, any man who stood in his shoes for awhile, might be inclined to say he was goddamn close.

One thing was for certain, Bill Haines was not going up to Cougar Gulch alone. When the time came to go up there looking for Crazy Randy, he would definitely take some back up assistance. If Randy

Halston was a guilty man, there would be a real good chance he wouldn't go quiet. In this part of the world, most every man seemed hell-bent on maintaining his outlaw reputation, whatever its status or consequence. And men like Crazy Randy Halston, more so than others. It was the simply the Pollard Creek way.

During the afternoon, Bill Haines had talked to the hippie kids at the Pollard Creek Inn. Crazy Randy had indeed been drinking in the bar most of the night. No one seemed the least bit surprised about the possibility of Randy starting the fire. But Randy had been no more trouble than usual, they said. And nobody had seen Randy commit the suspected deed. So Ralph and Betty Swanson would just have to wait until the slow wheels of justice took their course. Returning home, Bill Haines put in a call to headquarters in Grants Pass. Later that evening, he received a call in return.

The response was not what Deputy Bill Haines expected. Usually, those boys in Grants Pass were all fired up and ready for action, looking for a fight. It was too often left to Bill Haines to try to calm them down, keeping them from getting jacked-up and full of themselves. Those dumb bucks thought all the power they needed was to be wearing a uniform and holding a gun, expecting the rest of the world to come to a halt. The truth was they had watched too many cop shows, and didn't know their ass from a hole in the ground. Uniforms didn't mean shit up here in Pollard Creek. In fact, it was frankly just the opposite, an invitation for target practice. Shoot first, ask questions later. Then lay down your gun and plead self-defense. "He came onto my property and I was just defending myself." How many times had Bill Haines heard that excuse over the years? All the while, a gung ho, but utterly stupid officer of the law would be lying dead in the weeds. So much for uniforms.

But this night, the boys in Grants Pass were singing a different tune. Let's take this one slow, Bill, they advised. Keep the suspect under surveillance the best you can. Tell the victims that we are presently gathering evidence. Tell them to call you if they see Halston in town. Tell them we have gone undercover on this one, and we need their help. It was a bit of an odd request, not standard procedure. Normally, the suspect would be questioned as soon as possible. Bill Haines hung up the phone, shaking his head. Just when you thought you'd seen everything, here comes the eephus pitch, that slow high-arching junk ball falling out of the sky. Whatever the reasoning might be, Bill Haines knew one thing, something else was up. It might just take him a wee bit of time to figure things out.

Albert Krieger stood in the kitchen of the Pollard Creek Inn, dressed in a white bath robe and bare feet. He held a cup of coffee in one hand, in the other a bank pouch holding the receipts from the previous day's business sales. Darla Bloom and Laura Hale worked nearby, prepping vegetables and fruit for the restaurant day ahead. The women chatted about the arson attempt at the Country Store two nights before, the suspicions that Crazy Randy Halston had started the blaze late that evening, after leaving the Inn.

Albert Krieger was concerned. Some of the men from Cougar Gulch had become nothing but trouble. For them, Pollard Creek meant a chance to live out some kind of Wild West cowboy fantasy. It was an opportunity to carry guns on their hips, or loaded rifles in the racks of their trucks, as well as treating the Pollard Creek Inn as their own personal saloon. It was not quite what Albert Krieger expected when he had purchased the property. In Albert's vision, he saw the Inn as a business where good healthy food could be served, where people could come to drink and share the camaraderie of their daily lives, to dance and live freely in this beautiful mountain countryside.

Strawberry Fields had been his previous dream, to build a communal farm where people could make it on their own, to live peaceably together in the shared visions of a new alternative lifestyle. They would leave behind the bullshit of the city and the suburban life of America. They would run from that straight world of material desire, or parental expectations of a job in the corporate business machine. They would escape from the *Ozzie and Harriet* version of Middle America, the notions of a boring nuclear family, where in the end everything was happy and safe.

In fact, a serious chunk of the young Americans were no longer buying the sales pitch. As far as they were concerned, the government and the corporate elite of America were simply operating a con game. They were feeding the military-industrial complex, using fear to preach that communist domination was right around the corner, while mashing their boot heels on anyone who might beg to oppose them. These forces would use their power to keep in check those being left out of the American Dream. The shacks of a Mississippi Delta, the housing projects of Detroit, the desperate street corners of an Oakland, the wasted junk piles of a Wounded Knee reservation, all had become nothing more than a dangerous nuisance needing to be controlled.

So who could blame the disbelievers for wanting to get away? To emigrate to another land where things could be altogether different, where a more genuine and sincere self-realization might be achieved. That had been Albert Krieger's initial desire, his original intent. Blessed with a trust fund that could help make it happen, he had left New York and San Francisco, finding his way to Oregon, eventually leading others toward Strawberry Fields. Forever.

But forever is a long long time. And getting away is not as easy as it seems. A lifestyle with little privacy and no hot water begins to wear after awhile. The ideals of a shared vision and commitment to self-sufficiency are difficult to establish, and even harder to maintain. Especially when everyone has their own definition of 'doing their own thing'.

The Pollard Creek Inn allowed for a more unique possibility. It would require a commitment each resident could see and understand. The food and beer had to be bought, work shifts had to be filled, schedules met. There would be an economic engine needing to be fueled. In exchange, you would have your own room, your own personal space. Your time would be your own. The Pollard Creek Inn would offer a modicum of structure that Strawberry Fields had failed to provide, despite its best efforts to succeed.

However, there was one big problem which Albert Krieger was now just beginning to foresee. It was a problem he should have been wise enough to anticipate, but somehow had missed. At least at Strawberry Fields, the personal and communal issues had been internal ones, generated by people with a likeness of mind and intent. Both the good and the bad that confronted them had been entirely their own. On the other hand, the Pollard Creek Inn experience was becoming a different ball of wax. The Inn faced the possible consequences of external forces, incidents and events that could be out of their control. Life at the Inn had returned one step closer to the outside world, to the inherent dangers such proximity could effect. Nobody wanted to pay attention to those perils, to be forced to confront them in some serious way. Nevertheless, despite such denials, the dangers were all too present and real.

Whether it was the native Oregon loggers, or the Cougar Gulch desperadoes living in the bar, whether it was the hardcore rednecks or truckers passing through, or even the self-righteous religious fanatics living in fear, the Pollard Creek Inn was exposed to the vagaries of the greater American world. Toss in a road-weary host of American wanderers, looking for salvation and something to eat, amidst a strident local conservatism wary of change, and every day Albert Krieger could hear a quiet but constant ticking in his head. He tried hard to pay it no mind. Whether this ticking was a bomb waiting to explode, or simply the sound of his own fears, he didn't know. In the end, what did it matter? And what could he really do?

Meanwhile, upstairs at the Inn, Guitar Glenn lay on the bunk in his room, fingering the strings of his instrument. For Guitar Glenn, his guitar was an additional appendage to his tall long-haired anatomy. Guitar Glenn awoke with his guitar. He showered with it, he ate with it, he drove with it, he even worked the bar with it. He took a big healthy shit with it, before closing his weary eyes and going to bed with it. He even shook hands with it. Guitar Glenn was a man in search of a band, waiting for his rock and roll destiny to come.

Back in his own room, Jimmijay Connell could not be interrupted. He was currently on the air. Or at least his alter-ego, Jerry Fisher, was working the show:

"You're listening to KEGG 102.4 FM on your radio dial, the hottest rock and roll in Southern Oregon. The late great Jerry Fisher is at your service today. You just heard "Don't Eat the Yellow Snow" by the incredible Frank Zappa and the Mothers of Invention. Before that, "Down to Seeds and Stems Again", by Commander Cody and His Lost Planet Airmen. Which by the way, I just happen to be. So if you've got some of that Southern Oregon thunderfuck just laying around the cabin, be sure and drop by the studio and give your favorite DJ a little puff."

"Now don't forget you listeners, here at KEGG 102.4 FM we are always ready to play your requests. Just write down your name and the name of your favorite tune, include a check for twenty-five dollars to Jerry Fisher Productions, and your song will go out to our thousands of listeners throughout the Rogue Valley. And remember, all our request line participants get a free complimentary bowl of oatmeal at the finest restaurant in Jordan County, the infamous, I mean to say famous, Pollard Creek Inn. The Pollard Creek Inn has been given a five-star rating by the Grants Pass Tribune newspaper, and its dry oatmeal cuisine was voted best in the entire State of Oregon. Brown sugar and milk are extra, of course."

"It's a beautiful summer day here in Southern Oregon. Expect high temperatures today of about a hundred and seventy-five, and a low tonight of a hundred and forty-five, so you truckers out there be sure and carry a jacket this evening."

"Now remember listeners, don't forget to support our sponsors, the SLA, the FBI, and the SDS. And be sure to visit the Frankly Flat Dance Hall, where you can really learn how to kick out the jams, located just down the road in Twisted Ankle, Oregon."

But let's get back to the show. Here's a little something for all you game show lovers, titled "Beat the Reaper" by the Firesign Theater. Good luck to all our contestants. Although I would strongly encourage you to draw up that Last Will and Testament before you play. And be sure to name Jerry Fisher Productions as your one and only heir."

"So don't touch that dial, stayed tuned to 102.4 FM, the best rock and roll in Southern Oregon, twenty-four hours a day, seven days a week. Live from our mountain top studios here in Pollard Creek. And never forget what your favorite host, Jerry Fisher, always says. 'Who would ever want to be sane in an insane world?'"

Speaking of insanity, experts might say that such a diagnosis can only be seen through the eyes of the beholder. Although from a legal perspective, insanity might be harder to prove than any particular witness of first impression. It might be easier to simply use the label sociopath, and then let any empirical data speak for itself. As for Crazy Randy Halston, he didn't know one way or the other. Much like alcoholics, the insane are often the last to know.

One thing for sure, Randy Halston hadn't gotten the label 'Crazy Randy' due to some inexplicable bureaucratic error. No, Crazy Randy had dutifully earned his reputation through many long hours of dedicated effort. There was a lifetime rap sheet of inter-departmental documentations trailing behind Randy Halston, like toilet paper stuck to his ass. It was a trail no doubt, that if adequately measured, might truly be a mile long.

Was Randy Halston the brightest bulb on the block? Most outside observers would venture not. But was Crazy Randy the meanest angriest bulb in Pollard Creek? On that count, the man would undoubtedly get a few votes. The reasons for Crazy Randy Halston's particular human predicament would probably take a full semester of intense psychological research, complete with many studious hours of lab experimentation. Inside the lab, tests would be run for the effects of an alcohol-related pregnancy, or an economic deprivation. Other tests would be made for a harsh and uncaring childhood development, as well as domestic violence in the home, or the effects of an eventual adolescent stigmatization. There were so many critical elements to measure and pour into the pathological beaker, it would be extremely difficult to pin down the formula where it all went wrong. But wrong it had gone all the same, and it had only taken a few brief years to get there. And today, Pollard Creek, Oregon was finding itself blessed with the chemistry of its nefarious results.

Had Crazy Randy Halston started the fire that sought to burn down the Pollard Creek Country Store? Well, nobody knew. But the word was out that the authorities were looking for him, and so Randy had holed up on Cougar Gulch for the better part of a week, waiting on an outcome. Strangely, it had never come. It was a quiet Sunday evening, the last days of July shedding off the calendar. The days and nights remained hot and slow, with only a few vagrant cumulus clouds sneaking across the sky. The dog days of August lay ahead. August can be a precarious time, where the oppressive days of a summer heat can drive some human beings to go one way or the other. One might fall into a stupor of passive fatigue and sluggish unconsciousness, appearing listless and dehydrated. Another might be overheated to a maddening frustration of violent intent, waiting on the vagary of an unintended spark in order to explode.

Either way, Crazy Randy Halston was restless. His old beaten trailer house was like an oven inside. Maybe the insufferable heat of Mother Nature was pressing on his thinking, but what the hell. On a dusky Sunday evening, the town of Pollard Creek would be deader than a doornail. All the cops would be home with family. It was time for a ride with the windows down, followed by an ice cold beer away from home.

"Hey, Buck," Randy Halston roared. "Get off your fat ass. It's time to go to town, time to get a cold one at the Inn."

"Are you sure, Randy?" Buck warned. "What if somebody sees you and calls? There could be trouble. Are you sure you're ready for that?"

"Shit, did I ask you for any questions, Buck? I'm always ready. Like I said, I'm ready for a cold beer and a ride to town. Or am I repeating myself, you tell me."

"Whatever you say, Randy," Buck Thornton sighed. "But I think I better do the driving."

It didn't take long for Deputy Sheriff Bill Haines to get the call. And sure enough, it came just as he and his wife were sitting down for dinner. So what the hell else was new? Bill Haines' current career was twenty-four seven, and much like Murphy's law, bad things usually happened at the most inconvenient times. This guy, Murphy, whoever he might be, was getting to be a real pain in the ass. Bill Haines wasn't getting paid for twenty-four seven, you could take that notion to the bank. But it came with the territory. And his territory was Pollard Creek, Oregon. That was all that needed to be said. So Haines took the call.

The caller was Ralph Swanson, the owner of the Pollard Creek Country Store. He had stepped out onto the front porch of his grocery store to get a little air. Looking over at the Pollard Creek Inn, he'd spotted a very familiar pick-up truck parked outside. Randy Halston was drinking in town. Bill Haines stood in his kitchen, the phone receiver and cord hooked to his ear, watching as his dinner went chilling on the plate.

Bill Haines went through the same standard rigmarole he had warned Ralph Swanson about earlier in the week. Don't take the law into your own hands, Ralph, the investigation is moving forward. Randy Halston was beginning to show himself. He was obviously thinking that things were not pointing at him. This was a good sign, Ralph. You have to continue to be patient, and let the law takes it course. Certainly, if Halston comes to the store for any reason, call immediately. Otherwise, keep your distance and stay out of the way. Maintain your cool.

Mashed potatoes were never meant to be eaten cold. Bill Haines forced his way through the meal, wanting to talk of retirement, but knowing that particular dream remained several years away. He would have to continue with this dirty profession he had chosen. Or perhaps the profession had somehow chosen him. It didn't matter, he couldn't remember anymore. So, unless the Publishers Clearing House people showed up at his door, with a check in hand and the cameras rolling, Bill Haines would have to continue marching on. He would have to continue settling troubles, dealing with this trash heap of a world. All the while praying he didn't get caught in a crossfire before his time might finally become his own.

Finishing his dinner, Bill Haines got up from the table, dialing into Grants Pass. He filed the news that Randy Halston had been reportedly spotted at the Pollard Creek Inn. Bill Haines presumed a response would not come until the following day, when the regular work week would begin. Perhaps he could relax for the rest of the evening, before starting again tomorrow. But the phone rang again within the hour. This time, not from headquarters, but from that little prick of an Oregon State Police detective, a man named Barry Walton. Walton was a real piece of work, a guy who loved nothing more than to fuck with the bad guys, to kick some ass when nobody else was looking. That was Walton's rep, and from everything Bill Haines had ever seen or heard, it was damn well earned. However, the call now gave him a clue of recognition in regard to the Halston matter. Indeed, something else was up. Still, for the life of him, he was at a loss to figure what it might be.

"Haines, I'm calling back on the Halston arson investigation. You reported the suspect in Pollard Creek this evening. Give me the details."

Bill Haines did not have much to say. He had been requested to report to his superiors whenever Halston was spotted in town. And that's exactly what he had done.

"Okay," Walton responded. "Maintain the surveillance over the next few days. If he is showing up in Pollard Creek for any reason, I want you to call my office, in addition to your superiors in Grants Pass. But particularly, call whenever he might be spotted at the Pollard Creek Inn. It sounds to me like Halston feels the heat on him is growing cold. I want you to keep your distance, but stay on top of anything you hear. We want Halston to feel that it is safe to be in town, while we gain enough evidence to take him down. Got that?"

"Yeah, I got it," Bill Haines answered. "But tell me Walton, what's got everybody all hung up on Halston? We haven't even gotten the arson report complete. He is simply a suspect at this time. I need to know what's up here, so I can act accordingly. I need some background from you."

"Listen, Haines. There is information on our end that I cannot divulge at this time. But to help you out, let's just say there is a parallel investigation in progress that involves Halston. Right now, it's only on a need to know basis, so for tonight that's all I can say. However, we will let your department know all the details as things progress. For now, I just need some eyes and ears on Halston whenever he appears. Trust me on this. I will bring you up to date as things develop."

There was no sense in Bill Haines trying to get anymore out of Walton. The Oregon State Police ran their own show, especially the farther you got away from the City of Portland, or the State Capitol in Salem. The local county enforcement agencies were looked upon as suspect, as second-class policing districts, and thus treated accordingly. If the state boys were involved in something, the Jordan County Sheriff's Department would be out of the loop until they were needed, and especially a small-town deputy sheriff like William 'Bill' Haines. It was the way of the world, and it wasn't likely to change anytime soon.

But as he lay in bed on another hot summer evening, something else was surely on the burner in Pollard Creek. There had been one particular piece of information revealed by Walton, and it rang in Bill Haines' mind. "Particularly, the Pollard Creek Inn." Bill Haines didn't know for certain, but he now felt a suspicion. Perhaps another battle line was being drawn, and there was a good chance it involved the hippie kids at the Pollard Creek Inn.

CHAPTER TWENTY-EIGHT

THE NIGHT THEY DROVE OLD DIXIE DOWN
Take Down / Pollard Creek / August, 1974

THE BRIGHT BLUE THERMAL SUMMER OF JULY, 1974 turned a calendar page in the rough mountain terrain of Southern Oregon. The month of August entered onto the stage of time, barefoot, its feet covered in red volcanic dust. The evergreen trees of Ponderosa pine and Douglas fir breathed heavily, searching for oxygen, thirsting for hydration. The creeks, once bursting with the bounty of a winter's rain and snow, crawled scrawny and narrow through the canyons, shorn naked, their river rocks exposed. Swimming holes began to dangerously shrink away. Spring boxes trickled, gardens wilted in the heat. Everywhere, the fear of wildfire was on the lookout. The image of one tiny ember glowing in the dying grass, could cause a sleepless night or nightmare, where all might be lost.

The first day of August was a typical Thursday morning, typical in the sense that for weeks now, each heated day from dawn to dusk had appeared exactly the same. At the Mulcahey Farm, Sean McAllister helped move the garden water pump deeper into a pocket hole in a suffering Pollard Creek. Valerie Williams, having received her welfare check, dressed in a long sleeveless flowered chemise, preparing for a town trip to Grants Pass. Tom Sullivan tramped up the hillside above Railroad Bridge, checking on the spring box that brought water to the property below. At the Pollard Creek Inn, Jimmijay Connell removed the hinges of the kitchen's exterior double-doors, moving them to the outside lawn to paint. No one in Pollard Creek had much to say, as if to speak even a few words would cause the body to break out in sweat. For anyone who had spent a winter in Southern Oregon, it was unimaginable to consider complaining about the incessant sun and parched earth. It would be a sacrilege to entertain such thoughts. Consequently, silence was the necessary alternative, rather than to ever wish out loud for rain to come. But the circumstances were growing graver now, so quietly and secretively, those wishes could be heard.

Through no particular fault of their own, two men who had never met each other, were out of town for separate reasons. Back in New York City, Albert Krieger, the majority owner and unelected leader of the Pollard Creek Inn, had flown home to see his ailing father. Reading the front page of the New York Times, Albert marveled at the picture of a young French tightrope walker, suspended a quarter of a mile above the city's streets, strung between the two massive towers of the World Trade Center. Closer by, Wilton Parker, Chairman of the Jordan County Board of Commissioners, was vacationing with his family on the edge of a dark and cool Diamond Lake, high on the ridges of the Cascade Range. For Wilton Parker, it was good to be away from the tumult of paperwork and public criticism of his current political profession. Today, he would be free from the necessity of having to behave in a controlled and respectful public manner, those required characteristics that came with his job. These two men would be connected by the history of the moments to come, not so much by their personal proximities, but by their conspicuous absences on a hot August day.

Unknown to almost everyone in Pollard Creek, the day was waiting upon itself for time to pass. At one-thirty in the afternoon the call came through to Detective Barry Walton. Uncharacteristically, the call was not from Deputy Sheriff Bill Haines, but rather Ralph Swanson at the Pollard Creek Country Store. Crazy Randy Halston, and his ever present sidekick, Buck Thornton, were now in town. They had entered the Pollard Creek Inn, much like they had done at a similar time on the previous afternoons. Detective Walton was feeling particularly proud of himself. His plan was working so far. Walton had intentionally kept Deputy Bill Haines out of the loop. He knew Haines was a good cop, but he was too good a cop for the matter at hand. Bill Haines was definitely too close to all the locals in town, including the hippies at the Pollard Creek Inn. Bill Haines would have objected to the plan, and certainly the specific intents of Barry Walton's mission. Instead,

Walton had made Ralph Swanson his set-up guy. Walton knew that Ralph Swanson would do anything to see Randy Halston arrested and eventually charged with arson. Events were now in motion.

Walton's unmarked police car was parked near the north entrance ramp of Interstate 5 in Solace Valley, four miles and one mountain pass south of Pollard Creek. Beside him was another Oregon State Police detective. Nearby, were two Jordan County Sheriff vehicles, each with two men inside, awaiting direct instructions. On the north end of Pollard Creek, in another unmarked vehicle, an Oregon State Police special-weapons team of four men waited patiently, ready for the plan to ensue. If perhaps by the infamous chance that Patricia Randolph Hearst, a wanted fugitive for bank robbery in the State of California, might be hiding inside the Pollard Creek Inn, the State of Oregon would be prepared for such a possibility. In addition, at a booth in the Hungry Dog Café, two civilian public servants sat biding their time. One was from the Oregon Liquor Control Board, the other from the State Board of Health. Detective Barry Walton was anxious to give the orders to proceed, and so he did.

The unmarked Oregon special-weapons team moved first. They drove the shorter distance into the center of town, while Walton and the Jordan County vehicles drove north from Solace Valley. Within minutes the weapons team positioned itself in the open triangle area at the center of Pollard Creek. As Walton's vehicle arrived at the Pollard Creek Inn parking lot, the armed men exited their vehicle. Two of the men braced high-powered rifles on the top of the car, aiming toward the building's entrance. The other two officers walked toward the target to back up Walton. The Jordan County Sheriff' vehicles took position on opposite sides of the Pollard Creek Inn, one parking in the middle of the access road, the other where Lower Pollard Creek Road and Keto Road met near the post office. With two Jordan County deputies inside each vehicle, one from each proceeded toward the facility, the other two setting up for traffic control. In the heated somnolence of another summer afternoon, with so many citizens resting inside, at first nobody seemed to notice.

Detective Walton and his partner, both in plain clothes, pushed themselves from their sedan, quickly entering the Pollard Creek Inn. Turning left, they entered into the barroom. Laura Hale stood behind the bar, working her afternoon shift. Walton approached her, flashed his badge, asking for the whereabouts of one Randy Halston. For a moment, Laura and the several patrons in the bar froze in silence. Then a man at one of the tables spoke, saying, "He's not here." Walton turned and approached the man, asking him to identify himself. As Walton's partner stepped forward to join him in the interrogation, another man at the table, sensing the opportunity, suddenly jumped up, escaping out of the bar. The fugitive bolted into the empty dining room, running through the kitchen and out the open back doors. As Walton radioed the escape, his partner chased after the fleeing man. Walton then ordered the man who had spoken to step outside.

Jimmijay Connell, standing in the lawn, paint brush in hand, caught sight of Randy Halston flying through the vacant kitchen door, before racing toward the back of the building. A moment later, another man followed with a pistol in his hand. Jimmijay turned toward the front of the building, seeing the police cars and other uniformed officers approaching. Jimmijay, acting on the impulse of a kid from Chicago, threw up his hands as the officers ran toward him. "I'm just a workman," he said urgently, as the officers flew by toward the back of the Inn. But just as quickly, Jimmijay sprinted up the back stairway toward the second floor. He rousted those slumbering in their rooms, then ran into his own, before racing to the bathroom to flush his stash. Guitar Glenn undressed his guitar, feeling naked, but quickly scrambled through his clothes bureau, doing the same. With their emergency missions complete, everyone rushed down the back stairway of the building, seeking some form of safety outside.

Meanwhile, Detective Walton escorted the man who had spoken to him, out through the front door of the premises. Two uniformed officers met Walton outside. Walton asked the man if it was Halston who had run from the bar. The man rudely answered that he didn't know. In response, Walton whirled the man around, pressing him against the front side of the building, before delivering a hard body shot to the ribs. Walton pulled a knife from the man's belt, throwing it to the ground. When provided with handcuffs, Walton secured the suspect. When the man asked what he was being arrested for, Walton simply said "concealed deadly weapon". Another man, who had been sitting at the table inside, followed onto the porch. He demanded to know why his friend was being arrested. Walton pushed the second man in the chest, ordering him to turn toward the building, taking his sheathed knife as well. With the second man cuffed, the officers led the men to a police car. Walton slammed the head of one of the men against the top of the car, shoving the man inside. The doors were shut, automatically locking down.

Tension and fear, those two major chemical elements of violence and mistrust, swept through the heavy-baked air of a Thursday afternoon. Suddenly, as if strangely dropped from the sky, a crowd of bystanders appeared from nowhere, children included, surrounding the chaotic scene. Sheriff Bill Haines, unknowingly performing his daily patrol on the back road from Solace Valley to Pollard Creek, heard on his scanner a call for backup at the Pollard Creek Inn. Haines accelerated his vehicle, speeding the five miles back into town.

Valerie Williams, driving her station wagon, her son Canyon sitting beside her, exited the interstate at Pollard Creek. She turned onto the access road leading into town. As Valerie began passing the Hungry Dog Café, she saw the flashing lights of a police car, a uniformed officer waving her to the right. An immediate sense of concern overtook her, wondering what it might be. Valerie stopped and explained to the officer where she needed to go. In order to get to home to Main Street, she was told to drive to the far end of the triangle, then circle back, staying clear of the Pollard Creek Inn. Valerie worried. As she circled back toward Main, she could see other police cars and a crowd of familiar faces scattered in small groups outside the building. Reaching home, she debated whether to go, but grabbed Canyon by the hand, walking quickly but protectively up the street towards the danger ahead.

Darla Bloom had a different mission. She took the car keys that were handed to her, walking hurriedly to the back parking lot of the Inn. She told a policeman she needed to get her children. But instead, she sped out of town toward London Ridge Road and the property of Robert Sage. Sage was a co-owner of the Inn, but he lived on his own eighty-acre piece of timberland four miles out of Pollard Creek. For Darla, the first two miles were paved, but the last two would be a winding and bumpy ride into the mountains. With Albert Krieger back in New York, everyone needed Robert Sage to come, and come quick. With the summer dust billowing behind her, Darla rushed over the potholes and hairpin turns, speeding her way with the news.

With the two men from the bar secured in the police vehicle, Detective Barry Walton focused his attention on finding the suspect he had come to arrest. His partner and another officer had searched the outside grounds, including the little caretaker's house behind the Inn, before sweeping through the upstairs rooms of the building. There was no sign of Randy Halston. Walton ordered an all-points bulletin. But just as Walton was about to have the building searched again, an officer noticed a small open access space in the foundation of the building. Kneeling down, the officer pointed a flashlight inside, spotting movement deep within a corner of the dark interior. He called out for Walton to assist. With Walton's flashlight adding to the illumination, they could see the face of a huddled figure crouching inside. Immediately, the two officers pulled back from the opening. Walton nodded to the officer to pull his firearm, before ordering the suspect to exit immediately.

Arriving at the scene, Bill Haines pushed through the crowd of bystanders, quickly striding toward the crouching pair of men. Walton looked up. "Talk to him, Haines," Walton commanded, "or we'll have to flush him out with gas." Bill Haines just stared at Walton, wanting to tell the little prick all that the felt about him. Haines held his stare until Walton's expression acknowledged that he understood. Then, Haines spoke into the opening. "Randy, there are women and children out here, young man. You've got nowhere to go. If you are armed, tell me right now." Bill Haines waited for response. The answer of 'no' came from inside the crawlspace. "Randy, don't make us have to gas the building to get you out. At this point, you will only be charged with resisting arrest." Haines looked up at Walton, desiring confirmation. But like the little puissant he was, Walton only shrugged. Bill Haines just shook his head, but continued speaking. "Don't make it any worse for yourself, Randy. You know the drill here. If you continue to resist, no one can help you."

For a long moment, nothing was heard, but what followed were shouted words out of the hole. "All right, I'm coming out, you fuckers. Not you Haines, but the rest of those fucking assholes." At that remark, a devilish smile crossed Walton's face. "Hands first, Randy," Walton urged, sounding appreciative, "then we'll help pull you out." However, the minute Randy Halston's hat and shoulders scrunched through the opening, Walton nodded to the other officer. They grabbed Halston under his armpits, forcefully dragging him into the yard. Lightning quick, Walton was on top of the suspect. He secured Halston's wrists, jamming his knee into Halston's back. "Handcuffs," he shouted. Once the other officer had wrestled the handcuffs onto Halston's wrists, Walton released his grip on the forearms. But Walton didn't stop there. He swatted off Halton's brimmed leather hat, before violently yanking the long hair on the back of his head.

"Got you, you fucking hippie asshole," Walton muttered only to Halston, but he continued to hold Halston's head back as if displaying his prey. "You're under arrest for arson in the first degree, and whatever fucking else we can think of along the way. Now get the fuck up." Walton released his grip on Halston's hair. He dragged the suspect up from the ground, quickly turning Halston around to face him, the other officer strongly securing him from behind. Randy Halston looked down on the smaller detective, the anger and spite of his own particular life searing like a burn into Walton's eyes. But Walton only smiled his wicked grin. "Answer me, you are Randall Gray Halston, is that correct?"

For another long moment Crazy Randy Halston maintained his piercing look of hate leveled at Walton. Then his face relaxed, replaced by a satiric grin of his own. He lowered his gaze, smiled, then spit at Walton's shoes. Looking back at Walton, he said, "No motherfucker, I'm Donald Duck". Walton appeared to look away, but cocked his right arm, landing a punch into Halston's gut. A burst of air and saliva exhaled from Randy Halston's mouth, as he doubled over from the hit.

With the punch, an impulsive roar emanated from the center of Pollard Creek, casting its echo down the narrow valleys and timbered rock canyons of this mountain community. It was a roar of visceral realization and shocked response, of men tightening their fists and crying out, of women aghast at such a physical act, of young children cringing close to their mother's side, their breath sucking in with fear. Detective Barry Walton heard the rush of the action's consequence, feeling the arc of a dangerous wind. But unlike someone recognizing their own mistake, and seeking the cover of excuse, Walton's defenses only caused him to smile ever more. Bill Haines stepped forward, "That will be enough, Walton, right now."

"Stand down, Haines," Walton shot back. "This is my collar. This is my operation. You will step back immediately. You will secure this crowd, do you hear me?"

Deputy Bill Haines steadied himself. He looked to the officer who held the bent over Randy Halston, but the officer stared away. Walton felt for the firearm at his side, before grabbing the slumping suspect. Along with the other officer they wrangled the stumbling Halston to an awaiting police car. The crowd continued shouting its discontent at what they had witnessed. After forcing Randy Halston into the cruiser, Walton stepped toward the angry crowd, shouting that if they did not disperse they would be subject to arrest. The crowd quieted in response, but not a single person moved. Bill Haines had no choice but to interject himself further into the situation before a riot might ensue. He began trying to calm the crowd while Walton ordered the two police cars of arrested men off to Grants Pass for booking.

When owner Robert Sage finally reached the scene, Randy Halston and the others had already been transported to Grants Pass. However, the special-weapons team remained standing in the triangle out in front of the Pollard Creek Inn, their high-powered rifles held across their chests. Sage stalked toward them, angry with intent. But the cops turned the guns toward him, ordering him to halt. Sage demanded to know who was in charge. One of the gunmen pointed to a man standing in front of the building. Sage turned around, heading for a man not dressed in uniform. But before he could reach the man, Guitar Glenn and Jimmijay Connell met Sage in the middle of the road. They informed him that the building was being searched upstairs. Also, that two other men, one from the liquor control board, and another from the state health department had begun to inspect the premises. No one else had been arrested, they said, but nobody was allowed into the building until the search was complete.

"Robert, you won't believe this," Jimmijay Connell said excitedly. "Someone said they are really looking for Patty Hearst."

Robert Sage humped a laugh, but it was not a laugh of humor or pleasant response. Instead, it was a laugh at the recognition of such a strange yet indelible absurdity, and all the unbelievable bullshit that had gone on recently in this crazy crazy town.

"Jimmijay," Sage mused disappointedly, "you and your goddamned bathroom humor." But there was little else to do but shake his head.

Robert Sage continued forward, aimed at the man in street clothes. Upon reaching Detective Walton, Sage got right to the point. "I'm one of the owners of this building. And I want to know just what the hell is going on?" Sage began. "You better have a goddamned warrant to search this property, and if not, you will call off these people and exit the premises immediately."

Detective Barry Walton quietly smiled. "One of the owners, are you? And what might your name be, if I might ask?"

Robert Sage bristled at the arrogance of the man. "Sage. Robert Sage. Now where the hell's the warrant?"

Walton reached slowly into his shirt pocket, pulling out a document. He neatly unfolded the paper, taking his sweet ass time. "Let's see," he spoke, as if to question himself. "Who do we have here? We have Krieger, and we have Rucker, and what do you know, we have Sage." Then he paused and looked at Robert Sage. "Mr. Sage," Walton intoned, as if a teacher explaining to a child, "based on complaints filed with the authorities in Jordan County, and concurrent with laws administered through the State of Oregon, the warrant states that we have reason to believe that there are numerous safety violations currently ongoing at this commercial liquor and dining establishment. More particularly, the possible existence of weapons in the facility, as well the sale of liquor to minors under the legal age. In addition, we believe that certain food safety and sanitation issues exist on these premises that could endanger the public welfare. And what do you know, I have here the signature of the Superior Court Judge for Jordan County, Oregon, J. Stewart Bream." At that point, Walton gracefully handed the document toward Robert Sage.

Robert Sage took the warrant in hand, seeking confirmation of its authenticity. For a moment he scanned the document, but he was too upset to read it word for word. Sage raised his head, staring at the man. They were both about the same size in height, but this guy was older by maybe ten years. Robert Sage wasn't worried, he knew he could wrestle the man to the mat if necessary, or out in any parking lot at any appropriate time. "And who may I ask are you?" Robert Sage asked sharply.

"Me?" Walton drawled. "Me? Well, I'm nobody special. Just Detective Barry Walton of the Oregon State Police, Special Operations Unit for Southwestern Oregon. Like I said, nobody very special."

Sage could feel the hot blood rushing through his body, boiling at the insolence of this man standing before him. Then Sage held out the warrant. As Walton's hand reached to claim it, Sage raised it up until Walton's eyes met his. Sage motioned the paper higher, tight in his hand. "Bullshit," Sage answered, before letting the document float to the ground.

Walton didn't make a move to retrieve it. "I'm sorry you feel that way, Mr. Sage. However, as unfortunate as this may be, it is the order of the Court. But let me tell you one thing, Mr. Sage. And this is strictly off the record, mind you. Just between you and me. But let me be very clear." Walton hesitated, pausing for effect.

"Nobody, and I mean nobody, especially the State of Oregon, will ever let you hippies take over this town."

CHAPTER TWENTY-NINE

ALL THAT YOU DREAM
The Aftermath / Pollard Creek / August, 1974

BY EARLY THURSDAY EVENING, the afternoon's twisted events at the Pollard Creek Inn seemed to have disappeared into an historical moment in time. Following the drama, the Inn's residents closed the business for the rest of the day, nervously trying to ascertain the consequences. The streets of the town appeared asleep, solitary, like the measured silence that often follows a crowded holiday parade having come and gone. Only the passivity of the summer heat remained.

Throughout the evening and following day, the communication of what had occurred spread up and down the famished creeks and asphalt arterials of Pollard Creek and Solace Valley. Outside of town, with telephones at a premium, word of the bust passed its way between driver-side vehicle windows, while motors idled in the middle of the road. The gossip mill started to grind away, with human perceptions beginning to elevate the story, coloring the truth with painted strokes on canvas. The gossip talk began to make mountains out of mole hills, creating fiction novels out of accurate journalistic reports, until the telling itself had taken on a life all its own.

The Grants Pass Tribune newspaper reported its own prejudiced view, which could only be ingested with shakers of salt. A suspect in the case had been arrested and jailed on felony charges of arson in the first degree, with bail set at $105,000. The Tribune declared that a dozen police officers had been at the scene, along with forty 'longhairs', who shouted obscenities at them. Two other men had been arrested for harassment and third-degree assault. The newspaper made no mention of concealed deadly weapons. There was no mention of anyone slamming Buck Thornton's head on the side of a police car, no mention of high-powered rifles pointed at the Pollard Creek Inn. There was not a single written word detailing Detective Barry Walton's sucker punch of a restrained individual, which had electrified the onlookers. And conveniently, there was no reporting of the search of the premises, either by police, or state liquor and health officials. According to the police report, the court-ordered warrant had been for the arrest of Randal Gray Halston, nothing more. Not even Patty Hearst could get her name in print, when it came to the truth about the Pollard Creek Inn.

When Albert Kreiger received the news by telephone back in New York City, a helpless sense of foreboding overtook him, but there was nothing he could do. Albert's father lay seriously ill in the hospital, his prognosis in doubt. Albert could not return. In the days that followed, Jordan County Commissioner Wilton Parker returned from his vacation. Despite knowing the real inside story, Wilton chose to follow along as the designed events continued to unfold. The State had already managed to get to the other two commissioners. Everything was locked and loaded for bear. Although the Pollard Creek Inn continued to operate, the fix was definitely in.

On the following Thursday, August 8th, 1974, the next step in the plan was implemented. The Director of the Oregon State Liquor Control Commission ordered the suspension of the beer and wine license, acting under the emergency powers of the State. The suspension would be in response to complaints lodged by the Oregon State Police, the Jordan County Sheriffs Department, and finally by the Jordan County Board of Commissioners, Wilton Parker included. Reports had been received that indicated a myriad of safety and sanitary violations. The charges complained of "numerous children wandering in and out of the tavern section of the Inn, unauthorized person's serving liquor, as well as the existence of weapons inside the facility, including the presence of men sitting outside the Inn during the early hours of the morning with shotguns in hand." The Oregon State Health Department kept the mud flying, stating that the "existing sewer facilities were considered inadequate".

By late afternoon the same day, state police and sheriff's deputies accompanied liquor control and health officials to the establishment in Pollard Creek, where notice of the suspension was served. The second major piece of the puzzle had now been set. The scandal was legally in progress, and the Pollard Creek Inn was closed. Yet, throughout the mountain hills and valleys of Jordan County, as well as the extended traverse of the American continent, hardly a single citizen paid attention. For across the land there was a greater and much more indelible moment at play. The President of the United States of America, Richard Milhous Nixon, had resigned from public office.

The Watergate Scandal had reached the highest political seat of power on the planet earth. However, as he made his last parting statement as President, Richard Nixon continued to keep to his script. He admitted no wrongdoing, only the single admission that due to events he was now unable to lead. Still, a sense of temporary vindication crossed the hearts of many in the land. Richard Nixon had been expelled, his reign of deceit finally coming to a close.

Sean McAllister was pleased with the news that Richard Nixon would now be forced into a powerless obscurity, shorn of his arrogant command of the nation that McAllister called home. For almost six years Nixon had dominated the conscience of America, his scurrilous mendacities resulting in the unnecessary killing of thousands. He had jailed and marginalized many others, all for an enterprise lost. In the mind of McAllister and many others, Nixon, Kissinger, Agnew, and Hoover were criminals in the first degree, masquerading as public servants, adorning themselves as men of character and trust. For many in this country, nothing could have been further from the truth.

The Nixon cabal had taken the best of America, attempted to destroy its ethical foundations, and circumvent its rule of law with a fraudulent carelessness bordering on treason. These particular men had blood all over their manicured white hands, deserving nothing more than a set of iron bars staring down their face. Mercy was not a word whose meaning these men had ever understood, and surely it should never be an emotional fate they should ever receive. If Sean McAllister was certain of any one thing at the age of twenty-four years, he believed he would always be certain of these feelings. They were a given. No pardon or forgiveness ever need apply.

But strangely, after so many years of frustration and anger, the wringing of hands, the helplessness in the face of such power, this day should have been one for celebration and relief, for the wicked witch was finally dead. But after so much time and so much angst, Nixon's ending seemed short of elation, worn down by the slow process of its own inevitability.

Yes, Richard Nixon was gone. But realistically, only from a job he could no longer keep. Beyond him, lay an American public that refused to see themselves as an accessory after the fact. Sending Nixon home would be the sum total of their responsibility in the matter. Sooner or later a new snake oil salesman would come along. He would herald America's sacred sense of Christian hegemony. He would drape them in a flag of red, white, and blue. He would cater once again to their fears of things unknown. Deceit is like a cockroach. Uninvited, it moves at night and is almost impossible to dispel. Kill one, and another arrives to takes its place. Richard Nixon was gone, one big fat cockroach eliminated. But it could never be a day for celebration. Sadly perhaps, Nixon's fall from grace might just become another rest stop on the road to oblivion.

Ironically, over three thousand miles away from Washington D.C., the Pollard Creek Inn had lost its bar and restaurant license. The enterprise of its economic life and survival would be latched up tight. Cunningly, another malevolent bug had risen out of the sink drain. And nothing much had changed.

Darla Bloom brought the news of the Inn's suspension down to the Mulcahey Farm. Darla was picking up her children to spend a day or two at the Pollard Creek Inn. Upon her leaving, McAllister walked her and the children across the swinging bridge back to the parking turnout by the road. As he helped Darla pack the sleeping bags and clothing into the car, she turned to him and spoke.

"You know, the kids are staying for the weekend. And then on Monday, my friend Taylor, who owns the school bus is coming to stay for a visit. I'm going to be really busy and won't be able to see you for a time. Plus, things are going to be different now at the Inn. Taylor will be taking the bus when he leaves, and I need to move into a room upstairs. So there will be a lot of things going on for awhile."

McAllister understood, but wasn't sure how to respond. Darla's statement was matter of fact, which didn't surprise him. She wasn't a woman who minced words when she knew what she needed to do.

McAllister had felt the sheer unemotional imperative of her words before. They were always practical and direct, as if to say that sexual intimacy was one set of circumstances, the rest of her daily life quite another. Her reddish brown hair rested straight along her arms and shoulders, thinly crossing the front of her laced white blouse, her firm breasted cleavage exposed to his sight. Raising his gaze to her stiffened facial expression, he fixed a furtive glance into her deep brown eyes, before looking away.

"Whatever is best, Darla," he managed to respond. In a manner of speaking, Darla's words were not unexpected. McAllister had come to understand his role in this new scenario, this involuntary part of his life he had chosen willingly to play. Maybe he did expect that more would be said between them, a more sincere discussion of the message being sent. They had indeed shared some personal level of intimacy during the previous weeks of time. But Darla simply let a thin smile cross her face, before giving him a short embrace. With that gesture of affection complete, she circled to the front of the car to be on with her way. Opening the door, she looked at him standing alone on the other side.

"When do you leave for Washington, for the apple harvest?" she asked.

McAllister had to take a moment for the question to sink into his mind. He had become temporarily detached, as if watching a movie scene play out on the theater screen. Then he realized he was actually an actor in this film. He answered Darla's question.

"A few weeks, I think. I'm not really sure."

"Oh, still a while yet," she responded. "So we'll see each other in town, or perhaps when I bring the kids. No need for any farewells tonight. Goodbye, Sean," she said, then slipped into seat of the car

"See you, Darla." The car started and pulled out onto the road, pointing back toward Pollard Creek. Darla and the kids waved, McAllister waving back as the vehicle motored away. He stood still for a time, listening as the car headed up the road, its metallic glare flashing through the trees, reflected by the lingering evening sun. Yeah, he thought to himself, the Pollard Creek Inn is closed, in more ways than one. Yet strangely, although there was a slight empty feeling in his stomach, it wasn't stretching deep. Certainly, the shock of rejection is often a pointed arrow that usually finds its mark. But in a weird way, this particular arrow had not found his heart. It felt more like a glancing strike to his side. No doubt, some emotional blood would be drawn, but he sensed he would be able to pull out the arrow's sharp tip, before methodically treating the wound.

It wasn't as if the reality of Darla's firing him had come totally out of the blue. He sort of had sensed its inevitability, maybe as far back as their first morning together. Now, standing by the road, he turned himself west, taking in the reflected light of a setting sky. So here he was, living in this high summered paradise that seemed to continue unabated day after day. It occurred to him that in the past two months he had been keenly observant of everything around him. Yet, on a different level, the time had been spent as if walking through a dream, waiting for his number to be called. The sharp pointed tip of Darla's sailing arrow now seemed to cut him awake, a certain wave of recognition taking hold.

Since his arrival in Pollard Creek, he realized he had been living a daily life of reaction. With everything around him being so different, each day had been spent tagging along amongst the lives of others. He had been drawn into following the script, engaging whenever necessary, finding his place. The arc of his own life had strangely been put on hold, but not in a negative way at all. It was more like being a tourist on holiday, or a curious stranger visiting a foreign land. Darla Bloom had pulled him into her own life trajectory, and without a second thought he had willingly followed along.

Now suddenly, his past, which had become so disconnected from him since his entry into Pollard Creek, grabbed hold of his present with a firmly held grip. In doing so, it demanded his future join the party, refusing to take no for an answer. And even though the future can never really be told, its bold predictions often as ambivalent as a restless thought, the future does demand one thing, it demands belief. It demands a certain volition, whatever the outcome might be.

Okay, he reminded himself. I'll go to Washington and work the apple harvest as long as I can. After that, I'll return to the Mulcahey Farm and Pollard Creek. I'll continue my journey in this beautiful mountain community. I'll try to save enough money to visit my family for Christmas. And finally, I'll write that letter to Mad. I'll make good on reconnecting this aborted trail of her painful loss in my life. Once and for all, I'll wipe the slate clean. All the while, I'll begin to live my life in my own direction, whatever that direction might become.

Emboldened by these new resolutions, McAllister turned back across the railroad tracks. He walked the dusty fire road down toward the swinging bridge. He figured he would probably be too late for the communal dinner, but it really didn't matter. He had some food at camp. But coming up to meet him was Rita, 'Lovely Rita' as Mookie James referred to her. More than likely, Rita was on her way home. She lived a short distance down Lower Pollard Creek Road, caretaking a cabin for a man from San Francisco, who was rarely ever around. Rita worked for the Forest Service, performing long summer stints at a fire lookout tower somewhere in the forest. But it seemed that whenever Rita was home from her job, she liked to visit the Mulcahey Farm, taking in the lives of its residents in her soft-spoken inquisitive way.

Much like Darla Bloom, Rita had long brown hair, but much darker and full. It cast in curly waves down her shoulders and back. Unlike Darla, however, Rita was often dressed in halter tops, her worn blue jeans torn at her knees, her heavy work boots cinched at her feet. She was an outdoor girl who genuinely fit the landscape of this rough rocky land. Yet, surprisingly, in contrast to her rugged appearance, Rita's real persona was shy and reluctant. For Rita, it seemed as if the world of people was far more elusive to her than the solitary dangers of animals and wildfire high in the Cascade Range. In McAllister's perception, it seemed like the unusual circumstances of the Mulcahey Farm had become Rita's own personal research project. It was as if she was testing her ability to exist within the dangerous element of an anarchistic social order, in opposition to her more trusted preference of living alone.

During the last several months, McAllister had observed this woman during her occassional visits to the Farm. Rita appeared to display some personal internal struggle within her, a silent tug-of-war of disparate desire and motivation, which she was unable to keep hidden from public view. It revealed itself in her body language, like another piece of clothing she wore each day. She would appear so strong and deliberate in one moment of perception, then so weak and fragile the next. But don't be mistaken, Rita's particular conundrums concerning the world were attractive as hell. Rita made McAllister want to divine the depths of these eternal questions that beset her. It made him want to sleep with her, to prospect the gold of her emotional uncertainties.

Of course those notions would be mostly an intellectual distraction, and deep down McAllister knew the real truth. Rita was thin and athletic, her body firm and contoured, perfectly aligned. Suddenly, all of McAllister's philosophic meanderings about the state of his being; his musings on the past, the future directions of his life, of Richard Nixon's fall from grace, the disappointment about the Pollard Creek Inn, Darla's perfunctory abandonment of his intentions, as well as his pontifications on Rita's personal dilemmas were mostly a crock of shit. It was time to throw the baby out with the bath water. He knew right then he would walk her home. And maybe, just maybe, see what his new future might bring.

The course of human life on earth, which is all that is truly known, is framed within a continuum of human events. Life appears to be a continuing trail of ongoing circumstances, one following the other. The dynamic of the human enterprise is one of motion, of cause and effect, which only seems to rest with sleep. And the context of this motion is governed by one fundamental law. It is the law of duality, which seems to always be at play. There is the good and the bad, the high and low, the happy or sad, the love or the hate, winner or loser, in sickness or in health, the lost and the found, and eventually, the dead or alive. Essentially, it is the yin and yang of all things. But most important is the moving, always the moving, toward either the next declaration, or the next contradiction, including all the shades of coloration wedged somewhere in between.

Human memory allows the story to be told, to fashion a history of this incredible journey through time. But its telling cannot escape that fundamental law, the duality of its observation by man. Even the truth can become nothing more than belief, perhaps accepted by some, or rejected by others. Within such an unknown and confusing reality, human beings have sought a myriad of constructions in order to answer the mysteries of life, all to no avail. Primarily, only the instinct for survival prevails. And should even that primordial objective become extinct, there tends to be the recognition that the motion of the universe would remain eternal, forever moving on.

Meanwhile back at the ranch, just the facts, ma'am. In Pollard Creek, Oregon, USA, in early August, 1974, certain truths were known. Randy Halston remained incarcerated in the Jordan County Jail. Crazy Randy, by virtue of his own set of life's circumstances, was entirely lacking of any friends with deep pockets or living in high places. This particular truth seemed to suggest that Randy Halston would continue to enjoy three squares a day in a small green cinder block cell, awaiting a trial date to be penciled on the superior court calendar. Buck Thornton had gotten released. He went home to Randy's rundown trailer on Cougar Gulch. Whenever he visited Randy, he conveniently failed to mention that he was sleeping in Randy's own bed, instead of on the couch. In his more selfish moments, Buck figured what the hell, you snooze you lose. Nevertheless, Buck Thornton did miss his friend and questionable mentor. For Buck, it was pretty darn hard making decisions for himself.

Commissioner Wilton Parker went forward with his business for the people of Jordan County. Wilton was old enough to know the world wasn't fair. And there were times when the issues of right or wrong simply had to be ignored. Unless, of course, they found their way onto the Commissioners' weekly meeting docket, where Wilton Parker might be forced to take a vote.

Deputy Sheriff Bill Haines knew the difference between right and wrong quite well, at least in his own opinion. But his opinion didn't mean shit on the matter of Detective Barry Walton. Sure, Bill Haines could have raised a stink on what had recently gone down at the Pollard Creek Inn. He could have chosen principal over personal survival, by filing a report of complaint against Walton, then patting himself on the back. But in so doing, he would have been getting out the shovel to dig his own occupational grave. A police officer only broke the unwritten code when he was about to retire, or had another job waiting in the wings. And that wasn't the case for Deputy Bill Haines. The only silver lining was that Barry Walton had conveniently and quietly been promoted north to Salem to avoid any further misunderstandings. For Haines, this predictable bit of inter-departmental news would never lessen the emotional murder in his heart for that little smart-ass prick of a man. God have mercy on the good people of northern Oregon for what they were about to receive.

Jake Beecher sat on his front porch near Pollard Creek, pulling on a last sip of Blitz beer, before tossing the empty aluminum can out into his yard. He lay back in his rocking chair, hooking his thumbs under his suspenders.

"Well, damn if those hippie queers ain't in the shithouse now," he said to nobody in particular.

The particular nobodies to whom Jake Beecher was speaking, just happened to be those cracker nephews of his, Solly and Jed. The two boys sat below Jake, lounging on the steps of the porch, sitting as if royal attendants at the foot of the great man. They laughed at Jake's pronouncement, before tipping their beers in agreement. But then a wandering thought of recognition crossed over Solly's face. This restless idea surprised Solly a little. It wasn't often that his mind made any kind of singular effort to think for itself. On the one hand, Solly was kind of spooked by his mental observation. On the other, he was feeling particularly proud he might have something to say.

"Only trouble now, we got to go all the way to Solace Valley, or even up to Glendale, just to get a drink. What do you think of that?" His younger brother Jed looked up at Solly in unadulterated awe, as if to acknowledge that Sol had just discovered a cure for cancer.

"No shit, Sol. Damn, what do you think of that? All the way to Glendale!"

Even Jake Beecher felt a nervous twitch at Solly's clearly intuitive remark. Jake had been so overly riled at those damn hippies in Pollard Creek, so focused at running them out of town, he hadn't given much brain time to what the consequences might be. His wife, Shirley, usually went down to the Inn every afternoon for a couple of drinks with the girls. Now, with the bar at the Inn completely shut down, well shit, that could only mean she'd be back here at home every afternoon, interfering with his own personal happy hour. Damn sure that was going to be an uninvited circumstance, one Jake Beecher hadn't much reckoned with.

"Just hand me another beer, Solly, you shit-eating billy goat," Jake Beecher ordered. "Nobody's raining on my parade today, especially you." But despite the cooling mountain evening rising to dusk, Jake Beecher could sense several mysterious drops of precipitation pursing onto his thin balding top.

As for Tom Sullivan, he hadn't been off the Railroad Bridge property all day long. Tom had been helping Freddie Jones nail off some freshly milled cedar siding on the new addition to his cabin. With the late summer evening beginning to sink toward twilight, he could hear Marty Johnson bouncing his pickup through Laughlin Creek. Halting at Freddie's place, Marty rolled out of the cab, a six-pack in hand. He had stopped at the Solace Valley Tavern on the way home from Grants Pass. For some reason, there had been twice as many cars parked out front on a Friday night as Marty Johnson had ever seen. He'd thought maybe somebody had died or something. But no, it was simply the fact that the Pollard Creek Inn had gotten the proverbial axe. At least for the near future, the Solace Valley Tavern would be the only drinking game in town.

Sullivan and Freddie Jones expressed their dismay. The Thursday night musical jamborees at the Pollard Creek Inn would be put on hold. The Saturday night dances shut down. And nobody knew for how long. No doubt about it, the loss of the Inn would be a huge void to fill. Each of the men felt ready to blame the old locals, some who had nothing better to do with their time than complain about other people's lives. But equally as guilty were those redneck cowboys from Cougar Gulch. They were men whose ignorance and low self-esteem made it necessary for them to make their own problems a problem for everybody else. All in all, it was one fucked up deal. Tom Sullivan's thoughts went to Valerie. How would she feel about Pollard Creek, now that things had become so inflamed?

What Tom Sullivan didn't know, was that Valerie Williams had already made up her mind. Valerie had seen enough of the prejudice, having personally endured the angry responses of both the police and the crowd on the day of the bust. She'd certainly had enough of the Cougar Gulch crowd, always wearing their guns and knives, with their constant complaints that they were the victims of an unfair world. The truth was that they were the goddamn problem. It was they who were constantly strutting their macho personas for all to see, needing the attention they had never gotten as a children. They reminded Valerie of the deadbeat druggies who had taken over the Haight-Ashbury so long ago, fouling the truthful days of love and peace she had once so much enjoyed.

However, Valerie would keep her decisions to herself. She would only tell Tom Sullivan whenever he came to the house. Canyon would be in kindergarten soon, and then into regular school. There was no way she was going to send him to Pollard Creek Elementary. She would not allow him to be exposed to the children of this bigoted and narrow-minded town. Although Grants Pass might not be much of an alternative, at least there would be a token expectation of civility and focus on learning. Perhaps Valerie could get some quiet sideline work to supplement her welfare, maybe even take a few courses of her own at the community college. Meanwhile, for the near future, she would harvest her garden, before looking for a place to live in the fall. She knew she could still visit Pollard Creek at anytime. And her friends would surely stop over when making their town trips for groceries and supplies. Sadly, sometimes the beauty of a place like Pollard Creek, much like the perceived beauty of a human being, was only skin deep.

The following day, on another sunny Saturday, the heat wave of the last month finally took a break. The residents of the Pollard Creek Inn awoke to a cool August morning, although distracted by strange feelings of uncertainty and communal angst. Today, there would be no need to prep the kitchen for a day of food service, no demand to sweep and mop the barroom floor. There would be no need to clean the bathrooms, or recycle the bottles and take out the trash. With Albert Krieger away in New York, everyone felt like survivors of a sunken ship without a captain to show them cause. They were cast in a lifeboat without oars to row, the distant ocean horizon desperate and empty, no rescue in sight.

Laura Hale could not bring herself to practice her dance, her congas lying unwanted in the corner of her room. Guitar Glenn sat in his bed, his back against the headboard, his guitar re-strapped to his body, but with nothing to play. Slick Bell was a man who loved to work the night shift. He enjoyed bantering with the loggers and truck drivers, as well as the Cougar Gulch crazies. Slick got his kicks living on the edge of other people's emotions, observing the eventual effects of alcohol intoxication and the misadventures it could cause. Yet, on this unusual morning, he tossed and turned in his bed, as if suffering from a jet lag, of having gone to sleep way too soon the night before.

Jimmijay Connell, never one to be short of a joke to tell, a radio show to host, or a piano to play, wandered the property inside and out, looking for something, anything to occupy his active mind.

Only Darla Bloom had chores to do. She needed to feed her two children, and clean the school bus before her friend Taylor's arrival.

And she needed to start fixing up one of the empty rooms in the Inn for a place to move when Taylor was finished with his visit. He would be driving the school bus away. On the edge of her thoughts was the worried concern that things were not well, that her future was precarious, her own security in doubt. Darla Bloom had grown from an innocent teenage mother towards a young woman hardened by the facts of life. Derrick Mulcahey had seen to that almost instant maturation. She knew now, as many a woman eventually comes to know, that the myth of until death does us part, was simply that, a myth. At the end of the day, when it came to men and love, it was every woman for herself. That was the new reality of Darla's world, and it was fine with her. And with so much of her future to consider, any thoughts of Sean McAllister never once crossed her mind.

At the end of London Ridge Road, on his eighty acres of timbered hillside, Robert Sage packed a suitcase for the California trip ahead. His wife, Tiffany, was down in West Marin, living near her younger brother and other friends. Robert Sage hadn't really planned on being married, but sometimes circumstances give one very little choice. Tiffany's parents were deceased, having been killed in a terrible car accident some years before. Her younger brother had only been fourteen at the time of the tragedy. When Sage had met Tiffany in Mendocino, her brother had gotten into trouble with drugs and arrested by the cops. In order to save her brother from juvenile incarceration, Sage had married Tiffany and adopted the boy. At that moment in time, perhaps love had something to do with it as well. But love has a way of changing color as time goes by.

Robert Sage had met Albert Krieger shortly after his marriage, while visiting family back in New York for the holidays. Sage needed to find riders for his return trip back to Mendocino, to help pay for gas. Albert Krieger had responded, and then fate stepped into the breach. Sage had driven Albert all the way back to Pollard Creek and the Strawberry Fields commune. Immediately, he decided this was the place for him. He brought Tiffany and her brother up to Oregon, but the results were not as he had hoped. Tiffany retreated back to California, and the relationship abruptly came to an end. Unfortunately, the legalities of marriage don't cease when the love has escaped. They remain like a rope tied around the waist, until someone takes the knife and cuts the ties that bind.

California was a community property state. In California, with marriage, you didn't just split the sheets without your checkbook in hand. Robert Sage did not want to lose his eighty acres, or his investment in the Pollard Creek Inn, but something might have to give. Meanwhile, he would have to keep his dangerous day job for some time to come. The job paid well, and it was time for another mission. Once the work was over, he would stop by West Marin and meet with Tiffany. He would try and do his best to come to terms.

Only Tiffany and Albert Krieger knew the nature of his employment. From time to time, Sage would get the call, and he was expected to respond. His job was simple, to carry things, to carry things from Point A to Point B. He was a delivery man, nothing more, a delivery man who didn't ask questions and didn't want to know. Often, he would travel from safety deposit box to safety deposit box. Other times, he buried things in the ground, until told to dig them up and finish the job. In this particular occupation there would be no shop talk after work, no union protection if trouble arose. His job resume might only be interesting to the DEA or the FBI.

He and Tiffany needed to move on with their lives. And she would want some financial settlement, a settlement that California didn't need to know. He would begin his drive south, aware that the liquor license suspension at the Pollard Creek Inn was now a fact. As well, the terse judgmental provocation of the Oregon State Police detective was still ringing in his ears. With his own need for the divorce funds soon to become a necessity, Robert Sage might have a decision thrust before him, a decision he had no desire to make. When both he and Albert Krieger returned to Pollard Creek, they would have to sit down and see what lay ahead, and what it might cost. It angered Sage to even have to consider such unwanted possibilities. He enjoyed being a part-owner of the Pollard Creek Inn. Even though the love for his land at the dead-end of London Ridge Road was equally dear, the daily aura of life at the Pollard Creek Inn had colored his life, for himself and so many others.

But an evil wind was blowing, and he knew what it might bring. The previous owners of the Inn, Dave and Laverne Standard, had asked only one thing of them at the time of the building's purchase. At that particular moment, the request had seemed totally insignificant. It was a passing verbal request for which Laverne Standard would never need to worry, and Robert Sage had readily agreed to comply. One thing, she had implored, as if there was some unknown truth that only she might have been aware, "Please," she had requested, "should you ever sell the property, please don't ever sell it to the State of Oregon".

On this perfectly comfortable Saturday morning, the sun a cool August bright, the sky scratched in thin cirrus streaks against an angelic blue, for Robert Sage a cold darkening thunderhead took hold of his thoughts. He was not necessarily a righteous man, no more or less than anyone else. But he expected himself to be a man of his word, whatever the outcome might be. It brought Sage no peace to think that he might be forced to betray such a delivered trust, even though such a difficult act might be out his control. To have to sell the Pollard Creek Inn to the State of Oregon, well it just couldn't be possible. There could be no doubt that the whole situation seemed clearly unbelievable. And yet today, sadly, only time would tell.

CHAPTER THIRTY

BOX OF RAIN
Pollard Creek / November, 1974 / Thanksgiving

ALTHOUGH NEVER IN A HURRY, time went by. The long hot Oregon summer packed up its suitcase. It purchased a plane ticket to Mexico and flew the coop. In the vacuum left by its escape, long blankets of brooding gray clouds slipped furtively into the narrow Siskiyou valleys. Rain began to fall over the big timbered forests. For days on end, Pacific fronts ran rough and ready over the countryside, pouring pitchers of water onto the marginal hills, turning the thin red dust of beaten roads into slick potter's clay. The rocky creek beds, steep with evergreens and hardwood, ran loudly through the forest divides, hurtling their liquid bounty down to the Rogue River and back out to sea.

The blood veins of the Great Northwest pulsed their way through wild Indian imaginations of returning salmon and sleeping bear. Wood smoke rose languidly out of stovepipes. It hung like pancakes amidst the unforgiving gray sky, slow, heavy, and predictably uncaring. Clothing and footwear grew musty and dank, wet against the skin. Kerosene lamps flickered in the early darkness of shortened afternoons, prompting long black hours of dampened expectation. The Oregon winter was back in town.

For Sean McAllister, it would be his first, and it was already becoming quite a surprise. During the last of August, he had loaded up the panel truck, driven north across the mighty Columbia River, deep into the desert country of Central Washington state. Under brilliant late summer and autumn skies, he pushed heavy wooden ladders into the interiors of sparkling green trees, heavy with pears and apples. Amongst sharply chilled mornings and tee shirt afternoons, he picked and picked and picked, filling plywood bins leveled to the top, turning bin tickets into paychecks, day after day. When the harvest was over and Halloween past, he returned to Pollard Creek, deciding to continue the communal adventure of which he had engaged. But the high flight of an Oregon summer was nowhere to be found. The easy life of heat and sun had become unmistakably absent, replaced by a harsher natural reality for which he needed to prepare.

With a stash of harvest pay in hand, Sean McAllister delivered half the proceeds to the Mulcahey Farm account, keeping the other half for himself. Mookie James had remained at the Farm, working to get his cabin complete before the winter rains. McAllister knew he could crash with Mookie and Annie until he figured something out for the winter ahead. But as luck would have it, a guy named Roderick and his pregnant wife were pulling up stakes. Roderick and his old lady had not lived on the Mulcahey Farm during the previous summer. But they had intended to make it their home. Roderick had taken a job with the Forest Service. In between, he had been building a cabin on the Mulcahey property, planning to move there when the cabin was finished. Unfortunately, Roderick and Derrick Mulcahey were birds of a feather, although neither of them knew it at the time. Something bad had gone down between them while McAllister was away.

Roderick had incorrectly expected that his view of a communal democracy would be shared by all. He argued for a structure that gave everyone a vote on matters of economics and finance, an egalitarian methodology where each individual had a voice. Whenever decisions had to be made, each person would possess a marker to place on the table. It would be majority rule. Roderick didn't understand that the Mulcahey Farm was based on the cooperative technique of consensus. With consensus, issues were discussed and shaped until everyone agreed to the outcome in final form. What Roderick hadn't considered was that the agenda would be stacked against him. It would be an agenda in the persona of Derrick Mulcahey, including his loyal brother, Jack, as well as the others who had come up from Santa Cruz since the purchase of the property.

In a one sense, Roderick and his wife had not missed the point. They had simply missed the reality. As for Mookie James and Sean

McAllister, neither had been born yesterday. Like Roderick, they too understood that idealism was a worthy goal for which to strive. But they also understood the nature of the game at hand. That sometimes the hierarchy of the tribe might play by a different set of rules. And Derrick Mulcahey was indeed the hierarchy of the tribe, make no mistake about it. Suggestions were appreciated. They would be given credence in the open forum of opinion. But the age-old smokey back rooms still existed. And even if you occasionally got to go inside that room, you would never be allowed to light up a cigar. In the end Derrick Mulcahey charted the Farm's daily course, and with his partners in concert, the Mulcahey Farm was just that, the Mulcahey Farm.

As is often the case, when human interaction finds itself in conflict, the real issues sneak around in the dark, silently growing in mistrust. Individual emotions begin to seethe inside, but remain unspoken. When the eventual blowup ensues, it's never really over the crux of the matter at hand, but instead over some little spark that lights up the fuel, exploding into the sky.

For example, take the incident of Derrick Mulcahey poaching a deer in the black heart of night. The issue is not really about the deer, or the night, or using a rifle with an automatic clip to bring down the prey, which just happens to be an unfair fight right from the gate. Is such a purposeful killing an amoral act? Goddamn right it is. But is the act itself simply Derrick Mulcahey doing what he wants to do, on his own land as far as he is concerned? You bet it is. However, this incident would be the spark in a political stand-off between two young men, a communal tug of war between two separate factions of intent? At least that was the essence of a story Sean McAllister heard upon his return from Washington.

By now, McAllister didn't have any misunderstandings about the Mulcahey Farm. It was indeed a working communal enterprise, with the intention of growing and raising your own, of sharing a common experience with others, and that was a really cool thing. But the politics of the Farm's direction was an entirely different story. As a result, it was not a question of either being 'on the bus' or 'off the bus'. The best thing about this whole commitment, as far as Sean McAllister could see, was that you could always get off the bus at any time you desired. And there would be no nagging responsibility or guilt regarding the cause, should you choose to do so. In the end, it was Derrick Mulcahey's trip, and you could come and go along for the ride, or take your departure at any time. And so Roderick and his old lady were gone. Roderick had chosen to make a stand and Roderick had lost. Consequently, left behind was an unfinished cabin standing alone at the far-end of the property. Sean McAllister figured what the hell. There might come the day when McAllister himself would purchase a one-way ticket down the road. But this wouldn't be that day, at least for now.

"Can I ask you a question?" Rita's voice inquired.

McAllister could hear heavy drops of rain hammering onto the metal roof above him. With both hands, he gripped the blanket cover of the comforter close to his neck. Soon enough, he would have to burst out of the bed, hustle over to the woodstove in the corner of the cold morning cabin, begin stoking up the fire. Rita leaned close beside him. She was hunched up sideways on her elbow, the curls of her lush hair partially disguising her face. She looked down at him with serious expression.

"Sure," he yawned. "What is it?"

Rita brushed the hair away with her fingers, before lying back down beside him. Gazing at the ceiling of the cabin, McAllister could feel the warmth of her arm pressing against his torso.

"So, what do you believe you want to do with your life?"

Sean McAllister turned his head toward the woman beside him. Her expression hadn't changed. Shaking his head, he smiled at her, trying not to laugh. "Did you just ask me, what I want to do with my life?" he joked.

Rita caught his attempt at humor, softly punching him with her hand. "I mean it," she followed, trying to remain serious. "What would you like your life to be? You know, like your future, and thoughts like that."

"Geez, Rita. I mean, I just woke up," McAllister answered. Chuckling, he pulled his right arm from under the covers. He let his hand gently rub along her wrist. "I'm not sure I have an answer right now. Do you? I mean, do you know what you want to do with your life?"

"No, not really," she answered, looking into his eyes. "But I think about it a lot. What my destiny might be, my purpose in this world, the person I should want to become, those kinds of things. Don't you think about those things, I mean, at least now and then?"

McAllister could sense the sincerity in Rita's voice. He needed to give her inquiry some credible answer. "Yeah, I do," he agreed. "Maybe not so early in the morning, I guess. But yeah, I do think about those questions in my life." McAllister paused. "But not as much as you probably do, I suppose. Like right now I was thinking about having to get up and stoke the fire, to get the cabin warm for us, a more practical kind of thinking."

"But don't you wake up sometimes in the morning, lie in bed and think about where you are in your life? Like the way your life is going, your directions, and where you might want to be with things? Like maybe the dreams that are most important to you, and the people you care about?"

McAllister raised himself up on his elbow, softly looking down at Rita. "Actually, I do," he said. "I do a lot. Maybe I just don't realize how much. But I know that I like being with you this morning." He smiled down on her, before kissing her on the nose, then on the lips.

Looking up at him, another question came. "So what is your birth date, Sean?"

"June 17th."

"So, you're a Gemini. What year?"

"1950."

"What time of day, do you know?"

"Around six o'clock in the evening," McAllister answered. "My mom used to joke about it with her sisters. Mickey always shows up just in time for dinner."

"Mickey?"

"Yeah, that's kind of my family nickname. My middle name is Michael. Everyone calls me Mickey at home."

"I like it," Rita said. "Well, if you'll get up and keep the fire, I'll make us a cup of tea. Then I'll do your astrological chart." Rita's face relaxed, smiling up at him. "Have you ever had your chart done? Maybe we can find out who you are, and then perhaps the answer to what you should want out of your life. You know, maybe a guide to this future of yours, that you're so dying to find out about," she snickered.

"Okay," McAllister said. "I sort of had it done once in Colorado, but I was half-drunk and the girl was kind of crazy. I don't really recall anything she said."

"Did you sleep with her?" Rita asked, as if truly wanting to know.

"No, she was just the neighbor across the street," he answered. But I'd like for you to do it, if you would."

"I do," Rita said. "I want to know, too."

McAllister rolled out of bed, stoking the wood stove with dry kindling from inside the cabin. Rita got up, putting water on for tea. Sitting near the fire, Rita got out her astrology texts, a pad of graph paper and pen. She made a circle on the page, drawing lines toward the center. After that, she began reading her books, writing down the signs of the zodiac, placing annotations and numbers throughout the paper. "This will take awhile," she said.

McAllister dressed, stepping out into the rainy November morning. He split some of Rita's firewood, packing her wood box full by the stove. Drinking his tea, he quietly perused her library. There were books on the I Ching, the Tarot, numerology, and biofeedback. There were worn copies of Richard Alpert's *Be Here Now*, the *Autobiography of a Yogi*, and *Seth Speaks*. There were books by Edgar Cayce, Scientology, and Eckankar. From time to time, Rita would speak to herself, as if relishing a new observation. But when McAllister asked for reference, she would simply smile and say he would have to wait. Finally, the chart was complete.

Rita seemed to get great pleasure out of the results. McAllister heated more water, pouring a second cup of tea for each of them. As Rita delved into the depths of his astrological soul, Sean Michael McAllister began to get sunned and mooned, as well as risen. After that, he was trined and squared, made opposite and sextiled. Then he was cusped and put into houses. By the time the reading was over, he had become a terribly sensitive and intuitive young man, yet also practical and responsible. In addition, he was independent, gregarious, fair, communicative, empathetic, clever, emotionally mature, solid and well-reasoned. As far as Sean McAllister could tell, he was one hell of a guy.

The best part of the reading was Rita, herself. She was positively excited by the investigation. The beauty of her long brown hair seemed to shine with her brilliant white smile, her lips curling at their edge, her voice expectant with each revelation, as if opening a gift on Christmas morning. In this moment she was as beautiful as he had ever seen her. "Does that sound like you?" she inquired, uncovering one affected human gem after another. Rita was as ebullient as a gold miner in these hard rock Oregon hills, beaming with each nugget of her discovery, as if striking it rich.

Later, as McAllister walked the Southern Pacific tracks back to the Mulcahey Farm, he was taken by Rita's lovely transformations. He hardly noticed the continued gray drizzle of the late morning sky. He hadn't expected to sleep with Rita, and yet somehow the stars had aligned, as they sometimes must. Rita was such an enigma. One moment she seemed so open and free, as the last night had been. But there were other moments when he had seen her so distracted, when her solitary quest of the spirit weakened her with its overwhelming uncertainty. In those times, her beauty would fade under a darkening cloud, gripped by the eternal questions she felt compelled to petition.

This spiritual quest endeavor was not an easy task. It demands a leap of faith, which for some, like Rita, is a puzzle piece that can't be placed. And what about religion, or astrology, and all the rest? Are they a certain guide to the fears and unknowns we as human beings cannot seem to answer or understand? Are they a path towards reconciling the mysterious questions before us, of who we really are? And why? Sean McAllister was quite sure he didn't know. Nonetheless, to wonder about these things is a beautiful avocation in life. Beautiful, as long as it doesn't bring one down by their determined ability to remain unknown. Rita was a pioneering soul. And although she held certain beliefs, many questions remained before her, questions in her heart and soul needing to be resolved. But if there was anyone in Pollard Creek who might find the answers to these riddles of the human dilemma, it would be Rita. And because of her own special beauty, everyone could be certain that she would share them with all of us, whatever she might find.

At the Farm, except for Darius, no one had known that McAllister had been away overnight. As a result, the pigs remained unfed, which was his job to complete. He headed for the barn, filled two pails with grain, before trudging through the mud out to the pens. The post and barbed wire fencing of the pig pen was all beaten to hell. Inside the large pen, the ground was rooted and slimed with Oregon muck, the pigs snorting and squealing upon his approach. McAllister poured the grain into the feed bin. Standing back, he watched as the swine wrestled and pounded against each other, their squeals heightening, their snouts hungrily fighting for all they could get for themselves. Looking upon this scene, there was absolutely no mercy, no generosity, no heavenly beneficence. It was nothing more than a no-holes-barred battle for survival of the fittest, or perhaps the survival of the largest in this particular case. If there was ever a photographic representation of at least one glimpse of animal reality, this was the place.

McAllister could only laugh to himself, as the caged rumble played out before him. "What do you want to do with your life?" he joked to the pigs. But the wallowing mud only continued to fly, while the evergreen trees dripped, and the rain fell steady on the back of his neck. No thoughtful answer ever came, just more grunts, snorts, and high pitched screams. As he thought to himself, an easier question might have been just the opposite. For example, what do you 'NOT' want to do with your life? As for that question, Sean McAllister could easily make a very long list. With the pig feeding over, it was time to eat some lunch. Empty pails in hand, McAllister headed for the kitchen to see what he could find.

In the weeks before Thanksgiving, Sean McAllister did what he could to batten down the cabin that Roderick and his wife had left behind. He found several windows in Grants Pass, framing them into the openings that Roderick had cut. With Mookie's and Darius's help, he completed a sleeping loft to make more space. He located an old trash-burner wood stove to install, fireproofing it with sheets of tin against the wall. He insulated the interior of the cabin with burlap feed bags and newspaper, and anything else he could find. In between, he and Darius cut and split firewood, stacking the fuel underneath the cabin to keep it dry.

Darius and McAllister would share the cabin together. They scavenged a table and chairs. They bought a wash basin, and several kerosene lamps to keep the place lit at evening. McAllister moved in a car battery and his eight-track tape machine for tunes. Still, the key to survival would be the wood stove, to keep the fire going most days and nights. Darius would be the fire tender most of the time. He was a laid back stoner of a guy, the quiet Zen master of the Mulcahey Farm. Darius moved slowly through each and every day. He could roll the perfect joint, like nobody McAllister had ever witnessed. Darius could smoke a number right to the nubs, rarely using a roach clip when the marijuana cigarette burned to its stub. The index finger and thumb of his right hand were constantly black with tar and THC. He could have been busted for possession, just on the skin residue alone.

In a somewhat similar way, Darius was a lot like Rita, a searcher of the unknown spirits of life. He appeared like a yogi in street clothes, speaking in low comforting tones, a caring and sweet soul of a man. His daily presence spoke to an ultimate deference and willing generosity toward others. Somehow, Darius seemed to have the bigger picture of things. Like most human beings, he could occasionally share his distaste for the violators of this world. But unlike the others, especially McAllister, he seemed incapable of showing the least bit of anger toward any human device. The Mulcahey Farm was a place of doing, of macho action and intentional energy. It was a communal attempt to carve a simplicity of survival in stark contrast to a selfish materialistic world. Darius was the yin to the Farm's working yang agenda. Not in opposition, but in the complimentary spirit and balance of the Tao.

It seemed strangely ironic that Darius had been picked up hitchhiking north from California by none other than Derrick Mulcahey. It was as if Darius had been brought to the Farm by the whim of some predetermined fate. His mission would be to act as counterpoint to the rugged reality of men being men, to help keep the waters calm with a measure of peace and genuine acceptance of all. If there were ever a Mulcahey Farm popularity contest, perhaps to be held after a communal dinner on a cold winter night, there would have been no need for a vote, no need for any long hours building a consensus. In the end, Darius would have won the undisputed title, hands down.

Even Derrick Mulcahey would have seen the writing on the wall. Darius was a comfort for each and every man and woman on the Farm. And more particularly for every child, with a special care he so easily bestowed. For is it not through the innocent eyes of a child that the blessed can be more truly seen.

On Thanksgiving Day, a subtle breeze from the Pacific coast pushed away the low clouds of Oregon gray. It bathed the holiday with an angled light of autumn sun, revealing the beauty of a colored afternoon. A concerted sense of optimism spread through the Farm. Everyone found a task to perform in preparation for the dinner ahead. The women and children held court in the kitchen, making all the preparations. A turkey was in the oven for the meat eaters, a tofu stir-fry for the vegetarians. Fresh baked bread cooled on racks. There were homegrown potatoes and beans from the garden, salads and cranberry sauce, a feast in the making. The men puttered outside, welcoming the invited friends who had wavered across the swinging bridge. They drank beer, took hits of whiskey, enjoying the sun. They shared their personal stories, or conversed of building projects underway.

In the chilling mid-afternoon breeze, amongst yellow oak and maple leaves floating their way toward the forest floor below, everyone came together for a family picture to remember the day. A ragtag group of young Americans collected themselves together. The children sat in front, their wide mouths clowning for the camera. The adults, dressed in their mackinaws and coats, their long hair streaming in the sun, held broad smiles for an instant, becoming a photographic snapshot of a moment in time.

Immediately following the photo, everyone wedged inside the kitchen, without an inch to spare. Around the communal table, one by one, each adult and child shared with the others the reasons for their gratitude, before diving hungrily into the feast. For an hour or more, the singular troubles of any particular life were suspended, replaced by the gleeful repartee of the children, the sarcastic jokes of the men, the intuitive perspectives of the women, so happy to have a family together. They were free as one tribe, safe from an outside world they had purposely chosen to avoid.

Sean McAllister sat on his tree round seat, stuffing himself, sipping on a glass of wine. Further down the table, Rita sat across the way, engaged in conversation. He watched as she conversed happily with the children, then caught her glance and smiled. She smiled back at him, seeming light in her spirit. She wore no larger questions on her brow, no prodding uncertainties sought to distract her. It was a pleasant sight to see. Within himself, he gave thought to his other family, the one he had left behind. He saw his father at the head of the dinner table in

Northland Hills, bantering with his brothers, Uncle Franny and Uncle
Joe. He saw his mother Connie hovering around, making sure everyone
had enough turkey, peas, and mashed potatoes. He saw his sister, Mary
Jane, sharing with her aunts the stories of her life in New York City, or
challenging her old-guard uncles with her strong opinions, whenever
necessity should demand.

He missed each and every one of them. And he wondered how this
gathering would seem to them, so distant from their own traditions,
so far and far away. But if he had been forced to make a choice today,
this moment would be his place and time. The past was one thing,
the present and future another. In his own life, he was right where he
wanted to be.

At the Pollard Creek Inn, the spacious dining room was buzzing
with similar intents. Darla, Laura, Valerie and the other women
fluttered throughout the commercial kitchen, bringing a large
communal Thanksgiving meal to its culinary height. Jimmijay Connell
sat at the piano. Guitar Glenn, wearing his favorite guitar, provided
musical background. Tom Sullivan, Marty Johnson, and Freddie Jones
had arrived from Railroad Bridge, joining the group of holdouts still
living in the Big House at Strawberry Fields. Everyone appeared in good
spirits, although for those that lived at the Inn the future remained in
doubt.

Robert Sage had been sent upstairs to bring Albert Krieger down
to the party. Dinner was soon to be served. Sage's mission was to rouse
Albert from his seclusion, where he had spent much of his time since
returning from New York. The death and burial of Albert's father,
the concurrent suspension and closing of the Pollard Creek Inn, had
sadly managed to push Albert into a swirling descent of depression,
a troubled loss of motivation from which he was battling to recover.
Sage could only focus on raising Albert from his ennui, to get him
down with the others, to put on a face, ignoring the darker realities
that might be before them.

In the coming weeks, people would have to sit down and attempt
to make some decisions. There would be unwilling choices that
the current circumstances were forcing them to discern. But for the
moment, everyone needed to see Albert at dinner, in his quiet and

gentle leadership role. Albert rallied, pulling himself off the bed, dressing as he and Sage shared some personal time together. Making their way downstairs, Albert's presence invigorated the group. They surrounded him with genuine love and attention, their silent worries for him eased by his appearance. Albert Krieger brightened with the energy and care. For at least a little while longer, everything would be the way it should be. The youthful beauty and energy of the Pollard Creek Inn certainly might be down, but not necessarily out. Surely not on Thanksgiving Day.

CHAPTER THIRTY-ONE

NOBODY KNOWS YOU WHEN
YOU'RE DOWN AND OUT
Pollard Creek / December, 1974

ON OCTOBER 12TH, 1973, Gerald Ford, the Republican House Minority leader, was chosen by then President Richard Nixon to occupy the position of Vice-President, following the resignation of former Vice-President, Spiro T. Agnew. Agnew had resigned the position following his no contest plea to tax evasion and money laundering charges, having taken bribes during his tenure as governor of the State of Maryland. Ford was confirmed by the House and Senate, and on December 6th, 1973 took the oath of office as the new Vice-President. Just over eight months later, Gerald R. Ford had become President of the United States. America had a new leader. Gerald Ford was a man whom former President Lyndon Johnson once characterized with these words; "Jerry Ford is so dumb, he can't fart and chew gum at the same time."

As far as Sean McAllister was concerned, the present state of affairs in the American nation spoke for itself. Still, it burned McAllister's ass to find out that less than a month after becoming President, Gerald Ford had signed a proclamation granting "a full, free, and absolute pardon unto Richard Nixon for all offenses against the United States, which he, Richard Nixon, has committed or may have committed or taken part in during the period from January 20, 1969 through August 9, 1974."

Gerald R. Ford had let Richard Nixon walk. He had pardoned the man before a single charge or indictment had ever been brought. This event only strengthened McAllister's belief that words like justice and equal protection under the laws were simply emotional constructs to distract the true reality of the time. The United States had become the province of a very powerful and self-protecting elite. An elite who would always take care of their own when things got tight, whatever the consequence. A minority of freedom-loving Americans could stomp and scream all they wanted. They could make themselves daffy as hell over such open displays of malfeasance. But in the end, the game was always the same. You were not invited to play. In other words, don't let the door hit you in the ass on the way out. Be sure and come back when you can't stay so long. Case closed.

Thankfully, news of the pardon had raised something of a stink across America. Thousands of citizens, like a pack of unlicensed dogs, had barked outside the windows of Ford's new home at 1600 Pennsylvania Avenue. As Ford tried to wax poetic about healing a divided country, he raised his window sash and tossed the unruly dogs a bone. The bone was called Executive Order11803, establishing a Presidential Clemency Board.

In a nutshell, this is how it went down: 'Calling all you Vietnam draft evaders hiding in the brush, and all you military deserters who had walked off the job. If you will give us a call and say you're sorry, we'll consider putting down the leash. We know you made a mistake. But just like Tricky Dick Nixon, everyone makes bad judgments now and then. So, if you are willing to put your tail between your legs, perhaps we'll see fit to let you dogs run free. Although we may be an imperial, militaristic bunch of money-grubbing savages dressed in suits and ties, damn if we aren't forgiving ones, too. So, like we said, if you promise to be good, and clean up a little around the dog pound, if you promise to do as we say and not as we do, we'll try to appear merciful and let you go home. But remember, this generous offer has an expiration date, and will expire soon. Make those calls now, before January 31, 1975.'

Whoops, what do you know? By the first of December, 1974, gosh darn if those unrepentant canine delinquents had hardly shown their snouts. Even though operators were standing by, the phones just wouldn't ring. Where in hell was the appreciation for such genuine beneficence?

If there was one thing true about Derrick Mulcahey, either by the birthright of his Irish genetics, or the hardscrabble experiences of his personal life, Derrick Mulcahey was nobody's fool. He made the telephone call from a pay phone in Grants Pass. As he listened to their excited spiel, Derrick could tell they were beside themselves that the phone had even rung. Ford's clemency program was looking like a total bust. They were desperate for any warm body to turn themselves in, and they needed them bad. Derrick Mulcahey had dodged the authorities successfully for almost six years. But he had been the guy always on the run, not them. Maybe, just maybe, he was currently sitting in the catbird seat. And damn if he wouldn't milk it for all he could.

Derrick told them he was broke, with two kids to support and he didn't even have a car. That would be fine, they answered. We'll come and pick you up, and we'll feed you well all the way through. The whole matter will only take about three to five days, and then we'll return you safely back home. And don't worry right now about the two years of alternative service. We have hardship exemptions, and you will certainly qualify. Initially, your discharge papers will state 'Undesirable'. But after your alternative service, or the acceptance of your hardship review, we'll change it to a 'Clemency' designation. Now listen up, you will have to sign the loyalty oath, and there will be no Veteran's benefits in your future. We're sorry, we can't help you there. But remember, Mr. Mulcahey, you will no longer be subject to any criminal charges. You will no longer be a wanted man on the run.

Derrick arranged for the authorities to pick him up in town, at the front driveway of the Pollard Creek Inn. There, at least, he would be surrounded by others in public view. Two young soldiers arrived in a sedan, opening the door for him to climb inside. They promptly drove him to the air base at Klamath Falls. Despite his long red hair and beard, his scruffy woodlot clothes, Derrick Mulcahey was fed and treated with appropriate military respect. Within hours he was on a huge army transport plane headed for Indiana. Upon landing, he was driven to another military base to begin his repatriation.

For two full days he was put up in quarters, given three squares and asked to fill out paperwork. And it certainly wasn't as if Derrick Mulcahey was worried about signing a loyalty oath. He had previously signed one some years before, and they could take a wild guess how that had turned out. His processing completed, the board would get back to him on the alternative service and hardship application, but thanks so much for coming. Your return flight is waiting. The following evening,

Derrick Mulcahey sat in the communal kitchen at the Mulcahey Farm, telling his story at dinner. After six long years on the run as a fugitive from justice, having been labeled a traitorous scourge on the body-politic of the American majority, Derrick Mulcahey comfortably ate his meal at home, a man unchanged in any observable way.

America is one hell of a crazy place. But sitting at dinner, Derrick did make one thing clear as a bell. If he did a single minute of community service, it would be on his terms, not theirs. There would be no retribution on the government's part, no matter how hard they might try to apply it. Derrick Mulcahey had his own game plan, and he would only play theirs when the outcome favored him. In a way, it was no different than any other day.

On a cold December morning, Jimmijay Connell stood on the front porch of the Pollard Creek Inn, watching as an Oregon State health inspector pasted a label in the shape of the letter 'D' onto the window glass by the front door. The kitchen and restaurant would be allowed to reopen. But the rest of the world would need to know that this particular establishment was by no means a Class A joint. Hell, even that grease pit down the road, the Hungry Dog Cafe, had a 'B' rating, for crying out loud.

So here they were, a hippie enterprise in the middle of nowhere, the Oregon winter basking in its full depressing majesty, trying to entice some lonesome hungry customers off the Interstate highway for a bite to eat. The 'D' rating would essentially be a warning to them, that after eating their meal, they might just get sick and die. More than anyone, Jimmijay Connell had a penchant for the comedic appreciations of life, but this particular act of black humor was indeed beyond the pale.

Albert Krieger and Robert Sage, as legal owners, had appealed the liquor license suspension. A hearing had been held in Grants Pass. But as often is the case, the truth never had its day in court. The Jordan County Commissioners, including Wilton Parker, voted not to recommend the license be restored, and that's all the State of Oregon wanted to hear. There would be no further alcohol served at the Pollard Creek Inn. The result would be that the economic underpinning of the business, thin as it was, had now been completely yanked away. The old roof of the historic building was beginning to leak, the upstairs windows drafty and damp, the cost of constant heat far too high. A conspiracy of bureaucratic sabotage was virtually complete.

And so, in December, 1974, the permanent residents of the Pollard Creek Inn woke each day from a cold overnight sleep, seeing their breath escape in the morning air. They dutifully put in their time working the restaurant kitchen, pretending to operate, but hardly anyone came. The bar had been the focal point for cash flow and food. But now, the barroom would only be occupied by tenants, playing pool in their winter coats to idle the time. When they weren't pretending to work, they huddled in their rooms upstairs. With the electric heaters running, they played cards, smoked joints, or watched the single-channel black and white television deep into the night. Albert Krieger had returned to his room and his depression, sleeping most of the days, unable to respond. The long Oregon winter stretched before them, with no end in sight. The Pollard Creek Inn was cornered and beaten, ripe for the picking to come.

In the ultimate of ironies, Crazy Randy Halston was put on trial for arson, but the prosecution hadn't found enough evidence to convict him. A jury found Randy not guilty. He walked out of the Jordan County Courthouse a free man, returning to Cougar Gulch, back to his guns and his way of life. The only thing lost was a stretch of time he had often done before.

Meanwhile, in the interim months since the bust at the Inn, some calmer heads had tried to bridge the cultural divide that had infected Pollard Creek, with a measure of success. Several public meetings were held at the community center behind the post office. Emotions and feelings were expended, the troublemakers castigated, with almost everyone on both sides angry at the authorities and police. The catharsis had done some good. Putting people in a room together, allowing them to see each other's humanity close-up and personal, was never a bad thing.

However, the increased civility in Pollard Creek had not changed Valerie Williams' mind. She had not been able to make the move by autumn as she had hoped, but her intentions remained. She split the firewood that Tom Sullivan had brought her from Railroad Bridge, keeping her yellow house warm. Two days a week she opened her home to a preschool, teaching the hippie kids who came, allowing them to learn and share together. But she knew this winter would be her last in Pollard Creek. When school approached the following September, her son Canyon would be of age. It would be time for a change from this roughneck reality that Pollard Creek might never be able to escape. Valerie loved her friends and the beauty of these timbered hills, but her son needed his education. From time to time, she had spent several nights with men from Pollard Creek. But passion and love were two separate kinds of emotion. One was only physical, the other from the heart. Valerie had no expectations that Prince Charming would be pulling off the freeway at Exit 76 anytime soon.

Sean McAllister and Mookie James sat in the Solace Valley Tavern, sharing a table with Tom Sullivan and Marty Johnson from Railroad Bridge. The Tavern was now the place to drink, with the Pollard Creek Inn down for the count. McAllister and Mookie were trying to figure out a way to get back east for Christmas. Neither had visited their families in over two years. Mookie had pretty much drained his savings building the cabin at Mulcahey Farm. McAllister still had some dough from the apple picking trip, but not much more. Marty Johnson said he knew a guy in Grants Pass that had gotten a big reforestation contract out on the coast near Coos Bay. The man was looking for tree planters and needed guys who wanted to work. If Marty could get a crew together out of Pollard Creek, the contractor would give them a crummy truck to make the trip.

Back at the Mulcahey Farm, the men told the commune at dinner of their plans. Jesse Simmons was all ears and wanted to go along. The crew would work for two and half weeks, then break for the holidays. Mookie and McAllister still weren't sure if they could pull off the east coast bid, but needed to give it a try. Others would be staying on the Farm over the holidays, so their plan had a chance. Three days later, the crew pulled out of Pollard Creek. Packed into an old yellow passenger rig, stuffed with their gear and planting tools, the men headed north to Roseburg, then due west for the coast. Marty Johnson was at the wheel, with Tom Sullivan beside. Along with a kid from Grants Pass named Kooskie, there was Mookie, McAllister and Jesse from the Farm. The gang of six was on the road.

Planting trees in the coastal mountains of an Oregon winter is something every man should be required to do. It should be a mandatory form of universal service, or at least a right of passage towards some higher status in life. One thing for was for sure, it certainly got your attention. It made one value their education. It made one dream of warm sunny territories, or hot showers and peaceful nights sitting by the fire. The fact is, it would make one think about almost anything but what they are doing at the time. It was one hell of a way to make a buck.

And so, this is your tree planter's dream: It begins in the black winter of dawn, located at an ugly sheet-metal trailer park. This is followed by a long dark ride that eventually gives way to an overbearing gray water-ballooned sky, with trails of foggy mist hanging through the tree tops. You travel over slick and rutted logging roads, a thermos cup of coffee sloshing in your stomach like a storm at sea. Reaching the unit, you begin to witness the wicked sins committed by others, the slashed clear-cuts of whole mountainsides in the early morning light. All the virgin timber is gone, with only its excrement left behind. Once pristine Oregon creeks remain piled with debris, where healthy salmon used to return and spawn. Your breath is taken away by the sight of such destruction. Stepping outside the crummy, you are stunned by the eternal silence of death, the total evacuation of every living thing, marked only by the sound of a Pacific coastal wind passing through your ears.

This is your workplace, a land of unnatural disaster you have been called upon to heal and repair. Instead, you feel like a man torn with guilt, an accessory to a crime you feel compelled to report, a travesty of environmental justice waiting for arrest. But you know full well, there's not a cop in sight. Only Marty Johnson handing you a planting tool called a hoedad, and a belt full of genetically-processed seedling trees, their roots damp and hungry for their own chance at survival. You wake up from the dream and get your ass to work.

Up and down the hillside, you climb over broken dead logs and branches. You kick at the ground for topsoil, before raising your arms and slamming the hoedad into the earth. In one singular motion, a seedling in your right hand, you pull back the scar, gingerly swinging the tree into the opening, its tap root straight and its laterals spread. Once set, your foot carefully stamps the hole shut, before measuring a particular distance in your mind, and repeating the maneuver. All day long this repetition continues. You rarely look up, your back hinged at the hips, face to the ground. Under your rain gear, the body is constantly damp with sweat, your hands blistering from the hoe.

With the purpose of the work, the nightmare surrounding you is forgotten, the devastation ignored. A new reality emerges. Your thoughts now only care about the degree of the slope, the amount of slash left behind. Your personal issues are no longer moral, but industrial in scope and reference. And why? Well, because trees in the ground equal money in the wallet. Trees in the ground equal a trip to see your parents, your sister, and your old homeboy friends. Trees in the ground become the thing, the only thing. The rain and these ravaged hills become nothing more than hardships that must be confronted, to be battled against to get trees in the ground.

In the evening, you sit in the cramped trailer house, eating beans from a pot. Everything is damp, inside and out, body odor steaming with no escape. You drink cheap quart beer, smoke cigarettes and weed, with human conversation being only of the work. Numbed by alcohol and THC, the body dulled with fatigue, you curl into a sleeping bag on a narrow cushioned bunk that sinks with your weight. The next day will be the same routine, the same gray rain and pall, the same blistered sores and numbers count. Picking apples in the warm afternoons of Central Washington seems like a breeze in comparison.

But just like bin checkers in the orchards, the corporate Weyerhauser boys monitor your work. They check that the taps root are straight and not curled, the root stock safely covered with soil, the trees not too close or too far away. If things get too lax, monetary penalties will result. McAllister and Mookie go slow, needing to perfect the work. Young Jesse picks it up fast, motoring across the unit, lithe and quick. Marty Johnson keeps things on track, an able leader, direct but supportive. Tom Sullivan remains quiet and cool. After more than a week, they finish the first units. They discuss whether to run home for a couple of days, before returning for the next assault. It's a Friday afternoon, the darkness already beginning to creep as the winter solstice nears.

As Marty Johnson bumps the crummy down the logging road, Jesse Simmons catches sight of something out the window. "Hey, Marty, whoa, look at that!" Marty slows the rig as Jesse points to his right. The other passengers snap from their daydreams following Jesse's direction.

"Shit, man," Marty Johnson peers through the windshield. "It's a fucking bull elk. And from the looks of it, it ain't doing too well."

Marty brings the crummy to a stop, everyone inside staring at the sight. The huge animal struggles in the ditch below the road. Its back legs appear injured, its front legs attempting to drive itself upright. Marty turns off the engine, jumping from the vehicle. The rest of the crew follow right behind. From the roadbed above, the men look down upon the animal, struck by its size, the piercing sound of its pain snorting with each heaving breath. The elk continues trying to pull itself up, but the damage looks grim. For a time the men watch in silence, the elk's front legs beginning buckle, its torso leaning over, slumping to its side. Its breathing grows intermittent, gasping for air. Its eyes are glazed with a distracted recognition, as if realizing its fate.

Marty Johnson speaks. "It must have been hit by a logging truck, that's all I can figure." Marty continues to stare down at the animal. "But it's not going to make it, I'll tell you that."

"What do we do, Marty?" Jesse asks. Marty doesn't answer, but his mind seems to be working, a decision before him.

"Tommy," Marty begins to ask. Sullivan stands on the far side of the crew, like the others, looking down below.

"Yeah, Marty," Sullivan responds, almost matter of fact.

"Are you thinking what I'm thinking?"

Tom Sullivan takes a long pause, before responding. "I imagine so. It could take hours to die, we know that much. Nobody is going to save it. I don't see any reason to linger."

"What about the meat?" Marty asks.

Sullivan continues to watch the animal. McAllister turns his head to view Sullivan's response. Tom Sullivan's gaze seems to be far away, as if lost in some unknown memory. Without moving a muscle, he answers. "I don't know, Marty, first things first."

"I'll do it," Marty says. He goes to the back of the crummy, opening the double doors. He reaches inside, pulling out the long handled axe. The rest of the crew shuffle in distraction, waiting. Only Sullivan holds still. Marty slides down into the ditch, positioning himself behind the bull elk's massive head and rack. He leans down, pressing his hand against the animal's pulsing neck. The elk stirs, but its eyes never move. Satisfied, Marty stands up. He spreads his feet, raising the axe handle high above him, before coming down with the full force of his arms. The blade splits through, severing the target, the elk's whole body lurching on impact, dark blood gushing out of its neck. For what seems like forever, the elk's body shutters, the blood continuing to flow, before finally shaking still.

Sean McAllister's face is blank with expression, his eyes forced to watch, his mind empty of thought. Marty Johnson steps back, letting the axe handle fall to his side. "I guess that's it."

Upon his remark, the group jumps back to life, as if letting the pent-up air out of their lungs, relieved by the outcome. Only Tom Sullivan doesn't move, just staring down, lost in thought.

Jesse speaks. "I can help skin and butcher it. I've got my skinning knife in my pack. We've done lots of deer at the farm. We could just take the large cuts and cover the rest."

Marty Johnson looks over at Sullivan. "Tommy, what do you think?"

Hearing his name, Tom Sullivan raises his head, looking over at Marty Johnson on the far side of the ditch. "Do you think those loggers are off the show up there?" Sullivan asks. "It's been quiet for awhile, but they could be working on their equipment or something."

"True enough," Marty responds, "but it's getting late. We probably only got an hour or so of light. It would be a shame to waste it. It's not like we poached it or anything. But I guess we couldn't report it, as far as that goes."

"Anybody got a problem with this?" Sullivan asks, speaking to the group.

McAllister turns toward Mookie, who catches the glance and simply shrugs his shoulders. The kid Kooskie nods without speaking. McAllister looks at Sullivan. "I've never butchered anything, but some chickens we've done at the Farm. You'll need to tell me what to do."

Upon McAllister's response Marty Johnson jumps across the ditch to the other side. "Okay, we have to go quick. Jesse, get your knife. Sean, you and Mookie pull out all the work tools from the rig. Get out the tarps. Look in the toolbox. There should be a hammer and short-handled axe. If there is a hacksaw, get that too."

"Now, if we hear any vehicles on the road, stop what you're doing," Sullivan commands. "We'll cover up and act like we're just making a piss stop."

The group went to work. Jesse sliced and gutted the huge elk's midsection. Marty Johnson and Tom Sullivan chopped and sawed at the bones with the axe and hacksaw. Mookie James and Kooskie spread the tarps, taking the hacked sections of meat, wiping them of blood and entrails. McAllister used a shovel to dig a hole in the ditch to bury the guts, gathering a pile of brush to cover the carcass when the job was done. The late afternoon light grew thin, the body heat of the dead animal steaming into the air.

Suddenly, they heard sound of a vehicle engine coming down the logging road. At Marty's direction, McAllister scrambled the gear back into the crummy, closing the door. Mookie and Kooskie pulled the tarps closer to the crummy so as not to be seen. Marty, Sullivan, and Jesse dropped their implements, jumped from the ditch, turning to appear as if relieving themselves. The vehicle appeared in sight, its headlights on. The four-wheel drive pickup slowed as it approached, with three shadowed figures inside. Marty, acting like he was pulling up his zipper, turned toward the vehicle, giving a wave of salutation.

The pick-up stopped, the engine idling. "You guys all right," a voice asked from the truck. Marty approached the passenger window, trying to block their view. "Yeah, we're fine, just taking a piss break." Marty continued to speak with the men inside the truck for a time, the group holding still. As Marty stepped away, the truck rolled slowly forward, its passengers peering at the men, before accelerating down the road.

"Shit, that was close," Marty said. "Let's wind things up and get the fuck out of here."

"Do you think they suspect anything?" Sullivan asked.

"I'm not sure, Tommy. I guess we'll find out sooner or later."

The men finished the job as quickly as possible. Wrapping the meat in the tarps, they covered the cargo with their hoedads and tree belts as best they could. Disguising the carcass with branches and slash, they jumped into the crummy, speeding down the hillside, back to the trailer park in Coos Bay. Once there, they replaced the tree planting gear with their backpacks and personal items, before driving the three hours home. The elk meat was unloaded at the Mulcahey Farm. Using their flashlights, Jesse, Mookie, and McAllister hung the meat in the woodshed outside the kitchen. Marty and Sullivan drove Kooskie back to Grants Pass, before returning home to Railroad Bridge. It had been a very long eventful day.

The official letter came the following week, reaching the Mulcahey Farm mailbox, at 3100 Lower Pollard Creek Road. The letter was addressed to Timothy Moore, in whose name was the legal owner of the property. Tim Moore had been Derrick and Jack Mulcahey's pot smuggling friend from Santa Cruz. Moore had helped Derrick and Jack buy the Pollard Creek property, which they were still paying off. The letter bore the heading of the Jordan County Planning and Building Department. It got right to the point.

Dear Mr. Moore:

It has come to the attention of this office that you are in the process of constructing a number of residences on your property located on Lower Pollard Creek Road. This area is zoned Single Family Residential and allows only one residence per lot. The minimum lot size in this district is five acres and each lot must front on a public road.

Under the present zoning regulations for Jordan County, you are required to partition your land to accommodate the residences or remove all but one of the residences from the property. Either of these alternatives must be accomplished within sixty (60) days of this notice.

You will be required to bring the remaining structures up to the Oregon State Building Code. Please contact this office as soon as possible so that this matter may be resolved.

Yours sincerely,

James Smith
Planning Director

Perhaps in translation, the letter could have been written in another way:

"Dear Mr. Moore. We've got you hippies up in Pollard Creek by the proverbial balls. And now it's time to go for the squeeze. We've got the Pollard Creek Inn dead to rights, and so we have decided that you and your so-called residential family are next on our list. By the way, how do they feel right now? And we don't mean your feelings you long-haired faggots, but your fucking balls. You might as well pack it up and go. There's no way you're going to squirm out of this little grip, not in a million years. Especially not in Jordan County, that's for sure."

Richard Milhous Nixon may have gone away. The Vietnam War may have been finally winding down, and the political battles of the past decade appearing to abate. But the cultural wars between two generations in America would not go down so easy.

The 'back to the land' phenomenon was one of those cultural wars. Young Americans were leaving behind the bad guys and their capitalistic material world, their global corporate imperial agendas, their patriotic one-Christian-god national orthodoxy. They were choosing to take their own desires for life and the human condition back to the hills, to live within their own progressive ways of thought. They were sailing away in their wooden ships, saying you don't need us. You can have all your useless stuff, and your useless beliefs. Just leave us alone.

But the fact of the matter is this, the bad guys can't leave anything alone. Not a buffalo, not a tree, not a river, nothing. And especially not someone who disagrees with them, someone who might call into question their own sick view of the world. The *Easy Rider* fable was still very much in play. Only the tactics were a little less demonstrative. Instead of a shotgun, it was better to make a law and send you a letter.

The women at the farm took the letter terribly to heart. They worried about the kids, about the homes they shared. Derrick and Jack Mulcahey worked to console them, but privately they knew there would have to be a fight, perhaps a battle they might not win. Still, they decided they would ignore the letter and its request for consultation. They would wait the sixty days, let the red tags come, then figure their response.

Back in Coos Bay, the timing of many events in life can cut both ways. In some moments, events can be serendipitous, positive in their consequence. Other times they can be most unfortunate, appearing at the worst possible moment. For example, cue up the elk salvage incident:

If an elk doesn't cross the road at the same moment a logging truck comes barreling down the grade, then the Coos County Sheriff's deputies are not parked in front of an old rental trailer house in Coos County on a rainy December night. They don't take statements from the suspected violators, who tell them the honest truth. They don't immediately call the police officials in Jordan County. Police officials who send a cadre of officers with rain gear and flashlights over a swinging hippie cable bridge on a dark moonless evening to impound the evidence necessary to make their case. In Oregon, the simple possession of wildlife out of season, and without a permit, is prima facie evidence of the actual taking of that wildlife, regardless of the circumstances.

If the logging truck and the elk do not collide, a story doesn't get picked up by a beat reporter for the Grants Pass Tribune newspaper, whose editors see fit to twirl the charges into a front-page poaching incident at a hippie commune in Pollard Creek, known as the Mulcahey Farm. Then later, in a follow-up story, the paper labels the four men and one juvenile arrested as the Pollard Creek Five. The fact that concurrently, a letter of civil complaint by the Jordan County Planning and Building Department had arrived at an eerily similar time, was nothing more than pure coincidence. But it sure didn't help the cause.

The men were cited in Coos County despite their full cooperation. They argued that Kooskie, the twenty-year old kid from Grants Pass, had not been involved, and the cops saw fit to let him go. They also tried to protect Jesse Simmons as well. But Jesse would have none of it, telling his story exactly how it occurred. Jesse wanted to be treated just like the rest. When returning from Coos Bay the following week, the men contacted a public defender, pleading not guilty, requesting a jury trial. They argued that they had done the humane thing, putting the elk out of its mortal distress. Call them scavengers if you must, for preserving available food for their own survival. But poachers they were not, there had been no intent to commit a crime. They would tell their story to the court, whatever the outcome. But they had no reason to believe they would get a trial by their peers, whether in Coos or Jordan County.

Sean McAllister had never witnessed the type of mercy killing he had seen. Nor the difficult butchering of the animal that followed. He found it oddly ironic to be charged with the implicit crime of taking wildlife, when he hadn't fired a gun since rifle training at YMCA summer camp. He had owned no more than a pellet gun at the age of ten. However, his consideration of these unusual circumstances, including the legal threat of eviction from the Mulcahey property would have to wait. Mookie had found someone from Solace Valley heading for the east coast. Marty Johnson came by with their money from the work. They cashed their checks and packed their things. Hopefully, nobody was going to arrest them for wanting to be home for Christmas.

CHAPTER THIRTY-TWO

NEW YORK STATE OF MIND
New York City / Pollard Creek / January, 1975

ON A SATURDAY MORNING IN EARLY JANUARY 1975, Sean McAllister sat on the couch inside a basement brownstone flat in the Upper West Side of New York City. The apartment's interior was dark, the ceiling low, the only natural light casting through a small iron-barred window in the bathroom. Mary Jane's home was filled with the strange curios and knick knack items she was always picking up at thrift shops, or things she brought home from her job as a designer and window dresser for Bloomingdales. Mary Jane's politics had not changed, but her penchant for art and eccentricity was flourishing. Her wardrobe was almost completely second-hand, even down to her shoes and boots. She had taken to New York in a big way. Mary Jane had learned how to move quickly through the city, flagging down a cab with the best of them. She had friends and associates all over town. She could easily stay out late, wake up early. She was engaged in everything life in the Big Apple could toss her way.

In comparison, her brother, Sean McAllister, felt like a troglodyte, a cave dweller from out of town. In his worn jeans and rugged boots, his shoulder-length hair and flannel shirt, he felt like a sore thumb on the streets of the city, a true-to-life stranger in a strange land. The day before, while Mary Jane was at work, McAllister had spent the afternoon riding buses here and there, doing nothing more than people watching, which was a full-length movie all its own. There were human beings of all shapes and colors, yacking, clawing, and swirling through the asphalt jungle in a million assorted ways. There were Wall Street brokers pushing their way to the next possible deal, attractive women spiked to the heels, their sexual hips rocking from side to side. Everyone was racing towards their next destination, while dodging the worn-out bag ladies meandering along, peering expectantly into sidewalk trash receptacles. Homeless men staggered through their alcoholic dreams, engaged in lively conversation, if only with themselves.

For the inexperienced of this blackboard jungle, a nervous sciatica might run through the body, wishing to escape the sensory overload. After two days in the city, Sean McAllister was ready to run for the big country, the open skies of western America, back to the relative quiet of a smaller but wider world. He was impressed with Mary Jane, how she could cope with such a dissonance, even thrive in this mass of human hysteria. It seemed to him that it took a peculiar strength of character to survive this urban milieu, an inner fortitude he no longer possessed. New York was a city where an unsuspecting ego could be crushed like a grape on the pavement. He was more than ready to hit the road, to return to Oregon, back to a land where his sense of self would not be challenged by such overwhelming odds.

"Disco," Mary Jane said, as she stood at the kitchen drain board, pouring cups of coffee.

"Disco? What's that mean?" McAllister asked.

"It's short for discotheque, a place to dance," Mary Jane answered. "Don't you know, Mickey, the peace, love, and rock and roll scene is dead already. Hippies like you and your friends are old news these days, little brother." His sister laughed as she brought him the coffee. "Nowadays, you work all day, then snort cocaine and dance all night. At least here in New York City. There isn't even a band onstage anymore. Just a DJ with a box of dance tunes to play. You don't dress down. You dress to the hilt, go out and shake your booty. A few places have these big electric strobe lights that look like hanging balls. They flash all over the dance floor. It's the next big thing. You watch."

"I guess I can't wait," McAllister muttered. "Do you like it?"

"Sort of," Mary Jane answered. "It's new. Something to do, I guess. The music is kind of redundant, but everybody is getting into it here. I enjoy it because I get to dress up in some of the outfits I find. And it's a real good workout, dancing all night. Of course, doing the coke probably makes it seem better than it really might be. Have you ever tried it?"

"Yeah, from time to time. It's not like I can afford it, though. Most everybody in Oregon is into the weed. But I wouldn't turn it down if offered, that's for sure. Makes you feel pretty swell, if only for awhile. Then you always want more."

"That's for sure," his sister responded. "You always want more."

"Is David still around? Do you see him much?"

"I do," Mary Jane answered. "We've become friends now. He's about to finish law school this spring. David's a pretty serious guy these days. But it was best we separated. It was hard for us at first, but I'm glad we can still talk and remain close. What about Mad? Did you see her while you were home?"

"No, she's up in Pennsylvania somewhere. I did finally write to her, though. Pretty much told her I was sorry for what happened between us, but that I was happy to be in Oregon. I tried to make up with her, I guess, at least from my side. It was something I needed to do."

"Did she write back?"

"Yeah, she did. She said she was glad that I was okay and doing well. I guess she is still living with Willie Chambers, although I don't know for sure. She didn't mention it, and I sure didn't ask. She said she'd like to come to Oregon sometime, to travel out west. I don't think she realized it, but those words kind of cut me up some. Shit, it was the travel thing that kind of broke us apart in some ways. I always wanted to go, and she didn't at the time."

"Do you still miss her?" Mary Jane asked, in her sisterly tone of voice.

McAllister paused. "Yeah, a little at times, but really not that much. You know, once in a while there are those questions about what might have been, especially when something happens that brings her to mind. They usually come when I hear a song by Gram Parsons or Poco, or even Neil Young." McAllister chuckled, as if to himself. "That kind of sucks."

Mary Jane nodded and smiled. "It's the *White Album* for David and me. It had just come out when we first met at school. And it sure doesn't help that there were so many great songs on that album. Mary Jane paused. "But those memories are better these days. One day it will be the same for you. Better."

"I'm okay with it," McAllister answered. "Sometimes it still kicks me in the ass, but those moments are pretty rare anymore."

An hour later, Mookie arrived from his parent's home in Jersey. McAllister hugged and kissed his sister, saying his good-bye. Mookie and he caught a bus to the auto transport place, where Mookie had arranged for them to deliver a car across country to Los Angeles. Going through the checklist and paying the hundred dollar deposit, they headed out of the city, back on the highway to California. Sean McAllister was once again leaving his old roots, returning to the new home he had chosen to continue. But more than anything, he was heading west, back to the farmlands, the prairies, the mountains, and towering cumulus skies. He still loved the journey as much as ever, that American wanderlust of being on the road.

As the miles went by, he reflected about the holidays behind him. Overall, things had been good. His mom had been exhilarated by his return. For Connie McAllister to have her two children home together, was the best gift the world could give. As for his dad, Bill McAllister appeared to have given up the fight, at least the fight for the future of his son.

For McAllister himself, he was happy to be back home, sharing holidays with his family. The best part was that his parents seemed to have overcome the consequences of an empty nest. Luckily for him, Mary Jane got down when she could. She helped to take the pressure off this long distance reality of their departed son. McAllister was pleased that his parents appeared to have found a pattern of living without them. They still had their work, their sibling families and friends, the beach and other things they loved to do. Yet, with each milepost passing on the road, leaving his family further behind, there was an empty feeling in his stomach. But thankfully, there was no ache of guilt in his heart.

Often, when returning home from an adventure, you want to tell the ones you love all that you have seen. It was only human nature to want to share the experience, to tell the new story as best you could. But with the drift between two generations, the canyon divides of time, the effects of culture and change, of war and its consequence, the truth of the telling cannot be told. Just try to name a Vietnam veteran who could share such an ultimate and dramatic experience to anyone outside of his own. Name a hippie child from the Haight-Ashbury who could honestly tell her forbearers all she had witnessed and engaged. Sadly, these were two generations that could not be bridged, nor shared in a way that might not provoke fear and worry, if not anger and concern.

So Sean McAllister had not told his folks the whole story. Instead, he told a tale of travel and beautiful country, of good people and hard work in the apple orchards and timber country of the Great Northwest. In the manner of his telling, he could easily have been journeying through Europe, before coming home and settling down to the expected mores of a good job and climbing the ladder of success. He conveniently left out the food stamps, the steady use of marijuana, the naked bodies at the swimming hole, and the overnight sexual liaisons. He spared them the disgruntled battles between hippie and redneck, or the criminal charges for the taking of wildlife. In return, his father had not asked him if he was trying to make some form of statement with his lifestyle, or what in the world was he searching to find. Bill McAllister refrained from going into his occasional soliloquy that life is not easy, that you have to be able to support yourself, that your beliefs don't put food on the table. As a result, the time spent had been a fair exchange between them. It was a peace with honor of sorts, a benevolent cease fire for all concerned, especially for his mom.

As for his old friends, there came a surprising realization. Although Sean McAllister could have told his old homeboy buddies about every little nugget of his journey so far, nobody seemed to ask. It was great to see Bruiser and the other boys from his youth. Johnny Howard was back from Boulder, Snark Rosenbloom home from Wisconsin. He even caught up with Reggie Disalvo down in the city. Everyone had their stories, which they all shared to some degree. But in the end, what is happening with one's own life is the most important thing. Perhaps this is how it should be, because if you're not living your own life, then you might be living for somebody else. And that would be such a powerful mistake. But the overall lack of interest McAllister felt from others about his travels west, and probably he for theirs', was a clear reminder to him. His present course of adventure was his and his alone. It might seem trivial, but there is that moment when you realize that the past has come and gone, that much of what has been shared before must now be left behind. Thomas Wolfe's famous words rang true:

"You can't go back home to your family, back home to your childhood, back home to a young man's dreams of glory and

fame. Back home to places in the country, back home to the old forms and systems of things which once seemed everlasting but which are changing all the time. Back home to the escapes of Time and Memory."

Mookie James pushed the car forward, speeding into the stark January afternoon. Cold gray clouds cast the sky, the western horizon a pale banding of tarnished white. For McAllister, a final memory of his leaving squeezed its way within him. He closed his eyes and let it come. It was the vision of he and a beautiful young women, seated together on a water tank under a warm summer sun, their liquid bodies holding close, the taste of red wine on their breath, their lips softly pressing, one against the other. Perhaps the moments of first love are never really forgotten. And perhaps they never should be, especially when the pain of their escape has tempered with time. Such moments are the linchpin between who we have been, and who we might become. But as the memories begin to fade, the door to the future springs open, and once and for all we let the memories go.

County Commissioner Wilton Parker sat in his office at the Jordan County Courthouse, looking out the window at the large wet snowflakes drifting by the glass. The outside temperature was just warm enough that the snow was turning to mush on the streets of Grants Pass. But Wilton Parker knew that at the higher elevations out of town things would be a little more difficult. The necessary response by his Public Works Department would be underway. The snow plow rigs and dump trucks of sand were heading for the mountain hamlets throughout the county. The weather reports were predicting as much as a foot or more in some areas. The Jordan County Schools Superintendent had just announced an early closure, so their buses would be on the road getting the children home. With so much action going on, he sure didn't need to be sitting here with this officious pale-faced crew-cut man of a State Building Director, Craig Benson. But it came with the job, like it or not.

Benson, as usual, was all business. There was not a shade of humor or personality to the man. He was like one of those human robots you might see in some science fiction movie, with a demeanor so cold it breathed a chill in the room. Wilton Parker was pretty sure that Benson, and the obsessive behavior he had toward his job, would one day be a danger with which Wilton Parker would have to contend. Maybe not today, but at some point down the road.

Benson began his spiel. "Commissioner, I am here this morning to give you an update on the progress of building compliance issues in your jurisdiction. In conjunction with James Smith, your director over at Planning, we soon will be moving forward on several property inspections county-wide. Based on our research and investigations, we fully expect that these direct inspections will result in serious conditions of non-compliance. The result will be that specific enforcement measures will have to be taken to redress the violations."

Wilton Parker knew this crap was coming. The County had been forced to get their ordinances in line with the statewide zoning and growth mandates coming down from Salem. The majority of residents in Jordan County were opposed to such regulation and restraint. They had said as much in a county-wide vote sometime back. No matter, the State of Oregon had prevailed on the issue, and the chickens were coming home to roost. But as anyone knows, legislation is one thing, the enforcement of that legislation entirely another. Wilton and the other commissioners would have preferred to drag their feet on the implementation, taking their time to let the recognition of the changes slowly sink in with the citizens. The Commissioners wanted to focus only on new residential and commercial construction without stirring the pot. But Craig Benson was a wild card, a bureaucratic maverick from outside the county. He was a man hell-bent on full and complete application of the law. And Benson didn't give a damn about the political consequences, for Wilton Parker or anybody else. So, this was not good news.

Benson quickly reviewed the two initial complaints that his department would pursue. They were initially focused on two hippie communes, one in Pollard Creek, the other located at the far southwest end of the county, near Cave Junction. Wilton didn't have much of a problem with those situations. The hippies had suddenly infiltrated Jordan County in recent years, bringing their new lifestyles and immorality into his homeland. They were getting on food stamps and welfare, growing their marijuana, and staking out mining claims wherever they might live for free. Wilton Parker didn't have much sympathy there. But Wilton also knew that one or two missteps by Benson's department could blow things sky high.

Jordan County had a long history of anti-government sentiment. And private property rights were at the heart of that political reality. Jordan County was full of rural homesteaders, Birchers, eccentric prospectors and constitutionalists, many with a shoot-first mentality when it came to government control. The outfit known as the Posse Comitatus was strong in these parts. They believed that the County itself was the highest form of government order, not the State, and certainly not the Feds. In their view, there was no higher legal authority than the County Sheriff, but it was an authority whose only mandate was to carry out the will of its citizens. But who in the hell would want that job? In the Posse Comitatus' literature, should the Sheriff actually refuse to carry out the will of the county's citizens, then "…he shall be removed by the Posse to the most populated intersection of streets in the township, and at high noon be hung by the neck, the body remaining until sundown as an example to those who would subvert the law".

Suffice to say that for many in Jordan County, they would not take kindly to government interference, particularly if it was aimed at them. When it came to that possibility, Craig Benson, boy wonder, wouldn't have a clue. As far as some were concerned, Benson could screw his little book of rules and regulations. With these particular folks, should Benson even try and red tag an outhouse or shed, there was a good chance he might be pushing up daisies in a shallow unmarked grave somewhere in these forbidden hills. As for Wilton Parker, he could kiss his ass good-bye, at least as a Jordan County Commissioner. At best, he might still be at his ranch in Hugo, about ten miles north of town, rustling up a living, with his own thick neck barely intact.

So Wilton tried to be as diplomatic as he could. He let Benson know that this building crusade might be dangerous in certain quarters. That sometimes, certain things in life are better left alone. But Craig Benson did not appear to be getting any hidden messages, no recipes for survival that might not cook his goose. One could say that as a culinary expert, Craig Benson couldn't par boil shit for a sled dog. And it appeared as if Wilton Parker would just have to wait and see when his own Last Supper might come.

"Let me ask you something," Wilton inquired, as the meeting drew to a close. "Benson, were you ever in the military? Did you ever serve?"

"No," Benson replied. "I never got the call."

"That's too bad," Wilton Parker answered. "You would have made a damn good soldier, Benson, a damn good one, I believe."

"Why thank you, Commissioner," Benson returned. "I'm pleased you would think so."

Wilton Parker smiled across at Benson, as if planning to speak again. And although he held his words, he didn't hold his unspoken opinion. 'Yeah, a damn fine soldier, you fucking dressed-down son of a bitch, all spit and shine. A damn fine soldier, but more than likely, a dead one too.'

On a Saturday in late January, Sean McAllister fed the pigs their grain and some leftover roughage out of the Mulcahey garden. He shoveled and wheel barrowed manure out of the large chicken coop, keeping the manure pile dry with plastic sheeting. The winter day was cold, with a low ceiling of heavy gray sky. After a noon lunch, he and Mookie James started an outdoor fire near the banks of Pollard Creek. They cut and snipped branches of alder, willow, and vine maple that rimmed the creek bed, amidst the sound of rushing whitewater, loud from days of winter rain. With Jesse Simmon's help they weaved the branches into an igloo shaped hut, before covering it with old blankets and tarps. As the fire pit blazed then settled, they set river rock into the coals to heat.

Throughout the chilled dry afternoon, others from the Farm, as well as friends from Pollard Creek, came down to enjoy the sweat lodge they had built. Naked kids and adults excreted out their toxins inside the steamy hut. The more courageous found a safe hole in the bend of Pollard Creek to cool themselves from the sweat. The women poured buckets of cold water over the children's heads, who went screaming in delight. Afterwards, people sat circled by the fire pit, sitting on tree stumps or empty five-gallon containers, draped in blankets or towels, passing quarts of Olympia or Rainier beer between them. Small town gossip shuttled across the flames, the incestuous updates of life in Pollard Creek passing from one ear to another on a slow winter day.

That evening, with the communal dinner over, Mookie, Darius, and McAllister trudged up to Betsy Simmons one room cabin, their flashlights in hand. Betsy's home had been the very first structure built on the property, back when Derrick and Jack Mulcahey had initially bought the land. Derrick had stayed on alone, to be free from the FBI dragnet that was closing down on him in Santa Cruz. The cabin's meager foundation consisted of large tree stumps, the framing was built of old scrapped two by four lumber. The siding of the cabin consisted of stripped log tailings scavenged from the mill in Glendale. The roof was sheathed in battered corrugated tin, with roofing tar spotted over the nail holes. The stovepipe stuck at an angle out the side of the cabin wall, secured by baling wire to keep it in place.

Betsy Simmons was the mother of the three boys, Jesse being her oldest. Although her days in Los Angeles were far behind her, Betsy's party spirit remained intact. She was the oldest person on the Mulcahey Farm, in her late thirties or thereabout. Betsy collected her welfare for the boys, gave some to the farm, keeping the rest for herself. She liked her Jack Daniels, her cigarettes and her books. Once in a while, she would disappear for a night up to Cougar Gulch, partying with the hardcore redneck men and women who lived over on the east side of Pollard Creek. Betsy had a great sense of humor and some Cherokee blood. Suffice to say, Betsy Simmons was not afraid of having a good time.

Mookie had begun to call Betsy's cabin the USO Club, because the Mulcahey Farm sometimes felt like a boot camp. Jack Mulcahey was a great guy, but he was stoic and closed, not a man who could enjoy the camaraderie of others, his inability to communicate so difficult to overcome. And Derrick Mulcahey was the renegade master of ceremonies, who kept his distance in order to maintain his hegemony, his charming purity, and the constant manipulations he held close to his vest.

Betsy had known Derrick Mulcahey since his student days in Hermosa Beach. She would be forever grateful to Derrick and Jack, for having taken her son Jesse under their wing, giving him guidance and plenty of male direction in his life. But she was plenty experienced in Derrick's penchant for grandiosity and control. Betsy had the maturation of age on her side, and when Derrick got angry or weird in his intents, she didn't get upset, she simply blew him off. And although no one saw fit to give her credit, despite her bathroom humor and sometimes careless ways, Betsy Simmon's cabin was a port of call during the occasional storm. She was a hardened voice of realism whenever the histrionics of Derrick Mulcahey's personal vision and exploitations got way out of line. Betsy had the larger and longer perspective that others lacked, that nothing on the Mulcahey Farm was as serious as it certainly might seem.

Hence, the USO Club. It was a cozy warm establishment to smoke cigarettes and pot, to take a hit from a bottle of whiskey, before washing it down with a swallow of beer. It was a safe place to complain and make fun of things, without getting bent out of shape. The Club acted as a shelter of security from the rugged survival of an Oregon winter, the pitch-black rain of weariness on a Saturday night, with nowhere else to go. Sometime later, with their shoulders hunched and flashlights leading the way, the men took their leave, before wrestling into sleeping bags on hard cots of wood, to bravely dream until the coming of another day.

As January, 1975 reached its end, a growing tension began to take hold at the Mulcahey Farm. In a couple of weeks, the sixty-day waiting period on the letter sent by Jordan County would be reached without response. What might happen next, nobody knew. From Glendale to the north, to Solace Valley in the south, there were at least seven other intentional communities in varying states of communal operation, each one with numerous non-compliant structures. There were the stragglers left behind at Strawberry Fields, and the boys up at Railroad Bridge. There was the educational commune near Glendale, the environmental and lesbian groups up on Robertson Creek, as well as the new gay commune purchased only recently by men out of San Francisco. And of course, there was Brave New World, who some called the first hippie community in Southern Oregon. Its inception dated back to 1968, when the politics of Berkeley and the Vietnam War had driven it founders back to the land.

However, no other commune appeared to be presently under the Jordan County gun, just the Mulcahey Farm. The Pollard Creek Inn folks had surely taken their own weird hit, but that was a story all its own. Still, the incidents at the Inn had seemed like a harbinger of more bad things to come. The Mulcahey Farm had a reputation for hard work and sustainability, of building toward a goal of self-sufficiency, a

Mother Earth News work in progress. So, if the Mulcahey Farm could be run off by the forces of authority, there was no doubt that others might follow. The clock was ticking, as if Cinderella was waiting, for the other shoes to drop.

Sean McAllister busied himself with the daily life of the Farm, while waiting for his criminal future to come. Marty Johnson and Tom Sullivan had secured a public defender in response to their poaching arrests. They would fight the charges as a group and see what happened. No court date had been set.

McAllister spent the early darkened evenings and long rainy nights reading Ken Kesey's *Sometimes A Great Notion*. With Kesey, he sank deeper into the heritage and roughened independence of the Oregon timbered life. He witnessed the hell-bent exteriors of his characters. He felt the deeper secrets and fears of their interior lives, which they were never allowed to show. He read Brautigan's *In Watermelon Sugar*, Kerouac's *The Dharma Bums*, and Tom Robbin's eccentric *Another Roadside Attraction*.

He read Henry Miller's *Tropic of Cancer* for a second time, embracing Miller's caustic rebellions against the greed and hypocrisies of his fellow man. Miller raged against the human corruptions of its institutions, the soiled imagery of its fallen and disenfranchised masses, all of whom Miller both hated and loved, while allowing his own incredible vulnerabilities to be placed on display. It was therefore not surprising to think of an American government that would need to ban *Tropic's* publication for over thirty years after the book was written. Miller was a rough and tumble guy from the streets of New York. He had left his homeland for the city of writers, Paris, needing to write the craziness of his own life and take a literary shot. He would spill out his provocative opinions and feelings, his lusts and loves for all to see. He would hold no quarter when it came to his art.

> *"It is now the fall of my second year in Paris. I was sent here for a reason I have not yet been able to fathom. I have no money, no resources, no hopes. I am the happiest man alive. A year ago, six months ago, I thought that I was an artist. I no longer think about it, I am. Everything that was literature has fallen from me. There are no more books to be written, thank God."*

As far as McAllister was concerned, Henry Miller had become a man horrified by the American Dream, its hypocrisies and weightless pronunciations, its prejudices and provincial constraints. He was Kerouac before Kerouac, Ginsberg before Ginsberg. And he was as American as apple pie. But America did not know him, only the pornographic myth his detractors sought to portray. But Henry Miller was good, real good. For anyone with nerve enough to take the ride.

The winter coastal fronts continued their barrage, pounding one after another through the tough Siskiyou terrain, forcing the mountain country to endure their wrath, for the simple mistake of getting in their way. More wood was cut and chopped to feed the stove, kerosene sales were at an all time high. Mildew threw a garden party every day, while a swollen Pollard Creek roared through the night. Eventually, February slipped quietly through the backdoor cabins of these Oregon hills, but no one seemed to notice. For it is sometimes hard to see certain things, when your head is forever down against the wind and rain.

CHAPTER THIRTY-THREE

PERFECT IMPERFECTION
Pollard Creek / February, 1974

Bite the bullet. Before the discovery and widespread use of anesthesia, army doctors would have the patient stick a bullet in their teeth, biting down hard as the wound was treated, enduring the pain from which there was no escape, no escape unless you wanted not to die and live another day. Whether by being a victim of circumstance or its own personal misjudgments, the Pollard Creek Inn was on the operating table, fighting for its life.

The State of Oregon held the scalpel in its hands, perched over the dying soldier. Fate had taken its course, the injury was critical, the surgery must be done. The irony was that it was the doctor who had fired the shots. Somehow, he had become both the perpetrator and now your saving grace. But in your innocent suffering, you have no choice. You bite down hard on the metallic shell, looking up at a wicked grin gazing down above you, before passing out as the knife pierces inside your skin.

Within the unconscious dream that ensues, you vision the history of your past:

You are on a horse-drawn stage coach, pulling up to the Six-bit House, two bits for dinner, two bits for bed, and two bits for breakfast. You are on your way to Portland from Sacramento, a long week's journey heading north through the wilderness of the Great Northwest. Dragging your satchel upstairs, you pass the open doors of occupied rooms. Jack London sits at a desk working on a book. President Rutherford B. Hayes stands in front of a mirror, practicing a speech. Clark Gable and Mary Pickford laugh and drink whiskey together. Outside your window, you see a horde of slant-eyed Chinamen swinging sledge hammers, laying steel for the railroad to come.

Waking in the morning, you go downstairs. The building has fallen into disrepair. Looking in the tavern room, you see short-haired tree fallers in their suspenders and large heeled boots, taking swings at each other just for fun. Cakes of reddish mud lay broken on the floor. You enter the dining room where the wood stove burns. At a large table a group of younger men and women sit across from each other. Their long hair hangs across their shoulders and down their backs. They are dressed in strange colorful clothing, but their expressions are sadly forlorn, as if pressed with a decision they would rather not make. You take a seat at a table nearby, beginning to listen as the discussion unfolds.

Albert Krieger and Robert Sage sit next to each other at the table's head. Jimmijay Connell, Guitar Glen, Slick Bell, Laura Hale, Darla Bloom, and several other brothers and sisters sit anxiously together. Outside, the cold February rain continues its mission, its ear held to the window glass, awaiting the moment of truth.

As expected, the State of Oregon was making its play. Fifty thousand dollars for the property, the same amount as the original purchase price, it would make the owners whole. The kicker was the offer of relocation money paid to the residents, the amount based on their length of time living at the Inn. Excepting the owners, who were not included in the offer, the residents would get up to four thousand dollars in exchange for packing their things and walking on down the road. Four thousand dollars! It might as well be a million when one's pocket is empty of cash. The problem was this, there was so much more at stake.

Four thousand dollars to give up your home, to leave your family and friends. Four thousand dollars to give up your dream, a dream that before the bust last summer, you had lived every day without thinking of the future. You had awakened each day to a new adventure in living your life, completely in the present, without a single thought of a purpose or consequence.

Now, the present hung around your neck like a stone, and the future so very much a concern. As for the dream itself, it had turned black with soot, as dark as a lump of coal on Christmas morning. Face it, this thing was dead, killed by forces out of your control. The only thing left was the money on the table, immersed in a puddle of blood. Principles and ideals are beautiful emotions, and one should hold to them whenever they can. Yet, survival trumps all, time and again.

There was no question that if Albert Krieger and Robert Sage had run the flag up the pole, if they had rallied the troops to battle against the enemy, the story might have been different. But Sage had already moved on, and Albert had become weakened by feelings and emotions he could not dismiss, an emptiness he could not manage to fill. The sense of regret was enormous, but there were not enough provisions to carry on the fight.

And so it was settled. The bullet bit. They would take the offer and accept defeat. With the decision made, there was a sense of collective relief among them. This terrible emotional trauma would finally come to an end. They would have until June to figure out their futures, when the sordid money would come. But tonight, no champagne bottles would be popped in the room. It's not the beverage of choice at a wake for the deceased. If there would be any drinking at all, it would require a bottle of Irish whiskey and tears.

In the middle week of February a high pressure system crashed like an ocean breaker onto the Oregon coast, spilling over the inland mountain valleys of Southern Oregon. High above, the temperate heat of a winter sun shined bright and clear. Unfortunately, the warmth of the atmosphere above was higher than the chilled wet ground below, capping the narrow valleys of Pollard Creek and Solace Valley with an impenetrable misty fog. Only hundreds of feet above, the sun shone, its rays spreading like the warmth of a Chinook wind on the skin, giving hope, accepting gratitude, raising spirits with its presence. But unless one was living on a mountaintop, or cutting wood off a logging road at higher elevations, the musty indifference of an Oregon winter remained, the inversion continuing to barricade most of the populace inside a wintry gray tomb.

On this type of socked in February morning they arrived, the three bureaucrats in a blue and white Chevrolet Blazer, accompanied by two Jordan County police officers from Grants Pass. Unannounced, the bureaucrats waddled their way across the swinging cable bridge. Their feet were spread wide, their arms outstretched keeping their balance, film cameras strapped and bouncing off their chests. The police officers were dressed in brown and tan, their Stetsons looking as if welded perfectly to their heads, their five-star badges fitting prominently over their hearts. Someone beat on the metal gong that hung outside the communal kitchen. Everyone halted upon whatever chore they engaged, hustling to the kitchen as if called to a fire.

Immediately, everyone knew this was the day. Derrick Mulcahey took the warrant handed to him by the police officer, but didn't bother to read. It really didn't matter to Derrick. In his mind they could do whatever they were expecting to do. The family had already decided they would not resist. There had been full consensus agreement that any type of zoning or building conformance was out of the question. The Mulcahey Farm would continue to fight them until the day the bulldozers arrived. They knew full well that such an eventuality would be a longer time in coming.

Unbeknownst to the intruders, a different response was in play. Mookie fired up the pick-up, heading the back way to Solace Valley and the commune known as Brave New World. There, Lou and Gary strapped on their rifles, following Mookie back to the farm. Arriving nearby, the men entered the property from the adjoining residence next door, planting themselves and their weapons on the hillside above the cabins below. It would be a measure of protection should something dangerous occur.

As the bureaucrats were led from cabin to cabin, taking pictures with their cameras, the women engaged the officers in discussion, acting courteous and demure, their children in tow. Meanwhile, back at the kitchen, Jesse filled two plastic pitchers with sugar, before grabbing a funnel. As the troupe of police and investigators, women and kids, went from house to house, Jesse made his way across the bridge, then up to the roadside turnout where the vehicles were parked. The Blazer got doused first, the sugar poured freely into the gas tank. The second vehicle would be a little more dicey, especially parked so close to the road. But the police car's gas tank was locked shut. Jesse returned to the Blazer, giving it a second helping, before dashing down the railroad tracks, across the bridge next door and back to the farm. His secret guerilla mission was complete.

Annie took pictures of men taking pictures, recording the history of their presence, for whatever it might be worth. In short of two hours the intrusion was over. The forces of public safety and welfare had completed their task. In their convoluted minds, they were saving the Mulcahey Farm from the apparent dangers they were inflicting on themselves. Although Jordan County might argue that the law was the law, there was frankly no doubt of its purposeful political intent.

As the authorities drove away, a mid-afternoon sun pierced itself through an opening of gray-blanket sky, embracing the evergreen hills in resonant yellow light. The members of the commune chatted about the event. They had survived the enemy's first attack. A new mission was banding them together as one, to protect each other and the homes they shared. The internal distractions of individual personality were forgotten for a time. The men joked and speculated about how far the Blazer would go, hoping it would die on one of the mountain passes above, right in the path of a barreling tractor trailer on Interstate 5. The women and children felt the energy of a family integration, easing their worries of the future. Again, there seemed a singleness of purpose, one that the difficulties of a winter survival can often separate and divide. There would be peace in the valley, at least for a time.

The small one-room bungalow cabin that stood out in the back of Valerie Williams' yellow house on Main Street shook like hell. The roar and compression of the Southern Pacific evening freight train sounded like a disaster event in progress. Its initial passing overwhelmed any chance of natural or conversational sound, followed by the high screeching of the wheels on the rails, the heavy dull thumps of the cars rocking with their loads of milled lumber and wood chips, thundering through the black of night.

As the lights from the caboose flashed in the back window of the cabin, the long haul of freight was past. The voices emanating from the television set inside the cabin returned to the room. Marty Johnson took a drag off a joint, handing it back to Tom Sullivan.

"Shit, man. That's a fucking ball buster. How could any human being sleep through that?"

Sullivan took the joint, drawing in a hit, before passing it to Mookie James who sat beside him on the couch. He exhaled the smoke.

"Guess Rita won't be going to sleep before nine in the evening," Sullivan said, matter of fact.

"You guess?" Marty asked satirically.

Tom Sullivan watched as Mookie James passed the marijuana cigarette to Sean McAllister. McAllister took a hit. Getting up from the couch, he walked the joint back to Marty Johnson. Marty reached into his shirt pocket, attached a feathered roach clip to the smoke, taking a final hit before passing it on. The television once again became the center of attention, as the men watched a Saturday night episode of *All in the Family.* Sullivan had strung up an aerial onto the roof of the old shed structure. He had moved a couch and a couple of chairs into the room, hooking up an old television set he had found in Grants Pass. Otherwise, the cabin was empty of any other furnishings.

Over the past month, Sullivan had emptied the shed of old tools and miscellaneous garbage. He had cleaned it out, installing a wood stove he and Marty had fashioned out of a fifty-five gallon drum. He was making it ready for Rita to occupy when she returned from California. Rita had ended her caretaking gig on Lower Pollard Creek back in December, storing her stuff for a time while she went down to San Francisco for the holidays. She had remained down in the Bay Area while taking some sort of Zen Buddhist training course. She was due back sometime in March. Rita and Valerie had known each other in San Francisco, and Valerie could use the extra fifty dollars in rent income that Rita would pay. In the meantime, the empty shed was doubling as a something of a boy's club until Sullivan finished the job.

The four men sat in the cabin facing the television, still dressed in their winter coats and heavy boots, each with their own quart of cheap beer, occasionally rolling a cigarette out of the yellow Top can that lay on the floor in front of them. The setting was the best these men might hope for on a rainy cold Saturday night in the middle of February. Their bonding had developed with their time spent working the tree planting contract over on the coast, sharing the worn out trailer house where they had stayed in Coos Bay. They also had become the fab four of the infamous Pollard Creek Five. Only Mookie James had a girl at home. As for the rest, none had a female squeeze whom they were required to feel responsible towards, so some scratchy television viewing would be the sum total of their current weekend entertainment.

"So, Sean, are you still hanging out with Rita?" Marty Johnson asked, leaning forward off his chair.

Sean McAllister looked over at Marty, readjusting his position on the couch. "Uh, not really," McAllister answered. "We hung out a couple of times before she left. But that was all, I suppose. She liked coming by the Farm a lot. But you know Rita, she's always got a lot on her mind."

Mookie James and Tom Sullivan snickered at McAllister's perspective. Marty Johnson continued to lean forward, looking at McAllister.

"I mean, don't get me wrong, she's as nice as she could be," McAllister continued. "You know, she's just different, that's all. She worries about things a lot. Like things maybe you can't do much about. It's just a little hard sometimes to keep up with her, that's all. She's okay, I mean she's great, inquisitive as heck, but it's not like we are serious or anything."

Marty Johnson leaned back against the chair, looking over at Sullivan. "So when is she coming back, Tommy? When do we lose our little crash pad in town?"

"About a month," Sullivan answered. "I've got to get a cook stove hooked up, and something of a kitchen in this place before she gets back."

When the television show was over, Marty Johnson and Tom Sullivan went out into the rain, heading back to Railroad Bridge on the moonless winter night. Mookie James and Sean McAllister rolled another cigarette, finishing their beer.

"Where's Valerie tonight?" Mookie James asked.

"I think she went with Laura and Darla up to Eugene for the weekend. That's why Canyon is down at the Farm, staying with Derrick and the kids. I think Laura is looking to move up there, now that everyone has to leave the Inn."

"When do they all have to move out? I can't believe they had to sell it. What a bunch of crap. It's a raw deal, through and through."

"Yeah, it sucks," McAllister answered. "But I guess there was no way they were going to get the license back. The forces of bullshit win again, so what's new in the world?"

"Got that right," Mookie agreed. Mookie took another swig off his beer. "Hey Sean, there is something I got to tell you, bro. And I suppose now is as good a time as ever."

"So what's up?" McAllister asked.

"It looks like Annie and I are going to split the sheets sometime soon. I thought you should know before you hear it from her or from somebody else."

McAllister's head pulled away from the television set, looking at his friend. "What? You and Annie? You're kidding me. I mean you almost got the house built and all. I mean, damn."

"She says she needs some space, you know, the normal stuff. Says she's not feeling happy right now, that maybe a break between us would be good for awhile."

McAllister pushed himself back against the couch. "Damn, brother, I'm sorry. I guess I can't believe it."

"Me either," Mookie answered, "but I guess I got to."

McAllister took a drag off his cigarette. "You know, maybe it's just the winter, Mook. This kind of weather can get anybody down for the count."

But McAllister worried it might be more than that. Annie had been acting different, even to McAllister himself. Something had changed after her time in California. Maybe it was her parents, or maybe worse, somebody else. He wondered what Mookie had been feeling. Much like himself a few years ago, you sense that something isn't right, but you don't believe it. You try to put it out of your mind. But in the end, you're simply the last to know. Not because you shouldn't know, only because you were afraid to really look. He could feel a deep sympathy for his friend, and those sad uncertain feelings that would come with this consequence. He wished he could do something to make it better, but he knew it wouldn't matter. He'd been down that road before.

"You're not going to leave the Farm are you?" McAllister asked.

"I don't want to," Mookie answered. "There is so much more to do. But with this building code shit coming down, and now Annie, I don't feel much like doing anything more on the house. I don't know. We'll see I guess."

"Does Annie want to stay, or what?"

"She says she does, but I don't think she really knows what she wants. I mean, I'm not going to kick her out or anything. But I really can't say. It's all too new and weird right now. It's going to be sort of day to day for awhile."

The two friends turned off the television, latched the door to the shed, driving back to the Farm in the rain. McAllister followed his flashlight through the darkness out to his cabin. He undressed, climbed into the loft, going to sleep for the night. Upon waking in the morning, the latest block of cold rain had passed. The morning sun cut through the evergreens, reflecting off the moisture of wet trees, shimmering in the light. Oregon could sure get you down sometimes, but you just had to make the best of it. McAllister lay in his sleeping bag, thinking about things that came to mind.

Women were so hard to figure out. For that matter, sometimes life itself was so hard to figure out. Now, Mookie and Annie were on the outs. You look at friends like them, who seem on the outside to have such a good relationship. They appear to be so together, you think of them as one and the same. Mookie and Annie, their names roll off your tongue as if one inclusive persona, you hardly think of one without the other. McAllister had once experienced that similar collective reality, Sean and Mad, for most of two years. But things are often never as they seem. When it ends, at least for the one left behind, there is a stripping of identity that must be confronted and endured. Mookie would now have to climb into that boat, and the seas would be rough for a time.

The one good thing about Pollard Creek was that monogamy and fidelity were no longer an expected pattern of human behavior. Although both the women and the men still occupied the traditional roles of their gender, the culture of the times had begun to obscure the difference. For many women, the love and devotion, till-death-did-you-part syndrome was waning. Women no longer feared the insecurities of not having a man, a bread winner by their side. No doubt that the luxury of welfare and food stamps had aided the liberty of their cause, but the changes occurring ran deeper than simply income assistance. Women now had the opportunity for personal freedom in their minds. They could act more independently on their own impressions, make a wider range of choices about sex and compatibility.

And in Pollard Creek, the women were not about to waste these new opportunities. They could now take men for whom and what they were, satisfy their needs as necessary, then let them go. Free love was no longer a one-sided affair, solely the province of men in society. Women could now do the same. As a result, many men were having to adjust to these new circumstances, having to give their female counterparts the benefit of the doubt. Without question, it was not an easy thing to do. For men, such traditional expectations and paternalistic mores don't give way at the drop of a hat. Nonetheless, they were beginning to understand. The jealousy of the heart is an unconscious knee-jerk set of emotions, an almost instinctual response of historical origination. Yet, the die had been cast, whether you liked it or not. There would be no more grabbing by the hair, dragging your woman back to the cave. Personal freedom now had a wider social arc. Hypocrisy would no longer be tolerated. In Pollard Creek, the boys would either have to 'live it', or 'live with it', there was no going back. They would just have to figure it out.

Mookie was a damn smart guy. He was also a man with a gentle heart. McAllister knew that Mook would survive the difficult changes ahead. Still, McAllister couldn't help but feel sorry for his pal, knowing the sharp pain and sense of loneliness that would test him, the confusion he would feel in trying to be a stand-up guy.

McAllister had failed in that regard, he had run away from the pain, the anger he felt, the loss of self that consumed him. He couldn't face the reality of his own culpability, or the simple fact of life that people change. But he was younger then, inexperienced in the loss of love, unable to overcome rejection. Last summer, when Darla cut him off from their affair, he had handled it well, taken it in stride. But today, he remained unsure. With Darla, he hadn't necessarily been in love. Everything was so new, it was like he was on a roller coaster ride. Darla's leaving was just another rush down the track he was expected to survive.

What worried him most, was whether he had grown hardened inside, incapable of putting his heart on the line when the right woman came around. Would he be able to overcome his fears, let himself go, step off that cliff into the void that true intimacy demands. Eventually, one day, he would have to try and open his heart again.

CHAPTER THIRTY-FOUR

CHANGES
Pollard Creek / June, 1975

SURVIVING A NORTHWEST WINTER is not necessarily deserving of an Olympic gold medal or a Nobel Prize. A Northwest winter doesn't require the stone-cold hardness of a Minnesota, a Buffalo, or the windswept desperation of a North Dakota snowdrift piling over your door. It doesn't come at you with the powerful punch of a George Foreman right cross knocking you to the mat. No, a Northwest winter is more insidious in its consequence. It has a gradual and cumulative effect. It entraps you. It plays you like the Muhammad Ali 'rope a dope' strategy. It bobs and weaves, pulls its gloves together, taking your best shots. It slowly and deliberately wears you down. Then suddenly, you are looking face-up from the canvas. Through your dazed vision, you see the referee holding the Northwest winter's right arm high in the air. The Northwest winter has regained the championship of the world!

Defeated and depressed, you retreat to your dressing room to lick the wounds, to treat the psychic damage. The next morning you roll over in bed, not wanting to get up, the curtains drawn. But somehow, finally, a ray of sunshine slips its way into your room. Someone gently raises a window. You hear the forgotten sound of a returning song bird, you breathe in the sweet scents of lilac and rose. The window curtain flutters with a warm morning breeze pressing against your skin. You pull yourself up, throw off the covers. You step out into the sentient expanse of a lovely blue June sky. You are ready again to live the romance of your life.

Pollard Creek had survived. Things were still a little problematic in certain quarters, but this business of living in the twentieth century would forever have its challenges. The defeats of winter couldn't keep a good village down. It was time to get back in the ring.

At the Pollard Creek Inn, Jimmijay Connell returned to the studio. He cranked up the stereo, started rolling the tape, he was back on the air. Guitar Glen re-strung that accessory appendage that hung from his neck. He wrote a new song. Laura Hale fetched her conga drums from the corner of her room, went out into the side yard of the building, pounding away. She would arrange for one more dance class, until the Inn was forced to close. Darla Bloom drove herself to Ashland. Darla was going to become a midwife, and needed some training to begin. The taste of spring, the elixir of growing evening light, the bloom of mountain wildflowers had become a natural medicinal high.

The buzz of these new adventures pulled Albert Krieger out of his cave. The beginnings of a smile returned to his face. Soon, the Pollard Creek Inn would be his no more, and Albert needed to prepare. Decisions on the next chapter of his life, on everyone's life, would have to be made. There was really nothing more to do. Nothing more than to forgive his regrets and look to the future. Strawberry Fields was behind him. He would not return there. Despite the pleasant memories of its past, he would list it for sale. The financial proceeds from the sale of the Inn would be coming soon. Albert needed to search for another property to buy. He began to feel much better with each decision he made. The remainder of the Inn family would soon get their relocation money, before moving onward in their own separate ways.

Valerie Williams continued to keep her true intentions close to the vest. She would move to Grants Pass when the summer was over. Until then, she would start her garden. She would enjoy the mountain summer with the many friends she had come to know and love. It felt unusual to Valerie, how a belief in the future made the present so much easier to accept. So often in the past, Valerie had tried hard to hang onto the present, to her mischievous days in the Haight-Ashbury, even her early days in Pollard Creek. She had always hoped that her present situations would match her dreams, only to become disappointed and restless when her current realities failed to provide.

Valerie had always been practical and strong in her own presence and understanding of others. What she didn't realize, was that her particular aspirations were colored with her own expectations of peace and love. She had always wanted to believe that genuine human care and acceptance would follow her wherever she might go. Although these numerous past circumstances were trying to prove otherwise, Valerie knew she would not give up on her desires. They were too important to ever forsake. But the rough uncut stone of youth becomes polished by the weather of time and experience. Valerie was no longer the starry-eyed teenager with flowers in her hair, not the dreamy young woman stirred by the romance of eternal love. She no longer believed that the geography of place might offer all her hopes could inspire. If this was what people referred to as innocence lost, so be it. She was not so foolish in her beliefs to fail to comprehend.

Grants Pass would be Grants Pass. It would be a place to put her son in school. It would be a location to find some part-time work, a proximity to some additional training and skills. No more, no less. This time, her move would not be shaped by the dreams of her heart. Nonetheless, she vowed to never leave those dreams behind. Like a rabbit's foot, she would keep them in her pocket, bringing her good luck and fortune when better times might come.

If Tom Sullivan could have read Valerie's thoughts, he would have stood beside her time and again. Sullivan knew better than others that Valerie had touched both the roses and the thorns, and always chose the roses whenever she could. But Tom Sullivan was not reading anyone's mind today. The Southern Oregon spring was beginning to blossom. He, Freddie Jones, and Marty Johnson were running the Alaskan mill, setting logs with the boom truck, cutting rough cut two by four and six, sticking and stacking them orderly in a pile. Along with the boys from the Mulcahey Farm, he and Marty had finished the Weyerhauser tree planting contracts over on the coast. Sullivan was glad that difficult work trip was over, along with everybody else. It wouldn't be long before Laughlin Creek began to settle down from the winter runoff. They would once again be able to get the trucks in and out of Railroad Bridge. Until that day arrived, they would cut whatever they could off the log deck, keeping the finished product covered and stored until sales and deliveries could be made.

Marty Johnson was still running hot and cold. His girl from California, Celia, had never returned, despite Marty's desperate attempts to get her to reconsider. There had been only one true communal summer at Railroad Bridge. Ever since the cruel winter that followed, the property had become nothing more than a boy's club for Marty, Freddie, and Sullivan. Little Kenny, Celia's younger brother, had joined the Hoedads' tree planting cooperative out of Eugene. He had met a girl there. And more recently, he had gotten a chance to fall timber in the woods out toward the coast. Little Kenny had written a letter to Marty, telling him that he planned to stay north. Whenever he got the chance, Kenny would come down to Railroad Bridge to get the remainder of his possessions.

So any romantic connections to Celia had begun to pass away. Marty had mostly recovered. The painful rashes that had plagued him for a time had begun to dissipate, his drinking had gotten more under control. He could still get crazy now and then, but overall he had returned to the tough minded ex-Marine that Tom Sullivan had first met so long ago. Marty had used the GI bill for only a quarter last year, barely completing the first segment of the welding program at the community college. But with the tree planting contract over, and the summer growing season ahead, Marty intended to return to school in the fall, hoping to get his certification sometime down the road.

But first things first. It was time to get the garden started. And by those words Marty Johnson didn't mean vegetables or peas. With nobody else but the three of them expected for the summer, the pot patch holes were being dug, the drip lines stretched, the seeds planted in their funky hotbox greenhouse. Marty had procured a different seed stock over the winter. It was called cannabis indica. The new strain would not grow as tall and stringy as the more familiar sativa variety. The plants would be shorter and bushier, with their growing season shorter in duration. Plus, the result would be a different kind of high.

Meanwhile, Tom Sullivan was simply going from day to day. He was happy enough being at Railroad Bridge, there was always plenty to do. He continued to work on the interior of his cabin. He remained constant in keeping his journal notes describing the practical elements of his daily world. He didn't have a woman in his life, but tried not to let it bother him. The ambivalence he felt toward his friendship with Valerie still gnawed at him, sometimes wishing he could say that he loved her. Sometimes wishing that he could step forward and make a commitment to a family, and all the predictable responsibilities and expectations such a leap of faith would require. But, he couldn't. It just didn't feel right. He didn't love Valerie in that particular way. Still, deep inside, he worried. Whenever Valerie found somebody else, how would he feel? She continued to mean so much to him.

Back at the Mulcahey Farm, Sean McAllister was happy that the Oregon winter was on the wane, the tree planting contract complete. Yet, he was having a hard time being sure that this communal experience at the Farm was really where he wanted to be. When the county building inspectors had invaded the property last winter, the initial result had created a sense of unity and patriotic intent amongst the group. Everyone had emotionally banded together to battle the enemy and protect their homes. McAllister helped write a letter to the newspaper. He had also researched ways to fight the county on a legal and political front. The good news was that over the last several months, the building department had gone on an excessive search and destroy mission of compliance throughout Jordan County. The citizen response had been swift and emotional. A much larger battle had begun to ensue. The Mulcahey Farm's difficult circumstances were no longer isolated.

Several hippie land trips, including the Farm's, were facing indictments for not responding to the initial directives for compliance. Collectively, these communes had secured an attorney in Medford to represent them in the coming fight. The issues to be challenged were beginning to take shape. First, the search warrants regarding the properties had not been signed by a judge. Dubiously, they had only been administrative warrants signed by the County Commissioners. Second, there would be a challenge to the zoning definition of the term 'family'. The current ordinance, which had been rushed through by the Commissioners, stated that a 'family' could be no larger than five persons not related by blood or marriage. No one was particularly surprised by the political intent of that requirement. It was clear to everyone that the authorities were out to bust the communes, and the definition of family would be one of their weapons of choice.

Further challenges would be made to the new building codes themselves. There would be a legal fight against the enforcement of the new codes, seeking to protect any construction that had occurred before the effective dates of the legislation. In addition, the defense would challenge the constraints of the new requirements against persons who were constructing structures simply for their own personal use and habitation, where no public safety and welfare concerns could be argued to exist.

But the more intense circumstances of the battle were not necessarily legal ones, they were political. The building and planning departments in Jordan County had unwittingly stepped into a pile of conservative shit. The building department had gone onto the property of certain citizens who had no time or belief in government interference on the rights of property. Those actions had stirred an angry response throughout the constitutionalist community. The good old boys in Jordan County were now raising their voices and their threats against the county administrators. The new ordinances and codes were raising hackles on both sides of the political spectrum, from the right as well as the left. The situation had fostered an utterly strange confluence of political and cultural agreement, with both rednecks and hippies finding themselves on the same ironic side .

No doubt, Commissioner Wilton Parker was fried to his hat. Wilton's own private fears were playing out right in front of his eyes, with his office and home phones ringing off the hook. That bureaucratic bonehead, Craig Benson, had ignored Wilton Parker's warnings, just as Wilton had feared. Benson had gone on his own obsessive tirade to clean up Jordan County, to enforce any code violations wherever they could be found. The goddamn hippies were one thing. But now, Benson's foolishness had every land owner who had ever posted his property, who had ever built a barn or outbuilding on his ranch, or who had ever listened to the Allan Stang report on the Grants Pass radio station, fuming and hungry for bear. Wilton Parker's stomach needed another bottle of Tums, and it needed them right away.

Wilton Parker put in a call to Assistant Attorney General, David Hinson, who was hiding up in Salem. This time around, Wilton didn't mince his words. He sternly reminded Hinson that he and the other commissioners had played ball with the state. They had done their part when it came to the issues of the Pollard Creek Inn. With Jordan County's help, the State of Oregon had managed to starve out the current ownership, before proffering the owners with a purchase offer they had no choice but to accept. In addition, the Commissioners had passed the emergency zoning measures necessary to get in compliance with land use directives issued from the capitol, despite local opposition. But Craig Benson had become the goddamn joker in the deck, an insufferable obsessive titmouse who needed some restraint. Wilton Parker argued that Hinson needed to slow things down in Salem. Surely, other rural counties in Oregon had to be feeling similar heat. But Hinson was coy in response, appearing to understand, yet offering nothing of certainty. The man was his usual ambivalent self.

Wilton Parker slammed down the phone, reached for the bottle of antacid, finding nothing but air. He got up from his desk, putting on his suit coat. He would head out to the Shop-Rite to find some relief. In a less than a year and a half from today, Wilton Parker would face re-election, that is, if he didn't have to face a recall vote sometime before. If these matters continued to get out of hand, Wilton might as well start marking the calendar while searching for another job. The internal combustion roiling inside his tummy made him wince again at the thought.

It was hard for Sean McAllister to watch his good friend Mookie James go through the pain. McAllister and Mookie went way back to the days when they had first met in the rooming house at college. Mookie and he had always shared a similar political interest and disgust at the Vietnam War. They had taken the trip to Miami Beach for the Republican National Convention. And it was Mookie who had encouraged him to come to Boulder when McAllister had been looking for a place to escape. Then later, Mookie had called him to come to Oregon, to this new adventure that Mookie James had found. Politics aside, they had become fast friends. It was a friendship that Sean McAllister valued deeply, one of the few that had grown beyond his life in the east coast. Unfortunately, there was only so much one friend could do for another, especially when it came to a woman's love.

Mookie and Annie continued to share their cabin at the Mulcahey Farm. But for how much longer it was difficult to tell. On a daily basis, each acted as if nothing was wrong, but McAllister knew better. He understood that Mookie was dealing with the inevitable. For Annie, it was inevitable as well, only easier. She would be the one doing the leaving, whenever circumstances would permit. Part of the current problem was that each of them loved the Farm, and did not want to exit. McAllister was certainly happy not to be standing in Mookie's shoes. Mookie was a straight up guy, there was no question about his friend's particular honor. Even now, Sean McAllister doubted he could have endured such a diplomatic and yet painful reality. Running away would probably have been McAllister's cowardly device.

McAllister's devotion to the Mulcahey Farm was not as strong. Derrick Mulcahey was indeed a piece of work. Derrick managed to persist in his manipulations of people and direction. Derrick Mulcahey had that constant power of persuasion. It derived from his peculiar ability to make you not want to cross him, to not want to be the target of his anger and derision. Derrick had honed his practiced skill at finding the weakness in others, then using that weakness to dishonor you in some personal way, to make you question yourself.

This character trait was indeed a subtle weapon of control. The result was that you didn't want to engage Derrick Mulcahey in any substantive way. Instead, you became adept at tip toeing around any troubles that might arise, any behavior Derrick might choose to act out in your presence. Sean McAllister had definitely gotten to know the lay of the land. And confrontation would be a losing proposition. Derrick Mulcahey was a highly attuned master of conflict resolution. In other words, your conflict, his resolution. Somehow, his brother and the rest of the Santa Cruz crowd had come to grips with this condition over time. Except Darla, of course, who had obviously been on the front line of Derrick's histrionics until she could take it no more. For McAllister, this constant unsettling drama was beginning to take its toll. It was no way to live from day to day. He was beginning to believe that his own future lay in some other location. Only right now, he didn't know where.

John Fiske, a late nineteenth century American historian, in writing about early colonial religious-based communities, spoke to the necessities inherent in their ultimate survival. "No liberty of divergence can be allowed to the individual without endangering the community." Fiske was speaking to the need for conformance as a necessary requirement for a community to sustain itself, against the greater odds of every man for himself. The Mulcahey Farm understood the particular responsibilities inherent in maintaining its own survival goals. But the most significant danger to this sustainability did not appear to derive from the divergence of its individual parts. Rather, it came from the eccentric divergence of its leader, Derrick Mulcahey. There could be no question that within an intentional community, there must be some adherence to the group, to the greater good, to the safety and security of the whole. But the confirmation of such adherence, the giving up of certain elements of individual liberty on behalf of the community, must be initiated from the individuals' themselves, either by a consensus of its members, or perhaps the democratic majority of the collective.

Every social order that must by its formation continue to survive, demands that some level of hierarchy be established to maintain its existence, to prevent the dangers of anarchy from devastating its agreed communal intentions. But by that very structural formation new dangers arise, the dangers of leadership and the powers so entrusted to the same. The loss of liberty becomes ever more threatened by the flow of power and persuasion to the few. And so, the concentration of this power becomes both a necessity and a curse. When it becomes a curse, it is not a pretty sight. To borrow a phrase, "power tends to corrupt, and absolute power corrupts absolutely". With such a happenstance, the darker vagaries of the human condition, of greed and self-possession, begin to take their hold.

The terrible chronology of human history has endured the results of such corruptions. The community then becomes endangered, not by the liberty of individual divergence, but rather by the necessity of the hierarchies it was forced to create for its own protection. The irony of Fiske's declaration is that the consequence is like a double-edged sword. The liberty of divergence must both be given up on behalf of the greater good, and yet, at the same time held forcefully dear, in order to protect its survival from the damaging effects of its own surrender.

Sean McAllister was not necessarily grappling with these philosophical incantations of the human condition. He was simply trying to figure out a few things in his own mind. After spending a year on the Mulcahey Farm, both engaging and observing the mechanics of its daily life and direction, he was having second thoughts. They were thoughts about divergence, and the liberty of such thoughts he might be allowed to entertain.

The Mulcahey Farm was not a cult. It was not the Manson Family, or the Moonies. It was not the Church of Scientology, or some other crazy religious sect fleecing its membership or promising eternal salvation from the sins of a dangerous world. The Farm did not require adherence to a master of ceremonies, an iconic figure that must be obeyed. It was a plain and simple hippie commune. Its intentions were to create a sense of collective identity and a level of sustainability, free from a lost American culture of materialism and imperial authority. It was an extended group of individuals searching for a new methodology for living in their world. These intentions would be in concert with its natural surroundings. It would attempt to promote a new form of rural progressive conservatism, including a native regard for spiritual pursuits and human interaction, away from the conformist economic structures and expected societal behaviors of the mythical American Dream. Actually, the discovered history of white America had initially begun with similar intents. It was really nothing new.

Nor was the Mulcahey Farm alone in such pursuits. The Farm was just another dot on an agrarian and forested map of America, part of a larger emigration away from the urban rat chase for material wealth. The purpose was to find a future away from a single family home in some lifeless suburban enclave, where the only reflection of your personal values was evidenced by a shiny new car sitting in the driveway. Should any neutral observers look at things from such a weary perspective, they could hardly blame many young Americans for wanting to run for the hills. We've been there, we've seen that, they had begun to say. It was time to stick out the thumb, or pack the Volkswagon bus. Time to hit the road in search of a better life.

Perhaps the biggest surprise to these inclinations to find a new frontier, was the antipathy it generated amongst the rest of modern America. Were the first colonists, or later the westward pioneers, lambasted for such desires and motivations? Hell no! They were celebrated! Throughout its history, these seekers have been heralded as icons of rugged American individualism. There are statues placed everywhere across the sovereign of the national enterprise, of men on horses, sticking flags in the ground, of immigrant minorities in covered wagons heading out into the majestic panorama of the unsettled west. Had something changed in America? Was a peculiar resistance emerging? If so, what were the reasons?

Unfortunately, the angry modern response usually went something like this: "Celebrate them folks? Yeah, whenever hell freezes over. That will be the day. They're just a bunch of ungrateful middle class kids, who wouldn't fight a war against those damn commies trying to take over the world. Those kids have rejected everything we have done for them, good schools, food on the table, nice clothes, jobs in our corporate economy. We even gave them Disneyland and Ozzie and Harriet, all the things we didn't have when we were their age. They wear their hair long just to spite us. They resist the price of freedom that we were forced to protect. They run away from their obligations to America. They hide up in the mountains, saying they are 'doing their own thing'. Meanwhile, they collect food stamps and welfare, engage in premarital sex, and try like hell not to work. Well, you can either love it, or leave it, you coddled little whiners. Celebrate you? You're lucky we don't exterminate you."

It might be fair to say the following; it was very unlikely any bronze statues of some long-haired hippie pioneers, going back to the land in order to save America, would be gracing a public park anytime soon. And one can be certain that if any such attempt had been made, the corporate advertising men down on K Street in Washington, D.C. would have been racing through the halls of Congress waving their arms. Anti-materialism and certainly anti-war were definitely not good for business. "Consumerism and militarism are the holy future of America, Senator Smith, and you best not forget it."

Geez, you would think they had better things to do than get all bent out of shape about a few kids preferring a different road to travel. Obviously, the time-worn traditions of celebrating diversity were no longer important to the American creed. The right of the individual in the hallowed halls of American freedom certainly had a nice mythical ring to it. But definitely not when it came to the newly crowned ethnocentric values of 'my country right or wrong'.

One thing for sure, a whole lot of America was still mad as hell. They were mad about the Vietnam War going sideways on them. They were mad about the belief in their democratic institutions getting robbed by the saga of Watergate. They were definitely upset about their very own kids taking a hike. It was a personal affront to their cherished fidelity towards the American Dream. And it damn well pissed them off to have to question themselves about its current modern veracity. So if Jordan County, Oregon, a bastion of the god-fearing fundamentalist notions of American hegemony, might be out there kicking some hippie ass, well that was just fine and dandy. Spare the rod, and spoil the child. The eventual punishment was more than likely well deserved.

However, what this common clave of America didn't understand, was that other truly American forces were at work. The real truth was this; you didn't need to create a conspiracy to eventually cut off the legs of the Pollard Creek Inn. You didn't need to create land-use rules and regulations to disperse those ragged strangers off their land. You didn't have to fire gunshots onto their property, or scribble slogans of prejudice onto telephone poles, or castigate their immoralities from the pulpit on Sunday mornings. Nope, it was none of the above. All you had to do was have a little patience. All you really had to do was wait.

For this was the heart of the matter. Communalism was simply not part of the American psyche. Individualism would eventually become the paramount concern. The intentional community had a valued ideal and purpose, with guiding principles that would always be important in the hearts and minds of good human beings. But the actual reality was shockingly clear. Nowadays in modern American society, even the nuclear family could barely stay intact. As long as rapid individual mobility might continue to exist, as long as there was a capitalistic engine with gas in the tank, there would be no need to fear. For it was the freedom of mobility that had become the primary instinct and impulse of the American character. As long as the heritage of American mobility could sustain itself, the individual would continue to reign supreme, and no guiding principles or intentional philosophies could ever overcome its effect. Maybe for a short period of time, but in the long run it would never have a chance. In the end, the needs and desires of the individual would dissipate the power of the communal enterprise in America. This single truth, more than anything, was the current American Way.

As for Sean McAllister, he wasn't going anywhere, at least for the moment. With the arrival of summer, the normal distractions of living day to day took hold. The Mulcahey Farm once again became a way station of human activity and things to do. There would be friends and travelers passing through, the garden to grow, kids and animals to nurture, repairs to be made, milk and eggs to deliver, and other work to be done. In summertime, it is easier to shelve for a while those nagging questions of personal conscience or future orientation. The fear and danger of building inspectors, the possible personal confrontations over the Mulcahey Farm's very existence were easily put aside. For now, fate was in the hands of lawyers and a political firestorm raging throughout Jordan County.

Concerning the elk deal and the charges for illegal possession of wildlife, Coos County let the charges transfer to it neighbor. A court date had been set for July. The Jordan County Public Defender was not only lame, he was seriously overworked. But thankfully, the attorney had at least managed to get Jesse Simmons deferred to a juvenile status with a slap on the risk. As a result, only the four adults remained. There was the possibility of a pre-trial settlement, but the lawyer felt it might not come. The Jordan County Prosecutor appeared anxious to proceed, feeling confident a jury and judge would not look kindly on hippies poaching wildlife in the Oregon hills.

There was a standing joke in Pollard Creek; that a man was hippie-rich when he had twenty bucks, a full tank of gas in the truck, and a pick-up bed full of empty beer bottles. As for the latter, the bottle return law in Oregon had created a new economy of scale. Any beer bottle just lying around was fair game for the wily entrepreneur, a whopping five cents of personal investment wealth. People were known to scavenge through trash barrels at every opportunity, especially at the rest stops on Interstate 5, searching for nickels made out of glass. But even that economic boom paled in comparison to the third Friday in June, 1975. On that particular day, the gross national product of Pollard Creek, Oregon spiked to an unprecedented all time high. The Pollard Creek Inn relocation money had arrived.

Albert Krieger and Robert Sage painfully signed the closing documents with the State of Oregon. They got their purchase money back, but deep down there was no joy in 'Mudville'. However, they would manage to deal with their resignation. The two men could now go on with the next steps in their individual lives. Still, the loss of a dream, the memories of so many good times, would be a harder void to fill. As for the Inn's residents themselves, the feeling was mutual, but what could they do? Open a bank account and deposit the check, that's what. Head for the liquor store and have one last party together. Along with family and friends, a wake would be held far into the night. The end of the Pollard Creek Inn had come.

The next morning, they would endure their hangovers and begin to pack. By Monday afternoon they would be gone, each alone with their own singular futures tasked before them. They would be richer in pocket, but poorer in spirit. Only then, would the depression of their familial loss begin to take hold. As well, there would be no television cameras taping the event, no written journalistic reports of the Inn's demise. Recorded history would ignore them and the story of their time together. Sadly, only their personal memories would endure. By Monday evening the Pollard Creek Inn stood alone and forlorn. For many in this town, it felt like the emptiness of a loved one leaving home, the aching sense of loss that a mother abides as her child pulls away, knowing full well that her life will never be the same. The heart of Pollard Creek skipped a beat, a vacant moment of uncertainty holding still. Then it fluttered again, marking life and time.

CHAPTER THIRTY-FIVE

HELLO, GOODBYE
Pollard Creek / 1975-1976

TIME HAS A WAY OF SLIPPING silently through the night. Even during the hours of sleep, it continues to travel its constant predetermined mortal road. Imperceptible in its stealth, you awake in the morning, feeling that nothing has been lost. Still, the hours have passed, never to return. Life is best when the theft has not been recognized, when one's days are spent in living in the moment, or looking ahead. In these times, memory is nothing more than a recollection, an ephemeral mile-marker along the road, short of regret or wistfulness. These are the good times in life. You are content with their current interaction, lacking any need for personal reflection. History remains unnecessary, and the future is of no concern.

For Pollard Creek, with the passage of time, a hell of a lot had gone down. Not always easy, but not often hard. Without forced bussing, the school integration of two states of mind had unconsciously begun. Yes, a cultural separation continued to exist between the two points of view. But slowly, an unintended acceptance had begun to take shape. An undeclared truce was forming, borne more out of proximity than any change in personal perspective or social mores. You buy food at the same market, you get gas from the same pump, you claim your mail from the same federal post office.

With the commonality of the every day, similarities begin to emerge. Other sides of the human dynamic take shape, and a troubled distance begins to narrow. You start to leave politics, religion, and morality alone at the doorstep, and the tension begins to ease. Although in the privacy of your own home, the other side might still be viewed as a hippie or a redneck, something familiar has taken hold. Unconsciously, the others have become 'our' hippie, or 'our' redneck, and that subtle difference is more than enough. The need for human prejudice seems almost as necessary as food and water for the human condition. And certainly that is a sad reality when compared to the greater aspirations of the human enterprise. The Red Sox hate the Yankees, and the Yankees hate the Red Sox, but life would be so much less if they didn't play the games.

Meanwhile, the authorities in Jordan County had given the newcomers their best shot, and the hippies had not gone away. Jordan County was a world full of conservative Christian fundamentalists, whose value system included telling other people how they should live. It was also peopled with expatriate republicans from places like Orange County, California, who saw greater conspiracies around every corner, where anyone different was a reason for fear. The original white natives weren't much different in outlook. They were generations of families who had sawed and bucked their homesteads, mined and fished their waters. They continued to struggle in a hard-rock country whose riches had been stolen from them by timber barons and railroad entrepreneurs. In times of stress, everyone needs someone to blame. Yet, through all the dissonance, these new youthful immigrants, the hippies, had begun to take root.

The kicker was the thread of independence that everyone shared. Southern Oregon had always gone its own way. It may not have celebrated diversity, but it certainly celebrated a righteous individualism to be left alone. And so, if the government could come and tear down your neighbor's home with a simple piece of paper, then 'sure to shootin'' it might tear down yours. "We might hate those goddamn faggot longhairs," they probably said to themselves, "but it's none of the government's business to do the same."

One thing was for sure. Southern Oregon was a melting pot of ironies, so convoluted it was hard to get one's head around. Sardonically, this 'back-to-the-land' hippie migration fit like a glove into Southern Oregon's kooky culture of human belief. And there was no hypocrisy here. Hypocrisy, by its initial definition, means the intent to deceive. Outside of their political and religious hierarchies, the everyday locals were not practiced in the art of deception. The best way to describe Southern Oregon was a state of utter social confusion, devoid of any consistent rationale of political, religious, or cultural thought. That could only be the reason why any self-respecting group of Grants Pass business boosters would purposely choose a 'Caveman' as their community mascot. The only thing missing in Jordan County was an announcement by the roughest logger in Jordan County, stating that he was coming out of the closet, declaring he was gay.

The year of 1975 came to an end. Patty Hearst had been arrested at an apartment in San Francisco. Muhammad Ali had managed to narrowly defeat Joe Frazier in a brutal fourteenth round TKO, retaining the championship title he had won from George Foreman a year earlier. New York City, on the verge of municipal bankruptcy, was bailed out with funds from the Federal treasury.

The Vietnam War finally crawled to an infamous and costly end. Over fifty-eight thousand American soldiers were dead. Almost forty thousand of the deceased had been between the ages of eighteen and twenty-two years of age. If they had lived, they would have been part of Sean McAllister's generation. Dead and wounded Americans combined, totaled over two hundred and eleven thousand. Yet, these terrible numbers paled in comparison to the wanton death and destruction of Vietnam itself. Estimates of combined military and civilian dead for both North and South Vietnam totaled over five million human beings. Such terror and destruction had destroyed one nation, and divided another. What thoughtful human being could help but question, whatever in the name of life had been achieved? What beneficent consequence could ever be inferred? What thin silver lining of understanding might ever be recognized? What lesson of experience could ever be learned as a result of such error?

Again, one is reminded of Santayana's declaration, "Those that cannot remember the past are condemned to repeat it". But what in hell were the chances that America's memory would be capable of such a task? Any disciplined study of history itself, appeared only to deny such an evolution. Karl Marx had been more to the point. "History repeats itself, first as tragedy, second as farce". One could only ask themselves this; when and how soon the next farce would return.

In Pollard Creek, personal histories continued to revolve. Valerie Williams moved out of her home on Main Street, finding a small house in Grants Pass. She put her son, Canyon, in kindergarten. She took a class in bookkeeping at the community college. To supplement her welfare, she found part-time work under the table, cleaning several homes in the neighborhood. Valerie's new house continued to be a way-station, a place to stop by and visit, to take a shower or sleep on the couch after a day or night in town.

Albert Krieger took his money from the sale of the Pollard Creek Inn, buying the old Harkness' place adjacent to the Mulcahey Farm. Darla Bloom and Jimmijay Connell joined Albert there as roommates. For Darla, it was the perfect scenario. She would be right next door to her children at the Farm. Darla had completed her training as a midwife. She had begun to assist an associate in delivering home-born infants throughout Jordan County.

Jimmijay Connell set up another studio at his new home. He continued to make his Jerry Fisher radio shows, but he had to make a living one way or another. With a surplus of marijuana coming out of Pollard Creek, there was a need for a middleman, a small town dealer to work the streets. There would be workers in Grants Pass, and rednecks in the hills that needed a connection. Jimmijay Connell was a people person as they say, a high energy personality who was easy to meet and greet. He knew the growers in Pollard Creek, and he could easily handle the bar scene in Grants Pass. Jimmijay was the perfect man for the job. He used some of his relocation money to get started in his new career.

Although Albert Kreiger tried his best, his days in Pollard Creek were numbered. The loss of the Inn had really knocked him down for the count. And as hard as he tried he couldn't get up. But there was another contributing factor as well. Albert Krieger was a man who loved men. For that reason, Pollard Creek was a lonely and difficult vista to maintain. Sure, there were the San Francisco gays who had purchased some land as a getaway from the City. But these men were a different breed. They paraded their sexuality for all to see, often dressing as women, expressing their personal identity in colorful public ways. Albert admired them for their courage, but this was not his own demeanor. Albert was more gentle and quiet. Despite his political and cultural idealism, he was in truth a homebody, a man of family and heart.

Everyone loved Albert for his spirit and generosity, his ease of leadership and commitment to peace. But they couldn't give him what he needed most, an intimate love and companionship in his life. Albert began to make plans for a return to New York, to find something more than Pollard Creek could give.

Guitar Glenn and Slick Bell had taken their money and moved north to Portland. In Portland, they could find more music to play, their own dreams to pursue. Laura Hale had jumped at the news of Valerie's move to Grants Pass. Laura took over the yellow house on Main Street, forsaking a move to Eugene. She was engaged in a torrid romance with a wild and crazy guy named Rickey Rucker, who never seemed to be in town for long. Rickey Rucker had been the third, but silent investor in the purchase of the Pollard Creek Inn. Maybe if Laura settled into the house, something more stable with Rickey might occur. She loved her dance and her conga drums, but she was beginning to love her Black Velvet a little too much. Her growing wild side with Rickey needed some balance, and the house might help that cause.

As for Sean McAllister, in his own particular life he had spit the bit. He had quietly decided to leave the Mulcahey Farm. The previous summer had been an unfortunate period of complaint and growing dissatisfaction. The spark had been a fall out between Derrick Mulcahey and the young man who had for years been his protégé. Jesse Simmons had now turned eighteen, and he wanted to experience his own life. Derrick attempted to demand Jesse's adherence to the Farm, but Jesse now had a place to run, the fruit orchards of Central Washington. Jesse left the Farm early in the summer, heading north, uncertain of his return. Jesse also found a job for his closest brother, who soon followed with Betsy's blessing. McAllister watched as the Santa Cruz core continued its fracture.

Annie seized on the opportunity to move into Jesse's small rough-cut shed that was attached to the barn. This would be her big break, and there was no doubt in McAllister's mind it would be final. Mookie James remained perseverant. Mookie appeared to take the change in stride, but McAllister knew the serious hurt his dear friend was managing to suppress. In late July of 1975, McAllister and Mookie, along with Marty Johnson and Tom Sullivan, accepted a plea deal on the illegal possession of wildlife charges. They accepted fines without probation of five hundred dollars each. Each man scrambled to find the money necessary to pay the penalty. McAllister was able to borrow the money from his sister, Mary Jane. But now he would have to pay it back. Coincidentally, at almost the exact moment, a grand jury in Jordan County came calling. The grand jury passed down indictments against the Mulcahey Farm and five other properties for building and zoning ordinance violations. Battle lines seemed to be drawn on so many fronts.

Throughout the previous winter of tree planting, including the legal drama over the killing of the elk, Sean McAllister had deepened his friendships with Marty Johnson, and particularly Tom Sullivan. McAllister, like them, was a single man. Railroad Bridge was a beautiful and remote piece of ground, difficult to maneuver, but the men who lived there were relaxed in their individual pursuits. They lived separately, but together, sharing certain expenses, but otherwise on their own. In early August, Little Kenny came down from Eugene, removing from the old miner's cabin what possessions he could pack in his truck. Tom Sullivan had already read McAllister's mind.

"You can live there if you want. Marty and Freddie are cool with it. The cabin might as well be used if you need it," Sullivan advised.

"I've got to go north to Washington for the work," McAllister said. "And I'll need to work the whole season. It might be Halloween before I return. I could only do it then, if that's okay."

"Yeah, sure. Just let us know if you change your mind." Tom Sullivan remained a man of few spoken words. But he had a way about him that let you know he'd like to have you around.

In late August, McAllister made ready for his trip to Washington State. He told no one, not even Mookie that he would not return to the Farm. Meanwhile, each day at the Farm was becoming a struggle for Mookie James. Every interior board that Mookie cut, each finish nail he hit, was a reminder of a once shared dream with Annie that was now forever changed. The reality of their separation was taking its toll. Days before McAllister's departure for the harvest, Mookie walked out to McAllister's cabin. He sat down and asked if he could go along. There surely was no reason for Mookie to inquire, but McAllister was elated at the prospect. The two men packed their vehicles, caravanning together to the desert sun of the grand Columbia River, Meatball along for the ride. They put up shop in a one room picker's cabin at the orchard where McAllister had spent the previous harvest. Settling in, they worked long days deep into October, before saddling up and returning to Pollard Creek.

In November of 1975, McAllister said his good-byes to the Mulcahey Farm. Emotionally, the move to Railroad Bridge was not without a sense of guilt and regret. In the broader perspective, the Mulcahey Farm was a group of people doing good things. Under the auspices of Derrick Mulcahey's dreamy intents, merged with the quiet and firm practicality of his brother, Jack, the Mulcahey Farm was a truthful experiment in creating an alternative American lifestyle, where the shared purpose and sustainability of the congregation was the ultimate goal. The necessity and desire for such a social structure was as old as man himself, the practice of survival by banding together as one. It is the prerogative of the tribe against the elemental forces of nature, the instinct to live and endure.

The value of this human enterprise could not be questioned. To grow and raise your own in order to support the greater whole. To conserve and re-use the resources that surrounded you. To share the bounty of your efforts with others, where the strong protect the weak for the mutual betterment of all. There is something uplifting and secure in the human heart when engaged in such a common purpose. It is an elemental thread of the human dynamic that will forever seek to be realized.

But that same human dynamic is much more complex. There are other threads of aspiration that must be satisfied, elements of individual fulfillment that search for their own liberty and fruition. But these are often desires the requisite of the tribe cannot provide. Therein exists the rub. The thread of longing for personal freedom contradicts the communal imperative. It is the wrench thrown in the works of the utopian construct, disabling its societal preponderance in the world of man.

There was no debating the facts. Late-twentieth century America was the global poster child for the emancipation of the self, whether it be the impulse of capitalism, the freedom from the paternalism of gender and color, or the basic human right of personal conscience and decision. The result was the confluence of two tidal forces, pulling the human dynamic one way, then another. It was an existential reminder of the many mysteries of life, seeming to remain forever unsolved.

Therefore, the reasons for guilt and regret that Sean McAllister felt within. He believed in the community of the group, the satisfaction inherent in being part of the team. To quit and walk away seemed like a violation. He would be letting his teammates down, a responsibility forsaken. The personal regrets ran deeper, for there is always the human element. Mookie and Annie, Darius, Jack and Christine, Betsy and the boys, all the others he had come to know and share. But on the other side, he would have the greater freedom to engage in the larger world of Pollard Creek. He would be able to venture further on his own particular journey, as uncertain as that might be. In addition, there was one particular reality that remained very clear. Derrick Mulcahey was Derrick Mulcahey. Things at the Farm would always be the way Derrick would want them to be. In the end, it was time for a change.

CHAPTER THIRTY-SIX

GOOD TIMIN'
Pollard Creek / 1976

TIME AND ANOTHER OREGON WINTER went by the boards. On a sweet lilac Friday afternoon in late May of 1976, Jordan County Commissioner Wilton Parker unlocked the lower drawer of his office desk, pulling out a bottle of scotch and a shot glass. His work was done for the day. The curtains in the windows rustled with a thin warm breeze. The forecast was for a glorious weekend ahead. That kind of sunny expectation would normally be enough to celebrate. But today, the weather was not the primary reason for Wilton's particular toast with himself. Wilton poured the shot glass full. Leaning back in his leather chair, he sipped on the hot bite of liquor. Nodding his head upward, he let the shot go down, feeling a sense of relief he had not enjoyed for a long long time.

That sneaky little weasel, Craig Benson, was finally gone from his world. The public announcement was direct, to assume a higher position with the Department of Commerce in Salem. But Wilton Parker knew better. Finally, something had broken his way. Maybe he would take the old lady out for dinner tonight, wherever she wanted to go. His wife wouldn't necessarily understand the reason for such a festive occasion, but she would definitely know it was good. County Prosecutor, Jeremy Morris, had dropped all six charges against Jordan County property owners for violations of the County and State building ordinances. And Benson was heading back north with his tail between the legs. Goddamn if Wilton Parker might just get himself re-elected

in the coming November. Smiling to himself, he put his feet up on the
desk, taking another sip. It was indeed a beautiful day.

As usual, the Grants Pass Tribune printed the news. Prosecutor
Morris had cited the expected high cost of the prosecutions, as well as
the need for more cooperation between citizens and the Jordan County
Building Department. The newspaper reported that Benson was being
promoted, but the real truth was political and nothing more. For
more than a year Jordan County had suffered through a public assault
from all sides of the political spectrum. Hippies, ranchers, farmers,
and most everybody who owned a piece of ground, all had banded
together in opposition to Benson's war of compliance. They had taken
over the Fairgrounds for public meetings, had formed citizens councils
throughout the County. Recall petitions had been circulated against
the Jordan County Commissioners. Even state legislators and the
Governor had been dragged into the fray.

In addition, the criminal matter would not have been a slam
dunk. Craig Benson, himself, had surprisingly never been certified as
a building inspector. And there were serious irregularities in the local
ordinances that were ripe for legal reversal. And so, predictably within
the old back rooms of cigars and whiskey, there were other decisions
that had to be made. It was time for the big boys, including Wilton
Parker, to save their ass.

Undoubtedly, Wilton Parker was not the only celebrant. At the
Mulcahey Farm and other communes throughout the jurisdiction,
there was ecstatic joy and relief. Homes and buildings would be saved
from the threat of abatement and removal. Once in a while, the voice
of the people is finally heard, no matter how devious the intent, or how
lame the excuses when the wind suddenly changes direction. It was
May, it was spring, it was indeed a beautiful day.

As the Gemini sun turned to Cancer, Pollard Creek hit its stride,
settling into its own little world. It found an easy rhythm, a comfortable
sense of self. Sure, the town remained as eccentric as its strange history
appeared to demand, but the heat of summer softened its hard rugged
edges. There were bright vernal mornings of absolute blue, when
Pollard Creek would awaken to emerald tree tops soaring against the

sky, to songbirds welcoming the day, to the music of the Grateful Dead calling it to play. Leaping out of bed onto its feet, Pollard Creek felt free from a single care.

Especially on Volleyball Saturday. Volleyball Saturday never waits for Godot. Haul ass mister, get the lead out, we're going to be late. It's first come, first serve. Volleyball Saturday is the one true religion in Pollard Creek. If you have to work, you don't give two-weeks notice, you quit right on the spot. If the babysitter's late, you make a citizen's arrest. If your car won't start, you learn to fly. To miss Volleyball Saturday would be to come undone.

In the high heat of a summer afternoon the white-stitched ball flies through the air. Half-naked bodies rustle underneath, subtly pitching it one to the other, before rudely hammering it to the opposing side. The powdered Oregon dust rises like a cloud. There are no referees. Rules are frowned upon. It is mountain ball only, a game of reckless abandon. There are no organized teams, just the shuffle of new bodies after each final point. Spectators surround the games. They lounge on the grassy perimeters, shaded from the sun by ponderosa, cedar, and fir. Beer after beer is pulled from coolers of ice, while hand-rolled cigarettes are passed from mouth to mouth. The children run wild in the nearby meadow beyond, playing their own imaginary games amongst themselves.

Not far away, pairs of men match up for a game of horseshoes. There is the clank of metal against spike, the soft flat thud of a ringer, the pause while points are measured, before the verbal report of score. Music blasts out the doors and windows of a nearby house. There is early Fleetwood Mac, the Allman Brothers, Hot Tuna, Santana, and Jackson Browne. At the back of the property, a wood-fired hot tub cooks under a shady grove of timbered trees, waiting for late afternoon. After the games, clothes are stripped and hung over a bench, bodies slipping slowly into the hot soothing water. Weary muscles become softened by its heat. Gradually, the sound of truck and car engines begin to start. People drift away into dusky twilight evening. Another Volleyball Saturday tempers toward rest.

Some days in life have a genuine fortune to them, from start to finish. Of course you never know when they will come. As she stood over the butcher block of her kitchen countertop, a knife in her hand dicing vegetables, Suzanne was a woman lean in figure. A long thin flowered chemise hung loosely about her. The dress stretched to the tops of her ankles, her bare feet showing beneath. Gentle blonde hairs fell down off her shoulders, her features narrow, her soft white skin stretched tight. Shards of fading sun beamed through the window glass, highlighting her deep dark eyes, while she focused on the chore at hand.

Sitting in a burgundy-stuffed easy chair, Sean McAllister took in the sights of her modest cabin home, a glass of red wine in hand. The interior walls smelled of cedar planking, a guitar and mandolin hanging by their straps. Fruit boxes were nailed to the wall, acting as libraries for special books and culinary instructions. Muted stuffed pillows rested on the floor, waiting for multiple guests, or to sit closer by the wood stove in the corner of the room. Near the door, an antique French mirror gave final approval before heading outside into the world. Below the mirror rested a lonesome row of footwear; huarache sandals, hiking boots, a pair of shiny dress shoes waiting for the call. Hanging above, a raincoat, a light flannel outer, a brown suede vest, anticipating cooler nights to come.

McAllister sipped his wine, conversing easily as Suzanne swept delicately about the kitchen's L-shaped corner across the way. There were no cabinets, just open shelves above. There were glasses and dishes, wooden mixing bowls, clear gallon jars of grains, containers of vitamins, and green Little Mickey beer bottles full of spices and herbs. A silver grinder was fixed to one end of the counter, a five-gallon bottle of propane resting on the floor near her modest kitchen range, a box of wooden matches nearby. On a fine crafted chest rested a basket of sea shells, a conch shell, an ornamental tea pot, a wooden candelabra. On the walls hung a Japanese print, small framed watercolor paintings, and bird feathers stuck within the cracks of its planks. The kitchen table was adorned with a basket of summer fruit. Another basket was filled with colored paper and pencils, several more candles as well. Hanging planters draped by the windows.

Behind the chair in which he sat, a sharp angled ladder led to a sleeping loft above. Underneath the loft rested a spinning wheel and several cardboard boxes for the things that couldn't find a place. Suzanne lit the candles. She spread utensils wrapped in dark blue linen, serving a steaming stir-fry of rice and vegetables with dark brown bread. The couple sat and enjoyed the dinner, followed by the opening of a small box of mints. McAllister helped Suzanne with the dishes. Pouring the last of the wine, they found the sentient feel of their arms, the sweet breath of moist lips coming together. Later, through the open windows of the loft, he could breathe the fresh coolness of the mountain night, hearing the silence of darkness waiting for a sound. Closing his eyes, a final thought did come. Could there ever be better days than this?

And so the life of Pollard Creek trundled along. Vegetables grew in gardens, wildflowers along the road, pot plants hidden in the hills. There were potluck dinners on Friday nights, card games of cribbage and hearts. Town trips were made to Grants Pass to watch *Chinatown*, *Blazing Saddles*, or *One Flew Over the Cuckoos Nest*. There were occasional group excursions to the Wonder Bur liquor bar, or the Palace Hotel to dance the night away. At home, the women canned their food, made crafts and clothes, raised their kids, braided their hair, read *Fear of Flying* and talked of men. The men worked the woods, built cabins and barns, tended to their pot patches, or fixed up small sheds for a place to eat and sleep. They drank Blitz, Olympia, and Rainier at the Solace Valley Tavern. They rolled dice games of ship, captain and crew, to see who would buy the next round. Occasionally, poker games were dealt until the sun came up. Vehicles were repaired at Friendly Frank's Auto yard. They ate hamburgers and French fries at the Hungry Dog Café, and sometimes talked of women.

Everyone made trips to the Bay Area, Eugene, or Portland, for friendship or family, for concerts and the taste of urban civilization. For those folks with a television, they tried to stay up late watching 'Live From New York, It's Saturday Night'. They laughed along with George Carlin, Richard Pryor, and Andy Kaufman. They cracked up at John Belushi's impersonations of Joe Cocker, Beethoven, Ray Charles, or working as a desk clerk at the Samurai Hotel. They watched as Gilda Radner became Emily Litella and Roseane Roseannadanna. They waited expectantly for Chevy Chase to crash over a restaurant table, or tumble over a lectern while playing Gerald Ford.

In the sexual world of Pollard Creek, monogamy became like a four-letter curse word. It made men reach for rifles in knee-jerk response. It made women grab their children and run for the welfare office. Monogamy breathed of authoritarianism, a threat to individual liberty, a barrier to personal growth and experience. Commitment was like a restless rubber ball bouncing in a vacuum. It was a form of social hypocrisy, a challenge to the freedom of individual intents. Relationships were often short and sweet, before souring in the face of new temptations. Indeed, there were always a few partners who managed to ward off such alluring notions of non-committal sex and love. But it was hardly an easy task when others were at play.

Still, you couldn't have your cake, and eat it too. If your heart suddenly got the best of you, your deeper need for security and intimacy searching for expression, you couldn't just wish to call a halt to the game. If you play with fire, then you're going to get burnt. Jealousy did not have a place in Pollard Creek. If you mistakenly fell in love in the more traditional sense, and the object of your wishful attraction was in bed with another, you suddenly couldn't cry foul. Whether a man or woman, you had to suck it up and take it like a trooper, acknowledge the rules and accept the consequences. Much like monogamy, free love came with a set of responsibilities. Coming down with a broken heart was your singular cross to bear. There was no one else to blame.

This was the rhythm of Pollard Creek. It was a land of little money, but lots to do and share. Pollard Creek seemed like a motley troupe of character actors thrown upon a stage, having been left behind by a theatrical director who had quit in disgust, skipping town as fast as his Cadillac could wheel. And time was of little circumstance, the future uninvited. Pollard Creek seemed forever young, filled with an innocence it refused to abandon. Meanwhile, the rest of the world went flying by, all day and night on Interstate 5, possessed with their singular life pursuits. Perhaps they might pull over to gas up and eat, to stretch their legs for a moment and take a look around. But they too had their own lives to live, their own fish to fry. With their tanks now full, the world outside put pedal to the medal, accelerating up the exit ramp, leaving Exit 76 behind. All the while, never knowing for an instant, that Pollard Creek, Oregon was the only place to be.

CHAPTER THIRTY-SEVEN

ROLL YOUR OWN
Pollard Creek / Halloween, 1976

SEAN MCALLISTER DROVE HIS WAY SOUTH, leaving behind the sun-bleached desert hills of Central Washington. The panel truck was packed with gear, plus weathered gray boxes of freshly gathered apples. Golden, Red Delicious, Winesap and Rome. The mountain draws and water courses of his journey were bright with the yellow of cottonwood, paper birch and aspen, the burnished orange of other deciduous hardwoods. These were the autumn colors of the Great Northwest. He crossed the Columbia River at Biggs Junction, skirting the rugged farm and ranchland country of Central Oregon. He climbed the Cascade Crest out of Bend, before winding down the Umpqua River drainage to Roseburg. He picked up Interstate 5, motoring the final miles toward the Rogue River watershed and his home at Pollard Creek.

Exiting the freeway, he pulled up to the Country Store, purchasing some groceries and beer. Sitting himself down on the bench of the porch outside, he took in the brilliant autumn afternoon. Next door, the Pollard Creek Inn stood silent and alone, vacant of the life and loves that once stirred with human activity. The front porch of the Inn seemed to lean awkwardly in pain, its white paint and black shutters beginning to peel away. Like a lost dog, it emanated a sense of sadness and regret, while waiting for the State of Oregon to come and transform its life forever.

McAllister stretched his legs, chewing on a package of cookies, taking in the fading angled light, not quite ready to drive the final miles to Railroad Bridge. He hoped he would still be able to motor across the rocky wash of Laughlin Creek. If so, he wouldn't have to hump and wheelbarrow his loaded possessions over the trestle to get to Little Kenny's cabin. The center of town was quiet, but for a passing car or truck heading this way and that, or over to the Post Office to pick up the mail. He decided to drive down Main Street to see if Rita was home. He would bring some apples to her, perhaps catch up on the news and gossip of things during his time away.

Valerie Williams was no longer living in the yellow house out front, having moved to Grants Pass a long time ago. But Rita had kept the small shed-room building behind, the one that Tom Sullivan had remodeled way back when. If Rita wasn't on the road herself, she might be home. Her firewatch job for the Forest Service would be over for another year. Their short fling together was far in the past. It was just one of those things. Rita remained a steady and energetic woman, but she continued to wear so much of life's questions on her brow. She was a woman always searching for something, and the burden of that search often seemed to pull her down. Sean McAllister was not on a similar quest. For him, the mysteries of life were just what they were, a mystery. Worthy of consideration and reflection, no doubt, but not to be carried to the point of uncertainty. Rita was different in that way. For Rita, understanding the meaning of life was a serious endeavor, a spiritual task she could not let go.

And so McAllister had drifted away. Things between them were a little complicated for a time, but eventually an understanding took hold between them. That was the one thing about living in the small incestuous world of Pollard Creek. One couldn't just take their personal histories, dig a hole and stash them away. There was no place to escape in this town, the music was always playing. If you intended on staying around, you better be able to live with that reality. It wasn't always easy, but those were the rules.

And so he and Rita were okay. He still really liked Rita in many ways, and she was accepting as well. But when it came to love, Pollard Creek was a continuing grand experiment. It was like being in a commune without really being in one. Or maybe, it was just the normal existence of a small town life. Perhaps there were secrets you wished to keep to yourself. But such an individual volition was not in the cards. You were naked as a jaybird in Pollard Creek. You best get used to it, or hit the road back to a more crowded world.

As McAllister began to pick himself up, an old blue Valiant pulled up to the store, with Jimmijay Connell behind the wheel. Jimmijay jumped from the car, ready for his next interaction with life. "Sean McAllister," he cried. "I haven't seen you since before the beginning, man. Where you been?"

"Jerry Fisher," McAllister answered, calling Jimmijay Connell by his more familiar radio persona. "How's it going, brother? I just rolled in from the apple harvest in Washington. Geez, I figured you'd be headlining in Hollywood by now," McAllister joked, poking fun at Jimmijay.

Jimmijay laughed, shaking off the repartee. "Yeah, something like that. That's right, I forgot you were gone. But hey Sean, you're back just in time. I'm hosting the Tops Swap at my place on Friday night. Marty is bringing his best bud from up on the Bridge. You're still living up there, right?"

"Cool, the Tops Swap. I've missed it all these years, getting back too late. Yeah, I'm still at Little Kenny's cabin up on the Bridge," McAllister answered.

"Hey listen, could you help me tabulate the votes since you won't have an entry? I'm going to need some help with the scoring, in case things get out of hand. It doesn't take long to lose track if you know what I mean."

"You mean like dazed and confused," McAllister laughed. "Just a wee bit I guess. Sure, bro, I'll help you out. But nobody can cry foul if Marty happens to win, right?"

"Don't worry," Jimmijay answered. "It's a blind taste test and I've got it all set up. Hey, we can say that all ballots will be counted and verified by the accounting firm of Connell and McAllister. That will really shake their tree. So just bring some whiskey or beer, and some munchies of course, and you'll be ready to tabulate."

"I'll bring my visor hat and be ready to go," McAllister said. "By the way, I've got something for you to take back home, for you and Darla."

McAllister went to the back of the panel truck, loading up a bag of apples for Jimmijay. Saying his farewell, he drove over to the post office, picking up a packet of mail being held for him, before swinging down Main Street to see if Rita was home. Arriving at the yellow house, a red late-model Cadillac was parked in the driveway. A Caddy was a bit of an unusual sight in Pollard Creek any time of year. He filled another bag of apples before walking behind the house to Rita's shed. But Rita wasn't home. He left the bag of apples on the doorstep, heading back for the truck.

As McAllister returned past the side entrance to the yellow house, the slim wiry figure of Rickey Rucker stepped outside. Rickey the Rocket, as he was known by almost everybody in town, appeared at little nervous at McAllister's presence, but Rickey always looked a little nervous most of the time.

"Hey, Sean. What's going on? Rita's not here. She and Laura went into Grants Pass. They won't be back until late."

McAllister could feel right away that something was up. Rickey was talking faster than normal, with the kind of edge that spoke for itself.

"How you doing, Rickey?" McAllister asked. "Yeah, I just got back from up north, picking the fruit. I left some apples for Rita. Would you and Laura like some? I got plenty. They're fresh off the trees."

"Oh, yeah? Not today, Sean, but thanks. Maybe next time." Rickey the Rocket was not in the mood for casual conversation and McAllister could feel the vibe. It wasn't a concern. McAllister knew he wasn't a threat, even if Rickey wasn't so sure.

"Nice looking ride out there, Rickey. You got some new wheels?" McAllister kept walking toward the panel truck, with Rickey the Rocket following right behind.

"Oh no, it's not mine. Just a couple of friends passing through for a visit. I'd invite you in, but they're getting ready to go."

Walking by the Caddy, McAllister ran his hand over the smooth shiny fender of the car. "Hey, hang on for a minute." McAllister went to the back of the panel. He opened the doors, quickly grabbed another paper bag, placing some apples inside. He turned and handed the bag to Rickey Rucker.

"Here. I know Laura would want some. And hey man, not to worry. Sort of bad timing I suppose, but things are cool, Rickey. Relax, will you. I know it's that time of year." McAllister smiled as he handed him the apples.

"Hey, sorry, Sean. Nothing personal. I know it's cool. Just that these guys inside don't know you from Adam. That's what it's all about."

"Got it, Rick. You can't be too careful, I understand." Rickey Rucker's facial expression eased. "So, you going to be in town for the Tops Swap on Friday night?" McAllister asked. I just ran into Jimmijay at the Country Store. He says it's down at his place this year."

"Yeah, I plan to be there, unless something comes up."

McAllister closed the rears doors to the panel truck. "Jimmijay wants me to be a judge or something, to help him count up the votes. So if you've got an entry, I'm accepting all the bribes I can get."

Rickey Rucker snickered at the comment. "A judge? With you living at the Bridge? If Marty's got an entry, is that really fair?"

"Guess not," McAllister shrugged. He watched as Rickey Rucker settled down a little. "I'm not a judge, really, just a bean counter. You know Jimmijay. He'll be in full performance mode. I'll just be helping him keep the scoring right. Do you have an entry this year?"

"Not this time around," Rickey answered. "I'll be an innocent bystander, like you I guess."

McAllister stretched out his right hand, thumb up. Rickey got the message and clasped it with his own. "You always got an entry, Rickey," McAllister followed. "It may not be your own, but it surely will be a good one no doubt. As for an innocent bystander, that's one thing you will never be, Rickey. I'll see you on Friday." With that, McAllister turned toward the front of the truck.

Rickey the Rocket shook his head. "Thanks for the apples, Sean. I'll let Laura know." As Rickey walked back toward the house, McAllister climbed into the cab of the panel. He fired up the rig, heading for Railroad Bridge.

It was indeed that time of year. Even big-time middlemen like Rickey Rucker had symptoms of the harvest-time fever. McAllister was glad he generally wasn't around for most of it. He'd never had a chance to grow his own. Maybe someday he would get the opportunity, but for now the apple harvest was his money thing, and he dug the trip. But each succeeding year in Pollard Creek, the pot was getting better, the patches bigger, the fear and loathing greater, the stakes that much higher.

There was a new cash crop in the mountain territories of the Pacific Northwest. Small communities from Garberville, California to the Canadian border were not just timber and mill economies anymore. An illegal agribusiness was taking root. It was a four to six month labor of love, from tiny seed to dripping gooey bud. For ten months of the year, towns like Pollard Creek and Solace Valley were wild enough. But from Labor Day to Halloween, these hills were becoming a land of tight-lipped hermits, living amongst a dangerous den of thieves.

The pressure was great. Not a single dollar could be made until the harvest and delivery were complete. Thus, the heavy stress and paranoia that came toward the end of the season. At this time of year, every strange vehicle was a question mark, every unfamiliar face deserving of identification. McAllister couldn't blame Rickey the Rocket for feeling his worried concern. That's what made the Tops Swap so much fun. It was like an illegal holiday of sorts, when the crop was secure and the pressure finally relieved. Only then could everyone let down their crazy vigilant guard.

~~~

The wheels of justice turn slowly. Especially slow for white men in positions of power, notwithstanding the nature of their crimes. In title, John Ehrlichman had been the Assistant to the President for Domestic Affairs. Since 1971, in addition to his day job for the United States, John Ehrlichman had become Richard Nixon's hatchet man in the Oval Office. He was the head of the notorious White House Special Investigations Unit, later referred to as the 'Plumbers'. Erlichman had also been the lead man in the Watergate Cover-up two years later.

Now, in late October of 1976, almost twenty-two months after his conviction in January of 1975, Erlichman was finally entering prison. Even Patty Hearst had already beaten him to the jail cell. Patty hadn't even been kidnapped until February of 1974. She had been caught and charged with bank robbery in September of 1975, then tried, convicted, and sentenced to seven years. Patty had already been in the slammer a month before Ehrlichman would get to hear the bars slam shut. That's presuming there were even metal bars wherever Erlichman would do his time. More than likely, his new home would be a minimum security country club of sorts, with a brand new mattress and a color TV.

Meanwhile, the man responsible for the most devastating bombing campaign in the history of man, and whose crimes of deceit and slander had abridged the most fundamental rights of civilian Americans, was resting comfortably at home, free as a bird. Maybe Richard Milhous Nixon was a bird who couldn't fly as easily these days, but he was still goddamned fucking free.

McAllister's only hope as he listened to his small transistor radio on a frosty cold late October morning, was that the man who had pardoned Richard Nixon, might get his own comeuppance in a matter of days. Gerald Ford was in the late stages of a Presidential election, against a more progressive Democratic outsider named Jimmy Carter. McAllister would begrudgingly vote for Carter, but not with any particular expectations. His own faith in America had sunk so low, it was no longer even a concern to him. As Wavy Gravy had suggested, it might be better to vote for 'Nobody' for president. For 'Nobody' tells the truth, 'Nobody' knows all the answers, 'Nobody' knows the trouble he'd seen, and most important, 'Nobody' cares.

McAllister stoked up the fire in his woodstove, placing a chunk of dried oak inside. The fire would burn slower and longer now, not having to be tended for awhile. He poured another cup of coffee, turned off the radio, sitting down to read the mail he had picked up the day before. There was a letter from Johnny Howard, his old boyhood friend. Johnny was finishing his chiropractic training in Boulder. He had met a girl and was moving to San Diego. Johnny had also been back east during the summer. He'd seen Bruiser and others, and everyone seemed to be doing well back home.

Then came the highlight of the correspondence, or the low light, or the mid light, whatever. There was word from Johnny Howard of the rumor that Mad had left Willie Chambers. She had moved back from the Susquehanna to her family home near Philly. The news stirred McAllister with a confusing mix of emotions.

On the one hand, he felt a sense of negative redemption against Willie Chambers, the devious asshole who had stolen his girl. On the other hand, there was the return of those difficult feelings of loss from so long ago, of being rejected and left behind. But that wasn't all. There still remained that little stir, a crazy sense of hope that the void that now existed between he and Mad would somehow be crossed, that a long lost love might be born again. At the same time, in almost complete contradiction, he felt a passionless distance from the circumstances that had occurred. It was as if he was looking into a crystal ball, seeing the history of prior events unfold, but without the pain and suffering endured once upon a time. McAllister figured he might need about three or four hands to work out the emotions of this unexpected surprise.

Right now, there was no other woman in his life. If there had been one, it would have been easier to put these mixed-up feelings back on the shelf. Instead, a pinch of loneliness tried to force its way into his heart. But he was stronger now, older and wiser than before. The past had lost its grip. He put the letter back in its envelope, went on with his day. Still, the effect of the news followed him around in the hours hence. Why he kept thinking of Mookie's dog, Meatball, he didn't know for sure. Perhaps because Meatball had been his companion through the toughest part of those difficult times. Maybe, just maybe, Sean McAllister needed to get a dog of his own.

'Too Tall' Tim Wilson stood on the deck of his homebuilt cabin, the morning frost beginning to soften with the day. The autumn sun was rising above the ridge tops, bathing the property in warm amber light. Tim looked down at Laughlin Creek. The hard rains of November had not yet come. The creek still ran low toward the Rogue River, its larger rocks remaining exposed. The flattened gravel and sand bar below him waited for higher water to come. Tim took another hit off the joint in his hand. He lightly stubbed out the roach on the handrail, sticking its remains in the chest pocket of his shirt for a later burn. He took a hair tie out of the pocket of his jeans. Pulling his waist-length head of hair together, he secured it down the length of his back. Unconsciously, he raised a hand, smoothing the edges of his handlebar mustache. He raised the arms of his six and a half foot frame above his head, beginning to stretch. He was ready to do some work outside the cabin, although it hadn't occurred to him what the first task might be.

Lately, it had been hard for Tim Wilson to stay motivated. The Bureau of Land Management was climbing up his ass again, looking for reasons to invalidate his unpatented mining claim. The Jordan County government had been trying for a couple of years to tear down structures the hippies had been building on their own land. Everyone in town knew how the State of Oregon had managed to close and starve out the Pollard Creek Inn. The Feds were no different. Too many people were filing claims on BLM land, putting up shelters and pretending to be locating gold in the watersheds of Southern Oregon. Tim Wilson had been on his Tujunga Claim since 1972. He had built a sluice box to show his intentions, and always paid his annual improvement fee, but the pressure was increasing. Regardless of his compliance, when it came to many claims like Tim's, the Feds would never fail to have the ultimate hammer.

In order to survive, one had to work the claim, then show mineral deposits that would pass the 'prudent man rule' and 'marketability tests'. In laymen's terms, the miner had to show that a prudent man would be "justified in the further expenditure of his labor and means, with a reasonable prospect of success in developing a valuable mine". The marketability test was even tougher. "The mineral locater, to justify his possession, must show by reason of accessibility, bona fides in development, proximity to market, existence of present demand and other factors, that the deposit is of such value that it can be mined, removed, and disposed of at a profit".

Based on those two requisites, the Tujunga Claim would be literally between a rock and a hard spot. Tujunga had always been a placer claim, working the sand and gravel of Laughlin Creek. Tim had shown some flake from time to time, whenever he chose to sluice the creek, but not much more than that. To really get at some possible bedrock gold, Tim would have to make a heavy investment of money and equipment, neither of which he could afford. The improvements he had made to the claim were not so much for mining, but for his own personal subsistence. He had cut and milled timber off the land, but only for his own cabin, nothing more. He had improved the road to the mine for easier access. Still, there was little chance he could pass the continuing legal tests for mining the claim.

Tim had already spent twelve hundred dollars with an attorney to fight them off on the first go round. But it would be little more than a pyrrhic victory. As soon as you fought off one rubber-necked bureaucrat, there was a new one at your doorstep. And the new guy would just begin another investigation on the same battle you had previously won. If the BLM wanted to bring a little guy down, they had the time and constancy to do so. In other words, you couldn't fight City Hall. Therein lay the reason for Tim Wilson's lack of motivation. It was the simple realization that one day you could arrive home and see that the claim was posted by the Feds. You would have very little time to clear out all your shit, then get the hell out of Dodge. Other claimants who had ignored or resisted the Feds, sometimes had arrived home to find everything burnt to the ground. Lately, these circumstances didn't do much for Tim Wilson's belief in future expectations.

Tim Wilson's spouse and two boys had fled to Eugene. Early on, his wife, Sarah, had become fed up with the uncertainty. Truthfully, the break up wasn't really over the BLM thing, there were other good reasons as well. Just having to drive fifteen miles to get to Pollard Creek was a big one for sure. Unless a person was really committed to living every single day like the little house on the prairie, it was a difficult style of life. Sarah grew tired of it. Tim hadn't. In the end, the whole situation was probably for the best. The rest of the family had grown happy and content in Eugene. And the boys were still able to visit from time to time.

Standing in the middle of his parking area in front of the cabin, Tim could hear the sound of a vehicle far up above on Laughlin Creek Road. October was hunting season. This time of year, strangers would pass by, bungling along in their fancy four-wheel drives, dressed in their new camouflage and orange vests, usually lost as hell. But on this particular morning, the vehicle sounded like a car, racing fast. Tim waited to see what was up. Today, he sort of had the time.

Rickey the Rocket fishtailed the big red Caddy around a curve on Laughlin Creek Road, almost losing control. The gravel spit, knocking against the undercarriage of the car, prompting the man riding next to Rickey to shout inside the Caddy.

"Damn, Rocket. Slow the fuck down. It ain't that important. We don't need to be getting killed over this shit."

Rickey the Rocket Rucker let his foot slide back from the accelerator. He took a quick look over at the man named Charley, his dope connection from San Francisco. With a mischievous shit-eating grin on his face, his black eyeballs appearing to be popping out their sockets, Rickey the Rocket reduced his speed. "Sorry, man," he apologized. Guess I forgot about that curve. I haven't been down here in a while."

The dope connection, Charley, shook his head. "Last fucking time I let you drive this rig, I know that. Am I right, Andy?" A third man, sitting in the back seat, echoed his approval.

"Shit, Charley. I figured you guys were in a hurry, that's all," Rickey the Rocket responded. Rickey pulled his foot further off the accelerator, slowing the car to an idling crawl. The Caddy bumped along the gravel road, barely moving forward.

"Come on, Rocket, cut the shit. This deal better work out, that's all I got to say, you cranked-up son of a bitch."

"Okay, okay," Rickey answered. "Just pulling your chain, that's all. Don't worry, Charley, everything's cool." Rickey Rucker picked the car up to a normal safe speed, pushing the Caddy further down the road.

Rickey the Rocket was feeling the buzz. The coffee, the taste of the morning bud, the two big lines of coke he had done while making the deal, were coursing through his system. Rickey had purchased three burlap bags of the dried crop far up on Robertson Creek less than an hour before. But the grower didn't want them breaking it down at his place, so they had returned to Laura's yellow house on Main Street to clean things up. But Laura would have none of that plan. Not in her house, she demanded. So Rickey had been forced to think quickly. He had thought of Too Tall Tim's place down near the Rogue River. From Tim's location, once the job was done, Charley and his buddy Andy could either circle down over the river and into Grants Pass, or double back through Solace Valley, before returning to San Francisco.

When Rickey slid the Caddy down the dirt access road to the Tujunga claim, sure enough Too Tall Tim was standing in the driveway, trying to figure out who the hell was coming. Rickey parked and jumped from the car. He gave Tim the scoop, plus a fifty dollar bill, promising to leave some stash behind when the deal was done. With that, Tim Wilson drifted away towards his truck barn that stood nearby. Rickey and the two men took the burlap bundles from the trunk of the car, a box of plastic bags and a suitcase, heading inside the cabin. Tim Wilson killed some time, puttering over his two old Chevy pick-ups. He rambled around the property, picking up some things here and there, before smoking the last of his roach down by Laughlin Creek.

In just over an hour the visitors had completed their work. They exited with the suitcase, placing it deep in the bowels of the Caddy's trunk. Too Tall Tim just shook his head when Rickey asked him if he would shuttle Rickey back to Pollard Creek. The two men from San Francisco saluted a good-bye, driving the Caddy away. The deal was done. Too Tall Tim fired up his pick-up, driving Rickey back to town. Rickey the Rocket apologized for leaving a mess inside the cabin, but he placated Tim with the news that it would definitely be a mess worth cleaning up.

With the pleasant buzz from two snorts of cocaine coursing his brain, Tim Wilson picked up some groceries and beer at the Country Store, before driving back home. Back at the cabin, he shook out the burlap bags, sweeping up the remains of top leaf and broken chunks of bud. He placed the leftovers in his cigar tin stash box, before breaking up the branch stems of the plants and burning them in the woodstove. All was well. Tim Wilson had awakened this morning, slightly at a loss as to what his day would bring. A half day later, he had fifty bucks, a short cocaine high, a town trip complete, and had increased his stash. It occurred to Tim that life in Pollard Creek was sometimes a hell of a lot like the weather in Oregon. For a moment or two it might be heading one way, but wait five minutes and it was likely to change. And with guys like Rickey the Rocket in the social circle of your everyday life, well, even the weather would be hard pressed to be as temperamental as the world of Pollard Creek.

Jimmijay Connell loved being the master of ceremonies. A Commander Cody album played in the background. Most everyone sat around the kitchen table at the old Harkness' homestead, the starry darkness of an Oregon night outside. In honor of Halloween only two days away, Jimmijay was dressed in a corduroy sport coat, a purple scarf, and a mask of Richard Nixon over his face. Albert Krieger had retreated back to New York, perhaps never to return. Darla Bloom had taken her two young children south to California, visiting her family down in Los Angeles. Her kids would get to do their trick or treating in a busier world. As a result, Jimmijay Connell had the house to himself with no one else to worry about. The annual Tops Swap was underway.

Marty Johnson, Tom Sullivan, and Sean McAllister were present from Railroad Bridge. There was Robert Sage, Too Tall Tim, Rickey the Rocket, and several others. There was Joe Joe Gifford, one of the last holdouts from Strawberry Fields, and the favorite to win. Last but not least, there was Caroline Reynolds, the single female entry. Whiskey and bottles of beer sat on the edges of the table. In the middle, the eight entries in the competition lay on folded dinner napkins, each with a number below. The individual colas of bud rested tantalizingly under the overhead kitchen light. Tightly bound in soft green and purple color, their crystal resins sparkled, their tiny hairs aging in sentient burnished orange. Resting together, the sweet odor of skunk filled the kitchen, ready for the test.

Sean McAllister knew early on that Jimmijay Connell would not be much help in the scorekeeping. Jimmijay's alter ego, Jerry Fisher, was already into his Nixon stage show, mimicking the jowl faced former President's voice and delivery. McAllister handed out index cards with an entrant number and four category descriptions on each card. Both the entrants and observing bystanders would vote. Category #1 was Appearance. Category #2: Scent. Each cola would be closely viewed and sniffed by the electorate. A score of one being lowest, to five being highest, would then be entered on each card. Following the first round of scoring, the second round would begin. Joints would be rolled from each cola and passed through the room. Voters would now choose a score based on Category #3: Flavor, and Category #4: Smoothness.

Sean McAllister realized he would not be able to participate in category numbers three and four. Smoke was already hanging heavy in the kitchen air, and with the beer and whiskey in assistance, the marijuana high was quickly taking its toll. The scene was very similar to a hippie poker game, where everything was fine until the bong pipe was passed around. Then each player would start telling jokes and stories, until nobody, including the dealer, could remember what card game had been called. In other words, things at the Tops Swap were debilitating fast. McAllister began to take his job seriously. He knew he had to be in control if an annual winner would be judiciously crowned. The necessity of his temperance was certainly uninvited, but was absolutely necessary.

Caroline Reynolds sat at the kitchen table, a bottle of fresh-squeezed carrot juice beside her. Caroline didn't drink. In fact, she didn't even smoke her own crop. Caroline was small and hard-bodied, a lot like Rita in size and appearance. But unlike Rita's long wavy brown hair, Caroline's was short blonde and curly around her head. Everyone was aware that Caroline Reynolds was the green goddess of gardening in Pollard Creek, a human book of knowledge on all things grown. Still, she had to be brave as hell to be in the same room with this current bunch of crazies.

McAllister asked Caroline to collect all the index cards. Being the only sober man in the house, he asked that she assist him in reading the numbers to him for each entrant and category. Although his request met with a chorus of boos and smart remarks, by this point nobody cared. They retreated to the living room, where Caroline read off the numbers for each particular entry, excepting her own. McAllister marked down the scores on a clipboard, with Caroline returning to the kitchen to await the outcome. McAllister continued adding up the final scores for each contestant.

When he was finished with the totals, McAllister called Jimmijay Connell into the living room. Jimmijay bounced into the room, taking off his mask. "So who is it?" he quickly asked in his regular voice. McAllister was pleased that Richard Nixon had finally left the building.

"Well, you're not going to believe this," McAllister began, "but it's Caroline in a landslide. She got fours and fives in every category."

"No shit, that's great," Jimmijay beamed. "It's perfect. Which one was her entry? Was it the longest one in the middle? Number four, I think."

McAllister looked at his clipboard. "Yep, number four, that's Caroline.

Joe Joe came in second. And Marty got third."

Jimmijay had purchased prizes for the winners. For Marty Johnson, third prize was a huge orange pumpkin. For Joe Joe Gifford in second place, a ten dollar gift certificate at the Hungry Dog Café. Everyone cracked up at this announcement. After the certificate was handed to Joe Joe, he sent the envelope sailing toward the garbage basket in the corner of the kitchen. But when Caroline was announced the victor, the place went nuts. The men cheered and hugged her over and over, with Caroline beaming from ear to ear. Jimmijay handed her the first prize, a bottle of Bailey's Irish Cream liqueur. Caroline looked at it funny, but hugged it to her chest.

With the evening winding to a close, McAllister volunteered to drive Marty Johnson's rig back to Railroad Bridge. Marty sat beside McAllister on the bench seat of the rig, Tommy Sullivan pressed by the window. On Marty's lap sat the plump orange pumpkin Marty had won. Marty's head bobbed along as they drove down Lower Pollard Creek toward home.

"I tried to trade Caroline for the bottle," Marty nodded, "but she wouldn't go for it. I bet she steals a sip or two. That stuff is sweet as sin."

"I'd like to carve that pumpkin tomorrow, Marty," Tom Sullivan asked, "if that's okay with you?"

"Sure, Tommy, what the hell. What's it going to look like?"

"I don't know yet, maybe a self-portrait of myself, what do you think?"

"Get out of here," McAllister cracked.

There was a short pause as they drove along. "Vincent Van Sullivan," Marty croaked, and all three men laughed together.

Again, moments of tired silence passed as McAllister headed home. Making the turn onto Laughlin Creek Road, the headlights pierced the blackened night as he slowed to cross the railroad tracks.

"You know what this means, don't you?" Marty Johnson mumbled.

"What does what mean, Marty?" McAllister asked.

"Halloween."

"No, I don't know. What?"

"The next day will be the first day of another Oregon winter. Another fucking Oregon winter, that's what it means."

McAllister steered the truck down the logging road toward the entrance to Railroad Bridge. The head lights pointed into Laughlin Creek and the slow rocky crossing ahead.

"Can't argue with that," Tom Sullivan agreed. "You know, Marty, those good old days in Baja sound better and better all the time."

"Man, you got that right, Tommy. Those were the days."

CHAPTER THIRTY-EIGHT

IT SHALL BE
Pollard Creek / 1976-1977

ON NOVEMBER 2ND, 1976, Jimmy Carter, a Democrat and former governor of Georgia, was elected President of the United States. Carter's victory ended the interim occupancy of the White House by Republican Gerald Ford, who had ascended to the office upon the resignation of Richard Nixon two years earlier. Many believed that the absolute pardon of Richard Nixon was instrumental in Ford's defeat. Perhaps that observation was true. But Sean McAllister didn't believe it. In McAllister's view, when it came right down to it, the voters of America generally didn't know their ass from a hole in the ground. Only four years before, they had elected Richard Nixon to the Presidency over George McGovern, giving Nixon a 61 percent plurality. Richard Nixon had won a near complete electoral college sweep. Only the single state of Massachusetts, and the District of Columbia had given McGovern the nod. No, America, it wasn't the pardon.

Rather, the 1972 Nixon landslide was simply your way of beating your chest and telling anyone who cared to know that you couldn't ever be wrong. Re-electing Richard Nixon was your way of fooling yourself into believing that Vietnam was an honorable endeavor, and no one was going to tell you any different. And if you couldn't bomb and burn those slant-eyed gooks into submission on the battlefield, you sure could show them how to win at home. And win big.

But when the Watergate shit hit the fan, what do you do? Instead of taking a good hard look at yourself, you conveniently lose your memory and start looking for someone else to blame for your own misdeeds. By then, Nixon and his cabal had become an easy enough target. So you take down all the mirrors in your home. You follow that expedient chore by seeking to impeach the godless idol you had only recently crowned as king.

No, America, you only elected Jimmy Carter because you needed to wipe your own sins clean, to forgive yourself without admitting a lick of responsibility. But after a time, when no one else is paying attention, you will surreptitiously put those mirrors back on your wall. You will arrogantly return to admiring yourself as god's holy gift to the planet earth, waiting patiently for the next false prophet to lead the way.

Sean McAllister's cynicism toward the politics and leadership of his country had grown strong roots, fed by the events of his time. Like the bully boy in the neighborhood, the United States had gotten used to taking whatever it desired. Arrogance has a hard time admitting its mistakes. Using the blame game becomes a rather convenient forte. The American character had become quite accustomed to forgiving its own hypocrisies. And that courageous trait was unlikely to change anytime soon.

As for Jordan County Commissioner, Wilton Parker, well, he had mistakenly put his money on the wrong horse. Wilton had ignored his certain personal proclivities for better judgment and fairness, casting his lot with the politics of the time. Although he had done his best not to do so, he had stepped into a pile of political horseshit. An ill wind had followed, and the stink in the air had taken Wilton down. With his re-election campaign lost, Wilton would soon be back at his ranch in Hugo. He would be cleaning out his barn, driving his wife batty with his nervous energy, while looking for another job.

To Wilton Parker's credit, he was not a man to blame others for his own mistakes. He refused to blame that bureaucratic lackey Craig Benson, that Assistant Attorney General David Hinson, or the plethora of other state bureaucrats Wilton had sought to appease. Wilton Parker didn't know a damn thing about what those hippie kids called 'karma'. But if bad karma had indeed come his way, Wilton was man enough to accept that he alone was at fault. Wilton Parker had gotten his own comeuppance, but he wasn't afraid to look in his bathroom mirror, accepting his fate.

The State of Oregon itself was a classic study in incongruity. Independent as hell, it hated all things Californian, wanting to preserve its own identity in the face of a constant immigration it could not prevent. Oregon had long been a jurisdiction of bow-legged loggers, marginal ranchers, as well as hard-rock miners who wanted nothing more than to do their own thing in their very own way. Ken Kesey had captured Oregon's rugged streak of individualism in his portrayal of Hank Stamper's constant eternal scrap against the forces of both nature and men. Stamper's careless and obstinate defiance spoke to a character trait that was all things Oregon. *Sometimes a Great Notion* was the bible book for the Oregon state of mind. It was a state of mind that was always tough, restless, and unforgiving in face of relentless danger.

There was a reason that timber logging was a most dangerous occupation. Logging was ranked second only to race car drivers in the premium ledgers of every insurance company in America. The timber trade could kill or maim a man in an instant, before even a final thought might come to mind. The cracking and breaking of towering branches in the sky, the concussive power of a giant virgin Douglas fir thundering when it met the earth, was always a ceaseless reminder of a mortal fate one could not control. Loggers hadn't named certain unseen broken tree tops as 'widow makers' simply to coin a phrase. Even the safest looking conifer in the forest had the potential for a final terminal result.

In the face of such dangers every working day, an otherwise reasonable man must give his due to the whims of fate. But such a perceived reality begins to take its toll. One becomes careless in his concerns for self-preservation, because what difference does it make? You work hard, you drive hard, you fight hard. You have long ago accepted the fact that the next moment is never guaranteed. You drink hard or fuck hard until its time to eat or sleep. You wake up each morning, put on your corks, grab your round aluminum helmet, climb back on the hill. Perhaps you sit in church on Sunday, but you have already accepted both heaven and hell. It no longer matters on which side you might fall. More than anything, you speak your mind whenever it speaks to you. Everything you say, except maybe to your wife or your kids, is done without concern or remorse. Time and future are always waiting in the wings. But if the worst should happen, you'd prefer to be killed right on the spot. Rather that, than being busted all to hell, a forgotten man, sitting alone in a wheel chair on a street corner in Grants Pass, having to wait out your final days.

This was one side of the Oregon story, but there was another side as well. The persistent specter of mortality, and its assurance of inevitable loss, breeds a strange element of forgiveness and acceptance of all things before you. You battle fist for fist in the barroom until somebody falls, then you pick them up and buy them a drink. You roust a hippie or a nigger just for kicks, but you give them a job if they show they can work.

Oregonians take the bounty of their land for survival, but stand firm against outsiders taking it for their own possessive wealth. Somebody may have called it 'god's country', but even god knows better than to call it his own. Oregon is our state, and we will mess it up or make it better in our own peculiar way. You can come and visit us, but don't be bringing your goddamn garbage across our border, or throwing your bottles out the window while driving through. And don't be thinking you are going to scarf up our coastlines, then fence them off and call them your own. We are the best country in the country, with the country's best beer.

That was Tom McCall. As Governor of Oregon for eight years, from 1966 to 1974, McCall understood the identity and independent mind of his people. He also felt the thirst of California for new worlds to conquer, of new lands to reshape in its own desirous image. McCall rallied his troops against the invaders. At the same time he couldn't allow Oregon to harm itself with its own mistakes. Oregon would protect its magnificent coastline for all its residents to share. It would refrain from tossing litter onto its own roads. It would seek to keep its rivers clean, while protecting its lands from mass-produced development and sprawl.

By no means could Tom McCall stem the tide of late-twentieth-century American mobility and consumption. But he was able to set Oregon on a path of progressive response, an independence of mind where its citizens would call their own shots. Oregon would not become the rat race of California, nor become the military-industrial complex of Washington state. Oregon would make its own destiny, whether right or wrong. McCall sought to preserve Oregon's own native identity, but challenge them to protect their future as well. Tom McCall was a turning point in the state he called home.

But nothing along the trail of the human dynamic is black and white. Complexity is the true color and spice of life, although it is rarely observed on first impression. Jordan County saluted Tom McCall's statewide missive for an autonomous and self-reliant identity. But Jordan County's own geographical separateness from Portland and Salem remained distant and distinct. For many natives in Southern Oregon, there had long been the desire for a separate sovereign jurisdiction to be called the State of Jefferson. Jordan County would align with other counties in southwestern Oregon, as well as the northern timber counties of California. Residents of this mountainous hinterland had long felt separated and ignored by the politics and public funding of their two state legislatures. The idea of some form of secession and individual self-governance had an emotional response in the hearts of many citizens of the Siskiyou and Shasta regions of the Great Northwest.

Tom McCall's bugle cry gave solace to that similar long-held passion for regional liberty. But it might come at a price that Jordan County had a more difficult time in reconciling. If it meant establishing uniform criteria for the appropriate use of private land, as well as a larger public right for resource and wilderness protection, this would be a harder pill to swallow. McCall's missive would require a merging of conservatism and liberalism in thoughtful understanding, a negotiated settlement between personal freedom and the public welfare. For Jordan County, that might be too much to ask. Jordan County's first knee-jerk response would be to resist, whatever the consequences might be.

'Eclectic' is a word of Greek derivation, described in Webster's as an adjective meaning "composed of elements drawn from various sources". By the early nineteen seventies, Jordan County had become a wild menagerie of personal and political notions. It was indeed a mix of generally white pioneer emigrants, from old time loggers and miners, hermetic survivalists and religious fundamentalists, to rogue troublemakers and cops. In addition, now throw in tribes of wandering hippies or after-shocked Vietnam Veterans, as well as normal aging transplanted squares from California, and the word 'eclectic' had a new meaning all its own.

Jordan County was a misfit band of Americans, colliding in a mountain backdrop river valley called the Rogue. It had a county seat whose mascot was a Caveman, and the rain-drenched temerity to exclaim, if you pardon the French, "It's the 'fucking' Climate". If one had to scratch their head, and try to figure out which way the wind was blowing in Jordan County, they would surely end up with a balding dome as smooth as a bowling ball. Even Tom McCall didn't have clue about the wild and wooly world of Jordan County, despite his best intentions for the oneness of an Oregon mind.

But wasn't that just the point? Southern Oregon was a beautiful and exotic land of gracious American knuckleheads, looking for their own romantic destinies, or simply a place to be left alone. But in the end, everyone was an Oregonian, terribly tried and true, and boasting full of provincial pride.

In the early winter of 1976, Sean McAllister put his panel truck in hibernation. He bought a three-quarter ton International pick-up for five hundred dollars. With his Stihl chain saw and files, his oil and gas cans, a splitting mall and axe, he took to the hills above Pollard Creek and Solace Valley, cutting firewood for sale to the locals. The wood cutting trips took him alone to the higher mountain country above the valleys. Often, he would get to sweat beneath the winter sun, well above the somber gray fog of weather inversions below. He felled and cut fir and pine, or the slower burning hardwoods of Pacific madrone and Oregon oak. He split and stacked, split and stacked. On the wetter days, he steamed inside his rain gear, his West Coast boots caked with slick red clay, the wood truck bathed in mud from fender to fender.

Similar to his life at the Mulcahey Farm, he lived a Railroad Bridge existence of kerosene light and car batteries, of damp clothing evaporating in wood stove heat, of books and beer and pots of stew, of hand rolled herb and tobacco cigarettes. In the depths of winter, Railroad Bridge could have easily been situated on the moon, the darkness of a rainy winter holding sway. For a time, the woman Suzanne would take him in, feeding and comforting him in her lofted lair. But eventually, something grew old between them. Suzanne had greater expectations and McAllister became the odd man out. The notions of enduring love seemed to elude Sean McAllister in Pollard Creek. But he was not the only victim. Sexual companionship in Pollard Creek was like a game of musical chairs. Here today and gone tomorrow. No one seemed immune from the temporary nature of its condition.

On a cold dark evening in January 1977, Sean McAllister sat at a table with his buddies Marty Johnson and Tommy Sullivan, drinking beer in the Solace Valley Tavern. It was a Friday night, the barroom crowded with patrons surviving the Oregon winter, one moment and one drink at a time. Outside in the parking lot, several loggers stood together, sharing hits off a bottle of McNaughton's whiskey before returning inside. Others stood around the pool table, or rotated on red vinyl bar stools, jabbering away. Enough time had gone by. The battle lines between hippies and locals had long ago merged into a familiar understanding and acceptance. Sooner or later, everybody's money is good. Sooner or later, things get figured out, and people no longer become strangers to fear.

Blanche Hayworth, the dayshift bartender, stood over the tavern jukebox, her arms outstretched, gripping the machine, holding herself up. On Fridays, when her work was over, Blanche stuck around to catch a little buzz, and perchance a man to take home for the night. Blanche was older, fortyish, with a couple of kids now on their own. Everyone knew the sorrow of her history. Her husband, Bud Hayworth, had been knocked dead by a busted snag ten years before. Blanche had every right to drink a little longer than she should. Blanche Hayworth had a heart of gold. She had always treated her long-haired patrons with a cordial respect from day number one. Blanche felt like a mom to all the young men who came to sit and chat with her on restless gray afternoons, making them feel at home.

So if Blanche had a few too many glasses of wine, it was just okay. And someone would always would look after her, that was a given. Southern Oregon could be damn hard for anybody at certain times. But especially hard for an aging single woman, with a future that might only be in the past. It wasn't necessarily sad. It was just the way it was.

Sean McAllister snickered to himself, before speaking at the table. "I bet she plays it again," he said, smiling at Marty and Tom.

"What?" Marty Johnson asked. "Who plays it again?"

"Blanche," McAllister answered. "The same song. She's already played it twice tonight. I got a feeling she's going for the triple lutz. It's her theme song when she gets this way."

Marty Johnson and Tom Sullivan turned their heads toward the jukebox, catching sight of Blanche slowly slipping the quarters into the machine. Returning his gaze, Marty Johnson grinned at McAllister, catching his drift. Tom Sullivan, as usual, didn't say a word, just sat in his chair, shaking his head.

"Which one?" Marty asked quickly.

"You know which one," Sullivan deadpanned, looking at McAllister.

"The "Behind Closed Doors" song, right?"

McAllister nodded his head at Sullivan, smiling in fun. "Yeah, that's the one. "Behind Closed Doors".

"What's the other one called, the other one she always plays?" Marty Johnson asked.

"The Most Beautiful Girl in the World", Sullivan answered, matter of fact.

"That's it," Marty said. Then he turned his head and shouted over to Blanche. "Hey, Blanche, play "The Most Beautiful Girl in the World" song, would you. I love that tune." He turned back to McAllister, wearing a shit-eating grin.

Blanche rolled her head in Marty's direction. "Oh, okay," Blanche slurred. "Isn't he great. I love Charley Rich."

"A beer," Marty said to McAllister. "A beer that song comes first."

"You're on," McAllister answered. "She's already got the other one picked. You'll see."

Sullivan looked at Marty. "He's right, bro. She's already got it picked."

"No way," Marty answered. "No way, three times in a row."

The men watched as Blanche put in the last quarter and made her final pick. Sipping their beers, they waited. It only took the first few bars. McAllister knew right away and started to sing. "My baby makes me proud, Lord don't she make me proud…." Then he laughed as Marty Johnson let his head rest on the table, banging it up and down several times, before raising back up.

"Three times in a row, I can't fucking believe it," Marty whined. "Goddamn. So what the hell do you want?"

"Whatever you're having, Mr. Johnson," McAllister answered, grinning.

Per their expectation, Tom Sullivan just stared at Marty Johnson, once again shaking his head.

A short while later, the men got a huge surprise as longtime friend, Mookie James, came walking through the door of the tavern. Mookie was back in town. He had been down in California for several months, helping a guy build a house in a town called La Honda, south of San

Francisco. It was like old home week for the boys, a reunion of sorts
that brought new inspiration to the dark January night. Mookie had
spotted their rigs at the tavern from the freeway exit ramp, interrupting
his intended destination towards Railroad Bridge.

Mookie James was no longer a member of the Mulcahey Farm.
At the end of the previous summer, Annie had moved back to her
parent's home in Southern California. She had decided to return to
Santa Barbara to complete her education. She and Mookie's romantic
detour to the communal experience of Derrick Mulcahey's world was
officially over, much as McAllister's own residency had come to a close
over a year before. And like McAllister, Mookie's own personal leaving
had not been without regret. Despite the strange machinations of
Derrick Mulcahey, there had once been a happy dream and bonding
they had all shared together. There were people they had grown to love
and cherish, an ideal of living they had wishfully hoped to realize. But
sometimes the road of life has other plans.

Mookie had hung on as long as he could. He had put so much
emotional effort into both his relationship with Annie, and the cabin
he had built. For Mookie, to pull up stakes was to suffer more than one
defeat. But eventually, it had to be accepted and done. With Annie's
departure, the last rites were final. Mookie's cabin became a prison of
the past, with nothing more to give. The job opportunity in La Honda
had given Mookie his release, until a new future would reveal itself to
him, wherever it might be.

The men continued to drink and bullshit with themselves and other
friends at the Solace Valley Tavern. As closing time neared, they paraded
into the winter night, firing up their vehicles, before driving the interstate
pass over to Pollard Creek. The Hungry Dog Café was a twenty-four
operation, a familiar place to eat a midnight breakfast or a healthy plate
of burger and fries. Truckers were scattered on stools at the counter,
eating, drinking coffee and smoking cigarettes, taking a break from their
working routines on the long haul runs. At other truck stops, it was likely
no hippies would be seen. But Pollard Creek was a different story.

The group stumbled into the café as if they were home. Dressed in
their down vests and wool coats, heeled mudded boots, their long tied-
back hair and bearded faces, they crashed down into a booth. Drunk,
they laughed at each other's jokes, pouring down coffee and cleaning
their plates. Marty Johnson, as sometimes occurred, started having a

hiccup fit which wouldn't halt. McAllister, Mookie, and Sullivan tried not to do so, but couldn't help laughing as Marty drank gulps of water trying to stop. Pushing his way out of the booth, Marty lay on the floor of the café, closing his eyes, his body stirring with each jerk, until finally the conniption stopped. Everyone inside the cafe had been staring at the scene before them, as if watching a movie unfold. Then Marty got up, asking for his check. With the bills paid and the show over, the men returned outside, heading for home. It was just another winter night in Pollard Creek.

Mookie followed the caravan back to Railroad Bridge. Parking on the access road along the tracks, the men hiked over the trestle in the black moonless night. A fading flashlight guided them through the returning rain. McAllister carried Mookie's pack and sleeping bag, while Mookie leashed and coaxed Meatball over the metal grating of the bridge. Deep below, the roar of Laughlin Creek cut the silence of the night. Reaching his cabin, McAllister stoked up the fire, laying out a foam pad and pillow for Mookie to sleep. He found an old wool blanket for Meatball, placing it by the stove. Meatball circled over the blanket, before plopping down to rest. Mookie spread his sleeping bag and took off his boots. Rolling final cigarettes out of a can of Top, the men spoke in lowered tones amidst the flickering kerosene light.

"Did you drive all the way from La Honda, today?" McAllister asked. "You must be bushed."

"No, I just came up from Grants Pass," Mookie responded. "I actually got in late last night, and stayed at Valerie's house in town. Then, I just hung out with her for the day, fixing up some things around her place. She said to say hi to you guys."

"No kidding," McAllister said. "How's she doing?"

"She's doing good, Sean. She's doing real good. You know, bro, I really like Valerie a lot."

"You've always liked Valerie a lot," McAllister responded. "I've always known you had a thing for her." McAllister stubbed out his smoke, climbing into his bunk. "So what are your plans now?"

"I don't know. Get the rest of my stuff from the Farm I guess. Valerie offered to let me stay for awhile if I needed a place. But I wanted to ask you guys first."

McAllister stretched out in his sleeping bag. "Tell her we said no, and kicked you out. I'll write you a note if you need one."

"Yeah, like she'd believe that story," Mookie laughed. "But after I go to the Farm tomorrow, she said to come back into town and she'd make me dinner."

"That sounds like a serious invite to me," McAllister acknowledged. "You know, Mook, Valerie is damn nice woman. And I've always figured she liked you, too. Tommy and her are really close, you know that. But it's not the same thing, and it has always been that way. I think Tommy would be happy that Valerie might find someone she cared about. And lately, he's been skulking up a girl named Carley who lives up on Paradise Creek. Anyway, if that's what you might be asking, I'd say not to worry. You should spend some time with Valerie. You can always come back and stay here with us if necessary."

"I like her son," Mookie said. "Canyon's a good kid."

"All the more reason," McAllister answered. McAllister turned on his side, pulling up his sleeping bag tight to the shoulders. "Good night, Mook."

"Thanks, Sean. See you in the morning."

The Northwest winter battled its regiments deep into the spring of 1977. But the sun began marshalling reinforcements, sending budding leaves of oak, alder, maple, and madrone marching forward. It mustered flowers of lily, trillium, butterweed, camas and wild rose to the rescue. Cadres of Indian paintbrush, iris, purple loosestrife and azalea answered the call. The wild rivers of the Siskiyou joined forces, gathered ammunition from melting snowcaps, before tearing across the territory in frontal assault. Victory came late, but come it did, arriving to cheering crowds of shirtsleeves and shorts, of serpentine garden soils turning over in relief. The song birds again sang praises of joy, and waterfowl soared overhead in triumphant salute. The gray somber darkness of the enemy had been vanquished, the liberty of warmth and light restored for all to share.

For the first time in years, Sean McAllister dug out his baseball glove from a wooden crate in his panel truck. He oiled up the leather, joining a team of similar misfits from Pollard Creek and Solace Valley, itching to play. He put in a small garden of vegetables at Railroad Bridge. He helped Marty with the pot patch, Sullivan and Freddie with the Alaskan mill. He took a three day rafting trip down the Rogue River with friends. He made a trip to Ashland to see a Shakespearian play. He drank and danced on warm summer evenings in Grants Pass, played volleyball on Saturdays when there wasn't a softball tournament to compete. From time to time, he met a new girl, getting lucky as they say. Always, he worked whenever he could, whenever word of mouth brought a job to do. He had no bank account, just the frivolous money in his pocket that came and went. He read more Miller and Brautigan, and Robbin's *Even Cowgirls Get the Blues*. He had no interest in politics, ignoring the issues of the ERA, of South African apartheid and nuclear power.

In between, he smoked weed while tapping to the music, went barefoot, and sometimes lazily studied the deep blue sky. He listened to crickets and frogs, the bees buzzing in the heat. He lounged by the swimming hole, walked the railroad tracks, wrote letters and took long naps in the heated afternoons. In the evenings, he played pool at the Solace Valley Tavern. He slept late on Sunday mornings. Sean McAllister was twenty-seven years old, and his life was on a vacation of intent. His future stretched no further than the very next day.

But deep deep down, a faint shallow voice tried to call to him. McAllister was never quite sure when it might speak. He didn't want to listen, and that was that. Still, it kept coming now and again. He knew the voice had something to say, but it would just have to wait, he was having too much fun. In late August, he began preparing for going north again to Washington. He pulled the panel truck to Friendly Frank's Auto Yard on the edge of Pollard Creek. With Frank's help, and the other guys working on their rigs, he replaced the head gasket and radiator. The panel was ready to go. He called Ivan Jakes at the Lucky Girl Orchard, saying he was on his way. A cabin would be waiting. Once again, he crossed the great Columbia River. He was headed for the apple country, the work and the new people it would bring. The voice grew quiet, at least for a time.

Valerie Williams sat on the living room couch at her home in Grants Pass. Across from her, leaning forward on a cushioned chair, sat her dear friend, Tom Sullivan. Valerie watched silently as he rubbed the palms of his hands together, staring at the floor, taking in the news.

Raising his head, his eyes met hers and he spoke.

"I guess I always knew this day would come, but I suppose you are never prepared when it finally arrives." Tom Sullivan paused for a moment, before continuing. "You know how happy I am for you, for Canyon and Mookie, too. He's such a good guy. But it will be hard not having you around, not being close. I can't exactly explain it, but it will feel like something big will be missing in my life." Sullivan let his body fall back into the chair, his hands gripping the arm rests. "Have you told your son?"

"Not yet," Valerie replied. "There will be plenty of time for that. Mookie won't start school until January, but of course he's been accepted, and we have arranged for some married student housing. Hopefully, we won't have to show them proof. And the elementary school is within walking distance of the complex, so Canyon will be close. But there's no need to worry him now. If he begins to figure things out on his own, then I'll sit him down."

Tom Sullivan sat silent, lost in thought. Then he continued. "You know, I just saw this memory of you. You were out in the back of the yellow house on Main Street, trying to split that damn oak firewood that I brought you one time. You didn't know I was standing in the driveway watching, but you were cursing like a sailor." Sullivan chuckled. "It was funny as hell. I guess you won't have to do that anymore in Tucson." He looked up and smiled her way.

Valerie laughed. "That wood was brutal," she sang, "but it burned so good. I did make you chop the rest of it up, thank god."

"Has Mookie told Sean? You know he left for the apple harvest just the other day."

"No, we weren't sure about things until after he left. Is it true you are going to follow him up to Washington and do the work? That's what Mookie has heard."

"Yeah, I'm going to go. Sean's always talking about how much fun it is to be up there. Said he could hold me a spot if I wanted, and stay in the cabin with him. You know, Val, I haven't been anywhere in so long a time. And Marty and Freddie can hold the fort. The crop is looking really good. Marty won't be going very far for awhile, which is probably okay in more ways than one."

"Is he still drinking too much?" Valerie asked.

"Yeah. And being a whore whenever he can. So staying at home until the patch is pulled will be good for him. Of course, after that is done, look the hell out."

"Do you worry about him?"

"Sure, I do. He's as reckless as ever. But Marty is Marty, you know that."

"I guess so," Valerie mused. "People will be who they are. There isn't much anyone can do. I just know he's never been quite the same since Celia went away."

Tom Sullivan rubbed his chin back and forth with his hand. "Yeah, you're right about that. But like you said, what can anyone do, it is what it is." Sullivan looked up and met Valerie's eyes. "You know, Val. It's just a lot of us guys dealing with the shit. And each one of us in our very own way. Nobody has the right to tell the other what's best, if you know what I mean."

"I know," Valerie answered. "I understand. I've seen it with you."

Valerie got up off the couch to change the subject. She poured two cups of coffee off the kitchen stove, brought them back into the living room. She handed one to her friend, sitting back down. "And, Carley?" she asked. "It's going good I hope. Is she okay with you going to Washington?"

"Yeah, I guess so. We get along pretty well. In fact, in many ways she's a lot like you. She does her own thing. Carley doesn't need a lot from anyone most of the time. And she puts up with my moodiness, I suppose."

"You're not moody," Valerie responded. "You're just distant sometimes, like you went to another place. But it's always another place that no one else is allowed to go. Still, you are getting a lot better, Tom. You really are. I can tell."

"Am I? Well, that's good to hear." Sullivan paused. "Valerie, do you really truly know how much I will miss you. I've always felt that you, and me, and Canyon, we came to this place together. I mean, not exactly, but close enough. It's something that we have always shared. It will be so different now, with you being so far away. Like I said, I'm happy for you, but so goddamned sad at the very same time."

Valerie held still for a moment, her head down. "I'm not leaving tomorrow, you know. But you're making me cry." She sniffled before rising from the couch. Sullivan did the same. They embraced. Nothing was said as they held each other firm. Valerie finally pushed back from his shoulder and looked him the eyes. "Little did we know when we met on that very first day, what it would become. That we would still be here today, together, with so much time gone by. That two people like us could begin as lovers, and yet care about each other enough to become best friends. Like a sister and a brother, for ever and ever. It's so unusual, but for some crazy reason, I feel it was meant to be. I'm so grateful in my life that you have never gone away."

Sullivan pulled her close again, resting his chin on her hair. "I know it sounds foolish to say, Val," he began. "But it's true, it's really true. You saved my life. After what had gone down before, you gave me a reason to find something, something worth looking forward to. I can never really explain. But if I hadn't given you a ride that day, I'm not sure I would have tried so much to make it happen. You were always the first true inspiration, you always were." Tom Sullivan closed his eyes and held the woman strong.

Part Three
Orondo
(The Blonde)

*"I keep following this sort of hidden river of my life,
you know, whatever the topic or impulse which comes.
I follow it along trustingly. And I don't have any sense of
its coming to a kind of crescendo, or of its petering out either.
It just keeps going steadily along."*

- WILLIAM STAFFORD

CHAPTER THIRTY-NINE

DOWN BY THE RIVER

Orondo, Washington / 1977

On a late September afternoon, the mighty Columbia River quietly courses its way through the dry barren highlands of central Washington State. To the west, the North Cascade range rises towards the horizon, casting majestic shadows across the landscape, blocking easy access to the city of Seattle and the western border of United States, some one hundred miles away.

Along the coast, the Pacific Ocean fronts are forced to pay their toll of rain or snow. They collide against the mountain heights, releasing their fluids upon the coastal rim. Unburdened, they rise over the Cascade ridge tops, once again catching the jet stream, before riding further across the breadth of America, leaving the land of Central Washington a dry desert terrain.

Within this rain shadow country of arid rock and sage, the Columbia River is king. It was not so very long ago, before the march of civilization and the eventual conquest of the American way, that this forbidden possession was the province of thousands of years of geologic time. As the era of the Ice Age began to warm and melt, the legendary Lake Missoula burst its incredible banks, raging west in a tormented assault of surge and power. Huge floodwaters scoured the deep Columbia canyon, creating a slice of exposed basalt and granite cliffs, carving its way to the Pacific sea. Left behind from this momentous assault, a desperate thirsty wilderness took hold. It became a land bathed in sunshine, but vacant of green fertility, a godforsaken place but for the River king itself.

Fed by mountain streams from Canada and seven states, the Columbia River took no prisoners. Its singular impulse was to tear through this fast and rugged land, acting like a dangerous whitewater bully, solely intent on its ultimate geologic imperative, to reach the salted ocean further to the west. But fresh water, whatever its own particular calling, is the nurture of natural life, the first commandment of human survival. Despite the River's ferocity, the earliest of men had no choice but to settle nearby, to fish and drink from it tributaries, to risk its perils in order to live. At the confluence of the Wenatchee River and its mighty superior, the first Native Americans made themselves a home. These people called their settlement Wenatchee, 'the place of boiling waters'. Despite their many hazards, these rivers contained a bounty and sustainability for which the people were forced to persist.

The concept of time is another of the many mysteries of life. The evolution of the universe, the creation of this holy planet known as earth, is of a history so dramatically long that the human mind cannot truly conceive. Most scientists agree that planet earth is close to 4.5 billion years old. The average life of a man or woman is but a pin drop in this haystack of such an unfathomable understanding. In comparison, the pace of a human generation, from the time of birth to the average expectancy of an eventual death, is much easier to comprehend.

At even the shortest duration, it is believed that the human migration to North America began only as far back as eight thousand years ago. In North America, roving bands of tribal homo-sapiens lived off the landed earth in the barest of survival for most of these eight thousand years. How could it possibly be, that as recently as 1876, the natives of this Wenatchee and Columbia confluence were living as they had for thousands of years, catching and drying their salmon, hunting for mammals, foraging for roots and berries, in order to endure. How could it possibly be that just a single century later, the once wild and eternally free Columbia River, including its main watershed tributaries, would be strapped down and lobotomized by over forty fortified dams, never again to run.

In what only could have been the instant of a momentary restless thought, the length of a wayward glance, or the flick of a match stick, the explosion of modern civilization had struck. And with its incredible ignition, the billion-year histories of sun and moon, of sky and season, of water and spirit, were transformed asunder. As the smoke cleared and blinking eyes found clarity and sight, the world of natural men had forever changed. This 'place of boiling waters', Wenatchee, had suddenly become a city of mortar, steel and glass. Passageways of asphalt and towering electric wire now crisscrossed its geographical domain, marked by human shelters of concrete, tin and wood. Metallic spheres of carbon-fueled elements roamed its dimensions, occupied by people of white skin, adorned in cotton fabric and synthetic cloth. Wenatchee had become a blonde and blue-eyed Christian expression of heavenly evolution, striding forward with determined resolve. What now existed was an incredible new reality, so sudden in its shape and presence, that the measure of its past seemed almost as if it could never have been.

It was indeed a new Wenatchee World, as the local daily newspaper was so aptly named. It would no longer be called the 'place of boiling waters', for a new description had taken hold. 'The Apple Capitol of the World, Nestled in the Power Buckle of the Great Northwest' the paper's banner read. The phrase had a proud and glorified ring, all its own.

Should the casual observer be blessed to view this new desert realm from high above, to look down upon its almost instantaneous metamorphosis, they might become awestruck by civilized man's technological expertise. They would be stupefied by his boundless and energetic ability to tame and control his earthly surroundings, to take nature by the force of will and creative anticipation, and thus to build a system of human provision and security never before imagined. But more than any single task, civilized man had managed to harness the unruly River king, this aortic blue-blooded artery of the Inland Northwest. Man had forcefully succeeded in wrestling the Columbia River into an economic submission for all to share.

Continuing this view from winged heights above, tripods of electrical transmission lines would be seen racing across the desert hills in every direction, humming with light and power. Checkerboard squares of green agricultural production, of potato and bean, of alfalfa and vegetable, would spread throughout the Columbia Basin as far as the eye could see. Finally, along the banks of the Columbia itself, green ribbons of orchard fruit coursed the gray-blue River's margins for miles and miles, spreading into the tarnished khaki hills as far as the water might reach. The impact of such a perspective becomes a fantastic visual expression of the productive human enterprise. It becomes a late-twentieth-century testimonial to the hegemony of man over beast, of a commanding and permanent victory over the infinitely slow and dilatory rhythms of nature herself. Civilized man had come to put the pedal to the medal, to whip into shape the lazy inertia of geologic time, to get the lead out of nature's turtle slow ass. The sands of time were now on high alert, and expected to be dutifully prepared for more of the same.

In all this fast-paced excitement, no one had even a minute of time to pay much attention to that familiar poorly-dressed woman holding a placard sign along the shoulder of the highway. But there she was again, Old Mother Nature, always protesting one thing or another. Damn, they might say, she's always such a stick in the mud. Still, one couldn't help but catch sight of her latest peculiar written missive, so stark in its orthodoxy, as the carbon burning spheres went flying by. The words were simple enough. 'Speed Kills'.

U.S. Highway 2 is the most northern route of national highway in the continental United States. If one were to begin their transcontinental journey at its western terminus, they would do so near the city of Everett, Washington, a municipality north of Seattle along the banks of the Puget Sound. Heading east, the highway ascends the heavily timbered Cascade Mountains over Stephens Pass. Crossing the pass, the highway begins a descent through the sharp alpine canyons of the Wenatchee River, until reaching the city of similar name. At Wenatchee, the highway turns north for about twenty miles, flanking the Columbia until reaching the tiny hamlet of Orondo. There, the highway turns east, leaving the River behind. Climbing up through a steep rocky canyon, it crests upon a high wheatland plateau. Under this grand reach of western prairie sky, Highway 2 continues its eastern traverse across the breadth of the American destiny.

But what of Orondo, that eye-blink of a roadside junction left behind on the River's edge? The village is remembered as nothing more than a tiny speck of human populace, garnished with a zip code, a couple of gas pumps, and an old weathered grocery store surrounded by a dozen modest clapboard homes. On a sky blue and warm September afternoon, the community hardly registers a gentle pulse, a faint but collective beat of the heart, almost silent, yet somehow distinct. At this junction with US 2, a more meager stretch of two-lane blacktop has continued along the River's eastern shore, pointing north toward Canada. On each side of the road, acres and acres of green apple orchards bracket its trail, heavily laden with spectral reddish orbs, waiting to be picked. Perched above this ribbon of green, tarnished desert hills surround the River canyon, hammered dry by a summer of heat. The geography of this locale seems comfortably sheltered from the rest of the world. Yet, a quiet beat goes on. Yes, there is life here. Amongst this strangely beautiful dominion, the harvest has begun.

Off the quiet highway, a packed gravel road pierces through a curtain of trees, finding the Lucky Girl Orchard. As if entering a cocoon, the gravel path opens to a wide section of hardened dust and dirt, of open sheds and outbuildings, amidst the scurried activity of men and machine. Overhead, the midday sun revels within a background tarp of azure blue. Ivan Jakes stands alone in the center of the action, an apple picking bucket hanging from his shoulders. Before him rests a chorus of plywood fruit bins, filled with freshly picked golden delicious apples. As Ivan inspects and levels the fruit, his main ranch hand, Lonnie Mosher, runs the fork lift. With the speed of an experienced operator, Lonnie slides the forks under the bin pallets, raising the cargo aloft, gingerly stacking the bins onto the open bed of a semi-trailer parked in the yard. As Lonnie does his work, the beaten dust of a fading summer hangs like a fog in the afternoon air.

Today would be the last of the Golden Delicious harvest, these remaining bins the final load for the season. Once the loading was complete, Lonnie would drive the semi-trailer rig to a contracted packing shed located in the city of Wenatchee. There, the fruit would be culled, washed, waxed and graded, before being boxed for storage in huge refrigerated or controlled atmosphere warehouse buildings. As time went by, the fruit would later be trucked or railed for sale across the country and the rest of the world. Yet today, here in Orondo, these last moments of the Golden crop were only an early juncture in the harvest routine. Many more acres of the Red Delicious, Winesap and

Rome varieties remained ripening in the orchard trees. Much more work lay ahead in the coming weeks.

So far, the annual harvest at the Lucky Girl Orchard had gone pretty smooth. The Goldens had come to fruit in fair time and pleasant size. This year's picking crew had done a good job of getting the fruit off the trees with little bruising, and at a healthy measured pace. Ivan Jakes, the longtime manager of the Lucky Girl, had only been forced to run off three male pickers so far this season, men with no respect for the fruit or the work. Ivan didn't enjoy the task of sending a picker and sometimes his family down the road. But years of experience had made the unwanted chore easier, and Ivan was quick to spot those with a careless intent.

An apple grower could not afford to be forgiving this time of year. The quality of the fruit was the bottom line in this business and could not be compromised. The perils of weather alone were enough of an uncertainty, not to mention the growing competition and market forces of the industry. Those were factors that were out of Ivan Jake's control. But quality and condition were an absolute must. The apple harvest was the bread and butter of the Orondo Valley, as well as the value of Ivan Jakes work and family for a long many years.

Ivan backed away from the final bin as Lonnie slid the forks underneath. He swung the fork lift up and around, before speeding off toward the trailer bed. Ivan checked his watch. It was just past one-thirty. His wife, Sally, was in the house totaling bin tickets for the crew. Ivan had told the pickers to come by between three and four o'clock for their checks. Ivan hoped this would give Sally enough time to finish her work. The timing would also give the crew enough of a window to cash their checks by evening. Many of the pickers would be up to the house by three o'clock sharp, you could always count on that. Either way, Ivan would make sure the pickers got paid.

Ivan caught sight of a hawk swooping across the back edge of the orchard. He watched the raptor glide low over the tree tops, before rising up into the harsh rock of the desert hills beyond, disappearing into the glare of the afternoon sun. In another six weeks Ivan himself would be deep into the scattered pine hills of this Okanogan country. He would be away from the busy work pressures of the harvest, hunting with his rifle and pack supplies, perhaps enjoying the peace of an early winter snowfall. Ivan Jakes looked forward to those quiet days ahead.

Still, there was much work to do, this work that made things good in life. The work put food on the table, helped raise the kids, made possible the little pleasures that his family could afford. Ivan Jakes had been raised with this work, and often prayed that it would always remain. Years before as a child, when the wind blew dust thick across his daddy's Kansas farm, they had been forced to leave for the work. In between, there had been years of miles and migrant camps, until the family could finally settle in Orondo, and things had gotten better. Although those days were long in Ivan's past, a deep fear of uncertainty would forever haunt his reflections. God willing, he would never have to move again. But he knew full well that the vagaries of the future would never be his to say. And God was never likely to give you even a peak of what might be in his heavenly plan.

Lonnie ran the forklift over to the open equipment shed, parking the machine underneath. Climbing down off the lift, he walked over to Ivan, smiling a craggy grin through several missing teeth. Lonnie Mosher had been with Ivan and the Lucky Girl for most of ten years. Lonnie was a damn good field man since finally giving up the bottle. His simple sense of humor, born of a naive ignorance, endeared him to Ivan and many others.

"What do you say, boss? I reckon we got those tough old green ones just about licked. And I sure like the sound of that."

Ivan Jakes returned Lonnie's smile with his lips pursed thin. But his raised eyebrows and a gentle nodding of the head displayed his satisfaction. "Things look good, Lon, real good. We've done pretty well so far."

Lonnie Mosher yanked a kerchief from his back pocket. Pulling off his baseball cap, he wiped his head of sweat. "I can tell you those hippies down in the cabins are pleased those green ones are over," Lonnie snickered. "They were saying all kinds of crazy things this morning. They were topping off their bins like they were putting a baby down to sleep. Telling me to tractor those last bins out real slow, Lonnie. We don't want those New York City people to have a dented apple you know. Funny stuff like that."

Ivan Jakes cocked his head toward Lonnie, giving him a questioning look. But he let his mouth curl upwards to show he understood. "Pretty good crew so far, Lon. But you know, today is payday, and that will be the test. We'll just have to see how many we got come Monday." Ivan checked his watch. "Listen Lon, you go ahead and get some lunch. I'll strap down the load. After you make the run to town, you're off for the day. I'll be sure Sally has your check by the time you leave. And the kids can make the irrigation moves this evening. I'll have you take care of that tomorrow night, since Sunday will be a school night now."

"Thanks, boss," Lonnie returned, unconsciously tipping his hat. And it's okay for the wife to ride along?"

"Sure, Lon, there's no need to rush back home."

Ivan watched as Lonnie Mosher turned, walking out toward one of the tractor paths leading into the orchard blocks. Further down the path was the single-wide mobile home Lonnie and his wife Esther had shared as husband and wife for the last seven years. If Lonnie Mosher hadn't given up the sauce, hard to say where he might be today. Lonnie was a good man, but he was a better man without the drink. Ivan walked over to the tractor trailer, strapping down the load. Climbing into the cab, he pulled the truck over to the corner of the yard. When Lonnie Mosher returned, he would be ready to make the run to town.

"New York City," Ivan Jakes said to himself, heading back toward the equipment shed. Yeah, there was a damn good chance that some of the Lucky Girl fruit would end up in that big eastern city that Ivan Jakes had never seen. In fact, Ivan had never been east of the Kansas state line, and he guessed he never would. But Lon was right. Those young hippie pickers down at the cabins were surely a different lot. They had started coming around the last several years. The men, wearing their long hair and scruffy beards, the women walking along with bare feet and colored dresses. This season, there seemed to be hundreds of them looking for the work.

Someone had said, perhaps it was Lonnie, there had been some big hippie festival over in Montana. Lonnie said they called themselves a tribe, as if they were Indians or something. Ivan didn't have time to pay much attention, but these kids seemed to be from all over the country. Some were traveling in big painted school buses, with curtains in the windows, and stove pipes sticking out the top. Others were driving old commercial delivery trucks, or pick-ups with campers, station wagons, just about anything they could sleep inside and get down the road. This year, Ivan had to place three of the big buses down in a bin stacking area at the south end of the orchard.

Ivan knew that these kids came for the work and the money, but they didn't necessarily follow the fruit. They were different from the old white tramps and their families that had worked these orchards for so many years. But those men and women were aging now. And many, like Ivan himself, had settled into this and other valleys as the Washington fruit business had grown in size. The tramps were slowly being replaced by these wandering hippie kids, as well as the Mexican illegals who were showing up in greater numbers every year.

Ivan went to his pick-up truck, hooking up a smaller flat trailer to its rear. There would be ladders and empty bins to move to the red blocks. There would be some vehicle maintenance and irrigation to do, his two cows to milk, as well as other chores before the end of the day. Tomorrow, Bob Hunter, the packing house field man, would be out after church to check on the fruit. As far as Ivan was concerned, the reds would be ready to go by Monday without much wait. Things looked good. The cooler nights in the past week had brought on the color, and he was pretty certain the sugar content was right.

It was time to get some lunch at the house. Ivan would see how Sally was coming along with the payroll. The harvest work was pretty much dawn to dusk this time of year. Every day, but Sunday. Sundays were a different day and always would be. Sunday was a day for the Lord, and perhaps a little rest.

Down at the picker cabins and camp, work was done for the day. Trees and apple buckets had been traded in for bottles of cheap beer and a sandwich or two. The sweet aroma of marijuana hung in the air. Somewhere, a music box sent out sounds of rock and roll into the warm afternoon. Spirits were relaxed, ready for some time away from work. Pay checks would be coming soon.

Sean McAllister and Tom Sullivan shared a thinly rolled joint in the soft orchard grass, away from the cabins. The afternoon sky was a high desert blue. Tomorrow would be Sunday and a full day off. The Golden harvest was finally over. There wasn't much lot to be cranky about.

McAllister took a last hit from the joint, passing it over to Sullivan to finish. He untied and removed the blue bandana that wrapped his head when he worked. He ran his hands through his long stretch of curly light brown hair, pulling its rough tousle back behind his ears. He let himself lay back onto the warm orchard grass, lazily closing his eyes to the light of the sun. He could feel the sagging muscle fatigue of his body, the buzz from the marijuana beginning to relax his adrenaline from the long morning's work.

He could hear Sullivan rustling in the grass beside him. "I'm headed up to the bunk for awhile."

"Sure," McAllister yawned, his eyes peaking up at his friend. "I'll be up in a bit."

Lying alone in the warm afternoon sun, McAllister could hear the wiry edge of a Neil Young song spilling out from one of the cabins nearby. The song's mournful whine took him back to a memory from another time in his life, a life that now seemed so long ago.

He had thought of Mad less and less these days, it was pretty much down to little moments like this. Usually it was a song, or the tone of another woman's voice, maybe pieces of conversation or expression, little things that brought upon reflections of his times back east, and often her to mind. But Mad was easier to think about now, the deeper sense of loss having long ago been conquered by the intervention of time and distance. And though sometimes he might still feel guilty about his failures, these feelings had become easier to accept, the pain of her rejection having evaporated with the time gone by.

No one in McAllister's recent world of the Great Northwest really knew about this quiet burden he sometimes carried inside. Except Mookie of course, and Mook knew enough to let it be. There had been other women since Mad's leaving, short things, but no one with whom he could truly feel involved. Mostly, it had been more the attraction of sex and companionship, mixed in between the travels and other interests he had pursued since his migration west. But from time to time Mad's memory might appear, especially upon hearing the sound of music they had shared. And he figured it probably always would. But these days, it really wasn't so much about Mad anymore. Rather, it was more that he had failed to find a relationship with a woman with whom he could share his life. With the ending of the song, his dreamlike reverie slipped away.

As for Tom Sullivan, he sometimes had this reflection that his life was like a movie he was watching from afar. Sullivan was thinking these thoughts now, feeling a little stoned and sleepy from the morning's work. He lay propped up on his bunk in the small orchard cabin, making notes in his journal book. He had pulled off his work clothes, stretched out in his underwear, leaving the cabin door open to any fresh breeze that might come along. As he rested, making some notes of record, he felt again that recurrent sensation. What the hell was he doing up here in Washington? Was he really in this one room shack along the Columbia River on a warm September afternoon?

Shouldn't he really be back down in the hills of Southern Oregon, up on Carley's homestead at Paradise Creek, putting up wood for the winter ahead? Wouldn't he be surrounded by a similar beautiful afternoon, with a measure of sweat hugging his skin as he worked. And wouldn't Carley be nearby, this focused and practical worker bee he had somehow chosen to leave behind. He could see her now, moving with purpose throughout the property. She would be canning the last of the garden produce, harvesting herbs to dry, fixing a fence, or ordering a load of gravel for the road. There was a lot of 'doing' around Carley's place. She was the most driven woman he had ever met. As he had dutifully learned from his time at Railroad Bridge, Sullivan understood that one could spend a lifetime homesteading a piece of Oregon mountain land. There would always be something to do. In fact, that was the beauty of the whole thing, the best consequence possible, because you didn't have to think about other difficult things. There would always be a chore to distract you from too much reflection or consideration, and the uncertainties they might engender in your life.

So how the hell did he get up here, hundreds of miles north from his home in Oregon? And why? Back when he had told Carley that he was thinking of going up for the harvest, she had given him this look of discontent. But just as quickly she had said he could probably use the money. Outside of those few words, she had mentioned nothing more about it. Sullivan still wasn't sure how he felt about that response, but he knew right then he wasn't going to get any reasons why he shouldn't go. So here he was again, possessed with this feeling of watching himself go through the motions of his life. It had all started with Vietnam, and it didn't look like it might ever go away. Carley, or no Carley.

Sullivan glanced down at the journal book he held in his hands.

These thoughts of Carley, or for that matter anyone else, even this strange abstraction of watching his life unfold before him, such considerations never made his daily written pages of observation. Tom Sullivan's journal was not a diary. Rather, it was a compendium of events and factual minutia, a written record of information. There were expressions he had heard in the orchard. There were pasted pictures, matchbook covers, or torn out newspaper articles. There were bin totals, weather reports, lists of one kind or another, any kind of unique data or knowledge he found important to record. Sure, there were a few occasions when he might inject a cryptic anecdotal comment, something that might reflect some measure of emotion or perspective, but such events were rare. For the most part, the journal book was simply a detailed account of his presence at a particular place in time.

This journal keeping thing had started during his stint in Nam. He had found the exercise a necessary form of release in observing and recording his time there. But always, it had been too difficult to try and express any form of emotion within that deadly insane world. Those were thoughts he could never allow to possess him. When you're in the shit, certain feelings had to be suppressed at all costs, and there were no exceptions. To let them escape might have courted a final jeopardy, the survival of self, or the survival of others on whom one had to rely. Like most of the others, Sullivan had absolutely needed such intense denials. It helped to keep his anger and rage intact, permitting him to be fully capable of the highest final act. And that anger needed to be sustained, because it always led to action, whatever the consequence.

What Tom Sullivan had not anticipated was the plane ride home, and the stranger set of consequences to come. To return to America from where he had been, and what he had become, had been a hell of a transformation. To be expected to act like everybody else, as if nothing had happened in between. He had actually understood this ultimate irony from the moment he stepped onto the streets of Oakland. And he still knew it today, that living your life, and then trying to understand it, are two distinctly different forms of comprehension. The toughest problem was in learning how to cope with that understanding. In the years hence, all the guys who had made it back home, had been dealing with this crap in their own convoluted ways. Perhaps, for those who had not seen the shit face to face, maybe it was a little easier. But for others like himself, another battle had ensued.

For example, look at Hokey Cruthers, who spent most of his time wandering the woods of Pollard Creek, or babbling one thing or another while sitting in front of the Country Store. Then, there was Marty's close friend in country, a vet who had come home and locked himself up in his parents' garage for most of six months. Or take Rickey the Rocket Rucker, who couldn't sit still for five single minutes, always racing north and south, up and down, driving himself cuckoo most of the time.

And now there was Marty Johnson, his own dear brother, who had helped save Sullivan from the darkness of his own mind. Marty had seemed bullet-proof upon getting back from Nam, as if nothing could even faze him. But when Celia disappeared from his life, the cracks had begun to show. Each day that Marty spent closer to the edge, there was a danger for which Sullivan worried. Thank god for Freddie Jones. Freddie had been a motor pool guy, and the impact had been less. Freddie had always kept some sense of stability at Railroad Bridge. He was good for Marty to have nearby. And so Sullivan had brought this form of record keeping home with him. But he continued to leave himself out of the writing. Things might be getting better, but there was still so much more to try and reclaim.

Sullivan closed the journal firmly between his hands. He took a deep breath, laying his head back against the pillow and the bunk. So McAllister was still out there snoozing in the orchard grass. Hell, that guy could fall asleep just about anywhere. Tom Sullivan wished he was capable of such an innocent form of fatigue. Sean McAllister would probably die behind the wheel one day, just driving to the grocery store. Sullivan laughed to himself, thinking such a thing.

But that was the good thing about Pollard Creek and Solace Valley. He had met a bunch of friends and companions seemingly untouched by the troubled memories he kept hidden deep inside. They shared amongst themselves a certain innocence and belief in their lives, in their politics and view of the world. Sure, everyone had their issues and creaks of personality, traits that obviously distinguished each from the other. But hard feelings were rare, and even if so, they didn't last for long. Sullivan felt lucky to have found this place in Oregon, and he would always be grateful to Valerie for her directions, even if she herself didn't know what it would eventually become.

As for McAllister, Sullivan was happy that Sean had come to live at Railroad Bridge. McAllister was pretty low-key and easy to get along.

Although Sean didn't know all the shit, he knew he was lucky and appreciated the fact. He was an ex-college boy who had escaped the trip to Nam, and Sullivan knew it would always set them apart. McAllister had fought the war as a protester. Sean had his own stories to tell about the stateside end of the war, but he knew it was all bullshit compared to what Sullivan and others had been through. Sullivan understood that Sean always wanted to know more, to try to understand what he'd missed. But Sean also respected the secret alliance between those who had gone, that the real talk would only remain amongst those that had been. He begrudgingly accepted the fact that the outside world never need apply.

McAllister was two years younger than Sullivan, and that too accounted for some of their differences. But it was more the fact that Sean wasn't scarred by some of the bitterness that Sullivan felt within. And that made it healthy for Sullivan to be around him. McAllister was sort of playing at life these days, not giving much thought to his future, and more often than not in a positive space. It was this kind of thoughtlessness about things that Sullivan often found missing in himself. So, it was comfortable having McAllister think of things to move him. Sean had often spoken of the working fun of the apple harvest. Although Tom Sullivan remained somewhat uncertain as to why he was here, without some other compelling reason to find, he had to figure that his companionship with Sean McAllister had a lot to do with it. And for now that was good enough.

Sullivan's serious wanderings were halted by the sight of Sean McAllister, sticking his head through the open cabin door. He looked at Sullivan while letting out a heavy yawn.

"Hey, what's up? Writing in your diary again?"

"I told you, it's not a diary. I bet you fell asleep with that beer in your hand." Sullivan shifted in his bunk, putting down the journal.

"How'd you guess?" McAllister asked.

"Narcolepsy," Sullivan returned, "a recurring, irresistible, and uncontrollable desire to sleep. There is no known cure. Pharmaceutical drug treatment is the only prescribed antidote for the condition."

"So, what's the script, Doc? I'll try anything, you know that."

"Amphetamines, I'm afraid," Sullivan answered.

"Speed? Really? No shit? How lucky can a guy get? Yeah, go ahead Doc, write me up." Still standing in the cabin doorway, McAllister turned his head away from Sullivan. He raised his voice, speaking to someone outside. "Hey, Joe. Did you hear what Tommy just called me?" Joe Hulbert, the neighbor at the cabin next door, sat on the ground beside his BMW motorcycle. His toolbox was open, as he ratcheted a nut on the vehicle's rear frame. Hulbert stopped what he was doing. Turning his head toward McAllister, he answered. "No, what did he call you?"

"A nymphomaniac, Joe. No, wait a minute, I mean a narcoleptic. He called me a narcoleptic."

Joe Hulbert shook his head, but kept his focus on the task at hand. "A nymphomaniac? I don't think so, Sean, unless I've been missing something. I don't know what the other thing is, but if Tommy says it's so, I'm sure he's got it right."

McAllister turned back toward Sullivan, his arms still spread across the doorway. "A sleeping disorder, Joe, an incurable sleeping disorder. The good doctor here, he'll say just about anything to hurt a man's feelings."

Sullivan stared back at McAllister in mock seriousness, speaking quietly. "The truth shall set you free."

McAllister laughed, pushing himself away from the doorway. He walked over to Joe Hulbert and the motorcycle, looking down while his apple picking neighbor worked on the bike. "Sorry, Sean," Joe Hulbert said, "you're too freaking ugly to ever be a nymphomaniac. Perhaps a narco whatever maybe, but a nympho, no. You can forget about that."

"Thanks for the testimonial, Joe. I really appreciate it. So, are you and Linda going to town tonight?"

"Yeah, we're going to make a run to Wenatchee after the checks come out. Get some groceries and dinner. How about you guys?"

"We're going up to Chelan. Do some laundry, get some food, take in the sophisticated night life, I guess."

"Be sure and wear your black outfit, buddy. Those cowboys up there get a real hard on for a nympho in black."

McAllister laughed. "Fuck you, Joe. Shit, between you and the damn doctor in there, you have no respect for the afflicted."

Joe Hulbert finished his work, before raising his bulky wide frame upright, ratchet in hand. "How many did you get today?"

"I got four before it wound up," McAllister answered.

"Four? No shit. Yeah, I did hear you guys get out pretty early."

"Yeah, we went for it, I guess, being the last day of Goldens and all."

"Heck, Linda and I were lucky to get two between us," Joe admitted. "Neither one of us was really into it today. Fuck those Goldens anyway, they're a goddamn headache. Have you heard anything about the Reds?"

"Not yet," McAllister answered. "Maybe we'll know when the checks come out."

"Hell," Joe returned. "They'll tell us we're going to start on Monday, whether it's true or not. They don't want anybody pulling up stakes at this point in time."

"Can't argue with that," McAllister agreed. "Say Joe, how many miles did you and Linda put on this bike since last year?" Both men stood staring down at the motorcycle.

"Would you believe thirty thousand miles since we left here last harvest?"

"Jesus H. Christ," McAllister exclaimed. "Really? Where in the heck did you go again?"

"California, then Mexico, then Texas, Florida, and up the East Coast. And pretty much everywhere in between. Then we came all the way across Canada to make it to the Gathering in July. But after here, that's it. Linda says enough. We'll likely winter in Humboldt this year. She needs a house of her own for awhile."

"Man, that's a damn long time to be on the road. Guess I can't blame Linda after such a long trip. McAllister stretched his arms over his head. "Well, it's bedtime for bonzo for me. I need a nap for awhile. Have a good trip in town, Joe."

"All right, Sean, you too. But remember, black will do the trick. You'll be fighting them off all night."

McAllister popped back into his cabin. Tom Sullivan remained eased on his bunk, reading. McAllister stripped off his tee shirt and jeans. "Well, this here narcoleptic needs more rest," he joked. Fronting the end of the bunk bed, McAllister climbed up on the rack above Sullivan. The mattress and metal frame sagged as he lay himself down.

"What's up with Joe?" Sullivan asked.

"Doing some preventative maintenance, I guess," McAllister answered. "They're going down to Wenatchee. Can you believe that he and Linda have put thirty thousand miles on that bike since last year. No wonder she is ready to settle down for awhile."

"He's ready too, I bet," Sullivan responded. "He just won't admit it."

"The Easy Rider goes home," McAllister yawned. "Hey, I got to sleep for awhile, then we'll get ready to go, is that okay?"

"Fine with me," Sullivan answered.

Sean McAllister, his eyes beginning to close, watched as a fly landed on the strip paper that hung from the ceiling in the corner of the cabin. The fly began an accelerated buzz as it fought against the sticky adhesive of the strip. All to no avail. It would just become another dead fly in a long season of dead flies. McAllister's eyes closed and he fell again to rest.

CHAPTER FOURTY

ONE OF THESE NIGHTS
Orondo, Washington / September, 1977

THE KING OF ROCK AND ROLL WAS DEAD. A bloated human carcass, found prone on a bathroom floor, amidst a humid August afternoon in Memphis, Tennessee. For Elvis Presley, there would be no more childhood memories, no more gospel hymns to sing. No more recollections of his first audition, or the youthful joy of hearing his voice on the radio for the very first time. The King and his resonant croon were now silenced, the hips stilled. Fame had come calling for Elvis Presley, like a traveling salesman with a knock on the door. And with its appearance a boyhood innocence was lost. With fame, a devil's bargain is consummated, beginning with the very first Cadillac driven off a showroom floor. A celluloid dye is cast, and the rest is all downhill.

Sometimes, with fame, the pain of living grows harder every day. It leaves you alone amongst the delirium of an outside world, seeking from you what you cannot find for yourself. Happiness, or at least contentment, is the cost that must be paid. No amount of Cadillacs, nor homes, nor sequined capes that glitter in the light can stiff the bill. Fame demands the ultimate price. Fame is a loan shark, where no excuse can avoid its demand for repayment. And so, the heart is broken. It stiffens and grows cold. Only the legend and the music are able to live on. Elvis Presley was dead. At the time of his passing, Elvis Presley was forty-two years old.

As the Saturday afternoon passed, the Lucky Girl migrant camp awakened from its slumber. Whether in small groups, or by themselves, the pickers herded toward Ivan Jakes' ranch house to collect their pay. As quickly as a check was handed over, a car or truck engine would crank to a start, heading down the dusty lane to the highway beyond.

Sean McAllister didn't move as fast. Sluggish from his afternoon nap, he packed his bag of laundry before heading for the shower. The Lucky Girl bath house was like a concrete bunker, with a cold cement floor, exposed lead water pipes and rusted drains. A single light bulb illuminated the dark interior. Everyone in the picker camp called it the 'bomb shelter'. It was not the place for a warm lazy cleaning, nor a comfortable shit and shave. Those finer things in life weren't necessarily available in this low-end working world. Orchard housing accommodations made a cheap motel appear like a gilded palace, any day of the week.

Dressed in a light sweater and jeans, his curly brown hair brushed out long, McAllister cut through the weathered row of orchard cabins up toward the ranch home of Ivan Jakes. On his way, Tom Sullivan approached, returning. Sullivan looked tanned and cleaned. His hair was pulled back in a pony tail. He was dressed in a colorful shirt and Levis, stretching down to his huarache sandals and dark socks. In his arms, he carried a gallon of fresh milk, complements of Ivan Jake's dairy cows.

"We'll take the panel," McAllister spoke. "You can load your laundry, I'll be right back." Reaching the house, Sally Jakes sat at a picnic table in the yard of the home, surrounded by bundles of bin tickets and other paperwork. A lone remaining picker stood over her, waiting as she counted the bin tickets, before writing up the receipt and check for his labor. McAllister entered the gate of the white picket fence, waiting his turn. When it was time, he received his pay.

As McAllister returned to the gate, Ivan Jakes was heading towards the house from the loading yard above. Watching the man approach, McAllister could feel the strength of Ivan Jake's persona as their paths neared. An orchard farmer like Ivan Jakes was the ultimate jack of all trades. There was little in the daily mechanics of the Lucky Girl Orchard that McAllister hadn't seen Ivan Jakes handle in his previous years of the harvest. Dressed in his gray coveralls, his worn boots and John Deere baseball hat, Ivan Jakes was the boss of his world, and he wore the title well. With his broad physique and serious expression, Ivan exuded a sense of strength and capability that might be intimidating on first impression. Although for Sean McAllister, this impression had long ago waned with familiarity. What remained was Sean McAllister's abiding respect for the man's honesty and decency of character.

"How's it going, boss?" McAllister asked. Ivan Jakes held a binding tool in his hands, appearing to be lost in thought. McAllister's gaze was often drawn to the size and power of Ivan Jake's meaty rough hands, which were browned and weathered with age.

"How you doing, son?" Ivan responded. Then, returning from his distraction, Ivan Jakes realized he was speaking to McAllister. "Oh, Mr. McAllister," he nodded in recognition. "Don't tell me you want more money again? It surely couldn't be another payday already, I can tell you that." Ivan Jakes let a thin smile purse his lips.

"Yes, it is, boss. Another payday. Sorry, but it's true."

"Well, a man deserves his wages, Mr. McAllister. I suppose that is true as well."

"Will we be getting to the Reds on Monday, Ivan, do you know yet?" McAllister took the opportunity to ask. Ivan Jakes paused at the question.

"Well", Ivan drawled, "we probably won't know until tomorrow. Tomorrow, the field man from the co-op will be out to check some of the blocks. But I'd say from the looks of things, we should be able to get started."

McAllister was sure that Ivan Jakes knew from his years of experience that the color was good, the sugar content acceptable, at least in a few of the orchard sections. It just wouldn't be Ivan's call. "Are most of the crew sticking around, Mr. McAllister? Do you happen to know?"

"Far as I know, boss" McAllister answered. "Haven't heard any talk."

"Well, I've seen them come and go on a paycheck, so you never really know."

"I guess you're right," McAllister responded. "But I'm good, Ivan. You can count on me. I'll be with you till the last one comes off the tree."

"I'm always pleased to have you, Mr. McAllister, always pleased indeed."

McAllister rumbled the panel truck out the dusty gravel drive of the Lucky Girl Orchard. He pulled onto the highway, heading north toward Chelan. The late September afternoon was beginning the hint of evening. As the panel truck began to reach speed, the fresh air of the canyon blew through the open windows of the cab. The dry odor of desert sage mixed with the sugary smell of ripening fruit. Highway 151 was a medium two-lane haul along the east side of the Columbia, past acres and acres of deep green orchards, set in sharp contrast to the rough scrub and rock desert hills beyond. On both sides of the River canyon, the rugged ridges and cliffs began to darken in shadow, the sun making its final fall over the unseen Cascade rim to the west.

Five miles north of the Lucky Girl, the drive began to pass the expansive orchard operation of Dale Austin. Here, the roadside became lined with the tall green sway of Lombardy poplar trees. The trees circled the perimeter of the vast orchard complex, stretching down along the River, a bordered canopy that guarded the precious blocks of fruit from the periodic harsh canyon winds. To the left and below the road, the Austin Fruit Company swept gracefully down to the River's edge, a grand design of trees and buildings set in perfect order and time.

If there was to be a kingdom in this Orondo world, the Austin Fruit Company would fit the characterization. Not so much for the size of Dale Austin's orchard complex, but rather the man's commercial impact on the industry of the apple. Within the larger arena of an accelerating corporate fruit-growing market, Dale Austin was indeed a pioneer.

The Austin Orchard was where young Jesse Simmons had made his new home. Although Jesse still spent some time at the Mulcahey Farm in Pollard Creek, these days he mostly resided in Orondo, working and learning the trade of the orchard life. Jesse had described to McAllister how Dale Austin was cutting out old blocks of the Red and Golden delicious varieties. He was replanting those blocks with dwarf and semi-dwarf trees of newer varieties, the Australian Granny Smith, the Japanese Fuji, and the New Zealand Gala. Austin was leading the way in grafting new stock onto older root systems, experimenting with trellis growing techniques of post and wire, and raising the ante in specialty market production.

But Dale Austin was not a man prone to the desires for organic agriculture. Austin spurned the movement toward a potentially safer production of the fruit. He remained a firm believer in the science and application of pesticides, insecticides, herbicides, and other chemical interventions. These products were the savior of the apple. They made the bloom safer and disease-free. They allowed the apple to grow faster, redder, and stay longer on the tree until it was picked. As often denotes a man of such renown, certain myths gather in the transfer of tales through the language of human exchange. Jesse didn't figure it was really true, but the gossip of the valley told a story of how Austin had once swallowed a full glass of the controversial herbicide 2-4D, just to prove the safety of its righteous application. One thing was for certain, very few people could spend much time in the Orondo Valley, or work its orchards and packing houses, without having heard the name of Dale Austin, then forming an opinion of the man, whether it be of fiction or of truth.

The panel truck continued its hum over the asphalt blacktop, heading toward the Saturday night ahead. At the turnoff to Bray's Canyon Road, two battered gas-guzzling American sedans sat waiting at the stop sign by the highway. The cars were stuffed with men wearing jet black hair, their skin a rugged shade of brown. The cars rode low with the weight of their foreign cargo. The California plates revealed an identity that was growing increasingly common in these northern orchards of fruit, not more than two hours away from the Canadian border.

The first Mexican braceros were arriving in the Orondo Valley. Although many had come to America over the last couple of decades, few had ventured this far north from their border to the south. But the fruit business was growing fast, and the need for additional labor was increasing. Possessing no more than a battered suitcase and the clothes on their skin, the braceros came ready to work one final harvest, before returning south toward home.

The Bray's Canyon Road wound itself east off the highway, climbing to a higher bench of orchard fields. This was where the true migrants of the harvest toiled for the man by day, before sleeping in empty wooden bins at night. Situated above the River valley, the Lucky Badger Orchards were emblematic of the fast-growing corporate farms of America. Hundreds of acres of dwarf and semi-dwarf trees were reaching production, capitalized with tax-sheltered limited partnership investors, flooding a now global market with apples from Washington State. There wasn't what one might call blocks in the Lucky Badger Orchards, more like sectors. An apple picker would be given a bucket and a number, before disappearing into the industrial state. Alone amongst the trees, he would be left to hope for an empty bin, a tractor, a single moment of personal attention. But more than likely he would be blessed with a bad lot of ragged trees and an asshole for a bin checker. As far as most hippie pickers were concerned, the Lucky Badger was lucky all right, lucky for somebody else.

Forging further north, the tightness of the River canyon began to give way, opening to the big broad skies of the west. McAllister watched as the dark shadows from the falling sun inched higher up the slopes of the distant hills. Sunset strands of orange and red reflection colored the thin clouds of a cirrus sky. As the chill of evening began to take hold, he and Sullivan rolled up the open windows of the truck. With the exiting sun, the sky lost its brilliant blue, replaced by the soft pale white of twilight. Sean McAllister loved this country and the mysterious sense of lonesomeness it could evoke. The landscape seemed to stir with a sense of the spiritual, of something grand and eternal in its breadth, imbued with other-worldly notions so far beyond the mundane idiosyncrasies of a daily mortal life.

In moments of reflection like this, it was hard to comprehend one's own mortality. Hard to conceive that the length of your lifetime was nothing more than a single breath, when compared to an awesome geologic history measured in millions of years. It was difficult to imagine this River canyon, carved by shifting continental plates, seared by glacial ice, and scoured by raging floodwaters, would so swiftly have to endure the arrogant human presence of a late-twentieth-century America. Yet here they were, he and Sullivan, crossing this enormously infinite territory in a tiny metal sphere of internal combustion, smoking their way like a couple of unwanted insects across the desert floor. Who could have blamed Mother Nature for lifting her foot, then stamping out this nuisance within the home of her beloved creation. In a way, their presence was an infestation of human activity. They were unwelcome intruders amongst a grander beauty of universal intent.

For McAllister, it was a little confusing to be contemplating such vast and unknowing considerations. In one way, such speculations were interesting to consider. On the other hand, they were notions he did not want to be burdened with trying to grasp. He could imagine his friend Rita pondering every minute of these eternal questions, with her face worn weary by their constant unknowing. Unlike Rita, McAllister's own contemplations could only go so far. Otherwise, he didn't feel compelled to finding the answers. The day to day complexities of regular life were intriguing enough. Still, in these peculiar moments when he inhaled the incredible natural beauty and mystery of this earth, he couldn't help but wonder.

As for the social and cultural intricacies of the people that now held sway in this land of North Central Washington, that was a different story. Much akin to its tanned desert scablands and the deep blue River, this was surely a blonde and blue-eyed country. Here, the dominant white ethos of American culture continued to persevere. McAllister could sense the conservative individualism of a Calvinist doctrine, secure in its belief, clear in its conscience. Like his boss, Ivan Jakes, it was a neighborhood strong with the presence of a righteous god, comfortable with the professed orthodoxy of a fundamental and moral Christian order.

Throughout his four seasons of work in this orchard country, McAllister had witnessed and engaged the character of its people. He had seen the hardened cut of their faces, their red-tanned complexions born of bright sun and the farmer's work. Make no mistake, this was farm country. It might be a little different in setting from one's more familiar farmland vision, but it was farming all the same. These people had made their lives here, immigrants all, as field hands and tractor drivers, spray men and fruit packers, truckers and merchants. Ever so slowly, they had become the Grange, the town hall, the congregation, and certainly the cops. Over time, many had become owners of their stock and trade. It was easy to sense the moral certainty of their calling, the fundamentals of a safe and sacred life.

But what made these folks particularly unique, were the peculiar ironies with which they had to contend. It was simply called the harvest season. And it brought to this insulated inland world a rogue's gallery of exotic transient peoples each and every year. There were the gradually disappearing fruit tramps of a hobo generation, who hadn't yet given up the migrant life. There were the hippies of the Rainbow Family, whose own beliefs predicted the coming of a new spiritual age. There were other unaligned hippies, like McAllister himself, who had chosen to drop out from an oppressive mainstream world. There were veterans of the Vietnam War and the psychedelic revolution, wandering the planet in search of finding solace from trips gone awry. And finally, the increasing immigration of the Mexican braceros, further pushing north from California, honestly pursuing a piece of the American Dream. All were hardened, or lost, or searching souls, entering this church of the Jeffersonian ideal. And yet, none were cast aside. Instead, they were welcomed for the important assistance they could give.

Much like McAllister's adventure into the human conundrums of Pollard Creek and Jordan County, the milieu of the apple country was a similar invigorating escapade in both persona and expression. The journey might be akin to going to a different AA meeting each day, in a different location. You never knew who might be present, but each visit would be filled with new stories to tell. And all the stories were truly American, in their own way and time. Yet, unlike Pollard Creek, there was one thing about the harvest world and its melting pot of diversity, one thing that kept it from coming apart at the seams. And that was the work. When everyone here got right down to it, they got down to it for the money. This was the singular defining purpose, to get the fruit off the trees and the bucks in the pocket. For the one true gospel of America was clear. It was green in color and fat in the wallet, six days a week. The harvest clock was running. There was little time but to get the fruit off the trees and into the bin. And when it was over, get the truck back on the road before the cold strike of winter started freezing your ass. All in all, it was no more complex than that.

"Somebody give me a cheeseburger," McAllister spoke to the windshield, his eyes fixed ahead on the highway, the truck continuing up the road.

Sullivan had been quiet for most of the trip, which wasn't unusual. But he shifted in his seat beside McAllister, turned and looked his way. "Now, what the hell does that mean? If you're telling me you're hungry, well, thanks for the tip."

"Living in the USA", you know, that song by Stevie Miller. I was just sort of thinking how weird living in America can seem sometimes."

Sullivan held a stare at McAllister, with that feigned expression of mock seriousness he often wore. "Weird, huh," Sullivan mused. "You mean weird like the off-the-wall comments that come out of your

brain half the time. You mean, like that kind of weird?"
McAllister shook his head as he drove. "Yes, that kind of weird.
Okay? I was just thinking about some things. Geez, Tommy."
"That can be dangerous, Sean, you thinking about things.
Especially when you're driving. I get worried about you. Your mother
worries about you."
McAllister glanced at Sullivan. Then he mimicked Gilda Radner's
'Emily Litela' character from Saturday Night Live. "Never mind…."
McAllister geared the truck down as he approached the hard turn
to cross the Columbia River at Chelan Falls. The panel truck traversed
the Beebe Bridge over the River, before accelerating up a steep grade
to the plateau above, rising toward the town of Chelan. Turning on his
headlights, it was the beginning of a Saturday night.

The metal shopping cart bumped along the grocery store parking
lot, racking along with a thin cagey sound. Bags of groceries and
miscellaneous supplies pushed toward a yellow painted Volkswagon
van. Two women accompanied the cargo. A darkening night sky was
closing in on the town of Chelan. The outline of the surrounding
desert hills were drawn in shadowed contrast against the last strips of a
paling white horizon. The clear chill of evening was beginning to settle.
In the distance, the broad blue silence of Lake Chelan lapped against its
shores, settling down for a pensive night of rest.
One of the women opened the sliding door of the van before
climbing inside. She pushed out a large wooden box and drink cooler,
the other woman hefting the containers outside onto the asphalt. They
began to sort the purchases, packing the food where it needed to be.
The shorter woman poured a bag of ice into the cooler, before packing
it with perishables. The taller woman separated the dry goods in the
cart, placing them into the wooden chest. Each of them was intent on
their duties, failing to notice a dark green panel truck pulling into a
parking spot nearby.
Sean McAllister turned off the key, letting the panel rumble to a
halt. "Oh boy," he blurted, speaking to Sullivan. Tom Sullivan had his
head down, pencil and paper in hand, preoccupied with making a list
for the shopping trip. The men had already gotten their dirty clothes

washing at the Laundromat. Next stop was the grocery store, to cash their checks and purchase food for the work week ahead. "What?" Sullivan questioned, his focus still on the list.

"Oh, nothing," McAllister drawled. "Just girls, that's all."

"Where?" Sullivan raised his head. McAllister pointed through the driver's side window.

"Right there," McAllister said. "A rare species, don't you think. Two women, absent the company of men."

Sullivan leaned forward, peering through the window. "Oh yeah. I like the way you park," he responded, before returning to the list.

McAllister sat watching the women work beside the van. "Do you mind if I engage in a little picker talk? I know how much you hate such conversation, but this could be an extenuating circumstance. Okay?"

"I don't care, have at it," Sullivan answered.

Picker talk was an annual orchard addiction. There wasn't a day during the harvest season, whether you were with a fellow worker or even a new acquaintance, that picker talk was not the opening topic of discussion. But Tom Sullivan was new to the neighborhood, spending his first year in the orchards. For some reason the incessant conversations grated upon him, all this talk about good trees versus bad trees, of who was paying what amount, the often constant yackety-yack about the business of the fruit. Yet, it wasn't until Sullivan had initiated a ban on picker talk inside the cabin that McAllister realized how much picker talk dominated the daily social interaction. So much so at first, that McAllister had a hard time thinking of something else to talk about. The truth was that Sullivan actually was no less able to steer clear of such conversational exchange than anyone else. As a result, the edict had become something of a standing joke between them. Sullivan had eventually realized that it was easier to kick a heroin habit than not talk about the work.

McAllister eased his way out of the truck, a little nervous with his intentions. Talking with girls was sometimes hard, especially when one's true motivations were hardly that sincere, more truly driven by that primordial need for sexual companionship. Nonetheless, he put on his best face of false motivation and approached the van. "Excuse me," he started, "would you happen to be working the fruit around here, or are you just passing through?" The taller woman was closest to him. She looked up from the box on the asphalt, her eyes meeting his. However, it was the other woman who spoke.

"Both," the shorter woman answered, stooping over a drink cooler. She didn't look up. "We've been working in Manson, but we're about to meet friends and moving up north." The woman's tone of voice was terse and matter of fact.

McAllister heard the woman's response, but kept his eyes on the taller woman, as she rose to her feet. She had long blonde hair and an angular frame. The hair was pulled together on both sides of her ears, banded close with colored ties. The ends hung down to her shoulders and over her breasts. A blue-print dress stretched below her knees, her lower legs were clothed in long johns down to her socks and sandals. Her bare arms and hands wore the copper brown of a late summer tan. In the darkness, McAllister could not see the color of her eyes, but it mattered little, she was terribly attractive all the way through.

"How was it up in Manson," he asked? "Was it Goldens you were picking?"

Their eyes meeting again, the tall woman answered. "This is our first time," she began. "The trees were big and hard to pick."

"I'll say," McAllister responded, "especially when you first start out."

"Are you picking around here," the other woman asked? As she raised the question, Tom Sullivan came around the rear of the panel truck, walking over to the van. Before McAllister could answer, Sullivan interjected.

"Is this man bothering you?" Sullivan asked in his mock serious tone. His sudden presence drew the group's attention. The shorter woman by the cooler chuckled at the question, standing up. She didn't have an answer, so Sullivan continued. "Hello there, we're together," nodding toward McAllister. "What a nice van you have. They sure are great traveling rigs I bet. Is it yours?" The shorter woman answered yes. She and Sullivan became engaged in conversation about the vehicle. For McAllister, Tommy Sullivan's timing couldn't have been better.

"So where are you picking?" the taller woman continued.

"South of here about twenty miles, on the other side of the River near Orondo. We just finished Goldens today, and it looks like we will start into the Reds on Monday."

"Oh, that's good," the tall woman said. "We finished Goldens too, but the owner said they weren't going to start on the Reds right away, so we decided to move. We're thinking of driving north towards Tonasket."

"Well, I don't know," McAllister mused. "It might be even a later start up there."

"What do you mean?" the tall woman asked.

"The apples, they might still be into Goldens right now. Tonasket is further north, and I think the elevation is a little higher than along the River. So it could be a little later on the Reds up there. Plus, they don't have as much semi-dwarf fruit, so the trees might be bigger as well. I'm not positive, but that's what I've heard."

"You seem to know a lot," the woman responded. But we also heard they have some organic orchards in Tonasket. Terri says we should get away from so much sprayed fruit."

"Well, she's probably right about that. I've heard about those orchards, too. But I've never been up there, so I don't really know. You'd probably get lynched if you went organic in these parts. Did you happen to get sprayed?"

"No, but we heard it can happen. Mostly, we just wanted to go up there and see."

"And to meet your friends?" McAllister asked.

The tall woman looked over at her companion. She was showing Sullivan the inside of the van. "Terri just said that," the woman confessed. "We've been traveling for about a month, and we've had to be careful about things from time to time."

"I understand," McAllister said, nodding his head. "I don't blame you. By the way, my name's Sean, and that's my friend Tom." McAllister offered an outstretched hand.

"Paige," the woman returned. Their hands met gently, McAllister feeling the soft touch of a woman for the first time in a long while. The woman looked down at her groceries. "Sorry, but I've got to get this packed up. Then we need to find a place to park for the night. Are you shopping, too?"

"You know," McAllister began, "the city park is just across the street, and they have camping. It costs something, but it's pretty nice. I stayed there once before."

"Actually, that's what we were thinking, too. It would be better than starting the drive so late." Paige began to focus on packing the remainder of the groceries.

McAllister could feel the presence of this woman slipping away. There was nothing to do but go for it, to see what might happen. "If you stay at the park, perhaps you'd like to walk down and meet us for a beer in town. We've got to finish our laundry and shopping, but we're going to hang out for awhile before going back. What do you say?"

The woman looked up at him, showing a warmth of expression that wanted to say yes. "Well, thank you for the offer, but I couldn't say for sure. It depends on Terri, it's her van you know. And it's sort of been a long day. But you should tell us where you are working. Maybe we'll stop by and visit sometime. And do you know about the Barter Fair? We'll be staying around for the Fair before heading home."

"Where is home?" McAllister asked.

"Seattle," the woman answered.

"No kidding," McAllister responded. "You know, I've never been there."

"Well, you should come and visit sometime. I could show you around."

That was all Sean McAllister needed to hear. He headed for the panel truck, wrestled pencil and paper out of the glove box, drawing a map and writing directions to the Lucky Girl Orchard. As he returned, Sullivan was lifting the wooden storage box into the van. McAllister went over the map with Paige and Terri, telling them if things didn't work out up north, there was probably immediate work in Orondo, even possibly at the Lucky Girl. McAllister felt confident if he asked Ivan Jakes to take them on, Ivan would do it for him. If nothing else, maybe he would see her again at the Barter Fair in later October. With the van loaded, the women said their good-byes. Walking toward the grocery store with Sullivan, McAllister spoke. "Boy, I sure hope they come by the tavern. She is really nice."

"That might be a long shot," Sullivan answered. "I'm not sure they would come alone. But in talking with her friend, it wouldn't surprise me if they came to the orchard sometime. Who knows, it's hard to say. But I've got a feeling they really don't have a place to go."

"Well, the Barter Fair is surely on my calendar now," McAllister said firmly. At least it will be something to look forward to, rather than staring at your ugly mug every single day."

Sullivan laughed and shook his head. "I doubt it would surprise you much, but the feeling is mutual."

"See, Tommy, sometimes picker talk can have positive results. It sometimes can open doors to many beautiful things."

"Yeah," Sullivan mocked. "Whatever you say."

Chelan, Washington was like most small western towns, with a single retail corridor perched on both sides of the main street. The tops of the buildings appeared low and jagged when viewed from a distance. Chelan's downtown core had three or four taverns sprinkled within its midst. None of them were hard to find during a Saturday night in harvest season. The energy of alcohol and music spilled out the open tavern doors into the otherwise quiet night. Entering the Saturday night buzz was like joining a party already in progress. Although a little intimidating at first, there was little to do but cinch up your ego before diving right into the tumult.

Gale's Tavern was the place to start. The establishment had never really intended to become a bar. It was a former diner, now transformed into a beer and wine emporium. Its left flank was lined with booths, its middle scattered with wooden tables and chairs. To the right was the former lunch counter, bordered with rotating stools and a Formica topped bar. The taps were filled with the usual; Olympia, Rainier, Coors, and Hamms, including a harried bartender with a white apron coursing his waist. At the end of the bar was a kitchen, complete with deep fryers and grill. To the rear, three pool tables sat side by side, busy with men and games. The tavern's wall décor was adorned with beer distributor freebies, wall plaques and posters of beautiful women in swim suits, their hair long and windswept, smiling with beers in their hands.

Cigarette smoke hung like a fog below the bright restaurant lights above. The jukebox's volume was turned up high, with two options to choose from. Country and Western, or Western and Country, take your pick. In the background, the sound of frozen French fries and chicken strips sizzled in the scalding grease. Two older women, the weight of their torsos swelling with age, rushed to and fro. They carried pitchers of beer and red plastic baskets of hot food throughout the cacophonous room. Last but not least, all the players were set to the stage. They were the human menagerie of the harvest season in the

Great Northwest. There were cowboy locals, hippie pickers, Mexican workers, and Chelan tavern regulars, all with a story to tell. McAllister and Sullivan got lucky, finding two vacated stools at the end of the bar. They ordered a pitcher of beer, overcome by the scene, but ready to drink and settle within.

Pouring each of them a glass, Sullivan swiveled away from the bar, taking in the crowd. "Almost reminds me of Baja," he half-shouted to McAllister.

"Baja, Mexico? How do you mean?" McAllister shouted back.

"What's the place? Oh yeah, Hussong's in Ensenada. You know, lots of gringos, Pendleton jarheads, the Mexican locals, even vendors selling their wares. That place was wilder than this, but it sort of reminds me tonight. Marty and I had way too many shots of tequila that night. We got pretty fucked up."

"When was that, anyway? McAllister asked. "I've heard you guys talk about it from time to time."

"Baja? Just after I got out. We went on a road trip down there. I was pretty fucked up in more ways than one. But the travel helped a lot. That's when we decided to head for Oregon, to look for the property."

"Huh, I never knew that. I always thought you just came up from California."

"Yeah, we did. But that's how it all got started. And I met Valerie on the way up to look. She was actually the one who steered me to scope out Solace Valley and Pollard Creek. That's how I found Railroad Bridge. I got Val to come up later, after we settled in."

"So that's how it all went down," McAllister said, taking another sip from his beer. "You know Tommy, it's really hard to believe that Mookie will be gone soon, and Valerie too. Mookie and I go way back you know, like you and Valerie. I'm going to miss him big time, like you will Val. I sure am glad they will still be around when we get back, so we can say our good-byes. Valerie is sort of like your best friend, bro. She's like a sister or something. That's going to be different for sure."

"Yeah, but what do you say, no, you can't go," Sullivan responded. "Val has always deserved to be happy with someone. It just couldn't be me. And Mookie is good, real good. I know he'll look after her and the boy. But you're right. Things will surely be different after she's gone."

"Well, at least you have Carley," McAllister returned. "And that's more than I can say for myself these days."

Sullivan looked over at McAllister, a questioning expression on his face. "Hey, you know well enough, Sean. It's not always what it's cracked up to be. Carley's great, I like her a lot. But what the hell would I being doing up here, if I really knew for sure? At least you don't have to worry about those concerns, so don't go all slobbering in your beer over things."

"I get it. I figured as much. You know, it sure would nice if those girls showed up. Probably won't happen though."

"Have a little faith, buddy. You never know. The worst that could happen is that you'll never see her again." Sullivan joked. "At least the blonde will never have to be labeled as your future ex-old lady." Sullivan laughed, bumping McAllister with his elbow.

"Gee, thanks," McAllister whined. "Thanks a lot. Why the hell would I need a new girlfriend when I got you around? Tell me that, mister no picker-talk."

Sullivan drank down the remainder of his beer, before pouring another glass "You wait, brother. I bet you'll see her again. Maybe not tonight, but trust me, I got a good feeling. Like I said, I talked with Terri. We hit it off. I'm counting on a certain possibility that doesn't include you, but it just might benefit you all the same. So stay here with the beer. I'll put a couple of quarters on the table and be right back."

Sullivan got up and walked away toward the pool tables. McAllister turned on his stool, fronting the bar, pouring another beer. He hoped that Sullivan was right. Maybe he would get to see the girl again. But more remarkable was Tommy Sullivan's frame of mind, and the length of his conversation. It wasn't very often he had that much to say on one occasion. Actually, it felt really good. Sometimes, with Sullivan, you almost felt as if you were talking to yourself, he had so little to say. Deep down, McAllister knew Tom Sullivan was a real friend, one he could count upon. Just that sometimes he was so mute, you weren't really sure. This was better, way better. As McAllister began to surface from his thought, he heard a voice speak beside him. "Sure are a lot of granola heads in this bar, tonight." McAllister turned his head to the right, uncertain of what he might find.

The rugged face of an older man stared into McAllister's grill. The look wasn't angry but more mischievous in its expression, like a smart-ass grin waiting for a target to find. "Excuse me," McAllister questioned?

"Ah, nothing pal. Just pulling on your chain a little. How you doing? You up here for the fruit? What's your name?"

McAllister felt relieved that the man's initial comment wasn't forcing a predicament. He answered the last question first, raising his right hand open as a greeting. The two men shook hands. "Sean," McAllister said.

"Sean?" the man queried. "Is that like an Irish name, or what? Not many fellas with that name around here. What's your buddy's name, by the way, there in back?"

McAllister was going to need a crib sheet to jot down all the questions he needed to answer. "Yep, it's Irish. My mom is as Irish as they come." McAllister nodded his head toward the back of the bar. "And my friend's name is Tom."

"Tom. All right. That's more like it. A good Christian name. What's Sean stand for, I mean in English?"

McAllister felt the urge to crack wise, but he held back just in case he might have misread the man's intentions. "It's actually Irish for 'John', just a different spelling from the English word."

"No kidding," the man said. "Well, that's something. I'll have to remember that."

The man was older, his hair cropped short, graying on the sides. His facial skin was stretched tight and deeply weathered from years in the sun. He wore a cowboy shirt, tucked into blue jeans that looked almost new. A brass buckle held center at his waist, with pointed gear jammer boots enclosing his feet. If he wasn't a Chelan local, he surely couldn't have been from far away.

"Hey Ray!" the man cried to the bartender passing by. "Get this long-haired boy and his friend another pitcher. On my tab."

The bartender, who now had a name, passed right by them, hurrying with a handful of beers toward the end of the bar. "Hold your horses, Olin," the bartender demanded. "Jiminy Christmas!"

"There's no need for that," McAllister tried to say. "We can get our own...."

"No, no, it's my treat," the man interjected. "It's only money, that's what I always say."

Like it or not, Sean McAllister figured he had a new friend, and probably a story to come.

"Well, okay, thank you very much. Olin, is it?"

"Yessiree, boy. Olin Larson." The man stuck out his hand this time,

McAllister and he shaking once again.

"You're from town here, I guess," McAllister asked?

"Not these days," Olin answered. "I used to live down here with my wife and kids. But I moved up to Brewster after the divorce. I came down to watch my boy play football today. Ray there, he's my ex-brother-in-law. I just stopped in to see him and say hello. But I suppose I should have known better. There's no time for idle chit chat this time of year. Do you know Brewster?"

"That's just up north, right. I've been through it once, but that's all."

"So you been picking the fruit, I reckon. This is about the only time of year we see you longhairs around these parts."

Feeling safer, McAllister answered back. "You mean us granola heads?" McAllister asked, not being able to help himself. "You know, Olin, someone once told me. If you don't let your hair grow outside your head, then it just grows inside and clutters your brain." McAllister gave the man a gentle looking smile as he spoke. For a moment, Olin appeared stumped, not sure how to respond. So McAllister quickly got out ahead. "Just pulling your chain a little, Olin, that's all."

"Well, damn son, you got me there." The man raised his bottle of beer in salute, taking a long sip. "So where you boys working at around here?"

"Actually, we're down in Orondo."

"Which orchard?"

"The Lucky Girl, you know it?"

"Ivan Jakes' place? Damn, right. Hell of a running back, Ivan. And a good god-fearing man to boot. You won't find a better man to work for than Ivan Jakes. But I'll tell you what. That old Arkie could run you over in a heartbeat. He played up in Waterville. They were tough as hell in his day."

"No kidding, Ivan was a running back?" An image of Ivan Jake's large hands and broad shouldered strength crossed McAllister's mind. It was hard to imagine Ivan as a young high school boy, but it surely made sense he would have been as hard as nails. "I thought Ivan was from Kansas?" McAllister asked.

"Southern Kansas," Olin corrected. "Might as well be Arkansas when you're down in those Ozark hills. There are a lot of boys from back that way living in this neck of the woods. Ivan had a lot of family in those parts.

Ray, the bartender, dropped the pitcher on the bar and another bottle of beer for Olin. While they chatted, McAllister leaned back from his bar stool, looking through the plate glass window that fronted the street. There was no sign of who he was looking for. Turning toward the back of the bar, he could see Sullivan standing near one of the pool tables, engaged in conversation with some other men. McAllister figured that there had to be some kind of picker talk going down, no doubt about that. Tommy Sullivan would just have to suffer through the night.

Drinking another glass of beer, McAllister listened to the life story of Olin Larson. Olin was born and raised in North Dakota, of Norwegian heritage. His father had moved the family to this Columbia River country with the construction of the Grand Coulee Dam. Upon its completion, the family had come to Chelan. His father had gone into the irrigation business, selling and digging water pipe for the fast growing fruit business. Olin's older brothers had followed in the business, which was now headquartered in Brewster. But Olin had taken to local and long-haul trucking over the years. He had rarely been at home, his marriage failing as a result. As Olin told his story, McAllister could feel a sense of loneliness exuding from Olin's words. Perhaps it would be another Saturday night where Olin would later drive home to an empty house. Another Saturday night filled with certain regrets yet to be extinguished, waiting for the day when better times might come.

Tom Sullivan returned, having lost his pool game. The tavern continued in its heated recreation. McAllister eventually pulled away from his Nordic companion, retreating to the back of the bar with Sullivan, engaging in other interactions. From time to time, he continued to scan the front of the barroom in hopes of a particular arrival, but it did not come. However, a new acquaintance confirmed for him that the Barter Fair would be located at a small fishing lake northwest of the town of Okanogan, occurring the third weekend in October. McAllister quietly presumed he would be left with only that possibility, of perhaps finding the woman there. But as he continued to drink and shoot pool, such wishful considerations began to fade away.

On the midnight drive home to Orondo, the panel truck's headlights pierced the cool black night. The moon was approaching full, rising over the canyon hills, its light reflecting off the pensive course of the muscled River to his right. Silently, he couldn't help but wish that the evening might have allowed him a different distraction. He was hungry for the calming influence of a woman's presence. It would have been a chance to talk of things in life that men rarely chose to share. He was a little more than drunk, with the desire for sleep challenging this turn for home. At least tomorrow was Sunday, with lots of nothing to do.

CHAPTER FOURTY-ONE

SUNDAY MORNING COMIN' DOWN
Orondo, Washington / September, 1977

McAllister awoke from the night before, his body tinged with sweat. Upon first thought, he couldn't remember what day it might be. Then it occurred to him, it was Sunday. Thank the Lord. He rolled over in his bunk, his mouth dry with thirst, a thumping pressure gripping his head. A hangover was definitely underway. He tried to recall driving home, but the only image that came were white headlights aiming down the road. He squirmed with the realization that he must have been pretty fucked up, certainly a dangerous enterprise whenever behind the wheel. Instinctively, he rose, peering over to the bunk below. Sullivan's bed had been slept in, but was already empty. Lying back down, he could feel his body heavy, sluggish with the effects of the alcohol, the heat of the cabin rising with the mid-morning sun.

Another recollection crashed upon him. The woman. He could see her lovely face and brown tanned frame, the length of her torso, the strands of her pig-tailed blonde hair falling about her. Paige, such a nice name for a woman. He grabbed the pillow in his arms, rolling to his side, trying to imagine holding her in his grasp. For several moments he sunk deeper in the mattress, but the wishful thoughts couldn't last. A harsh nausea overtook him, pushing him off the top bunk and onto the floor. He wrangled with the bottled cap of aspirin, hurriedly drinking down two with a glass of water. Rubbing his face and eyes with his hands, he pushed his hair back behind his head. He slowly dragged on a pair of shorts before starting a pot of coffee on the hot plate burner. Each move was a fumbled attempt to recover and get into the day.

He opened the cabin door to the warm Sunday morning sun. Coffee in hand, he placed himself down on the front stoop outside. The orchard was quiet. There was no Tom Sullivan or other humans in sight. Then he remembered why. There were pancakes being served down at the Rainbow camp, which had become a recent Sunday ritual. Pulling himself up, he walked barefoot down the tractor path toward the circle of buses hidden in the trees. As McAllister neared, he saw the group of fellow pickers sitting together in the sun, with plates of pancakes and coffee in hand. Sullivan was sitting on an empty five-gallon bucket looking his way. Cat calls picked up as McAllister approached, his co-workers getting their kicks at his bedraggled late appearance.

Sean McAllister had never heard about the Rainbow Family until his initial journey to the apple harvest world. Many of Family's members had been all over the fruit country in the last several years, seemingly in concert with McAllister's own arrival from Oregon. The Rainbows' appeared to be a loose confederation of individuals, bonded by a general belief in the coming of a 'new age'. Their tenets spoke to the banding together of all peoples, celebrating the differences between nations, races, religions, ethnicities and cultures. They sought to collect together in the eternal oneness of all humanity, seeking tolerance, love and peace throughout the planet. By their own decision, the Rainbow Family had no hierarchies of leadership or direction, nor any commonly owned piece of the earth. These notions were in particular contrast to so many other intentional communities, ones that were built around a preferred goal of survival on a designated piece of property. Instead, the Rainbows' were a community of wanderers, forming a tribal bond based only on their beliefs.

Beyond such an emotional tether, there were no responsibilities or scriptures required to be dutifully obeyed. Each summer, over the week of the Fourth of July, their annual Rainbow Gathering was held on a requested site of Federal government land, most recently in the northwestern states of America. This was a time for the Family to join together, to confirm their tribal alliance of being, while praying for the onset of a lasting peace in the world. Many lived the migratory lifestyle of the gypsies in Europe, traveling from place to place, always finding each other through word of mouth and postal communication, until the next annual Gathering would ensue.

As well, the migratory life of an agricultural America suited their needs for basic economic survival. They came for the work, but not to stay. Unlike the wanderings of a previous Dust Bowl generation, whose homes had been dispossessed by the disasters of weather and depression, the work was not their end, only the means to their next destination. The apple harvest of North Central Washington certainly fit their bill, before moving on to places like Florida or California for other harvests, and predictably escaping the harshness of a continental winter. There's was a transitory lifestyle, each with their personal directions and pursuits, until the location of the next annual gathering was announced. Each summer, they would begin to drift like lemmings to the Mecca of their spiritual coming together, always on the Fourth of July.

McAllister accepted the offer of pancakes and another cup of coffee. The food would certainly help to cure his present alcoholic affliction. Of all the members of this roving band, he especially liked Santos, one of the Rainbow men who had settled at the Lucky Girl for another season of the fruit. McAllister and Santos had met the year before, while working the harvest. Santos' home was his 1959 Ford school bus, painted in burgundy color, a peace sign artistically inscribed on the top of its hood. Santos was a handsome man, with long brown curly hair and striking aqua-blue eyes. His young four year old daughter was a specimen of beauty and delight, the treasure of her father's love. Santos was a spectacular carver of soapstone pipes, a hunter for picture jasper and turquoise, a rock hound wherever he went. Like many of the others, he lived for the Gathering. Santos was interesting, curious, and so easy to get along. There was not an angry bone in his body, not a harsh word to his name. He was truly a gentle soul. Santos reminded McAllister of Darius, his dear friend and Zen master of the Mulcahey Farm.

Yet, sometimes, therein lays the irony of an otherwise romantic life. Santos' partner, Regina, the mother of his lovely child, appeared just the opposite in gentleness and character. Regina was a brooding self-possessed woman, extreme in her opinions, so difficult to be around. From McAllister's perspective, it was if he was experiencing night and day, good and evil, the black and white contrast of yin and yang, the poles of their two personas so contrarily defined. Regina was Santos' undeserved cross to bear. Somehow, Santos endured, blessed with an astounding measure of patience, or perhaps a remarkable well of ambivalence, either one or the other. McAllister could only wonder how the masters of fate could have put these two people together. Obviously, no doubt, for the child. Still, it was a mysterious sense of reasoning for which McAllister could not fathom. But here he was again, witnessing this unnecessary personal angst for a second harvest season. The circumstances could only leave a neutral observer scratching their head.

It had to be the hangover, the reason he was feeling so cranky toward Regina on this particular morning. A beautiful Sunday in late September, and just the sound of her voice complaining about some minor triviality, was making the silent pounding in his head more intense. But hell, he reminded himself, it wasn't as if Regina was acting out of character. It wasn't as if her difficult behavior was something he had never witnessed before. Hadn't she just put a plate of pancakes with butter and syrup down upon his lap. For crying out loud he chastised himself within, show some respect and gratitude to the woman. Still, if only she would give poor Santos a break once in a while.

After chatting for a time with the tribe, finishing his food and coffee, McAllister made his way back to the cabin. He had some chores to complete. He put up his freshly cleaned laundry from the trip to Chelan. He washed some dishes and swept out the cabin. On an old table outside, he set up his apple peeler and core device. Grabbing his picking bucket, he headed into the Golden blocks, salvaging a load of apples that had fallen to the ground. Upon his return to the cabin, Tom Sullivan was starting the engine to his pick-up camper. He and Santos were headed for a trip up Pine Canyon to the Waterville Dump. There, they would scavenge for some items of value, before driving a few desert trails looking for stone. Using the corer and peeler tool, McAllister spent some time turning the apples into connected strips of apple flesh, before hanging them with string in the afternoon sun. By the end of the harvest, he would have produced several gallon jars of sugary dried apple fruit to take home for the winter.

After cleaning up his mess, McAllister checked the oil in the panel truck. He put on his boots and a shirt, before driving out of the orchard to the highway. His hangover was finally beginning to give way. He steered the panel north to the Austin Orchard. Today would be a chance to visit Jesse Simmons and say hello. When McAllister arrived, Jesse's stubby yellow school bus was parked outside his makeshift quarters. Dale Austin had allowed Jesse to inhabit an old concession stand down by the River. Jesse had transformed the small white building into a modest little home. Jesse called it the 'Snack Shack'. A metal Coca Cola sign remained attached to the siding.

Jesse Simmons was growing older by the day. His facial features had now become more mature, although his jet black hair remained tied behind him, stretching almost to his waist. Jesse grabbed a couple of metal folding chairs, setting them in the shade out of the direct gaze of the sun. McAllister thought for a moment to defer, but then accepted Jesse's offer of a beer. Sitting down, Jesse rolled a joint. The two men passed the cigarette back and forth, catching up on the harvest, as well as news about Mulcahey Farm.

Two years had passed since McAllister had left the Mulcahey Farm. But even before he left, Jesse Simmons had gone north to Orondo, intent on leaving Derrick Mulcahey's land trip and the family behind. During the intervening period, Jesse had worked every type of orchard labor there was to perform. He had thinned, propped, and picked the fruit, even working Dale Austin's packing shed during the cold winter months. But the ties that bind blood and family always run deep, in spite of a young man's genetic need to find his own way. Jesse had returned to Pollard Creek several times, to see his mom and youngest brother, as well as others from the Farm.

Both Derrick and Jack Mulcahey had begun to acquire the orchard skills of budding and grafting fruit trees in the late winter and spring. Whenever Derrick and Jack would come to Washington, Jesse would join them to work the contracts at various orchards in the valley. Although breaking away from Derrick's authority had been a necessary circumstance as Jesse had come of age, the emotions and family bond of the Mulcahey Farm could never be forsaken. The two older men were still the only father figures that Jesse had in his life. And your family is your family, despite every crazy form of love and dysfunction that it might possess.

After finishing the joint and exchanging their requisite picker talk of the harvest, McAllister told Jesse about Mookie James' and Valerie Williams' impending move to Arizona. Jesse had continued to refer to McAllister and Mookie as the 'college boys', and they joked together about Mookie's chosen return to academia. But Jesse's own remarkable news did McAllister one better, a whopper that McAllister could hardly believe. Jack Mulcahey, the eternally loyal and supplicant younger brother of Derrick, was making a break. He was moving with his family north to the Yamhill Valley, a farming area southwest of Portland near the coastal range. Jesse explained that it was really Christine who was forcing the issue. She was pregnant with their second child, and had grown weary of Derrick's insistent manipulations. She now wanted Jack and her family to begin a life of their own. And Jack Mulcahey had finally been willing to comply. But there was more, Jesse said, and the following news seemed generally par for the course.

Derrick had blown up at the decision, his control of all things Mulcahey again showing their stripes. Jack and Christine would only be able to take their personal possessions, along with the beaten Chevy pick-up Jack had worked so hard to maintain. Everything else; animals, farm tools, food stores and money would be left behind. According to Derrick, everything on the property belonged to the Mulcahey Farm.

It didn't matter that almost everyone who had helped build the commune was gone. Jesse's mother, Betsy, and his youngest brother had long ago moved up to Cougar Gulch. Jesse's middle brother was living with an orchard family nearby in Orondo, only miles away from where McAllister and Jesse sat today. Darius had returned to San Diego. And Jerry, Christine's longtime friend, had been back and forth to the Farm, but he soon would be following Jack and Christine north to Yamhill County. Mookie and Annie were no longer present, after contributing so much to the commune's success. Finally, Jesse himself, this little kid worker bee, whose constant effort and youthful exuberance had been instrumental in the Farm's day to day operation.

And so, Derrick Mulcahey would inherit it all. Not even his brother, Jack, who more than anyone had engineered the reality of the Mulcahey Farm, would get a slice of the pie. McAllister, now slightly stoned, was lost for words. An odd sense of loss tugged at his heart. It was a feeling like one of those beautiful dreams a person enjoys, shortly before awakening from sleep. But just as quickly, the dream begins to slip away, fading so fast from memory that one is unable to recall the event. The Mulcahey Farm was over. At least over in its incredible gestation that Sean McAllister had been so fortunate to live and breathe. This sad and consequential news seemed to carry reflections that would take some time to truly comprehend. Thankfully, here was

Jesse Simmons sitting before him. Jesse was a younger man than he, and McAllister had watched as the boy had grown into his own. Jesse was like a little brother, one that Sean McAllister would always have, thanks to the Mulcahey Farm. Gratefully, something more than the difficult memories would always remain.

"So what do you think will happen now," McAllister asked?

"You know," Jesse answered. "You know Derrick, and what he will do."

McAllister paused to consider. It didn't take long. "He'll find others, am I right, other people to support his dream?"

"That's what I meant," Jesse said. "He'll do whatever it takes, at least until he finds a better place to go. Then he'll go there, and start again."

"He is who he is," McAllister mused. "I guess we got to give him credit for that."

Driving back to the orchard, McAllister wanted a cigarette. He only smoked from time to time, but for some reason he wanted to smoke and ponder the impact of this news he had so recently heard. He had the money, so he drove on past the Lucky Girl down to the Orondo Store. Pulling up to the gas pumps, he poured five dollars into the truck, before going inside. The store was pretty empty, but for Mr. Funky, the owner, and a group of Mexicans pickers, probably from the Lucky Badger. The Mexican men's grocery cart was packed high with packaged tortillas and refried beans. He'd never seen such a load. But thinking what the hell, he bought a six-pack of Ballantine beer to go with the smokes. At least he could try and figure out the pictograph riddles that Ballantine inscribed inside the caps of their bottles. Figuring these riddles always helped to pass the time. The beer he had earlier shared with Jesse had worked to cure the hangover he had awakened to start the day.

At the register, McAllister watched as Mr. Funky went through his disabling physical contortions. The man had some sort of nervous disease where his hands shook all the time, and his head never stopped moving. It was a strange sight to observe, being so odd that when McAllister had first come to Orondo, it seemed almost funny. But Mr. Funky was a good and decent proprietor, and quickly only a sense of sympathy prevailed. Mr. Funky's constant disability reminded Sean McAllister of the blessings in his own life, blessings he should never forget. On a quiet late Sunday afternoon, what better time to remember and be thankful for his own particular fortune in life.

When McAllister got back to the cabin, he decided he would take a walk up to the large flat rock that rested up in the scrub desert hillside just above the orchard. Sitting on the rock, one could gaze over a sea of treetop green, beyond to the deep blue drama of the Columbia River, and further towards the burnished blonde hills that rose toward the western horizon. In the settling light of the sun, it was a beautiful spot to be alone, to be closer to the rhythms of this gorgeous reality. It also allowed some reflection upon things falling behind, or perhaps to give some consideration for what might be ahead. He would take along a beer and a cigarette, enjoying some moments of repose before the start of another working week to come.

But pulling into the gravel road of the Lucky Girl, everything suddenly got put on hold. A yellow Volkswagon camper van sat parked behind his cabin. The beat of McAllister's heart quickened, a surge of nervous emotion rushing inside. His breath grew shallow at the sight.

As he slowed the panel truck to a halt, all his previous plans or thoughts of intent were quickly forgotten. A more fearsome but exhilarating moment was about to unfold.

CHAPTER FOURTY-TWO

QUEEN OF HEARTS
Orondo, Washington / October, 1977

THE SOLITARY EXPOSED LIGHT BULB RADIATED from the ceiling above, lighting the interior of the orchard cabin. Through the window, the October morning remained black, as the onset of a dawning sky was growing later each day. Sean McAllister sat on wooden chair, dressed in his long johns, jeans and boots. He wrestled his unruly hair back behind his ears, tying the blue bandana over his head. In his lap was a thin roll of adhesive tape. He cut the tape with his teeth, wrapping strips over the tips of his index fingers on both hands, which had been sliced red from days of rolling apples from the branches of trees. Tom Sullivan jammed newspaper and kindling wood into a small flattop wood stove, lighting it to temper the cold chill of the room. On the hot plate, water boiled for coffee and oatmeal. Another day of work was getting underway, without the necessity of a single word to speak.

After breakfast, the coffee thermos full, McAllister rolled a tobacco cigarette, staring at the grey slats of the wooden floor, smoking. As grayish light grew in the sky, the sound of tractor engines could be heard starting in the equipment yard of the Lucky Girl Orchard. He and Sullivan grabbed their brown cotton gloves and picking buckets, stepping into the chipped air outside, returning to the familiar daily routine. Finding his row, McAllister strapped the picking bucket to his chest, felt the steely nip of the aluminum ladder in his hands, the frosted dew of the orchard grass attacking the warmth of his booted feet. Things would surely go cold and slow for awhile.

Eventually, the autumn sun climbed its way over the desert hills to the east, wetting the dew with its immediate heat. The icy grip of the red delicious apples began to warm, the pace of the work picking up speed. By coffee break, the chilled wet of the orchard began to dry, circulatory systems starting to simmer, the first voices of the day opening to speak. As the morning sun moved higher, the skin pursed towards sweat, coats and gloves were stripped to the ground, lightening the load.

McAllister and others were now in full picking mode, slicing ladder sets into the trees, hands smoothly rolling apples up and off their branches, keeping their stems intact to the fruit. With each apple bouncing softly off his chest and into the bucket, he raced up and down the ladder until the bucket was full. Waddling over to the nearby plywood bin, he laid his load gently across the top of the other apples, careful not to bruise the crop. Quickly returning time and again, he would clear a tree and move on to the next, shouting for a tractor move or another empty bin. Priscilla, one of Ivan Jake's bin checkers, hardly paid him much mind. She would simply scan the bin to see if it was full, write out the ticket, then staple it to the bin, exchanging small talk before disappearing into another row of trees. She knew that McAllister was not here to damage the fruit.

If the trees were good, McAllister would often pack his lunch and stay in the orchard, rather than return to the cabin to eat, always pushing himself to keep up with the Mexicans working nearby. But such competitive intent usually ended in defeat. These men were just too damned fast. In their helmets and baseball caps, their work shirts, Levis, and second hand coats, the Mexicans could almost breeze through the trees with eyes closed, singing and chattering away. It was as if these men were born to the work. Much like superb athletes, they made the skill of the harvest look easy, effortless in their performance of the job at hand. Still, the challenge gave McAllister a goal to achieve, to try and stay up with them as best he could.

The warm afternoons of October were like a scrumptious dessert on a plate. The deep green orchards, the sentient azure sky, the sage and bunch grass hills above, the ebullient joy of solar heat and light. His body felt slim and muscular strong, his attitude loose with a carefree state of mind. High on his ladder sets, he could view the midnight blue Columbia River, quietly shining in the midday sun. On autumn days like these, the harvest was a heavenly cornucopia of beauty and peace, surrounded by a community of friends, all sharing the same together. On days like these, there was once again no better place to be.

Or perhaps the wonder of his mind was because of the woman, Paige, who McAllister couldn't wait to see. Sullivan and he planned on meeting Paige and Terri after work, to drive to Wenatchee for dinner and watch the World Series. When the women had arrived at the Lucky Girl in late September, Ivan Jakes did not have an open cabin to put them on. But across the road at the Stinson Orchard, Terri and Paige had found a job and a small white orchard cabin to set up their home. Something of a friendship had developed between the four of them. With Paige, McAllister hoped for more, but she was quiet and distant when it came to anything more than a harvest companionship.

Recognizing this reality, Sean McAllister had been forced by circumstance to still his sexual desire. He had accepted the facts of only a possible friendship, although he ached to find intimacy with Paige. Nonetheless, spending time with her was so much better than nothing at all. Paige did not deny him the interest he showed, but her response was non-committal, keeping things at bay. McAllister figured there must be somebody else, although he feared to inquire. In his heart he wished for more, but acknowledged the hand he was dealt. Surprisingly, Tom Sullivan appeared to have more of a shot with Terri, even though he had a girl back home. As a result, the two men kept their feelings to themselves, as to what might be going on inside. At least the girls were using Sullivan and McAllister's fellowship to keep other men from sniffing around. As male companions, they were mainly playing a more significant role of protectors, and that singular role might have to be enough.

There was nothing to do but keep on cranking with the fruit, in a land where dollars grew on trees. About twenty-five bags to a bin, up and down, down and up, the afternoon sun warm to the touch, the apples flush-red and ripe for the picking. This was the time to make the big bucks. McAllister topped off his sixth bin, looking to push for one more. One more would mean a fifty dollar day, and although he knew those damn Mexicans were kicking his ass again, he continued to push. Unfortunately, the afternoon sun was beginning to angle lower in the sky, mixed with a light chilling breeze lifting off the cold blue River nearby. It was getting late. Halfway through his seventh bin, Sullivan appeared below McAllister's ladder, saying it was time to go.

Disappointed, McAllister walked the last bucket to the bin, calling it a day.

Wenatchee, Washington was a railroad town, a dry rugged western city spurred by the transportation of agriculture, equally empowered by the hydroelectric control of the deep bully River rustling along its flank. Above, on the upper benches of the city, away from the River and commercial district, god-fearing residents lived the life of the late-twentieth-century American West. They were people of the desert terrestrial, white in complexion, Christian in belief, listening to Paul Harvey at noon each day. Wenatchee was an eight to four-thirty ordered life, five days a work week, hunting and fishing on Saturday, praying and resting on the Sabbath. It was a city milieu of conservative pride and progress, imbued with a flag-waving and boot-strapped patriotic state of mind. Wenatchee was a place where homogeneity was valued above all other traits of character, purposeful in its display. It was a product of manifest destiny, a geography of expressed belief and preferred orthodoxy. Deep down, Wenatchee kept its darker secrets well hidden, its peculiar afflictions safely secured behind closed doors.

Yet, railroad towns like Wenatchee, despite their adherence to a holier view of themselves, must endure the transgressions of America's dispossessed. They are forced to accept the devil's residue, the weathered and cracked faces of an outcast nation of desperate souls. They must endure this wayward minority, who often travel the American rails in search of some worldly redemption. Such acceptance is the consequence of Wenatchee's link to the outside world, its need for cheap labor and the transport to economic markets far beyond. Along the River's edge, lined with tracks of steel, the city tolerates the presence of men in tattered clothes that do not fit, burdened by worn suitcases and alcohol breath. Wenatchee must provide this labor with cheap hotels and poker rooms, tacitly receive the painted faces of women leaning against red brick walls. It must suffer the solicitations of panhandlers and cripples in Salvation Army soup lines, shivering in the cold.

For Wenatchee, this is the price of a faithful Calvinism, where material success is glorified in the eyes of God. Sadly, in America, the winners must always beget the losers, who just won't fade away.

Like many cities of the frontier west, Wenatchee is a town of terrible economic confliction, fraught with the effects of a capitalistic system that cannot be ignored. The only choice is to move further up the hills above the city, while praying to the Lord to cleanse the sins of the fallen who must struggle for its crumbs.

Sitting in the restaurant bar of the Columbia Hotel, the minions of a migrant destiny drink cheap wine and wander by, seeking some solace from the perils of an unjust world. Meanwhile, the World Series of baseball acts as a great and timely equalizer to the deprived reality of a disenfranchised republic. A republic that despite the contradictions inherent in its creed, everyone knows the power of the Yankees. And everyone knows the history of the Dodgers, those lovable losers, who had pioneered their way to Los Angeles, seeking a better life. On the green and red clay diamond of this autumn night, young men of common American extraction have found their way to paradise by catching, throwing and hitting a ball. Upon this field of dreams, the hopes of human equality are realized, at least for period of time. Despite color or standing, or which side of the railroad tracks or national borders one might have crossed, there are tonight no barriers to one's belief that victory and eternal recognition can possibly be achieved.

On this night, from sea to shining sea, much of the country revels in the drama, even restless hippie fruit pickers with two women at their side. It will be a night where a poor, half-Black, half-Hispanic man from a Jewish community in North Philadelphia, steps to the plate. And on the very first pitch in each of three different at bats, he drives the ball far into the seats. He will circle the bases to the roar of the crowd, making baseball history with each footfall toward home. Reggie Jackson has led the dreaded New York Yankees to another World Series championship, while putting an exclamation point on his personal journey to baseball's Hall of Fame. In America, it still rang true. One could be blessed to raise themselves beyond the constrictions of poverty and class, to attain the American Dream. Everyday, someone, somewhere, might find their way to overcome. But a sadder reality remained perfectly clear. In America, in October, 1977, the chances for such heroic opportunities would continue to be so few and far between.

Returning the twenty miles north to the Lucky Girl, the desert night was clear and cold, the waxing moon rising above the dark outlined hills surrounding the valley. Walking the women home, Paige suggested to McAllister that they detour to the River to view the stars. As they strolled, the moonlight glistened on the darkened surface of the placid water. In the ambient light, they followed along the orchard periphery to the River's edge. In the distance, across the Columbia, the electric glow of the town of Entiat pierced the blackened horizon. The night was silent but for the lapping of the River against its banks, the occasional sound of a distant vehicle passing on the highway beyond.

They spoke to each other about the Barter Fair, now only ten days ahead. Paige told him of her plans to return to Seattle immediately after the Fair. Paige and Terri's trip would be over. Paige would be settling back into her future, taking up nursing school again in January. She would be moving on with her life as planned. There wasn't much Sean McAllister could say. He would remain until the later apples were picked, before packing up and crossing the border to Oregon, returning to his own life in Pollard Creek. As the couple circled back to the Stinson Orchard cabins, he took her hand in his without resistance, walking the rest of the way. On the road outside her cabin, he took his chance and kissed her on the lips, she holding firm to his. Upon release, she said good night, slipping away.

Sean McAllister stood quietly, watching as the shadow of the woman entered the lighted orchard cabin, hearing the door close behind. Heading home, McAllister walked past the metal equipment sheds of the Stinson Orchard, then further out to the highway. Crossing the pavement, with his night vision better set, he found the orchard tractor path that led to the Lucky Girl housing. He tiptoed silently past the Rainbow bus camp, following up to his own silent home. In the darkness he sat down to take off his clothes, hearing Sullivan turning over in the bunk beside him.

"Was it good?" Sullivan's voice spoke into the black unseen.

"Yeah, good," McAllister answered. "Better than I expected."

"She really likes you, you know," the unseen voice returned. "I can tell."

"Really? You think so. Cause I really like her."

"But, hey," the voice spoke again. "Don't try to rush time with this one. Let it take its own course."

McAllister stood on the chair, climbing into his bunk above. He settled into his sleeping bag, his gaze peering up into the black. "Is there something I don't know about her, that you do? Something Terri might have said?"

"Possibly," the voice said from below.

"So, are you going to tell me now, or make me wonder all night?"

"It will keep till morning. Like I said, you can't rush time."

"Thanks a lot, buddy. I knew I could count on you." McAllister turned on his side, the metal bed springs creaking. "You can't rush time. Is that something you came up with?"

"No, it was something an old out black man said to me one time, way back when. Back at a moment when I didn't think I had any time at all. The advice has always stuck with me. I thought I might pass it along."

"In the war?" McAllister asked. He waited, but no answer came. "Well, it's good advice, I suppose. It makes you think."

"Good night, Sean," the voice returned, trailing away toward sleep.

The harvest hustled to its peak before beginning its final descent. The apple growing season had been six months of destiny reaching its last hurrah. From the initial white blossoms of spring, the bee buzz of pollination, to the burning of smudge pots and the whir of wind turbines to protect the bloom, to the chemical and hand thinning to control the size. It continued with the spraying of insecticides, pesticides, and herbicides, battling to the death the coddling moth, the aphid, the mice, the maggots and scale. There were the applications of auxins and ethylene to regulate growth, to increase the color, or retard early drop. Onward, towards the last chore of propping the sagging branches of trees laden with fruit. At its peak, the busy surge of the human dynamic, of picking buckets, ladders and bins, of tractor trailers and packing houses, of cement cold-storage and controlled-air buildings, to railroad cars and grocery stores across the continent. Further on, to tubs of water-bobbing apples on Halloween night, or the teacher's desk on a late autumn day at school. The apple, symbol of love, of knowledge and immortality. This was the cycle of the apple's birth and passing, time and again.

Soon the silence of winter would cast itself across the valley, the first snowfall sneaking down into the canyon draws. Human voices would drift away to warmer climes, leaving this naked land to its cozy slumber of hibernation, the only sounds being the quiet clip of a pruner's sheers. With little more to do, the local men would trudge through the rattlesnake hills, their rifles in hand, searching for deer. Their women would gas up the big sedans, heading for Nevada, seeking one-arm bandits to pull. This was the world of a magnificent late frontier, hidden in a northwest corner of America that many of the nation's citizens would never see or know.

McAllister could sense the harvest's ending, the slippage into a tranquil peace. Each year, like a siren's muse, the coming winter would call to him, urging him to stay. Perhaps he would hunker down in his one room cabin, with a heated stove and cords of apple wood stacked outside. He would have a bottle of brandy and plenty of books to read. He would imagine himself becoming a man of ultimate solitude, fasting from the busy expectations of living in a modern daily world. It would be a gracious and forgiving hideout, away from those thoughts of future intentions always demanding to be met. But he knew better than to fall prey to the siren's wail. All too quick, he was certain his youthful impatience would grow. In less than a week and one good novel, he would surely be pacing the floor, his head heated with a cabin fever, seeking to escape.

It's funny, all the dreams of ourselves that we seek to pursue. Those imagined personas and particular circumstances we wish to create. Often, only to find that they were not really what we thought they would be. Perhaps such dreamy inclinations are only the purpose, and not the end. They prod us to keep on dreaming, to continue to see ourselves as becoming someone else in some other place. But really, they are but the fuel to keep us moving, enticing us along towards whom we honestly must become, onward to our next individual chapter ahead. We are who we are, but by seeing ourselves as becoming something anew, we continue the journey toward life's eventual end.

McAllister watches as Paige loads the last of her things into the panel truck. Today, her hair hangs in a single blonde braid down her back, escaping from below a crocheted winter hat, hiding her ears. She turns to him and smiles, saying she is ready. As he closes the rear doors, it occurs to him there might be only one thing missing. If only Meatball was hopping inside the truck, the picture would be complete. For Sean McAllister, today there is no past. There is no Delaware, no Washington D.C., no Colorado or Pollard Creek. There is simply a beautiful woman, a road trip, and perhaps a missing dog. Tom Sullivan fires up the yellow Volkswagon van, with Terri sitting beside him. McAllister starts his engine, following behind Sullivan down the orchard drive. At the highway, the caravan turns itself north, north to the Okanogan Barter Fair, a gathering no one wants to miss.

Someone called the location the Okanogan Highlands, a dusted rocky rangeland country of treeless angled slopes, bedded in faded grasses tanned blonde by the weathered cold of autumn. Looking upward, the ridgetops run even against the sky, scattered in Ponderosa pine, Douglas fir and spruce, amidst pockets of the paling yellowed needles of western larch. Below the camp, a small fishing lake rests in the folds of a narrow valley, surrounded by the riparian species of alder, willow, and birch, fast being shorn of their weathered brown leaves. The valley itself is known as the Sinlahekin, an awesome topograhy void of the civilized world, populated by mule deer, bighorn sheep, and wandering cattle on the open range.

The title of the gathering fit the proceedings. Barter Fair, the trading of commodities, seeking an equal exchange. There would be a circling of twentieth-century wagons: buses, pick-up campers, step vans, flat beds of varied length, old station wagons and cars. People would be setting up their produce and craft products, or simply hauling in garage sale items they could no longer use. The ideal exchange was one needed thing for another, although the currency of the US dollar would never be turned away. There were boxes of pears, apples, gourds, banana squash, winter squash, and a truckload of potatoes. There were canned fruits and vegetables, specialty cheeses, cookies, nuts, even dried sunflower seeds by the bag. Craftsmen would market their stained glass, or carvings of bone and antler, uncut serpentine, turquoise, and jade. There would be lambswool handbags, jars of honey, dried flowers, incense sticks, feathered earrings, candles and holders, leather products, or homemade beer and wine. There would be farm equipment, box saws, stoves, grinding wheels and other tools.

There would even be llamas for sale, donkey rides for the kids, performance theatre by Reverend Chumley, and a magic show by Magical Mystical Michael. In the back alleys of this tribal town, there would be weed for sale, or dried psychedelic mushrooms direct from the coast. In the late afternoon, a spiritual circle would spread across the meadow, with the Rainbow tribe and others chanting together, praying for love and peace.

McAllister and Paige spent the day arm in arm, drinking hot coffee and Kahlua, traipsing the huge circle of produce and wares, laughing at Reverend Chumley's remarkable show. Stealthily, he bought Paige a pair of turquoise earrings, to gift to her upon her leaving. Camping near their Rainbow friends from the Lucky Girl, they sat huddled by a campfire at night, listening to mandolin and guitar, passing wine and reefer around a sparking, crackling blaze. All the while, the stars and the near full moon watched silently from above. Growing weary and cold, the couple snuck away to their panel truck home. Under sleeping bags and blankets, they made love for the very first time.

Upon the initial light of dawn, Sean McAllister crawled outside to relieve himself. Naked but for a heavy coat over his shoulders, he looked down upon the lake below. The Sinlahekin Valley spread further into the paling distance, the burnished grasslands tinged in cold white frost. As he breathed in the tight short air of dawn, Sean McAllister felt as healthy and at peace as a man could be, as happy and rested as one's human contentment might ever allow.

This was the Great Northwest, the best that America could give. This was his Ecotopia, the fulfilling dream of a new and progressive world. Right here, right now. Alone in the frosted cold field, a solitary dog sat on its haunches, perfectly still but for the breath that escaped from its mouth. The dog appeared to be waiting, not unlike the peace of a yogi in deepest meditation. For some reason, the famous painting by Andrew Wyeth came to mind, *Christina's World*. Andrew Wyeth could have done this western landscape justice, if Wyeth had ever entertained the thought of leaving his eastern home. Shivering, McAllister scampered back to the panel, diving into the warmth and love within.

There wasn't much more to say. It had been talked out as best it could. They sat on the big flat rock in the back of the Lucky Girl Orchard, the mystery of the desert hills behind, the more known drama of a harvest season sitting quietly below. The distant Columbia River rested calm as a mirror, reflecting the western rim of the canyon horizon. Hours away, the city of Seattle lay beyond the rising Cascade peaks. In the morning she would be going home.

Tom Sullivan had eventually told him the earlier secret, about a long relationship having only shortly come to an end. She was just beginning to find her own way. In January, she would return to school at the University of Washington, living for a time at her parent's home nearby. At the end of her plans, she would have a nursing degree, and then would decide about other things.

Paige was a jet city girl, born and raised. Her dad even worked for Boeing, the aircraft company that had coined the phrase. Her brother fished in Alaska, her mother a housewife before working in the schools. Paige seemed to have the evenness of demeanor that understood the rain, the cold waters of the north. Her Nordic beauty had captivated him upon first sight. Now she would be leaving him behind. The time had come. He held her hand in his, her long blue jeans stretching beside him, the heels of her working boots pressing together. Each passing moment came closer to goodbye.

"When you come, I'll take you to the Pike Place Market," she said. "And I hope you can meet my brother, too. For some reason you remind me of him. I know you will like him, he likes baseball too."

"I want to see the Space Needle," McAllister said. I saw a television show on it once, the World's Fair. You can see the whole city, right?"

"Uh huh. And we'll take a ferry boat ride across the Puget Sound.

Sean McAllister sat silent for a time, watching the tips of her boots tapping one against the other, feeling the warmth of his grip in hers.

"I'm glad we got to spend this time together," he began. "After meeting you in Chelan, I was hoping so much that I would see you again. And then unbelievably, you and Terri came. It was like a little dream come true for me. It's made the harvest season really good."

Paige turned her head toward his, waiting as he did they same. They kissed. McAllister put his arm around her shoulders, her head resting on his own.

"I'm glad we didn't go to Tonasket," she responded. "We both wanted to meet you and Tom again. Actually, we weren't really sure where we were going. It's been so much fun to get to know everybody, to be part of a family of sorts. I'll miss it all going back home."

"I'm glad you are going back to school," McAllister lied. "It's what you want, and it's a really good thing. I just wish you weren't leaving so soon. It's strange, but a part of me doesn't want to go back to Oregon."

"It will be okay," she answered. "Let's think of this time as a beginning of something, whatever that might be. It will give us both something to look forward to. You can visit me, and I'll come visit you when I can. But right now, I just need to move towards something besides a relationship. I really just need someone who cares. You can understand that, can't you? Can you do that for me, for both of us as friends?"

That dreaded word again. 'Friends'. A thin blade of pain sliced inside him. It was a word that could take the love out of romance, turning it upside down. But he sort of knew better now, and he tried not to be afraid. "I understand," he answered. "I mean Oregon is still home for me. I have so many good friends there. And I've never given much thought about leaving to go anywhere else. It's just that I'll miss you, and sad that you have to go."

"It's sad for me too," she softly agreed. "But you will come sometime. I'll write to you. You will keep me going, unless something else happens for you." Paige paused before speaking again. "Sean", she started firmly, "I didn't expect this. It was just supposed to be a fun road trip with Terri, before getting serious about going back to school. But I'm so happy it did, and I don't want to lose it so soon, for either of us. And I don't want us to ever be sorry we met. It means too much right now."

"I hope nothing else happens," he believed. "I don't want something else to happen. Not for awhile, not till I see you again. And I won't be sorry at all, never. I mean, I have an old truck, a cabin in the woods, and until meeting you, no thoughts for what might be next. And I'm okay with that. But more than anything, I am thankful for the time we've shared. I really can't tell you how much. He pulled away from her shoulder, kissing her again. Looking into her eyes, her beautiful gray-green eyes, he made a decision. "I'll walk you home. Terri is probably wondering if you've run away." He smiled. "Tomorrow, you'll be on the road home. And I've got Winsesaps to pick. I want you to be happy when you go." They got up from the rock, walking through the orchard hand in hand.

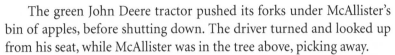

The green John Deere tractor pushed its forks under McAllister's bin of apples, before shutting down. The driver turned and looked up from his seat, while McAllister was in the tree above, picking away.

"Sean McAllister, you still here? Where the hell is that pretty little thing I been seeing you with lately? Is she keeping the bunk warm for you? She waiting to fix you biscuits and gravy back at the cabin?"

"Donny Jim Cade," McAllister responded from his ladder set. "The man with two first names. No, Donny Jim, she's flown the coop back to Seattle, left me here all alone. It's just you and me now, Donny Jim, picking these damn saps."

"Damn, boy. You crazy, or what? I would have crossed the Texas state line to stay with that little darlin'. And let me remind you, I'm not one to ever cross the Texas state line."

"Why's that, Donny? Texas got the goods on you, or what?"

"Hell, was just a little scuffle, that's all. But you'd think I'd shot the governor or somethin', the way they made somethin' out of it. No, Texas and me not likely to get along for awhile."

Donny Jim Cade, the last of the fruit tramps. They were a dying breed. It had been four years now for McAllister, and each season less and less of the old boys were around. The harvest was giving way to young hippies like himself, as well as the Mexicans, more and more coming in to the valley each year. You could also throw in the old senior couples, who would camp out and work for a time to supplement their pensions and social security. But in the old days, it was mostly the tramps and the families of the growers who picked the fruit. Nowadays the industry was beginning to catapult in size. More and more labor would be necessary, and the kids needed to stay in school. Something told McAllister that the Mexican invasion would continue, in order to meet the increasing demand. The immigration cops would still make some raids now and then, busing a few of the illegals back across the border. But those moves would only be for show. The real story would be to simply look the other way. The growers would continue to take whatever social security number was given, before writing out the check. With a previous generation of transient labor seriously on the wane, the growers would have no other choice but to hire the men who were standing before them, whatever their name and address might be.

Donny Jim Cade, dressed in his baseball cap and coveralls, a constant cigarette hanging from his lips. He was an aging symbol of a time whose days were numbered. Unlike many of his peers who had found a way to settle down, Donny Jim was one of the few who still enjoyed being on the move. If his beater car had gas, if there was some fruit to pick or a tractor to drive, Donny Jim Cade would be on his way. Although he had plenty of extended family in Orondo, there was no keeping Donny Jim down. His next stop would be to visit his aging mother in Arkansas, or maybe a couple of the kids he had long ago left behind. After that, he would be on the road to Polk County, Florida for the winter orange harvest. In late spring, he would head back west to California's Central Valley, before returning to Orondo for another season of apples and pears.

McAllister wondered how much longer Donny Jim could continue the run. Gray hairs were creasing the sideburns of his hair, the weathered lines of his face cutting deeper and deeper each season. His jowls were beginning to sag, and his hacking cough could rock the cold November air. As well, the price of gas was beginning to take a toll. One day soon, Donny Jim would have to stop, and with it an American grapes of wrath story would come to an end.

McAllister stepped down off his ladder, his bucket full, the tree almost picked. He leveled his cargo of Winesaps into the bin. Donny Jim pulled a thermos of coffee from behind the seat, unscrewed the cap, poured himself a cup. McAllister grabbed his own thermos from under the tree, doing the same. There was no reason to rush the work any longer. There would only be a few more rows to pick and the season would be done.

"You know what they say," Donny Jim started, sipping on his coffee.

"No, what do they say, Donny? Whoever 'they' are."

"They say you got to be a sap to pick saps," Donny Jim laughed, as if telling the joke to himself.

McAllister chuckled at the man's simple love of humor, shaking his head. "You got that right, Donny Jim," McAllister responded. "They're goddamn hard to get off the tree. But at least they're big and can fill up a bin."

"A damn good keeper, these Winesaps," Donny Jim followed, "A little tart, but crisp and clean. Not like those lousy Red Delicious apples. These boys in this valley will eventually rue the day they bet so heavy on that variety. A Red gets mushy real fast, and they got no flavor once they get to storage. They think people prefer them because they look so red and shiny. But one day the people will figure it out, that they ain't no good at all."

"Give me a sunburst golden any day," McAllister returned. "Beautiful to look at, crisp and sweet right off the tree. It's a bummer that they don't last too long."

"Like the girl," Donny Jim asked, "the apple of your eye?"

"Like I said," McAllister returned, "a bummer they don't last too long."

"Good one, McAllister," Donny Jim chuckled. "So you gonna to chase her down, right? When it's all over here?"

"Hmm, that may not be the story, Donny Jim," McAllister mused. "Not the way you'd like to think."

Donny Jim Cade lit another cigarette, climbing back onto the tractor. At the very same moment, a picker a few rows over shouted his name, with the word "Tractor" right behind. "You only got a bucket or so left here," Donny Jim decided. "I'll move you up yonder to finish the bin. You know, McAllister, there ain't no state lines between here and Seattle. It's all the state of Washington from here to there. Don't you forget that now." Then Donny Jim Cade fired the tractor to a start.

McAllister smiled and nodded his way. Donny Jim Cade lifted the forks, pulling the bin forward toward the apple tree ahead. Setting it back down, he accelerated down the row of trees, around the corner to the next move at hand. McAllister finished his coffee, strapped up his picking bucket, returning to work.

At the end of the day, before the early darkness of a gray November night, McAllister picked up some additional buckets of grounder apples that had fallen from the trees. He transferred them to cardboard boxes for fruit to take home. Tom Sullivan had packed up and left several days before. The Rainbow camp had disappeared. Joe and Linda, Terri and Paige, all were long gone. A few hardcore pickers remained, getting the last of the harvest before hitting the road. The hirsute busyness of the season was giving way to the silent hibernation of a winter ahead. At his cabin, McAllister built a fire in the wood stove, made some dinner, stripping down to his thermals in the growing heat of the room.

With the night pitch black outside, he wanted to write a letter to Paige, to tell her of his day. Instead, he began a correspondence to his sister, Mary Jane. It had been awhile since he had been in touch. In a day or two, he would pack up and be on the road to Oregon, having fulfilled his promise to Ivan Jakes to complete the Lucky Girl harvest. He looked forward to going home to Pollard Creek. But only because Seattle just didn't seem right for now. Sullivan's missive, "don't rush time", and Paige's own words "think of it as a beginning", played within his head. Both statements seemed to underscore the truth. Donny Jim Cade's earlier declaration was certainly correct. There were indeed no state lines between here and Seattle. Unfortunately, there were a lot of unseen lines standing in the way.

On a final chilled overcast morning, he packed up the panel. Picking up his check, McAllister stopped to say his good-byes to Ivan and Sally Jakes, to Donny Jim Cade, to Lonnie Mosher and others. Donny Jim, as he was prone and loved to do, needed to crack wise. "Well, boss," he said to Ivan Jakes, "you're finally getting rid of that young 'bird dogger', sending him down the road." 'Bird dogger' was a pejorative apple term for pickers who only picked apples from the bottom of the trees, stealing the low-lying fruit. Ivan Jakes ignored the remark. McAllister just smiled, winking at Donny Jim Cade.

"Well, you have a good year, Mr. McAllister," Ivan Jakes said. "And you just call me next season, whenever you want to return."

"Thanks, Ivan. I appreciate it," McAllister answered. "So, was it a good season, all in all?"

"I think we did okay," Ivan answered, then paused for effect. "Everyone tells you, Mr. McAllister, they say that crime doesn't pay. What they don't tell you, however, is that neither does farming." Ivan Jakes let a rare smile cross over his face.

Donny Jim walked McAllister to the panel truck. "Well, son, you got all your white-line money now, and you're ready to set those tires a humming. Just don't be looking in that rear view mirror, cause you'll soon be seeing ole Donny Jim Cade cruising right behind."

McAllister turned the engine over, pulling for a last time down the gravel drive of the Lucky Girl Orchard. It would not be without a tinge of remorse. Ivan Jakes and Donny Jim Cade were good honest men, each in their own separate ways. Although the world of their own lives was different from his, he couldn't help but feel a quiet sadness in leaving them behind.

At the Orondo junction, several women stood outside a packing shed, smoking cigarettes. Today, inside the shed, the last of the season's fruit was being washed and waxed, then packed in forty-two pound boxes, before loading to some ending destination. Surrounding the shed sat numerous bins of fruit that hadn't met the grade. These apples were the losers in the grading game of perfect acceptance and beauty. They had been declared unfit. Soon they would be trucked to a nearby juice plant, before being crushed, bottled, and sent away. These were the losers, the culls. They would never get to bask in a grocery store produce section's glorious light of fame.

In school, while you're still young and impressionable, they tell you how lucky you are, lucky to be part of a land of equality and opportunity, that you will always count as much as the boy or girl beside you. But really, it's just a scam to keep you in your place. Economic democracy long ago had been given over to the inherited few. And one could be sure they weren't about to give it up. As you slowly mature and come of age, you begin to understand, to accept the hand you're dealt. All the while, the propaganda machine of America keeps reminding you of how lucky you are. They hand you a flag with fifty white stars. They put a bible in the drawer of every room you sleep. They glorify you as part of the team. But when the real game begins they never let you play.

Still, somehow, the economic losers always manage to persevere. There would always be more to human life than monetary security and social status in the world of men. That's another thing they often preach, but in that advice they are surely square to the mark. Still, in the end, the winners often miss out on the beauty of such special moments, of a life that includes men like Ivan Jakes and Donny Jim Cade. The winners are too busy trying to make their own private worlds into images of themselves. Too busy always trying to get over, all the goddamned time.

Throughout the day, McAllister worked his way south. He crossed the Blewit Pass to Ellensburg, down through Yakima and Toppenish, before heading southwest to Goldendale and the Oregon border. Washington was an amazing and beautiful state. But unlike Oregon, it sometimes felt like New York. The cops always seemed to have a serious hard-on. And there was Boeing, and a heck of a lot of military presence. Toss in that bitch of a governor, Dixie Lee Ray, a woman who would build a nuclear power plant in your own backyard whether you liked it or not. Washington was a state that knew which side its bread was buttered, and like all the other winners, it wasn't about to change.

Oregon, despite its crazy complications, didn't necessarily have an industry or military complex that defined its view of the world. Like any other place, it had its share of fruit and nuts. But deep down it was more of a 'live and let live' state of mind. You could hitchhike on its freeways without somebody getting bent out of shape. You were returning to a land that accepted you, no matter how strange you might appear. Down in Jordan County, they might want to kick your ass, but at least you knew who was doing the kicking and why. Maybe Oregon was simply a more out-front and easier place to understand. Perhaps Oregon had a broader reality in which to practice one's own individualism, whatever that might be. It was hard to explain, but there was no denying what it felt to cross the majestic Columbia River and return back home. Only this time, Sean McAllister's crossing was tinged with an empty recognition he couldn't ignore. If only he wasn't leaving such a precious feminine gem back on the other side.

Part Four
A Long and Winding Road

*One of the great dreams of man must be
to find some place between the extremes
of nature and civilization where it is
possible to live without regret.*

-Barry Lopez

CHAPTER FORTY-THREE

STAGE FRIGHT
Pollard Creek / 1978

SEAN MCALLISTER RETURNED TO POLLARD CREEK, settling back into his own life. Time and a typical Oregon winter went by. With each passing day, the moments of living were realized, before being placed on the shelves of memory's library. Occasionally, a volume might be pulled from the bookcase, opened to a chapter and revisited, both the good and the bad. Yet, most of these moments would be left unread and forgotten. They are quite often trivial and redundant, filled with only routine thoughts and daily connections from one day to the next. But they remain part of the book, all the same.

Mookie James and Valerie Williams were gone, off to Arizona. New chapters were being written of their own lives. They would stuff their Oregon rain coats into a closet, beginning to work on their tans under a Southwest sun. They would become firm believers in air conditioning on hot summer days. Pollard Creek would have to carry on without them. But Sean McAllister would miss one of his closest friends. He was happy for Mookie, yet sad for himself. There would be more empty space needing to be filled.

McAllister toughed out the winter at Railroad Bridge. He planted some trees again on the coast. He set some choker for Hank Swain's logging show on a couple of units. He cut some firewood in the hills, washed dishes for a vegetarian restaurant in Grants Pass. He did whatever it took to get by. On winter Friday nights, he went to the pot luck dinners, playing cribbage and hearts with his extended family and friends. He drank at the Solace Valley Tavern or the Wonder Bur liquor bar in Grants Pass. Meanwhile, he kept the cabin fires burning, staying up on Saturday nights to watch the Not Ready For Prime Time Players on his scratchy black and white television.

From time to time there was a sexual interlude with someone he met, perhaps out of the bar on a cold winter night. However, he continued to reread the chapter of the previous year's harvest in Orondo. He would write an occasional letter to Paige, reporting to her of his regular life, although it seemed so boring in the telling. She would respond when she could. She was busy with school, yet doing well. There was nothing much to do, but not rush time.

In the early spring, he traveled with Tom Sullivan to San Francisco and Santa Cruz. The best thing about Pollard Creek was the wide extension of friendships that everyone shared, one with the other. He and Tom stayed with Sullivan's brother near the Castro District of the city. Both men were blown away by the San Francisco gay scene that was reaching its height. On Saturday nights, gay men would line up along the Castro in a meat market parade, looking for sex and love. On Sundays, they would dress in flamboyant feminine attire, bar hopping from place to place, living the theatrical dreams of their personal expressions. These men had come out of their closets for all to see. There was no question that San Francisco appeared to be a city of retreat for men who loved men, where acceptance and possibly romance could be found. Like the Haight-Ashbury only a decade before, San Francisco was a calling card for people looking for something they could not find at home.

In May, he jumped on the Green Tortoise, busing on an overnight run to Seattle. He awakened to a gray overcast of evergreen hills, the rising towers of an emerald city almost touching the low-hanging cover of clouds above. McAllister was nervous and uncertain at the prospect of his reunion with Paige. Thankfully, she was happy to see him. The memory of her beauty remained unmistaken, the pull of their sexual attraction still very much alive. Seattle was for the most part a working-class city of fisherman and airplane machinists, of longshoreman and bungalow neighborhoods, but wishing to be so much more. The city was becoming busy with new intents, of professional sports teams and Pacific trade. Seattle seemed to have an increasing pace that would surely grow with time.

With Paige still living at home with her parents north of the University, McAllister put up with her brother, Dane. Dane was a mellow guy of similar age. McAllister learned a little about the fishing business in Alaska, as well as the impact of the Alaska oil pipeline on the economy of this Northwest city. Paige took him to Seattle Center, home of the Space Needle. There, he was able to take in the incredible views of the city, this dramatic urban settlement on the banks of the Puget Sound. They went to Pike Place Market, before drifting down the urban streets towards Pioneer Square. They rode a bus out of the city center, walking through University of Washington campus, before hiking the final tree-lined blocks to her parent's home.

McAllister was charming enough with her parents, explaining his history of living in Oregon the best he could. However, trying to locate himself within Paige's current world was difficult. He liked Seattle, he liked San Francisco, but it was hard to imagine living in either place, or any city at all. This was Paige's home, her turf, her work and study, her life being lived. She was obviously comfortable in her element, intent in her motivations. Her brother was cool, a working stiff like him. But the bustle of Seattle surrounded him. He felt underdressed and futile, a man without a mission in life.

On their last night, they slept together in her brother's bed. Dane had stayed on the fishing boat in dry dock, allowing them some space to be alone. Things were still really good between them, despite the distance and time. But Paige did not bring up the future, and neither did he. They both understood that such a discussion could only lead to nowhere. Things were obviously more complex than the romance of the harvest season only months before.

It didn't dawn on McAllister until his leaving, that for some reason he was measuring himself, taking himself to task. Between Pollard Creek and the orchards of North Central Washington, he had been living in the wilds for over four years. He had become a hippie of the woods and farm fields, away from the everyday normalcy of a regular job, the standard beats and rhythms of a structured America. Part of him wanted to grab Paige, to pick her up, throw her over his shoulder like a rug, escaping back to the protections and security of a home and lifestyle he had come to know. Pollard Creek was a place where the rest of the world only flew by on the freeway, day after day, stopping momentarily for gas and a gander, as if visiting a zoo. The bottom line was that McAllister had become unfit, disengaged from the expectations of society, living his life in a tiny sheltered reality, which he undoubtedly preferred.

Maybe a woman like Paige deserved better than him. This was what he began to think of himself. He really had nothing of substance to offer her. What did they call it, 'prospects'. He had no future 'prospects'. For some odd reason, the trip to Seattle had shaken him up. What Sean McAllister might have considered the next step in something he desired, had instead thrown him for a loop. It was by no means Paige. She had been warm and comforting, keeping alive the companionship and intimacy they shared. She remained as lovely as ever, a woman who cared for him in some peculiar way. Why he suddenly felt like a fish out of water, he didn't know. But his emotional self-image had taken a hit.

Paige had two more years and hospital protocols to complete. Such a length of time seemed like an eternity. Returning back home, he immediately wrote and thanked her for the hospitality. Don't rush time, he kept saying to himself, don't rush time. He lied and said how much their friendship meant to him, but he knew his feelings were greater than such a general declaration. Was he in love? Damned straight he was in love. But was he in love with Paige, or in love with love, he didn't know. McAllister could only keep these troubling uncertainties strictly to himself. If Tom Sullivan didn't ask, then he wouldn't be forced to say. But a monkey was climbing on his back, and he needed to figure things out.

With summer on its way. McAllister let these questions go. He went back to his old ways, his familiar careless lifestyle. Whatever it might be that was bugging him, this strange crisis of confidence that had come out of nowhere, he needed more time to confront. For now, the truth could mean only one thing. He wasn't ready to leave Pollard Creek.

The Oregon summer has a way of trumping most cards, of overcoming the anxieties of winter, and the sometimes extended rainy springs of the Pacific Northwest. McAllister settled back into his world. He played competitive softball, enjoyed the heated camaraderie of community volleyball on hot Saturday afternoons. At Railroad Bridge, he worked with Sullivan and Freddie Jones at the Alaskan mill.

He helped water and tend the pot patch with Marty Johnson. Pollard Creek was still a beautiful place to be, full of friends and companions he had come to know and share.

Paige came down from Seattle. She was taken by the welcoming nature of his Oregon home, of Railroad Bridge, of Volleyball Saturday, the casual routines of living day to day. They went with a group on a one-day float down the Rogue River. He took her to the Solace Valley Tavern, where she could feel the sense of community of which he remained a part. They loaded the panel truck, driving for two days to the Oregon Coast, enjoying the incredible beauty of the Smith River canyon along the way. It was the best thing that could have happened for him, her feeling that he lived in a special place. It eased the earlier difficult denials he had stashed in the back of his mind. The saddest part was her leaving, returning to her own life away from him, and his life away from her.

As the summer began to wane, McAllister made ready to return for another harvest season in Washington. But this year Tom Sullivan would not be coming along. Shortly before the trip, Sullivan announced that he would be leaving Railroad Bridge. Carley had been accepted to law school at the University of Oregon in Eugene. Sullivan had made a major decision. He would divide his time between keeping up Carley's homestead on Paradise Creek, and living at her apartment at school. The news did not come as a big surprise. Tom Sullivan had not been on the Railroad Bridge property for most of the year, except to run the mill when necessary. But McAllister again felt the loss of another close friend.

The apple picking season of 1978 was nothing like before. McAllister returned to Ivan Jakes and the Lucky Girl Orchard. But there was no Sullivan, no Santos and the Rainbow group, no Terri, and obviously no Paige. Fortunately, Jesse Simmons was still working at the Austin Orchard, and like every other season there were new people to meet and share his time. Still, the fun and romance of the prior year went missing. And sadly, there was no Donny Jim Cade. Word from Ivan was that Donny Jim had taken sick back in Arkansas. The last of the fruit tramps might just be biting the dust.

McAllister grinded through the harvest toil. He made his money, attending the Barter Fair before heading back through Seattle. Paige was still two years from completing her nursing degree. The duration felt no shorter than it had before. Her brother was now living in a small town on the Olympic Peninsula. Paige and McAllister took a ferry ride, before driving for an hour to reach the town. Port Swan sat up on a hill, surrounded by water, a sparkling little spot of deep blue and green. Dane said he really liked the community, happy to be away from the busyness of Seattle. Although much larger than Pollard Creek, Port Swan felt quiet and laid back, seeming far away from the intense energy of the city. It seemed like one of those occasional places where one can see themselves living, it had that particular draw. Perhaps one day he would visit again.

Back in Pollard Creek, McAllister wasn't sure about battling another long winter at Railroad Bridge. Marty Johnson had stayed long enough to bring in the pot harvest, but he was checking out in other ways. Marty had met a woman while going to welding school in Grants Pass. He was making new friends and partying in between. For the most part, Railroad Bridge was being left to McAllister and Freddie Jones. Shortly after his return from the harvest, there came an offer from Robert Sage. Sage needed someone to caretake his property up on London Ridge. Sean McAllister had a decision to make. He went to Freddie and asked if he would mind the move. Freddie Jones pretty much kept to himself at his cabin by Laughlin Creek. There was less and less timber to mill, and the winter was upon them. As far as Freddie was concerned, it was no big deal. In Pollard Creek, change was as constant as the Pacific fronts rolling off the coast. It was not unusual for people to be moving from one place to another. And for the most part these days, everyone was doing their own separate thing.

Sage's London Ridge property would be easier for the winter. McAllister would be able to drive all the way home, not have to haul his ass back and forth across the trestle night and day. Marty Johnson had given him a share of the pot stash from the harvest. At London Ridge, he would have a bigger cabin, including better television reception with three different channels. Most of the time, he would have eighty acres all to himself, and still be closer to town than Railroad Bridge. Whenever Robert Sage came and went from his travels, there would be an old drying shed just above the cabin where McAllister could stay. So McAllister accepted the offer. He wasn't really moving away from Railroad Bridge, at least that's what he tried to tell himself. But deep down, if he was forced to consider it, maybe he was. It didn't matter for now.

Another chapter in Pollard Creek was coming to an end. Mookie and Valerie had ridden off into the Arizona sunset. The Mulcahey Farm days seemed like ancient history. And now Railroad Bridge was scattering with the wind. Fortunately, newer blood continued to find their way towards Pollard Creek. There would always be people looking for the rural escape. But this time around, the newcomers would not be motivated by a desired collective intent. Rather, it was becoming couples for the most part, buying land or vacated property, then building a home and settling in. Pollard Creek had a reputation on the word-of-mouth circuit as a place that was cool. This new influx had more money in their pockets, some being benefactors of the marijuana and cocaine trades. Others appeared to be trust funders, without visible means of support, yet searching for the satisfaction of their own particular dreams. No matter. Although the temperament of the community might be different than before, these new arrivals added some economy and new vitality to the community, replacing others who had begun moving on.

Still, the underbelly of Pollard Creek remained as rough and tumble as it had ever been. It continued to be a town where the no-counts could hide away from the law, stashing their artillery high in the hills. It was a place where one could grow weed for profit. Due to the economic distresses of this hard-rock world, it was a place where one could collect disability, welfare, and food stamps, or perhaps drink to excess without feeling the pressures of the outside society. By no means had Pollard Creek lost its edge, or the mean streak its history had always obliged. Peace, love, and a communal idealism had always been only a portion of its fabric. Mountain jurisdictions like Jordan County would forever be a vortex for ass-kicking ruffians, as well as the dreamers of a new-age progressive world.

For McAllister, Pollard Creek still held this particular fascination, a strange and kinetic attraction of beauty and trouble, of extremes in personality and motivation, like nowhere else. Nonetheless, from time to time he had pondered other possibilities, of potential places to be. But he knew it wouldn't be San Francisco and the expensive drama of a Bay Area lifestyle. Despite its winsome beauty, it would not be North Central Washington, its conservative mediocrity so tight and closed. And there had never been a single thought of returning east, to a world so burdened with social expectation, so conventional in its purpose and behavior. Perhaps a place like Seattle could be endured, but that would only be a choice of love over preference, and for now that was an option McAllister was not allowed to entertain. Those were just the facts, ma'am, despite any wishes to the contrary. For the moment, and the string of successive moments that make up a lifetime, it would have to be Pollard Creek, until some unexpected personal redemption might point the way.

Nothing could have prepared the City of San Francisco for the dramatic events of November, 1978. On November 18th, news began to reach the United States, reporting the deaths of 918 Americans in a mass murder-suicide in the country of Guyana, where People's Temple leader Jim Jones had led his congregation from its home base in San Francisco. Among the dead were two hundred and seventy-six children. United States Congressman Leo Ryan from the 11th District in California was among the dead, having been murdered while investigating conditions at the Jonestown compound. The murders and the following mass liquidation by Jones and his cadre of security personnel stunned the nation, particularly the city that so many of the dead had previously called home: Jones, too, was found dead at the site, from a believed self-inflicted gunshot wound to the head.

The incident was a terrifying illustration of the dangers of how emotional propaganda and the impact of charismatic leaders can control the human mind. The strange powers of religious cultism were becoming a troubling consequence of the times. Modern civilization had no answer for the psychologically dispossessed. Human beings would forever search for some fellowship of belonging to something, to give the confusion of their lives some measure of hope and reason to believe. But to try and understand the calculated murder of innocent children? The psychosis of such a deed was just too incredible for any ethical human understanding to conceive. To date, Jonestown was the largest single loss of civilian life in a non-natural disaster in American history.

Nine days later, as the impact and mourning of the Jonestown trauma gripped the city, a second shocking incident occurred. On the morning of November 27th, Dan White, a San Francisco City Supervisor, who earlier in the month had resigned from the Board, climbed through a first-floor window at the San Francisco City Hall, armed with a loaded police service revolver. White had petitioned San Francisco Mayor George Moscone to reappoint him back to the Board of Supervisors, saying he had changed his mind. Moscone had declined, intending to announce another more favorable political appointee to the position.

In a private conference area beside the Mayor's formal office, White pulled his gun, firing two rounds into Moscone's chest and shoulder. As Moscone lay on the office floor, White fired two additional bullets into Moscone's head at close range, killing him instantly. Reloading the handgun, White left the office, walked down the hall, accosting City Supervisor, Harvey Milk, the first openly gay supervisor in San Francisco history. Milk, unaware of the shooting, stepped into White's former office, whereupon White blocked the door from escape. He fired five more shots into Milk, again the final shot fired into Milk's head at close range. White, who once had been a San Francisco police officer, escaped the building. But a short time later, he turned himself in to two city detectives from his former precinct.

San Francisco, a liberal city whose history and best intentions had forged a sensitivity toward progressive change and understanding, had become another victim of the self-delusion and bigoted hate of a diseased human mind. Sean McAllister was shaken by the emotional impact of such incredible events. And Jordan County, despite its nativist Oregon distaste for all things Californian, was closely tethered by its own history and settlement to this grand city by the bay. Few were immune from some connection to the Bay Area, whether they were direct descendants, or refugees from the tumults of its population and pace. Despite any common cultural and provincial prejudice, the human orbit of the Bay Area extended deep into Southern Oregon. The San Francisco Chronicle and Examiner newspapers could be purchased in Grants Pass. The Oakland Raiders and San Francisco 49'rs were Southern Oregon's favorite teams. And much of the economics and tourism of its timbered backlands was linked to the California enterprise.

Even McAllister had begun to feel the connective tissues of this milieu. From his earlier California hitchhiking journey years before to Berkeley, his occasional travels to the City, to all the friends he now engaged who called San Francisco their home, Southern Oregon was attached to pulse of San Francisco's world. McAllister had seen the People's Temple. He had walked by Harvey Milk's camera shop on Castro Street. He had been within the reach of City Hall. More than anything, he had felt the vibe of the city's California dream. He had witnessed the pastel beauty of its neighborhoods, the Haight, the Marina and Sunset. He knew the gritty urban zones of the Fillmore and Mission. Like many others in Southern Oregon, the percussive tragedies emanating from San Francisco in November 1978 seemed close, terribly hitting home, as if right next door.

The deathly events in San Francisco coincided with the heavy onset of another Oregon winter. The all too familiar pounding of heavy rains and long dark nights began their assault. With the onslaught, life again would become the cold-chiseled splitting of oak and madrone, the heavy slick of orange-red mud caking to your boots, the mildewed odor of rain-drenched clothing drying by the wood stove. Winter returned like the repeat of another televised sitcom on a useless gray late afternoon. It would be a time for trading in your empty bottles for another quart of beer, eating redundant meals of homemade soup and vegetable rice. It was the season for coffee and smoking a bowl on a heavy downpour morning just to pass the time. The heights of recreation might include boring nights at the Solace Valley Tavern with nothing to say. Winter in Oregon was generally akin to falling asleep in bed with a book in your hand. The sad combination of such forsaken activities, mixed with the chilled coarse rain, could make the dreamy unconsciousness of a blanketed afternoon nap the most desired activity of a Southern Oregon day.

With Robert Sage expected to return to his London Ridge property in mid-December, Sean McAllister purchased a ticket for a holiday trip back to see his family. McAllister landed in Philadelphia, his father there to greet him. Both were happy to be together, to talk Eagles, Flyers, and Sixers. His mother, Connie, was ecstatic to have him close. The prodigal son had returned, at least for a time. Mary Jane came down from New York. He and Mary Jane stayed up late after the parents had gone to bed, catching up on the broad strokes and intimacies of their obviously different lives.

"So, you were right," McAllister said. "Disco is like the big thing everywhere these days."

"Disco? You're kidding. Disco is like old news now, little brother," Mary Jane answered. "At least, in New York. Punk rock is the latest craze. Although that music doesn't do much for me. It's just a bunch of angry noise as far as I can tell. But disco, no, that scene is fading fast. I still love to dance, but lately it's gotten pretty redundant. No, little brother, punk is what's happening now in the city.

"Why's everybody so bent out of shape," McAllister asked? "It's not like they're sending kids like us off to Vietnam these days."

"I don't know," Mary Jane answered. "New York is a mess. No money, no economy, a lot of crime in the streets. The city has always been tough, but lately things have gotten pretty extreme. You kind of have to watch yourself wherever you go."

"Huh," McAllister mused. "I guess I'm so out of touch these days. It's like I'm living at the end of the world or something. Or maybe it's the past, I don't know. I mean, some of the young people in Pollard Creek still wear white socks and black shoes, with their jeans rolled up at the cuffs."

Mary Jane had to laugh. "No kidding. You are in a time warp, Mickey. I've got to tell you, even hippies like you are ancient history back here."

McAllister and his sister continued to discuss the politics and personal ventures of which their lives revolved. Mary Jane was making good money. She had a wide circle of friends, as well as a boyfriend that she liked, although nothing was serious yet. His sister appeared to be settled, not looking for something else in her life. She had become less involved in politics, but still held strong opinions about nuclear power, the tragic issues of apartheid in South Africa, and the failure of the Equal Rights Amendment for women to reach constitutional status. It was interesting to see her sharp edges and matter of fact expressions. She was really becoming more and more a New Yorker in character and tone.

McAllister told Mary Jane about Paige, this distant but desired attraction that lived so far away. He didn't let on too much about the confusion their relationship was causing him, only that she was a woman he liked very much. Mary Jane might as well have been Sullivan, or even Paige herself. Take it as it comes, Mary Jane had advised. It will be what it will be. McAllister wished he could be as casual about the circumstances as everyone around him seemed to be. But Mary Jane's comments were once again a subtle reminder to continue on with his interests and pursuits. Okay, sure, although it was a little more difficult when you didn't know what those interests and pursuits should be.

The best news was that in Mary Jane's view their parents continued doing well. His dad and mom were pretty steady with their work and leisure lives, so McAllister didn't have to worry about any particular family concerns. Just like their mom, Bill McAllister missed his only son, but he had become more resolved with the reality of the situation, more at peace with the fact that for now his boy would not be near. Mary Jane's assessment was like music to McAllister's ears. He didn't want to face a difficult time, of having to defend himself against the concerns of his parents. But this good news had its own kind of irony. Strangely, his dad was becoming more relaxed about his worries for the future of his son. Yet, at the very same time, the son himself was beginning to feel just the opposite. McAllister was starting to quietly raise the same apprehensions about his future that his father had delivered not so long ago. It was surely a funny circumstance to consider. But in a way, maybe this was what it's all about, as time and people change.

A couple of days after Christmas, some of the guys got together for a holiday reunion at a bar on the outskirts of Wilmington. Johnny Howard was back in town from Boulder. McAllister and Johnny reminisced about the old days at the docks, and all the men they had worked beside packing bananas and transporting cars. Bruiser was putting on the weight, getting larger than ever before. He must have been sneaking extra product home from his father's beer distributorship. Others were beginning to move up in the world, getting married, settling for jobs with Dupont or some other chemical or banking corporation. To McAllister, it seemed like everyone was on their way towards the safe secure world, something even they might have rejected only several years before. He felt seriously out of touch, misplaced in his long hair and blue jeans, as if he was a figment of some former foolish days gone by. No one was particularly interested in hearing about his adventures out west. Those events did not relate to the present circumstances of their own singular anticipations, where the conventional world of their high school days was extending out before them.

McAllister would never have imagined that the height of the evening would be the appearance of Steve Rosenbloom, the Snark. The Snark was back from Wisconsin, his black wiry hair neatly trimmed, his full dark beard clipped with care. He looked the part of a college professor, which was exactly what he had become, after obtaining his PHD in history and continuing to teach. In the old days, McAllister would have done anything to avoid the Snark, dodging the guy's clinging offbeat ways. But after the Woodstock trip, McAllister had formed a changed opinion. On this night, years later, Snark Rosenbloom was in McAllister's view the most interesting man in the room. As the evening began to slow, he and Snark shared some time at a booth in the bar, catching up.

"You know, Sean, I've never forgotten that trip we took to Woodstock, and that you let me come along."

"Damn, Snark, you were the only one who got off his ass and was willing to go. If it wasn't for you and the Bruise, I wouldn't have had the balls to go it alone. I should be thanking you. But we did it, and that's the most important thing."

"I wish we had stayed for Hendrix. Gosh, one more day and we would have really been part of history. Who would have known he would leave such a mark, and then be gone a year after the concert. I still think about that trip from time to time, and I always get to tell my students I was there."

"You know, Snark, when I look back at that trip, I think more about the things you spoke about on our ride, your views on politics and America. I sort of knew then that you would make a good history professor. Now here you are, beginning to teach."

"Yeah, it's been good. I enjoy what I'm doing, and I even get paid. But I'll tell you Sean, things aren't the same on campus these days. The new students aren't listening much to what we were trying to say back then. Nowadays, they don't have a war staring them in the face, trying to take them away. It's different on campus now. It's kind of hard to explain. Everyone seems to want to return to the way things were before, to not be bothered by the need for change."

"Huh," McAllister mused, "You know, Snark, in a way I've become as guilty as them. I've become a political agnostic of sorts, mostly choosing to ignore the whole damn thing. Living out in Oregon, I mean it's not like you can disappear and everything, but at least you don't have to confront the bigger bullshit every day."

"That's what I mean, that's part of the problem," Snark began. "A lot of people from our generation are trying to escape from the system, trying to make their own way. What they unconsciously don't understand however, is that they are creating a vacuum, allowing others to fill the void. You haven't been on campus as I have. I can see the changes in intent. Other forces are beginning to fill that void, with a contrary set of ethics and motivation."

"How do you mean, Snark? As I said, I haven't been paying much attention. So what's happening that I don't see?"

"Well, it's not like there are no longer any progressive forces on campus, or anywhere else. But there is now a new element gaining more attraction. Some of the new students feel like they've missed out on something, so they are rejecting a lot of what we believe. It's probably just human nature, but at the same time it's not good. Economically, we are beginning to pay off the costs of the war. Concurrently, the rest of the world is getting hip to America's imperialistic ways. The oil producing countries are tired of getting ripped off, that's a big one. And at home, the fat cats are in the back room again. They have split up their profits gained from the war, while leaving the rest of the country to foot the bills."

Snark continued. He sure hadn't lost his natural ability to see things as they were, and what might be ahead. "In tough economic times, people look for something to blame, especially in America. And you can bet that the last on the list would be to blame themselves. Jimmy Carter is absolutely right in trying to promote the need for austerity, especially our national necessity for energy independence. However, what we fail to confront are the addictions that have become ingrained in the American reality. We have become a nation of speed freaks, from prescription drugs to electronic images, from instantaneous food to quick fixes for any problem that presents itself. The fifty-five mile an hour speed limit is a nice idea, but what a joke. You think some guy in a big hopped-up Detroit car is going give a shit about that restriction. In fact, most of those American made automobiles simply idle at fifty-five miles an hour. The only way you could cure that obvious problem, would be to mandate that everyone has to own a Volkswagon bus."

McAllister had to laugh at that remark. Chalk one up for the Snark.

But the Snark wasn't done. "Like I said, in difficult times, we look to find someone else to blame. When cultural change and confusion begin to ensue, fear is the consequence. In America, our normal response is to beat our chest and look for a fight. But the impacts of the Vietnam War remain too close. The big boys know they couldn't get away with creating another foreign enemy for awhile. But don't be mistaken, that particular tactic will return again. The military-industrial complex will be sure to promote another foreign danger sometime down the road. For now, they intend on focusing on the next best thing, our very own government. But it won't be the part of our government that led us into the Vietnam War. Instead, it will be the part of government that seeks to provide for those left on the roadside shoulder of the American Dream, the social welfare state. That's soon to become the new enemy, just you wait and see."

"Watch out for Reagan. He is the perfect political caricature of this John Wayne mentality. Watch out for his anti-government agenda, his bullshit morality fable of personal responsibility. Beware of his fairy tale that it is the black welfare mother in Harlem that is the problem, not the right-wing greed merchants that are personally financing his ascendancy. There is a stir of this ultra-conservative view of the world beginning on campus. There is a certain segment of the student population who need to see the vacuous reality of their personal lives in strictly black and white. That's the sum total of what their mind's can grasp. And we will pay the price if we discount their influence, if we cast their particular obsessions out of hand. They will seek to merge fundamental religion and the flag, while continuing the drum beat against a dangerous socialist world."

"But even more significant, they have seized upon Marshal McLuchan's missive that the medium is the message. They are becoming experts in creating televised images, paid by corporate benefactors, to sell America a bill of goods. Before you know it, they will have convinced you that only the rich are able to get us out of any particular mess. They will tell you that it's in the best interest of our country to leave the rich alone and let them do their thing. And Reagan is their designated set-up man. He is the perfect incarnation of their status-quo, unregulated, anything-goes orthodoxy. The reason Reagan is so perfect for the job, is that he's the quintessential believer in these myths they seek to continue. It's all a Ponzi scheme they can't afford to let falter, less their house of cards come tumbling down."

McAllister was intrigued by the Snark's cool but firm analysis. But was Snark really serious about Ronald Reagan? Not that asshole former Governor of California, the classic enemy of free speech in Berkeley, the cowboy warrior against peace and environmental protection. Not that former actor and Screen Guild president, who had reportedly turned a blind eye to his fellow actors being labeled as Communists during the Red Scare of the late nineteen forties. Not the man who had spoken out against civil rights, or was constantly blaming the federal government and welfare mothers for every single evil in the world of man.

Surely, America would not turn back so far as to make a man like Ronald Reagan, President of the United States. Not after so much destructive war and internal strife had finally been overcome. Could America once again deny its best intentions, to divert itself from the difficult course of striving to live up to the creed of economic opportunity and liberty for all? Could it really succumb again to the fear mongers seeking to create paper tigers, or allow its future leaders to plot one against the other?

Had not the costs of Vietnam and racial inequality been spent for a higher purpose we now all understood? America was just beginning to turn a corner, and despite the terrible loss of Martin Luther King and Bobby Kennedy, it had a real chance to heal its wounds, to once again begin to practice what it preached, both at home and around the world. But McAllister was smart enough to believe that Snark Rosenbloom was always a step ahead of the curve. He was reticent to refute Snark's perspective. Sadly perhaps, Snark was correct. It would be just another bump in the road, before business as usual would inevitably be restored to those who had never really lost control.

And what about the rest of America, the America who forever seemed to be in direct conflict with their own best interests? Would they again sit like monkeys in their televised living rooms, with their appendages humbly covering their eyes, ears and mouths? Would they once again start believing they should not see, hear, or speak any evil, afraid for themselves and waiting for direction? Would they be content to wait until the next snake oil salesman came along, stocked with plenty of bottles of cure? Would they once again fall prey to another swindler riding into town, or dancing like puppets for some words of entertainment, while the real puppeteers were never ever seen?

Sean McAllister had grown old enough to learn the factual reality of modern human cynicism. And he was as guilty as the rest, when it came to its dysfunction. But he also knew that the art of cynicism had no redeeming social value. It was akin to cocaine or heroin. It might give you a temporary high, but it would leave you empty and wanting after its passing. Yet, with Steve Rosenbloom's salient analysis playing like a broken record in his brain, he could feel the power of cynicism's constant seduction gnawing within his gut.

When she came into the restaurant, a little rush of fear ran through him. It was that fear that an actor feels before taking to the stage, that his words would fumble, that he might lose his train of thought. McAllister stood up and waved to get her attention. When she approached, they fell into a gentle embrace. She held onto him a little longer, in her own way letting him know how much he still meant to her. Slipping into the booth, she remained as attractive to him as long ago, her cheeks still full and tinged in red. But her hair had changed. It was shorter with a different cut, not thin and long as it once had been. She wore a skirt with dark stockings, flat pump shoes, and taking off her coat a soft green blouse. It was a much straighter look than their previous time together. But she was now working in a legal firm, so it was not unexpected. Nonetheless, she did not appear to be the woman with whom he had once fallen in love. She no longer reflected the past images he had carried around in his head for the last five years. Yet it was Mad all the same.

They managed to talk around the pain of an earlier time, speaking of their work and parents, and people they had known. She was surprised to hear the news about Mookie, but happy about his being back in school. It was hard for McAllister to speak about Oregon. Sitting in this restaurant in southeastern Pennsylvania, the state of Oregon could easily have been on a different planet, its culture and world so radically strange from this east coast reality. But it was a good experience, he explained, a small town with beautiful mountains. Pollard Creek was like a big extended family of sorts, with all the people he had come to know. Finishing their meal, he worried about her need to get back to work, but she said it was of no concern. It was Christmas week she reminded him, with hardly enough work to make it through the day. All the attorneys were on vacation. Finally, it got down to why they were really here together.

"Sean, I'm really glad you called. And I can't tell you how happy I was to get your letter, whenever it was you wrote. Everything until then seemed so unresolved. It made me feel so good to know you were okay, and doing what you had always wished to do."

"I'm sorry, Mad, sorry it took so long. But it did. I was so tripped out by what had happened between us. And angry, too. At you, at Willie, at myself for being such a shit. I had to get as far away as possible, and hope that it would pass."

"But that was it, Sean, you going away. From the very beginning, after your trip to California with Johnny, you were always talking about returning, to going out west. Part of me always wanted to go with you, but another part wanted to stay at home. But you were constantly distracted with those intentions. I know I should have spoken up sooner, but I chose to just hang on to the things we had at school. As the time got closer, I didn't want to confront it. The thing with Willie wasn't planned, believe me. He just kept finding excuses to be with me. And he wasn't about to go anywhere, to force me to make a decision I didn't want to make. I will always be sorry to you about any deception, but I was afraid to be honest with you, you wanted things so much. Instead, I just started to fade away from you, from us, from telling you I didn't want to leave home, that I didn't want to go."

McAllister's eyes rested on the table, listening. Then he looked up and tried to smile at Mad in understanding. "I guess I was always in denial about that, you never really wanting to go. I suppose I believed that once we were on the road together, you would become excited about everything, about a new adventure we were going to share."

"No, Sean, I wasn't. I wasn't excited at all. I was scared. Maybe the decision to be with Willie was an escape, I'm not sure. He was good to me after you left. But in the end, he made a lot of promises he couldn't keep. I'm glad things are over with him. It just wasn't meant to last. But at the time, I needed to be with somebody. I felt so insecure. And I feared you would eventually leave without me, and it would be over between us. It was bound to happen eventually, and it did, yet so much sooner than I ever wanted it to be." She paused. "But you should know this. The time we spent together was so good and so fun, for such a long while. I loved you then, I really did. I want to feel good about that time for us. But after you left, I couldn't at all, until you finally sent me your letter. Your letter allowed for things to feel easier for me, if maybe not resolved. And I knew you were happy and safe."

McAllister was at a loss on how to respond. It seemed in a quiet way that an unfinished picture was complete. Maybe now, this could be the honest explanation that would tie up the uncertain loose ends of his memory. The final answer that could forgive all those nights of grieving, the many lonesome moments of wondering, the hours and hours of trying to project some speculated outcome, of attempting to fill the emptiness in his heart that would never go away. And now, today, it was all down to this, sitting in a restaurant on a late December afternoon, listening to the sound of Mad's voice put things into their designated place. It seemed like such a high price he had been forced to pay, in exchange for the direct practical reasons now being revealed before him.

The measure of time and distance of course had a lot to do with it. But more so, perhaps, it was also the intuitive and frank dynamic that many women possess. Maybe not in the beginning for Mad, but today she was being clear and honest in her current perspective. Perchance, that is the difference with women. They actually learn something from relationships. Eventually, they begin to deeply understand those that are right and those that are wrong. Their own problem sometimes, is all the other worries that possess them. They hold on to their eternal hopes that things will get better. Or if they have children, their maternal concerns take precedence over the impact of a leaving, their terrible fear of the consequences of a broken home. But in the end, whenever their final decision has been reached, they rarely if ever look back. Whenever what's done is done, they are able to move forward with little remorse or regret.

Men don't take such loss that well. A woman's leaving becomes a tremendous threat to their own self-image. It challenges their manhood in a perceived world of men. Losing is not an option that they can handle without response. For some men, possessiveness is a right that cannot be abridged. Sadly, certain consequences can be very troubling, with verbal manipulations, or physical attack. Still, that kind of behavior has no place, never under any circumstance or any excuse. It becomes a chicken-shit and cowardly reaction, a shameful act of desperation short of a single defense. The methodology of running away may not be very brave, a cowardly and weak response. But it is not immoral or illegal. Rather, it is simply a means to an end. Sean McAllister had run away with his tail between his legs. Today, he was trying to make up for that prior disability, his youthful incapacity to honestly accept what he couldn't understand.

Outside the restaurant, standing by his car, McAllister watched as Mad headed down the street, walking away. He would always feel a deep sense of fondness and desire for this woman in his life. But he also understood such feelings were for the Mad he knew so long ago, not the woman he now encountered today. Separation, and the strange consequences of passing time, had produced their peculiar transformations. But Sean McAllister could only ponder whatever had happened to his former intense emotions of love and romance for this woman, back to those days when Madelyn Kelleher had been singularly the most important person in his world. How can such remarkable affections, so incredibly significant at a particular moment in one's life, have so fully evaporated and disappeared from one's heart? Reaching this indescribable point, where today, years later, it was if nothing had ever happened between them. As she turned the corner of a city street, perhaps forever gone, he could not fathom ever having an answer, believing only that these dramatic questions would always remain.

Bruiser sat behind the wheel of his car in the Philadelphia Airport parking lot, the engine still running. Sean McAllister sat beside him, not quite ready to say good-bye.

"So this is it," Bruiser said. "Back to the west coast. Back on the road, like you always seem to be."

"Yeah, I guess so," McAllister mulled. "Thanks for the lift Bruise. It's always a little easier leaving my mom crying at home, instead of feeling the hole in your gut as you get on the plane. I appreciate it."

"I suppose it will be awhile again, before you get back."

"Yeah, it seems like every couple of years or so. But I'm sure ready to get back to Oregon, I know that."

"I don't like it much," Bruiser began, "you being gone all the time. You were always so good at getting me off my ass. Getting me out there, doing one stupid thing or another. I guess, thanks to you, I can always say that I was at Woodstock, whenever the subject comes up. And of course, crazy Miami Beach. Although I'm still not sure about that fucking trip. Don't forget to say hello to Mookie when you talk to him. He'll remember when I was cursing your butt up and down the block for ever getting me to go on that dumb-shit excursion. Me and Mookie being stuck for hours on some hot fucking highway in the middle of the Confederacy."

"Couldn't have done it with out you, Bruise, you know that. And remember, you saved my ass down there, from those Cuban ass kickers that day. I still got the scar from taking the header on that punch."

"No shit, let me see."

McAllister leaned forward, showing a short indented line just above his left eyebrow. "It could have been a lot worse if it wasn't for you."

"Damn, you got a keepsake, Mac. Yeah, those boys were serious that day, wherever the hell they fucking came from."

"Seriously paid, no doubt," McAllister answered. "At least that's what I always thought."

"Maybe so," Bruiser said. "Well hell, perhaps it wasn't such a bad trip after all. A lot more exciting than the stuff going on these days, I'll tell you that much."

"You know, Bruise, maybe one day when Mookie and I get back together, maybe you and Johnny Howard too, you can come out west, and we'll do a road trip together, the four of us."

"That would be cool," Bruiser answered. "Yeah, I'd like to think about that, I really would." Bruiser paused, before speaking again. "I miss you guys, every damn one of you. But I miss you especially, Sean. You know that, right?"

"Always, Bruise, I know that. We go so far back, nobody even knows. We're hard-wired, brother. And it will always be that way."

"Hard-wired. I like that, Mac, hard-wired. It means a lot."

"I better catch my plane," McAllister confirmed.

"Yeah, Mac, you better catch your plane."

CHAPTER FOURTY-FOUR

IT'S NOT MY CROSS TO BEAR
Pollard Creek / 1979

ON JULY 15, 1979, President Jimmy Carter made a speech to the nation. He spoke to the effects of a sinking US economy, recently sparked by a huge increase in foreign oil prices. He spoke to the impacts of monetary inflation and rising unemployment that had become a consequence of the United States' incredible consumption of imported oil. He spoke to the stagnation of representative democracy, how special interests in Washington D.C threatened the ability of the Federal government to perform the public good. He spoke to a crisis of confidence in America, an America that having suffered through the assassinations of its vibrant leaders, the conflict and angst of the Vietnam War, as well as and the criminal conspiracy of Watergate, had begun to lose its way.

He called on America to buck up, to strengthen itself from within, to face up to the difficult challenges ahead. He called on America to take some personal responsibility for its actions in the past, to tighten its belt and conserve its resources. He called for its legislative government to get off its butt and do what's best for America's future, in a time of peace, not war. He called on everyday Americans to make some measure of sacrifice for the future of the country's economic destiny and democratic institutions. The speech was a spiritual and political warning to the United States. The country needed to change its ways.

But America did not want to listen. It had grown fat and sullen with the spoils of prosperity during the post-war decades. It had extended itself beyond its means, but remained in denial about giving things up. And for those who had prospered the most, the greed merchants of whom Snark Rosenbloom had often spoke, they surely were not about to return to preschool and learn how to share. America was in no mood to face these truths. It preferred the fairy tale of its arrogant hegemony, that the spoils of the American Dream would never leave its midst. Jimmy Carter was exhorting America to begin to face a necessary reality, to change its course for a continued future prosperity based on self-control and a communal effort of national intent. Instead, it was a monologue of warnings that a majority of the nation did not prefer to hear. In fact, the President was roundly criticized for the speech's stern measured tone. Jimmy Carter had done his best, but sometimes your best is not enough.

Was this reaction really a surprise? White America didn't care how many innocent victims lay dead in the streets of its nation, it would never curtail its guns. It wanted the electricity that ran its alcohol blenders, and kept its air conditioners humming. The Three Mile Island nuclear meltdown was a bummer for sure, but if it meant they couldn't have their Christmas lights, they weren't so sure about that. White America had bought the Vietnam War hook, line, and sinker. It had only turned against the war when too many of its own children came home dead in a box. White America had anointed Richard Nixon with a crushing second term victory, without a thought to the possibilities of his criminal misdeeds. It only later jumped ship when the indisputable truths became known.

White America could be trusted to get things wrong almost every single time. Just give them a flag and some old time religion, and you could count on them to drink the Kool Aid more times than not. White America lived like lemmings on the surface of the body politic, swimming to the beach whenever the next hypocritical illusionist might give them a call. Hip hip hooray for the general intelligence of most of White America.

Jimmy Carter was a good man, just a bit naive. He was a good man who had ventured into a very bad neighborhood. Morality, honesty, truth, and clarity of mind would not be enough to save his ass. Not in the capitalistic political world where he had ventured to play. For James Earl Carter, steely knives were being sharpened, ready for the cut.

~⌒

Driving his wood truck past the Hungry Dog Cafe on a warm August morning, Sean McAllister noticed the Railroad Bridge flatbed sitting in the parking lot. Next to it was Too Tall Tim's Chevy pick-up. McAllister pulled over and got out of his truck. It would be either Marty Johnson or Freddie Jones inside, maybe both, and he hadn't seen them for several weeks. Pasted to the back of Too Tall Tim's truck was a bumper sticker that read 'I Lost It'. It made McAllister laugh to see it. Where in the hell had Tim found that? The sticker was a sarcastic response to a multitude of bumper stickers seen recently in Grants Pass and on the freeway. 'I Found It' was a fundamentalist Christian advertising campaign claiming the finding of God.

Inside the cafe, McAllister joined Marty Johnson and Too Tall Tim sitting in a booth. Sliding in beside Marty, McAllister ordered some breakfast and coffee, mentioning the bumper sticker to Tim. Too Tall Tim said someone in Grants Pass had given it to him, acknowledging that it seemed to fit.

"It's great," Marty Johnson agreed. "I'm so sick of seeing the other ones. Those goddamn religious Jesus freaks are everywhere in these parts." He turned to McAllister. "Hey, did you see the Schludwiller truck out on the road?"

"The Schludwiller truck," McAllister asked? "You mean from the television commercials? No, is it out there? Cool. Are Vern and Earl here in the Dog?"

"Yeah, they're sitting over there at the counter with our best friend, Jake."

McAllister looked over at the restaurant counter. Jake Beecher was sitting on his familiar morning stool, talking to a couple of truckers who sat nearby. "Don't look like Vern or Earl to me," McAllister turned back grinning. "But old Jake looks as happy as ever to be alive."

Vern and Earl were two truck driver characters in a Henry Weinhard Brewery advertising campaign spoofing a beer called Schludwiller. Schludwiller was a clever combination of the Schlitz, Budweiser, and Miller brands. In the commercial, Schludwiller was a product of the California and Eastern Brewing Company. Vern and Earl were trying to sneak Schludwiller beer into Oregon because there was too much beer in California. In one particular ad, the truck is stopped at a weigh station after crossing the border from California. There, the Oregon State Police turn the truck around, telling Vern and Earl that Schludwiller was not allowed to be sold in Oregon. In a similar ad, a driver's car is searched, and a six-pack of Schludwiller is found in the trunk of the car. The cop arrests the driver for a misdemeanor, as Schludwiller is contraband in Oregon. When the cop asks the driver what his purpose is for coming to Oregon, the driver admits that he is a developer from California. In response, the cop arrests the driver for a felony.

The commercials were a comic hit in Oregon, playing upon the deep-seated mistrust of Californians, and the knee-jerk prejudice of any further development by the residents of that evil state to the south. The Weinhard Brewing Company, located in Portland, had even painted some of their tractor trailers with the Schludwiller logo to further parody the advertising campaign. From time to time, a Schludwiller tractor trailer could be seen at the Hungry Dog Cafe.

"Old Jake is over there pretending to be in serious discussion," Too Tall Tim joked. "Actually, he's just wondering when Marty is going to walk over and bust his balls like he always does. Am I right, Marty, or what?" Too Tall Tim laughed.

"Listen, that dumb-shit redneck will forever rue the day he took a pot shot at me and my girl," Marty confided. "There's no statute of limitations on that kind of bullshit. Like my Marine staff sergeant used to say, don't ever get mad, Johnson, just keep getting even. Maybe if Jake ever apologizes, that would be one thing. Until then, he remains fair game."

"I wouldn't be holding my breath," Too Tall Tim said. "I bet Jake Beecher has never apologized to anyone in his life, including his mother."

"Then the game goes on," Marty Johnson responded, "the game goes on."

The men got their breakfasts delivered, eating and drinking their coffee, talking the normal gossip about Pollard Creek. When the food was down, Marty Johnson popped the question that McAllister had been thinking to ask of Too Tall Tim. "What the hell is going on with Joe Joe Gifford? Is he really going off the deep end, or what?"

Too Tall Tim took a sip off his coffee. The expression on his face turned to deep concern. "Man, he's getting crazier than a loon. And there isn't much anybody can do. I've been trying, but he isn't listening. It's getting pretty fucking weird."

"Is he just fucked up all the time, not coming down, that kind of thing?" Marty asked. "Shit, I saw him in Grants Pass at the bar the other night. I don't think he even recognized me. Eventually, the bartender had to ask him to take a hike, he was so out to lunch. He was talking stupid shit and laughing his ass off. He was kind of nuts, Tim."

"Was Dirty Dino and that crew with him? You know those guys, right?" Tim asked.

"Yep. He was hanging with those dudes, as if they aren't enough trouble on their own. Do you think he is just coked out? That's what everybody else is saying."

Too Tall Tim shifted his long frame in the booth. "Yeah, he's been running with those creeps for a while now. Buying and selling the blow, and partying in between. He sort of comes and goes. He's still got his crop going above Strawberry Fields. But whenever I stop by to check on him, he's going like ninety miles an hour, talking all weird. I don't think he is sleeping a lick. Like I said, I've tried to talk him down, but it doesn't do any good. And I bet those guys are ripping him off, too. Hopefully, he'll come down off this jag, but I don't know."

"Is he getting violent or anything?" McAllister asked.

"Not that I know of," Tim answered. "But it feels like he might explode anytime you are around him. It's like having a friend who is shit-faced and looking for a fight. You don't know what could happen next. It seems like Joe Joe might flip out on you at any minute, but he never does. I just know I can't reach him right now. And I've been trying for Christ's sake, I can tell you that."

"Well, if you can't reach him, Tim, I don't know who else could," Marty Johnson agreed.

"I even called his sister, Paulette, down in Ashland," Tim Wilson continued. "She came up last week, but he wouldn't have anything to do with her. She just went back home shaking her head. I mean, she doesn't know what to do either. It's getting pretty bad. I'm just hoping he snaps out of this thing before something dangerous occurs. And that could be any moment."

The waitress interrupted the conversation, dropping off the bills for food. With that, the discussion about Joe Joe Gifford ended. The men got up, heading for the gift shop to pay their checks. As they neared

Jake Beecher at the end of the counter, Marty Johnson gave McAllister a wink, before speaking to the old man.

"Hey, Jake, how's it going today?" Marty Johnson asked.

"What do you want with me, hippie? Are you lost maybe, or do you just need a shower or something?" Jake Beecher smirked, turning to the truckers beside him.

"Nah, Jake, not today. But I wanted to ask you about those socks you're wearing. They're pretty stylish. Where'd you get them? I'd sure like to get a pair for myself."

McAllister and Too Tall Tim caught sight of Jake Beecher's pure white socks, resting on the foot rest of the stool. The socks were located between Jake's black Frisco jeans, and his equally black street shoes. They immediately understood Marty Johnson's jab, but moved ahead into the Hungry Dog gift shop, so as not to laugh in front of the old man.

"They're only made for human beings, Johnson. Guess you're shit out of luck."

"Well, they sure make the man, Jake," Marty Johnson responded sarcastically. "And you're the man, am I right. In fact, you're one hell of a private citizen. Yeah, I sure wish I had a pair of those socks. You have a nice day now Jake, a real nice day."

Marty Johnson came into the gift shop smiling. The men paid their bills before going outside. Too Tall Tim had to run. He got in his truck and drove away. Marty Johnson and Sean McAllister stood by the flatbed, saying good-bye.

"You been in touch with Tommy at all?" Marty inquired.

"Sullivan? Yeah, I talked with him last week. I'm going to stop and see him on the way to Washington later in the month."

"Apples again?" Marty asked.

"Yeah, one more time. But I think I'm getting kind of tired of it. Still, I need to make the dough. Have you been out to the property much?" McAllister asked.

"A few days a week to water the crop," Marty answered. "And today I'm taking a load of firewood back to town. I've been getting some welding work here and there. But I might come out on Saturday for volleyball. Are you still going to be around?"

"More than likely. We're done with the softball tournaments now. But you should come out," McAllister said. "Did you know that it's going to be the last year for volleyball at Butch and Lainie's?"

"No shit, man, no more volleyball at their place? That's a bummer. What gives?"

"They're just burned out, I guess. Too many people are starting to come around that they don't know. People going in and out of their house for the bathroom, some even taking food out of their refrigerator. Others are letting their kids run all over the property without any supervision. Pretty much, it's time for them."

"Guess I can't blame them," Marty responded. "But a Saturday without volleyball, man, that will be different."

Marty Johnson was right. Things would be way different. McAllister said his farewell to Marty. He started the wood truck, heading through town. A few days earlier, he had run into Jimmijay Connell at the Country Store. Jimmijay said he had some cash, and needed to start getting some wood for winter. McAllister had a half cord of dry madrone in the truck. It wasn't wood burning season yet, but the winter would be coming soon enough.

McAllister drove past the Pollard Creek Inn. The remodel of the building was recently complete. The State of Oregon had gotten what it desired, an historic bed and breakfast landmark, and obviously a new concessionaire. All the rehabilitation work had been performed by a general contractor from out of town. The good money had never really come to Pollard Creek. Sure, a number of the women in town would be getting the service work in the kitchen and dining room now that the Inn was open. Others would get to make the beds and do the laundry. But that would be the sum total of the Inn's economic boom.

McAllister had taken a quick look inside the building about a week before. There would definitely be no bar, no chance for the locals to have a place to drink and make trouble. Instead, it would be an overnight old hotel and restaurant. It would be a white tablecloth dining experience, with stark period accommodations furnishing the upstairs rooms. For McAllister, this newly revised version of the Pollard Creek Inn had all the charm and ambiance of a sterile tomb. That was the story of a revisionist America for you, as if a typical night at a nineteenth century stage stop would have been so morose. As well, the former energy, the real life hubbub of young people living and working the place, the camaraderie and reckless edge of the Pollard Creek Inn had been dutifully scrubbed away.

And you could bet the Pollard Creek Inn's recently past incarnation would never even be mentioned in any boring renditions of historical note. The marketing brochure would have no descriptions of Guitar Glen's music licks, nor Laura Hale's dance and drumming classes. There would be no mention of Jimmijay Connell's creative radio shows making fun of the everyday. The Pollard Creek Inn may have gotten a face lift, but the building had become as generically dead as any moment in its pioneer history. A shopping mall and a Motel Six would have more color and life than the new abridged edition of the Pollard Creek Inn. When Sean McAllister had first arrived in Pollard Creek, the Inn had been the rotating axis of a vibrant and special world, around which his new adventure had begun. The Inn's premature closing had been a serious bummer, but somehow the town's ebullient cultural life had found a way to continue. But now, Volleyball Saturday was reaching a saddened terminus as well. Something cold was in the air, even on this warm August morning.

Sean McAllister tried to let his discouragement pass. Yet, delivering the wood to Jimmijay Connell and Darla Bloom would take him by the Mulcahey Farm. McAllister slowed the truck as he past the wooded enclave, the place that had been his very first home in Pollard Creek. Through the trees he could see the pointed top of Mookie James' circular lofted bedroom, the everlasting home where Mookie had sought to build his dream. But that was all McAllister could see, as if the momentary sight of the structure was like a distant memory or a passing thought. It was a little hard for him to believe that more than five years had past since his arrival from Colorado. In some reflective way, the images of those moments were seared in his subconscious, as if they had only occurred just hours before. It surprised him how clear those memories remained.

Today, only Derrick Mulcahey, his second wife, Marlene, and their children continued to inhabit the property. Over the years, McAllister knew there had been others who had come and gone. He had met them from time to time in Pollard Creek. But all the original residents had long ago moved on with their lives. Still, there would have been moments during that earlier time, despite Derrick Mulcahey's peculiar whims and manipulations, when Sean McAllister might have believed that every one of them would have lived there together for the rest of their lives.

McAllister pulled down the driveway of the property next door to the Farm. Jimmijay Connell and Darla Bloom were still living at the old Harkness' place, the property that Albert Krieger had purchased after the Pollard Creek Inn's sale to the State of Oregon. Once Albert had left to go back to New York, he never returned. But he had kept the property as a rental, where Jimmijay Connell and Darla Bloom continued to reside. McAllister crossed the bridge over Pollard Creek, parking the truck by the woodpile outside the home.

Darla Bloom came out of the house, holding her new baby son in her arms. Darla and McAllister had always remained friends. With her reddish brown hair lying straight and smooth over her shoulders, Darla continued to be one of the most attractive women in Pollard Creek. Although their time together had been so short, it had planted a degree of intimacy that assured a genuine friendship between them. Pollard Creek had a way of overcoming difficult moments in relationships, before moving on together with no hard feelings. Pollard Creek had become like one extended counterculture family, mixing and matching as time went by. It was a strange sort of intimacy, based on the camaraderie of experience that everybody shared.

That was the funny thing about Pollard Creek, or similar small towns so incestuous in their geography. Everyone knew each other's warts and particular histories, at least the histories of their living together, where no secrets went unknown for very long. If you were an asshole, eventually you were accepted as an asshole. If you were a saint, you were accepted as the same. Privacy of self was not an easy commodity to preserve from view. It could never be hidden for long. You were accepted for whom you were, or who you were becoming. The inevitable results made it easier to accept yourself without disguise. That would always be Pollard Creek.

With Darla's direction, McAllister unloaded and stacked the wood. As he worked, they caught up on the rumors and gossip of the day. McAllister would never have figured that Darla and Jimmijay Connell would become a couple, but now they had a child to share. Their individual personalities were so distinctly different in source and expression. Jimmijay Connell was so dramatically comedic and out front, a constant stage presence for all to see. Darla was so incredibly frank and cynical, never letting a truthful word be wasted should it need to be heard. The couple had not consummated a marriage, so neither had been forced to declare until death do them part. It was an unwed partnership of convenience, with the bond of a child now at hand. It would have been absurd to describe their relationship as a marriage made in heaven, but then how many relationships really were?

Darla went into the house to get McAllister some money for the wood. As he waited outside in the late morning sun, the August heat beginning to rise, he looked across the nearby field adjacent to the Mulcahey Farm. He caught sight of Derrick Mulcahey walking along the fire road beside the tracks, heading his way. For a moment, a sharp current of anxiety cut through him. Even though he had not seen Derrick for a long while, those old waves of uncertainty continued to register. One never knew what might be on Derrick Mulcahey's mind. But whatever it might be, whether it was his high charming spirit or the onset of trouble, it was sure to come at you and not be left unsaid. Derrick's long straggly red hair and beard still roamed about his head, his walking gate wide and open, his expressive intent always full of purpose. That had always been the thing with Derrick Mulcahey, the uncertainty. And predictably, it always made you prepare for the worst.

The screen door banged shut as Darla appeared outside with the money in hand. She still held the baby in her arms, but by her side was Darla and Derrick's oldest daughter, Jessica. Jessica Mulcahey was growing up fast. She must have been reaching the age of ten or eleven, no longer the young child that McAllister had once gotten to know.

"Well hi, little one," McAllister greeted the child. "Jessica, you're growing like a weed. How old are you now? Are you ten, yet?"

"Eleven," Jessica answered firmly. "Mom says when I grow up, I can move to the city if I want."

"The city? No, kidding. Is that what you'd like, to go to the city?"

"Uh huh. That's where Canyon is now, he lives in the city. And he likes it a lot. He says there's lots more things to do."

McAllister looked over at Darla, who quietly shrugged her shoulders. But McAllister could see her attention was focused on Derrick Mulcahey, who was closing in upon them.

McAllister got out in front. "Hey, Derrick. Long time, no see. How things going?"

"Sean McAllister," Derrick answered, "you still around these parts? I'd thought you be gone like everybody else." Derrick Mulcahey shifted his weight. It was easy to tell Derrick had something else going on inside. "How am I doing?" he followed sarcastically. "Well, we're getting along, despite what others may think." There was an uncertain pause that followed, before Derrick turned his attention to Darla. "I need to talk to you about something, right away," he said.

McAllister watched as Darla's expression changed, as if to say to the world at large, here we go again. She handed the cash to McAllister, expressing her thanks. McAllister took the cue, said his good byes, climbing in the truck. It was definitely time to go.

Driving back to town, some things never change. Derrick Mulcahey would never change. And as long as Darla Bloom's two children were too young to decide for themselves, Derrick would be a part of her life, like it or not. Darla's cynicism about life was not a becoming trait. But if you had to deal with Derrick Mulcahey every day, just to have your children nearby and in your world, what should one expect. Most guys were happy enough to let the woman deal with the kids, perhaps give money when they could, spending time with them as necessary. But eventually the women were allowed to go on with their separate lives. Not Derrick Mulcahey. For Derrick Mulcahey, control was the most important thing. And any thought of losing it would be no laughing matter, whatever the consequences. The death of the Mulcahey Farm had no doubt been one of those consequences. But sometimes, it just had to leave you wondering why.

The first of September, 1979 arrived. Sean McAllister again made ready for the fruit harvest in Orondo, before heading north alone. Somehow the journey had changed. It no longer was imbued with anticipation for new people and a new adventure. It had become simply a work trip that he would have to perform. He stopped in Eugene, visited with Tom Sullivan for an evening before moving ahead. At the Lucky Girl, he settled in for the season, but somehow he knew it would be his last. The Mexican immigration had continued in force. They were good people, doing good work, but it was a culture and language he did not share. There were still a few other young people passing through, and Jesse Simmons continued his work at the Austin Orchard operation. But most of this harvest was solitary and mundane, the joy and excitement of previous years long gone.

Time and separation slowly create the inevitable. McAllister had stayed in correspondence with Paige, but the length of their lives was stretching away. She would not be coming over to the eastern side, and he would not be going to Seattle upon his return. The adage of taking things slow, of not rushing time, has its place in life. But there are no guarantees when things are said and done. He continued to miss what he and Paige had shared so long ago. Did he really love her, or she him? He no longer knew. Perhaps it was just the way of the world, another of those unsolved mysteries whose importance fades as the days pass, one beyond the other. Sean McAllister was quite aware that he was drifting, engaged in something of a suspended reality, unable to grab his life and set a new course.

In the meantime, there was little to do but gut it out, make the money and return to Pollard Creek. A new course in life demands an imperative, it requires a destination towards which to sail. It wasn't as if he was in denial regarding the circumstances, they were just too plain to see. And he had already been there before. Whether it had been college, or his days with Mad, the merchant mariner gig, or the disappointment of Colorado, he knew full well how to live with his uncertainties. Okay, so he didn't know his ass from a hole in the ground. What the hell else was new?

Living in the present is not a bad reality, when things are going good. But hope is an emotion inextricably bonded to the future, to seeing oneself in a better place and time. Dreams are more tied to the moment, more bonded to desire. Hope is better suited for the long haul, although you sometimes have to wait your turn. Nevertheless, at any moment fate can intervene. Fate is the ultimate requirement for which you cannot defer. Fate sometimes demands that you get crushed by the bus, just crossing the street. But hope has a different prerogative. It gives you the chance to look both ways before crossing, perhaps have a better shot at making it to the other side. For now, McAllister would at least cast his support with hope, and any future that might transpire. Meanwhile, he would look both ways upon crossing, and give himself a chance.

CHAPTER FORTY-FIVE

SUPERFLY

Eugene / Pollard Creek / 1979

SEAN MCALLISTER RETURNED from the Washington apple harvest season, perhaps for the last time. He pushed the panel truck down the back side of the Cascade Range to Bend. He crossed over the pass, then down the McKenzie River drainage into Springfield and Eugene. In Eugene, he spent a couple of nights with Tom Sullivan and his girlfriend, Carley. Carley was busy with law school. Sullivan had started working with a building cooperative, engaged in residential and light commercial construction.

McAllister always liked Eugene. It was a college town, the main campus for the University of Oregon. Eugene shared the liberal nature of much of what Oregon was becoming. It was home to the Saturday Market and Renaissance Fair in the summers. It was the home base for the well known Hoedads organization, an economically democratic and environmentally focused tree-planting cooperative. Near Eugene's sister city of Springfield, was located the little town of Pleasant Hill. This was the home of the patron saint of Oregon, novelist and Merry Prankster, Ken Kesey. Centered along Oregon's western Pacific side, between Portland to the north, and Ashland to the south, Eugene was a progressive crossroads for an Oregon state of mind.

During the day, McAllister walked the downtown streets of the city. He went to see John Belushi in Animal House, a film shot in and around Eugene. The film was stupidly funny and raised his spirits. It was hard to imagine getting through life without the seeing the comedy of the troupe from Saturday Night Live. There were the fabulous talents of Belushi, Dan Akroyd, Bill Murray, Jane Curtain, Laraine Newman, as well as the other-worldly Gilda Radner. There was Garret Morris as baseball player, Chico Escuela, and Don Novello as the incredibly clever Father Guido Sarducci. By their artistic genius, these young comedians lessened the angst of living in a politically devious world, easing that sense of powerlessness one felt surrounded by the American way. It felt good to laugh with them, while sharing the same with others.

That evening, McAllister, Sullivan, and Carley had dinner at home. They were joined by the neighbors next door, a woman named Tara and her five-year-old daughter, Feather. McAllister was attracted to this woman, her easy-going quiet demeanor, the bond she shared with her child. It was obvious that Tom Sullivan had taken to the young girl, playing and joking with Feather, almost acting as a temporary father figure. It seemed to brighten Sullivan in ways that McAllister had never seen from his friend, a stark contrast from Sullivan's often distant internal self. Tom Sullivan had always been good to Valerie's son Canyon, substituting then as a mentor and friend during their days in Pollard Creek. But this young girl seemed to bring out a sense of playfulness in Tom Sullivan, a persona that McAllister had never witnessed before.

McAllister had rarely given much thought to children, at least children of his own. Sure, like any man, he had entertained the intangible emotions of possibly having one of his own, and what it would be like. The rational idea of being a parent, of being able to teach a child what you knew and understood about life, was appealing. But in Pollard Creek, McAllister had also seen the responsibilities that such a reality imposed. There were the constant demands of focus that children required, not to mention the financial cost that their care consumed.

Pollard Creek had introduced him well to the world of children and their development. One of the best things about Pollard Creek was the ethic of a communal sharing of all the children's needs. Everyone was involved in their daily life, looking after them, keeping them safe and together. Despite any number of broken adult relationships, and the obvious lack of concern about the nuclear family household, the kids remained a primary source of attention and protection, shared by everyone in the community.

Still, it was hard to predict what deeper unseen effects the loss of a two-parent family might be creating. On the surface, there did not seem to be a problem. McAllister didn't know one way or the other. It had been by no means his direct experience. And he surely didn't know the details of Tara's singular parenting circumstance. But he could easily see the impact of Sullivan's attention to her daughter, the happy effect it had on her child. The evening had an influence on McAllister, giving him pause. He wondered what it would be like to have such a focused demand in his life, to be concerned with the needs of another human being who depended so seriously upon you. Perhaps raising children was the more traditional way of experiencing a purpose in this world, something to live for beyond your own concerns. However, it remained a perspective that Sean McAllister had never given much thought.

Later in the evening, McAllister and Sullivan took a walk through campus, finding a neighborhood bar where they could have a few beers. McAllister didn't have much to tell about the apple season. The harvest experience that Sullivan and he had enjoyed only two years prior was no longer the same. Tom Sullivan had not missed a thing. And the long distance relationship, or friendship, or whatever it had been with Paige, was waning. It felt just too far away to continue. It wasn't a bad thing. Again, it was only the circumstances, that time and distance thing which rarely can be sustained. It was surely something he didn't want to talk about, even with Tom.

As for Sullivan, Pollard Creek and Railroad Bridge were falling farther and farther away from his life. Each trip he had made to check on Carley's property at Paradise Creek had become shorter in duration. He would stay only long enough to keep the place in shape, nothing more. He missed everyone for sure, but he was making new friends through his work and Carley's school. Eugene had more things to enjoy and engage. Carley was now planning to sell the property on Paradise Creek. She was getting extremely involved in the world of law. It appeared as if Sullivan's previous homesteading passion was fading into the past.

McAllister wasn't surprised. Yet, the thought of Tom Sullivan not returning home was another silent kick in his rear, another close friend who had moved away. Sullivan had also recently heard from Valerie by letter. Valerie had written that she and Mookie were doing well, but that Arizona would not be the place for them when Mookie was finished with school. According to Valerie, Arizona was filled with rednecks trying to live the cowboy myth in the late-twentieth century. The world to them, she said, was still a screenplay in a Hollywood western. And the winter influx of the walking dead was driving her crazy. 'Snowbirds', she called them. They were boring aging Americans, with narrow minds and all the god-awful materialistic trappings from head to toe. It was like being in a rest home for the ridiculous every single day. Whenever Mookie got his degree, they would head back to the Northwest, wherever he could find a job.

Sullivan laughed at the telling. For a girl who had grown up in San Francisco, having experienced the Haight-Ashbury at its height, and lately Pollard Creek as well, Valerie's current circumstance had to be like an American version of hell. Especially for a woman who liked to dress up as Valerie preferred to do. She could only have stuck out like the sorest of thumbs.

So that was Arizona. Still, the news made McAllister feel really good that Mookie might be closer to him one day soon. "Maybe I'll send them a Reagan for President bumper sticker," McAllister joked. "It might help keep them safe until they can get the hell out of Dodge." He looked over at Sullivan with a wry smile. "You get it? Dodge! Dodge City."

"Yeah, I get it," Sullivan responded. "But it's Tombstone, buddy, not Dodge City. Dodge City is in Kansas. At least you haven't lost your sense of humor, Sean, despite all your other lost wanderings."

"Lost wanderings? What's that supposed to mean?"

"You know, don't you?" Sullivan countered. "Well, maybe you don't see it. But everything you say the last couple of times I've been with you, hangs like a question in the air. You're like a dangling participle, if that's what they call it. You're like a sailor without a compass, a hiker without a map. I mean, you're always on the move. But lately, it's like there is no destination, no certainty of direction."

"That easy to tell, huh," McAllister admitted.

"For me, yeah, it's easy to tell. Only, it takes one to know one, that's all. Like you, I've been that same exact guy since I got back from Nam. Wondering all the time where the hell I'm supposed to be. That is, once I realized I wasn't dead, or that I should be dead, like so many of the other brothers that didn't make it back. It's been a goddamn pain in the ass. Trying to figure out what you're supposed to be doing, when you don't even know why in the first place."

McAllister remained quiet, letting Sullivan continue. "It's not exactly like you these days, but it's damn close enough. The problem for me is that it may never go away. And it hasn't yet, I can tell you that. At least whenever I think about it, which happens to be now. But I see it in you, and I know what the hell it means."

McAllister was caught off guard by the turn in the discussion. He took a long sip off his beer. "You know, Tommy, this is the first time, the very first time you have ever said anything to me about Vietnam. Anything! In all these years of me wanting to know, and hoping one day you would talk to me about it."

"There really isn't anything to tell."

"No," McAllister demanded, raising his voice. "You know that's not true. You guys share it with each other all the time. I saw it that one night in Grants Pass. You, Marty, and a couple of other vets were sitting in that restaurant booth, after we were drinking one night. I still remember. You guys were crying like babies together. It was serious, I could tell. But we're not allowed. I'm one of your best friends, but I'm not allowed."

McAllister wasn't finished. "We shared it too, you know. Perhaps in a different way, a huge different way for sure. And I understand, or at least I think I do. But does it have be a goddamn secret forever? That we can't talk about it from time to time? Don't you see, but for the grace of god go I? Or that I was in Washington D.C., even with your brothers in Miami, making it all part of our lives, to be part of yours. It's just goddamn unfair, I'll tell you that."

Tom Sullivan held still for a long moment. "I'm sorry, Sean, but that's the way it is. And that's the way it has to be. You'll just have to accept it, that's all I can say." Sullivan turned his face toward McAllister, his expression filled with determination. But there was a hint of moisture in his eye. McAllister watched it well a tear, before slipping down his face. "I want you to know. I appreciate that you care that much. And I love you, man. You're like my innocent little brother. You have always helped me be myself."

McAllister's own emotions rushed toward his eyes, escaping. "I'm sorry, too," was all he could say. The two men turned and raised their arms over the other, embracing, probably making a scene. But it was a scene that spoke for much of a generation. And what that goddamn war had done.

Heading the hundred and twenty-five miles back to Pollard Creek, Sean McAllister didn't have any trouble coming up with lots of stuff to ramble through his head. There were a few meager harvest memories. There were thoughts of Mookie and Valerie, images of the woman named Tara and her lovely daughter, Feather. And of course, Paige, the woman he wanted so much to keep alive in his heart. After the Vietnam thing, he and Sullivan had traded shots and drank more beer, until closing time had come. It was all so true. Tom Sullivan was like the big brother McAllister had never really experienced in his life. Still, there were places you couldn't go with Tom. And McAllister knew that the previous evening was as close as he was going to get. He wouldn't try again, enough was enough. Their friendship was too important.

'Lost wanderings', the phrase Sullivan had used to describe his unconscious state of mind still nagged at him. And 'dangling participle', geez, he laughed to himself, where the hell had Sullivan come up with that little turn of a phrase. McAllister knew that a dangling participle was a grammatical term generally used to define a sentence that by its construction created an unintended meaning. Perhaps the phrase didn't apply in its proper context, but the word 'dangling' sure hit home. 'Dangling' certainly wasn't the best situation for a person's life to be, but it would have to do for now.

Okay, so he was engaged in a bit of lost wandering. And his present state of affairs did appear to be 'hanging like a question'. But what the hell does one do when the dangle is in progress? Sure, all it takes is an answer. A simple answer might do the trick. There was only one problem, where was the hell was that answer? Right now, right this holy frigging minute, there was no particular answer to be found. So what the hell do you do then?

Well, what you do then, is dangle, baby. Dangle until something better comes along. And there's no sense in beating yourself up about it, you've got to embrace the damn occasion. Get into it. McAllister wouldn't be the first to be a dangler. Shit, half the people he knew in the world were doing some form of dangle or another. So he was dangling. Okay, already. Thanks to Sullivan, now he knew. Meanwhile, he would dangle until the answer to the question came. And when it did come, he would climb safely back to the top of the wall, and everything would be great. Life would be a breeze. He'd be on his way to some grand personal evolution, and become a contented purposeful man of the world. He'd have his proverbial shit together. Cue the spotlight and the drum role, please.

One thing for sure, all this ridiculous mental exercise wasn't do much for his hangover. That was a fact. But he felt okay. There was nothing better than getting a little perspective on things. That favorite phrase from the Firesign Theatre boys came back to mind. 'Live It, or Live With It'. It had become one of McAllister's eternal mottos, whenever things conspired to get him down.

And McAllister had surely been 'living it' lately, all caught up in worrying about the way things maybe were supposed to be. So screw it, he would just 'live with it' for awhile. He clearly understood that he was ready for something else in his life. But what the hell it was going to be, he didn't have a single clue. In the meantime, he would just try to get back to being himself, playing the disinterested observer role he felt comfortable in performing. It sure was funny how the human mind can get the better of you. But enough of this nonsense. The panel truck was coming into Canyonville. He was not very far from home.

Tragically, life's future was not going down so easy for Joe Joe Gifford. The boy was becoming one sick dude, and it was not a laughing matter. Too Tall Tim was flat worn out, and had given up the cause. McAllister had returned to Pollard Creek to hear the stories. Everyone who cared about Joe Joe Gifford was on pins and needles, wondering what to do. It was like watching someone sink into madness right before your very eyes.

No one disputed that the cocaine was the accelerant. It had become the tipping point for a human mind gone haywire. And this was not just a regular cocaine habit, if there ever was such a thing. 'Biblical' amounts, Too Tall Time had confirmed, every living day. Sooner or later, something had to give. Joe Joe Gifford's brain had gone snap, like a giant fir branch under a heavy snow load. But the man wasn't dead. On the contrary, he was a living breathing beast out on the streets of Pollard Creek, a human tornado all over town.

While McAllister was away, Joe Joe's elevated state of mind had almost reached the breaking point. Somehow, he had gotten his pot crop harvested, with the help of some dubious friends, and probably a few secret enemies as well. On the final Volleyball Saturday, he had shown up like a whirling dervish, talking in tongues and smoking hugely rolled joints. He was like a chain smoker gone crackers, lighting up one joint with the burning roach of the one before. Needless to say, the circumstances threw a final damper on a long and beautiful Pollard Creek sporting ritual, one that now was ending its celebrated run.

The diagnosis from Nurse Donna, a woman who lived in town and worked at the hospital in Grants Pass, was 'word salad', or more medically defined as 'thought disorder', where the patient's scrambled brain placed words completely out of context, one from the other. It was a symptom of a psychotic episode, a marker for a diagnosis of schizophrenia. Underneath, Donna said, there could be the possibility of a more regular onset of mental illness, which often began to show outward signs in early adulthood. Still, there was no way to really tell, especially when the patient is charging freely through the everyday world, utterly fired up on cocaine, alcohol, and high concentrations of THC. And Joe Joe Gifford was definitely charging freely through the world of Pollard Creek. Unfortunately, he had not yet been busted, had not threatened anyone physically, nor made any traditional attempt to hurt himself. Until such a definitive event occurred, it was 'Katy bar the door'.

Sean McAllister did not know Joe Joe Gifford well. But from what McAllister could gather, Joe Joe had come of age as a very young man. His parents were a cross between the beat and the hippie generations. As a result, Joe Joe had been given many latitudes and experiences not granted to his peers, many of whom were children of a suburban white middle-class generation. By the age of sixteen, Joe Joe was already a free spirit in Pollard Creek, living an independent hippie lifestyle, something of a genius for a boy so young. Joe Joe knew how to do things, and do them well. Whether it was mechanics, building construction, or marijuana agriculture, Joe Joe Gifford could see something once and understand it completely. He was a husky, strong, and capable teenager, commanding an equal presence with men and women beyond his years. He was something of a man-child amongst all that surrounded him.

Too Tall Tim had taken the boy under his wing, and a brotherly relationship ensued. Tim Wilson loved the old pick-up trucks from the early fifties, working and modifying them constantly, with what money he had on hand. Joe Joe was equally fascinated with the trucks as well. He shared hours with Tim rebuilding engines from scrap, looking for parts or vehicles to purchase and restore to the road. A similar attraction was the cultivation of the herb. Early on, Tim and Joe Joe dug their holes in the woods above Strawberry Fields. They made manure tea from cleaning out barns and chicken coops, running their water lines from a mountain spring. Joe Joe Gifford read everything he could get his hands on regarding the science of horticulture, particularly the ganja weed.

When Tim Wilson had met Hank Swain's brother, Howard, the agricultural experience had taken another step forward. It was certainly the height of irony, that a brother in one of the oldest logging families in Pollard Creek might be secretly engaged in the smuggling of pot out of Mexico. But anyone who had witnessed the daring of the Swain brothers would hardly be surprised. According to many, Howard Swain was larger than life, a brawling cantankerous man of the woods. He was interested in everything, afraid of nothing. But he was also a man with a wife and four kids to feed, and not enough virgin timber to cut.

So Howard Swain had bought himself a plane, learning how to fly. After a while, he began disappearing for a couple of weeks at a time, always on business he said, and very hush hush. But a small town is a small town. Quietly, the rumors circulated. Like his brother Hank, Howard Swain enjoyed the hippies coming into Pollard Creek. They brought new energy to a world that was often too small for Howard, too redundant in its pervasive prejudice and mediocrity. The hippies well understood Howard's new part time job. Rickey Rucker, the "Rocket", saw an opportunity to be Howard's man on the ground, striking up a partnership with this man in the air.

Although Too Tall Tim was only on the outside, he had heard Howard talk of a specialty growing technique called sensimilla, where the male plants were pulled from the pot patch as soon as identified, leaving only the female plants to grow. As harvest time approached, the female plants would seek the male pollen, desiring to seed. Their resins would pour forth with this desire, straining to procreate as nature intended. The results became long hairy colas of bud. They were sticky, sweet, and heavy to the head. Too Tall Tim and Joe Joe Gifford didn't waste time. They seized upon the technique as soon as they could, and soon began to harvest the best bud in the valley.

But their partnership was hardly underway when news came that Howard Swain was gone, found with the wreckage of a small plane on a California mountainside. On behalf of the extended family, no one said a word about the circumstances. Sadly, there would be children left behind, who had lost a father and needed to come of age in peace. But Howard Swain's legend would remain, another myth in the wild and wooly history of this Oregon mountain town.

Meanwhile, a newer community myth was underway, and perhaps intending toward the same result. Joe Joe Gifford had become a voracious lion, and his close friend Too Tall Tim, a tamer without a whip and chair. Sitting in the Solace Valley Tavern one evening after McAllister's return, Tim Wilson told his story. He had tried to stop Joe Joe from acting out wildly, attempting to physically constrain him from taking any more cocaine. He reported that Joe Joe had been up for several days without sleep, bouncing from one place to another, talking his gibberish, completely out of control. People had come to Tim, requesting help. Too Tall Tim was a big man, but when he tried to subdue Joe Joe Gifford, it had been like wrestling with a wild animal, his strength was off the charts. Joe Joe had tossed Tim into the brush with little apparent effort. Then, Joe Joe had stared down at his friend with a defiant look of hate, a look Tim Wilson could not get out of his mind. There was a hardened look of intense paranoia in Joe Joe Gifford's eyes. It was a look that said Tim had deceived him, that he was now part of the enemy that surrounded Joe Joe's maddening world.

In between, there were apparent moments of strange lucidity, Tim explained, periods when Joe Joe seemed to be coming back. But his threatening presence always remained, like a hidden bomb waiting to detonate. During one of those sporadic intervals, a so-called friend of Joe Joe's had suggested they take him to the coast. The friend knew a place that might settle Joe Joe down. Tim had agreed to drive them to the location to see if this might help. Perhaps if Joe Joe was away from his current routine and pattern of drug use, things might ease. When they reached the location and set up camp for the night, Tim locked his car and kept the keys. But in the early morning, Joe Joe had awakened Tim, saying he needed to get something out of the car. Half asleep, and with Joe Joe seeming normal, Tim had given Joe Joe the keys.

According to Tim, this event was the final straw. Joe Joe and his friend had driven off in the car, leaving Tim stranded on the coast. Tim Wilson had to hitchhike back to Pollard Creek. But he quickly found out where Joe Joe had run. He called and told them to return the car the next day, or he would be forced to alert the cops. Apparently, the pair had driven to California to buy more cocaine. The car was eventually returned. But Tim Wilson now washed his hands of any attempts to help his old friend. It would be up to Joe Joe's sister and her boyfriend, or the parents, somebody else would be forced to intervene. McAllister could feel Tim Wilson's desperation, his intense anger at Joe Joe's deceit. But at the same time, he could feel Tim's deep sense of regret at forsaking the situation. All in all, another fact was true. In some quarters, the use of cocaine had taken over in the world of Pollard Creek.

Sean McAllister was not an innocent when it came to the blow. From time to time he had gotten to share the mirror, the lines of cocaine chopped and shaved with a razor blade. Noses would hover over the drug, with a cut off straw or rolled up bill of currency in hand. This would be followed by the snort, the ingestion of the white powder into the nasal passage, the head rising up, followed by a tightly rushed sniff to pull it all within. Shortly after, an incredible sense of well-being would course through the mind. It was a happy and fulfilled resonance of thought and feeling, free of anxiety or concern. The ritual was incomplete without the sidekicks of alcohol, cigarettes, and thinly rolled bud. The immediate effects were exhilarating, a pleasure dome of existence. Life was indisputable in its comprehension and understanding. For a time, everything was as perfect as perfect could be.

Only one problem, this sublime adventure of certainty and well-being did not last long. The body would suddenly send a frantic message. More would be needed to keep the pleasure ship at sea. And if it didn't get it soon, there might be consequences to pay. Waves of reality would begin to surge, tossing the boat this way and that, ready to take one down. For most cocaine sailors, the eventual storm was accepted and endured, for there was no more money to continue the ride. The party cruise would have to end, it was time to turn for home. Most of these sailors would accept their hangover and sleep it off. Once again, they would pick up their own uncertainties, and continue with the obligations of everyday life.

But for some of the others, they would refuse to turn for port. The siren call of cocaine would not let go. They would find a way to pilot through the storm, whatever it took. The pleasure ship could not go down. It was becoming the only way to live. Through the mist of their concentrations to keep the party going, they would never see the rocks. The inevitably of a sinking vessel lay perilously in wait.

The old hippie days of Pollard Creek were changing with the times. The days of a quart of Rainier and a homegrown fatty were no longer enough. In these new times, more was required, a few grams of flake and a quarter pound of skunk to sell for cash. People now had only so much to share. They huddled in tavern bathrooms or behind closed doors, snorting a line, separated from each other by the greedy necessity of enough for themselves. Harvest time was no longer imbued with the joy of the process. Nowadays, it was a time of hiding away and protecting your own. A gun became as equally important as a shovel. And silence and suspicion were necessary to keep the wolves at bay. A single pot plant had slowly become an agricultural commodity. It was worth thousands of dollars if grown the right way, and securely processed into tiny zip-lock bags.

For every action, there is an equal and opposite reaction. This is Newton's Third Law of Physics. But Pollard Creek now had its own extrapolation of the law. When marijuana equals money, the rip-offs will show. There had always been thieves in Pollard Creek, in one form or another. One only needed to ask a Rogue River Indian, if you could find one to ask. In Southern Oregon, claim jumpers, timber rustlers and wildlife poachers had roamed these mountain canyons for years and years. By the end of the nineteen seventies, a new kind of land shark had found its way to town, and he knew exactly what time of year to arrive. Indian summer in Pollard Creek was no longer a sweet time of extended sun and warmth. Rather, it was a time for trip wires and shot gun shells, a place where unfamiliar vehicles, deer hunters, and strange looking faces best not come around.

Sean McAllister had not been a frequent witness to this new transformation. Every fall at harvest time, he had been working north in Washington picking the fruit. But he could feel it in the air, growing in intensity each year before leaving for the apples. Although pot growing was becoming an economic necessity in a subsistence mountain world, there was no denying its effects on the once communitarian lifestyle everyone had enjoyed so much. Now certain people like Joe Joe Gifford were going crazy as a result, and the vibe was taking its toll.

Joe Joe was crazy all right, loopy enough to leave his best friend stranded on the Oregon coast. And a couple of weeks later, on a cold rainy November night, loopy enough to stumble into the gift shop of the Hungry Dog Cafe. Like the proverbial bull in a china shop, Joe Joe began purchasing a couple hundred dollars of useless knick knack items, while frightening the young cashier out of her wits, talking gibberish all the way. Carrying bags of the purchased items out into the evening rain, Joe Joe simply threw his cargo into the asphalt puddles of the truck stop parking lot, before driving away. Yet once again, he had failed to threaten any person, or commit a single crime of perpetration against the public safety.

Desperately, with Too Tall Tim and others having had enough, it was down to Paulette and her boyfriend to try and constrain him. Paulette finally called her parents, who stubbornly conceded their son had a problem that would not be going away. Legal arrangements were put in motion, and a judge was convinced that the Joe Joe was indeed becoming a danger to himself. The capture of Joe Joe Gifford wasn't pretty. He was physically subdued, then strapped to a plywood frame. Screaming like a banshee, he was shoved into the back of a waiting van, before being driven straight to a psychiatric facility in California. The talk of the town wondered if Joe Joe Gifford would ever again be the untroubled young man they once had known.

The early winter of late 1979 was a dark time. Joe Joe Gifford had been hauled away. The strange sickness of his illness coincided with the national trauma of the American hostages being held at the US embassy in Tehran. President Jimmy Carter, despite his best intentions, could not negotiate their release. The US economy was in the tank. Inflation, high interest rates, unemployment, and surging oil prices were conspiring against him. Despite his calls for conservation and patience, America was in an ugly mood. Per the usual, the United States was practiced at blaming everyone else except themselves. They blamed the President. They blamed the Iranians and the rest of the camel jockeys of the world. It was the perverse freedoms of civil society, of women seeking equality, of Black Americans wanting economic justice, of gay and lesbian citizens sinning against the dictates of a Christian god. The Soviet invasion of Afghanistan only added to their discontent and fears.

The desperate folly of Vietnam was quickly being forgotten. The oil companies, the military-industrial complex, as well as the merging corporate heavies, were getting their ducks in order. Energy independence, human rights and peaceful restraint were too high a price to pay. Business as usual was necessary. Enemies needed to be created, a divide and conquer theology was required in order to maintain the status quo. It was time to cue up a quality front man to carry the torch, a man who could symbolize a bully America, while protecting the wealth of a nation in the hands of the few. It wouldn't hurt if this man might look good in a cowboy hat and boots, a Marlboro man who could ride a horse off into the sunset. The casting department had found the perfect actor for the part. His name was Ronald Reagan.

CHAPTER FOURTY-SIX

DEACON BLUES
Pollard Creek / 1980

WITH THE COMING OF 1980, life in America dragged its butt into a new decade. In Pollard Creek, the rain seemed to never stop. When it did, the sun refused to make an appearance. Temperature inversions once again cast a foggy pall across the valley sky, compressing the town in a cave of cold depressing gray. Orange-red mud caked the wheels and fenders of every car, clung to the footwear of every boot, lay drying on the floors of every business establishment. The odor of wood smoke hung inside the cavern, trapped by the repressed barometric of high pressure systems that no one could ever see. A serious outbreak of cabin fever could not be contained.

Work and money were as thin as a wallet. Bills were never paid in full. People ate oatmeal, root crops and chicken pot pies every day. Gas tanks never reached further than a quarter of the gauge. Credit accounts at the Frontier Market and the Pollard Creek Country Store surpassed all time highs. The only fun on weekends was at the first of the month, when welfare and disability checks hit the post office box. Food stamps might as well have had George Washington imprinted on the bills, they were traded for dollars so many times. Televisions burned all evening, becoming the cheapest entertainment anyone could afford. Soap operas became the main topic of interaction on the gossip mill, there was so little new to exchange. One didn't have to play the blues in Pollard Creek, living it was plenty enough.

The mechanic's garage of the Union 76 gas station was as crowded as a theatre during the day. Men huddled around the wood stove, bemoaning the state of the economy while sitting on their ass. Outside, a fifty-five gallon trash barrel burned away. Other men stood outside warming their hands, passing a bottle of Mad Dog 20-20 between them. They would smoke and curse for something to do. Hugh Preston, the new owner of the station and the Frontier Market next door, let it all go. At least he was making some cash off the liquor sales. Everyone called this meeting place the '76 Club. It had all the charm of a prison yard, but at least it was warm inside the garage. Travelers along Interstate 5 didn't stay long. They left the wife and kids locked in the car, before gassing up and speeding away. The beauty of an Oregon winter was never much to see.

Randy Halston had taken the steepest fall. Once upon a time, he was the hard-assed gun toting cowboy from Cougar Gulch, whose reckless behavior had helped upend the Pollard Creek Inn. But Randy Halston had become a shadow of his former self. He had grown overweight and constantly inebriated over time, a helpless alcoholic. Randy had lost his ramshackle trailer and guns up on the Gulch. Nowadays, he wandered from shed to shed, at the mercy of those who might feel sorry for him from one day to the next. Lately, he had been sleeping at night in the bathroom building that sat behind the station. Hugh Preston did his best to look the other way, knowing full well that Randy Halston had no other place to go.

Sean McAllister had the unwanted pleasure of watching it all unfold. Everyone knew that eventually the winter would pass. Still, it was not a pretty sight. Reluctantly, McAllister did what he could to keep his own blues at bay. He cut firewood to keep himself in cash. He attended the potluck dinners on Friday nights, made occasional trips to the Solace Valley Tavern or an evening in Grants Pass. He had books to read, afternoon naps to dream away, or a basketball game to watch on the tube. But there was no real woman in his life, no one to share moments of intimacy through the long hard nights. Pollard Creek, the Pollard Creek he once knew and loved, the place he called home without a second thought for so long a time, was now missing in action. Missing in action it seemed, with little chance of return.

Paige Lindstrom, the girl he so much wanted to love, but didn't know how, drifted like a distant memory he was unable to recall. Time and distance can often be an appropriate necessity, allowing one to heal certain wounds and go on with their life. Time and distance can be a therapeutic catharsis whenever something is lost. On the other hand, time and distance can be unjust. It can take something beautiful and free, and by the duration of its absence leave it far behind. It can force the thrill of expectation, the desire for an imagined reality and purpose, to become closed inside. Once enclosed, it chips away the wishfulness of hope. It erodes the strength of love's belief like water over rock. Slowly, love is worn to sand and dust, left forever to scatter in the wind.

Paige's most recent correspondence, a few practical words of care and concern before the holidays, seemed to reflect a similar loss of emotion. She expected to be graduating with her degree at the end of the year. The last of her clinicals would begin in the months ahead at the university hospital. Upon graduation she would begin looking for work, or maybe take some time off, she didn't know. She hoped to see him again soon and hoped he was well. It was a letter of friendship more than love. And if anything might have been left unsaid, it didn't filter through.

McAllister had responded in kind, lying through his teeth that things were okay, wishing her the best. Paige was a beautiful woman, a woman that part of him wanted so much to be near. But he refused to rock her boat, to tell her how much he needed someone like her. He wouldn't burden her with his own truthful misgivings. She deserved better than such foolish concerns. Whatever he was to make of his life, he would have to make it on his own. One of these days he would hopefully figure things out. Meanwhile, the present would have to do, although he continued to be restless for some kind of sign to appear.

The United States was in no better spirits. Jimmy Carter had tried to recast a modern America, an America that needed to break its addiction to oil, to work together to help the helpless, while promoting personal responsibility and conservation. America needed to proffer a more even hand in its relationships with the rest of the world. It needed to drop its big sticks of interventionism, to halt cutting deals with despots and criminal states to protect its own economic interests. Carter tried to broker a Middle East solution, to reverse the costly arms race, to engender respect and support for human rights, to promote the rights of others for their own liberation. But the sins of America's past and present were conspiring against him.

The big boys of America were not on his side. They had too much to lose. They had made their economic riches on the status quo, and were not about to give them up. Guns and bombs were their major stock in trade, along with gas guzzling vehicles throughout the land. Savage dictators like the Shah of Iran and the Somoza regime in Nicaragua needed to be sustained. The arms race was good for business, the protection of oil and other commercial interests vital to maintaining power and control. But the dastardly effects of such brazen influence were taking their toll.

The rest of the world was beginning to figure out the shell game America was playing on them. The Organization of Petroleum Exporting Countries (OPEC) cartel wanted in on the spoils. United States support for the murderous repression of dictators like the Shah began to backfire, and all hell had broken loose in Iran. Throw in that maddening variable of religious fundamentalism and look the fuck out. It really didn't matter if it was Christianity, Islam, or any other godlike orthodoxy that believed in the sword. Spike any conflict with some old-time religion and things could get brutal fast. Jimmy Carter, and any other forms of progressive intelligence were getting caught in a cross fire, and likely to catch a bullet.

By the late-twentieth century, America had gotten used to its easy ways. Its middle class had grown comfortable in their prosperity, a prosperity forged at the costs of an unsuspecting third world. The United States had already shown it was more than willing to kill fifty thousand of its own to keep the engine running, to keep its rubber on the road. But in 1980, the country lived in fear of losing what it had gained. The bulk of America could only afford to be generous and progressive when things were going well. Sadly, as the world began a new decade, hard times were upon them. The economy was suffering a reallocation, while the rest of the world was getting hip to the game.

America remained divided in a serious and fundamental way. The greater nation had been sold a bill of goods that economic democracy and opportunity still existed in the twentieth century. But the facts were clear that most of the available wealth in the country had long ago matriculated into the hands of a few. The only mechanism that remained to stem this tide was a tax code that could act like Robin Hood. A tax code was necessary to force the aristocracy to pay a greater share into the pot for all to share. Short of a revolution, that was the way it needed to be. Franklin Roosevelt understood this necessity. Under the circumstances of such a wide disparity in wealth, a social welfare responsibility needed to exist. Private industry would be welcomed to thrive, but those that already had the gold would be required to pay some back for the public good. It was a workable scenario that allowed for free enterprise not to be thwarted, while allowing for the aged to survive, the helpless to be helped. Unfortunately, Snark Rosenboom's long ago assessment still held sway. Greed remained at the heart of the division. Social responsibility would continue to face an assault in the face of this greatest of human ills.

It was like a boxing match for the soul of American democracy. In the red corner, the survival of the fittest. In the blue corner, the general public welfare. The mismatch went something like this: "Pull yourself up by your bootstraps, boy. And get yourself down to the mine. This is your land of opportunity, so don't miss out." Perhaps a few years later; "Well, we're real damn sorry you got that black lung, that you don't even have enough breath to answer the door. Guess things didn't break your way after all, despite busting your ass six days a week. As for that grimy air your kids are breathing, and the water supply that's been contaminated, well you know, that's not our problem. But we do hope that lung gets better, we really do."

"And look, who is that man over there on the white horse, wearing the red trunks? Is that John Wayne? Why no, damn if it isn't Ronald Reagan. Now there is a man you should stop and give an ear. He'll tell you where your problem lies. It's your government that's the goddamn problem, feller, interfering with your inalienable right to be sick on your own. And don't forget to blame those lazy welfare queens sucking off the tit of your hard-earned tax dollars. Don't forget those commies, too. They're hiding at the edge of town, just waiting to take your precious freedoms and guns away. Hey, take this here Reagan/Bush yard sign. Put it out in front of your dilapidated shack. Ronald Reagan is a man who feels your anger. He's on your side, all the way."

"Well, we got to go now, back to our little houses on the hill. Aren't they swell? And so strategically located where the black smoke never blows. We can't be late for dinner. We're sure you would agree, it's never good to let the prime rib go cold. Hey, like we said before, take care of that lung."

"And don't forget to vote for Reagan, the Ronald Reagan, in his shining armor on the mount. He's got that practiced homespun delivery that will make all the bad times go away. However, please ignore those elderly white men standing behind the curtain, dressed in their corporate banking suits and ties, with their manicured fingernails, processed hair, and fat wallets bulging out their ass. No, look over here at this beautiful flag, and this picture of a big sturdy farmhouse surrounded by waving fields of grain. And in the distance, can you see it? It's the steeple of our church. Isn't it holy? God Bless America. And remember this one final thing. Propaganda and hypocrisy are not propaganda and hypocrisy, as long as they remain unseen."

The Oregon winter grinded onward. McAllister had left his living situation up at Robert Sage's property, finding another caretaking gig at a residence on the edge of Pollard Creek. The owners', George and Helen, were parents of a friend. They had moved to Pollard Creek to be closer to their daughter. George was a union electrician from California, who had hoped to retire soon, but planned to keep working in Oregon until it was time. However, the economy was in the straights. As a result, George and Helen needed to fire up their motor home, heading back south for available work in the Golden State. During their absence, McAllister would be able to live in their double-wide trailer house. When they returned, he could retreat to their bunkhouse cabin behind the home. It was a great deal, minimal rent and comfortable accommodations, a television set and electric heat. Physically, it was the best living situation Sean McAllister had experienced since his arrival in Pollard Creek.

Out the plate glass window of the trailer, McAllister could watch the traffic on Interstate 5, speeding north and south every day and night. Unconsciously, he was being drawn closer to the constant drumbeat of a mobile America, going to and fro. The view was like witnessing another world, a world he had chosen for some time to live without, never paying much attention. It made him ponder how large and expansive the world outside remained. As well, it was a constant reminder of how small his own uninspired life had become. He could be anywhere, be here or be gone, and the pulse of daily life would never skip a beat. All his personal opinions and cynical political notions mattered very little when push came to shove. The rest of the world would go right on passing by, roaring up one mountain pass then down another, uncaring but for their own individual destinies.

Such a realization could be strangely depressive, or highly inspiring, depending on the point in time. One day, it could feel like his life might never change. The next day, perhaps filled with a beneficent portent of things to come. But the bottom line was that something was missing in his own existence, and the awareness of this void was playing like a skip on his favorite album. You wanted to hear the song, but damn, you knew the scratch was coming. When it skipped, it would play over and over, until you got up and lifted the needle to let it play on. It sucked, but he knew a lot of things sucked in life. Still, whatever the trouble might be, the music needed to continue. And for sure, any existential thoughts of halting the chorus could never be entertained. The blues were an integral part of living, whatever their cause.

As for Pollard Creek, it is sometimes believed that bad events often come in threes. And events in the early winter months of 1980 appeared to be holding true to that cultural aphorism. First had been Joe Joe Gifford's illness. Joe Joe had been transferred back to the Oregon State Mental Hospital in Salem. Apparently, his drug use had acted to precipitate and hasten an organic disorder of schizophrenia, one from which he would likely never recover. Legal drugs would now be substituted to balance his manic delusions. Sadly, one thing seemed clear. Joe Joe Gifford would never be the young man he once had been.

In the middle of January, the weather inversion lifted. Clear blue skies rose above, but were bitter with cold. Randy Halston was found dead, lying on a picnic table in Pollard Creek State Park, a frozen bottle of Mad Dog wine nearby. The boys on Cougar Gulch gave Randy a drunken send off, but outside of them, no one much cared. Over time, Randy Halston had made his own bed in Pollard Creek. The flag at the post office would not be lowered to half mast upon his passing.

Nonetheless, death marks a significant moment, especially for the young. It makes one consider their own mortality, to reflect for a moment on their own eventual demise. However, such perceptions are difficult to maintain, and life goes on. Lucky Rogers, one of the good old boys at the '76 Club, had flatly put it in words. "That boy Randy just had the mad dog grip, and there wasn't a single thing anybody was going to do about that."

The third event was a little harder to swallow, and definitely unexpected. No one is ever prepared for the death of a child. Emmit Logan wasn't exactly a child, but seventeen was close enough. The kids in Pollard Creek lived in an unusual world. They were openly exposed to all their parent's predilections, right or wrong, good or bad. And much like the elders that surrounded them, these kids had a greater sense of freedom and carelessness as they came of age. They were allowed to run wilder than many of their peers in kind. As for the boys, guns were a big part of their upbringing, a childhood fascination easily given credence at an early age. Learning to hunt was an obligatory right of passage in this Southern Oregon world.

On a winter Friday night in February, parked beside the Pollard Creek Country Store, a couple of teenagers had gone inside. The others, including Emmit Logan remained in the car. Cruising the logging roads of Pollard Creek was something you did for something to do, whether it was to drink with your friends, or maybe hit a homer with your girl. On other evenings, perhaps you loaded your rifle, then grabbed your big flashlight to go looking for deer. Poaching out of season was never a crime unless you got caught. It was a typical teenage weekend in the world in which you lived.

Somehow, the safety must have been off, but no one knew for sure. Was it horseplay or a simple mistake, it didn't matter in the end. The sound of the gunshot pierced the inner confines of Pollard Creek, a little too close it was easy to tell. The rest was history and a hell of a mess. Young Emmit Logan was killed instantly and at short range in the backseat of the vehicle. Later, Sheriff Bill Haines called it one of the worst nights of his career. Haines had seen a lot in his time on the job. There were fatal car wrecks on the freeway, or an occasional murder scene in a family home. But to lose a kid in this manner required a particular strength that was difficult to summon. It was especially hard when you had raised children of your own.

Pollard Creek mourned. Despite the often juvenile antics of its own adults, the loss of a child hits home with chilling effect. It causes even the worst of the world to say a prayer at the gravesite, wishing it didn't have to be true. Still, it wouldn't be the first time such sadness had prevailed, nor the last time a life would be shortened by circumstances beyond one's control. In a land of dangerous logging, amidst a town populated by more than its share of rebels without a cause, death had its place in Pollard Creek. But for a kid on the verge of his own independence and youthful creation, it wasn't easy to take.

For Sean McAllister, to this trifecta of death and disease, one more could be added. On January 19th, 1980, retired Supreme Court Justice, William O. Douglas died at the age of eighty-two. McAllister still remembered the presence he felt at seeing Douglas years before, while a student in Washington D.C. William Douglas had grown up in Eastern Washington, in the fruit country of the Yakima Valley. Douglas' love of the Cascade wilderness country of the Great Northwest, his support for environmental issues throughout his career, was well known within the burgeoning movement to protect America's natural resources and habitat.

Equally important was Douglas' constant judicial adherence to protecting first amendment rights. He voted against attempts to strengthen the power of government against political thought during the McCarthy era. He was active in trying to codify the rights of privacy, free from interference by the state. In his earlier time as Chairman of the Securities and Exchange Commission, Douglas had also attempted to reign in and regulate Wall Street speculators. He sought to stop Richard Nixon's attempts to allow the US military to spy on domestic citizens. And throughout the trauma of the Vietnam War, Douglas had worked hard to find a way for the Court to hear a case that just might challenge the legality of the conflict. In August, 1973, Douglas actively went out on his own, granting a judicial stay that would immediately halt the expanded bombing raids on the sovereign country of Cambodia. Although the stay was promptly reversed by the full Court, Douglas had done what he could. It was not surprising that earlier in 1970, that familiar political knucklehead, Gerald Ford, while serving as House Republican minority leader, had made efforts to impeach Douglas' tenure on the Court. Then four years later, in the height of irony, Gerald Ford would pardon a man whose complicities in crime were an open and shut case, Richard M. Nixon.

On the day to day, the conscious mind goes through its regular routines. The body wakes in the morning, takes a shit and a piss as necessary, feeds itself as required. The conscious mind formulates the day's activities for good or ill. But deep inside the interior basement of the brain, the unconscious mind is hard at work. Like a boring accountant with a visor hat, it tabulates certain amounts of emotion, of memory, the piles of happiness and pain. The unconscious mind never hurries with its duty, it sticks to its calculations based strictly on the data being compiled.

When satisfied with its results, the unconscious mind is expected to file an analyzed report to the conscious mind, complete with opinions on the best direction ahead. Sean McAllister's unconscious mind was working long days and nights, collecting a hell of a lot of data, and a hell of a lot of overtime pay. Eventually, the day would come when it had to present its findings. But when a twenty-nine year old conscious mind has been relegated to watching soap operas on rainy winter afternoons, or staring out a window smoking a joint, counting cars and trucks passing by on an interstate freeway, well then, the unconscious mind had better get its ass in gear and send up that report. Meanwhile, Sean McAllister could only take some aspirin for his cabin fever, and wait patiently for a courier to knock on the door.

Another difficult Oregon winter fought its way into spring. The seasons on the coastal side of the Great Northwest are never cut and dry. Instead, they morph slowly one into the other, refusing to let go. Eventually, spring was able to untie the tether, bathing Pollard Creek in wildflowers of warmth and sun. McAllister, knowing he would not be picking fruit the following fall, planted a marijuana patch on a hillside above the property where he was caretaking. This would be his job number one for the summer. In between, he continued to cut firewood, and also got a job painting the Frontier Market. Anything to keep the cash flow running.

Freddie Jones, at Railroad Bridge, had purchased a couple of draft horses, selectively logging trees that were ready to cut, using the horses to pull them down to the mill site. Marty Johnson continued to spend a lot of time in Grants Pass with his girlfriend, while partying in town. But Marty also had gotten his welding certificate in between, and was setting up a small welding shop in Solace Valley. From time to time, both Marty and McAllister would help Freddie with the timber and the mill, but Freddie remained the last true holdout up on Railroad Bridge.

With the onset of summer days, McAllister felt the baseball bug kicking in. Although the game had changed to slow pitch softball, he joined a tournament team in Grants Pass, playing first base and outfield. It was fun to be playing for keeps beside other good players. With the community draw of Volleyball Saturdays now in the past, McAllister was free to fully replace this loss with the game he loved. But the consequence of this pursuit found him taking another baby step away from the day to day life of Pollard Creek. He was not alone. Everyone seemed to be finding new things in their lives that they preferred to be engaged. The intangible sense of oneness, which for so long had characterized McAllister's allegiance for living in Pollard Creek, was beginning to fade. It wasn't like he was grasping for straws, but his personal doubts continued whenever he chose to consider them. Fortunately, with a long active summer in his sights, the doubts were of little concern.

On a Monday morning in early June, McAllister sat alone in a small breakfast eatery in Grants Pass, reading the newspaper. After ingesting the sports page, he turned to the news section. A quiet personal disappointment befell him. The American novelist, Henry Miller, was dead at the age of eighty-eight. After reading the obituary, McAllister looked up from the newspaper, as if wishing to tell someone of this momentous event. Predictably, there was no one to share the experience.

And even if there were such a person, they would have likely known the name of Henry Miller only as a marginalized pornographer, instead of one of the great American writers of his time. Ernest Hemingway, they would have known for sure, even though they may have never read a line of his work. But Henry Miller, no, Miller was not to be read. He was a rude, anti-feminine subversive, whose angry pessimistic tirades against the American way deserved to be disregarded and ignored. Henry Miller's books were more likely to be burned than to be put on a library bookshelf. One could count on that.

What went missing in this onslaught of government sexual repression, and the lack of mainstream literary acceptance, was the fullness and incredible expansiveness of Miller's art. Readers would never get to perceive his indelible optimism, despite all the unbelievable sins of mankind he chose to confront. Miller never spared the reader the torture of seeing such misgivings, of calling a spade a spade, or raising his hackles against the hypocrisy of the American experience. He spoke to America's reactionary primitivism against the true diversity of art, culture, and human expression. Miller had figured out America's penchant for a doctrinaire conformity early in his adult life, long before he found his voice as a literary rebel. "I have never been able to look upon America as young and vital," he once wrote, "but rather as prematurely old, as a fruit which rotted before it had a chance to ripen." Yet, Miller's love of life was unmistakable. "Develop an interest in life as you see it," he would proclaim, "the people, things, literature, music, the world is so rich, simply throbbing with rich treasures, beautiful souls and interesting people. Forget yourself."

Amongst the literary euphoria of a pre-war Paris, Henry Miller found his muse and the calling of his life. And he took to it with the voracious energy and interest of a superbly conditioned athlete. Some years later, chased from Paris by the coming of Hitler's diabolical fanaticisms, he returned to his homeland, finding solace and company along the Pacific coast of Big Sur, California. It was at Big Sur where he wrote and painted for the remainder of his active life.

Perhaps Miller was too harsh a critic of the country to which he was born. But he remained unrepentant in his freedom to critique its faults and lassitudes, to challenge the distorted visions of what it was becoming. Henry Miller was framed and rejected by those that sought to silence him, but he never gave up the honesty of his perspectives, nor his clarity of mind. He would always be one of Sean McAllister's heroes, a voice in the wilderness of modern America that would always remain. Henry Miller had lived a long and interesting life.

The last six months in Pollard Creek had been edged with death. It's often peculiar how in the western cultures death becomes an indelible marker of time. In eastern cultures, death is more of a gentle passing toward an eventual rebirth and the beginning of new life. In America, birth is sanctified as god's blessing to all mankind. But as soon as birth occurs, the newborn child is thrown to the wolves of life, expected to survive by its wits and make its own way. A person's status is viewed through the prism of others, most often measured by what material attachments they can accumulate during their time on earth. Although birth is given such holy moral credence, it is death that becomes memorialized. Heroes and victims of killing are celebrated. Moments of silence are codified to give one pause. Flags fly at half mast upon death's finality, and statues are sculpted in honor and victory. All the while, necessary assistance for dispossessed children is debated on politically marbled floors. Death seems to bring more attention and devotion to the memory of a human life, than one might ever receive while alive.

The summer of 1980 rambled along, with work, swimming holes, softball, and other games to play. The rehabilitated Pollard Creek Inn catered to tourists of another economic dimension, strangers who came and went on their way. From time to time belated wanderers traveled through the town, looking for something that once had been, a dreamy utopia of which they had previously heard. No one paid them much mind. The thieves, no-counts, and snitches, all hung out by the creek near the center of town, wasting their days with alcohol and crazy talk. Still, plenty of long-haired men and women lived the day to day. The gay men from the San Francisco pranced within their mountain retreat. A strange religious sect of people in white robes and camouflage vehicles began preaching in town. Pollard Creek may have drifted toward a mediocre reality, but it by no means had given up the ghost. It would always be a vortex for eccentricity, with a sharpness of blade that could never be dulled. Henry Valentine Miller would have felt right at home.

CHAPTER FORTY-SEVEN

MAGIC
Pollard Creek / August, 1980

JAKE BEECHER WAS FIT TO BE TIED. Not that Jake's nephews, Solly and Jed, were about to don white coats, wrestle the old man to the ground, then force him into a straitjacket. As far as Solly and Jed could ever tell, Jake Beecher was always having a conniption fit over one thing or another. Does a bear shit in the woods, or what? It was the same old Uncle Jake, no big deal. At least it was no big deal until the boys heard the reason for Jake Beecher's latest manic distemper. And damn if the news wasn't one big deal, a really really big deal.

The news concerned Jake Beecher's very own granddaughter. She was the apple of the old man's eye, the only human being who could make Jake Beecher go as soft and fuzzy as a teddy bear. Petunia Jensen was Solly and Jed's very own little niece, the sweetest flower of the Beecher clan, the princess of the county fair. But little Petunia making whoopee with a goddamn Swain? What the blazes! A Swain? Grab your hat and hit the deck, feel the earth quake on its axis. Scramble under the house, pull your arms over your head. Don't bother looking up as an atomic mushroom cloud rises into the sky. In comparison, the prospect of a Beecher and a Swain would make Armageddon look like a harsh word between friends. This was not good. This could be as near to the end of the world as Solly and Jed Beecher might ever see.

Jake Beecher stomped through his house on the outskirts of Pollard Creek, leaving his boot prints etched in the floor. His wife Shirley, being out of regular booze, reached into the kitchen cupboard, pulling down a bottle of cooking wine, before taking a fast gulp. Her husband's face was as red as a beet, his flattened sparse hair smeared with sweat, his mouth forming curse words even the Almighty had never heard before. Solly and Jed quietly tip toed off the front porch of the house, before disappearing into the woods. Meanwhile, Jake Beecher reached into his gun cabinet, yanking out his shotgun, starting for the door. Billy Swain, the youngest son of Hank, was about to get a load of buckshot in his ass. That little rascal would be picking out metal for weeks. His little shaver of a butt wouldn't know a chair until calving time came next spring.

"Jake Beecher," his wife shouted at him. "Don't you dare pull a trigger on that boy, you hear me!"

Jake Beecher stopped in his tracks, turning to his wife. "It's a Swain, mama. It's a goddamn Swain," he shouted. "Over my dead body will there ever be a Swain in this family. Over my dead body, you hear me!"

"You shoot at that boy, and you will be a dead body," Shirley shouted back. "Hank Swain will bury you. And if Hank doesn't do it, one of his brothers will. I swear, Jake, if you get in that truck, I'll call Missie Swain right now. And Hank and his brothers will be waiting on you. Waiting on you with that goddamn smirk they wear. I warn you, Jake Beecher, if Solly and Jed get involved, they won't eat as much as a slice of bread in this house ever again. Now you listen to me. Petunia is a big girl now. She can marry who she wants, even if it is a goddamn Swain."

"You wouldn't, woman? You wouldn't do that?"

"You watch me," Shirley Beecher stated. "You hurt that boy, and our little sweet thing will never speak to you again. She'll hate you for the rest of your life. And I will, too. I won't have it. I just won't have it."

Jake Beecher let the shotgun drift to his side. But he couldn't keep his body still, his booted old frame turning circles inside the house. "Goddamn sons of bitches," was all he could say.

"You put that gun up, Jake. Quit flying off the handle. Our little princess isn't knocked up or anything. Maybe she is just having a time. Maybe the two of them just like the danger of it all. They know how the familys' feel about the other. It might be nothing more than that. Go down and talk to your daughter and son-in-law. Tell them how you feel. But you touch that boy, or even threaten our little sweet, and that will be the end of all of us, and you know it."

Jake Beecher took a few steps, slamming the shotgun back in the rack. He kicked open the front door, shaking the house as it hammered shut. Shirley Beecher heard the truck start, revving loud, before tearing down the drive. She reached back into the kitchen cupboard, unscrewing the cap, swilling down another nasty snort.

At the Solace Valley Tavern, Marty Johnson heard the story. Along with others in the bar, everyone laughed until the cows came home. There was one sure thing about news in Pollard Creek and Solace Valley, it traveled faster than the phone lines of AT&T. Petunia Jensen, the hot little granddaughter of the one and only Jake Beecher, had gotten knocked up by young Billy Swain. Could it really be true? But that was the funny thing about news in Pollard Creek. Once it got underway, it tended to take on a colorful life and mystery all its own.

When the hilarious patter slowed, Marty Johnson smiled to himself. The next time he saw Jake Beecher at the Country Store, the Frontier Market or the Hungry Dog Café, he'd have one hell of a zinger for the old fart. Marty couldn't wait for that opportunity to come. Jake Beecher was nothing more than an aging bullshit merchant these days. He was a man who hated most everything and everybody who didn't dance his tune. Back in Nam, most of the gooks who had taken rifle shots at Marty Johnson, Marty had never seen. But years ago, when Jake Beecher had shot at him, Marty was pretty damn sure Jake had aimed to miss. Jake Beecher was not a total fool, hippies or no hippies. Nevertheless, he had fired the shot. Marty Johnson was wise enough to forgive certain things. It was something you had to learn to do, in order to live in a cranky little burg like Pollard Creek. But forget? Nope, you didn't have to forget. And Marty Johnson was never about to let Jake Beecher forget.

But if the latest story was true, it would be the highlight of the summer, a shotgun wedding between the Beecher's and the Swain's. Everybody in town would be like a fly on the wall at that little gathering of the tribes. Plus, there would be little doubt that every male participant would be armed to the teeth, whether a Hatfield or a McCoy. There was a damn good chance that even that little shit brain of a pastor, Roland Whitman, would be dressed in a suit with a bullet proof vest. The strangest thing about living in this crazy neighborhood, was that sometimes the life here could seem as slow as molasses. But just when you thought so, something like this event would happen, and never a dull moment could be found.

The last Saturday in August, 1980, became a moment of truth in Pollard Creek, Oregon. Sheriff Bill Haines had put the date on his calendar as soon as it was known. He quietly prayed that he would not become an uninvited guest to the proceedings. Bill Haines had set his date for retirement at the end of the year. It was now just a little over four months away. He sure as hell would be kicking his own ass all the way to the heavenly gates, should he ever be stupid enough to get caught in a damn crossfire between a Beecher and a Swain. Bill Haines considered pulling the distributor wires on his marked patrol vehicle if any call did come in, then call for back up. Bill Haines was little more than a short-timer these days, and ending up in the middle of a backcountry feud was definitely not on his dance card.

Over at the Pollard Creek Alliance Church, Pastor Roland Whitman was wishing he could be on a family vacation. But Shirley Beecher, Petunia Jensen's grandmother, would have nothing of such a hopeful escape. Her dear grandchild would have a church wedding with all the fixings, and Roland Whitman wasn't going anywhere. And that was just how the deal was going down. The Beechers' would organize the church service, and the Swains' would host the reception. Billy Swain and Petunia Jensen would have little to do with the affair, except for their honeymoon plans. The couple had decided they were going to Disneyland after the wedding, and nobody was going to stop them.

As for Hank Swain, all this damn hullabaloo was something of a lark. Hank Swain didn't have a problem with most folks, and neither did his younger brothers, Odel and Teddy. Hank's heart still ached for his older brother Howard. But the loss had gotten easier over time. Howard Swain had been the leader of the family clan, the one most like their father, Howard Sr. The Swain family had worked these woods for several generations. As for the Beecher's, especially Jake, they always had a hard-on for something or somebody, and trouble seemed to be their middle name. Old Jake had never been able to measure up to Hank's dad in terms of smarts and respect. Jealousy was surely at the heart of Jake's anger and bullshit ways. But Hank and the rest of his family never paid the Beechers' much mind, unless it was absolutely necessary.

Hank Swain and Bit Jensen, Petunia's father, went way back. When Bit married Delores Beecher, Jake's daughter, things had gotten a little different, but were never strained. Petunia was a fine young girl, and she and Hank's son Billy were like two peas in a pod. Petunia was a Beecher, but what the hell of it. In a world like Pollard Creek, why would anyone be surprised they would not come together in lust and love. Such danger could be an attractive compulsion in an otherwise indifferent world. At least these kids hadn't run away, despite the big hurrah. And Hank wouldn't have stood for that with Billy. The young man would stand up and take the heat or the medicine, as every other Swain always had, Jake Beecher or no Jake Beecher.

But hell, life wouldn't be fun if Hank didn't have something up his sleeve for old Jake Beecher. Jake would be unaware that Hank Swain had quietly invited a host of the local hippies to join him in the reception celebration to be held on his property. Hank Swain had cut a lot of timber for these young men over the last number of years. And many of them had worked for Hank from time to time, on one logging show or another. They were the new locals he and his wife Missie had come to know. These young folks had begun to invite Hank and Missie to their potluck dinners and summer parties. Hank and Missie had always responded in kind. Missie had made friends with a lot of their women as well, sharing those things that women share together, kids, food, gardening, and talk of men.

These young people had become part of the town of Pollard Creek, its work, its land, its post office and stores. Sure, they were hippies and wore their hair long, but they were workers too. They had breathed a sense of youth into Hank's life, a youthfulness that had begun to fade with time. Hank much preferred their independence, their sense of humor and bravado, their natural desire to help one another for nothing more than barter or friendship. They had given this little dying logging town a kick in the butt with their presence, a place that had grown weary from the cold rain and nothing new to talk about.

The faggot ones were a different story. Hank got the willies and angry when it came to them. There was no way Hank Swain could go that far, in any acceptance of something so wrong. Except maybe for Albert Krieger. Albert was gone now, but he'd been unlike the rest, a genuinely kind and gentle man. Albert was just a little fucked up in the head when it came to his sex life. But most everybody else had been good for the town as far as Hank was concerned.

Old Jake, Hank smirked to himself, would just have to suck up the deal. When the church bullshit was over, it would be Hank Swain's celebration at his own damn property. He would share the marriage of his son with whomever he damned well pleased. And if Jake Beecher couldn't handle the heat, then he could just haul his bullshit ass out of the kitchen, and let the party go on. Hank laughed to think how tight Jake would get when the rug got pulled. You could bet Hank and his brothers would get a kick out of this one, seeing old Jake totally surrounded.

The Saturday afternoon was a tidy bit hot, but a beautiful day. And although boys could be boys, any verbal jousts of a shootout between the Hatfield's and McCoy's were just that, a lot of silly talk. Missie Swain and Delores Jensen were not about to let a bunch of cantankerous men spoil the wedding day of their children. Even that tough old bitch, Shirley Beecher, was on board. For this day would be her sweet and lovely grandchild's big moment in life. Sean McAllister hadn't planned on attending, but in the late afternoon Marty Johnson and Freddie Jones came rumbling up the drive to the trailer house. It was time, Marty announced, to go over and pay their respects to Hank. But more than likely, Marty really wanted to see if a border war had broken out.

The party was in full swing upon their arrival. Although there was a distinct separation in location between parts of the two families, an undercurrent of peace prevailed. Solly and Jed Beecher were on their best behaviors, knowing full well that to act out upon any direction from Uncle Jake, would mean they would be heating up Chef Boyardee and white bread for the rest of their days. True to form, Jake Beecher set up his perimeter around one of the picnic tables, and never cracked a smile. Dressed in an old black suit, white shirt and black tie, McAllister couldn't help but notice Jake's white socks and black shoes, remembering Marty's smart-ass remarks to Jake at the Hungry Dog Cafe sometime back.

When the cake was cut and speeches were rolled out, Hank Swain and Bit Jensen gave their obligatory toasts to each of their families and kids. But Jake Beecher never made a move, neither a word of support for Petunia, nor a single epithet toward the world at large. Jake Beecher was decidedly mum, outflanked on every side. For many it would be a day to remember, seeing old Jake Beecher roped to the ground like a calf at a rodeo show. But nobody was fool enough to think that Jake's trap would remain shut on the way back home. Jake Beecher was a human being who generally hated his world, and Shirley would surely hear a flood of castigation sooner than later. It might have been an embarrassing moment, one that Jake would not easily forget. But humble the old man, you could plum forget that possibility. An old dog like Jake Beecher wasn't about to learn any new tricks.

With the help of their mothers' and friends, the car was loaded and ready to go. Finally, the newlyweds began their drive to California, the tin cans tied behind, bouncing off the pavement heading down Robertson Creek Road. With their smiles of happiness and an unborn baby in tow, these two children of the woods were leaving together on an adventure one hoped they would always remember. For Billy Swain and Petunia Jensen, Disneyland would be their distant cultural mecca to the outside world. For other young Americans, such a honeymoon destination might be hard to fathom, but for two young innocent children growing up in Pollard Creek, the desired location was easy to understand.

Sean McAllister had never given marriage much of a thought. Still, it was compelling to witness the joy of the moment, to see two young people in flight on a journey of their very own making. They would be stepping together into a new reality, each with their particular hopes and dreams. Perhaps a wedding day was not a foolish ritual. Cynics would believe such a union was sarcastically destined for eventual decline and mistrust, lasting maybe a month, or several challenged years. Then again, maybe it would last forever, till death did them part. Maybe that was the reason mothers and fathers enjoyed the ritual so much. Could it be that the occasion took them back in memory to their own initial wedding day, to that day when their own love and life was filled with every possibility, and for a particular moment in time they would never feel alone?

It didn't surprise McAllister that Paige came to mind. And it would have to be Paige. There was no one else who had come into his own life since the love he had felt for her, seemingly so long ago. Caught for a instant in his own silent reflection, he wanted to rush home and call her, if only to hear her voice on the other end of the line. But the Beecher clan was leaving the grounds. Marty was walking over with a whiskey bottle in his hands, and Hank Swain was beginning to sing. Another Pollard Creek celebration was upping the ante on a warm summer night.

CHAPTER FORTY-EIGHT

THE LETTER
Tucson / Seattle / Pollard Creek / October - November, 1980

VALERIE WILLIAMS STEPPED ON THE PEDAL of her old turquoise Singer sewing machine, lining up the stitching, pushing the two pieces of fabric through the needle and bobbin as if driving a car. It felt a little sad for Valerie to be cutting up the calico material from some of her granny dresses. The clothing harkened back to a time gone by, of her innocent days in the Haight-Ashbury, when her life seemed so unfettered and free of necessity. They were special memories, and tonight she was stitching together what she could of the material, for either a quilt or some other personal creation. Valerie had just finished repairing a tear in her son's little denim jacket, and she didn't want to quit. Sometimes for Valerie, sewing thread lines to the rhythmic tisking of the machine seemed peaceful to her. For some precious moments of time, she could drift along reflecting on herself, alone with her thoughts.

Meatball and Fillmore were curled at her feet. Both dogs were aging with the years, yet so much a part of the family, so much a part of her and Mookie's individual histories. In the living room of the Tucson apartment, Valerie could hear the sounds of the World Series baseball game playing on the television set. Mookie James had turned her son into a sports fan, and the boy's wardrobe had definitely suffered as a consequence. Canyon would don his red Philadelphia Phillies tee shirt as soon as it came out of the wash, along with a set of pajamas that Mookie's parents had sent sometime back. Valerie smiled to herself at the apparent loss of her son to the world of sports. Earlier in the summer, Canyon had asked her to cut his long dark hair, wanting to be like the other boys at school and Little League, to not be seen as a hippie kid in his new Arizona world. She had been disappointed for a bit, but with the camaraderie and love between Canyon and Mookie growing so strong, it was a small price to pay. Canyon now had a man that loved him, who wanted to show her son a man's world. Valerie felt as lucky as lucky could be.

Mookie was getting close to his masters in architecture. Although he was sometimes stressed with the responsibilities of both school and a relationship, he was making his way. Valerie was doing her part, working as a waitress in a restaurant near campus. And with some financial help from their parents they were making ends meet. Tucson was okay, but so much of Arizona was nothing more than rednecks and strip malls, a land of desert basins and unforgiving heat most of the year. As soon as they could make it possible after Mookie's schooling was complete, they would return to the Great Northwest. Neither of them had realized how much they would miss the country from which they had come. Valerie never thought she would ache for gray skies and evergreen hills ever again. But it hadn't taken long to miss the world she had left behind. It wouldn't be Pollard Creek, but maybe Seattle or Portland, maybe Eugene or Bend, wherever Mookie might get a good job. At some point in time they would leave, and Canyon would have to make the best of the decision.

Suddenly, there were shouts from the living room, followed by her son running into the bedroom, telling her that the Phillies had won the World Series. Valerie was amazed at the thrill on her son's face, the overwhelming joy he seemed to exude at an event so fathomless to her. Mookie came in to hug and kiss her, equally stoked with happiness and bliss.

"You've turned my only son into a hopeless jock," she said to Mookie sarcastically. He could only smile and laugh at the remark.

"He's a hardcore Philly fan now," Mookie answered. "I'm sorry, babe, but there's no turning back. It's our first World Series championship," he stated almost seriously. "The pain of sixty-four is over and done. I feel like a new man, I can't tell you. It's a beautiful moment forever."

Before Valerie could ask about the pain of sixty-four, the phone rang in the kitchen. "That has to be either dad or Sean," Mookie informed her. Canyon ran from the bedroom to grab the phone.

"You're crazy," she said to her man, "both of you."

"Hey, Dad," Canyon yelled from the kitchen. "It's Sean, from Oregon."

Mookie looked at her with a smart-ass grin upon his face. "See, I told you so, babe," he laughed again. "There is nothing you can do." He kissed her quickly before heading for the call.

Valerie Williams rested back in her sewing chair. No doubt it was Sean McAllister. Mookie and he were like two brothers with a common thread, from where they had come. But Valerie wasn't sure if Mookie hadn't just missed the most important thing to her, more important than anything she could imagine. It had been eleven years since the days of her early motherhood in San Francisco, then on to Martinez and north to Pollard Creek. Eleven years of owning and taking care of her only child. Eleven years of wishing she might some day hear those beautiful words. Valerie Williams would always be a sports fan if it might come to this one moment. Two simple words emanating from her lovely son's lips. "Hey, Dad!"

The metro bus bumped its way north along University Avenue. A steady November rain revealed itself in the street lamps above, reflecting its light in the puddles pooling along the curb. In Seattle, this was the time of year for which the city was known. A quiet internal time, a time for books and televisions, of cooking and early to bed. Paige Lindstrom was familiar with this time. She lived it without complaint, for she had known it all her life.

Sitting next to a stranger, she was focused on the book in her hands. The book was only recently published. It was titled *Nursing: The Philosophy and Science of Caring*. She loved the author's approach. The intent was to bring a more holistic view of care to the nursing profession, of seeing beyond the standard elements of practical medical solutions. Although Paige had become weary of the stresses of school and study, the book reminded her of the reasons for choosing this profession, of her desire to honestly care for others in their time of need.

The bus journeyed over to 15th Avenue, passing through Ravenna Park up to 65th Street. Paige pulled the cord, placing the book inside her backpack. Exiting the bus, she pulled the hood of her coat over her head, beginning to walk the several blocks to her parent's home.

The route took her by her old school, Roosevelt High. Her time there seemed so long ago, but in a strange way it felt like she had not gotten that far. She quickly dismissed the thought, knowing full well it was only a means to an end. She was living with her parents for a reason, for a goal she was soon to reach. She was completing the last of her clinicals. In the middle of December she would graduate with a Bachelor of Nursing, then cram for her boards in early February. The end was in sight. If she passed the boards, she would receive her RN, the mission complete. She would then be able to consider other things, of where she might want to be.

Passing the high school, she thought of Sean. She remembered how he too had lived close to his high school, walking to school every day. She continued to miss him, worried that he might now have drifted from her life. Three years had passed since their first time together. They had tried to maintain the relationship, or the friendship, whatever it was. But time and distance had begun to take its toll.

Perhaps she was at fault. When they first met, the circumstances couldn't have been more prohibitive. She was still coming to grips with the loss of her time with Danny, and had made the decision to return to school. She had not anticipated meeting Sean in the apples.

She and Terri were simply on a fun road trip together. They had traveled to Yellowstone and throughout Montana and Idaho, before working the apple harvest and heading home. She had tried to resist at first, but a part of her wanted to be with him in a deeper and loving way. Eventually, she had relented. It was a time she would never regret.

Still, she had resisted any further temptation. She needed to acquire something important and secure for herself. And Sean had been stubbornly supportive, even though she knew the disappointment he felt inside. For most of two years, they had managed to keep it alive, enjoying their visits together, yet forcing the future out of their minds. Sean knew of her thing with Danny, of dropping out of school to go to Hawaii and Australia, before the relationship began falling apart. She knew of his loss of the girl back home, the depth of his own heartbreak way back when. In a way, the both of them were the same. Each fearing the potential for another mistake, of investing their hearts in a believed anticipation that might not endure. Sean was holding on to his life in Pollard Creek, and she to the objectives of her schooling, as well as the security it would bring.

But in the last year, things had begun to fade. The stress of school was significant, requiring her full attention. Sean was intent on finding his own way, and life in the city was not his cup of tea. So with time, their words had grown colder. Not in anger or mistrust, just in recognition of circumstances they could do nothing about. There was so much between them that remained unsaid.

Yet, within the confines of their silence her wishes remained. He was handsome, funny, a hard worker, caring toward others in an endearing way. Yes, sometimes he was moody, and he could be strongly resistant when he made up his mind. But he had never made her feel responsible to him. She was mostly thankful for that response, although sometimes she wished he would. But in her heart, with her future now opening again, she did not want them to fade away, at least not without an understanding between them. Thus, she had sent the invitation to see her graduate, to be part of her accomplishment, for him to be close at least one more time. If he came, perhaps there might be a chance for things to blossom again. If he refrained, then she would have to accept the consequence. She deeply wished for his presence, for she felt so ready to bring him near.

"Seven card stud, high-low split," Marty Johnson tried to yell amongst the haze of cigarette and pot smoke, the shot glasses of Jack Daniels whiskey chased with beer, amidst the din of human voices all trying to talk, one over the other. Marty pushed in his dollar ante into the middle of the poker table. He dealt two cards down to each player, then one up to start the betting.

It was a typical Pollard Creek poker evening. As usual, when marijuana and liquor were blended together, there would always be a player or two, not having heard the name of the game over the sound of their own voice. They would invariably ask "what's the game?" Rarely, if ever, was there studious and stern attention at a poker night in Pollard Creek. Once the pot and whiskey kicked in, poker night became a raucous collection of take-offs and put-ons, of suggestive one liners and teasing complaints. There were stories that just had to be told, one lie after another. In between, there would be High Chicago, or five-card stud or draw, jacks or better to open, trips to win. There were quarter bets, three raises, with fifty cents on the last raise.

"I'll call, and bump a quarter," Freddie Jones demands. Too Tall Tim fiddles with his cards, before nonchalantly tossing a quarter into the pot. "Shit, I'd watch turkeys fuck for a quarter," he answers in defiance.

It is generally a game without wild cards, or at least until it becomes Jimmijay Connell's turn to deal. Then the game turns wilder still. However, it would be far past midnight before anyone would let Jimmijay call his favorite game, Indian Poker. The game of Indian Poker could only show its face at a time when otherwise law-abiding men were capable of making fools of themselves. It was a time when the players, fueled by alcohol and cannabinol, had finally reached a misguided sense of immortality. Each and every one of these players sitting around a table, with a playing card plastered to their foreheads, one that everyone else could see but the player themselves. The men would grin at each other with muggy bloodshot eyes, their faces red from drink. They were a Pollard Creek ship of fools.

Jimmijay Connell had been in his latest 'Jerry Fisher' persona all night long. Tonight, he was acting suspiciously akin to Rodney Dangerfield. He would spread his arms, before reaching for his throat as if straightening a necktie, while cracking one-liners that he got no respect. Jimmijay was at the top of his game. He was living his comedic small-town dream of New York and Las Vegas night clubs, feeling as famous as the great comedians he often sought to portray. On this particular evening, the other men graciously let Jimmijay live out his fantasy of fame. For they knew a deeper secret, that Jimmijay was masking something painful he was attempting to ignore.

The word had come through Mookie, via Valerie. It was said that Darla Bloom, the mother of Jimmijay's son, was making plans to return to Santa Cruz. Darla had made a very big decision. She would move herself and the boy away from Pollard Creek, leaving Jimmijay behind. She would be moving on with her own life, leaving this current relationship of which she had gotten herself involved. More significant, but with intense regret, she would also be leaving her two older children, knowing full well that the remains of her time with Derrick Mulcahey was never going to change.

Tim Wilson, 'Too Tall Tim', was also at a crossroads. Tim had been fighting the BLM for years to stay on his mining claim. Each time Tim would think that he had won the battle, some new bureaucrat would be at his neck, with some nefarious challenge that Tim wasn't working the claim. Recently, another posting of the land had come, and Tim was finally throwing in the towel. He had rented a place in the town of Hugo, closer to Grants Pass. Everyone at the table had agreed to help Tim remove his cabin, stick by stick, board by board. Too Tall Tim would take his stable of old Chevy pick-ups, his tools and his clothing, before starting over again.

As for Too Tall Tim's adopted little brother, Joe Joe Gifford, he too was more than likely gone from Pollard Creek. Joe Joe had been released from the nuthouse up in Salem. Paulette, his sister, had moved him to Ashland, to be closer to her. People who had seen the new Joe Joe, reported that he was so pumped up with meds that he looked like a zombie. His former personality had been successfully shaved away. The worst fears had been realized for the life of Joe Joe Gifford.

Marty Johnson was all over creation, from Grants Pass to Solace Valley, or back to Railroad Bridge. One never knew where Marty might be, or what shape he might be in. Settling down did not appear to be on Marty's agenda these days. He had a girl and a group of people with whom he continued to party in Grants Pass. But the next thing you knew, he would be back on the property at Railroad Bridge, helping Freddie with the mill, or doing a local welding job at his little metal shop in Solace Valley. Marty was always on the move, a gregarious bundle of energy and quickness of mind. He continued to appear comfortable and in control in almost any quarter, remaining the same Marty who had been such a natural leader in moments of stress. Still, the pace of his life, and the hard drinking in between, made one wonder how long he could last. Marty Johnson was not a persona who had time for reflection or personal evaluation, only for the next thing to do or say. It wasn't as if Marty was larger than life, but there was a personal force about him that never seemed to slow.

Sean McAllister had always held a particular fascination for Marty Johnson. He admired how Marty lived the moments of his life with so little fear, or the need for any particular level of caution. If there was ever a guy who could think on his feet, Marty was the one, whatever the occasion. Although McAllister and Tommy Sullivan had their own strong friendship together, there was no doubt that Sullivan and Marty Johnson shared a companionship that was deeper and more understood between them. And it was a friendship that could often be exchanged without saying a word. It was more than a mutual respect. Instead, it was a peculiar bond forged by the common experience of their time in Vietnam, as well as the ensuing years joined together at Railroad Bridge.

As for Tom Sullivan, he remained so quiet and mysterious at times, so in contrast to Marty's personality of wearing everything on his sleeve. It was if the character traits of these two men were like a fork in the road. Marty might go one way, Sullivan another. Regardless, some unspoken communication and acceptance existed between them. It was a tacit comprehension of one for the other, upon which they both relied. It had always been an interesting dynamic for McAllister to witness between them.

Tom Sullivan, no doubt, was the better player at cards. While Marty Johnson would chase an inside straight until the sun came up, Tommy Sullivan would already have figured the odds, so purposeful in every deliberation. More than likely, in all those goddamn notebooks he so religiously kept at hand, were probably descriptions of previous situations in poker games, including statistical results. Tom Sullivan didn't need to develop a poker face, he was born with one. He never hesitated to fold early and often if circumstances required, then suddenly bluff the pants off right off your legs. The surrounding dramas of whiskey, smoke, or smart-ass remarks had minimal effect. You could have slipped a truth serum into Tommy Sullivan's drink, and at the end of the night you would have still lost your butt.

Sometime past one in the morning, Rickey the Rocket Rucker burst into McAllister's bunkhouse, and the poker game got a jolt it probably didn't need to have. However, it was a jolt no one would think of turning down. Out came the mirror and the razor blade, along with a tightly rolled hundred dollar bill. Rickey the Rocket's black hair looked like it had been plugged into a light socket, his huge dark eyeballs rimmed in white. A poker night that once had appeared to be counting down toward the final buzzer, quickly headed into overtime. There would be no end to the proceedings until the powder was gone, which by the appearance of dawn had finally come.

There is something strangely weird and disorienting about carelessly engaging in the occasional all-nighter. It begins with the initial realization of first morning light, when the night sky pales to gray in the windows outside. The shock of the next day starts scolding through the room, like an upset mother punishing her child. An anxious fear overtakes the neurons of the brain, hoping not to get spanked for such a juvenile transgression. Racing for sleep appears to be the only possible escape, but it is far too late even for that feeble excuse. One just might as well forget the crime, for the conventional continuum of daily behavior has already been completely disrupted. A night shift has turned into a day shift, a jet lag syndrome occurs, without ever leaving your seat.

Coming down from the cocaine high, as well as the onset of an alcohol and indica hangover, doesn't help matters. One is led to believe that eating breakfast at a twenty-four hour truck stop called the Hungry Dog Cafe will assist in creating some stability. Perhaps eating farm eggs and greasy sausage will help to right the ship. However, none of the above is true. And so, with the phone cord pulled and the curtains drawn, McAllister eventually attempts a restless sleep. He tosses and turns all through the waking day, while the rest of the world drives around outside in the cause of normal behavior. The fact of the matter is that an international dateline has been crossed. You've fucked up and lost a day, and you won't ever be getting it back.

McAllister awoke about three in the afternoon, his clothes strewn on the floor of the bunkhouse. The pounding of a bongo drum beat inside his head, the electric feel of his nervous system bitching about the poisons he had ingested. With his body as sluggishly heavy as a set of barbells, he looked about the room. A tornado had hit, pure and simple, the bunkhouse smelling of day-old smoke and leftover beer. So this was the price of fun? How easy it was for someone to forget the real price of such juvenile conduct. One had to figure that this kind of fun required a certain loss of memory. Otherwise, the fun might never get a chance to be enjoyed again. For any lasting memory of its gruesome paybacks would be so incredibly preventative.

McAllister bumped here and there within the room, cleaning up the aftermath while encased in a fog. He trudged out to the trailer at the front of the property, entered inside and took a long shower. The one lucky thing today was the weather. The autumn Saturday afternoon was a stoned cold gray and overcast sky. It was the kind of day perfect for hiding away from the rest of the human race, until recovery was complete. The shower helped. McAllister dressed and put on his boots. Pollard Creek was less than a mile away. He decided to get outside and walk to the post office. He would then cross over get some food at the Country Store, hoping to be unnoticed by the painful world at large. These single chores would be the most significant events of his day. He would follow their necessity with a couch and blanket, accompanied by the blue light of a television. This day might as well have been skipped on the calendar, for all it would be worth.

The walk helped him breathe some air, a feeble attempt to re-enter the land of the living. But if one doesn't watch out, hangovers can sometimes engender depression. Walking along the roadside, he knew deep down that his life wasn't really a piece of shit, but it sure felt like it today. Soon, another Oregon winter was on its way. He had no goals, no future, not even a distraction in sight. And there was definitely no woman to take him by the hand. He had enough cash for a half a pound of hamburger and a loaf of bread. The rest of his funds were in Tom Sullivan's wallet. There wasn't much choice but to silently sing the blues.

He changed his mind and went to the store first, sliding in and out with as few words as possible. He crossed the triangle of downtown Pollard Creek to the post office. The town seemed somber and internal in the fading afternoon light. Inside his post office box, there was no more than an advertisement or two, but also an envelope that looked like the size of a greeting card. Turning the letter over, he spotted a familiar Seattle address in the upper left hand corner. His weary mind suddenly felt the thrill of expectation, but quickly followed by a reverse sense of dread. His heart felt too fragile to open it now, of what news it might bring. He stuck the letter into his hip pocket, hurrying home.

The card was a commencement announcement which read: "The President, Faculty, and Graduating Class of the University of Washington, School of Nursing, announces the graduation of Andrea Paige Lindstrom, on Saturday the thirteenth of December, nineteen hundred and eighty, at eleven am, with a Bachelor of Science degree." Inside the announcement, a folded up handwritten note fell from the card into McAllister's lap. He opened the letter and read:

Dear Sean,

I hope you will think of this. It's hard for me to believe it's been three years since I started back to school. Where does the time go?

Sometimes, it has felt like forever. I finish my clinical work just before Thanksgiving. I think they would consider keeping me on at the University Hospital, but I'm not sure that is what I want to do right now. I guess I want to take some time and look around.

Dane has moved over to Port Swan. Do you remember that beautiful town on the peninsula where we went to visit? They have decided to put the boat up there. Dane likes living out of the city. Sometimes, I think I would too. They have a hospital in Port Swan, and public health services as well. I'm not sure. I'm just trying to consider what's next for me.

I hope you are doing well. I went over to Wenatchee with some friends a few weeks ago. It was harvest time. It was strange to imagine you not being nearby, working so hard and fast like you do. Whenever I think of Eastern Washington, I always think of you. Today, the Barter Fair seems so long ago. Almost like it never happened, like it was only a dream we had together. But it is always a good dream to remember. We had so much fun.

I just wanted to write and let you know. Please come if you can. It won't be a big deal, and it would mean a lot to me if you did. Maybe we could do something together after, but I'll understand if you are unable to come. Please say hi to Tom when you see him. Is he still in Eugene? Terri has moved up to Bellingham. She likes it there, and has a new boyfriend. She's coming down for the graduation. Write when you can.

With love,
Paige

McAllister put down the letter. Resting back on the couch, he ran his hands through the curls of his long brown hair. Could it be that Paige still wanted him to be with her on such a special day, this woman who had taken up residence in his thoughts for such a long while. Over time, he had tried to give it up, to let those difficult expectations that rise in concert with first attraction and love not to overtake him. He had tried to not rush time, as Tom Sullivan had counseled him so long ago. Along the way, he had learned that time has its own set of consequences. With time, attraction and love can begin to fade, and reality marches on. Eventually, an unwanted acceptance ensues, and hope is once again placed inside a little box. It becomes locked away. It is made to wait until another chance for escape.

Now this letter and the disquiet it provoked. The heaviness of his poker-night hangover made it difficult to think. McAllister got up, keeping the letter in hand. He heated water for tea. Sitting at the kitchen table, he read the letter again. Memories flooded his conscious mind. He could see Paige for the very first time, standing in the parking lot of the grocery store in Chelan. He could see the night along the River, when he received her first kiss. And of course, the Barter Fair, when he knew he was in love, waking to the length of her torso cuddling beside him. He wanted to return to those moments, to live them again if he might be given the chance. Yet, part of him felt the need to somehow hold back, to protect himself against the pain of some hidden yet foreseeable loss.

Bullshit! He set the hangover aside. Surely he would go. Nothing ventured, nothing gained. He had some pot from the harvest to sell. That would help pay for the trip. He had more than a month to get better tires for the panel truck and replace the clutch. He would go to Grants Pass and get some new clothes to wear. More than anything, he would try and maintain a level head. He would make it all about Paige, whatever the outcome might be. Most of all, he would have something to look forward to, a feeling inside him that had been missing for so long. He got up to look for paper and pen. He had so much to say.

Tuesday, November 4th, 1980, could have been any other day in Pollard Creek. The autumn sun had begun its lowered crossing through the chilled blue sky. A measured breeze gently sifted through falling leaves. It was a good day to work. For the last several days the crew had met far down Laughlin Creek toward the Rogue River, at the soon to be former home of Too Tall Tim. Freddie Jones had managed to pull the flatbed through Laughlin Creek one last time at Railroad Bridge, before the winter rains would come. The men had used nail pullers, hammers, and crowbars to do their task. They ripped off the cedar roofing shingles for kindling. They carefully removed the exterior siding. They took down the ceiling joists and framing lumber. They set the saved material on saw horses, pulling the nails, stacking the salvage into the flatbed, as well as the other pick-up trucks nearby. They were in a race against time. The Bureau of Land Management bureaucrats were coming, but nobody knew when.

Too Tall Tim would not have been faulted for working in tears, bearing the emotions of ripping down the home he had built over so many years. His personal belongings had already been moved to the rental property in Hugo. There were only the building materials which remained. But Tim Wilson had already dealt with his grief. By now he had a single solitary mission, to save whatever he could from those government assholes. The Tujunga mining claim had already been posted and the eviction date had passed. Still, he would take every decent worthwhile stick he could carry, until the Tujunga access was chained and locked. Even then, he would keep on going, whenever they weren't around.

It was late afternoon before McAllister unloaded his wood truck of lumber at Too Tall Tim's new place. He began his return to Pollard Creek. Crossing Sexton Pass, he might have normally pulled off in Solace Valley for a beer at the tavern, but today he had another responsibility to fulfill. He continued the drive over the next summit, dropping down into Pollard Creek. In the growing darkness of evening, there were a number of vehicles parked at the post office. People would be inside the community center annex, doing their civic duty. As he climbed out of the truck and began to head inside, Darla Bloom was exiting the building. She began walking toward him.

Darla was still as attractive as ever. Tall and thin, she wore a blue navy pea coat, her copper brown skin smooth to the eye. There would always an allure to Darla, her features Arabesque, the length of her torso long and graceful in its stride. Sean McAllister would be forever grateful to Darla for inviting him into her domain upon his arrival in Pollard Creek. She had helped restore his manhood at the time of his indecisive arrival. Darla had helped introduce him to the new and exciting life of Pollard Creek. Although their affair had not lasted long, they had become accepted companions in this world in which their lives continued to revolve. A friendship had carried on, short of intimacy, but enduring in its own way.

Darla remained as direct and practical as ever. The woman never wasted words, or attempts to soften a blow. Darla always got right to the point, and you could take or leave its emotional impact at your own discretion. "You're too late," she said matter of fact, before McAllister could even say hello. "They have declared Reagan the winner, and Carter has already conceded."

McAllister was stunned at her declaration. "What," he asked? "You're kidding, right? For crying out loud, I haven't even voted yet. Reagan? Fucking Ronald Reagan? What about California? He's even won the thing before California?"

"That's what they say inside," Darla confirmed. "Marty and Freddie just turned around and left. You just missed them."

"We've been down at Tim's all day, taking down his house. I fucking can't believe it." Darla said her farewell, leaving McAllister standing alone in the parking lot, shaking his head. Jimmy Carter might have been a good man whose heart was in the right place. But his political savvy and toughness of mind was a goddamn joke, leaving the whole Pacific coast to fend for themselves, without a thought to its political impact.

There was no doubt that Jimmy Carter was a victim of circumstance in so many ways. For all the reasons that did not have to be reviewed. But to let that cardboard cut-out of a cowboy, Ronald Reagan, chew him up and spit him out, now that was a goddamn crime. Carter lacked the courage and the credibility of a Bobby Kennedy, a man who would have easily pierced the bullshit of Reagan's bluster and mythology. Bobby would have kicked Reagan's ass down the proverbial block, win or fucking lose. But the Kennedy's had been murdered, and in their absence the Democratic Party had become a spineless congregation of worrywarts, who went into a back-peddle at the first shout of an angry taunt. Until they got some got some goddamn gonads and put some brass knuckles on their fists, the bullshit merchants of the Republican Party would have their day.

Ronald Reagan, you had to give him credit. He had the entire Twenty-Mule advertising script down cold. He was an expert at throwing the red meat on the table. He could find a whole host of red herring to blame, including poor black mothers in a white man's world. He would have blamed the Indians for living on the continent if he had needed to go that far. He had already blamed the trees for getting in his way. Wall Street would be pleased with his performance. Business as usual would soon be underway. Another episode of *Death Valley Days* was about to begin.

McAllister went inside the community center. He voted for what progressive statewide candidates he could give some assist, no thanks to Jimmy Carter and his prayers before bed. As for voting a President, it was a no-brainer for now. He would choose Barry Commoner and the Citizen's Party. His vote would be a small cry for the environment and economic equality, for a necessary future that the majority of America continued to disregard. Although it might take decades, one day the chickens would come home to roost. The plutocratic shell-game could only go on for so much longer, before the shit would really hit the fan.

Returning home, a sense of political depression began to sink within him. A disappointing personal realization began to take its hold. His ideals, any hopes for the future of his country had been dealt a crushing blow. The eight hundred pound gorilla was back in the room. Once again, the three wise monkeys were sitting in the corner, their tactile paws covering their ears, eyes, and mouths. This was probably going to be his America for the rest of his waking life. McAllister's particular vision and opinion of his country would always be in the minority, and he better get used to it. Still, it was not a particular recognition that was easy to accept. It was a goddamn bringdown to consider. And its effect would only serve to further a deeply entrenched cynicism he might never overcome.

CHAPTER FORTY-NINE

IN MY LIFE
Pollard Creek / Seattle / Port Swan / December, 1980

In early December, six inches of snow blanketed the sharp-edged hills of Southern Oregon, marked by freezing temperatures and roads packed in white. The front passed through, but the cold remained, brilliant with a silver-blue winter sky and blinding angled sun. The surrounding evergreen timber sparkled in the light of day, the sound of passing vehicles muted by the cover, the quiet tenor of footprints crunching underneath. At night, a frozen silence cast itself through Pollard Creek, the stars staring down from overhead, crystal in their clarity. The evening air was thin and keen to the breath, exposed human skin clean and tight. Like a moment captured in a photograph, the purity and beauty of this mountain country engendered a certain holiness that only nature could provide.

But the weather, like much of life, is subject to change. Such beauty should never be taken for granted. Rather, it should be celebrated while the moment prevails, for it does not last. This is a rule of thumb that should not be ignored, for there is always the fated possibility that it may not come again. The axiom of spring is to stop and smell the roses, to ingest the sweetness of creation before it begins to wither away. In winter, it is the compelling desire to reach down and grab a handful of new fallen snow, to pack it in your hands, before flinging it with joy high into the air. For tomorrow may be too late. It will swiftly harden with time, or quickly melt away. For the concept of time has a destination and schedule it is required to keep. Time fails to have the luxury of memory, of being able to stop and reflect on where it has been.

Human beings have the good fortune and opportunity of being able to both possess the moment, and then later to cherish it and keep it close. Sadly, they also have the innate ability to miss the point, or worse, to ignore the beauty once before him. These circumstances become another of those mysteries of life. Why, when blessed with such marvelous opportunities for the enjoyment of beauty, man chooses instead to rush on by, chasing after some expectant truth he might never find. Perhaps such behavior derives from a deeper anxiety of knowing that time is of the essence, that death is right around the corner, waiting for its chance. Everlasting faith remains so uniquely unknowable, despite all those who preach its certainty and creed. Could it be possible, that true faith is really only the moment itself, the sweet perfume of the rose, or the snowball flying in the sky? Perhaps time is only a trickster, whose divine purpose is to disguise these eternal truths of everlasting life. And because of its motion, we tend to seek it somewhere down the road, missing its presence in each moment that we live. Meanwhile, we stop and check our watch, continuing on our journey, not realizing that each moment of truth is passing us by.

By the weekend, the cold spell and snow had washed away, a more normal Pacific front melting the land. The liquid runoff filled the washes of Pollard Creek, its water running high and red with a volcanic tint, the surrounding ground sticky and smooched in slippery clay. A marijuana connection had come down from city of Portland, looking to buy. McAllister's marijuana crop had been small, but more than lovely in tightness and taste, filled with plenty of kick. He had planted his indica crop on the edge of the industrial power lines that ran behind the property. On the previous summer days when he had tended the patch, the constant hum of electricity could be heard overhead. It was impossible to say if being in such a hot location might have had an effect. But there was no doubt that his crop was one-hit shit. As a result, he had labeled his product Pacific Power pot, after the utility company that bore the name. It never hurt to have a sales pitch when setting the price. One might call him a hypocrite, but what the hell, he'd do anything to pay for the trip to Seattle.

On Monday, the eighth of December, he sloshed around all day at Friendly Frank's bone yard, replacing the clutch in the panel truck. Tom Sullivan found McAllister there, stretched under his rig in the early afternoon. Sullivan's pick-up truck was loaded with furnishings and gear, heading back to Eugene. Over the recent weeks past, Sullivan had been making trips back and forth. Carley had sold her property up on Paradise Creek. She would not be coming back to Solace Valley after finishing her law degree in the spring. Sullivan had been selling what he could, or hauling it north to a storage unit in Eugene. It was far too late to haul any stuff into Railroad Bridge, as Laughlin Creek had risen too high with the autumn rains and snow. McAllister planned to head north on Wednesday afternoon. He would visit with Sullivan before driving onward to Seattle for Paige's graduation.

Finishing the clutch repair, McAllister returned home to the trailer house as darkness began to fall. He did some laundry for the trip ahead, before making a dinner of beans and rice. Finishing his meal, he smoked a bowl, before turning on the Monday Night Football game between the Patriots and the Dolphins. Lying on the couch, he nodded off to sleep. When he awoke, the score of the game was close, late in the final quarter. He considered going to bed, but instead made a cup of tea, deciding to watch the rest of the game. With only three seconds to go, the Patriots called time out, preparing to kick a field goal with a chance to win the game. As the field goal kicker came onto the field, broadcaster Howard Cosell began to oddly speak to the television audience that this was only a football game. Then, he delivered the tragic news....

Suddenly, the heart of a world goes dark. A chest sinks into a stomach, as if falling into a bottomless pit. A breath halts upon its inhale, as if never to resume. There are times when words cannot be spoken, when feelings are stilled to stone by the shock of disbelief. The spirit of the living suspends itself inside an empty vacuum, a vacuum devoid of air, devoid of any light.

"John Lennon. New York City. Shot. Dead!"

Where oh where, does one go from here? Why oh why, would a pulse keep beating, a planet keep turning, a clock keep ticking, or an eye continue to see. For a fragile failing moment all is lost, there is no single answer able to survive, no single reason for believing in life that might ever come again. The sun is draped in black. Life becomes extinct. Dead! The dream is over. No living thing is ever left to tell.

And then, like the flickering of light from a power outage, the resuscitation of life returns. Alone at home, Sean McAllister gets up from the couch. He struggles to the phone, calling his sister Mary Jane in New York. But there is no answer, just the ringing on the other end. Almost breathless, he sits at the kitchen table, his head down. But he needs to talk to someone, to share this overwhelming moment of shock and loss. He hesitates to call Paige, afraid she might not know. Yet, his helplessness is much too severe. He dials the number. The phone picks up after a single ring.

"Paige. It's Sean. I needed to…,"

"Oh, Sean," she interrupted. "I just tried to call. But the phone was busy," her voice spoke haltingly. "I needed to hear your voice. Do you know? Do you know what's happened?"

"I know," he answered. "I know. I needed to hear you too."

"My god," she said, "it's all so devastating. Please tell me it can't be true. And for Yoko and their son, I just can't believe …." Then, she broke down in sobs.

Sean McAllister had yet to shed a tear. But the sounds of Paige's crying, the depth of its sorrow was all too much. He sat at the kitchen table, his eyes watering in grief at the sound of her tears. Momentarily, he recovered, trying to be strong as best he could.

McAllister stayed up late, watching the tragedy unfold, engaging in the morbid fascination that human beings are capable of involving themselves, the circumstances regarding seminal events their rational minds demand to understand. After a restless night, he awoke to the genuine sadness of another day ahead.

In the morning, he had reached Mary Jane. She was equally as distraught. Mary Jane had gone to the Dakota, singing and crying long into the night, a candle in her hand, her boyfriend at her side. It was all too hard to accept. The world, or at least the world that cared so deeply for this man, was left with nothing more than the sympathies they could share. Only one thing could sustain them, the most important thing of all. The music. Somehow, some way, the music would live on.

Throughout the day, McAllister made the final preparations for heading north. All the while, the music played, too beautiful and too numerous to count, too lovely and creative to favor. John Lennon was the most incredible artistic talent of a generation. No one would ever come close to such a masterpiece of personal human poetic put into a song. The political and social strivings of Bobby Kennedy and Martin Luther King would forever mark the history of America. They were men who had captured the hearts and best intentions of their country, with the human dreams they sought to inspire. But in the end, there would be no comparison. John Lennon's music spoke to the much deeper human condition, the personal journey of every human soul. John Lennon spoke to the frailty of a human life, both the goodness that lived within us, as well as the deceptions and selfishness that our humanity must overcome. He would never be a religious icon, never a Jesus, an Allah or Buddha, carved in the stones of a cathedral or temple square. He would simply be a man who wore the duality of his nature upon his sleeve. And yet Lennon knew deep inside, that love would always be the answer. In the end, John Lennon knew that to give love and to receive love was truly the heart's desire. Only then, would an eternal peace forever sing.

Reality demands that the living continue on. For without the living, reality would cease to exist. In the United States of America, a confused and troubled man is allowed to purchase a gun. The gun is an article of man's invention, whose purpose might be argued, but whose consequence is always the same. It is not an invention of life, only injury and death. Survival is a necessity of existence, by whose definition a gun can be conceived and built. But peace is also a necessity of existence, by whose definition the bullet must be removed. In between, doth the reality of man appear to reside. Caught within this tortuous middle ground, a man of peace is killed by a gun. Sadly once more, another of life's mysteries becomes so impossible to comprehend.

Driving north toward Seattle, McAllister watched the Oregon rain pool upon his windshield, before the wipers would sweep them away. They would swing in constant rhythm, like the beating of a heart, or the tick-tock of a grandfather clock, all the way to Eugene. Along the freeway, McAllister noticed the many trucks hauling the bundled Christmas trees heading south for California. In a matter of weeks, a celebration would be held for a man of Christian peace. A believing Christian culture would once again swear its allegiance to a wishful human aspiration it might never be able to achieve. It was difficult to consider such a momentous sense of irony, nor prevent that terrible emotion of anger from not rising in response. Deep down, McAllister felt that John Lennon would have been frustrated at such a consequence, for he had loved his life so true. Yet, he more than likely would have put his arm around the killer, before writing him a song. For anger and forgiveness both have their place in this unknown human drama, of which we will never understand.

In Eugene, he stayed over with Sullivan and Carley, borrowing a sport coat from Tom, before continuing his journey north. The panel truck remained without a radio, leaving time for more reflection, or imaginary worries of what was to come. He battled the traffic through Portland like a country hick, growing tense as the urban high-rise of Seattle loomed in the distance ahead.

With her long blonde hair cut short to her neckline, Paige appeared like another woman, until her smile, the sound of her voice, and the warmth of her hands drew him close. He tied back his hair, shaved the ragged peach fuzz off of his face, dressing in the sport coat for the first time in years. He was once again quiet and gracious with her parents and family. Working in the timber trade was his familiar refrain, whenever faced with the standard American question of 'what do you do'. Thankfully, Dane and Terri were nearby. Somehow he could blend in with them, trying to avoid the unspoken questions of who he might be.

She looked beautiful walking down the aisle in her tallish stride and purple gown, the graduation cap a wee bit large for her head. His desire grew strong at the slim sight of her nylons above her shoes. He had the urge to race up and steal her away, like Dustin Hoffman had gotten to do in the Graduate so many years before. But he was able to mask such intent as the ceremonial festivities coursed through the remainder of the day. On late Sunday morning, she climbed again into the panel truck, and they finally had each other all to themselves. They kissed long and hard, with her passion equal to his. He knew then, that maybe something was coming true, although he didn't know how it might be revealed. He had to remind himself to do his best to go along for the ride.

The town of Port Swan sat on a hill in the distance, surrounded by the dark blue waters of the upper Puget Sound. Dane had stayed behind in the city. McAllister and Paige would have his home alone for a night. He built a fire in the woodstove while she unpacked their things. As the late Sunday afternoon fell into darkness, quiet and unknown, they fell into each other as if one and the same.

Sean McAllister ran his hand up the length of her thigh, before slipping it under her nightshirt, rising to the warm heat of her breasts. Paige snuggled her head closer into his chest, her voice in soft murmur as she awakened from sleep. He let the hand roam over the course of her back, holding her tight, kissing her ear. It had been such a long time, but here she was, her body full in his arms, a precious jewel of soft white skin breathing beside him. He felt no single reason for ever letting go.

"Sean," she sighed quietly, her head still resting below his.

"Yes," he returned, stretching the word for effect.

"Is it already morning?" she whispered. "Really?"

"Well, there is something they call light coming through the window. And I can see a big orange ball rising in the sky. Outside of that, I'm not really sure," he joked.

Paige raised her head, looking into his eyes, before turning towards the bedroom window. Looking back, she kissed him on the lips before speaking. "You're still the comedian aren't you? How could I ever forget?"

"I was just filing a report," he smiled back at her sarcastically. "Upon your request." Their lips met again. Paige rolled over onto her back, lying beside him.

"I can't believe it," she spoke to the ceiling. "That here we are. I was always afraid it might never happen again, to be here with you this way. There were so many times when I always hoped it would." She turned to face him, waiting for a response. Her face grew intent before him. "Do you know what I mean," she asked?

Sean McAllister took a moment to answer, rolling over to face her, looking into her eyes. "Sweetheart, it's always been the same for me. But I can tell you this, I wouldn't want to be any other place in the world, or with anybody else, but with you right now. I could tell you a long drawn out story about things, lots of things, of how much I've missed you. But those things don't seem important now." Then he finally released his heart, making his long withheld confession. "I was always scared that time would come between us. Always worried that things would fade away, that something else would happen for you. To be here now, just the two of us here together, it's like a crazy wish come true. I really don't know how to say it, except that this is the dream that I had wished for, but of which I could never speak, because it seemed so far away."

She looked at him intently, before leaning in close and holding him still.

"Sometimes, I wondered why we didn't do this before. Why I didn't just take the chance with you. I mean with us, with me. So many times it felt like things had come and gone, for whatever the reasons might be."

"Paige," he began, "you weren't ready then. And that was okay. And neither was I, or at least I wasn't sure. But it really doesn't matter anymore. I promised myself before I came, that I would be however you wanted me to be. I would continue to not rush time, especially if I could be near you again."

"Rush time," she mulled. "Huh, that's a funny way to put it."

"It was something Tom said to me, way back when, during the harvest when we first met. 'Don't rush time', he said. At that point, I just wanted to grab you and take you back home with me to Pollard Creek. I think he knew it wasn't the right time for you, something Terri might have said, with school and your recent past and all." McAllister breathed out a sigh. "Of course, I was wishing Tom was wrong. But deeper down, I knew he was right. Still, the longer the time went by, I could feel us beginning to drift. I think I wanted it to go away, because I didn't want to feel the hurt. It's just so hard to explain. I guess I just lost hope. That's why it feels so good today, this trip, you, everything. And now you have graduated from school, which is what you needed to do."

Paige drew him close, kissing him deeply. "I love you, Sean. I want to be with you now. It's been too long for the both of us."

"And I love you. So much more than I can say. Paige, I'm ready to go wherever you want to go, to do whatever you want to do." He kissed her again, pulling her tight, as if pressing her within him. They both relaxed, sharing the warmth of their touch and affection.

"Tom is such a funny guy," Paige confided. "He's so cryptic, sometimes. I mean, even though I haven't seen him much in all these years. He's so much a part of my memory of us back then. He still feels so close."

McAllister chuckled at her description, rubbing her arm as he spoke.

"Cryptic? No kidding, cryptic. That's a great description for that trouble-making son of a gun. Did you get to read his card I brought along?"

"Un huh. It was really sweet. Did Terri ask you about him? She still talks about him whenever we get together."

"Oh yeah, but there wasn't much I could say. Only that he and his girlfriend Carley were still living in Eugene. But you know, sweetheart, when I stopped there on the way to Seattle, it felt like there was something going on between them. I'm not sure what it was, and I didn't get a chance to ask Tom. But it just seemed like they were passing each other in the night. Things were just so matter of fact between them. It's hard to explain."

"Oh," Paige responded, but did not continue. She snuggled in closer under his arms. "I'm glad you feel good," she said. "And so do I." She paused for a moment, a moment of silence prevailing. "Do you think we can make it last? What we have? You and me, together?"

Sean McAllister turned his gaze towards hers, smiling into her eyes. "I do," he said with all his heart. "Let's make it last for awhile, a long while if we can." He let his lips fall into hers, feeling the moisture, the intimacy of someone close. Then he pulled away and spoke. "So let's start with breakfast, what do you think?"

They packed up and made the bed, left their things inside, driving downtown to the main street of Port Swan. The center of town was lined with old brick buildings along the waterfront. At a breakfast place, they saw lots of other people the same age as themselves, eating and starting their day together. Outside, they walked the strip of businesses along the street. Some of the storefronts were empty or boarded up, but the people seemed alive and upbeat as they passed on by. McAllister liked the town, it had a good vibe. He could understand why Dane liked living here. It felt a lot like Pollard Creek, just larger and with perhaps more going on.

He and Paige drove out to the state park at the edge of the community. The park was an old World War I military installation, with large barracks and officer's homes, all resting on the water's edge. They walked a long beach towards a lighthouse and rocky point, the cold blue of the Puget Sound lapping at their feet. Dressed in blue jeans and a long heavy sweater reaching over her hips, her face fresh and blushed with cold, Paige appeared lovely and content. Hand in hand, they began to put their feelings together as one, investing in their future, whatever it might be.

After taking her boards, Paige would come back to Port Swan whenever she could. She would stay with her brother and look for a job. If something happened, that would be great. McAllister would return to whatever she could find, even Seattle if that's what it took. Meanwhile, he would go back to Pollard Creek, arrange for another caretaker to look after the property. He would continue to work, doing whatever until Paige said it was time to come. However, he wanted her to come down to Pollard Creek one last time. She could even take the train to Eugene. He would pick her up there. They could visit with Sullivan before going south towards home.

McAllister wasn't quite sure why a final visit was so important. Maybe he just wanted Paige to share it with him one last time, to understand what he was leaving behind. Or maybe he just felt the pull of a past he couldn't completely forsake. Although he was more than ready for a new adventure, and the beautiful chance to have someone close in his life, he knew he would be leaving something that would always be a part of him, something he would always miss. Perhaps he just needed Paige to know what it meant to him.

On the way out of town, they drove by the local hospital, just to take a look. He told her it would be a piece of cake, that they would hire her as soon as she walked in the door. And he would find some kind of work to do, as he always had done before. Dane had said he could always go fishing in Alaska, if push came to shove. But right now, that would only be a last resort. It was Paige with whom he wanted to be, not another crazy work trip so far away. On the ferry ride back to Seattle, a musician with a guitar was playing Beatles' songs in the passenger cabin. People nearby began to sing along. On this particular Sunday, across the world, a vigil in John Lennon's memory was taking place, a remembrance of all he had meant through his music and life. In one way, it was a sad and disturbing reflection. In another way, something new and peaceful was being born.

CHAPTER FIFTY

O LUCKY MAN!
Pollard Creek / Eugene / April, 1981

NOTHING COULD BE FINER THAN A WARM SPRING DAY in Southern Oregon. Spring is a time when the wildflowers bloom, the heat feels warm to the skin. The creeks and rivers run whitewater clear, the river rock glistens like jewels in the sun. Certainly, not everyone would agree, for spring is beautiful wherever it comes. For with the coming of spring, it is the effect on the heart and soul that really matter, and location is of little importance.

Upon the rebirth of one's natural surroundings, romance and hope awake from their hibernation. They slowly rub the sand from their eyes, excited about a chance to begin anew, eager to fulfill the wishful possibility of winter dreams. Belief in life reaches outward in exaltation, stretching its arms to greet the future. Romance and hope excitedly don their Easter bonnets, convinced with a spirit that happiness is right around the corner, waiting to be satisfied. Love, true eternal love, feels for a moment close and attainable. It becomes comfortable to the touch, under an ultimately forgiving deep blue sky.

Sean McAllister sold his wood truck and other personal items he would not be able to carry north. He arranged for a new caretaker to take over George and Helen's property. He paid the last of his bills, closing his meager bank account. Someone gave him a radio and tape player, which he wired into the panel truck. He would now have music to play. He asked the Postmistress to hold his mail until he landed an address for things to be sent.

There would be no going away party, no spoken tributes or heartfelt missives upon his leaving. Pollard Creek had never been that kind of place. Everyone had always believed in doing their own thing, whatever it might be. People had their own lives to live. One could be back in a month, or never again. Pollard Creek would forever be an extended family of sorts, but a family without any traditional obligations to send you on your way. You would always be remembered, if only for the incidental stories one might be able to recall, as time went by.

Still, it felt odd to pass through the center of town one last time. He passed by the Hungry Dog Cafe, with its usual bevy of tractor trailers parked along the road. To his left, stood the Pollard Creek Inn, appearing silent in the morning air, the history of its better times looking tight-lipped and sadly alone. The Country Store sat nearby, its front porch empty, basking alone in the sun. To his right perched the Frontier Market and gas station, the good ole '76 Club, waiting for its daily patrons to arrive. Across the triangle, a few people milled in front of the post office, their heads peering down, shuffling through their mail. For everyone else in Pollard Creek it would be just another day.

The panel truck steered out the access road to the northbound exit of the interstate. McAllister accelerated up the mountain pass. The evergreen hills were brilliant in the sunlight, strong and sturdy against the sky. Somewhere amongst them, tough-minded men would be cutting a timbered unit of trees. Long steel cables would be stretching down a steep angled slope, the yarder equipment tooting as it yanked the cargo up to the flat. McAllister could almost hear the crashing and splitting of brush, as the trees heaved upward across the forest floor. The panel truck peaked at the summit, sliding downward past the exit to Glendale. Closer still, the metallic roar of a sawmill would be toiling away, while acres of raw cut logs lay piled in heaps waiting their turn. Lumber trucks, their engines gearing loud, the diesel exhaust spurting into the air, would pull away from the loading yard, as the sweet aroma of sawdust and wood chips filled the nostrils of this busy industrial state. This was the day to day working tale of the Southern Oregon world he was leaving behind.

In his gut, Sean McAllister felt a small corner of emptiness inside, a place where all the reflections of these last seven years seemed jumbled and lost. A part of his heart began to sense the absence of a home he had come to know so well. His mind's eye was stocked images that contained the faces of friends and neighbors, of the people remaining, or those that had journeyed on before. All had become his durable companions. They had welcomed and accepted him on a similar spring day so many years ago.

But today, such emotional recollections remained outweighed by the adventure ahead. Standing before him was the chance at love, someone close to share all that might continue to unfold. With each mile passing under his wheels, there rose the expectation of something new and exciting, a reason for being that he had been so long awaiting. Any regrets would just be a tiny part of the coming equation. In the bigger picture of things, there was an undeniable certainty it was time to go. He would push all his chips to the center of the table. He would be like Marty Johnson, willing to take a risk. Paige would be waiting on the other end, and that was more than enough to make the bet. He would reach Eugene by early afternoon, enjoying some final moments of camaraderie with Tommy Sullivan, before saying his farewell.

Tom Sullivan sat on a stacked pile of framing lumber at the new home site, eating a banana, finishing his lunch. The midday sun was almost hot in its brightness and heat. For Sullivan, it felt good to be wearing a tee shirt, instead of being locked inside a rain slicker, dodging a cold precipitation. The rest of his cooperative construction crew had driven down the street to eat at a nearby restaurant. Sullivan poured a cup of coffee from his thermos, enjoying a few moments of quiet before things would crank up for the afternoon's labor.

If anyone might ask him, Tom Sullivan enjoyed the job he was doing. Building new houses or doing residential and commercial remodels was invigorating and challenging work. And being part owner of the business made it all the more worthwhile. He was learning how to bid each project. He was getting better at managing each day's purpose, dealing effectively with his fellow members when it came to effort and time. The only responsibility he didn't desire to perform was negotiating with the owners or clients. He would let someone else handle those administrative parts of the project. It wasn't that he couldn't handle those tasks if absolutely necessary, just that dealing too much with people was not his choice or forte.

Eugene was a good town. The city was growing busier than he might prefer, but at least there was available work. He missed Pollard Creek from time to time. He missed Marty, Freddie, and the others, the quiet days of solitude at Railroad Bridge. But Pollard Creek had always been a rough locale to try and make a living. Other things had changed as well. Valerie had been gone for quite awhile, and now Sean McAllister was even picking up stakes. Carley had sold her homestead on Paradise Creek, so things were over there. He'd never even bothered to get his name on the deed at Railroad Bridge. And truthfully, it never really mattered. Railroad Bridge was Marty and Freddie's place when you got right down to it. As long as they held on, he knew he could always retreat there should it ever be necessary.

Actually, something had already gone haywire, but it had nothing to do with economics or living in Eugene. Spring break at the University was underway. Carley was down south in Los Angeles. She would be visiting her folks, and making feelers for a job after her graduation in June. But he would not be going along. They had agreed to share the apartment until school was over. Then Carley would go on with her life, and he with his. Love and commitment might sound like durable foundations, made to last long and strong through any tempest and storm. But in these times, it was simply a myth on which to rely. The truth was that people change. Or maybe better expressed, that circumstances change. In his and Carley's case, no one was at fault. It was just a matter of things unseen as time went by, of personal expectations being left unfulfilled. Eventually, the husk sheds off the seed, becoming naked and clear. And no amount of denial can hide the fact.

Tom Sullivan remained unsure if love had ever really been at the heart of the matter. Attraction, yes, there was no doubt about that. And Carley had always given him things to do, goals to reach, projects to finish. She had kept him constantly preoccupied with many interests and new things in which to involve. Being with Carley he rarely had to look at himself, there was always something to distract him. Valerie had been forgiving and understanding. She was a master at letting him find his way, even if it meant they would only become friends. With Carley, he had someone to hide behind and follow along. She was the kind of woman who wanted the challenge of performing in a man's world, a new modern world in which she could engage. He admired her for such intents. But slowly he had turned away.

Sullivan hadn't told Sean McAllister the news. And he didn't intend to now. His friend was on all-time high. He was famously in love and pursuing a new direction in his own life, a direction that for quite some time he had been unable to find. Paige was the best thing that could happen for him. She was caring and practical like Valerie, yet appearing to enjoy the freedom McAllister was always wishing to maintain.

Sullivan was glad they were not choosing Seattle to give it the first shot. He knew that life in the city would be difficult for McAllister, in one fashion or another. It wasn't that Sean was some wandering free spirit, a rolling stone that gathered no moss. He was actually more easy-going than most, and down to earth in both thought and reflection more times than not. It was just that he needed to feel free at any time, and not controlled by the expectations of the world at large. As long as Sean could keep that vision of being free, he would be happy to stay safe at home. Paige had a little of that same confusing wanderlust herself, but she was much more down to earth. Sullivan hoped that their trail together would bind with time. But such trails could sometimes become a difficult road.

So there was really no compelling reason to blow McAllister's little pop stand, just for the sake of truth about his own situation. But if Sean did happen to ask, Sullivan would tell. In the end, it would never be a big deal between friends. Sean would be arriving soon, and to be honest Sullivan was quietly excited. The crew pulled up in the company truck. Sullivan yanked his tool belt back onto his waist, ready for work.

The two men sat at the kitchen table in Sullivan's Eugene apartment, the windows open to a comfortable evening outside. Sullivan had poured a couple of shots of whiskey to go with their beers.

"What time will you get up in the morning?" McAllister asked.

"About six," Sullivan answered. "But you can get up and leave whenever you want. Just lock the door whenever you go."

"No, I'll get up with you. I'm planning to stop up in Carlton to visit for awhile with Jack Mulcahey and Jesse. And I need to get to Seattle before dark. Her brother is coming over the next day to help us move her stuff."

"How are those guys, Jack and Jesse? I haven't thought about them in a long time."

"Good, I guess. They're really getting into the fruit grafting thing for money. They go back and forth to Orondo and such, but now they are getting some work near home as well. They're back in Carlton at the moment. That's why I'm going to stop and visit."

"Is Jack's brother still down on the farm in Pollard Creek?" Sullivan asked.

"Derrick? You know, I think so. Although Derrick Mulcahey is not the kind of guy I would necessarily go looking up." McAllister took a sip off the shot of whiskey, chasing it down with a swig of his beer. "It's funny how you can live in such a small town sometimes, and still never see some people you know. Of course, it's not like I've gotten around much, once I made this decision to move. I guess I'll catch up on things when I see those guys." McAllister paused. "You know Tommy, once Paige and I get settled, you and Carley should come up for a visit. Port Swan seems like a pretty cool place. And it's kind of different from Oregon. Actually, there's no oak and pine to speak of, but it does have pockets of madrone here and there."

Tom Sullivan poured himself another shot of whiskey. "I'm afraid that's not likely to be happening," Sullivan began. "I guess there is something I have to tell you, but you have to keep it only between you and me."

Sean McAllister was surprised at the news, but not overly shocked. In some ways, Carley and Sullivan always seemed like a strange match. She was certainly an intelligent woman, with a lot of energy for politics and stuff. She always had a real drive to work and make a difference in the world, even in Solace Valley. And Sullivan always seemed to be going along for the ride. He was so much more low-key and internal than her. It wasn't as if McAllister had ever witnessed anything difficult between them. But then again, he'd never seen much special affection displayed in their relationship. It always seemed so practical and business-like much of the time. Hearing that Carley would be heading back to Los Angeles didn't seem out of character for her. But for Sullivan, it surely would have been a little hard to believe.

"So the two of you are capable of living together here for awhile, knowing what you know? I don't know why, but that just feels so difficult to me. Mookie and Annie were like that too. I guess it all makes sense, I mean, if nobody else is involved. It just sounds so adult."

"Certainly not your forte," Sullivan cracked. "You'd be bouncing off walls, looking for some place to hide."

"Gee, thanks for the vote of confidence, brother," McAllister responded. "I really appreciate it. But then again, you're probably right."

"Don't take it personal," Sullivan began. "It's actually a good thing. Sean, you tend to live things all the way through, if you know what I mean. But don't ever try and grow up. It wouldn't be healthy for you. And if you ever started to get numb about things, I'd have to kick your ass."

McAllister shook his head. "Okay, whatever. You know, Tommy, you sound like my sister sometimes. My older sister, if you get my point. Pour me another shot out of that bottle, pretty please."

"I've seen your sister," Sullivan returned, "at least pictures of her. I'm not sure whatever happened to you, but she could eat crackers in my bed anytime."

"Talk about kicking my ass?" McAllister joked. "Mary Jane would kick your ass up and down the block. In fact, she's more like Carley than Carley. You wouldn't stand a chance."

Sullivan laughed at the taunt. He was catching a buzz, and so was McAllister. "You're probably right," he admitted. He went over to the refrigerator, pulling out two more beers.

"You know, I wasn't even going to tell you this shit. I didn't want to spoil what you are heading for with Paige. She's a damn nice woman, Sean, and I'm happy you are taking the chance with her. It will be a good for the both of you. I know."

"Lucky is more like it," McAllister responded. "And hey, by the way, I did what you said, Tommy. Do you remember, I didn't rush time. But more than anything, I got real lucky, and I'm sure okay with that." McAllister raised his glass to Sullivan, clinking in a toast. "Still, it is a bummer what's happening between you and Carley. But I know someone else will come along. Right now, I just feel like Eugene is your home, and for you it will be a good place to be."

"Maybe it already is," Sullivan smiled. He leaned back in his chair, sipping another taste of the whiskey, an odd look on his face.

"What? Now wait a minute. What does that mean?"

Sullivan gently nodded his head toward the apartment wall, as if pointing in a particular direction. McAllister wasn't sure, but he thought he was getting the message.

"Now, don't be cryptic," McAllister whined. "And that's not my word, smart ass. Paige said that about you not long ago. He's cryptic, she said. And then I told her, that's the perfect definition for you. In fact, I said he's cryptic most of the time. Presuming he says anything at all."

Sullivan delivered McAllister a half-looped grin, as if picking up on McAllister's response. But as he gave up the smile, he didn't say a word.

"Wow," McAllister breathed. He paused, taking a hit off his beer. "You know, it's funny. But that one time I was here, and we had dinner together, I felt something strange about that night, especially with you and Tara's daughter. You just lit up around the kid, in a way I'd never seen before. Geez, has it been going on for that long a time?

Sullivan shook his head, but his expression became serious. Finally, he spoke. "No, it's actually been only a very short time. Sort of when I knew Carley and I would be splitting the sheets. But I could feel it coming a long way back. You know, it's really what I want, Sean, and I think I'm ready for it now. It's a lot like what you are about to take on. It's a good time for the both of us."

McAllister was feeling the whiskey and beer taking its effect. But more than anything he felt a realization that his longtime friend was beginning to open up. Yet, here they were, about to embark on a new course in their lives, a course that would begin to take them away from each other for a long time ahead. And even though it was good for the both of them, it was somehow sad at the very same time.

McAllister answered. "Yeah, it's good. I know it is for me. It's something I'd been hoping might happen for quite a while. And for you, it sounds like the right thing, too. Something tells me that young girl loves you very much. And you feel the same. And now her mom is on your side. I hear it in your voice. And if that's so, then Eugene is definitely your home, and you need to make it happen in a good way."

Tom Sullivan leaned back in his chair, breathing out a long sigh. "Yeah, it's been a difficult time, lately. So much stuff has been going back and forth in my mind. Wanting to do the right thing, you know, but not hurting anyone in the process. But you're right, Sean, this is the best thing for me. For the longest time, I never believed I could be serious about anything again. In fact, it's no surprise that anybody who has ever come back from Nam could ever take anything serious. To be able to make a commitment, an honest commitment to anyone in a good and healthy way. How the hell do you make a commitment to anything real, when in the very beginning you're supposed to be dead?"

Sean McAllister wasn't sure how to answer. In a way, he had no right. He'd always felt that he was unable to advise on these terrible things, these terrible things he'd never had to experience. But this was his friend, a man for whom he deeply cared. Regardless, he had to try and respond.

"You know, Tommy, now is the time to let it go. That's just what this circumstance is telling you. It's a different kind of caring, it really is. But you have to do it without all this goddamn baggage that's been trailing behind. Do you really want to know something? I'll tell you something. They don't give a flying shit. They've already forgotten you. Nixon, the military, and all those pimps who have come before. They've already stolen something from you. They stole from you, and Marty, and Freddie, and all the rest of the guys. But don't let them have the rest of your life, Tommy. Fuck them! Don't let them have it, because they'll take it every time without giving a fuck. They fucked you once, brother. And you can never get that back. But don't let them fuck you on and on. Take the rest of your life for yourself, for this young child and her mom you have chosen to love. Let them have who you really are, and not all this bullshit that has come before."

Tom Sullivan stared at McAllister, a deep thoughtful expression on his face. He was silent for a time, his eyes occasionally blinking, as if letting the words sink in. Then he reached to pick up his bottle of beer, draining the last. "Okay, man, I hear you. And thanks, thanks a lot." At that moment, he smiled and changed character, taking the edge off. "You're a good friend I suppose, even for being such a pain in the ass. And maybe, just maybe, I'll miss you when you're gone. Perhaps I'll come visit you in Washington. But don't start counting the days or anything. You can tell Paige I'll come to see her. That's it, tell Paige. But now I'm getting hungry. We got to eat."

McAllister just shook his head at his dear friend and smiled. "Sure, whatever. Let's do it." But just as he spoke, there came a knock on the door. Sullivan looked up, yelling to come in. The door opened slowly. Then a small head of light brown hair and a face peered inside. It was the face of a young girl with shining eyes.

"Hi, little one," Sullivan greeted, "what are you doing?"

"Mommy says to tell you she is making dinner. Spaghetti with meat balls. She said to tell you and your friend to come over if you want to."

McAllister and Sullivan looked at each other. McAllister lifted his shoulders to say why not. Sullivan answered. "Tell your mom, little one, we'll be over in ten minutes, okay?"

"Okay," the child drawled, then backed herself out, closing the door behind.

Sullivan looked over at McAllister, slightly raising his head in acknowledgement. Sean McAllister chuckled in response. "Cool, Tommy. Very, very cool."

CHAPTER FIFTY-ONE

DOIN' FINE

Oregon / Washington / April, 1981

THE FAMILIAR CATCHPHRASE had its derivation with the Berkeley Free Speech Movement in 1964. The phrase became a rallying cry for students in protest against the University of California. 'You can't trust anyone over thirty'.

For Sean McAllister, there was once a time in his own experience when the catchphrase seemed to make perfect sense. However, back in those days, the age of thirty had felt very old and light years away. Today, back on the road, driving north toward Corvallis on the Old Highway 99, it seemed almost ridiculous to believe. Here he was, easily over thirty years old, soon to be thirty-one in a couple more months. Could it actually be true, that he might now appear so old to others just coming of age? He didn't feel old. In fact, he didn't think of himself as much older than any other day in his life the last ten years. Still, it was weird to think that others might see him that way. No doubt, perception would always remain in the eye of the beholder. But could it be that one's own self-image was capable of such a distortion, to not be able to see the consequent realities of age? Although the physical body might conspire against you with the passage of time, does not the human mind prefer to see oneself as forever young?

Sean McAllister certainly didn't agree that he might be viewed as a person not worthy of trust. But maybe this was a self-perception it was difficult to see in the bigger picture of things. Maybe this was what his last few years had been all about. Other friends were changing, and perhaps he was changing too. Yet, within the passing day to day, these changes are hardly ever considered. Such a picture is never clear when only the moment prevails. McAllister knew one thing for certain, he wasn't buying into that particular statement anymore. He still felt purposeful enough to defy such a point of view. Yes, perhaps the day would come when he might be old and in the way, a day when his views of the world would suddenly stand in contrast to the ways he thought before. But it wouldn't be today. It was way too early in the game to be getting that close to the grave.

McAllister had awakened early with Sullivan. They had coffee together before saying their good-byes. Sullivan had asked how Marty Johnson was getting along. McAllister had reported that Marty remained on his crazy fast-paced run through life. Sometimes it didn't look good. Other times, he appeared to be the same old Marty that McAllister and Sullivan had always known. But when McAllister had asked Sullivan how he thought things might go, whether Marty might ever be able to settle down again, the typical Sullivan answer was short and sweet. "It could go either way," he muttered, "it could go either way." Thankfully, both men knew they didn't have to worry about Freddie Jones. Freddie was the salt of the earth. Freddie seemed forever content living in the hills, and that would always been enough for him. And Railroad Bridge would always be a safe haven for Marty, as long as Freddie continued to make the property his home.

The Willamette Valley spread flat and wide around him, as McAllister headed further toward Corvallis. The morning sun was full and bright. Another lovely spring day was getting underway. The farm fields of spring were wrapped in a blanket of soft new green. The mountains of the coast rose in the western horizon, the foothills of the Cascades to the east. They surrounded the expansive valley in a cordoned perimeter. Lazy groups of cumulus clouds scattered aloft, bumping their way through the Willamette sky.

It always felt good for Sean McAllister to be moving, whenever traveling on the roads throughout the West. Such motion never failed to provoke a sense of romance, something strangely spiritual and eternal. Words would always fall short of expressing its effect. These were the other-worldly sensations that the vastness of nature could inspire, the eloquence they sustained. Perhaps it was more the expectations that such motion could create, of something new rising in the distant future, or something old falling further behind in the past. Whatever it was, these feelings cast the spell of a wishful timelessness he could not convey, a soulful immortality that beckoned to him from faraway. They were feelings always peaceful in their wonder and consequence, filled with a knowing that language could not impart.

The only failing was the solitary nature of their marvelous impact. For these miracles of beauty and heart could only be experienced alone. Maybe that is why love is so intoxicating, so addictive in the heart. For love is that everlasting attempt to share such experience with another human being, in ultimate fulfillment, at whatever the cost. Perhaps true love can bridge this gap that cannot be tethered in life. It becomes one last attempt not to travel alone. For deep down there is something we subconsciously understand, that death will always be an isolated enterprise, whenever the last moment comes.

So, why the hell not fall in love, when in the end, you have to go it alone either way. You can't take it with you, no matter what some others might preach. And the occasional blues are part of the game of life. So what if sometimes you fumble on the goal line, and your world looks like it's coming to an end. Well, it is coming to an end, sometime down the road. Sure, it sucks, but it's true as far as one can tell. Sometimes the rest of the world might spend a few minutes kicking your ass. But sooner or later, everyone has their own shit to worry about, their own mistakes to overcome. But whenever one is blessed to sense the horizon, to stand up in the high country and look out upon the grand vista beyond, to breathe in the crystal thin air of a mountain sky, it somehow reminds you. It tells you that one day there will be another game to play, another goal line to cross. And this time it will be crossed with ball in hand, possessed with the thrill of that very moment to enjoy. So, why not fall in love?

Sean McAllister gave thought to his mom and dad, and his sister, Mary Jane. He was reminded of how much they really meant to him, although so far away. Much like him, they were loved ones making their own way in life, making their own choices, either by circumstance or personal belief. But they were part of him in every way, and he a part of them. And the same could be said for so many others along this road so far.

He knew in his heart he would choose livability and friendship whenever he could. He would continue to learn, and try his best to do the right thing. That didn't mean he would give up on his cynicism or progressive beliefs, they would always be part of the game. For the greed merchants and bad boys would always be out there. They were not going away anytime soon. But one day, somehow, they would fade away. And the distant horizon would eventually be within reach. Mankind would reach the Promised Land, as Martin Luther King had expressed so clairvoyantly on the night before his tragic death.

McAllister motored through Corvallis, continuing north towards McMinnville, before branching off to the little town of Carlton in the heart of the Yamhill Valley. There, he found the rented farm house and acreage of Jack Mulcahey and his wife Christine. He had phoned them earlier that morning, and knew they would be home. Jack Mulcahey was the same as ever, his reddish blonde hair tied back in a braid, his beard full, his lips pursed straight, his spoken words as ever difficult to come. Christine still looked the spitting image of a hippie mother of two. She and Jack had remained people of the land, a farming family with kids and animals, and a host of other projects close at hand.

Jack Mulcahey had been both the pillar and the foundation of the Mulcahey Farm. He was continuing in this life he loved and found most comfortable. His brother, Derrick, had been the Pied Piper of the times, imbued with an idealism that Jack Mulcahey loyally supported and shared. It was an idealism of living, working, and committing together. It was an attempt to shed the individual propensities of a materialistic culture, a culture that by its nature and application, had so successfully separated one from the other in so many ways. Derrick's belief and desires were true, at least in their intellectual formulation. But putting them into practice had become much more difficult and complex. One could rightly blame Derrick Mulcahey's personal need to control and manipulate the farm's direction, as the reason for its eventual disintegration. But that reason was just a singular factor in a particular situation. The Mulcahey Farm was not alone when it came to the eventuality of a failed experiment. Many other forces were equally at play.

The culture of individual freedom, on which America had become so emotionally founded and expressed, was now ingrained in the soul of its becoming. Traditional and historical models of communal behavior, of the tribe or the sect, were no longer a necessity for safety or survival. A single man or woman could create their own economic and personal security in a modern world. But the more communal aspirations remained addictive to the human soul, and had sporadically found their manifestation in the American experience. Yet in the end, the strivings of the individual had carried the day. However, this singular American evolution had come with its consequences. Separation and loneliness were often the result. Unfortunately, the intense constant communalism of earlier models could not apply. Another model needed to be formed.

Community might be the better word in America. To give the individual their personal space, to allow their own nuclear world to express itself and thrive. At the same time, to satisfy their personal human need to bond with others, as well as providing for the shared social needs of their neighbors, their planet, and their common spiritual fulfillment. The Mulcahey Farm, and many other intentional communities, might be viewed by some as a lost cause in the search for a workable human dynamic. It had failed to meet the needs and intents of all concerned. But for Sean McAllister, that would never be the case.

If Sean McAllister could become an attorney in the court of such reflection, he would have argued for the defense. In his own experience, he had learned some lessons about personal commitment and understanding. He had learned about the difficult responsibility of working toward a consensus of mind with other human beings. He had learned how idealism and practicality must somehow be merged in order to progress. In addition, he had learned how to operate chainsaws, to grow and harvest food to eat and survive. He had learned building and mechanical skills, and how to exist without electricity or running water for long periods of time. He had learned how to cook for many, and to value the beauty and necessity of the natural world that surrounded him.

No, these things were not failures, nothing of the sort. They had become the building blocks of his maturation into becoming a man. They were the tools of his experience; practical, social, and personal, upon which he could always rely. Derrick Mulcahey may have been a pain in the ass, a man dealing with his own particular demons, and in doing so, had created an eventual demise. But Derrick Mulcahey had also given those that surrounded him an opportunity to explore and absorb a new and adventurous world. And upon their leaving, taking with them something they didn't have before.

For Sean McAllister, there were a few singular moments in his life when the joy of brotherhood had been so high in exaltation. One was the time when he and Mary Jane, on a cold crisp sunlit day, had marched together in Washington D.C. They had shared together, with thousands of others, a common belief for peace in the world. Equally, there had been moments on the Mulcahey Farm, when that joy of togetherness was revisited, and everyone had personally dwelled in the contentment such joy could provide. No, in the end there was never really a failure, not even close.

But one should never go to a gunfight carrying a knife. Trying to carve out some semblance of a living upon the marginal terrain of Southern Oregon rock and clay had been no easy task. And no one could ever argue that without a Jack Mulcahey, they could have ever persevered. This man would always have a special place of respect in Sean McAllister's mind, and equally in his heart. Nor should it be forgotten, that without his partner Christine, Jack might have ever been so dedicated to the task. Along with Derrick, they had been the circle around which everyone else revolved.

To see young Jesse Simmons in the flesh had its own kind of high. His long black hair continued in its pony tail, deep to his waist. But today, Jesse wore the features of man, no longer the precocious teenager that roamed the Mulcahey Farm. McAllister would forever enjoy being Jesse's 'college boy' older brother. Just the sight of Jesse's smile and devilish expression made McAllister feel warm inside. Jesse had become the perfect compliment for the taciturn Jack, even more so now that he was coming of age and confidence.

The three men spent some time walking the farm exterior, catching up on their time in between. Jack and Jesse were beginning to travel more. Their orchard budding and grafting work was beginning to expand beyond North Central Washington. As well, Jesse was getting into growing nursery stock for regional landscape vendors in the Portland area. McAllister gave them the update on Mookie James, Valerie Williams, Darla Bloom and others. They asked about Mookie's old girlfriend, Annie. She was back in Los Angeles as far as anyone knew. Rita was back in San Francisco. They could only figure Darius was somewhere near San Diego, but no one had heard from him. And it was much the same for so many others that had passed through the Mulcahey Farm, only to move onward to points unknown.

McAllister had lunch with the family before saying his farewell. He pushed the panel truck back toward the interstate, turning north once more for the final run to Seattle. The peaceful afternoon sky was softened by a thin mask of high white cover blocking the sun. With his new radio in the truck, McAllister found an FM station in Portland that was playing rock and roll. His visitations were now complete. His thoughts returned to the renewed anticipations of being with Paige, just hours away. Steering through the traffic of the city, he approached the River bridge ahead.

Crossing the mighty Columbia, McAllister looked down upon the wide stretch and white lap of the dark River below. Again those difficult feelings overtook him, the slight sinking in the stomach, the tinge of emotional regret. Oregon would be falling behind him, with no turning back. The emptiness was akin to that sense of leaving home for the very first time. Those moments when one has waited so long for the chance to be out their on their own, before suddenly realizing that they will be going it alone. Over the bridge, the panel truck grounded into Washington state, keeping pace with the traffic, forging its way ahead.

Yes, this was something of a leaving, and a serious leaving for sure. But McAllister would not be leaving the Great Northwest. Not by any means. He had read about a university professor in Seattle, who had coined the term 'Cascadia', defining both a regional geographic boundary, as well as a socio-political, environmental, and cultural state of mind. Much like the concepts of Ecotopia and the State of Jefferson, Cascadia would become its own sovereign land, free from the heartless and possessive rhythms of the current American union. Cascadia would seek a just and progressive construct for human civilization, a watershed moment in the evolution of the species, abandoning the selfish and destructive intents of the past, intents which continued to haunt the concentrated history of man on earth.

To his left, looking out the window of the panel truck, the huge cooling towers of the Trojan Nuclear facility rose high on the horizon. They appeared as if dark steaming cauldrons of death, wafting over the natural tellurian like a foreboding prediction for the end of the world. Yet, ahead and to his west, lay the incredible destructive remains of

Mount Saint Helens, a decimated forest that less than a year before had reminded the planet of the natural world's limitless powers to both live and die. In Cascadia, to die by the first would be a tragic mistake, filled with self-inflicted remorse, fraught with misgivings about what could have been. Tragic as the second might be, it would be spiritually accepted as part of the circle of life, as understood as the continuum of the seasons, where spring gives the birth of new life, and winter harkens the passing, silent for a time, before being reborn.

Cascadia meant 'land of falling waters'. McAllister loved the name, and the progressive belief in the future of which it spoke. The Northwest was both the land of the green, as well as the blonde. There could not be one without the other, the yin and the yang of life's ultimate reality, full of those mysteries that remained unknown. But at its heart, it would always be the water, the teeming blue of King Columbia, flowing within its midst, toward its forever destiny with the sea.

His thoughts turned to anticipation. The FM station began playing a tune by Savoy Brown called "Doin Fine". Listening to the song, he grew happier with each orbit of the tires. Yes, something in his life was coming to an end. But a new beginning lay before him, with someone he loved waiting for him at the end this road. Sean McAllister felt lucky to have come this far.

THE END

THE GREEN AND THE BLONDE
THE SOUNDTRACK
(Song Title / Album / Performer)

(*Author's Note:* The music of each generation carries with it the memories of a time gone by. It accompanies the living of life, and serves as a marker for reflections of the past. The songs in this soundtrack take their place for the telling of this story, although many other songs might serve as well. Literature provides for the sustenance of the heart and mind, but music always reaches deeper toward that romantic reflection of who we have become.) JTB

ACKNOWLEDGEMENTS

I would like to thank the following for their friendship and support in the creation and completion of this work. Michael Hale, artist, dreamer, and listener, for his early encouragement and bottles of wine during the work's early gestation. To Arthur 'Chef' Bell and Jeannie Moore, for their warm plates of food on cold winter evenings. To the many readers who were kind enough to read parts of the manuscript, particularly Mazzie Hale, Bill Kiely, Diane Diprete, Gail Harrington, Beverly Michaelsen, Mike McAndrew, Bill Kush, Eric Laughlin, Jim Daubenberger, Sam Gibboney, and Sarah Muirhead. To Adrienne Harun, writer, for her time and tips, and to the inspiring Gary Lemons, poet, whose uplifting spirit kept the creation energy alive. Also, to Kathleen Tellgren, Beth Krehbiel, and Char Wedin for their information on nursing and medical conditions.

In Oregon, so many who contributed their stories and memories: Mark Harry, Danny Metz, Steve Semmons, David Maranov, Dennis Mertz, Stephanie Potter, Doreen Gold Clayton, Vivian Murray, Sharon and Larry Gamble. Special thanks to Laurie Robertson for the same, and her ease of accommodation on my research excursions. To the newspaper morgue assistance personnel at the Grants Pass Courier newspaper in Grants Pass, Oregon. Finally, for the always noteworthy assistance of one, Jeff Curran, the real life 'Jerry Fisher', who will one day headline in your own home town, if only in your own mind. And to the many friends and neighbors of the fictional community of Pollard Creek, who by their living gave life to a special era in American time.

On the production end, to Julie Knott and Brion Toss for their assistance and information on self-publishing. To George Leinonen, photographer, for the author photograph. To Michael Hale for his beautiful cover art, Mary Rostad for her cartography skills, and to Marsha Slomowitz for her competent and professional book design. Finally, a special thanks to Pat Kenna, dear friend and co-owner of Printery Communications of Port Townsend, Washington. Pat's generous interest and support in leading the author through the maze of the self-publishing process is gratefully appreciated and acknowledged.

To anyone I may have forgotten to mention here, thank you for your care and support during the project.

Gratefully, Johnny B.

JOHN THOMAS BAKER has lived and traveled the Northwest for almost forty years. He currently resides with family and friends in Port Townsend, Washington, on the Olympic Peninsula

photo by
George Leinonen